Brok _____ Blues

JOYCE CAROL OATES

A *Virago* Book

Published by Virago Press 2000

First published by Virago Press 1999
First published in the United States by Dutton, an imprint of
Dutton NALI, a member of Penguin Putnam Inc 1999

Copyright © The Ontario Review, Inc., 1999

A CIP catalogue record for this book
is available from the British Library.

ISBN 1 86049 770 5

Typeset in Berkeley by M Rules
Printed and bound in Great Britain
by Clays Ltd, St Ives plc

Virago
A Division of
Little, Brown and Company (UK)
Brettenham House
Lancaster Place
London WC2E 7EN

Joyce Carol Oates is the author of numerous novels, stories, plays and poetry. Her most recent publications include *Man Crazy* and *Blonde*, a novel based on the life of Marilyn Monroe. Oates was a finalist for the 1995 PEN/Faulkner Award and a Pulitzer Prize, and the recipient of the 1996 PEN/Malamud Award for Achievement in the Short Story. She is currently the Roger S. Berlind Distinguished Professor of Humanities at Princeton University.

—for John Updike, a fellow time traveler

Contents

. . . Life is a dream a little less inconsistent.
—Pascal

I. Killer-Boy

John Reddy, you had our hearts.
John Reddy, we would've died for you.
John Reddy, John Reddy Heart.

—"The Ballad of John Reddy Heart"

1

There was a time in the Village of Willowsville, New York, population 5,640, eleven miles east of Buffalo, when every girl between the ages of twelve and twenty (and many unacknowledged others besides) was in love with John Reddy Heart.

John Reddy was our first love. You never forget your first love.

And where John Reddy wasn't exactly our first love (for after all, our mothers must've loved our fathers first, when they were young, in that unfathomable abyss of time before our births—and certain of our Willowsville mothers were in love with John Reddy) he supplanted that first love, and its very memory.

This time we most cherish isn't the tense "public" time of John Reddy's notoriety: those seventy-two hours when he was an actual fugitive from justice and the object of a statewide manhunt by New York State troopers and other law officers, to be tracked down in the mountains and arrested and brought home in shackles and most of it reported on TV and in the local papers, John Reddy Heart's face reproduced in the media daily for weeks: sixteen years old, good-looking even though battered and bleeding, stubborn, mysterious in his refusal to speak, his eyes heavy-lidded with secrets. Nor did we most cherish the drama of his trials in the fall, and yet more publicity, lurid screaming headlines: SUBURBAN TEEN TRIED IN SHOOTING DEATH OF MOTHER'S LOVER—16-YEAR-OLD TRIED AS AN ADULT, D.A. CALLS "VICIOUS MURDERER"—in *Time*, *Newsweek*, *Life*. And footage on network TV. (Even in English and European papers, we were told, there were articles, with accompanying photographs, of *John Reddy Heart*.) Nor did we most cherish the giddy weeks of "The Ballad of John Reddy Heart," by the rock band Made in USA, which was number one on the charts within a week of its release.

> John Reddy, you had our hearts.
> John Reddy, we would've died for you.
> John Reddy, John Reddy Heart.

Words you couldn't actually hear clearly, the amplified guitars, drums and general screeching were so loud. ("The Ballad of John Reddy Heart" sold more than any other single record—this was before tapes and CDs—in the history of Willowsville and vicinity. Though the music was kind of crude, you'd have to acknowledge, and Made in USA might be characterized as early, unintentional grunge. And we all resented the way, in the ballad, "John Reddy Heart" was portrayed. For he just wasn't the John Reddy any of us knew, our classmate.)

More distorting yet, and luridly sensational, was the CBS TV film in two parts *The Loves of the White Dahlia*, a docudrama supposedly based on the private life of Mrs. Dahlia Heart, John Reddy's mother—*the most controversial female to ever reside in the affluent suburb of Willowsville, New York, in its century and a half of history*. But this film, in our mayor's incensed words "a libel upon our village as upon the Heart family," wasn't aired until several years later, when we were all away at college, and the Hearts themselves long departed.

No, it's a quieter time we cherish. Those of us who knew John Reddy well. As Trish Elders would say, "He's someone you *feel*. Though he enters you through the eyes, he's someone you *feel*." This time when John Reddy, on probation, was living alone on Water Street, devoted to finishing his senior year of high school after twelve months' incarceration at Tomahawk Island Youth Camp (in the Niagara River) where he'd "maxed out" (as we'd learned to say casually) for getting into fights, failing to rack up a single day off for good behavior. The fights hadn't been John Reddy's fault, we were sure. He'd had to protect himself against other inmates, bigger, older guys, and guards, too; not just his physical self but his honor "as a man." So John Reddy's basketball teammates Dougie Siefried and Bo Bozer told us, incensed—"Because you know John Reddy, he's not gonna take any shit from anybody. John Reddy's the kind of guy you'd have to kill to make give *in*."

It was thrilling to hear Willowsville boys talk like this. The boys we'd gone to school with all our lives. Alluding to matters girls weren't supposed to know, though we could guess (we believed we could guess) what they were, sort of— "Forbidden acts," as Verrie Myers said gravely. Dougie and Bo were a year younger than John Reddy, in our class at school, but, speaking of John Reddy, they took on the elusive qualities of someone older, deeper into masculine experience. They frowned, brooded, sniffed, lit up cigarettes (forbidden for guys on teams) and shifted their shoulders inside their maroon Wolverine jackets in the way that John Reddy shifted his inside his black leather jacket. A signal they were restless, eager to be gone. Their aggrieved nasal voices were eerie echoes of John Reddy's voice. A slight drawl and sexy drag to vowels that wasn't western New York State but John Reddy's enthralling accent we'd been informed was west Texan.

Not that it was one hundred percent certain where John Reddy was from, still less where he was born. One newspaper, at the start of his trial, claimed he'd been born in Gila Bend,

Arizona. Another, in Las Vegas, Nevada. All we knew absolutely, as Bo Bozer said, with satisfaction, was, "Anywhere but *here*."

* * *

"On probation? What's that mean, exactly?"

"He's out of prison. But he's, like, still *in*. Under the surveillance of the state. He has to report to a probation officer. He isn't 'free.'"

"He's maybe—being watched?"

It was a melancholy kind of glamour: John Reddy back among us, in Willowsville, but not living in his family house on St. Albans Hill (though still furnished, the Heart house was empty); instead, he lived in a shabby two-room apartment (we'd been told, we'd never seen) on narrow, hilly Water Street, south of Main and a short block from the old Willowsville Water Mill. John Reddy would be eighteen the following February. (We knew of his birthday from the papers.) He'd lost a whole year of school; his own class had graduated and moved on while he'd been shut up in prison—"You have to know that injured his pride as much as being an ex-con. And being 'on probation' for another twelve months!"

John Reddy's family, the Hearts, had vanished from Willowsville. This surprised us—we'd always believed they loved him. They'd stand by him.

It was said that John Reddy was stubborn and "unrealistic"—wanting to reenter our school, which had the reputation of being possibly the best, the most academically demanding high school in upstate New York, to get his State Regents diploma. He'd personally petitioned to be reinstated to WHS and the board debated the issue heatedly, and after a close ballot voted to allow him back—with the mean proviso that he be barred from "all sports and extracurricular activities of any kind taking place outside regular school hours (8:45 A.M. to 3:15 P.M.)."

A slap in the face to all of us! Especially Coach Woody

McKeever and the varsity basketball team. John Reddy had been their star forward.

Of four hundred seventeen students enrolled at WHS at that time, John Reddy Heart was the only one not living with any family, any adult. The only one "on his own." It seemed strange to us, and wonderful. We spoke of him in hushed, reverent tones. It was enough to utter his name, to summon tears to our eyes. *Living alone? Alone? But he's only a boy.* Because John Reddy was a minor on probation, he had a nine p.m. curfew weeknights, an eleven p.m. curfew weekends, and was forbidden to associate with other persons on probation or on parole. He was forbidden to drive more than twenty miles from his official place of residence without permission and he was forbidden to drink alcoholic beverages or associate with people who did.

(Did this mean that John Reddy couldn't drop by the Haven for even a Coke, or hang out at Tug Hill Park if some of the guys were playing softball and somebody's older brother had brought along beer on ice?) Of course, John Reddy was forbidden to use drugs or to associate with people who did. "But John Reddy would never get lonely, like the rest of us," Verrie Myers argued. "He wouldn't be weak in that way. He doesn't need other people." Verrie had been in love with John Reddy Heart since the age of eleven years, two months, and eight days.

Quickly Mary Louise Schultz said, "If John Reddy seemed to need another person, it would be out of kindness to him. Or her."

Those stolen evenings in Verrie Myers's canary-yellow Olds convertible her parents had given her as a surprise present for her sixteenth birthday. Remember the sharp lovely smell of *new*: the leather interior of the hue of butterscotch, soft as human skin. And the gleam of flawless chrome like the purest of smiles. The glittering instrument panel. "I'm the luckiest girl in the world," Verrie would say, smiling, as if by rote, as if she'd been taught these words, this refrain, almost a song,

by her elders, "—and part of my luck is *I know it*. Except—"
And she sighed wistfully, yet happily too, and we sighed with
her, for there was John Reddy Heart and none of us had *him*.
Six or seven of us crammed breathless into the Olds. Skinny-
haunched Ginger McCord half sitting on Millicent LeRoux's
sturdy lap. We smoked a shared pack of Winstons, a secret
from our parents, who would've been shocked (though most
of them smoked too). As John Reddy Heart was a secret from
our parents. "God! I'd want to die if anyone found out. If *he*
found out," Trish Elders murmured. Her fair skin emitted a
feverish heat. She squirmed in excitement. We laughed but
we were thinking the identical thought. If our parents knew.
If guys at school knew. Shelby Connor said, "*He* wouldn't
tell." Millicent LeRoux said, "That isn't the point. The point
is, we've got our pride. Dignity. We are who we are. I mean—
aren't we?"

"No! No, no!"—we squealed like maniacs.

In Verrie Myers's canary-yellow Olds convertible swinging
into what was called the lower village from the hilly St.
Albans neighborhood at the northern edge of Willowsville
where we lived on the Common, Hampton Hill Drive,
Meridian, Castle Creek, Turnberry, Glen Burns Lane. Passing
at Brompton and Seneca the glimmering-pale Unitarian
church. The Frank Lloyd Wright–designed house where
Smoke Filer lived, slabs of granite, planes of glass, looking at
dusk like a seductively lighted cave. There was our school:
Willowsville Senior High School set back on its ten-acre lot,
bell tower lighted. There was Tug Hill Center, a Revolutionary
War landmark. We turned onto Main Street passing familiar
storefronts, some darkened, some lighted, the Willowsville
Sport Shop, The Bookworm, The Silver Shoppe, Harwood's
Stationers, the Glen Theatre where on weekend evenings we
were taken by our boyfriends often on double or even triple
dates casting sidelong shivery glances at one another and
biting our fastidiously lipsticked lips to keep from dissolving
into peals of unfeminine laughter. *Are you going to kiss your*

date tonight? That guy? That mouth? And what about his tongue,
ugh! And his hands! And—the rest. Zipped up inside his clothes
where you can't see. Verrie slowed the car to cruise past the
Avenue of Fashion (as it was called): our favorite stores were
Laura Ashley, Jonathan Logan, the Village Tartan Shoppe,
Pendleton. We were rich girls but we were kept on strict
allowances. Not one of us had her own credit card. No one at
WHS had a credit card. When money was spent on us, as it
would be, summer camp at Lake Placid, tennis lessons at the
Club, riding lessons, ballet lessons, SAT tutorials, our debuts
at the Buffalo Cotillion, beautiful birthday cars like Verrie
Myers's, our parents would spend lavishly but it was their
prerogative entirely, their generosity. We wouldn't have
believed we were entitled, for we were good moral Protestant
girls anointed with the virtue of *frugality*.

"God! I don't think we should be doing this. Last time—I
got scared we'd be caught. It's kind of—crazy, isn't it?"
Pattianne Groves pleaded. "—I mean, isn't it?"

And now past Spring Street. Mill Street. The Old Eagle
House Inn. The Willowsville Free Library in its 1838 granite-
gray wedge of a building. The Willowsville Police, the
Willowsville Fire Co., the colonial Willowsville Township
Building on Willowsville Green. Traffic was light on Main
Street at this hour of evening: almost nine p.m. Most stores
were closed. Even the Sunoco station was closed. Verrie deftly
timed the Olds to cruise through green lights block after
block at twenty miles per hour—"just like Daddy does." We'd
begun to breathe quickly. We fumbled cigarettes, coughed as
we exhaled smoke. We knew that Pattianne was right. Yet we
couldn't help ourselves. We'd lost John Reddy Heart to his
fate for a year and almost seven months of our young lives
while he'd been at Tomahawk Island and, before that, incarcerated in the Buffalo House of Detention awaiting trial; and
now he was returned to us; how could we help ourselves?—
leaning forward eager and tremulous as songbirds on a wire
in a fierce head wind. "He'll be there. I know." Verrie spoke

softly, as if, like a stage actress, she were uttering prepared words. She exhaled smoke in thin jerky streams. At North Long Street she turned right by Burnham Nurseries and so onto potholed Water Street and across a narrow plank bridge spanning Glen Creek. Our pulses leapt. "Now we can't turn back—can we?" We were in lower Willowsville, a no-man's-land it seemed to us, grassy vacant lots, a hulking railroad overpass, a used car dealer's and smudged-looking stucco buildings, row houses with cramped front yards—a neighborhood so different from the rest of our village it might have been in Cheektowaga, Tonawanda, or Lackawanna or the gritty urban edge of Buffalo itself. Hungrily we stared at the storefronts of John Reddy's neighborhood for we were determined to memorize John Reddy's exterior life. "This is so sad. He's alone. And *here*." Where once he'd lived like us on the Hill. Decades later, some of us could recite in unison the litany of names of Water Street: Gino's Grocery, Ace TV-Radio Repair, Midas Shoe Repair, Glenside Vacuum Cleaner Repair, North China Take-Out with its mysteriously steamed window and glaring fluorescent interior. "When I'm in danger of getting a migraine," Shelby Connor confided in us, at our tenth class reunion, "—it's signaled by a flash of that steam-and-fluorescent. Vague-and-dissolving light and blinding light. And blindness rising in my left eye. North China Take-Out!" We knew what Shelby Connor, through her life a gawky lovely bird-girl of fluttery hand motions and eyes so pale a blue you'd believe you could see through them, meant exactly; yet could not have explained. It was above the North China's perpetually steamed window that John Reddy Heart lived, and this was a fact that filled us with an excitement so immense it verged upon terror.

We were approaching John Reddy's building—three-story sandstone taking up most of the block. Behind it was Glen Creek, invisible from the street; a short block away was the old "historic" water mill, darkened at night. The creek made a murmurous whispering sound. It was Willowsville's single creek, with several waterfall drops, a creek so narrow and picturesque visitors believed it must be man-made, but in fact it was natural, it was *ours*. It seemed right that John Reddy lived by Glen Creek even if, from Verrie's car, we couldn't see the creek. We could hear it, like silk being shaken, shaken, shaken.

"I'm afraid. If he sees us—?"

"I can't believe we're doing this. Oh *God*."

"Who's going to know?"

"If—*he*—"

"*He* would never tell."

Verrie braked her car to a jolting stop. We saw she was excited, clumsy. There were cars parked along the curb and one of them was John Reddy's, a rust-flecked old Mercury that yet exuded an air of sinister seductive power. Just to look at that car, its darkened windows, a cobwebby crack in the rear window, a crooked radio antenna and dented right front fender—"You felt you'd been *in it*. Taken for a fast, rough drive somewhere *unknown*. With *him*."

The Mercury was there, John Reddy was home! We jostled one another leaning over to peer up at his lighted window on the third, top floor of the building. Or what we believed to be John Reddy's window. "Is that it? Are you sure?" "Of course I'm sure! Don't be ridiculous." "Who's being ridiculous? That's an insult." "Shhh! *Look*." We stared, breathless. We saw that the blind at that window had been pulled down carelessly and hung crooked. Possibly it had been tugged off its roller, broken, exactly what an impatient John Reddy might've done. (He had a short, hot, dangerous temper. This temper had been his undoing. We knew.) Anxiously we studied the blind, which was like none we'd ever seen in our homes: the blinds in our homes, selected by our mothers, or interior decorators, were custom-made, elegantly slatted venetian blinds; this blind was parchment-colored, soiled, riddled with cracks. Verrie cried, "Oh!—*look*." "What? Where?" "*Where*?" "Millie, damn—move your *head*." Passing across the inside of the blind there'd come a faint fleeting shadow, blurred like a bird in flight, that might've been the shadow of a human figure, a tall lean young male figure—but we couldn't be sure. Trish Elders said, as if in pain, "That's him. I saw. For a moment." (Trish was the one of us who'd come belatedly to adoring John Reddy, she who'd once laughed at us. Mingled in her feeling for him was a shaken sense of her own judgment, for if she'd been blind and ignorant only a short while ago, mightn't she be blind and ignorant another time?) Shelby cried, "But *where*? My eyes are staring but I can't seem to *see*." Mary Louise Schultz murmured something inarticulate, groaning. For suddenly there was nothing above us but the blank lighted window, a taunting rectangle of opaque light. A grimy window and soiled crooked blind. Pattianne, who was a good Christian girl and never, ever swore, even under her breath, was heard to say huskily, "*Damn*."

Verrie parked the car and gave the command—"Come *on*." She was the first out of the car, panting as if she'd run from St. Albans Hill to here. The rest of us climbed out timorously and were surprised to discover the night air so chill, moist and almost hurtful to our nostrils. "Like the very air, the smell and taste of the air, was different in John Reddy's neighborhood. Downhill, like at the bottom of a well." We realized it was November already, winter imminent. A hurtful bright moon like bone glared above us. "Oh, God. *Oh*." We clutched at one another. Hands grappled hands, icy cold. There seemed to be too many hands—too many icy fingers. From somewhere above (John Reddy's window had been opened by about six inches, you could imagine him shoving it up with his muscled arms, scowling, impatient because the room was overheated and stuffy) came a sound of blues music—heavy, percussive, *adult*. It wasn't the simple pop-rock music we listened to. In that instant we knew that our fates would be a single fate: we were virgin Willowsville girls and would remain virgin Willowsville girls all our lives. Though John

Reddy would be our first lover, our virginity would grow back. We were impenetrable. This virginity, like a curse, would persist through our brave, desperate attempts at adulthood. Through our marriages, our plunges into motherhood and adultery. Through separations, "nervous breakdowns," divorces, second marriages, further motherhood. (Mary Louise Schultz, seemingly not so competitive a cheerleader as the rest of us, would have the most babies: four.) We were virgins in memory of John Reddy Heart and those lovesick nights on Water Street, on the downside of town.

Thinking *Our fathers would kill us if they knew!*

Thinking *Our mothers would die of envy. We can't tell them.*

One of us, it might've been Millie LeRoux (of all good girls, a Sunday school teacher at the First Episcopal Church, a Girl Scout, a Student Council officer, with beautiful calm eyes) suddenly cupped her hands to her mouth and called yearningly, "John Reddy! John *Red-dy*!" Appalled, another of us, it might've been Shelby Connor, or Trish Elders, moved to quiet her—"Shhhh!"—and Millie whirled in frantic reaction, driving an elbow into the other's breast, which, fortunately, was cushioned by her WHS cheerleader's jacket. Mary Louise Schultz astonished us by moaning, "John Red-dy! *John!*" Verrie groaned as if she were being tortured, swaying, big-eyed, yanking at her wind-whipped blond pageboy hair. For what was to prevent us from calling for John Reddy Heart, screaming like young female cats in the throes of their first incandescent heat? What if? And why not? Did it matter that John Reddy Heart had killed a man, and a stark-naked man at that, discharging a .45-caliber bullet into his brain in an instant of passion never to be reversed, erased, or even comprehended? Did it matter that John Reddy Heart was condemned and feared by our elders, most of all our appalled fathers? Did it matter that though adoring him we were terrified of him? That his touch would have paralyzed us? There seemed nothing to prevent us from rushing up the dim-lit stairs of that shabby building on Water Street to pound on

John Reddy's door crying "Killer-Boy! Killer-Boy! Let us in! Help us!" How decent sane good-girl behavior was the thinnest of membranes that might be ripped in an instant the way, in the hope of minimizing pain, you tear a bandage off a small wound you believe has healed.

Next morning and all the mornings to follow for years! the tale told, retold! at our high school with its redbrick opulence and Doric columns that was our unacknowledged church in those heated adolescent years, over the telephone lines connecting individuals as in a massive X ray of a single brain's circuits every household of significance in and surrounding the sacred Village of Willowsville. And through the Village—on the streets, the sidewalks we'd memorized from early childhood. In Nico's, in the Crystal, in Greek Gardens, in the Haven, in La Casa di Napoli Pizzeria & Restaurant, at the lunch counter at Muller's Drugs, in the mirrored foyer of the Glen Theatre. Breathless the tale of that night John Reddy Heart opened his door to those unnamed girls of the Circle who'd come to him in secret. Their pale flowerlike faces, their fevered eyes. Taking these girls one by one by their chill trembling hands and leading them into his bedroom. Laughing at their fearfulness. Their shyness. Their luminous-beautiful young-girl bodies stripped of the disguise of their clothes. John Reddy Heart making love to each of the girls in turn. And more than once, in turn. The sexiest boy. The sweetest boy. And the most gentle, because so practiced. Six girls, or seven. In some accounts eight. Ten! A dozen! John Reddy would've been equal to the challenge. John Reddy would've grinned saying Sure, why not? Kissing the girls each in turn, and at that moment she was the sole girl of all the world. And afterward he'd keep quiet about it. That wild night on Water Street! John Reddy Heart wasn't the type of boy to boast about girls he made out with, ever. Or women. Not the type to boast about anything—if you were John Reddy, what need? You'd trust John Reddy with your virginity. With your reputation. With your life. A keeper of sacred secrets, John Reddy Heart.

It wasn't like that.

Instead, we lost courage.

A cold drizzle was perceived to be falling, blown slantwise by an unfriendly wind. Overhead the bone-bright moon that had contributed to our madness was being blown away like crumpled trash. On Water Street a car's headlights blinded us approaching and passing and we hid our heated faces in terror of being recognized. Except for Verrie who, in a trance, was rummaging through a filth-stained green plastic garbage can at the curb. We whispered, "Verrie, what are you doing? Verrie!" Verrie Myers had attained schoolwide fame the previous spring playing Shakespeare's Portia. Her presence on stage, unnaturally highlighted, had riveted us all. That moon-shaped face like a cameo we hadn't realized was *beauty* until then. The way in which, assured, dreamlike, she'd delivered her lines. Who knew if Veronica Myers could act, and who cared? In awe we'd stared and stared. Mr. Lepage, our sexy drama teacher who devastated us with his witty sarcasm, stared at her in awe. There was Verrie Myers who was our friend, a girl like the rest of us since kindergarten at the Academy Street School but up on stage she was transformed, a girl we hardly recognized. Now on Water Street, shivering beneath John Reddy's window, we stared in astonishment at Verrie dipping her hands into trash and sloppily bagged garbage. There was a strong smell of coffee grounds, a stink of rancid meat. Yet Verrie didn't hesitate, plunged to the elbows. Her pink-pearlescent manicured nails! the opal keepsake ring on her right hand her boyfriend since ninth grade Kenny Fischer had given her! The silver I.D. bracelet on her left wrist identical to the bracelets all the girls of the Circle, and other girls in emulation of us, owned. Verrie cried, "I got it! Here!" What had she snatched up?—we pulled her to the car, idling all this while at the curb, prepared to escape. (There were customers at the North China eyeing us curiously. What if someone knew us? And cars were passing in the street. John Reddy would hear the commotion and look

out his window and possibly recognize Verrie Myers's yellow
convertible.)

Verrie shifted the car into gear violently and drove us away,
to safety we thought, we prayed. Swerving on wetted pavement. She was driving too fast for these narrow roads, we
could scarcely recognize our surroundings—Beechwood? The
bottom of Mill Street? Chalmers? Taking the back way home,
the long way home, careful to avoid Main Street, crossing
Glen Creek over a sturdy metal bridge at Garrison, and now
past darkened, featureless Tug Hill Park and Battlefield from
which all visitors were officially banned at sunset—"The
Bloodiest Single-Skirmish Battle of the Revolution, August 2,
1777." What spiritual influence this bloody battle of nearly
two centuries before exerted upon our Willowsville generation was never made clear to us; what agitated ripples in
consciousness across the decades, what dreams of reckless
and even self-destructive heroism; what visionary hunger to
locate in the world the origin of our most vivid and powerful
dreams. *Even if the search is futile—even if!* The mysterious
lightweight object Verrie had discovered in the garbage can
was being passed among us with excitement, shyness, some
initial skepticism and even repugnance. As Verrie whispered,
thrillingly, "His mouth touched this. *His actual mouth.*" Not
many years after this luminous night there would float across
how many hundreds, thousands of movie screens in America
the gigantic so-beautiful face of Veronica Myers in her film
debut and we who gazed upon it with anxious affection
would recall this moment, the demented drama of this
moment, Verrie's whispered words which several times she
repeated as if in the presence of the deaf—"His mouth. *John
Reddy Heart's actual mouth.*" Ginger McCord whispered back,
frightened, "Verrie, you're crazy." Was Verrie performing,
merely? Or is *performing* our truest human nature? Less certainly, Mary Louise Schultz whispered, "You're all crazy." Yet
by degrees the realization was sinking in. Even as Verrie's car
sped homeward, away from the lower village. Of course. Of

course! One of us, it may have been Trish Elders, the least
likely among us, touched the can's opening, the mouthlike
aperture, with a reverent finger; as we stared, she brought
her lips to it, shyly. God!—we felt the visceral charge deep in
the pit of Trish's belly. Her soft lips, the sharp-eyed aperture!
And in that instant we saw John Reddy carelessly yanking off
the pull top, in that quick brisk matter-of-fact way in which
boys yanked off pull tops, so very different from the more
cautious, timid (for what if the liquid inside fizzes up, spills)
way in which girls yanked off pull tops; how many times
we'd surreptitiously witnessed such an act, John Reddy out
back in the school parking lot, at noon: the yanking-off of a
pull top, the tossing away, the lifting to the mouth, to drink.
Inside Verrie's can, which was slightly dented, there was a
pungently, sweetly chemical smell; if you shook the can
gently you could hear a remote, liquidy sound, a faint roaring
like the sound of a seashell pressed against the ear. An empty
Coke can, tossed away amid smelly trash. "His mouth. His
actual mouth!" We began to laugh, to hyperventilate. We
were choked, scandalized, incredulous. "*John Reddy Heart's
actual mouth touched this.*"

The Coke can would be Verrie Myers's to cherish, forever.
She was the one of us to have snatched it from oblivion.

2

John Reddy came out of the west,
John Reddy came out of the west.
John Reddy came to us out of the west.
John Reddy, John Reddy Heart.

Does God play dice with the universe? We knew better.
Not because we were rich men's sons. Anyway, not all
of us. There was a reason that John Reddy Heart came to live
in Willowsville, it couldn't have been just accident. Every
guy in Willowsville of a certain age, twelve through twenty,
and many unacknowledged others besides, liked it that John
Reddy Heart who was our classmate had killed a man, an
actual adult man, *an actual adult man like our fathers* (except
you could argue, like Dwayne Hewson, that Melvin Riggs was
more like our fathers than any of our fathers truly were), but
we didn't like it that he was caught. Tracked down by bloodhounds in the Adirondacks when we'd come to believe he'd
escaped to Canada, we'd wanted to believe he'd escaped to
Canada. Beaten by New York State troopers and hauled off in
handcuffs like a captured wild animal. And that picture of
John Reddy in the papers—his face bloodied, eye swollen
shut but there he was standing straight between cops with his
head high, defiant, unshaven and battered but that cool *Fuck
you* look in his face we loved and tried to emulate without
much success. Arrested, made to stand trial and winding up

in this crummy place in the Niagara River, Tomahawk Island Youth Camp. "The first boy ever from the Village of Willowsville to be incarcerated at any state 'youth facility.'"

It hurt us that John Reddy disappeared from our school for a year and a half. So many months! This kid that, as a sopho-more, already had his basketball and track letters. He'd come close to breaking the Wolverine record, dating back to 1941, for points scored in a single season in competitive basketball, and would've broken it his junior year if he hadn't killed Mr. Riggs instead.

If he'd kept on scoring the way he was, through senior year, as everybody expected, John Reddy would've had his pick of basketball scholarships to Syracuse, Cornell, Ohio State, Indiana. We just knew.

"It's a tragic fate. Like a Greek goddam tragedy like—Sophocles, Homer. My heart is broken for that boy." This was the statement our coach Woody McKeever made every time he was asked about John Reddy, and he was asked about John Reddy a lot.

We felt the same way, mostly. Guys at WHS who were John Reddy's classmates, or a little older or younger than he was. Not that we went around saying so. *My heart is broken*. Hell, no.

Still, our hearts were broken. It was like a death. Such tragic goddam bad luck, like Coach said.

The girls. The girls were all crazy for John Reddy, it got sort of embarrassing sometimes. Not that we were jealous. Maybe we were jealous, a few of us, like Ken Fischer who'd been crazy for Verrie Myers since kindergarten, like Dougie Siefried who'd had a crush on all the girls of the Circle, especially Ginger McCord and Shelby Connor, like Art Lutz who'd had a crush on Mary Louise Schultz since seventh grade and con-fessed of dreaming of her, every goddam night of his life—"And she doesn't know I exist! And doesn't care." Dwayne Hewson who was Pattianne Groves's steady under-stood that, deep in her "secret girl heart, that I or nobody else is gonna penetrate," Pattianne Groves was in love with John Reddy Heart, and so was Millie LeRoux, and little Trish Elders. And others. How many others! We were jealous but we could comprehend the logic. Like the song said, *John Reddy came out of the West*, and not one of us would've remained ourselves if we could have changed into John Reddy Heart so how in all conscience could we blame our girl classmates?—"They're only human, too."

Still, we didn't talk about it like the girls did—the arrest, the detention, the trials and the Tomahawk Island incarceration. We brooded. Years later our wives, these strange, somehow accidental females we'd end up marrying, having kids with, would accuse us of "refusing to share"—"refusing to communicate"—"bottling up everything inside"—"passive-aggressive manipulation"—and we'd protest, *Jesus Christ what do you want me to say? what do you want me to* say? but deep inside we'd understand, yes it was so. Some of us would remain married—like Bert Fox said (though maybe Bert wasn't a good example, he'd finally kill himself), it was like taking a deep breath and diving back down into the very water you'd almost drowned in because what the hell else are you going to do? where the hell else are you going to go? and some of us, the more reckless, the more desperate, the more luckless, and a few "problem drinkers," bankrupts and crazed adulterers would get divorced, not invariably of our own volition, but we'd never become hysterical, never displayed our emotions in public like girls do, or did back in Willowsville in the time of John Reddy Heart: wearing red sequin hearts on their sleeves, for instance, or scattered in their hair, during John Reddy's trials. And bursting into tears when nobody expected it. *We* coolly distanced ourselves from such behavior, knowing that John Reddy, never a guy to complain (say he'd pulled a muscle running track or got hit hard in the ribs on the basketball court, or even fouled to the groin—you'd see his face go white, and beads of sweat pop out, but that was all), would've been embarrassed as hell by such excess. Eyes averted, with a little frown he'd ignore the special cheers for him the varsity cheerleaders had worked up—

> John Reddy we're ready!
> John Reddy we're rea-dy!
> Mmmmm JOHN REDDY WE'RE REA-DDYY!
> YAYYYY!

And the crowd in the gym went wild cheering, clapping, whistling, stamping their feet till the floor rocked, the overhead lights vibrated. Dougie Siefried sighed and laughed sadly, saying in some dreams of his such a cheer was aimed at *him*, and his heart bathed in a feeling of such happiness he knew it was heaven, or as close to heaven as he'd be likely to get, but John Reddy scowled and wiped his face on his jersey in that way he had, like he didn't care if hundreds of people were watching, or wasn't even aware. "You don't play to the crowd. You play to the basket"—John Reddy once remarked to Dwayne Hewson.

So we liked it O.K. (even Artie Riggs, a nephew of the murdered man, thought it was "kind of cool") what John Reddy'd done, though we knew better than to say so publicly. But the way John Reddy's life was permanently screwed up afterward—that was something else, that made us think. That scared us. Like Mr. Cuthbert our social studies teacher said, lecturing at the front of the classroom, pacing excitedly about, his owl eyes mournful and bright behind his glasses— "Students! Consider! How the moments of your lives have been rushing toward you without your comprehension, like the Niagara River rushing above the falls, and you can't see the falls, and you make a split-second decision, behaving in a way we might designate as X"—and here Mr. Cuthbert chalked a swooping X on the blackboard, as if we couldn't follow his reasoning otherwise—"and just possibly X is no more and no less than you've been genetically programmed by millennia of ancestors and by the fact that you're Texas-born and reared in the West and conditioned by your familial and cultural environment to be hotheaded and impetuous and prone to acting spontaneously with your fists or whatever's at hand—so in that fatal split second you take up a gun you aren't even certain is loaded, drop to one knee as John Reddy Heart allegedly did and fire off a shot into your opponent's head—into his brain—and both of you are pierced by that bullet. *Your life forever afterward is changed.*"

Mr. Cuthbert had a point. A profound point. You do X, your life's X. So changed, you could say *it isn't your life any longer*.

* * *

The first person in all of Willowsville to set eyes on John Reddy Heart was—Ketch Campbell.

The sighting occurred right on Main Street, near Willow, at the heart of our four-block downtown as it's called. Thirty years later, Willowsville's downtown will have spread as far as Haggarty Road to the east and Burlingham Avenue to the west—with a shopping plaza set back on Spring Street, and a medical center on Garrison—but when the Heart family arrived downtown was those four blocks you could stroll in less than ten minutes or ride your bike through in three minutes. A succession of glittering stores and storefronts memorized as in a recurring dream of such comfort and assurance it seems not a dream at all but an inviolable and permanent reality solid as a substratum of granite. Ketch would claim it was precisely 4:08 P.M. by the tower clock at the Metropolitan Life Building. The day was warm-muggy like the inside of, say, a Coke bottle. No air stirring. A July afternoon when John Reddy Heart first appeared in Willowsville, approximately four and a half years before he would shoot Melvin Riggs, Jr., down dead in an upstairs bedroom in an old Dutch Colonial house in the most prestigious neighborhood of Willowsville, less than two miles from Main Street at Willow.

Ketch was downtown (with his mom who was taking him to Buster Brown's for new sneakers—but this never figures in the story) when he happened to notice "this weird, wild, bright-salmon-colored Caddie pulling a U-Haul trailer with Nevada license plates" moving a little too fast, sort of impatiently, weaving out of the ten-mile-per-hour lady-shopper traffic on Main Street. "You could tell immediately," Ketch said, "before even you saw the skinny underage kid who was driving, or noticed the plates, that these were folks from somewhere else. Somewhere *far else*." Ketch who'd been one of those nervous twitchy fattish kids always running and puffing trying to keep up with the rest of the guys. He'd learned to tell this story in the right way, like every factor in the equation, including of course eleven-year-old Ketch Campbell (he'd never mention his age if he could help it), had to be what it was, absolute and fixed. He'd speak excitedly sometimes, you couldn't interrupt but had to let him tell it start to finish. And each time the story got a little longer, more like a movie.

The Caddie was a Bel Air possibly five years old. Painted a Day-Glo pinkish-orange, a misconceived repaint job that made your eyes pinch but you couldn't look away. (Others on Main Street, including Ketch's mom, must've been staring, too. Willowsville's that kind of place, alert to intruders, invaders.) This Caddie, amid the boring beige, buff, matte gray, black-green, black-blue, classy black-black of the other cars on Main Street on this typical summer afternoon. Also, the front and rear bumpers of the Caddie were stippled with rust. The car was low-slung, dragging its muffler and listing just perceptibly to one side. There was a long wicked dent like a lightning zigzag running the full length of the car's left side and the left rear door (out of whose rolled-down window a fierce old white-haired and -whiskered man in a cowboy hat was gazing in Ketch's direction) appeared to be wired shut. "Yet, Jesus! The car was beautiful."

And there was John Reddy Heart behind the wheel. His name unknown.

John Reddy, only eleven years old! Seated on three Las Vegas phone directories so he could peer over the steering wheel and along the shiny-glaring hood of the car. Ketch had to admit he'd never have guessed that the boy driving the Caddie was so young—his own age—later he'd figure, we'd all figure, that, out West, kids grow up faster, with more purpose than those of us in the East—but it was obvious the boy was too young to be licensed. Unless he was a midget or a dwarf, and he didn't appear to be either. Ketch said, "He looked maybe thirteen. Kind of olivish-dark. Not foreign-looking exactly—well, possibly a little Indian—I mean, American Indian—I realize they aren't 'foreign,' but—you know what I mean. Anyway this kid's sort of—strange. Exotic you might say. Did I mention the sideburns? Like Elvis. With really dark aviator-style sunglasses like an adult man would wear, and a straw hat like a fedora with I think a red band"— though in alternate versions of the story told over the years and eventually decades Ketch would swear he recalled John Reddy wearing a cowboy hat (like his grandfather in the rear seat) or, yet more unlikely, a Buffalo Hawks baseball cap— "and a baggy white T-shirt. And a watch on his left wrist, sort of a big, pilot-style watch." The kid was maneuvering the Caddie and the U-Haul (a clumsy vehicle about the size of a Volkswagen) through Willowsville traffic like a quick, impatient creature, a fox for instance, through a herd of slow-moving sheep. Mrs. LeRoux was backing her Lincoln Continental out of a parking space in front of Fleda Vetch Intimate Apparel in that blind-cautious way of our lady shoppers and the kid in the Caddie punches his horn with a balled fist and eases past, just missing the Lincoln's rear left fender by a feather. And there's Mrs. Marsh maneuvering her bottle-green Mercedes into a tight space in front of Waterford Wedgwood like a woman maneuvering into a tight girdle, and the kid driving the Caddie coolly leans on his horn and eases past her—Jesus!—by a fraction of a feather. If you know Willowsville you know that during shopping hours in the

area called the Avenue of Fashion, there are always women—
wives, mothers, grandmothers—youngish, middle-aged,
elderly—the third fingers of their left hands glittering with
expensive stones, maneuvering their expensive cars in, and
out, of parking spaces. In, and out, of parking spaces. In front
of Scroop's Shoes, the Bookworm, Gucci, Jonathan Logan,
Waterford Wedgwood. In front of pink-mantled the Bon Ton
Shop. Village Florist. The Village Tartan Shoppe. Laura
Ashley. The Crystal Tearoom & Sweet Shop. Voss Jewelers.
The Gift Box. Fleda Vetch Intimate Apparel. The English
Shoppe. Pendleton. The impatient kid in the Caddie sounded
his car horn and our Willowsville ladies yielded.

Ketch watched fascinated. "It was, like, a historic moment
I guess. And none of us aware. Except somehow, it's hard to
say and I don't want to exaggerate, but—you *know*."

This was plausible. To a degree. But Ketch couldn't help
but push too far, claiming that he'd seen a gun, an actual
gun, lying on the rear window ledge of the Caddie. "It had to
be it—the murder-weapon-to-be. What else?" The .45-cal-
iber Colt revolver that would be revealed, in time, as
registered in Nevada in the name of Aaron Leander Heart,
John Reddy's grandfather. Bullshit, we retorted. Typical Ketch
bullshit. Say the old man might have been carrying the gun
on his lap (though that's doubtful), or the gun might've been
on the front seat between John Reddy and his sleeping
mother (even more doubtful), but why would it have been in
full view on the rear window ledge? Matt Trowbridge, the
Willowsville traffic cop shortly to flag John Reddy down,
would emphasize that there was *no firearm* visible anywhere
in the Hearts' car that afternoon—"You think I wouldn't have
noticed? Christ, I'm a police officer. I'm not *blind*." But Ketch
persisted: he'd seen the gun. Stubbornly through the years as
he faded from the muscular swagger and grating hee-haw
laugh of adolescence to the morose-ironic pallor-pudginess of
a middle-aged CPA at an undistinguished Buffalo money-
management company, acquiring a wife, children, the

incalculable complexities of adulthood, the one among us who'd first sighted John Reddy Heart and for whom this first sighting would be the defining feature of his otherwise insignificant boyhood—"I saw that gun. I saw it somehow. I saw John Reddy and I saw his mother and I saw the gun *and I saw them in the same moment.*"

Of course it was Willowsville patrolman Matt Trowbridge, at that time assigned to downtown traffic duty, whose testimony was more reliable. If you deducted some for a cop having to protect his professional reputation. Thirty-two years old on that July afternoon, not young, but youthful, up-and-coming in the small village police force, idealistic, energetic, slightly disappointed (in secret) that he'd ended up in suburban cop work and not gritty urban work, packed a gun he'd never have to use, and would rarely remove from its holster while on duty, Trowbridge would long recall staring in disbelief—"What the hell?"—as the Day-Glo pinkish-orange Cadillac tugging a swaying battered U-Haul with Nevada plates cruised through the intersection of Main and Willow even as the yellow traffic light turned to red, maneuvering its way with bold, insolent agility around a pigeon-colored Cadillac Eldorado that had just braked to a proper stop. Trowbridge blew his whistle—that loud, shrill, ear-piercing whistle that was like a sexual clarion call—and flagged the driver down, and stalked over to confront him. "And, Christ, it's a *kid*. I mean a young kid, not twelve years old." The boy cast Trowbridge a look he could only interpret as pissed, not scared. Annoyed, not worried. Trowbridge saw the boy's lips move in a silent but unmistakable expletive—*Shit*.

A kid wearing man-sized aviator sunglasses with almost-black lenses. A man-sized hat (a straw fedora, for the record, with a dark band). His Indian-black hair longish, sideburns on his cheeks. His skin tone olive-tan. Young, yet not young somehow: he hadn't the muscles of a boy but the sinewy shoulder and arm muscles of a man who's been doing outdoor work.

"It flashed through my mind, it's Police Academy training: *This kid, this car, these folks might be dangerous*. The Nevada plates sort of spooked me." Swiftly Trowbridge took in what he could see of the car's other occupants, just a family it seemed, kids in the back, oldish man, sleeping woman in the front passenger seat. No sign of trouble. There might've been something odd about these folks, but they didn't look dangerous. Trowbridge was staring at the woman in front, evidently sleeping, her blond head resting against a pillow and her face shielded from the sun by a thin white veil—"It came to me it was a bridal veil. The woman was wearing all *white*." Behind the sleeping woman was a scowling gentleman in his late sixties, hatchet-faced, with iron-gray eyebrows like fierce caterpillars, wearing a soiled cowboy hat and glaring at the traffic officer—"He looked like a real old-West character. But I could see his hands, he was unarmed." Beside the old man was a plump-faced girl of about six, who looked frightened; beside her, a boy of about nine, thin-faced and frightened, blinking at the patrolman through round, smudged eyeglasses. Both children sat hunched forward, their fists clenched on their knees as if the car's momentum had thrown them nearly off the soiled plush seat. (In time, Trowbridge would embellish this episode. He'd recall that old Mr. Heart "gave off an odor of malt whisky you could smell yards away. If he'd been driving, I'd have had to run him in for DWI." The boy, Farley Heart, in young adulthood to distinguish himself in a computer-related field about which Trowbridge would know nothing, had, he recalled, been "calculating on some sort of plastic gizmo" the way another child, restless and bored on a lengthy car trip, might play with a toy. The girl, Shirleen Heart, one day to be Sister Mary Agatha of the Sisters of Charity, was as Trowbridge recalled squinting into a "heavy black Bible in her lap and moving her lips—like begging God to intervene. And maybe He did.")

In fact Trowbridge hadn't paid much attention to the passengers in the back of the Caddie except to ascertain that they were nonthreatening. It was the sleeping woman, the gorgeous woman in white, who drew his interest. She was waking, slowly; murmuring something petulant to the boy behind the wheel, who grunted an inaudible reply; just possibly, the boy had nudged her in the leg to wake her. The veil still over her face, she yawned loudly, and stretched her shapely bare arms; she arched her back, with amazing results—her heavy, voluptuous breasts strained against a low-cut halter sweater of fine-knit white nylon, the nipples defined like beads. Trowbridge stared, mesmerized. His mouth had gone dry. There was a roaring in his ears. *She's somebody I know—isn't she? Somebody I know. Who loves me.* The woman wore white linen slacks that fitted her body snugly; her stomach was rounded, not plump but firm flesh like a peach; there was a scent as of ripe, or overripe, fruit about her; perfumy perspiration, talcumy deodorant; the halter sweater was low-cut, like no sweater any woman of her age would wear in Willowsville; it had ridden up at her waist to reveal the soft pale flesh of her midriff. Her hair, bone-blond, was frizzed to her shoulders in a girlish style. Trowbridge murmured, "Ma'am? Excuse me?"

"That's my mom. She's kind of tired," the boy said quickly. "We been driving a long distance today . . . sir." The boy was sitting as straight as possible, trying to appear taller, and older. He spoke in a liquidy drawl Trowbridge recognized as Southern, Southwestern. Trowbridge asked his name, and the boy answered, "John Reddy Heart, sir." Trowbridge asked his age, and the boy said, with a childlike dip of his head, "My age? I don't know exactly. There's a birthday coming up, I think. My mom would know. . . ." The boy had removed his sunglasses in a gesture of abnegation. Trowbridge saw he was sweating. Pinpricks of anxious sweat on his forehead, on his short upper lip. He'd have been a good-looking kid, with wavy black hair, deep-socketed thick-lashed eyes with irises so intense and dark they bled into the pupils, except for the strain, the anxiety. *Eyes of a child who's seen too much and knows it isn't over yet, he'll be seeing more.* "Well, son," Trowbridge said, "you don't have a driver's license, I guess?" The boy smiled hard, and said, "Yes, sir. I do." Trowbridge said, surprised, "You do? *You?* May I see it, please?" There was a moment's pause. The boy was still smiling but seemed not to have heard Trowbridge's request. "And the registration for this vehicle?" The boy glanced at the woman beside him, who was still not quite awake, and said, reluctantly, "Yes, sir." He opened a woman's straw handbag on the seat between them and rummaged about inside it, pushing aside jars of makeup, an inexpensive pressed-powder compact, bejeweled tubes of lipstick and kiss-blotted tissues (Trowbridge would dream uneasily of *kiss-blotted tissues*, that very night) and an alligator-hide wallet swollen with money, credit cards, and color snapshots; out of the wallet he extracted a driver's license and a car registration, which he handed to Trowbridge and which Trowbridge examined frowning. He said, "Son. This driver's license belongs to one 'Dahlia Magdalena Heart, blond hair, green eyes, five-foot five and a hundred nineteen pounds'—you trying to say that's you?" The boy who'd identified himself as John Reddy Heart fixed his deep-socketed eyes on Trowbridge's and said, still courteously, "Sir, you asked if I have a driver's license, and I do. Technically, it's my mom's. Dahlia Magdalena Heart is my mom."

Startled, Trowbridge laughed. He hadn't meant to, and not so harshly. "Yes, son, but you happen to be driving this vehicle, not your mother. *You're* in violation of New York State vehicular law." Stubbornly the boy said, "O.K., like you say I'm 'driving' the car, but my mom's directing me. It's her car. I was just doing what she told me. It's none of my fault if the light changed while I was under it, I'd have gotten through except somebody blocked me, people don't know how to drive here!—jeez. *I* didn't break any law." Trowbridge smiled, had to admit he was entertained by this cocky little fellow, touched by something desperate in the boy's face. By now Trowbridge's keen eye had taken in the stack of phone directories upon which the boy was seated, the wrinkled khaki shorts that appeared too large for him, his scabby knees, grimy bare feet. And the impressive, adult-looking wristwatch on the boy's left arm, its face complex with numerals and dials, its worn brown leather band wadded with adhesive tape to make it fit. Trowbridge thought, *His dad's watch.* He felt pity sniffing the rank animal smell that lifted from the boy, the odor of worry. But he was a police officer, knew his duty, and it wasn't to be sentimental over such folks, strangers to Willowsville and, who knew, a threat to law-abiding taxpaying residents, saying sternly, "'John Reddy Heart' you call yourself?—you've committed a moving violation, son, and you appear to be a minor lacking a proper license. And your mother is an accessory. I'm sorry, but I'm going to have to—"

The veil slipped seductively from Dahlia Heart's face.

So it would come to pass that Patrol Officer Matt Trowbridge of the Willowsville Police Department would be the first individual in our village to set eyes upon "The White Dahlia."

Except: by one of those mysterious coincidences that thread through our lives, arguing for, not mere chance, but fate, destiny, purpose, if but the cruel purpose of cosmic irony, at that very moment Mrs. Herman Skelton, Irma Skelton, happened to be driving her gleaming dark-green Lincoln past the offensively bright-hued old Cadillac parked at the curb, and would afterward claim that she'd gotten a clear look at a "heavily made-up, coarsely 'glamorous' woman making a shameful provocative appeal to a young traffic officer—obviously with the intention of being spared a ticket." How embittered Mrs. Skelton, Herman's wife of twenty-six years, would be, in time, by the role this "glamorous woman" would play in her life.

And, additionally: there came Suzi Zeigler and her boyfriend Roger Zwaart, hardly more than children at the time, though, thrown together by alphabetical seating since first grade at the Academy Street School, they'd long been a steady, devoted couple by seventh grade, and would afterward claim that they, too, had a fleeting glimpse of the woman to be known as Mrs. Heart—and the boy John Reddy—while pedaling their bicycles on Main Street in the direction of the Tug Hill swimming pool; they'd noticed the Cadillac and U-Haul and Nevada plates and a uniformed officer leaning in the car window "and these strange-looking people, these sort of freaky, misfit people," Suzi began, and Roger intervened as often he did, completing Suzi's wayward sentences, "—so we knew whoever they were had to be special. Freaky or misfit possibly but *special*."

In the Cadillac, Dahlia Heart was asking Trowbridge what seemed to be the problem in a warm, fluid Western accent more honeyed than the boy's, and Trowbridge, mildly dazed, began to explain, and the boy began to explain, and Dahlia Heart laid a hand, a beautiful beringed hand, on the boy's surprisingly muscled shoulder—"John-ny, you *hush*. This is between the officer and me now." And again Trowbridge tried to explain (the running of the red light, the boy's age) but his voice came out sounding, not authoritarian, but apologetic, for he'd have to admit afterward he'd never seen such eyes in any human face—"'Sea green' you could call them but actually more like some kind of jewel, what's it—emerald?—" Trowbridge would grope for words, not being by nature a man of words, and never had he seen such a perfect female face, a beautiful face, dazzling and luminous and of a kind to be magnified to gigantic goddess proportions on a movie screen; and all this while Dahlia Heart leaned earnestly in Trowbridge's direction even as Trowbridge earnestly leaned into the rolled-down window of the parked car, past the now silent, frowning boy, Trowbridge was like one being sucked into a vacuum, the V neck of the blond woman's halter top straining with the weight of her breasts. Dahlia Heart was pleading for understanding, and sympathy: she had "sensitive eyes" and a "congenital propensity for migraine headaches";

she'd been driving that morning since Cairo, Illinois, and was exhausted, so she'd asked her son to take over at the wheel as often she did, it was just a practical maneuver, he'd drive while she rested her eyes a little, covering them with the veil, but able to watch the road through the veil, and never sleeping of course, she'd been fully awake and fully conscious all the time. "My son is almost twelve, Officer. He has the intelligence and driving skills of any sixteen-year-old. Back home in the Southwest it's common for young boys to drive cars, trucks, tractors, combines—it's common for them to do a man's work. And Johnny is a better driver than I am, in fact." Trowbridge's face was painfully flushed. "Yes ma'am," he said uncomfortably. "But the boy is a minor and doesn't have a valid New York State license. And—" Dahlia Heart cried impatiently, her eyes shimmering with hurt, "Officer, haven't I explained? I was awake. I was directing him. It's a method we've worked out, Johnny and me, for long-distance driving. The boy may slide behind the wheel but it's really me, his mother, who drives. The boy is my medium behind the wheel. I'm the adult responsible. I'm the mother. I'm the mother of this child and of these two others"—she indicated the shy, cowering boy and girl in the back seat—"and if you must deal with anyone, it's me." This odd impassioned speech left both the woman and Matt Trowbridge slightly breathless. Those "sea-green" eyes. And a glisten of talcumy damp in the cleavage between her breasts. "And that is my father, Aaron Leander Heart, Officer. He doesn't say much but he's one hundred percent alert and reliable helping out if Johnny needs help—aren't you, Daddy?"

The old man, wild-white-haired, with deep ironic creases in both cheeks, a burnt-cork flush to his face, muttered what sounded like, "Why sure."

It did flash through Trowbridge's dazzled mind *That old guy might be armed* but in the next instant, staring at Dahlia Heart, who was smiling at him, so reasonably, so intelligently, he'd forgotten the thought, or any thought at all. Snapping shut his packet of traffic tickets and shoving them, quick and embarrassed, back into his pocket. Every word this woman Dahlia Magdalena Heart had said made perfect sense.

Omitted from Matt Trowbridge's account of his initial encounter with the Heart family was the fact that, as a Willowsville police officer, one of the younger members of a police force noted for its civility and courtesy to Willowsville residents, if not invariably to nonresidents, especially non-residents with darker than Caucasian skin, he'd felt obliged to escort the family to their new home in the St. Albans Hill neighborhood. For of course they were strangers to the village's tricky "lanes"—"drives"—"passes"—"circles"— "ways"—and "places." For of course they'd have gotten hopelessly lost without his assistance. Trowbridge leapt onto his motorscooter to lead the way; Dahlia Heart, who'd traded places with little Johnny, followed in the Cadillac, driving cautiously, the U-Haul in tow. North on Spring Green Lane Trowbridge led them, a quick right east onto Lilac Lane, again north on Meridian Boulevard in the direction of the old historic village and of the old, grand Willowsville estates, another uphill mile to elm-sheltered, sequestered Meridian Place where he might have been surprised, if he'd been thinking coherently, and not distracted by afterimages of Dahlia Heart like those mysterious, seductive yet elusive dream residues that continue to haunt us long after we wake from sleep, to pursue him through weeks, months and eventually years, for the primary and most enduring sexual organ in the human male is the eye—he might have been surprised to discover that the Hearts' destination was the stately if rundown old Dutch Colonial house at 8 Meridian Place between better-kept properties owned by the Aickley Thruns and the G. George Bannisters. Trowbridge would have assumed, like any Willowsville resident, that this landmark house had been owned by the Edgihoffer family since the death of the retired Colonel Esdras Edgihoffer, whose obituary he'd read a few weeks ago in both the *Buffalo Evening News* and the *Willowsville Weekly Gazette*.

"Is this it, Mrs. Heart? *This?*"

"It is, Officer." Splendid the woman Dahlia Heart stood in the sun, whitely blinding as a vision. Radiant face of no age Trowbridge could have stated with certainty (no more than twenty-five or -six, he'd have inaccurately sworn), the bone-pale luxuriant hair, her sea-green eyes that weakened his knees. And the shining key held aloft in her fingers—the key to Willowsville itself.

"Thank you for your kindness today, Officer, which I will never forget."

He murmured ma'am it was only just his duty.

Years would pass. If not tragically, for there is no tragedy in Willowsville, then sadly. Before Matt Trowbridge would again exchange words with Dahlia Heart. Or even come into her presence again. Though glimpsing the woman frequently, alone or in the company of men; less frequently, in the company of her own children. Observing her at a discreet distance with lovesick, yearning, yet unjudging eyes. As, by degrees, he aged, thickened at the waist and began to gray, and she of course did not. As her son the cocky little fellow "Johnny" matured by quick degrees into a lanky, good-looking adolescent astonishingly sinuous as an upright snake on the basketball court—the "John Reddy Heart" Trowbridge would read about in the high school sports section of the *Gazette*. Until at last the summons came as he'd known it would. For Dahlia Heart was a woman to inspire illicit passion, if not in Officer Trowbridge himself (happily married, with three children below the age of ten who adored their policeman daddy) then in other less disciplined men. Though he could not have anticipated the shocking nature of the summons, bringing him and three other police officers to the Dutch Colonial at 8 Meridian Place at 2:12 A.M. of a frigid March morning approximately four years and eight months after Trowbridge had escorted the Hearts to their new house. Pistols drawn, breaths steaming, crouched and prepared for a sudden eruption of gunfire, Trowbridge and his comrades cautiously approached the large fieldstone-and-wood house whose windows were luridly ablaze with lights and whose heavy oak front door, glaring an incongruous robin's-egg blue, was flung open. They had been summoned by a dispatcher in response to a 911 call by a distraught neighbor of the Hearts, Mrs. Irma Bannister, who'd cried into the phone, "Help! Police! Emergency! Hurry! Those white-trash Hearts—they're killing one another next door!"

3

John Reddy, so cool.
John Reddy's mom, burning-hot.
John Reddy, John Reddy Heart.

"Like it's her wedding day, every day"—it was said of Dahlia Heart, John Reddy's mom. Because the woman always wore white. Because if you saw a flash of white, a kind of hurtful, intense, dazzling-blinding white, a white whiter than most white, a white to sear your eyeballs and leave an afterimage that would burn for hours, it was likely to be Dahlia Heart.

But nobody in Willowsville ever called her the White Dahlia—a reference to some notorious never-solved murder case in Los Angeles in the 1940s. (Where the female victim, a beautiful young woman who'd always worn black, thus called the Black Dahlia in the press, was found murdered, sexually abused and grotesquely mutilated, her torso nearly severed from her legs.) "The White Dahlia" was meretricious made-for-TV sensationalism and not Willowsville's style.

John Reddy Heart and his mom never knew (for who would have wished to tell them?) that, before they arrived in Willowsville, Dahlia Magdalena Heart was a crude rumor in certain Willowsville circles—"that blackjack woman" she was called. Or, "that conniving blackjack woman." Or, "that

conniving criminal blackjack woman." In their emotional distress at the sudden death of retired Colonel Esdras Edgihoffer
(about which rumors also circulated), the Edgihoffers themselves must have spread the rumor, speaking unguardedly to
friends, even to their hired help, who naturally spread the
lurid story through Willowsville. It could be summed up in
its earliest phase as an outcry of shock, hurt and class
betrayal, as Reggie Edgihoffer remembers vividly, decades
later, his mother exclaiming on the phone to a relative. "Oh,
Bessie! You won't believe it! The Colonel is dead, and he's left
his fortune to *a blackjack woman in Las Vegas!*"

At first it was believed, or in any case declared, that the fifty-
nine-year-old Colonel had died in a hospital of cardiac arrest.
But where was the hospital? Palm Beach, where the Colonel
had allegedly been living in retirement? Washington, D.C.,
which the Colonel often visited? Then it came out, revealed to
Kenny Fischer's mother by her Monday–Thursday cleaning
woman Carlotta, who did housework for the Matthew
Edgihoffers, that in fact the Colonel had died in Las Vegas
where he'd been "gambling away his life savings." (This wasn't
entirely true. The Colonel was believed to have lost approximately $75,000 in the casinos, over a period of twelve days,
but he had assets worth much more than that, including property in Palm Beach and at 8 Meridian Place in Willowsville.)
Later it came out, revealed by a half-dozen sources simultaneously at a women's fashion luncheon at the Willowsville
Country Club, that the Colonel had died not in a hospital
room but on the floor of Caesars Palace Casino, at a blackjack
table where, ironically, he hadn't lost with a turn of the card
but had won—sums ranging, as the luncheon ladies told and
retold the amazing tale, from $5,000 to $50,000. But shortly
after this it was revealed, by an undisclosed source close to the
grieving family, that the Colonel had in fact died in a private
suite on the thirtieth floor of Caesars Palace Hotel where he'd
been staying for some time, registered under the name "Ike
Egan" of Washington, D.C.; and he hadn't been alone.

He had, though, died of cardiac arrest.

Discovered by a medical emergency team on the floor beside a "pharaoh-sized bed" (as the hotel described these mammoth beds), naked, amid a tangle of bedclothes partly torn from the bed in his death throes, the Colonel had been in close proximity to a woman at the time; and it was this woman who'd called the front desk to report the Colonel's collapse. This "woman in white"—as described by the medical emergency crew who'd rushed to the suite—had left the premises almost as soon as they arrived, slipping away without anyone taking notice; they'd had but a vague, confused impression of her, believing her to have been a nurse, perhaps; a nurse-companion of the stricken man who'd seemed, in the blue-faced paroxysm of such a death, to be much older than his age. Closely questioned by legal investigators in the hire of the Edgihoffers, who'd valiantly sought to break the Colonel's last, clearly demented will, the medical attendants said that deaths like "that old man's" occurred so frequently in Las Vegas, especially in the big hotels, it was difficult to remember one from another—"And the women sort of look alike, too."

"The Edgihoffer tragedy"—that was exclusively a subject for the older generations. Our parents, grandparents, relatives—and their hired help, too—spoke obsessively of it in the weeks and months following the Colonel's death. (His funeral was strictly private, attended only by close relatives, at the St. Luke's Episcopal Church where the Colonel had been baptized, as everyone remarked, almost sixty years before to the day. The funeral was so private that even the Amherst Edgihoffers weren't invited—the large, diverse family of Edgihoffers having split off, at about the turn of the century, into two generally rivalrous factions.) The Colonel with his drooping white mustache, polished-looking bald head and exaggerated military bearing was something of a local celebrity and a war hero; decorated for his valor in France, in World

War II; a friendly acquaintance of General Dwight Eisenhower during the war years and an occasional visitor to the White House when "Ike" was president; and the Edgihoffers were a well-to-do, much respected local family who owned property in downtown Buffalo, in those years a thriving Great Lakes city whose original name, Beau Fleuve (French, "beautiful river," meaning the Niagara), wouldn't have seemed so sadly ironic as it would in the economically depressed years to come. The Edgihoffer name was associated with Christian charity, goodness, high moral standards. It was boring and embarrassing to be an Edgihoffer, Reggie complained, even at Colgate where he went to college there'd be an aura attached to his name, or possibly it was just the sound of it—"Like some old echo out of the dead past." Reggie was stricken with embarrassment by any talk of the "Edgihoffer tragedy" because everybody knew that what was meant was sex; but sex involving a man of such an advanced age, beyond even forty, it was mortifying even to contemplate. "Whose business is it what Uncle Ez did with his money? Or anything any old guy does? Or tries to do? Christ's sake." We all felt the same way.

The sexual behavior of older generations—just to think of it made us queasy.

* * *

"But *I* have the key. Colonel Edgihoffer placed it in my hand, and it doesn't have to be probated in any will."

It was true. Colonel Edgihoffer had not only willed his family home at 8 Meridian Place to the woman named Dahlia Heart, of whom no one in Willowsville had ever heard, he'd presented her with the actual key to the house—"For safekeeping," he'd said mysteriously. As if he'd had a presentiment of death. Or a sense that things would shortly veer out of his control forever.

Naturally, the Colonel's children had expected the house, and other properties, to be willed to them. And, in an earlier will, they'd been the principal heirs. But now there was a new will, said to have been "hastily drawn up" in Las Vegas, Nevada, only a few days before the Colonel's death.

Since the death of Esdras Edgihoffer's wife Mildred a few years before, it was generally conceded that he'd begun to behave strangely. Unpredictably. Their marriage had not been a happy one—though, by the Willowsville standards of their era, it hadn't been an unhappy one; but it had endured nobly for more than three decades and had acquired, in the view of Willowsville society, the featureless stolidity of the most prominent obelisk grave-marker in the Episcopal cemetery, the black marble monument to J. W. W. Edgihoffer (1834–1910) who had established the family's early fortune in trading on the Great Lakes in the boom years following the Civil War. The Colonel and his wife had, in later years, traveled separately, belonged to separate clubs, and had distinctly different favorites among their four adult children. Never would they have established separate residences, nor would they have contemplated divorce, for such things weren't done in good society; but there was a collective sense of relief among the family when, after years of querulous illnesses and convalescences, Mildred Edgihoffer settled into a serious kidney condition, and died. "Now nothing scandalous can possibly happen between her and Esdras!" The Colonel had been genuinely stricken with grief, for several months.

Around this time, Colonel Edgihoffer was invited to speak at our high school for Memorial Day. The red-white-and-blue-striped and -starred six-foot flag was repositioned at stage center, behind the podium at which, in full dress uniform, his left breast gleaming with military decorations bright as tinsel trinkets from our breakfast cereal boxes, the Colonel spoke passionately of "patriotism"—"democracy"—"sacrifice"—"valor"—"vigilance against the Red Menace." You couldn't help but be impressed with the man's brisk rapid-fire speech, which emulated (we thought) the staccato rhythms of machine-gun fire and flak. And his fierce white mustache of the hue of Ivory White our moms, or our moms' Negro cleaning ladies, used on laundry day. And his ramrod-straight posture, and the flash of his bloodhound eyes. Sure, some of us were bored out of our skulls, since infancy we'd heard tales from our dads and other old guys about World War II, and other wars, but still the Colonel made a strong impression. And then at the conclusion of the Colonel's speech, when our principal, Mr. Stamish, invited questions from the audience, a swarthy sophomore named Ricky Calvo shot his hand into the air before anyone else and asked in a wise-guy voice, "Colonel, why did the U.S. drop A-bombs on Japanese civilians?" There was a shocked pause. Mr. Stamish, a pork-faced man with polished glasses, stared in dismay. The Colonel's face reddened. Who the hell was Ricky Calvo? A new kid, belonging to one of those Italian families who lived on the eastern edge of Willowsville on lower Spring, or Water, or Division. His father was a carpenter for Skelton Construction. Or worked for Moss Lawn & Tree Service. Ricky Calvo wasn't one of us and we sort of resented him for speaking up like that as if he was, but it was thrilling, too, to see the Colonel's reaction, glaring out at him, like an officer glaring at an underling before he orders him shot, saying in a blustery voice, "Why, son, to stop the war. Mr. Truman offered the Japs—Japanese—plenty of opportunities to surrender but they refused. And so—" But wise guy Calvo interrupted, continuing, "On children? on babies? on elderly people? on *hospital patients*? My dad says—" The Colonel interrupted, his voice rising, "The Japs—Japanese—would not surrender *un*conditionally! Their own pride destroyed them! Their madness! *They* gave *us* no choice, son." The Colonel had stepped from behind the podium to squint angrily into the audience at this defiant adolescent. Fearful of his bloodhound eyes, we cringed in our seats. "Who's been talking to you, son? You have been imbued with the wrong, wrong, *wrong idea*." Before Calvo could reply, Mr. Stamish quickly cut off the exchange.

(One by one four Calvo boys and three Calvo girls, all swarthy-skinned and good-looking, would attend our high school. Sasha Calvo, one day to acquire renown as John Reddy Heart's girl, was the youngest. We'd never forget Ricky, though he wasn't one of us and never would be. He lived at the wrong end of Willowsville. He'd come along years too early to be Italian.)

After this the Colonel began to miss golf dates with old friends. He was observed entering the enormous dining room of the Willowsville Country Club, halting in his tracks, turning, and walking out again. His vividly white mustache began to droop. He declined dinner invitations without offering excuses or, unforgivably shocking in Willowsville society as a breach of promise, he accepted and failed to show up. It was realized that he'd ceased attending church since his wife's funeral. And he'd ceased giving money to the church. Without informing anyone, including even his housekeeper of twenty years, he began to disappear from Willowsville for varying periods of time. He was rumored to be "gambling." He was rumored to be "drinking." The handsome old landmark colonial at 8 Meridian Place, in which Edgihoffers had lived since the late 1890s, began to be neglected, needing repainting, repair. The intricate rock garden in the side lawn, a much-photographed pride of the Gardeners' Club of Buffalo, began to be overgrown and weedy. The Colonel's old friend and neighbor Aickley Thrun remarked philosophically, "Even before the blackjack woman, Esdras was consorting with unsavory, treacherous people. The end was foretold."

The Edgihoffer family lawyers, the old Buffalo firm of Chase, Rush, Beebee & Pepper, fought to break the Colonel's Las Vegas will; but Dahlia Heart, following the confidential advice of Jerry Bozer, of Metropolitan Life, with whom she became acquainted (how closely, was disputed) immediately after moving to Willowsville, countered by hiring the aggressive Buffalo firm of Trippe, Schwartz, McVitter and Cranker to defend it. Since, it was acknowledged, Mrs. Heart was already in residence in the late Colonel's house, with her father and three children, and since the Las Vegas will appeared complete and duly executed, there was little the Edgihoffers could do. Public sentiment and a collective sense of justice were on their side, but the law, it seemed, was on the side of the blackjack woman. The case dragged on for months and was finally settled out of court with an undisclosed amount of money going to the "rightful heirs."

How much, in fact, did Dahlia Heart inherit from Colonel Edgihoffer? No one ever knew definitively. There was much speculation; estimates ranged from a modest $50,000 to $500,000. The property at 8 Meridian Place was worth approximately $250,000 (thirty years later, of course, the identical property in the prestigious St. Albans Hill neighborhood of the village would go on the market for not under $1.5 million) but it looked shabby outside and in; if Mrs. Heart wanted to sell it, as cynics expected, and hoped, she would have had to invest many thousands of dollars in it. But though she did make repairs on the house, to a modest degree, she showed no signs of wanting to sell. Instead, within days of moving into the house, she drove into the village in the salmon-colored Cadillac and, dazzling in a trim white silk suit with a bolero jacket and a short, scalloped skirt, a pert straw hat with a white silk band, in spike-heeled white leather shoes, she made inquiries at architects' and builders' offices about renovating the old Dutch Colonial. Everywhere she went, Mrs. Heart drew stares. Some were stares of startled admiration, some were stares of wonder and curiosity. Some were stares of hostility. (For already, in our close-knit village, "the blackjack woman" was known.) Some she acknowledged with a smile, most she coolly ignored. To Herman Skelton of Skelton Construction, who treated her to a two-hour business lunch at the Old Eagle House Inn on Main Street, she was reported to have said, with modestly lowered eyelids, "The Colonel wished for me to dwell in his house. 'It's the closest I can offer you, Dahlia, to dwelling in my heart,' he said. So I intend to stay in Willowsville. And I intend to be happy here. I hope to make lots and lots of friends."

4

John Reddy, eyes of icy blue.
John Reddy, whoever knew you?
John Reddy, John Reddy Heart.

(John Reddy's eyes were unmistakably dark brown. Made in USA hadn't ever seen John Reddy face-to-face.)

Most of us at WHS, even guys who'd played varsity basketball with him for two seasons, even the few girls who claimed to have gone out with him, would have to admit we'd never had an actual conversation with John Reddy Heart. It wasn't just that John Reddy wasn't the type to talk much, he wasn't the type to confide easily in others. At the Academy Street School he scared us in his navy blue or black T-shirts, jeans and battered boots, with his glowering looks that intimidated even our teachers. He was often absent from school and, in eighth grade, he was mysteriously suspended for twelve days. (Why? We never knew.) He was the first to have pimples. The angry-looking kind, the genuine article, glaring-red, hot-to-the-touch pimples that looked hard as berries. (We stared, mesmerized. We were envious.) And there was John Reddy's shadowy beard, yes, a beard—bluish like twilight, or razor blades, against his olive-dark skin. (A boy of eleven, twelve, even thirteen—was it normal for him to *shave*?) And John Reddy's genitalia—"If you were a kid that age, a boy, undressing for gym the way we had to, stripping for the shower, you'd be terrified to glance at John Reddy, there were these sprouting bristly-black hairs at his groin, and a sausagelike appendage bobbing between his legs, you'd be stricken with panic, thinking *Am I supposed to have one of those, too? But where will it come from?*"

Behind John Reddy's back, guys joked of "JOHN READY!" and brainy Chet Halloren came up with "ATTILA THE HUNG!" and we laughed till tears leaked from our eyes; we were scared shitless.

It was a gas: our parents cautioning us, "Stay away from that Heart boy"—"That Heart boy doesn't belong in school with you children"—"That Heart boy's a bad influence." As if it was a matter of our choice, not his, the distance between us!

One Saturday morning a few of us encountered John Reddy in an isolated spot in the Glen Creek ravine, actually not far from Main Street but hidden away from paths, not far from the rear of the old red mill, we were in ninth grade, fourteen years old, and Art Lutz poked us and whispered, "Look!"—it was John Reddy in rumpled-looking clothes, alone, squatting on a rock smoking like a grown man sucking at the cigarette and exhaling smoke in that brooding unsmiling *This is goddam serious* way of our dads if glimpsed unawares, and you never wanted to call attention to yourself if you came upon your dad in such a pose, such a posture, eyes staring yet turned inward. John Reddy was frowning down toward the water—Glen Creek is a narrow stream flowing across a sequence of shale outcroppings in this part of the ravine, splashing waterfalls, measuring maybe twelve feet across, and there was John Reddy staring at the white-sparkling water, we were shocked seeing he'd been injured, both eyes bruised, his mouth swollen, scratches on his face (a woman's finger-nails?—his mom's?—our crazy imaginations goaded us), and Ken Fischer who'd always been a good guy, one of these upright honest wide-eyed good citizens, though in middle age a shark of a "troubleshooter" (as they're called) for Motorola, Inc., surprised us by stepping forward, asking sort of shyly, "John Reddy? You O.K.?" and John Reddy jerked around, and said, "Yeah, I'm O.K.," and after a moment added, "Thanks." His voice wasn't a boy's voice but deep, resonant, sullen and mournful and his bruised eyes on us (damp? had John Reddy been *crying*?) beat us away, we retreated hastily, got out of earshot and began to run calling to one another excitedly, "John Reddy was in a fight! A fight! Got the shit kicked out of him, in a *fight*!"

A year or two later in high school, to be precise only a week or so before the shooting death of Melvin Riggs, Jr., at the Heart residence, Bo Bozer spoke of seeing John Reddy at his locker in the junior corridor, one of those mornings we'd see John Reddy in desperate haste scrawling homework on a sheet of paper torn from a notebook and pressed impracticably against the wall, sometimes against the uneven surface of lockers, that look of fury, bafflement, and resignation in his face, and deep shadows beneath his eyes as if he hadn't slept all night, and his jaws unshaven as an adult, desperate man's, and his clothes rumpled, smelly (Verrie Myers who'd memorized John Reddy's entire wardrobe, and was capable of distinguishing between T-shirts of varying gradations of faded navy blue, black, yellowed white, and frayed and holey jeans, even socks, said it was "self-evident, and sad," that John Reddy frequently didn't undress for bed, probably didn't go to bed or sleep at all some nights, for he'd wear the same clothing two days in a row, or even more, an inimitable and unmistakable John Reddy–odor wafting in his wake the girls would sniff after like alert, aroused cats)—that morning, Bo told us, there was a gouged-looking cut on John Reddy's left cheek, not a scratch but like something made with a knife, still bleeding a little, and how weird it was, and scary, John Reddy seemed oblivious of the cut, hurriedly drawing geometrical figures without the aid of a compass or triangle so that his homework looked like something done by a five-year-old. Bo told us, whining, "I figure I'm a friend of John's from the team, right? There'd been a few times when I scored and John would tap me on the shoulder to congratulate me so I figure it's O.K., it's cool, to say, 'Jesus, John!—what happened to your face?' But John Reddy sort of turns to me like he didn't know I was there, he wipes at the blood like he didn't know what it is, then sort of blushes, and shrugs, like to say, 'Shit, no big deal, what business is it of *yours*?' And goes back to his homework that I can see, over his shoulder, is gonna be D+ if he's lucky."

(Lots of us offered to help John Reddy with his homework lots of times, but he always said no thanks. Somehow, he managed to pull through without failing any course. And without cheating, either—"Hell, John Reddy's got too much pride for *that*.")

Because of basketball and so much attention, and girls (and grown women) looking after him with lovesick eyes, John Reddy began to mellow some his junior year at WHS. He was like a young wild horse beginning to be, not tamed exactly, because John Reddy never did get tamed, but less distrustful and edgy than he'd been. You could call out, "H'lo!" to him and possibly he'd acknowledge you though he wouldn't call out "H'lo" or "Hi" in turn, that wasn't his style and we respected it. If you had the nerve and your legs were long enough you could maybe fall into stride with him in a school corridor, or on the stairs, or pushing out through the rear doors (John Reddy only left school by the rear, where his Caddie was parked) and you could talk to him earnestly, breathlessly, maybe he'd reply and maybe he wouldn't but it was O.K., it was cool. And you're smiling thinking *Hey I'm walking with John Reddy Heart. Look at me!* Monday after a Friday night basketball game, for instance after the Willowsville Wolverines beat the West Seneca Indians 47–25, when John Reddy scored a fantastic record-breaking thirty-one points of which nine were foul shots, you could walk with him hurrying to keep pace with his long-legged stride and breathlessly recount every move he'd made, every basket, every rebound, every foul shot, and even if John Reddy didn't mumble more than "yeah" and "right" and "O.K., man" it was a fully satisfying exchange. You would feel the glow of it for hours, days. Twenty, twenty-five, and at last thirty years after it happened, in a tension-filled play-off game with our rivals Amherst for the Erie County high school basketball championship, which we'd win 58–49, Dwayne Hewson, another WHS star jock, would tell of how he'd been fouled by an Amherst guard, got tangled in feet and fell and broke his ankle and had to be helped from the court, near bawling with pain and dismay, and John Reddy grabbed him around the waist with his muscled arm slick with sweat and walked him from the court cursing and livid with anger as if Dwayne's bad luck and misery were his own, and at the sideline he'd squeezed Dwayne's hand like you wouldn't expect another guy to do and looked Dwayne in the eye—"Like John Reddy was saying to me, with all these other people screaming, he knew what I was feeling, how fucking shitty it was, I was out of the game, I was gonna have a lot of pain but I'd have to accept it, that's how things are." All this, John Reddy communicated without a word. Then turned, and was back in the game, to score the foul shot in Dwayne's place.

If there were girls John Reddy confided in, they kept his secrets.

If there were guys—Orrie Buhr, Clyde Meunzer, Dino Calvo, Jake Gervasio and others he'd hang out with back of school, talking cars, smoking, their laughter harsh and to our sensitive ears (we regarded these vocational arts majors from a distance, contemptuous of them as they were of us) derisive—John Reddy confided in, they too kept his secrets.

At class reunions Trish Elders would recount for us the story of how, driving the salmon-colored Cadillac he'd inherited from his mother (who'd moved on to a new silver-gray Mercedes, rumored to be a gift from one of her business associate friends—"Probably poor Herman"), John Reddy, at that time two years ahead of us in school, gave her a ride down-town to the library, in pelting rain; and Trish, who'd sneered at other girls' crushes on John Reddy (whom she'd considered just a jock greaser and not especially good-looking) fell pow-erfully and irrevocably under his spell during the six-minute ride. Her heart began to pound so violently, the front seat of the car vibrated and she was in terror that John Reddy would be aware of it; there was a roaring in her ears like Niagara Falls so that she could barely hear her own bright nervous idiot chatter—"Who did I sound like? Exactly like my mother, on one of her 'mood elevator' pills." John Reddy drove in silence. How at ease he was, in his lanky muscular body, in a grungy black T-shirt missing both sleeves and oil-stained jeans and his usual biker boots, the wristwatch that resembled a Swiss Army watch on his left arm, the face turned inward. Breathless, clutching at her 18×24–inch sketch pad she'd wrapped in plastic to protect from the rain, Trish was overcome by emotion, embarrassment, self-consciousness, excitement. *I am in John Reddy Heart's car. Alone with John Reddy in his car.* Her eyes misted over. She saw, blurred by moisture, the comically oversized dice, fuzzy, fleshy pink with pronounced black dots, swinging from the rearview mirror. A Buffalo rock station beat out sound so loud you couldn't hear what was being played. Scattered on the front seat of the car, and on the floor, and in the backseat as well, were numberless notes, some with bold lipstick-kisses on them, some with flashy red-inked hearts—love notes left in John Reddy's Cadillac by voracious senior girls. Trish forced herself to stare straight ahead, blindly, at the windshield streaming rain. *I am in John Reddy Heart's car. The very place my parents would forbid me to be. If they knew. But they don't. No one knows. I, Trish Elders, am alone with John Reddy Heart in his car.* She would marry young, have babies, and divorce in heartbreak (though as for most of us, divorce would be her decision) and remarry, all along pursuing the elusive mirage of her art into middle age and beyond, somehow knowing, that day in John

Reddy's salmon-colored Caddie with the ridiculous swinging dice, littered with love notes, that her subject was seated just a few inches away—"But just the *feeling* of John Reddy. It would be futile to try to draw or paint *him*." She was thinking, gloating, that never had any other girl of the Circle ridden in this car. Never had Trish's closest dearest friend, Verrie Myers, who confessed of dreaming of such rides with John Reddy, ridden in this car. *Wait till I tell Verrie, Verrie will die.* Already Trish was rehearsing how she would tell her story: she'd been caught in the rain without an umbrella, carrying the awk-ward-sized sketch pad, her purse and books, about to cry she'd been so vexed stumbling along the sidewalk at the inter-section of Main and Farber Lane and a car braked to a stop at the curb and a voice, deep, gravelly, not familiar, called out, "Climb in," as if it was the most natural thing in the world and since this was the Village of Willowsville at a time of such innocence in our history that a girl like Trish Elders might unhesitatingly, trustingly climb into any car whose driver was thoughtful enough to offer her a ride in the rain, Trish climbed in. And saw the driver was John Reddy Heart.

And so Trish Elders fell in love. Though John Reddy scarcely spoke to her, or glanced at her. Trish was one of the popular girls in her class, a JV cheerleader, secretary of Hi-Y, accustomed to attention from boys and even, though it was unwanted, unsought, from men, but John Reddy didn't per-ceive her in such a way at all—"It was like he'd have given anyone, possibly even a dog, a ride in such rain. As a favor. Just to be *nice*." The roaring in Trish's ears swelled. She could-n't wait to be alone in her room, in her parents' half-timbered English Tudor house on Mill Race Lane, to try to sketch, with shaky fingers, the phantom John Reddy Heart, not yet know-ing such an effort was doomed to failure; thinking *I am alone with John Reddy Heart, a fact that means nothing to him though my life will never be the same again*. And already the ride was over. Six swift minutes. It would've been shorter still, except for slow-moving Willowsville traffic. John Reddy didn't seem to know the exact location of the public library so Trish had to point it out to him, and gallantly he swung the Caddie into the library's drive so that Trish could get out beneath an over- hang and run to the door. "T-thank you," Trish stammered, unable to call him by name, though in dreamy recapitula- tions of this scene she would murmur *Thank you, John Reddy!* and John Reddy behind the steering wheel said, smiling, "O.K., honey. Shut the door hard, huh?"

Trish shut the car door as hard as she could and stumbled blindly into the library, nearly fainting. It was fortunate that no one saw her—one of the librarians, or a friend of her mother's. For John Reddy had called her "honey"!

"It wasn't until years afterward that I realized," Trish said, sighing, "—John Reddy obviously hadn't known my name."

* * *

For that was the hurtful, humiliating fact. The knowledge we had to accept: that these *intimate exchanges* with John Reddy Heart were intimate on one side only—ours.

For next time you encountered John Reddy, even if it was that same day, he'd be likely to ignore you; just not-see you. If, say, you called out cheerfully, "Hi, John, how's it going?" he'd be likely not to hear.

As Dwayne Hewson summed it up years later, in a tone unusually thoughtful for Dwayne, and not at all tinged with irony, "It wasn't out of cruelty or meanness that John Reddy ignored us. Nor even out of distraction or forgetfulness or because he smoked dope with his buddies or even exhaus- tion—you know, John Reddy never got enough sleep. But just because in some essential way, in his innermost world, the rest of us didn't *exist*."

5

So we were never to know. So many things. Even after both John Reddy's trials. Because we couldn't ask John Reddy and there was no one else.

For instance, this was a question that vexed our mothers more than it did us: why was Dahlia Heart always known as "Mrs. Heart"? With a fussy old-fashioned formality the woman persisted in signing her name *Mrs. Dahlia Heart.* When you met her, she shook hands and, smiling emphatically, introduced herself as "Mrs. Dahlia Heart." Yet she introduced her father as "Aaron Leander Heart"—evidently "Heart" was her maiden name? Unless, as Roger Zwaart's dad said, tongue-in-cheek, she'd married a man named Heart in addition to having been born Heart. We puzzled over such possibilities. We were led to wonder if Dahlia Heart had ever been married at all. It was not an era in which women who were mothers were without husbands designated as "fathers." It was not an era in which women who were without husbands were comfortably designated as "mothers." We didn't want to think that John Reddy was *illegitimate.* Yet it was an era in which, if you lacked a legal father, and your mom lacked a visible husband, it might well be murmured of you that you were *illegitimate*.

The cruder term, *bastard*, was not to be uttered.

In the Village of Willowsville, there were no *bastards*. Even on the slumping-down east edge of town, beyond Spring Street, Water Street, Division, women who were mothers were married.

Our moms pondered the possibility that the Heart children—John Reddy "and the two others," whose names no one could remember—hadn't the same father. For it was generally conceded that the younger brother and sister more closely resembled each other in their plainness, doggedness, and myopia than either resembled John Reddy. But then these two didn't much resemble their mother, either.

And with the passing of time, Farley and Shirleen would resemble Dahlia Heart less and less.

Among those WHS teachers who'd claim to have gotten to know John Reddy after he returned to school, sobered by his year at Tomahawk Island and shorn of his luster as a star athlete, it was Mr. Dunleddy our junior-senior biology teacher who relayed the information—"But it's confidential"—that John Reddy's father had died a hero's death in the Air Force, a test pilot who'd been killed in the line of duty and "lost somewhere in the vastness of a desert—possibly the Sahara." Whether John Reddy's father and Dahlia Heart had been legally married, Mr. Dunleddy said stiffly, "I wouldn't presume that such private information was any of my business." Our teacher's heavy bulldog face expressed a strange, touching protectiveness for John Reddy (whose grades in biology were barely passing) and scorn for gossip-mongers.

Miss Bird, our brilliant and caustic-tongued English teacher, was equally, strangely, protective of John Reddy. Perhaps she, like Mr. Dunleddy, perceived him as an orphan; as more vulnerable than we who were his contemporaries could perceive him. Her claim to intimate knowledge of the mysterious Heart family was based upon frequent after-school conferences with John Reddy (who was barely passing English, too) and upon a more curious episode: she'd given a lift one evening in her car to John Reddy's grandfather Aaron Leander Heart, whom she discovered "wandering by the wayside" several miles east of Willowsville on the busy highway Transit Road; the white-haired old gent appeared to be disoriented, like a sleepwalker, smelling of whisky and dressed in mismatched clothing and dragging a hefty burlap sack whose contents, clanking and clicking like glassware, he'd declined to identify. Old Mr. Heart hadn't known Miss Maxine Bird, of course; but Miss Bird recognized him, for she'd seen him once or twice in Willowsville in the company of John Reddy and deduced their kinship. (Was Miss Bird watchful of John Reddy even outside of school? It was an open secret in those days that ferocious Maxine Bird with her red-dyed skinned-back hair and intolerant green eyes and high-strung nerves and fervent idealism about all things literary had a crush on John Reddy; less clear was whether the thirty-five-year-old teacher was aware of it.) It took considerable cajoling, Miss Bird said, to convince this eccentric old man to climb into her car, though traffic on Transit Road was rushing by as usual, and the weather was miserable—rain laced with sleet, that perpetual cold wind from Lake Erie. But at last Mr. Heart was persuaded and slid into the rear with his bulky burlap bag, which must have weighed thirty pounds; and Miss Bird, fired with a sense of mission, drove him directly home. Old Mr. Heart reeked of alcohol and of something damp and rotted. He was stony-faced, with an affectation of deafness. But Miss Bird talked. Like all teachers she was ninety percent words. So she talked. "But only when I mentioned John Reddy—'Your grandson is one of my most promising students'—did Mr. Heart come alive. He snorted, '"Promising"—huh! That don't mean a hill of beans.'" Each time she told this story, Miss Bird laughed excitedly at this point. With the passage of time her red-dyed hair would retain its aggressive luster even as it thinned; her pale, plain face began to wither when she was only in her fifties, yet it was with girlish vigor she spoke of John Reddy—"Those remarkable years. That *saga*." Forever in our eyes she would be our beloved Miss Bird whom, when we'd been her students, we'd hated; from this authority she derived an air of the proprietary and the secretive. For instance, Miss Bird would only hint, yet would never come out and say explicitly, how startled she'd been by seeing the former Edgihoffer house, a village landmark, so transformed—its oaken front door, shutters, and trim painted a bright robin's-egg blue instead of black or dark green. And the beautiful rock garden invaded by painted plaster-of-paris gnomes and gigantic frogs. And John Reddy's salmon-colored Cadillac a glaring presence in the driveway where, evidently, he'd been repairing it, in the innocent way in which, in less prestigious neighborhoods than St. Albans Hill, teenaged boys worked on their cars and motorcycles in full view of neighbors and passersby. Of these distractions, Miss Bird would only exclaim, ruefully, "Well! The Hearts certainly made their mark on the community, didn't they." Of John Reddy's private life, Miss Bird invariably hinted that there was much she knew that she couldn't reveal. It was her conviction, though, that John Reddy's father had been married to his mother—"John Reddy is as *legitimate* as anyone in Willowsville." Whether the identical man was the father of the younger brother and sister wasn't so clear.

There was a way we admired that Miss Bird drew herself up to her full height of five feet one inch, jammed her harlequin-style maroon plastic glasses against the bridge of her narrow nose, and declared, as she was on record having declared to numerous inquisitive reporters, "Yes, the Hearts have been a 'tragic' family. But a thoroughly American family. 'Judge not, lest ye be judged.'"

It was Coach Woody McKeever whose claim to have known John Reddy intimately seemed the most plausible, though Coach had a reputation for hyperbole and even hysteria, like many high school sports coaches. His throat was raw from yelling at generations of oafish high school athletes but he spoke in a cracked, tender voice of John Reddy—"The son Mrs. McKeever and I never had, by God's inscrutable grace." Yet Coach too couldn't resist hinting that he too was in possession of "confidential information" about the Heart family he would never reveal. Of the faculty and staff of Willowsville High, including even our harassed principal, Mr. Stamish, it was Coach McKeever who was most pursued by reporters and TV camera crews; he complained of having to have his telephone number changed to an unlisted number, having to leave school by a different exit every afternoon, and having to wear dark glasses in public. He limited interviews to luncheon sessions at such excellent local restaurants as the Old Eagle House Inn where, though by degrees he became drunk, and maudlin-weepy, he gave nothing away that might have embarrassed or offended John Reddy. His favorite, much-quoted utterance remained, without adornment, "My heart is broken for that boy." (At our fortieth class reunion we'd still be quoting Coach with affection; it would be Art Lutz who could imitate him with eerie facility in that cracked, tender voice.) We admired Coach's reticence, his air of propriety. For it did seem, in fact, with the loss of the spectacular basketball player he'd been grooming for a big basketball school, that his heart was broken.

Except: at one of our early reunions, possibly the tenth, at a beer tent in Tug Hill Park where Coach, a guest of honor, had consumed ice-cold beer (to be precise, beers—light, dark, mellow, strong, domestic, imported, "gourmet"—our WHS jocks were beer fanatics) with a dozen or more of his favored former athletes, he turned emotional toward evening, hinting that he knew "a damned lot more than I would ever disclose to the police or the D.A.'s office" about what had happened in that bedroom at 8 Meridian Place on the night of Melvin Riggs's death. "Not half of it came out in the trial, you can be sure. Not one-third." By this time Coach surprised us, he'd gotten so drunk. Swaying on his feet so that Bo Bozer, Ken

Fischer, and Tommy "Nosepicker" Nordstrom (never a favorite of Coach's in the old days) had to hold him up. Coach's eyes were brimming with tears and his flaccid skin looked boiled. We expected him to shake us off and yell something comic and insulting, but Coach was deathly serious. We all knew, but would never out of tact have alluded to the melancholy fact, that since the departure of John Reddy Heart from varsity basketball, Coach had never led any team through a really satisfactory season and the school board and local alums had hired a younger, more competitive coach to ease him out; if he was kept on the WHS faculty it was for sentimental reasons and because he had tenure and belonged to the A.F. of L. teachers' union and couldn't be fired. He was saying loudly in our startled faces, in his cracked, husky voice, "That boy John Reddy was a damned good boy despite his background, a noble boy, y'know what I'm saying? Protective of his mother, eh? Y'know what I'm saying? Protective of that"—he was puffing, out of breath, eyes contracted with an unspeakable vision, almost choking on the word he was forced to utter so he spat it out like something foul and stinging—"*woman.*"

Nor did we ever learn if Dahlia Heart had been a blackjack dealer in Las Vegas. All information pertaining to Mrs. Heart's private life prior to her move to Willowsville was excluded from trial procedure and testimony, thanks to the aggressive tactics of the defense attorney Rollie Trippe, whom she'd hired to represent John Reddy, but anecdotal evidence seemed to suggest she'd been an employee of some kind at Caesars Palace. Mr. Trippe, who played squash regularly at the Buffalo Athletic Club with Blake Wells's dad, told Mr. Wells that Mrs. Heart had been "in public relations" at the casino. And that it was as she'd testified—"She fainted easily." Other men acquainted with Dahlia Heart refused to provide information about her private life, but it came to be believed, with scorn, that in fact they knew little—"It's easy to be discreet if somebody's pulled wool over your eyes." Melvin Riggs's assistant at the Buffalo Hawks, Inc., spoke with grudging admiration of Dahlia Heart as a "shrewd businesswoman if only she'd applied herself." From other sources, among them Herman Skelton's wife, Irma, it was said that Mrs. Heart had been, variously, a "photographer's model"—an "exotic dancer"—a "high-priced call girl." (Embittered by the ruin of her marriage, Irma Skelton was not considered, even by her loyal woman friends, a reliable witness.) The Thruns and the Bannisters, neighbors of Mrs. Heart's in the sequestered elm-shaded cul-de-sac Meridian Place, denied any knowledge of her and her family, though it was reported to Mrs. Thrun by her cleaning woman that the Hearts must have moved into the Colonel's house with next to no possessions. "Myrtle said that days passed and no moving van ever arrived. All that family's worldly goods were in the ratty U-Haul. Imagine!" Mrs. Bannister's cook reported having seen, carried out of the U-Haul by the Hearts, "spangled dresses on satin coat hangers" and a "huge big tumble, in a bushel basket, of fancy high-heeled shoes"—which bolstered theories of modeling, dancing and so forth.

Yet other reliable sources, including the assistant prosecuting attorneys who'd tried so hard to send John Reddy away for life like a hardened criminal, insisted that Mrs. Heart had a "shrewd legal and contractual mind" despite her public pose of being uninformed and confused and overwhelmed by legal proceedings. They insisted (though without confirmation from Rollie Trippe's side) that Dahlia Heart had helped direct her son's defense. It was said of the boy that he took after his mother in crucial ways. Despite his erratic school record, he was believed by certain of his teachers to have a "mind for numbers and abstract thought." He was certainly physically coordinated to a remarkable degree, with, as Coach McKeever liked to say, marveling, "reflexes swift and accurate as lightning." Of course, Farley Heart was immediately recognized by his teachers at the Academy Street School as a "math whiz"—"a budding genius." Shirleen Heart, that strange, shyly stubborn child, who in another, later era might have been diagnosed as mildly autistic, was acknowledged to have neither any aptitude for numbers nor much grasp of grammar and syntax and communication skills, but she could spell and precisely define "big" vocabulary words with astonishing accuracy—"Like an intense little robot," as one of her teachers said. John Reddy never spoke of his mother, of course. Not to us. Not in our hearing. Taciturn about all things, he would've been doubly taciturn about her, as about his family in general. (Dwayne Hewson insisted that John Reddy was proud of his younger brother, though. There'd been a photo in the *Gazette* of three prize-winning students at the Academy Street School, one of them Farley Heart, at the time in eighth grade, and Dwayne had mentioned this to John Reddy and John Reddy brightened and said, "Yeah. My brother's getting grades enough for us both. I'm glad.") But one day in the locker room after basketball practice, when they were sophomores, Dougie Siefried who had a crush on dazzling Dahlia Heart blurted out to John Reddy impulsively, "Was your mom ever in the movies, John? She coulda been!" and John Reddy, scratching roughly at a cluster of bleeding pimples between his shoulder blades, said, wincing, "Shit, man, why ask *me*? Our moms have their secret lives."

Our moms have their secret lives. This, too, became a much-repeated remark of John Reddy's. "Wow! Cool." We didn't believe it, though.

Years later, Scottie Baskett found himself in Las Vegas, Nevada, at a convention of the American Association of Plastic Surgeons, and decided impulsively—"Why the hell not?"—to try to track down the Vegas address of the mysterious Hearts. "See if I could find out something about Dahlia no one else knew." (The notorious woman had long since vanished from Willowsville, of course. Like John Reddy.) A less zealous, optimistic and dogged individual than he would not have even supposed that, so many years after the Hearts had emigrated east from Vegas, that city of all American cities phantasmagoric and insubstantial as a delirium tremens hallucination, there could be any trace, any vestigial memory of them. But Scottie went to the Las Vegas County Clerk's office and came away with several street addresses, for the appropriate years, of "D. Heart"; took a cab to the first, on Paradise Street, a commercial street behind the towering Flamingo Hotel & Casino, and was stunned to see that the entire block was now a low-rental Days Inn motel, a parking garage, and a Taco Bell; took the cab to the second, El Dorado, behind the shimmering Mirage Hotel & Casino, and was disappointed to see a car wash where a dwelling of some sort had once stood, in a bustling Latino neighborhood; took a cab to the third, on a more distant street near the dissolving edge of the city, and here, at 837 Arroyo Seco, Scottie discovered an adobe bungalow. He wasn't prepared for the impact of such a sight. "I thought, 'Jesus. Why didn't I have a camera. Dahlia Heart and John Reddy lived *here*.'" Years—as many as thirty—had passed since the Hearts had lived in this modest bungalow that looked as if rust-corroded, but it seemed clear that the residence, like the neighborhood, couldn't have changed much. Single-story dwellings with postage-stamp front yards and one-car garages like doghouses—built in the forties, or earlier. At 837 Arroyo Seco, the facade appeared to be cracking even as Scottie stared. The once-garish, now dulled orangish-red paint had peeled in languid patches; the small windowpanes had the milky lustre of glaucous eyes; the windows were further obscured, from the inside, by what appeared to be strips of aluminum foil. Yet there was a miniature, crumbling porch upon which (Scottie eagerly hypothesized) the lovely young mother Dahlia Heart might have sat, cradling an infant John Reddy in her arms. "I could see it, almost!" Scottie told us, with a look of pain. "And me, Dr. Baskett, kidded by the girls on my staff I'm always so overprepared, with no *camera*."

Next door at 839 Arroyo Seco, on the crumbling adobe

porch of a smudged custard-yellow bungalow, a replica of the Hearts' old bungalow, sat a grizzled old man with a bare, sunken chest and flaccid breasts, observing Scottie and sipping beer from a can. So Scottie called over cheerfully to inquire if the man had lived in this neighborhood for very long, and the man said sourly, with the deadpan air of a stand-up comedian, "Long? Only half my fuckin life, doc." Scottie asked if the man could remember a resident of 837 Arroyo Seco who'd lived there years ago, as many as thirty, or more— "A really beautiful, gorgeous woman named Dahlia Heart. She had three children, two boys and a girl; a father who lived with her, a white-haired old fellow with some strange name of antiquity—Leander, I think." Seeing the bare-chested man's look of disdain, Scottie added, "It's likely that this woman, Mrs. Heart, worked at Caesars Palace, or some other casino." Scowling, the man scratched both his breasts with spiteful vigor. He said, "For prostate cancer the fuckers give you fuckin hormones that grow tits like a woman. Kindly explain to me, doc, you make a million a year why can't you figure out the fuckin dosage?" Scottie said, startled, "How— do you know I'm a doctor?" and the man snorted with laughter, saying, "What? You gotta be kidding, doc." Scottie tried to steer the subject back to Dahlia Heart. He was convinced this old man had known her. Of course this old man must have known Dahlia Heart. "Then it happened my life was sort of passing before my eyes. I tasted panic, the way that guy was looking at me. *He's seen the Hearts, now he's seeing me. Soon I'll be gone, too.* It was unnaturally hot for November—the sun was wrongly positioned in the sky. A winter sun, you're thinking, but summer heat. My hair's thinning and I should've worn a hat. I'm so old—almost forty-five. Did you ever dream you'd get so old? I weigh thirty pounds more than I did in high school. I was such a skinny, hopeful kid in high school. Just four ballots short of 'Most Likely to Succeed.' After taxes and insurance I pull in about five hundred thousand a year. This practice in Westchester.

I've got four kids I'm proud of—more or less. I'm an officer of this plastic surgeons' association and I'm giving a talk the next morning at the Hilton. My marriage is O.K. I married a TriDelt from Cornell who was looking to marry, I guess, a doctor. But it's O.K. But here my life's passing before my eyes in Vegas, in this old lost neighborhood—'Arroyo Seco.' I mean I really was panicking, like going under anesthesia. I felt like crying—I'd never been friends with John Reddy Heart but I'd *lost him*. The girls I'd wanted to date, Pattianne Groves, Verrie Myers, never knew I existed. It came over me—nobody's happy anymore. Nobody's happy with their bodies, or with their spouse's body. We're too old too fast. We aren't ready to be so old. We're our *parents* for Christ's sake! I was thinking it might've been better for him—John Reddy—if the state troopers had shot him down in the mountains. It might've been better for all of us. Plastic surgery! Sure I do pro bono work, birth defects mainly, but the bread-and-butter is droopy breasts, hooter breasts, Dixie-cup breasts, bags under eyes, crow's-feet, jowls, turkey necks, liver spots, varicose veins, warts, acne scars, ripple thighs, love handles, hook noses, porky noses, double and triple chins, sagging eyelids, sagging upper arms, sagging potbellies, sagging butts. It's about stopping the clock—no, turning it back. *Un*winding it. It isn't what I was anticipating going into med school but it's what I got. Actually I wanted to be a musician. I played trombone, remember? And Blake Wells, clarinet. Pete Marsh fooled around with drums—not bad. We'd smoke cigarettes pretending it was marijuana and we were high and that's where the music came from. Mr. Larsen said, I quote, we were 'as good as any rock band' and maybe he was being sarcastic but I believe he was correct. But, hell. I'm one of the happy graduates of our class. I'm one of the lucky ones. There's guys like Bozer who've basically bottomed out. Dwayne Hewson was telling me Bo calls him at midnight sometimes, wants to talk about the old days, certain of the games, and what's there to say? 'He won't hang up. He makes me hang up. It's like killing him. I hate it,' Dwayne says. *He's* doing pretty well, old Dwayne. Running for mayor of Willowsville—man! But there's guys in our class who've killed themselves. I don't mean with cars—Smoke Filer, Steve Lunt. Or even Pete Marsh—that was a long time ago, he was just a kid. I mean a guy like Bert Fox. Remember Bert? Just a regular guy, one of us in the 'math, science' major, not a jock and not a geek and he's married, three kids, living in Batavia selling insurance and one day he's dead. You'd have thought—*Hell, Bert Fox doesn't have the depth to kill himself. Why's Bert Fox who used to screw around in Dunleddy's class taking himself so seriously, killing himself? Like he's impatient, can't wait for nature to do it for him?* That's what you'd have thought but you'd be wrong. Now Ken Fischer's the latest. You heard? Jesus. *Ken Fischer.* 'Best-Looking Boy.' 'King of the Senior Prom.' He'd gone with Verrie Myers since seventh grade—*Veronica Myers.* In Europe, someone said. In a hotel room where he was all alone. Or maybe wasn't alone. Who could predict—*Ken Fischer?* Someone was saying that Mary Louise Schultz was in the hospital. 'Maybe a drug overdose.' That terrific-looking girl—those *breasts.* Why'd a doll like that want to kill herself? Her husband's some big deal in Albany. Friend of the Governor's. *I* tried to date her, and no luck. Bibi Arhardt—remember that cool chick? Husband decides he's gay, divorces her and she winds up in a detox place in Minnesota. So I was thinking how happy I am—basically. How much I love my wife, my kids. Basically. It was like my life, my soul, was a substance thin as smoke that might dissolve into nothing if my will weakened. I stood there trembling in the sun that's like a furnace in Nevada on the sidewalk in front of a rundown shit-stained bungalow trying desperately to explain to a cancer-riddled old man what the Hearts meant to me. I was saying, almost begging, 'I went to high school with Dahlia Heart's son, John Reddy. Do you maybe remember him?' No, he doesn't. I tried to describe Dahlia Heart to the old man—but *how do you describe Dahlia Heart?* 'A beautiful woman, a stunning, unforgettable blond woman, a gorgeous body, sort of like—Marilyn Monroe, Kim Novak—but like Grace Kelly, too—' and the words echo in my ears *they're so fucking inadequate*. We're drowning, dying, *our words are so fucking inadequate*. So this old guy's sneering at me. He's enjoying this, I can see it. Like sometimes in my office I enjoy telling some rich old bossy bag it's essentially too late. He laughs, and rubs at his crotch, and says, 'Look, doc, you live long enough you learn there's no telling one c—t from another. Give it up.' And I was shocked. I mean—shocked. Like a kid might be shocked, some old Santa Claus pronouncing such words. I got out of there fast. No more Arroyo Seco for me. That night at the hotel I got drunk and lost seventeen hundred dollars at blackjack and next morning I gave my talk like a zombie and on the flight back to La Guardia I caught some vicious bug like dysentery I couldn't shake for weeks." Dr. Baskett yanked off his wire glasses and rubbed his eyes, there was nothing more to say.

We understood. We were gravely shocked, too. For it had to be false, a lie. It wasn't the truth. If there's but one truth we'd all learned from knowing Dahlia Heart, even if we hadn't known Dahlia Heart, it's that one c—t can certainly be distinguished from another.

6

John Reddy, pawn of fate?
John Reddy, at Hell's Gate?
John Reddy, John Reddy Heart.

W*as the shooting of Melvin Riggs accidental?*
     If you wanted to think that John Reddy was an inno-
cent pawn in some sort of cruel celestial drama, you'd want to
think *yes*. If you wanted to think that John Reddy Heart knew
exactly what he was doing when he ran to get his grandpa's
gun (which the old man kept wrapped in an oil-stained towel
in a cardboard carton at the foot of his bed amid a store of
empty bottles of all sizes, colors, qualities of glass and
designs) and ran back upstairs to his mother's room—the
"master bedroom suite" of the Heart residence as it would be
called—in which the naked, drunken, rampaging Riggs was
abusing Dahlia Heart, and kicked open the door, and dropped
to one knee (as Blake Wells said admiringly, "That's the John
Reddy touch") and fired a single shot between the man's eyes,
raising the heavy .45-caliber revolver (it was thrilling, we
could envision it!) steady in both his hands, uttering not a
word (for John Reddy's words were famously few, it was our
theory that when he was in action the speech center in his
brain shut down), merely squeezing the trigger—then you'd
want to think *no*.

Girls and women tended to think *yes*. The rest of us, *no*.

How many dates, gatherings, parties ended in shouting matches—girls on one side, boys on the other. Suzi Zeigler and Roger Zwaart broke up, were reconciled, broke up and again reconciled how many times, we'd all lost count, over the issue of John Reddy's guilt. So too with Verrie Myers and Kenny Fischer. Janet Moss and Steve Lunt. Mary Louise Schultz and Smoke Filer. Shelby Connor and Dwayne Hewson. Pattianne Groves and Dwayne Hewson. Babs Bitterman and Jonathan Rindfleisch. The Circle (that elite, some said snobby group of eight girls, five boys who'd started together in kindergarten at the Academy Street School and would graduate together, thirteen years later, from WHS, out of a class of one hundred thirty-four) was grievously shaken. At our senior prom, when we should have been celebrating, not picking at old wounds, old grievances, and theoretical issues, Ginger McCord in a daffodil-yellow chiffon strapless formal and her grandmother's pearls turned upon her date, Dougie Siefried in a rented tux, slapping and bloodying his nose so that his white shirtfront was splattered with red, crying, "John Reddy Heart is not a murderer. *He is not.*" Soon, a number of us joined in; how could we resist? John Reddy himself, rumored to have been elected King of the Prom by a flood of ballots, his election angrily denied by school officials, came very late to the prom, at nearly midnight, stayed only about half an hour, and spoke to few of us. Many denied he'd been there at all—"Just you drunks 'saw' him. 'Talked' to him. Come *on.*" Babs Bitterman, smoking pot with Steve Lunt in his gorgeous Buick LeSabre in the parking lot outside the gym, insisted she'd seen John Reddy pull up, park—"In that funky-sexy Mercury, I'd recognize it anywhere. Even without my glasses. Even with Stevie's hand between my legs and his tongue in my mouth." (Babs liked to shock us with her racy talk. We'd miss her in later years, as we'd miss Stevie, Smoke and Pete Marsh.) Decades later at our fabulous class reunions, the debate continued. The outcome of John Reddy's trial hadn't settled anything, it seemed. Nor had the passage of time that's said to "cure all wounds—almost." For this was an underground fire that smoldered invisibly and malevolently for years, never dying out but flaring up at unexpected intervals. At our tenth reunion, for instance, during a festive pig roast on the terrace of the English Tudor home on Ivyhurst Drive, Amherst, of Shelby Connor Strickhauser (Shelby's first husband was a Buffalo pacemaker manufacturer eight years Shelby's senior, and rich), the delicate-boned Shelby with her pale blue staring eyes and fair, flyaway hair forgot her role as hostess, demure in a pink floral Laura Ashley summer dress, and turned on Bo Bozer (with whom she'd gone out briefly in ninth grade) crying, "Damn you, Bo Bozer: John Reddy Heart was not a *murderer*. He was *not*."

We were startled by Shelby's vehemence. In high school, she'd been the frail-seeming waifishly pretty girl who wasn't quite so striking as her more spectacular girlfriends (Verrie Myers, Mary Louise Schultz, Ginger McCord, et al.) and had no outstanding talent or aptitude of which we knew, though she'd sung, in a sweet wavering soprano, a prominent role in Handel's *Messiah* at Easter of our senior year, and had thrown herself with fevered concentration into knitting a multicolored muffler, though possibly it had been a turtleneck sweater, for John Reddy Heart when he'd been locked up at Tomahawk Island. Shelby's dad was a banker, and rumored to be a shark among sharks, but Shelby with her fluttery hands and a mild propensity for stammering was a gawky lovely bird-girl we'd somehow never taken seriously. But we saw the stunned hurt in Bo Bozer's doggy eyes, as if, these years, in secret, he'd been in love with Shelby though married, as we all were, to other people; Bo shot back at Shelby, forcing a smile, "So what was he, then—an Eagle Scout?"

Roland Trippe, the suave, expensive lawyer Dahlia Heart had hired to defend John Reddy, argued eloquently that if the shooting was accidental, as he certainly believed it to be, the most the prosecution should have charged his client with was involuntary manslaughter, not second-degree murder—"Your Honor, this is a shocking and unconscionable case of the flagrant misuse of prosecutorial discretion." Trippe took his indignation to the press, gave interviews charging the district attorney's office with "extreme prejudice" toward his client on the bias of his client's youth and his family's "nonconformist lifestyle"; but the prosecution held firm, and the charge of second-degree murder held. In the eyes of District Attorney Dill, and numerous others besides, John Reddy Heart was a "vicious, precocious murderer"—a "shocking example of American teenaged lawlessness and depravity." It didn't help his case that John Reddy stubbornly refused to express remorse; nor did he offer any explanation of what had happened in his mother's bedroom, and why he'd fled Willowsville. Some of us admired John Reddy's refusal to cooperate with authorities but others, the more pragmatic-minded, like our *Weekly Willowsvillian* editor, Blake Wells, worried aloud—"Why doesn't John Reddy *say something*? Like, 'I shot the man to protect my mom.' That's all he'd need to say." Evangeline Fesnacht, one of several writers in our class, a beetle-browed, hulking girl, said scornfully to Blake, "That's what you would do in John Reddy's place; but *you* are not *John Reddy*." For months in Mr. Cuthbert's social studies classes, in Miss Bird's and Mr. Lepage's English classes, even in Mr. Dunleddy's biology classes, Mr. Salaman's and Mr. Alexander's math classes, Mme. Picholet's French classes, Mr. Schoppa's driver's ed classes, Coach McKeever's and Miss Flechsenhauer's gym classes, the subject was sifted, analyzed, argued. The WHS Christian Youth Group pondered issues of sin and forgiveness. The Debate Club pondered issues of free will, determinism and guilt. Where the majority of us cared primarily for the minutiae of the case, what John Reddy was wearing at the time of the shooting, for instance (which of his numerous T-shirts, which pair of worn, holey jeans, which of his gray wool sweat socks with the thin black stripes around the elasticized cuffs), and whether it was stained from Melvin

Riggs's blood, and the route he'd driven from 8 Meridian Place on St. Albans Hill to the stark snowy wilds of Mount Nazarene two hundred sixty miles to the northeast, in the Adirondacks, where he'd be captured seventy-two hours later (in the cafeteria at school, in the library during study period, in The Haven, in The Crystal, in pizzerias we pored tirelessly over New York State road maps we'd elaborately marked in red ink, with more ferocity of concentration than we could manage for our school subjects), the brainier among us like Clarence McQuade, Ritchie Eickhorn, Bart Digger, Dexter Cambrook and Elise Petko, as well as Blake Wells and Evangeline Fesnacht, were obsessed with metaphysical conundrums of accident and necessity, free will and determinism, Original Sin and redemption. Evangeline Fesnacht who proudly asserted she was a "lapsed Lutheran" insisted that, if you believe in Original Sin, you must believe in redemption. Dexter Cambrook argued pedantically that since the universe had recently been discovered to be "a concatenation of accidents arising out of nowhere and fated to disappear into nowhere, into a second cataclysmic Big Bang, all acts within it, for instance one living humanoid organism 'killing' another by firing a bullet through its brain, had to be similarly accidental, and without meaning." Katrina Olmsted burst into tears hearing Dexter's pitiless words. Reggie Edgihoffer denounced Dexter as a "godless agnostic." Elise Petko, Dexter's nemesis (since ninth grade when she'd transferred to our high school from the private Spence School for Girls in Manhattan, and who would in time edge Dexter out by .19 of a point to be named valedictorian of our class, relegating a chagrined Dexter to the rank of salutatorian) brilliantly countered his argument by saying, "If everything is accidental, then all of mankind is equal in the face of blind chance, and *we're all equal in terms of responsibility and guilt*."

("That cruel, cold-hearted bitch!" Verrie Myers fumed. "I hate her." "But Elise doesn't mean anything personal," Ken

Fischer said, squeezing his girlfriend's cold, combative fingers, "—it's just, like, the 'philosophical perspective.'" "Screw 'philosophical perspective'—we're talking life and death. *John Reddy's*.")

At the time of John Reddy's second trial, in November of the year Melvin Riggs died, our debate club sponsored a competition with our old rival Amherst on the subject: *RESOLVED: Man is a rational being and is capable of exercising free will*. The debate was publicized locally; where these competitions were usually argued in a kind of echo chamber in the auditorium, drawing only a few diehard friends and parents, and sometimes not even those, this debate filled half the auditorium of five hundred seats; a reporter covered it for the *Willowsville Weekly Gazette*. Ritchie Eickhorn, one of our writers, an honor student with a faint stammer, spoke with surprising eloquence. Evangeline Fesnacht spoke forcefully, if at too great a length. Blake Wells had done research into local and national crime statistics relating to "juvenile crime." Both Dexter Cambrook and Elise Petko shone. There were numerous interruptions of applause. Faculty judges lavishly praised the debaters and voted for a draw, and girls in the audience who'd been stricken with anxiety that John Reddy Heart would be discovered to be "guilty" fell laughing and weeping with relief into one another's arms.

Thank you, God. Nothing has been decided.

* * *

It's true, and this is fact not conjecture, the Hearts were mysteriously *accident-prone*. And so were others in their vicinity.

The workmen—roof-repair, painters, plumbers, electricians, lawn crew—who were hired by Mrs. Heart, through Skelton Construction, to make improvements on the house at 8 Meridian Place, for instance: one, a seasoned roofer, fell two storys from the edge of the steep mossy-rotted slate roof to seriously injure himself on the ground; another, a young

painter in his twenties, grew dizzy in the sunshine and toppled off a second-floor scaffolding, his fall fortunately broken
by an evergreen shrub; another painter was dismissed by
Herman Skelton for unprofessional behavior (he'd been discovered prowling the upstairs of the house, a silk
undergarment of Dahlia Heart's in his overall pocket, having
thought evidently that no one was home); an experienced
worker for Moss Lawn & Tree Service unaccountably lost
control of his chain saw (watching Dahlia Heart in white silk
shirt, white shorts, white scarf tied around her head, digging
in the rock garden?) and severed a thumb. A cleaning woman
hired by Mrs. Heart, on the recommendation of a new
acquaintance, scalded herself scrubbing one of the old, enormous ceramic tubs in the upstairs bathrooms; it would turn
out she'd been drinking, stealing sips from Aaron Leander
Heart's liquor supply. And there were mysterious instances of
pilfering, small items (like Dahlia Heart's champagne-colored
silk negligee with matching lace panties) missing, with no
way of tracing the thief. Crudely hand-lettered notes in the
Hearts' mailbox, addressed to "MISS DAHLIA"—

> You know I lovve you.
> I could eat your juicy Heart.

(Dahlia called Matt Trowbridge of the Willowsville Police
Department; he came at once to the house to examine the
note but declared that, so far as he knew, whoever'd written it
had not broken any law and could not be arrested—"But if we
can find out who it is, I could possibly speak with him unof-
ficially," Matt Trowbridge said grimly, clenching his fists. "I
could possibly discourage him from harassing you further,
Mrs. Heart.")

"It's as if some force is trying to drive my family and me
away from Willowsville," Dahlia Heart was overheard complaining to Skip Rathke, owner and manager of the Village
Food Mart on Spring Street, who on Saturday mornings, his

busiest morning, stood at the front of the store greeting customers and chattering like a master of ceremonies, "—but it won't succeed." Mrs. Heart spoke bravely and defiantly, as if well aware that her words were being overheard and memorized by strangers, primarily women, who, coolly assessing her in her stylish oyster-white silk-and-linen pants suit, cork-heeled shoes with straps that tied around her naked ankles, ropes of shiny cultured pearls around her neck and her bright makeup flawless as if she'd just strode onto the stage of a Las Vegas casino nightclub, did not wish her well.

"Yes. An actual force. *But it won't succeed.*"

And one day, approximately eight months after the Hearts moved into their new house (still known generally as the Edgihoffer house) while the Edgihoffer suit was still pending and extensive repairs were being made on the property of which not everyone in the Village approved (including all sixty-four members of the Village Historical Society who unanimously signed a petition to Mrs. Heart delivered by certified mail protesting the robin's-egg-blue paint, the felling of many beautiful trees and the "grotesque disfigurement" of the formerly prize-winning rock garden), Dahlia Heart in her usual white costume, white satin pillbox hat with a dotted-swiss veil perched on her lustrous white-blond hair fashioned into a French twist, was the conspicuous guest of Willowsville businessman and entrepreneur Jerry Bozer for lunch at the Willowsville Country Club as other diners stared ("That fool! Does he think we're supposed to believe he's having a 'business lunch' with the blackjack woman?"); and the youthful middle-aged Negro waiter serving the couple in the sun-filled dining room overlooking the golf course suddenly grunted, staggered, dropped the tray of plates he was carrying, gasped for air and fell heavily to the floor and began to shake, writhe, kick; and the beautiful Mrs. Heart leapt up, crying, "He's having a convulsion! He's an epileptic! Call an ambulance!" While every other woman in the dining room looked on in terror and repugnance, Dahlia Heart squatted beside the writhing man, whose eyes were rolling back in his head and whose lips were covered in froth, lowering herself so abruptly that her tight-fitting white skirt rode up her thighs, and her thighs and calves were revealed thickened with muscle, causing her stockings to burst into myriad runs. With strong capable hands, not minding if her elaborately lacquered nails broke, Mrs. Heart held the writhing man down and forced his jaws open and with "a wicked-looking long-handled steel comb" (as it was described) from out of her handbag pressed his tongue down flat to keep him from swallowing it. And all so fast! Without missing a beat! By the time the emergency medical crew arrived from Amherst General Hospital a few minutes later, the crisis had passed. The black man was breathing again, almost normally; his face, grayish, mottled with sweat, resembled a human face again and not a death mask. Panting, Dahlia Heart rose to her feet. No one thought to assist her. The pillbox hat was crooked on her head and a strand of synthetic-looking blond hair had slipped loose from her French twist. Both her stockings were ruined. Her stylish white suit with the bolero top and skirt slitted at the back was damp and smudged, as if by the black man's mahogany-dark skin. It was only when Mrs. Heart glanced up to see the dining room of white faces still staring at her, and Mr. Bozer's among them, that it might have occurred to her she'd made a blunder.

(There's a melancholy story in the background of John Reddy's life in our suburb that has to do with Dahlia Heart expecting to be invited one day to join any of our private clubs. After all, her affluent, influential business associates Mr. Bozer, Mr. Skelton, Mr. Wells, Mr. Pepper, Mr. Riggs and others belonged to these clubs and occasionally took her to them as their guest: the Willowsville Country Club, the Glenside Tennis Club, the Lake Erie Union Club, the Buffalo Athletic Club, the Country Club of Buffalo. And there was the Gardeners' Club of Buffalo, even the Village Women's League. And others. But even before the Riggs scandal, when the few friends she'd cultivated would drop her cold, this just wasn't going to happen. That day at the country club when the Negro waiter went into convulsions sealed Dahlia Heart's social fate in Willowsville—though she hadn't known, of course.)

Months later, Herman Skelton had a near-fatal accident, never entirely explained, on the Peace Bridge returning to the United States. It was past midnight of a weekday when Mr. Skelton's newly purchased Oldsmobile somehow skidded out of control at the crest of the long, magisterial bridge, swerved across the median and narrowly missed an oncoming car before it crashed into the railing; the car would have plunged hundreds of feet down into the rushing Niagara River if the railing hadn't held. Unconscious, badly bleeding, Mr. Skelton was rushed by ambulance to Buffalo General Hospital; he'd suffered a concussion, his collarbone and several ribs were broken and his handsome ruddy-freckled face was lacerated and would be badly scarred. The damage done to his car and his marriage of twenty-six years was even more serious: for Herman had lied to his wife Irma, telling her he was attending a business dinner in Buffalo when in fact, as it immediately came out, there had been no business dinner, and there'd been a woman in the car with him at the time of the accident—Dahlia Heart. Herman had taken Mrs. Heart "sightseeing" in Fort Erie and Niagara Falls, Ontario; they'd had a lengthy dinner at the Top of the Flame, the twentieth-floor revolving dining room of the Niagara Tower, and had gone drinking and dancing afterward at the Horseshoe Lounge, overlooking Horseshoe Falls from the Canadian shore; to add to his other injuries, Herman would be charged with reckless driving and driving while intoxicated. Dahlia Heart, his companion, who'd chosen not to ride with him in the ambulance to the hospital, but, for his own good, to return directly to her home, by some miracle hadn't been injured at all.

Yet Dahlia Heart was prone to accidents herself. A number

of times in the years this mysterious woman lived among us, Mrs. Heart wore conspicuous dark glasses in public because—we surmised—one or both of her eyes might be blackened. These glasses were Hollywood-style white-plastic frames with very dark lenses—"shades." These glasses had the power of riveting a guy's attention almost as much as Mrs. Heart's remarkable face itself. Once John Reddy began playing varsity basketball we saw her sometimes at home games, usually with John Reddy's grandpa (a character, white-haired and wearing a cowboy hat even indoors) and maybe with John Reddy's younger brother Farley and sister Shirleen (not that we knew their names, we didn't), she'd get to the game on time but often leave at the halfway point no matter how exciting the game was or how spectacular John Reddy was that night. Everyone watched Mrs. Heart enter the gym, clad in her trademark white, in cold weather a luscious white (ermine? though our moms swore it was fake) fur coat to her ankles, making her way in spike-heeled white shoes or in cold weather spike-heeled white boots to the reserved seating; and everyone watched her leave. Possibly she'd take time to shake hands with sweaty Coach McKeever and congratulate him in her husky, honeyed voice—"Coach, these boys are terrific. John-ny tells me *you are the best*"—leaving Coach blinking and shaken as if he'd been hit on the head with a sledgehammer. Possibly she'd exchange a few cheery words with our principal, Mr. Stamish, who came to all home games, our teachers Mr. Cuthbert, Mr. Larsen, Mr. Dunleddy, Mr. Schoppa. We observed these men staring at Dahlia Heart, the more transfixed if she was wearing her dark glasses, and we liked it that, for those fleeting seconds, our teachers' thoughts were identical with our own and the "generation gap" was bridged. Speaking for his less articulate buddies, Dougie Siefried rolled his eyes, moaning, "That woman is sex-y," making suggestive motions like he was trying his damnedest to keep his hands off his crotch. "You can smell her at one hundred yards. You got to wonder—who's banging her

around, she's got a black eye she has to hide? *Who's banging
her?*" Sometimes we'd trail her checking out the Avenue of
Fashion, Saturday afternoon. We'd sighted her in the Bon Ton
Shop, in the Village Tearoom, in Nico's or the Crystal—alone
or with her stumpy daughter. In a brave platoon of several
cars we cruised the cul-de-sac of Meridian Place, hoping to
catch sight of Mrs. Heart working in the infamous rock
garden (we thought the two-foot plaster gnomes, freaky green
frogs and sunbonneted little girls with sprinkling cans fashioned from wood Mrs. Heart had placed amid the rocks and
flowers were a nice touch—"Like Disney's *Fantasia*," Blake
Wells said thoughtfully. "It allows you to peer into the
woman's mind"). We hoped to hell the nosy old biddies who
lived on either side of the Hearts, Mrs. Thrun and Mrs.
Bannister, wouldn't call the cops on us. We hoped to hell
John Reddy wasn't around to notice us.

As time passed it became unclear in our minds if we'd actually seen or only just imagined Dahlia Heart's sexy blackened
eyes, bruised arms and (well, we couldn't have seen this)
breasts, belly, thighs. It was unclear whether we were normal
horny-crazed kids of sixteen and seventeen or sick perverts.
"What'd it be like, do you think, if your mom was—*her*?" Jon
Rindfleisch wondered. "If, y'know, you were in the same
house—bathroom, bedroom—with *her*?" We tried to imagine
John Reddy's domestic life but our imaginations failed. Ketch
Campbell startled us by saying with a lewd grin, "She's a
woman you gotta kiss—or kill." And Dougie Siefried would
moan as if in actual pain, "*Who's banging her?* It's gotta be
somebody." For hours we sat in Nico's chewing pizza crusts
and swilling Coke, speculating which one of our dads might be
Mrs. Heart's mystery lover. We'd heard plenty of rumors (overheard, our moms gossiping on the phone) that Mrs. Heart saw
married Willowsville men; we didn't know exactly what "saw"
meant, but we had hopes. Dwayne Hewson volunteered his old
man, a former quarterback at U-B and now a go-getter executive at Metropolitan Life. Smoke Filer volunteered his old man,

fattish but not bad-looking, "to hear him talk, a real stud." Art Lutz, Pete Marsh, Roger Zwaart—we all argued it might be our dads since they weren't home much, worked late at offices and traveled out of town on business. Only Bo Bozer whose old man was, in fact, long rumored to be one of Mrs. Heart's close male friends, shrugged off the subject like a bad smell. It was weird how Bo lit a cigarette and exhaled smoke through both nostrils with a sneer, saying, "My old man? Don't make me laugh. The poor sap couldn't get it up with a crank—if he had the chance."

Once at Nico's, making this statement, Bo started to cry. Tears just spilled out of his eyes and ran down his cheeks and the rest of us kept on eating pizza, swilling Coke, making dumb-ass jokes and never noticing a thing.

* * *

Girls never believed that John Reddy Heart was accident-prone in any careless, negligent sense. As Trish Elders argued, "John Reddy tries to keep things from going wrong." Brooding Janet Moss agreed, "He has a tragic soul." Verrie Myers, edgy, excited, making husky sighing noises like her mother, broke in, "'The tragic hero'—Mr. Lepage was telling us today—'is the force of action, and is acted upon.' Like Hamlet." Millie LeRoux objected in her nasal way, "But isn't Hamlet a 'sacrificial hero,' too? Because he has to die. Like Othello." Mary Louise Schultz said, lighting a Winston (she'd just begun to smoke, stressed by the drama of John Reddy's first trial, which had abruptly ended in a mistrial), "That is so damned *sad*. And so *unfair*. You get to be a hero but you must be *sacrificed*." Shelby Connor countered, "Look, Millie, say you're Ophelia, you're sacrificed, too. But you never get to be a 'hero.'" Verrie Myers said impatiently, her beautiful deranged eyes ranging across our faces, "What's any of this got to do with John Reddy Heart anyway? He's an American, for Christ's sake. *He's one of us*." But the remark hung tenuously in the air like curls and coils of smoke from our shared cigarettes. We didn't want to contradict Verrie but we couldn't believe it was so—that *John Reddy Heart was one of us.*

Swinging his legs up onto the lowermost rung of the fire escape at the rear of the Academy Street School, and hauling himself up, and beginning to climb. You wouldn't have said he was showing off. He was possibly restless, bored. A skinny-lanky boy of only eleven, with gnarly-muscled upper arms. That Western drawl you wouldn't want to smile at. A pack of Lucky Strikes stuffed in his back pants pocket. As every kid in the playground watched, John Reddy climbed swiftly, unerringly, monkeylike, up the fire escape ladder, over the edge of the building and disappeared. "Disappeared?" someone always asked, doubtfully. "He didn't *disappear*." "In fact, he did," we said. "He disappeared." "But that's impossible. You just didn't see where he went." "The Academy Street School is a building that stands by itself. John Reddy climbed up onto the roof, and we ran around the side, we ran around the front, we ran around the entire building—he'd *disappeared*." At once other boys tried to follow him, competing with one another to climb up the ladder. DeMott Duncan, a fattish eighth grader, slipped, fell ten feet onto the pavement, broke his left forearm and was half-carried away by one of our teachers, bawling. After this, John Reddy was observed with wariness and respect. Girls liked it that boys feared him. He had a quick temper, quick fists. He could attack without warning. He rarely spoke unless he had something to say and then his words were terse and matter-of-fact, adult. It would be many times recounted how he'd come into homeroom one Monday morning, this was in eighth grade, one of his eyes swollen and welts on his face and Miss Koithan, shocked, asked what had happened to him, and John Reddy said in his polite Western drawl, "Ma'am, I was coldcocked." The boys in the room laughed to disguise their anxiety at not knowing what "coldcocked" meant. The girls pretended they hadn't heard the actual words. After a moment, her cheeks reddening, Miss Koithan pretended she hadn't heard them either. A few years later, when John Reddy was a sophomore in high school, we heard he was in fights involving police—he'd been picked up one night in Niagara Falls. Who he'd been fighting, and why—we didn't know. At the age of fifteen, he was reported to have grown-up girlfriends, women who weren't in school, no one who lived in Willowsville or was known to us. In the spring of John Reddy's sophomore year there occurred the famous Tug Hill battle between guys from Amherst and guys from Willowsville: these Amherst guys were in the habit of cruising our streets after school, trying to pick up girls and yelling crude remarks, and one day they went too far whistling at Sasha Calvo, only a freshman, walking home on Main Street, "Hey wop-girl, wanna ride?" John Reddy heard of this and organized a dozen Willowsville guys, fellow team-mates of his, and there was a fight in Tug Hill Park, an actual fistfight. For years Art Lutz would marvel, "My God, John Reddy was fighting like a maniac. It was a profound sight." Smoke Filer said, "It never surprised me he killed anybody, afterward. Nobody who'd seen him use his fists would've been surprised."

"The worst was, when John Reddy almost died. On the Millersport Highway."

"He didn't almost *die*. He wasn't even hurt."

"He might've died! He said so himself."

"But that accident wasn't his fault. Not in any way."

And that was so: It hadn't been John Reddy's fault, except there was something in him that seemed to draw, like a magnet, such incidents. Three weeks before the shooting of Melvin Riggs, John Reddy was driving his glaring acid-green Cadillac north on the Millersport Highway when a carload of stoned guys in their twenties from South Buffalo drew up dangerously close behind him in a black Trans Am, yelling insults, hitting the horn in an effort to goad John Reddy into racing with them; but John Reddy wasn't in the mood and gave them the finger and the Trans Am retaliated by almost ramming his rear bumper, the two cars traveling at about seventy miles an hour on the three-lane highway, across which thin, wraithlike streams of drizzly snow were being blown; John Reddy sped up to try to escape, but of course this was what the driver of the Trans Am wanted, now swinging around to pass the Cadillac close as if to sideswipe it, the two cars roaring along, shuddering in the wind, as other vehicles braked, swerved to avoid them, fled bumping and bouncing onto the shoulders of the road. The Trans Am was in the process of passing the Cadillac and shifting into its lane—John Reddy was pumping his brakes by this time, praying the car wouldn't fishtail as he'd tell police—when it went into a skid, lurched off the highway to crash head-on into a concrete abutment near Dodge Road. "The most hellish thing I've ever seen," a witness, driving another car, told police. "That black devil-car just *crumpled*."

The driver of the Trans Am was killed outright, the top of his skull sheared away; the young man in the passenger's seat died in the wreck, and two other passengers in the back seat were critically injured. "You could see the blood, the actual blood, seeping out of the wreck," a witness said. "Blood, oil, gasoline! Some of us worried it might be combustible. The wreck might explode." How John Reddy managed to save himself, braking the Cadillac to a stop on the highway shoulder, he wouldn't afterward recall. It had all happened in a daze. It had happened in an evil dream. It had happened (he would tell Mr. Dunleddy this, though not until many months later) in the way his father had died, spiraling down from a slate-blue desert sky with such force that a crater measuring one hundred feet in circumference would be ripped into the sandy earth. When police and paramedics arrived at the wreck they would discover sixteen-year-old John Reddy Heart within a few yards of the twisted Trans Am, kneeling on the ground, his head bowed and eyes shut, lips moving as if he was praying. Other drivers stood about, shivering and staring, aghast at the carnage. Inside the smoldering wreckage of the Trans Am were mangled, lifeless bodies but the driver of the acid-green

Cadillac, a boy in a well-worn black leather jacket, jeans and battered leather boots, hatless, his black, oiled hair disheveled around his brooding face, was not looking. "That young man's face was dead-white," one of the paramedics said, "—I'd have said he was in shock but he insisted he was O.K., just wanted to go home." Luckily for John Reddy there were witnesses to the accident who would explain to police what had happened, absolving him of any blame. In the morning *Courier-Express* there was a front-page article, with a photo of the Trans Am and inset photos of the four young men who'd been in the car; no photo of John Reddy Heart, but his name and address were given. Everybody at school was talking about the accident but—where was John Reddy? He stayed away for days. And when he returned somber, frowning and distracted, he shrugged off talking about the accident even with his varsity teammates. "I was kinda hurt, to tell the truth," Dwayne Hewson complained. "I come up to John Reddy who's my buddy, give him a punch on the shoulder with the edge of my fist, not hard, and say, 'Close call, eh, John? I heard—' and John Reddy cuts his eyes at me like I'm Nosepicker Nordstrom *and just walks away*." Similar responses were reported from other sources, including those senior girls in the habit of boldly loitering at John Reddy's locker or begging rides from him in the Caddie after school. Verrie Myers who believed by this time that she had a "psychic rapport" with John Reddy slipped notes through the slats of his locker and affixed them to the windshield wipers of his car—without response. But Mr. Cuthbert encountered John Reddy at Farolino's Cabinets & Carpentry where John Reddy worked part-time, and bluntly asked him, for bluntness was Mr. Cuthbert's classroom style, what truth was there to the tale everyone was telling that he'd almost been killed the other day. "The boy wouldn't look at me at first, which wasn't like John Reddy who'd look anyone in the eye. Then he said, so softly I almost couldn't hear, like he was ashamed, 'Sir, I prepared quick to die. But it didn't happen.'" Smoke Filer, a popular jock, a state champion wrestler, told how his dad, a surgeon at Buffalo General, ran into John Reddy one morning in the hospital, asked what he was doing so far from home and John Reddy said he'd been there to give blood; he'd tried, too, to visit two friends of his but they were in intensive care and you can't visit anyone in intensive care unless you're a relative. Smoke said, "It's got to be those guys from the crash! We-ird! Giving blood, and calling them friends of his! My dad asked me if 'this John Reddy Heart' is a doper, his eyes were so strange, and I told him, 'Hell no, Dad, John Reddy is *one cool dude*.'"

Squeezed into our booth at the Crystal, Smoke Filer importantly recounted this story, with an already deft, practiced air. When he finished, he was surprised that none of us spoke. The clamor of the Crystal washed over us, we heard nothing. Mary Louise Schultz was wiping at her eyes. Verrie Myers was lighting a Camel borrowed from Smoke's pack, with trembling fingers. Ginger McCord was biting her lower lip, staring into the melting ice of her Diet Pepsi as into a vision of her own mysterious future. At last Trish Elders whispered, "His blood."

"His actual *blood*."

"Imagine: John Reddy's *blood*."

"In a transfusion. Hooked to your arm. *His blood*."

"Coursing through your veins. Your heart."

"Your heart!"

"Oh God. *Oh*."

"*Ohhhh. God*."

(Smoke grumbled to his buddies how pissed he'd been telling the girls of the Circle this story about John Reddy he believed would impress the hell out of them, only to have them go into practically a trance. "It was like being the only guy at a lez-orgy. There was this weird wild electric current between them. Like, suddenly, I didn't fucking *exist*.")

* * *

Then there were "the other Hearts," to whom few of us paid much attention. Though clearly they, too, were prone to mysterious accidents.

For instance, John Reddy's grandfather Aaron Leander Heart. It was he who owned the "murder weapon" though, as he was forced to admit to police, he had no New York State permit for it. "If that gun hadn't been in the house, John Reddy couldn't have used it. If that gun hadn't been loaded, John Reddy couldn't have killed a man." You could argue that the tragedy was Mr. Heart's fault, and it's possible that the old man suffered guilt and remorse for what had happened, if not to Melvin Riggs ("If there was ere a bastid that deserved death, it was Mel Riggs," Mr. Heart was several times quoted) then to his grandson John Reddy ("If there was ere a brave boy, our Johnny was him"). But he'd gone on record stubbornly testifying to police that the .45-caliber Colt revolver "hadn't been loaded, no sir, I could swear." He'd gone on record angrily protesting the confiscation of the revolver by police—"*I* purchased that damned gun in Nevada, *I* paid a hundred and five dollars for that gun, *I* say *that is my rightful gun.*" At John Reddy's trials he was a reluctant, uncooperative witness for the defense who seemed often not to know where he was, or why, and a stubborn, testy, only intermittently coherent witness for cross-examination by the prosecution. There were observers who believed Aaron Leander Heart to be "nutty as a fruitcake" and others who believed him to be a shrewd, practiced actor in a secret drama of his own devising.

Mr. Heart had the look and stance of an old Indian fighter. A pioneer of some long-vanished American Southwest past. His horse and his rifle had been taken from him but a veiled, sardonic vigilance glinted in his stony eyes. *Don't tread on me! Don't even turn your back on me.* His white hair that was almost too white, like Dahlia Heart's platinum-blond hair that was almost too blond, flowed to his shoulders. His soiled beige cowboy hat slanted at a jaunty angle on his head. White, wiry whiskers, tobacco-stained around his mouth,

partly obscured a windburnt, creased ruin of a face. ("But
you can see he was once good-looking, can't you? Like John
Wayne. Gary Cooper.") In profile Mr. Heart resembled a
hawk. His teeth were what you'd describe as "frontier
teeth"—with a look as if grit or sand had blasted them, wearing them down, embedded in the cracks. The canine teeth
were conspicuously long and pointed. When Mr. Heart
laughed (as he'd laughed several times, unexpectedly, on the
witness stand in the courtroom), he resembled a wolf laughing. His laughter was silent and hissing and possibly wasn't
real laughter. We heard it sometimes, alone in our bedrooms,
shivering, knowing it was the wind and not terrible old Mr.
Heart prowling the night like a ghost. "But if John Reddy
loves him, he's got to be O.K." It did seem clear that John
Reddy loved his grandfather for sometimes they were seen
together in John Reddy's car; John Reddy treated his grandfather tenderly, yet with respect, always calling him "Sir" when
we chanced to overhear.

When it was revealed at the time of John Reddy's arrest that
Aaron Leander Heart was seventy-three years old, the fact
was met with surprise and some disappointment. "Somehow
you don't think of a character like that being any fixed age."

Old Mr. Heart! We tried to see John Reddy in him, but it
required an effort of imagination that was beyond us. It made
some of us queasy just to contemplate our parents, let alone
our grandparents, seeing, like an unwanted sight in a mirror,
a glimmer of our fate in a mother's face, a father's profile. We
did not know, nor did we wish to guess, our parents' ages. We
did not know, nor did we wish to believe, that our parents had
once been young. That John Reddy had a hawkish, hungry
profile like old Mr. Heart—that the bony structure of his
young beautiful face was identical to the bony structure of his
grandfather's face—that the two, separated by decades, shared
certain unmistakable mannerisms, a cocking of the head, a
veiled sweeping gaze from beneath knitted brows—not to
mention the Texan drawl—were not to be acknowledged.

"There's no one like John Reddy Heart! *No one.*"

Since moving to Willowsville and taking up residence in Colonel Edgihoffer's house, old Mr. Heart had become a familiar if controversial sight. His St. Albans Hill neighbors strongly disapproved of him. The old man was "the worst of the pack." He was "little more than a vagrant. A ragpicker. And a souse." Yet his mismatched, slapdash clothes were perceived to be, by grudging eyes, of quality. Jackets, vests, stained neckties, mismatched gloves, the red kerchief knotted around his turkey-wattled neck. His boots, battered, with a look of being manure-stained, were believed to be of hand-tooled leather. Each morning he must have risen early, before dawn; taken up his hickory walking stick and his increasingly frayed, filthy burlap sack, and set out. He was seen everywhere. His ghostly figure might appear unexpectedly in a roadway, out of mist, fog, drizzle, light snow, oblivious of the screeching of brakes, a tattoo of horns. Mr. LeRoux, Millicent's father, who commuted from Willowsville to the Marine Midland Center in downtown Buffalo, leaving his home on the Common before dawn on winter mornings, told the tale of how one misty-drizzly morning he'd struck old Mr. Heart with his car's right fender and knocked him down—"I just didn't see the man! He materialized out of nowhere. But he got up immediately, refused to listen to me when I tried to speak to him, waved his hand at me and limped away, indignant. What a character!" For old Mr. Heart was a passionate man. A man with a destination. A man with a vision. (But none of us could have guessed at the time what Mr. Heart's vision was.) He prowled our placid suburb as far south as St. Peter and Paul Cemetery (where he sometimes also napped) and as far north as Amherst Hills Tennis Club. Scavenging tirelessly for discarded bottles and glassware, he tramped the manicured slopes of the Willowsville Country Club golf course as brazenly as if he were tramping through a weedy vacant lot. Visitors to Willowsville recoiled, seeing the apparition of an elderly white-haired gent with a walking stick, a burlap bag slung over his shoulder, a brisk limp—"My God, who's that? Father Time?" We didn't know how to explain Mr. Heart. We were embarrassed of him, protective of him, proud of him. John Reddy's grandpa! Sharp-eyed and voracious as a vulture scouring parks and paths and alleys for trash-treasure, perusing garbage cans in front of our houses, railroad under-passes, parking lots, Dumpsters. The tangled banks of Glen Creek and the nameless ditches that fed into it. Mr. Heart slept where sleep overtook him: his favorite bench was along the "One Hundred Weeping Willows Walk" of Glen Creek. Several of us sighted him on a warm spring day wandering, like an upright crow, the marshy no-man's-land beyond Tug Hill Park; we saw, through binoculars belonging to Shelby Connor's kid brother, that Mr. Heart was picky about his find-ings. Not just any discarded bottle or glass object would do. Frowning, he lifted and examined specimens, holding them to the light before deciding whether to add them to his sack or drop them carelessly down again. (It was shocking to some members of the community, and more evidence that the Hearts were lowlife stock, that Mr. Heart hadn't a glimmer of interest in picking up trash. Whatever he was up to, it was for his own purpose.)

Mr. Heart soon grew restless in our village where pickings were slim. Mr. Olmsted, Katie's father, reported sighting him scavenging miles away near the Naval Park exit of the Buffalo Skyway—"I called to him, tried to get him into the car so I could drive him home but he didn't seem to hear. Just walked away." At various times Maxine Bird reported driving Mr. Heart back from Transit Road, and elsewhere; one windy autumn evening, when John Reddy was a sophomore at WHS, Mr. Heart was found "dazed and incoherent" by a road-side in Batavia, and another time in Clarence Center; sometimes local police drove him home, sometimes John Reddy or Dahlia Heart hurriedly went to fetch him. One winter day (at a time when John Reddy was becoming a local basketball star), Mr. Heart was picked up by Thruway police for scavenging on the Thruway where pedestrians weren't allowed. His most dangerous episode occurred only weeks before the shooting of Melvin Riggs: he was scavenging at the Dodge Road landfill, eagerly climbed a small mountain of discarded Christmas trash and unleashed an avalanche, fell and was buried beneath debris for hours, in −5° F, before being discovered and rescued by sanitation workers. Treated for frostbite and hypothermia, Aaron Leander Heart who'd been so stubbornly reticent for years began to chatter excitedly, like one who has peered over the horizon into nothingness. "The Lord has demanded a Glass Ark! Beside a Glass Lake! I have a mission that *must be fulfilled*." And, clutching the wrists of anyone who came near, with an air of pleading, "I've been a craven sinner and I don't repent. I've been a cruel man to other mortals. But there is my mission that must be fulfilled." When Dahlia Heart and fifteen-year-old John Reddy came to take Mr. Heart home, and Dahlia was told by authorities it was her duty to supervise her father more closely, she protested, "'Supervise'? Him? How? Tie him down? What can *I* do, I'm only his daughter, d'you think that vain old man listens to *me*?"

So Mr. Heart was saved from freezing to death, and soon afterward resumed his wanderings. He continued them oblivious of our parents' stares of disapprobation and outrage. Until one day we realized we'd been seeing him for years. All our lives. Since we were children. And certain of our parents, too, who'd grown up in Willowsville, swore they remembered him from their own childhoods. "Old Mr. Heart? That white-haired old man with the sack? Oh yes, he's always been here. Some people say he's actually died, and it's his ghost now that's here, haunting us."

Then there were John Reddy's young brother Farley, and his younger sister Shirleen. About whom little was known when they were children in Willowsville. Both were awkward, uneasy children who shared in the family's penchant for accidents, but to what degree isn't clear—"Our knowledge of them, ironic in retrospect, was so minimal."

Farley was three years younger than John Reddy—thirteen at the time of Riggs's death. His teachers at Academy Street would speak of him as "quiet"—"withdrawn"—"intense"— "extremely bright in math"—"from a family like that, unexpected!" A ninth grader, Farley was taking a course in solid geometry at the high school a mile away; his teacher there, Mr. Salaman, spoke of him as "naturally gifted"—"very young for his age, though not 'immature.'" In both schools he passed among his classmates invisibly. "I know he must've been there, I sort of remember his name being called, and a sense in the classroom that, wow, *This guy's a brain, this guy's something special*. But if I try to summon back a face for this— is it Farley?—there's nothing there. A blank," Janie Zeiga, Norm's younger sister, told us.

At the high school it was said that John Reddy's very shadow was darker, more vivid and "solid" than ordinary shadows. (Photos in WHS archives taken of John Reddy on the basketball court seem to confirm this controversial asser- tion.) Yet Farley Heart, oddly, was said to have no shadow; at the most, a faint, fleeting shadow that rippled lightly over surfaces and readily vaporized. At thirteen he wasn't quite five feet tall; he weighed hardly seventy pounds; his hair was fair, not quite brown and not quite blond; already, it appeared to be thinning. His head was bulb-shaped, his eyes myopic and inclined to bulge. Yet there was a distant look in those eyes, an element of haze, as if his mind was elsewhere. "You wanted to knock gently on his head and say, 'Hello? Hello in there? Anybody home?'" one of his junior high teachers recounted. It must have been that the Hearts needed money, for poor Farley, shy and uncoordinated, had tried a series of part-time jobs for which Mrs. Heart brought him in person to apply. (Unsurprisingly, Farley was nearly always hired.) He worked for a week at Muller's Drugs—"We had to let the kid go. He was always dropping things, cutting himself on broken glass." He worked for a week at The Village Food Mart—"We had to let the kid go. He was always dropping things, cutting himself on broken glass." At La Casa di Napoli, where he worked briefly in the kitchen, Farley scalded his hands in steaming hot water—"Poor kid. We had to take him to emergency. Then we let him go." It was said that, some months later during summer vacation, when Farley was bicycling home from his job at Burnham Nurseries, he collided with a delivery van—"The kid just ran into me, skidded into my path like he's blind or something"—was knocked down, suffered cuts and a broken left wrist. It might've been that time, or another, that John Reddy was seen, in his Caddie (by this time painted a brilliant acid-green, with a subtle pattern of gold trim bordering the windows, and a prominent chrome tailpipe) arriving with a shriek of brakes to carry his sniffling brother, and his brother's crumpled Schwinn, home. He'd said, exasperated, "O.K., kid. Climb in. Wipe your nose. I'll shove the fucking wreck in the trunk."

And Shirleen. We'd rack our brains trying to remember Shirleen. Plain, pudgy, sad-faced, eleven years old at the time of Riggs's death and probably (it was surmised) she'd never laid eyes on Riggs, hadn't met any of her mother's "business associates." (Except it might've had a lot to do with her converting to Roman Catholicism, joining a convent and taking a lifetime vow of celibacy. That seemed plausible!) Her classmates couldn't remember her. Her teachers tried valiantly, in vague terms, as people will when trying to recall, years later, an individual who has received unexpected renown. Shirleen Heart was "a quiet girl"—"a good girl"—"jumpy, nervous"—"secretive." "You could see she had spiritual leanings, maybe." Or was she "stubborn, sometimes. An obstinate little mule." Shirleen's grades didn't reflect her soberness, they were only average to mediocre; she was too shy to speak in class; her weakest subject was math—"The poor child was incapable of comprehending the objective logic of math. She seemed to think that you could will a thing *to be*, or *not to be*, with your mind. As if, if you wished hard, and you were 'good,' whatever solution you came up with had to be right." Her sixth-grade homeroom teacher said of her, "Shirleen was the kind of shy, plain, young-old child you hope won't grown up embittered and filled with rage at the world in the guise of 'humility.'" Like Farley, Shirleen wore glasses from an early age, yet even with her vision corrected she appeared near-sighted and oblivious of her surroundings. She had a habit of walking with a book held up a few inches from her eyes, so that she was continually stumbling into things, bruising and cutting herself. If you spoke to her in such a state, she didn't hear. It was said that, at the age of ten, she'd tumbled down a flight and a half of stairs in the house at 8 Meridian Place, clutching an oversized, illustrated copy of *Alice in Wonderland* which she refused to let go even in the ambulance. Her right leg was badly broken and she had to endure a cast for eight months during which time she reverted to crawling on her hands and knees like a baby. Forced to leave the house, she had to be pushed in a wheelchair; she came reluctantly to use crutches, for her legs, she said, "scared" her. Dr. Groves, Pattianne's father, who treated Shirleen Heart, said, "It happens sometimes: the child loses faith in her ability to walk. She doesn't trust her legs to hold her up. And she's angry at her legs. Or at someone she imagines controls her legs." Long after the terrible cast was removed, Shirleen walked unsteadily, as if making her way across the deck of a tilting ship.

"You can see whose fault it is—*that woman's*." So our mothers sniffed to one another.

(None of us, their children, walked unsteadily. Except Chris Donner who'd had polio as a young child somewhere in Indiana, before the Donners moved to Willowsville.)

Though Mrs. Heart and John Reddy were often seen together in town, a striking couple, Mrs. Heart was rarely seen with her younger children. She did not, in fact, appear to be a woman who'd had children. There was something sculpted and tranquil about her beautifully shaped body: it did not have the look of a body stretched to accommodate childbearing. Yet Mrs. Heart took Shirleen, in her cumbersome cast, to the Crystal and the Bon Ton Shoppe; she took Shirleen to the children's wing of the Willowsville Public Library, helping the beetle-browed, perspiring child with her crutches—"Shirl honey, come *on*. You can manage these stairs. Mom's right here, aren't I?" For such excursions Dahlia Heart modified her ordinarily dazzling-white costume: she wore an oyster-white trench coat over slacks of a similar off-white hue; she tied a pale pink diaphanous scarf around her throat, or wore powder-gray gloves, a matching velvet hat. When at last the cast was removed from Shirleen's leg, Dahlia celebrated by taking the girl to Buster Brown's for several pairs of new shoes, including black patent-leather ballerina flats of the kind all the girls were wearing; she charmed the salesgirls at Junior Miss, bringing in the shy, finger-sucking fifth grader who had to be coaxed into trying on spring jackets and coats, obstinately refusing to contemplate her image in the three-way mirrors. "But you *are* a pretty girl, if only you wouldn't frown so," Dahlia encouraged Shirleen, as the salesgirls chimed in like a chorus, "—*Yes you are!*" Dahlia continued the celebration by providing a luncheon for Shirleen and eight of Shirleen's "closest girlfriends" from her fifth-grade class, at the Village Women's Club. (Frannie Reid, mother of one of the girls, marveled at how adroitly Dahlia Heart whom she scarcely knew finessed her into arranging for the luncheon, since she, and not Mrs. Heart, was a member of the club. "At least the woman paid," Frannie told her friends. "Paid *me*.") On another occasion, Dahlia took Shirleen downtown to Kleinhans Music Hall where mother and daughter saw a lively stage version of *West Side Story*, tickets provided by the Buffalo personality Melvin Riggs who sat with them for most of the performance. (We'd heard that, after Riggs's death, interviewed by police, Shirleen couldn't identify photographs of Melvin Riggs. We wondered if she'd erased the memory of *West Side Story*, too.)

At our fifteenth class reunion there was Verrie Myers, now glamorous Hollywood star Veronica Myers, on the eve of the opening of her seventy-six-million-dollar film starring Jack Nicholson and Clint Eastwood, recounting how in the Crystal one afternoon she, Ginger McCord and Mary Louise Schultz spied on Dahlia Heart and her mysterious daughter. That girl who looked nothing like her mother, or her brother John Reddy—"Sort of a gnomish creature, like something that'd crawled up from underground, blinking in the light. Yet she was appealing, too. When her eyes glanced up, through the mirror, you remember that ellipsis of mirrors in the Crystal? if you sat in a corner?—you'd feel an actual shock thinking *Why, that poor little girl* without exactly knowing why because, my God, we'd all have died to have a mother glamorous as Dahlia Heart. I mean—that's what we thought at the time." Verrie laughed, startled, as if she was having a new thought now. It was like music how Ginger joined in, though since marrying Dougie Siefried, with Dougie's drinking problems, which possibly she hadn't comprehended were actual problems at the time of marrying him, Ginger had lost most of her old flirty-teasing ways and was now almost somber, severe—"Yes. We were there in the booth watching John Reddy's mother through the mirrors seeking some clue to her, and through her to him. Because there was magic to her, as much as to him. So we were studying her, smoking our grown-up cigarettes and studying her, the way adolescent girls do, not just memorizing but absorbing, like through our pores. And then gradually it happened we were studying the daughter. 'Shirleen,' who'd one day become this remarkable nun, this teacher of autistic children, on *60 Minutes* they compared her practically to Helen Keller 'reaching into another's darkness and bringing in light'—only who could have imagined such a thing, then? My God. Like Verrie says, she was a gnome. Maybe we're exaggerating a little, we're drunk, but anyway we can say the kid wasn't any version of her mom. But we got riveted by her. A kind of spiritual tugging. This wasn't long after that pathetic ugly cast had come off her leg, and about a month before the shooting. This was winter. And as Verrie says the girl was appealing somehow. Her eyes. As a hurt animal is appealing." Verrie said, "But a hurt animal can be dangerous, too." We looked at her expectantly: there was such a vivid, electric intensity to her face, it was natural to imagine her in a film, and ourselves as mere background figures. Because of her public prominence, anything Veronica Myers said had a tone of authority. It seemed scripted; not, like our own language, improvised and faltering. "John Reddy's sister was one of those ancient children," Verrie said. "As if her soul had passed through many incarnations. Dahlia Heart looked and acted *young*; the girl looked and acted old. It didn't surprise me to learn she became a nun, to salvage not just her soul but her *life*." Verrie held her glass out for her host Doug Siefried, Ginger's husband, to pour champagne into; it was Verrie's second, or perhaps third, glass; she'd grown breathless with the recitation as if it held a special significance of which she wasn't herself certain. Shirleen had eaten her Crystal Banana Split (chocolate and strawberry ice cream, Reddi Wip and maraschino cherries) hungrily while Dahlia Heart spoke to her, calling her "hon"—"honey"— "sweetheart" with almost a pleading in her voice which the girl seemed to ignore. Ginger said, thoughtfully, "There was a glisten of hurt, or fury, in the girl's eyes. I recognized it years later when Jennifer, our daughter, was two years old. That sudden eruption of a child's *will*." Verrie said, "There was something desperate in Dahlia Heart's eyes, too. But no one ever saw. Publicly, I mean." "Her lover Riggs was abusing her. Threatening her." "But nobody knew." "John Reddy knew." "Oh yes—John Reddy knew. But maybe not exactly, not then." It was crucial for us to recall the exact sequence of events in the life of John Reddy Heart for we knew how, with the passage of time, our memories would melt and lose definition, like our muscles. We'd noted the frightening example of our elders who easily and even affably confused decades, mistook sons for fathers, and fathers for sons. In the Crystal that day the girls were compulsively pushing quarters into the jukebox. You had to be quick to get a quarter in, to beat out other booths. Verrie favored sentimental pop classics like Elvis Presley's "Heartbreak Hotel," Ginger favored down-and-dirty like Lollipop "Die Lovin' You," Mary Louise had a weakness for the Shrugs' rockabilly "Broke Heart Blues." (We were missing Mary Louise at this reunion. She'd come for the tenth, and she'd come for the twentieth, but she was missing the fifteenth—she had a new baby, her fourth, living in Albany with her politician bureaucrat husband we called Ice Eyes.) Verrie was saying, "When Mrs. Heart left the Crystal with her daughter, everybody stared. It was like a movie. And the girl who'd been waiting on them, Ray Gottardi's sister Gloria, told us how Mrs. Heart had been bringing the girl into the sweet shop twice a week, like she was trying to cheer her up—'You know, trying to be like other mothers and daughters. Especially in public.' We asked her what did Mrs. Heart say to her daughter, that she could hear, and Gloria said, 'She's trying to get the kid to smile at other kids in the place. "C'mon, honey, *try*. So they'll come over and talk to you. To us." But the kid can't smile. It's like you'd try to get a wounded animal to smile. But Mrs. Heart is a classy lady, leaves me real tips not pennies and nickels like certain cheap-skates.' Gloria paused to let that sink in. The three of us wanted to hide under the table! Then she says, 'And she's nice to me. Like I'm not a servant but somebody real. Just now she left me a two-dollar tip and says, "I know what it's like to be on your feet all day, Gloria—it's hell." And she winked at me. A woman who lives in St. Albans Hill, winking at *me*.'"

It was a remarkable performance of Verrie's. Not only could we hear Gloria Gottardi (whom some of us dimly remembered) we could see Gloria Gottardi. Verrie had become, for the duration of the anecdote, Gloria Gottardi. ("Why didn't Verrie continue with a stage career?" was a question sometimes batted about by her old friends. "She had talent. She could act. It was something that came over her, her voice, her eyes would turn liquid. She could make you doubt you'd ever known her.")

Of course most of us had heard this story, seen this performance, before. Even Wayne Butt who'd transferred to WHS in our senior year and had never seen the notorious Dahlia Heart in person had heard this story more than once. But we loved it. We were thrilled by it. Words precious to us as the words of an old childhood movie. *I know what it's like to be on your feet all day, Gloria—it's hell.*

* * *

Had gorgeous Dahlia Heart who'd inherited the Edgihoffer property on Meridian Place once been a *waitress*? We filed such a notion away for the record.

And for the record, too: certain remarks the Hearts made to one another in the Glen Theatre one Sunday evening a few days after news broke of Jerry Bozer's "nervous collapse" and hospitalization. (It was said that Mr. Bozer was drinking heavily, fired from his job at Metropolitan Life where he'd been a top executive for twelve years, and had moved out of the family home on Castle Creek Lane. Bo never spoke of his dad any longer, not even in derision, and none of his friends wanted to ask. In time, like others, Mr. Bozer would disappear from Willowsville.) Suzi Zeigler and Roger Zwaart spoke of how they'd happened to be sitting in their usual seats in the back row of the Glen Theatre at a second-run showing of *The Sound of Music* when who should file in two rows ahead of them but the Hearts—the entire family! They'd come at the most popular time for families, Sunday at seven p.m. (Friday and Saturday nights were date nights, of course. None of us would've wished to be caught dead at the Glen on Sunday evening with our families.) The theater was about two-thirds full and everybody, Suzi said, knew the Hearts were there within seconds of their appearance, stealing glances at them, or frankly staring if they were in a strategic position. Suzi and

Roger who ordinarily slouched in their seats, sort of partially collapsed worn-velvet seats in the middle of the row, by now fitted to their buttocks in the strained posture in which they sat for hours pressed together, kissing dreamily, now sat alertly upright and leaned forward to observe the Hearts. It was amazing—"How normal they seemed. I mean, like anybody else," Suzi said. John Reddy oblivious of eyes snatching at him from out of the semi-dark led the way, carrying a giant box of popcorn and a large Coke: he looked older than sixteen, needing a shave, his hair greasier than usual, slicked to the back of his head but falling down in quills; Roger thought, sure, John Reddy was embarrassed like anybody'd be, seen in public with his family at the Glen, but Suzi disagreed—"John Reddy always had such *poise*. You could never tell his thoughts." They did note that John Reddy was patient to the point of impatience with his younger sister, the beetle-browed girl of ten or eleven who walked stiffly as if her leg was still in a cast; she was slow to settle in her seat, puffing and fussing, carrying a Coke and what appeared to be a fifty-cent box of M&M's. Beside her sat John Reddy's younger brother, a pigeon-breasted boy with glasses and a skeptical look— "Sharp kid," Roger said. "My brother Jamie's in his ninth-grade class." Then there was glamorous Dahlia Heart, amazing to see her in the role of mother, not that she looked like anybody's mother, she might've been (this was Suzi's observation) John Reddy's slightly older sister or even (but this was weird to contemplate) his woman friend, the two glancing toward each other (so both Suzi and Roger noted) from time to time during the movie as if to check *How're we doing? O.K.?* Bringing up the rear was old Mr. Heart in his cowboy hat, rumpled jacket and noisy boots; both he and Dahlia had their arms full with Cokes, candy and popcorn boxes, one of which old Mr. Heart promptly spilled as soon as he sat down. "God *damn*." And Dahlia whispered, "Dad*dy*. *Hush*." The main feature began with a burst of Technicolor. Fortunately Suzi and Roger had seen *The Sound of Music* before, or in any case they'd sat through it; Suzi loved the movie, Roger couldn't bear it. This time, Roger said, he observed Julie Andrews's almost too luminous face reflected on as much of Dahlia Heart's face as he could see from his seat. Suzi marveled, "It was another amazing thing. How on the Hearts' faces, which were such rapt, uplifted faces, I could see *The Sound of Music* like ghost images rippling in water." (Except John Reddy must have grown restless, for he slipped away at least three times during the movie to use the men's room or possibly to step outside the exit, which you weren't supposed to do at the Glen, to have a quick smoke though smoking, of course, was forbidden for WHS team players during basketball season. Neither Suzi nor Roger dared follow John Reddy to find out what he was doing, nor did Mimi Duncan behind the refreshment counter know though she calculated he was out in the alley for "somewhere between five and eight minutes each time. Alone.") Of all the Hearts, Dahlia seemed the most moved by the sentimental story of children, dogs, nuns and love in the scenic Swiss Alps; she wiped at her eyes during crucial scenes, and laughed joyfully during others; though Mrs. Heart, too, slipped away from her seat several times, to use the ladies' room presumably, and, as Suzi subsequently learned, by querying Mimi Duncan, to make a telephone call in the manager's office—"Something Mr. Nordstrom doesn't ever let anyone do, but he let her. That real pretty blond woman. It must've been an important call, huh?" Old Mr. Heart, his cowboy hat in his lap, nodded off frequently during the movie but, when he was awake, could be heard responding to it emphatically, laughing, muttering, even groaning. And when THE END flashed onto the screen amid buoyant, deafening music, the very music of happiness, without a cue from Mrs. Heart all five Hearts burst into spontaneous applause. "What a lovely movie!" Mrs. Heart exclaimed, her eyes shining with tears. "What a wonderful, *true* movie!" The Hearts' enthusiasm was contagious; others in the audience joined in. Filing out of the theater, the

Hearts were heard to say to one another, as Suzi and Roger tried not to be too conspicuous about following after them, especially avoiding John Reddy's eye, these remarks:

"This was fun!"

"This *was* fun!"

"Let's do this again—soon!"

"Would anyone like the rest of my popcorn?"

"Would anyone like the rest of my M&M's?"

"Would anyone like the rest of my Coke?"

"Would anyone like the rest of *my* popcorn?"

"I love Technicolor, it's like real life."

"I love Technicolor, it's better than real life."

7

John Reddy looked his man in the eye.
Said John Reddy, Time to die!
John Reddy, John Reddy Heart.

Evangeline Fesnacht was our chronicler of disaster. Already in elementary school she'd exhibited those strains of precocious morbidity and hyperscrupulosity that would distinguish her, years later, in an adulthood forged beyond the leafy perimeters of the Village of Willowsville as *E. S. Fesnacht, a voice of disturbing but penetrating insight into the tragic human condition.* In seventh grade, elected secretary of our class, Evangeline insisted upon including in her fastidious minutes not only every minor transaction of our meetings but parenthetical synopses of events that had occurred in the weeks between meetings—accidents, illnesses, traumas, family woes and even deaths as they pertained, however obliquely, to members of the class. Miss Scholes, English teacher and seventh-grade advisor, looked on in amazement as Evangeline read in a somber, quavering voice of Bonnie MacLeod's "nine-day chickenpox," DeMott Duncan's "broken left forearm and facial lacerations, when he fell from a fire escape at the back of the school," the "near-fatal vehicular accident on Youngman Highway" of Ketch Campbell's older brother Ryan, our social studies teacher

Mrs. Carlisle's "miscarriage—her second in two years," Dwayne Hewson's grandfather's death "by coronary thrombosis while teeing off at the Willowsville Country Club" and the removal of a "cancerous lung" from Smitty, one of the school custodians. Evangeline's mild, suety eyes glowed behind the lenses of her pink plastic glasses as she recited these grave yet poetic facts that gave to the ordinary dimensions of our meeting room in the Academy Street School an air of opening out not onto the familiar rear of the rain-washed school grounds and freshly laid asphalt pavement but onto eternity. Miss Scholes interrupted, "Evangeline! Those items have nothing in the slightest to do with our last meeting!" and Evangeline replied, with equanimity startling in a twelve-year-old, "Miss Scholes, excuse *me*. These items are far more significant than the minutes of some silly old *meeting*. They are of the great world of chance and fate that *surrounds us*." Never again would Evangeline Fesnacht be elected class secretary though each spring at election time, year following year through our junior year, stubbornly, perhaps spitefully, she presented herself as a candidate, taping hand-lettered posters urging * E. S. FESNACHT FOR CLASS SECRETARY * TRUTH, TRUTH & NOTHING BUT THE TRUTH * to school walls and telephone poles nearby; she argued reproachfully, it seemed to us almost warningly, "I am taking 'minutes' on our lives whether you allow me to or not."

As Ritchie Eickhorn said of his old, abrasive schoolgirl-rival, "From the first, you knew that 'E. S. Fesnacht' was out for blood."

It wasn't generally acknowledged that Evangeline Fesnacht had started school in Willowsville in kindergarten: that is, she was a member of that élite (if unofficial) group of thirteen known, enviously by some, as the Circle. (Eight girls, five boys—by chance, it seemed, all well-to-do, from prominent Willowsville families. Yet those in the Circle claimed never to think of their special status; some professed to be embarrassed by it—"I think it's all just so ridiculously trivial and snobbish," Verrie Myers said. "I want to be known for *other things* for God's sake!—like talent." The five guys of the Circle—Dwayne Hewson, Ken Fischer, Smoke Filer, Roger Zwaart and Jon Rindfleisch—denied emphatically that the Circle existed and pointed out that there were a number of others in our class who'd begun kindergarten with them at the Academy Street School—"But their dads are nobody special, or they don't live in the right part of town, so, somehow, it doesn't count.") Evangeline Fesnacht's father was president of Fesnacht Electronics, Inc., her mother belonged to the exclusive Village Women's League, the Fesnachts lived in a large half-timbered English Tudor house on the Common between the Burnhams and the LeRouxs, yet none of this made any difference: "Poor Vangie. Not only didn't she fit in, *she didn't even know it*."

Decades later, a literary journalist preparing "E. S. Fesnacht: A Profile" for *The New Yorker*, would canvass us, Evangeline's old classmates, for memories, anecdotes, impressions. Of course we were tactful and duplicitous. We spoke of Evangeline's "early, budding talent"—her "strangeness"— "uniqueness." We did not say that Evangeline Fesnacht displayed no visible attractions whatsoever. "Not just she lacked 'personality-plus,' she lacked 'personality' altogether." "An ugly duckling amid Willowsville's glamour," Mr. Lepage once remarked. "A bold, strong-willed girl," Miss Bird recalled. "We *wanted* to like her." Evangeline's face was spade-shaped, with a fleshy wedge of a mouth. For years she wore glinting wire braces of a peculiar webbed complexity and when they were finally removed, just before graduation, her teeth were still mildly crooked, odd greenish-pale baby teeth that shone when she smiled. Evangeline's complexion!—a baby-smooth skin perversely stippled with bumps, pimples, pustules which with brooding nails she picked in class, often causing to bleed. ("Fesnacht sure grosses me out," Art Lutz said, admiringly. "And that isn't easy to do.") Evangeline's eyes, her most distinct feature, were yet small, beady, myopic;

watchful; shrewdly intelligent; of the color, as Dexter
Cambrook recalled, of "slightly tarnished zinc." Her hair was
a darkish nondescript brown, kinky rather than curly, always
cut short, exposing her large, creamy-pale ears. When, after
staying away for thirty years, Evangeline would return for
our thirtieth reunion, we were startled at her short stature, for
we'd remembered her as tall, hulking, and clumsy; in fact she
was about five feet three inches tall, and by the age of sixteen,
when other girls were acutely conscious of their figures, dieting to maintain perfection, Evangeline Fesnacht must have
weighed one hundred forty pounds and walked with a rolling,
flat-footed, swaggering gait—"Like, from behind, Clyde
Meunzer." (We laughed, but it was so: Clyde was one of a
number of North Country hicks bused into our school district
from outlying regions of Erie County.) Ken Fischer, urged by
his well-intentioned mother to be nice to certain girls (whose
mothers belonged to the Village Women's League) whom it
would not have occurred to any boy to "be nice to" otherwise,
went out of his way to speak with Evangeline at school; once,
as the rest of us laughed behind our hands, and Verrie Myers
flushed crimson, Ken asked Evangeline to dance with him at
a noon St. Valentine's Day hop. How comical to watch good-
looking Ken Fischer with his wavy chestnut hair and dreamy
eyes, one of the most popular guys in our class (whom no
one, not even his closest friends, could find much fault with),
pushing a perspiring, beetle-browed Evangeline around the
gym floor. Ken said defensively, "Evangeline isn't bad. She's
kind of fun, actually. If you get to know her. But it's kind of
hard to get to know her, and possibly not worth the effort."

We didn't tell the inquisitive journalist for *The New Yorker*
how, as a teenager, Evangeline Fesnacht wore her mother's
clothes—or so we believed. Mrs. Fesnacht was frankly
middle-aged, as plain and hulking as her daughter, though
more inclined to smile in public and to make an effort to be
friendly, gracious. Certainly mother and daughter eerily
resembled each other, like sisters, in near-identical black wool

tentlike coats with large shiny buttons that gave them the look of ungainly but enthusiastic vultures when they appeared, as they invariably did, at the homes of families in the St. Albans Hill area in which there was illness. Mrs. Fesnacht and her daughter were known for their casseroles and home-baked pies delivered to startled neighbors who hadn't yet realized what was in store. "We knew Uncle Harvey would never make it," Pete Marsh said, shuddering, "when Evangeline and Mrs. Fesnacht turned up with their tuna-breadcrumb-baked casserole." In ninth grade when poor Dickie Bannister who'd been such an outgoing, athletic kid grew thinner, paler and bluer-veined in our appalled midst, it was Evangeline who predicted his eventual demise. "He has that look in his eyes. I know that look." Evangeline spoke flatly, as if reading numbers from a blackboard. By the time Dickie died of leukemia over the summer, before we entered WHS, his death seemed secondhand even to his closest friends. But Evangeline was most notorious for keeping in her locker a large photo album with black satin covers she called *Death Chronicles*, which she allowed some of us to inspect, though only in her immediate presence, turning the pages and closely monitoring, with her small beady bright eyes of no discernible color, our reactions. In the album were pasted with schoolgirl neatness and in chronological order articles and photos from local papers; some were formal obituaries, but most were front-page stories with such lurid headlines as 4 BUFFALO TEENS KILLED WHEN CONVERTIBLE OVERTURNS—WEST SENECA PROM TRAGEDY: 3 DEAD, 2 INJURED—ENGAGED COUPLE KILLED AT TRAIN CROSSING ONE WEEK BEFORE WEDDING. It was exclusively girls to whom Evangeline showed these clippings and to whom she murmured huskily, "It's hard to feel sorry for some people. These girls out on dates with their boyfriends and 'fiancés.'" Evangeline also collected stories of girls and women murdered by men—husbands, boyfriends, stalkers and total strangers. She told Trish Elders, her wedge of a mouth contracting, "See? That's what being pretty and 'popular' gets you. Like you." Trish was too shocked to reply, and seeing the look in her face Evangeline laughed harshly, shut the album and said, "Oh who am I kidding? No man would ever kill *me*."

After Melvin Riggs was shot down dead less than a half-mile from the Fesnachts' house, Evangeline began to specialize almost exclusively in John Reddy Heart. Of course she'd been aware of him for years. She had dismissed the interest of other girls in him as "female adolescent infatuation" (which, after the shooting, would escalate to "mass-hysteria mode") while insisting that her own interest was pure, abstract, metaphysical. When the news broke she declared calmly, "It was fated to happen. I know killer eyes when I see them." Evangeline pasted into *Death Chronicles* clippings from local papers covering the crash of the Trans Am on Millersport Highway with which John Reddy had been involved; according to an offended Orrie Buhr, she'd "hung around John's locker trying to get him to autograph some of it, but John froze the goofy chick out." Subsequent to the car crash, in the approximately three weeks before the shooting of Melvin Riggs, we noticed that Evangeline Fesnacht was becoming transfixed by John Reddy Heart as she hadn't been before. In addition to hanging about his locker in the junior corridor, where she was conspicuously out of place, and vying for John Reddy's attention with other, more aggressive and glamorous senior girls, Evangeline dared to follow him to and from classes, trotting to keep up with his long-legged stride; in a kind of swoon she passed close by him whenever she could, on the stairs amid a stampede of feet, her pug nose twitching in his wake and her mild eyes widened and blinking moistly behind her pink plastic glasses. She panted; she sweated; her wool jumpers, in darkish lugubrious plaids, betrayed half-moons of sweat at her underarms. Several girls of the Circle whose mothers had admonished them to "be nice to" Evangeline Fesnacht complained of how, if they paused to speak with Evangeline, she scarcely seemed to listen but was "forever looking over our shoulders—looking for *him*." Shelby Connor and Pattianne Groves were particularly insulted when they invited Evangeline to have lunch with them, an enormous concession since our cafeteria tables seated only ten, and each seat was precious, only to witness Evangeline rushing off, leaving behind a bowl brimming with chili con carne and crushed oyster crackers—"She'd sighted *him*. She's *shameless*."

We'd recall, a decade later, the time we watched from a second-floor library window as Evangeline Fesnacht dared to approach John Reddy in the parking lot behind school. "Not one of us 'good girls' would've gone out there. *God*." John Reddy was talking with his buddies Orrie Buhr, Dino Calvo, Clyde Meunzer, leaning against the acid-green Caddie and passing a butt among them (a reefer? marijuana? there were rumors); we saw the rough-looking guys in their leather jackets, soiled jeans and battered boots, hair long and oiled to slick duck's-ass points at the backs of their heads, pause in their conversation to stare at Evangeline Fesnacht in amazement beyond derision and even beyond sexual belligerence. Hardly daring to breathe, we pressed close against the windowpane watching as the wide-hipped dark-clad girl spoke to John Reddy who'd separated himself from the others, thumbs stuck in the pockets of his jacket, head politely bowed as Evangeline spoke with him—how earnestly, we could judge by the puffs of steam, like exclamation points, of her breath. John Reddy, a full head taller than Evangeline, gazed not at her but toward her. He didn't appear to be speaking to her, only just listening. But he was listening. For those several minutes, on a March day less than four days before Riggs's death, John Reddy Heart listened to Evangeline Fesnacht as, we couldn't help but think, steaming the window with our own yearning breaths, he wouldn't have listened to any of us.

The cruder guys had a name for Evangeline—"Frog Tits." But John Reddy wasn't one of these.

(Years later, in Kenawka, Minnesota, Ritchie Eickhorn, now Richard Eickhorn, would ask Evangeline Fesnacht, now E. S. Fesnacht, what she'd said to John Reddy that day. Evangeline told him without hesitating, as if the incident had happened only the previous day, "I was trembling. I came up to him and I said, 'John Reddy, you will be the agent of your own destiny. I can see it in your eyes.' I was excited, stammering. I was afraid I might faint, John Reddy standing so close to me, and looking at me—he'd never looked at me before. And his buddies staring at me like I was a freak. I said, 'It's possible you can avert your destiny. I saw it in a dream and I've come to tell you. I—' But I ran out of breath. I couldn't continue. He must've thought I was crazy. He said, embarrassed, 'O.K. Thanks.' He didn't know my name, I don't believe he knew any of our names. That was all of it. I turned around and made it back into school and there was this roaring in my ears and whatever else happened—I didn't faint.")

* * *

"If the boy was going to kill any one of them, Mel Riggs was the man."

Passing by the living room of his home on Coventry Circle a few days after the shooting, Bert Fox told us how he happened to overhear his father make this remark to some friends at the house for cocktails, and Bert almost stopped dead in his tracks, he said, struck by a note of harsh jocosity in his father's voice, and by the laughing agreement of other men in the living room. (The women, including Bert's mother, made no response he could hear.) "You don't expect them to be cynical like us," Bert said, shocked. Yet Mr. Fox's opinion was general through Willowsville.

Pattianne Groves reported that her father, a doctor, actually said in her hearing, "Riggs! At last, somebody had the guts to do it."

In Willowsville circles, such a remark had a special resonance unknown elsewhere in America. It was a witty, perhaps cruel echo of a notorious remark loudly uttered at the Willowsville Hunt Club when news of the assassination of John F. Kennedy was announced to members: "Well. At last, somebody had the guts to do it."

(Though Carolyn Cameron would one day tell us that her husband, who'd grown up in Grosse Pointe, Michigan, reported that the same remark exactly had been made at the Grosse Pointe Yacht Club that day!)

In public, though, everybody said *What a shock, what a shame, what a tragedy*. A man like Mel Riggs shot dead. A sixteen-year-old boy arrested for murder. And Dahlia Heart— "Can you imagine how the woman feels, now? Now it's too late?" We'd hear till we wanted to puke *What a terrible thing to happen in Willowsville of all places. In Buffalo, maybe. In Buffalo, certainly. You expect people to shoot one another in Buffalo, in some* (that is, "colored") *neighborhoods. But—in Willowsville? Where there's practically no crime? One of the four lowest crime rates in any community in New York State, with no violent crime, ever?*

Melvin Riggs, Jr.! Shot down dead. A big funeral, to which a number of our parents and relatives went, but none of us, except Artie Riggs, the dead man's nephew. (Artie, who'd never much liked his uncle, kept a low profile on the subject. He never allowed himself to be interviewed, for instance. He'd say to us, shrugging, gazing off in a corner of the room, a little embarrassed, "Yeah. Shit happens.")

In the media, Melvin Riggs, Jr., was described as a "Buffalo-area personality"—"a local figure of controversy." For what seemed like all our lives we'd been seeing Riggs's fat face on billboards and in newspapers, we'd switched on the TV to see him being interviewed on local stations. First he'd run for Erie County treasurer as an independent, and lost; then he ran for one of eight positions on the Erie County Board of Supervisors as a Republican candidate, which he managed to win, after pouring many more thousands of dollars into the campaign than the token yearly salary would appear to justify.

(But the county board of supervisors ruled on zoning issues, and Willowsville real estate was a hot commodity, and certain of Melvin Riggs's friends were developers.) How familiar his face on billboards at the edge of the village where such advertising was allowed—a full, florid, brimming face like a sunflower in full bloom, with a big toothy smile. MELVIN RIGGS, JR. FOR COUNTY SUPERVISOR. QUITE SIMPLY THE BEST. Even in these carefully posed ads, Mel Riggs stared at you with a look of bemused animosity. His hair was sand-colored in a fluffy fringe around a bald crown that shone with imperial luster. His eyebrows were several shades darker than his hair, fierce and knotty; his nose was frankly big, with widened, dark nostrils as if he was perpetually sniffing. His smile looked like elastic—if it stretched too far, it would snap.

Melvin Riggs owned property in downtown Buffalo, including a well-known supper club, the High Life, on Elmwood Avenue; he was co-owner of the Buffalo Hawks; but he'd lived most of his adult life in Willowsville where he'd married a woman named Laetitia Palmer, from an old, revered local family. In Willowsville he'd soon become controversial— "notorious"—for buying a fieldstone colonial on Brompton Road which he razed to make way for an immense neo-Georgian house; to the fury and protests of neighbors he cut down dozens of elms, poplars and junipers, with the bluff explanation "They got in the way of the view" of the Willowsville Country Club golf course. For much of a summer that end of semirural Brompton Road was a nightmare of bulldozers, backhoes, dump trucks and chain saws, and Melvin Riggs would be known as "the man who brought carnage to Brompton Road." Yet he was most "controversial"—"notorious"—as owner of the Buffalo Hawks, our National League baseball team we grew up loving though the poor guys usually hovered in the bottom third of the league and hadn't been in play-offs since the last year of the Korean War. Still, we loved the red-hawk insignia on their gray caps and their red-and-gray-striped uniforms; we wore their T-shirts and sweatshirts though each of us, at least once, suffered bouts of revulsion at the Hawks' bad luck and destroyed such articles of clothing with scissors, knives or bare hands. (But was it bad luck, exactly? Talented players, hired by the Hawks, soon began to play "erratically"—to use the sportswriters' word—for Buffalo, while players who'd had mediocre seasons in Buffalo, shipped to other parts of the country, immediately improved.) Melvin Riggs was publicly sanctimonious about the role of baseball in American life, calling it our "natural American religion"—a "great game, a noble game, a 'sacred' game." To understand America, Melvin Riggs preached, you have to understand baseball: "Of all athletes it's baseball players who are models for American youth." Such were the speeches Riggs made regularly, often on TV. To some of us these speeches were uplifting though we could see in the man's eyes he was probably bullshitting. "But the best things adults say are bullshit. We've got to believe *something*."

Riggs's critics called him an "exploiter of dreams"—a "traitor to sportsmanship"—a "saboteur of baseball." He was accused of betraying his own team. Of not giving a damn about individual players, only about money. Every baseball season the sports pages of the local papers were enlivened with articles, columns and letters pertaining to Riggs and his luckless but scrappy team, Riggs and his quick temper, Riggs and his firings of managers, trainers and players. At about the time Dahlia Heart and her family were preparing to leave Las Vegas for Willowsville, several years before Riggs's death, he'd burst into the local media for trading the much-loved veteran pitcher Billy Florence to St. Louis after Florence had overcome knee surgery to pitch his best season in years, raising the Hawks from dismal eleventh place to almost-respectable eighth place; denounced on all sides, his Niagara Square office picketed by outraged fans, Melvin Riggs had boldly gone on the *Sal Morningstar Show* on WWBN-TV to be interviewed, saying into the camera, "Look, friends. I'm not running a charity. Nobody in the baseball business—nobody in any business—is running a charity. And the Buffalo Hawks ain't a charity hospital. The name of the game, friends, is *hardball*." For weeks furor raged in the media. Melvin Riggs appeared in caricature on the editorial page of the *News*, a rare distinction. More fans picketed his office and a Niagara Falls congressman charged him with "the hometown equivalent of the Nazi Final Solution." Garbage would have been dumped on the Riggses' elaborately landscaped front lawn and strips of toilet paper flung into the highest branches of their few remaining trees if alert security cops hadn't turned cars away at Brompton Road and Sheridan Drive. (Among the guys in these cars were Hank Siefried and his younger brother Dougie, Jon Rindfleisch who'd one day purchase the Riggs house himself at a price of $1.5 million, Jax Whitehead and Tommy Nordstrom—all of whom ended up that night, drunk, dumping the garbage across the stately steps of Amherst High and flinging the toilet paper into the highest branches of the trees in classy Westwood Heights near the Amherst Country Club.) Next season, Riggs coolly canceled the contract of an even more popular Hawks player, Jimmy O'Grady, a good-looking hotheaded twenty-six-year-old from Lackawanna with whom Riggs had "temperamental differences."

So it began to be noted and in some quarters admired that Melvin Riggs, Jr., had so strong a sense of what he called principle and others his own rampant ego. "You have to hand it to Mel—the S.O.B. is fearless." And, "The S.O.B. answers to no man but himself." Even in Willowsville there were women who found him "maddening, but attractive"—a man with "personality"—"personality coming out of his ears." In his trademark fedora, smiling broadly, a cigarette holder clamped between his teeth FDR-style, Riggs took delight in antagonizing others. His quarrels with his business partners, the public and the media became part of his legend. At home games, Hawks fans booed him with gusto. Obscene lyrics were chanted in his honor. If the Hawks played poorly, Riggs was to blame for "low team morale." If the Hawks played well, it was "despite Riggs." Picket signs abounded, and became part of the TV coverage. RIGGS, BUFFALO NAZI—RIGGS ARE YOU ASHAMED?—RIGGS DIE! Though upon strategic occasions Buffalo's longtime mayor, Democrat Budd Dorsey, joined in the chorus of Riggs denouncers, Dorsey and his entourage often sat with Riggs and his entourage in Riggs's elevated box at Pilot Field. Sometimes the governor and his entourage joined them. Riggs's grown children were sometimes included in the party but more often not; Riggs's wife Laetitia never appeared, with the excuse that baseball crowds "oppressed and frightened her"; it wasn't Melvin Riggs's style to pass himself off as a family man. Often in his Pilot Field box as often at the High Life Supper Club there were beautiful young women "assistants" with ambiguous duties. Though they looked like models or showgirls they were identified as "political aides," for instance, attached to Mayor Dorsey's office, or "public relations consultants," or "liaison officers." One of them was a "business associate" of Riggs's introduced as "Mrs. Heart"— a striking platinum-blond woman of perhaps thirty who wore very dark Hollywood-style sunglasses even on overcast days and entirely white, dazzling-white clothes. Through the baseball game, during lulls in the action, TV cameras would cut to Riggs's box providing closeups of the big gregarious man with the florid sunflower face seated beside the woman in white— "Controversial Melvin Riggs, Jr., co-owner of the Hawks. With a lady friend." Riggs too wore dark glasses, checked suits and conspicuous neckties, a fedora tilted on his head and his cigarette holder clamped between his teeth as he smiled into the camera, winking. *Eat your hearts out, suckers.*

On an August afternoon seven months and eleven days before Melvin Riggs would be shot down dead, naked, in her upstairs bedroom at 8 Meridian Place, Willowsville, Riggs and Mrs. Heart were seated together in Riggs's box at Pilot Field watching the Hawks, fueled by desperation, almost win against the Chicago Cubs, 4–3. It was a tumultuous game of roller-coaster intensity at moments and Mrs. Heart was observed jumping to her feet with the others, clapping, laughing giddily in the spirit of the occasion as Riggs, swaying on his feet, his face flushed more vividly than usual, slung an arm around her shoulders and squeezed her against him— "What'd I tell you, eh? These guys are O.K." A Hawks player with two strikes, two balls against him swung and connected with the ball hitting an almost–home run deep into left field where a Cubs player, as if by perverse magic, fumbled the ball. Screams, cheers! Two runs! You might have believed that Mrs. Heart was a baseball fan, or a fan in any case of the Buffalo Hawks, so vigorously did she applaud. A woman resplendent in white: white jersey dress with a matching coat, silk-lined; a white silk scarf knotted about her throat; a white satin slouch hat with a veil to protect her complexion from the sun; the dark glasses, crimson lipstick and crimson nail polish; on her slender feet, spike-heeled white kidskin shoes. The beautiful but mysterious Mrs. Heart had been introduced to other guests in Riggs's box as a "business associate–friend" of Riggs's whom he'd been advising, he said, on stocks and other investments; it seemed that Riggs's advice had paid off, for Mrs. Heart said, "I have reason to be very grateful to Mr. Riggs," with a sidelong smile at the beaming Riggs. After Riggs's death a friend of Riggs's who'd watched the game with them that day remarked, "Sure, it was pretty clear that Mel and the Heart woman were close. But Mel was always close with good-looking women if he could manage it. You don't plan on dying over a *hobby*."

Melvin Riggs, Jr., hadn't planned on dying at all, it seemed—he'd never gotten around to making out a will, and his accounts would be left in a complicated, disheartening snarl after his death, tied up in litigation for years.

He would be fifty-three years, seven months and fourteen days old at the time of his death.

Not even Evangeline Fesnacht was ever to determine how exactly Melvin Riggs, Jr., met his fate—that is, Mrs. Dahlia

Heart. Or when. Mrs. Heart herself couldn't recall the circumstances of their first meeting; questioned for hours by Willowsville police detectives, she burst into tears, suffered fainting spells, migraine headaches and what her physician pronounced to be "post-stress traumatic amnesia." ("We didn't want to upset Mrs. Heart any further," Willowsville police detective Leroy Stearns said. "She'd been beaten by Riggs and her son was wanted for murder, we figured she'd gone through hell enough.") It seemed, though, that Riggs and Mrs. Heart had not met in Willowsville but in Buffalo. Mrs. Rindfleisch, Jon's mother, claimed to have sighted "that adulterer Riggs" and "that blond blackjack woman" together in Riggs's red Fiat sports car only a few weeks after the Hearts' arrival in Willowsville—"They were just turning out of the drive at the Kingswood Inn, obviously they'd had a late lunch, and he leaned over to kiss her in broad daylight! I *swear*." Yet evidence suggests that Riggs and Mrs. Heart had not met, and certainly hadn't been lovers, for so long. Instead it was believed they'd met within a year of Riggs's death. Mr. McQuade, Clarence's father, liked to dramatize, for us as well as to older people his own age, how he'd been an "unwitting witness" to the very moment of the "doomed" Riggs pushing himself into Bob Rush's face asking to be introduced to Dahlia Heart sometime the previous spring. "I was having lunch with my accountant in the Niagara Room of the B.A.C."—the Buffalo Athletic Club—"when I heard someone say, 'There's Mel Riggs!' and I looked up, and there was old Melvin weaving his way across the dining room half tanked at two p.m., his eyes lit up, drawn to that woman as if by a magnet. You have to admire the poor son of a bitch—he knew what he wanted, and he got it."

(Months later witnesses reported Riggs and Rush quarreling in the exclusively male Jockey Club Bar at the B.A.C.; Riggs was said to have thrown the remains of his double malt whisky into Rush's face and stalked out. Dahlia Heart was presumed to be the subject of the disagreement, but she appeared to be nowhere in the vicinity at the time.)

An equally reliable source associated with Buck Pepper claimed that the lovers first met in Riggs's nightclub, the High Life, where Mrs. Heart had been brought one evening by a Buffalo money-manager named Hooks. (In terror of a grand jury investigation that might expose his private/professional life, this "Hooks" disappeared from Buffalo immediately after Riggs's death and was rumored to be living abroad.) The glitzy High Life, at last razed in 1991 to make way for a Four Seasons Hotel commandeering most of a block on lower Elmwood Avenue, had long been Buffalo's premier nightclub: "classic" singers and musicians presumed dead elsewhere in the country were booked there regularly, like Nat "King" Cole, Dick Haymes, Jo Stafford, Dinah Shore, the Kay Kyser and Tommy Dorsey bands. On the night of Riggs's meeting with "The White Dahlia" (who was wearing an allegedly eye-stopping white satin-brocade dress that evening, with a "dramatic cleavage," and a "mesmerizing" French perfume, L'Heure Bleue) it was the Mills Brothers who sang such old favorites as "Paper Doll" to waves of nostalgic applause. The High Life was crammed with patrons, many of them Buffalo celebrities, but Mel Riggs in his trademark tux and red-and-gray cummerbund made his way unerringly as a hound on the scent to Hooks's table to be introduced to the gorgeous Mrs. Heart—"Wel-come to Buffalo—'Belle Fleuve'!" He was said to have "fallen hard" for her and pursued her for weeks before she agreed to meet him for a "strictly business luncheon" at the Black Derby on South Street. The financial advice Riggs provided Mrs. Heart must have been valuable, for the two began to meet two or three times a week, usually downtown, for, as Mrs. Heart was heard to complain to Skip Rathke in the Village Food Mart, "Willowsville is all *eyes!*" After the shooting Mrs. Heart would vehemently deny she'd ever invited Riggs—or any other man friend—to her home at 8 Meridian Place; she made it a point to "separate my business life from my domestic life."

Yet Mrs. George Bannister and her housekeeper Tina spoke

of witnessing, from a kitchen pantry at the rear of the Bannisters' house, a sorry episode involving Jerry Bozer, drunk and disheveled, turning up one morning to ring the Hearts' doorbell and to call out piteously for Mrs. Heart to let him in, to no avail; another time, the mailman whose itinerary included St. Albans Hill reported seeing two "furious, grim men in expensive cars, a Lincoln and a Porsche, ramming each other's bumpers" at the foot of the driveway at 8 Meridian Place. (One of these men, the driver of the Lincoln, was almost certainly Mr. Bozer, by this time dismissed from Metropolitan Life and under investigation for embezzlement; the identity of the other was never established.) On the night of the shooting, Bob Rush had showed up uninvited at the Hearts' at approximately eleven o'clock; Dahlia Heart had unwisely let him in; he'd stayed for forty minutes and was on his way out when Melvin Riggs showed up, apparently without warning; the two struggled in the front doorway of the Hearts' house, and Rush was persuaded by Mrs. Heart to leave; Melvin Riggs was allowed to stay. (Proof that Riggs, of Mrs. Heart's several businessmen friends, was her favorite? Her preferred lover? Or proof that Riggs exerted some sinister control over Dahlia Heart the other men didn't?)

And by 2:10 A.M. Melvin Riggs was dead, and John Reddy Heart, fleeing the house with the "murder weapon," had become a fugitive from justice.

8

Said John Reddy, This will be the day I died.
John Reddy, our Prince of Pride.
John Reddy, John Reddy Heart.

He might've been killed by state troopers, it's true. Shot down like a hunted animal in the mountains. (Some of us expected this. We held a vigil death watch for as many of the seventy-two hours as we dared.) But it didn't happen that way, they tracked him down exhausted, starving and freezing in subzero temperatures and "using forcible means to subdue the prisoner who was resisting arrest" brought him back to Willowsville in shackles.

WILLOWSVILLE TEEN CAPTURED IN ADIRONDACKS
ARRESTED IN RIGGS SHOOTING

And

UPSTATE MANHUNT RESULTS IN CAPTURE
OF 16-YEAR-OLD MURDER SUSPECT

We hadn't wanted John Reddy to be caught but we loved it that, in photos on the front pages of the *News* and *Courier-Express*, our classmate glared out at us from bruised eyes, his unshaven face bloody and battered like a mask, his mouth set in a scowl like Brando's in *The Wild One*. (And Brando had been beaten, too.) Within days of John Reddy's capture, the interiors of at least two-thirds of all lockers in junior and senior high schools in Buffalo and vicinity contained copies of this famous photo, many of them laminated for preservation. (Lamination would preserve even a newspaper photo, some of us discovered, for decades.) Some girls, like Verrie Myers, taped duplicates to their bedroom walls close beside their pillows. Or, if their parents objected, hid them in secret places in their underwear drawers, between pages of Webster's Collegiate Dictionary, beneath their pillows. At the age of forty-one, Shelby Connor would bring her laminated photo of John Reddy's arrest twenty-five years before to discuss earnestly with her therapist in Bethesda, Maryland, where, the wife of a middle-rank State Department official, she was under treatment for chronic fatigue syndrome and depression—"Doctor, I realize this is an adolescent fantasy. I realize my marriages have been damaged by it. But if I outgrow John Reddy Heart, what will I have left?"

Frankly, it's bullshit that John Reddy ever uttered the words *This will be the day I died*. Anyone who knew John knew he was an individual of few words and these were carefully chosen words, never anything fancy. Where the rest of us chattered and goofed off continuously like monkeys in a monkey house, John Reddy had dignity. Teachers were wary of calling on him in class because, if he didn't know the answer, he'd stare at them unblinking and just barely move his mouth— "Guess I don't know. Sorry." He'd manage to look pretty tough yet at the same time courteous, like being a smart-ass was beneath him. It was known that, after his arrest, he'd refused to be interrogated by police. He'd told them, "O.K. Do what you have to do," like he was detaching himself from his own fate. Like even his own fate, his possible imprisonment for life, was beneath him to consider. He refused to answer his own lawyer's questions and at the start of both trials he stood silent, sullen and stony-faced in a dark blue serge suit too tight across the shoulders, a white shirt and dark-striped tie, declining to look up at the enraged judge when the man asked how he pleaded, so that Mr. Trippe at his side answered on his behalf, "My client pleads not guilty, Your Honor."

Maybe it isn't exactly bullshit that John Reddy was our "Prince of Pride." We admired like hell his refusal to cooperate with authorities, for even the most loudmouthed guys (Dougie Siefried, Art Lutz, Nosepicker Nordstrom for instance) would've panicked in the presence of actual police, especially the Gestapo-uniformed New York State troopers, who had a reputation for roughing guys up before bringing them into headquarters. We admired John Reddy's strange, stubborn silence. His stoicism through months of detention. *Because he was guilty of killing Riggs and didn't repent. Because he knew he'd done the right thing so the hell with explanations.* This was exactly how we'd have behaved if we were John Reddy Heart! For after all, we too were rebels. In Nico's, in the Crystal, in our cars cruising Main Street, Transit Plaza, the Millersport Highway, swigging beer, and our parents not knowing where we were, exactly—we were rebels! We just didn't want to jeopardize our allowances or cause our parents worry, especially our moms. Most of us got along with our moms really well. Or anyway O.K. Our moms took Valium and Librium and smiled a lot and were good-looking for their ages. Our dads might've been a different story but most of them weren't home that much. You could gauge your dad's success by how little you saw him. If you saw a lot of him, that was bad news. When Babs Bitterman's father was forced to resign as president of a plastics company in Niagara Falls he set up an office in the Bittermans' house, to do freelance work and to seek a new job, and Babs told us, "God, it's *weird*. Every day, Daddy's *home*. But we aren't supposed to acknowledge him. Like he's invisible. Mom and I go shopping all we can to get out of the atmosphere so we can *breathe*." At the other extreme, Scottie Baskett once boasted that he hadn't seen his dad, a corporation laywer, in seven weeks, and Jenny

Thrun, Pete Marsh and Steve Lunt whose dads were investment bankers at the same top Buffalo firm joked of not being able to remember clearly what they looked like—"Except, you know, sort of generically." We were proud of our dads and anxious for them. They flew constantly, even weekends, to New York City, to Washington, D.C., to Chicago, Dallas, Philadelphia, Cleveland, Tulsa, Atlanta, Los Angeles, San Francisco and Seattle. To Toronto, Mexico City, London, Paris, Rome, Madrid. Their flights left Buffalo International Airport at an hour when we were deeply asleep. What they did in those cities wasn't clear to us but we understood that they worked hard, "damned hard" (as a dad would sometimes sourly remark on those occasions when he was able to join his family at the dinner table) to maintain our Willowsville homes and "lifestyle" and so we loved and feared them at a distance. We understood Ritchie Eickhorn who confided in us in his cracked, tremulous voice after his dad had dropped dead at the age of forty-seven of a coronary thrombosis while negotiating a contract for a steel company in Pittsburgh, "I feel like I'll get to know Dad now, now he's settled down some. I can think of him clearer now he's in one place." When Bo Bozer's dad moved out of the house, at Mrs. Bozer's request, and the locks on all the doors were changed, Bo said with a grin, "So what's new? He was gone before, he's gone now." Ken Fischer cracked the guys up one night in the Haven telling about his dad he hadn't seen much of for a long time taking him hunting up at Scroon Lake where the family had a lodge, "It's, like, he knows I hate hunting, and he hates it, too, but it's this father-son thing to do, right? So we're tramping around in the snow with these twelve-gauge shotguns that weigh a ton looking for, what?—'The kind with antlers,' Dad says, puffing—and this weird scary thought comes to me *Dad hopes I'll shoot him in the back. To put him out of his misery*. I got the shakes, I was so scared I almost puked. So we interpreted it I had the flu and we came home early and Dad hasn't said a word to me about hunting since."

For such reasons we admired John Reddy Heart who had no father. (So far as we knew.) We admired his aloneness. We admired his courage. We believed it to be courage—his decision not to cooperate with anyone. Basically we didn't want to believe the way John Reddy was acting was self-destructive. We didn't want to believe that a refusal to express remorse for his crime on the part of a swarthy sixteen-year-old kid wearing his hair long and oily in duck's-ass style who'd killed a fifty-three-year-old millionaire known as an "area personality" might not be the shrewdest defense strategy.

How many hundreds, thousands of times in the weeks, months and years to come would we proud classmates of John Reddy Heart communicate with one another in John Reddy's words—*Do what you have to do.* In a stampede of legs and feet at the high school, in the sweaty quavering unspeakably sweet backseats of cars, downtown in the Village on Saturday mornings, on any Willowsville street, cruising the drive-in restaurants on Transit, leaning our heads out car windows as we burned rubber taking off from stoplights—"DO WHAT YOU HAVE TO DO!"

As if any of us had a clue what John Reddy meant.

* * *

"At last—democracy has come to Willowsville."

Mr. Lepage may have spoken in irony, for such was his style, like that of other WHS teachers who couldn't afford to live in our suburb, but it was true: overnight, after the shooting of Melvin Riggs, all social barriers dissolved. Suddenly you saw Verrie Myers, Trish Elders, Pattianne Groves and Ginger McCord huddled together at a cafeteria table earnestly conferring with Orrie Buhr, Dougie Siefried, Janet Moss, Dexter Cambrook and Ritchie Eickhorn. "Preppies, hoods, jocks, geeks"—as more than one observer noted. Evangeline Fesnacht, the sole geek-girl of the Circle, basked in her new-found popularity, moving confidently through all cliques with her data-rich ever-expanding black-satin *Death Chronicles*, now exclusively devoted to John Reddy Heart. Unshaven Clyde Meunzer and Dino Calvo in black leather and grease-stained jeans were glimpsed in the company of Dwayne Hewson, Smoke Filer, Ken Fischer. Norm Zeiga, a recent transfer to WHS from the Niagara County school district, would complain for the next thirty years that he was never able to grasp the social intricacies of Willowsville since, after that historic March day, the old class distinctions had dissolved, as in a violent seismic upheaval. Katrina Olmsted and Ray Gottardi began going steady, thrown together often at Nico's. And it was at Nico's, in a crowded, smoke-hazed booth, that Dougie Siefried came to realize he'd fallen in love with Ginger McCord who cried easily, seeing her pale freckled face streaked with tears and her pale red-lashed eyes shimmering with hurt as Dougie teased Ginger and her friends mercilessly—"Hell, you girls have got to face reality. Before Riggs was shot, that evening, John Reddy wasn't home, right? That's what his mom told police? He got back home around one a.m. when Riggs was already there, so—where was John earlier? With who? Dino knows more than he's letting on. You can't trust any wop. Dino says they were just driving around in John's car but what must've happened was Dino was not with John, John was alone with Dino's sister Sasha. It figures. John doesn't want cops questioning Sasha and the Calvos sure wouldn't so Dino is saying he was with John till about quarter to one but the fact is—*John Reddy's got a girl and that girl is Sasha Calvo.*" It was at this point that Ginger began snuffling and burst into tears and Dougie stared at her hearing his cruel bully's voice ringing in his ears and wishing to hell he'd kept his damned mouth shut.

Our teachers, too, crossed barriers. It was embarrassing. We cringed to see sharp-eyed Miss Bird lunging in our direction, or heavy-breathing Mr. Dunleddy loitering in the doorway of his classroom with its faint sickish odor of formaldehyde. Mme. Picholet daintily inquired of us before class, "Quelles nouvelles de John-Reddy Heart?" Mr. Lepage affected disdain of "tabloid journalism" yet was keen to know, nevertheless, the latest bulletin. (During the tense three days following the shooting when John Reddy was a fugitive from justice and no one knew his whereabouts apart from a wishful rumor that he'd escaped to Quebec.) Miss Flechsenhauer, a tall, rangy, sinewy woman with a foghorn voice, detained us in girls' gym. In driver ed., Mr. Schoppa who smelled of cigars instructed students to drive past 8 Meridian Place repeatedly, attempting parallel parking in front of the Hearts' very house, while keeping up a steady stream of chatter about the Buffalo Hawks and "Texas-style justice." In Mr. Cuthbert's social studies classes we began those painstakingly theoretical discussions that were to continue for months and be resumed in the fall and again continued until (it's said) Mr. Stamish spoke with Mr. Cuthbert urging him to move on from his idée fixe—the ironies of fate, the paradox of chance and destiny, the "interchangedness" of victim and executioner, and the ways in which, as Mr. Cuthbert expressed it with gleaming eyes, "countless tributaries feed into the great rushing river of Fate that leads to an irrevocable existential act like aiming a gun at another person and firing." We were particularly embarrassed to see Mr. Stamish himself, our ordinarily gruff and aloof principal, dawdling in the first-floor corridors with hopeful glances in our direction as if to inquire, with Mme. Picholet, *Quelles nouvelles de John-Reddy Heart?* Yet Mr. Stamish was too reserved to actually ask. We hurried past him averting our eyes as we might in our homes glimpsing a naked parent.

In time, we would know more about the Riggs shooting and John Reddy Heart's involvement than we would wish to know and more than would seem to have been healthy for us to know. More than our fevered adolescent brains could metabolize. Many of us memorized as much as we could learn of the chronology of events of the fatal March night and subsequent days through to the capture of John Reddy, on foot, in a desolate mountain area two hundred sixty miles northeast of Willowsville, on the slope of Mount Nazarene in the Adirondacks. A number of us maintained time charts and maps to which we added more information as it was revealed during subsequent months. Evangeline Fesnacht maintained the most elaborate of these, of course, yet there were others who startled us with their diligence—Janet Moss who'd once been so shy she'd never dated, Tommy "Nosepicker" Nordstrom who was famous for snorting No Doz to keep his starting place on the varsity swim team, brainy-neurotic Clarence McQuade who'd been our New York State High School Science Fair prizewinner the previous year for a massive project involving a homemade telescope and planetary charts. And there was swarthy Norm Zeiga with his "Transylvanian" looks and exotic accent like one of Sid Caesar's comic impersonations, except Norm was always deadly serious; Norm, a transfer to WHS, by the caprice of alphabetical destiny seated just in front of Suzi Zeigler in their classes and fated to be the instrument of her breakup with Roger Zwaart, who intrigued Suzi with his meticulous time chart and map in colored inks—as Suzi excitedly declared, "Like everybody else, I'd been thinking Norm was just a weirdo. A kind of interesting weirdo, but, y'know, a weirdo. Now, he spread out this fantastic time chart not just of where John Reddy was that night, but months leading up to it, and maps of Willowsville and the route John Reddy took into the mountains, he said, 'The search for truth compelled me. It is the most powerful human instinct second only to the instinct to reproduce the species,' in that accent of his, and, God!—was I impressed. I looked at Norm for the first time, really looked at him, and I saw. *Those eyes.*" (While Roger who'd been around forever, since first grade, Suzi's boy friend and familiar as an old sock, wasn't at all sympathetic with Suzi's interest in John Reddy Heart. He'd say, out of the corner of his mouth, to anyone who'd listen, "Jesus, why *care*? This is like mass hysteria or something. What's that guy to any of *us*? He isn't in our crowd, for Christ's sake." We knew what Roger meant, sure, and with a part of our brains we agreed; but Roger, like our fathers, just didn't get it.) Even Millicent LeRoux whom boys dreaded calling to ask for dates (Millie was so placid, so sweetly vague, "Who'd you say this is? Dougie? Oh—Cla*rence*. Oh, gosh, thanks. But I guess I'm busy Friday, and all the Fridays on the calendar. But, gee, *thanks*!") became aroused by new news of John Reddy and was several times seen actually trotting into the cafeteria, breathing quickly, swaths of color in her cheeks and breasts bobbing, to appeal to, of all bipolar personalities, Evangeline Fesnacht whom she'd been snubbing since kindergarten— "Vangie, what? What? *What?* People are saying you know *something that just happened*?"

In retrospect, Bart Digger would recall our collective anxiety on the third night of John Reddy's flight from the law when several of us brainy guys, members of the WHS chess team, sat up most of the night in the parking lot between Burnham Nurseries and Glen Creek, smoking and drinking beer. (Bart's older brother Tracy had bought the six-packs for us.) It might've been unspoken among us that this was a mode of guy behavior not typical of geeks so if we behaved this way we couldn't be geeks. Ritchie Eickhorn, who would become, like the more celebrated and controversial E. S. Fesnacht, a published writer in his twenties, a poet and professor of literature at a small Minnesota college, recalled being alarmed by the "wild, incoherent thoughts that buzzed my head" after a single can of lukewarm Molson's, but "I believed that a new, radical personality was emerging in me, at age sixteen, bound up somehow with John Reddy Heart. I didn't know him, *but I knew this fact*." Clarence McQuade who was the team's star chess player, destined to blow out by his own estimate not less than twenty percent of his brain on speed, meth, "crank" in graduate school at Berkeley, researching an abstruse problem in de Rham cohomology for a math Ph.D. that would forever elude him, recalled, "*I* was terrified, I don't know why. That I might shoot my own dad by accident somehow. We didn't

even have a gun in the house! Then I'd be hunted down like
a dog and shot, too. It was my first drunk but it wouldn't be
my last." Dexter Cambrook said broodingly, "Not that I knew
John Reddy Heart any more than he knew me. I sort of think
I'd been mixing him up with other kids who resembled him—
'hoods,' 'greasers' we called them—I never went to basketball
games, or any big-crowd sports. But I was scared, too. It was
like a vision of the next decade in America. A kid shot down
by police. I was sure they were going to kill him. Us against
them. And we didn't have any choice who 'us' was—it was
us." Bart Digger agreed, saying, "I trace the start of thirty years
of existential anxiety to those hours. Those beers, and puking
into Glen Creek at three a.m. while my mom was worried
sick where I was. Jesus, now I've been a parent myself, I
know." As the beers took hold the subject shifted from John
Reddy Heart to God, to "free will and destiny" and "whether
Christ died for our sins *really*." Blake Wells surprised us by
saying vehemently that he resented God for "all the evil He
permits." Petey Merchant who never talked, hardly five feet
tall at fifteen and a half, said, frightened, "That's wrong, to talk
that way. *Don't*." Dexter Cambrook who was drunk and laughing spoke of how he'd made an asshole of himself calling
Pattianne Groves to ask for a date though he knew it was
hopeless, she was going with Dwayne Hewson and she'd turn
him down and of course she did—"In this kind of whispery,
stricken way those girls have like you're a cripple they're
trying to be nice to, they *truly do wish you weren't a loser-geek
with pimples so they could say yes*." But none of the others
laughed. Bitterly we spoke of guys like Dwayne Hewson, Ken
Fischer, Smoke Filer and that crowd. Bart Digger said, his
voice heavy with sarcasm, "If they have pimples, pimples are
in." Clarence McQuade said, with a vulgar zest that surprised
us, "If one of them farts, it's a *big joke*." Ritchie Eickhorn
hadn't known he might be drunk until he heard his bitter,
flailing voice, "Their dads make more money than ours do.
Their moms are better-looking. They live on the Hill and we

live south of Garrison." Blake Wells said savagely, "But they won't get into Harvard, those assholes." Dexter Cambrook laughed, beer dribbling out of his nose, "Shit, will *we*?" This was met with shocked silence, a kind of sobriety that hinted of violent headaches to come, teary eyes and pissy-tasting bile at the back of the mouth. Ritchie Eickhorn would recall coming to a realization that night with his friends that none of them would ever forget the occasion though it wasn't exactly clear what the occasion was. A death watch for John Reddy Heart— though in fact John Reddy would not die in a hailstorm of bullets but would be captured and returned in shackles to Willowsville by ten o'clock that morning. A vigil on a starry March night, temperature –5° F. Eighteen years to the day later on a starry March night in even colder weather in St. Paul, Minnesota, Ritchie Eickhorn, now Richard Eickhorn, would begin to compose his lyric, lovely *America I Hear Your Heart Breaking* which would gain him a modest but respectable reputation in literary circles and the Walt Whitman Award from the Poetry Society of America. (Though none of Richard Eickhorn's several awards, nor even his per-durable reputation, would ever erase for him the exquisite pain of their original catalyst.) "The poem was an attempt to evoke a mood. A passion. Not an individual passion—something communal, collective. Our 'yearnings of infinitude'. It's the black hole in the firmament where God used to be. Americans are likely to feel it young, we're precocious *and we never grow out of it.*"

At first we knew only that Melvin Riggs, Jr., had been "shot down dead" in the Heart house. And that John Reddy Heart had fled with the "murder weapon" in his car but unwisely, impulsively, in confusion and panic he'd tossed the gun off the Castle Creek Bridge about a mile from his home—where it skidded along the ice, for of course the creek was frozen. Willowsville police would discover it in the morning—the .45-caliber Colt revolver registered, in Las Vegas, in the name of Aaron Leander Heart. "The kid's prints are all over that gun. It's an open-and-shut case."

"It must have been an accident."

"And the kid isn't too bright, is he? Tossing his gun out onto *ice*."

Verrie Myers, trembling, stared in dismay at her sneering, scornful father. Her Daddy! Her Daddy she'd adored since infancy! He was laughing. Laughing! Reading of the "shooting death" of Melvin Riggs in the morning's *Courier-Express* (of course, Mr. Myers acknowledged that Riggs's death was a "tragedy"—"but somehow not very surprising, considering Riggs's reputation with women") and shaking his head at her as if, infuriatingly, she were still a small credulous child. "I mean, hell, what can you say about a kid so dumb he tosses the 'alleged murder weapon' out onto *frozen ice*?"

It was the repetition that did it. The gloating, the rubbing-salt-in-the-wound as into tearful Verrie's aching eyes. *Ice. Frozen ice.* How could he! Suddenly, as in a movie scene where the music signals a crisis, Verrie realized she'd never truly seen her father *as a man and individual independent of their relationship* until that terrible moment.

Her voice was hoarse from crying. She whispered, "Daddy, I hate you."

It *was* a whisper! Mr. Myers would forever recall it as a "hysterical scream."

Then Verrie was running! running! running from that room and that suffocating bourgeois house! *running from my old dead false self, my hypocrite life as somebody's daughter. Forever!*

We vied with one another memorizing the chronology of the fatal night: the incident at the house, and John Reddy's flight to Mount Nazarene, and the capture. Quickly it became a movie we'd all seen. After John Reddy's second trial, in November, naturally we were able to fill in certain frustrating gaps and to add relevant remarks by various individuals (excluding John Reddy, who proudly refused to speak). In *Death Chronicles*, Evangeline Fesnacht, with a fanatic scrupulousness scarcely hinted when she'd been class secretary in grade school, divided the chronology into sections: "The Fatal Night"—"The Fugitive and the Manhunt"—"The Capture"— "The Return to Willowsville." In this, even Evangeline's detractors concurred. Here, much abbreviated, it is:

On March 18, a schoolday, John Reddy Heart, enrolled as a junior at WHS, cut all his morning classes, arrived in time for fifth-hour geometry (where his grade ranged from C+ to D–) and attended basketball practice from 3:30 P.M. to 5:00 P.M. ("playing competently, though he missed some easy shots and seemed distracted" as Coach McKeever told police); from the high school, he drove to Farolino's Cabinets & Carpentry on Chippewa Street where he worked until about 7:00 P.M. ("John was helping me sand down and stain a battered old cherrywood bookcase; he did a good job as usual but seemed distracted, got stain on his hands and on the floor"); from Farolino's he drove to his home at 8 Meridian Place, arriving, at Mrs. Heart's estimate, at about 7:20 P.M.; he showered, shaved, put on fresh clothes and hurried out again saying he was seeing his friend Dino Calvo and "some other guys, maybe"; Mrs. Heart urged him to sit down with the family and eat dinner ("Every night I prepare a hot, home-cooked meal for my family, every night I'm able to be home") but John Reddy left before 8:00 P.M., driving to the home of Mr. and Mrs. Joseph Calvo of 93 Division Street where he was evidently a frequent visitor ("No matter what they say about him, John Reddy Heart is a good boy—and a good friend to Dino" as Mr. Calvo told police). From about 9:00 P.M. to 12:40 A.M. of March 19, John Reddy was said to be in the company exclusively of seventeen-year-old Dino Calvo, riding in John Reddy's car with no special destination ("Just talking, no we weren't drinking, we maybe stopped at a few places just to hang out, got a pizza at Enrico's off Humboldt, I ran in and John stayed with the car, just the two of us," as Dino told police) then bringing Dino back to his home and returned to his own home at 8 Meridian Place. We didn't believe this! We believed that, on the fatal night, John Reddy had been with his girl Sasha Calvo, Dino's beautiful fifteen-year-old sister. It's possible that Dino and some other kids were with them, or just Dino, for all or part of the evening, the information provided us was vague and contradictory and anyone close to John Reddy who might've known, Orrie Buhr, Clyde Meunzer or Dino himself, surely wouldn't tell *us*. "It's a measure of how loyal these people are," Evangeline Fesnacht said, with the air of an anthropologist making an observation, "—they'd risk breaking the law to protect one of their own." The entire Calvo family clammed up of course. (What happened to Dino Calvo? He wouldn't be one of John Reddy's friends to testify for the defense, as a character witness. And beautiful Sasha Calvo disappeared from Willowsville soon after John Reddy's arrest, said to have been sent away to live with relatives in Brooklyn.)

Apparently unbeknownst to John Reddy, a friend of his mother's, Robert P. Rush (of the distinguished Buffalo law firm Chase, Rush, Beebee & Pepper) arrived at the house uninvited and unexpected at about 11:00 P.M.; insisted upon coming inside to speak with Mrs. Heart, to inform her that he'd asked Mrs. Rush for a divorce because he was in love with her; he'd been drinking, and was upset; Mrs. Heart felt she couldn't just turn the distraught man away, and so let him in—"For just a few minutes. He promised." Unfortunately, at about 11:45 P.M., as Rush was about to leave, Melvin Riggs, also uninvited and unexpected, also having been drinking, arrived at the house demanding to be let in. The two men, confronting each other in the front hall, got into a shouting, shoving match; Rush, his nose bleeding from a blow of Riggs's, was persuaded to leave, but Riggs refused to leave; and soon afterward, Riggs and Dahlia Heart retired upstairs to the privacy of her bedroom—"I swear, and my family will confirm this, it was the first time Melvin Riggs ever climbed any staircase in my house. Yes, we were lovers. But I'd never allowed him to come into my house, where my children are, I swear! The man had such power over me, I'm so ashamed! He threatened me, saying if he couldn't have me no other man would." Around 1:00 A.M., John Reddy returned home, saw Riggs's car in the driveway (did he know whose car it was?), came inside and was met by his grandfather Aaron Leander Heart who was still dressed, who told him about his mother's visitors and the fracas in the front hall— "John Reddy says, 'Is one of them here now? Upstairs?' and I says, 'Yes, but it's peaceful now. It's not our business, now.' So John Reddy went off to his room at the back of the house. I should've called you folks myself," old Mr. Heart gloomily told police, "—except law enforcement officers and me have had our separate views of things." Then at about 1:50 A.M. there was a commotion from Mrs. Heart's bedroom, heavy footsteps, thuds and sounds of struggle, and Mrs. Heart's cries; and John Reddy who hadn't gone to bed yet "might've run upstairs to investigate. Or maybe not. Everything became confused," Mr. Heart said.

Asked by police where he was at the time of the commotion, Mr. Heart said he believed he'd gone to bed.

From this point onward, the sequence of events became unclear. It would never be untangled. Dahlia Heart told police she wasn't able to recall what had happened in her bedroom during the minutes leading to Riggs's death: "That man tried to strangle me! I kept fading in and out of consciousness. I was on the bed, or on the floor. I was in terror of my life. I must have screamed for help and Melvin threatened to kill me and—it was a nightmare. I didn't realize my son Johnny had come home—I never had a glimpse of him, I swear. I don't remember hearing a gun go off. When I came to, a paramedic was reviving me. I didn't know where I was. Why there was blood all over. I was convinced something had happened to my children. My little girl. But I hadn't seen a thing. I *swear*."

Dahlia Heart's testimony to police was breathless, agitated. She said repeatedly that she somehow hadn't "seen" the body of Melvin Riggs on the floor of her bedroom, when she was revived; she might have heard a gun fired, but couldn't truly remember—"It was such a nightmare. It didn't seem real." There was no contesting the fact, however, that the murder weapon, the .45-caliber Colt revolver licensed to Aaron Leander Heart twelve years before in Nevada, had been discharged at a distance of less than six feet from Melvin Riggs, sending two bullets into the bedroom ceiling and a single bullet into Riggs's head at an upward angle, piercing his brain and lodging in the top of his skull, killing him within seconds.

Neighbors would report having heard "shouts, screams, slamming doors and cars" earlier that night as well as, just after 2:00 A.M., "gunfire." Irma Bannister of 10 Meridian Place was the first of several persons to dial 911 to report an emergency. By 2:12 A.M. of March 19, four Willowsville police officers arrived in two squad cars to discover lights blazing at the Heart residence. The front door was ajar, and upstairs, in a large, sumptuously furnished bedroom, lay the naked corpse of a man they recognized despite the damage done to his face—Melvin Riggs, Jr. The middle-aged man lay sprawled on the floor just inside the doorway, about twelve feet from an opened, rumpled bed where, apparently unconscious, in a blood-splattered white silk negligee, Dahlia Heart lay, the apparent victim of a beating.

On the stairs, dazed, the elderly Aaron Leander Heart babbled to police officers that there'd been an "accident"—"the gun hadn't been loaded"—he "hadn't seen, didn't know what had happened" or who even had been shot. A boy of thirteen, Farley Heart, in pajamas, his thin, childlike face drained of blood, stood barefoot in the hall rocking from side to side and whimpering, too, of an "accident"—"John didn't k-know the gun was loaded, he only meant to—" At this remark, as the officers looked on in surprise, old Mr. Heart turned sharply on the boy and shook him by the shoulders like a rag doll before one of the officers could intervene, saying, "You damned fool! *Johnny wasn't even here.*"

"The night Mel Riggs was killed."

Matt Trowbridge, by this time a Willowsville lieutenant, would many times speak marveling of that night. Of how, though John Reddy Heart had vanished, his car gone, the Colt revolver gone with him, neither of the adult Hearts seemed to know if he'd been in the house, at or anywhere near the scene of the shooting. It was like a mist had come over things. "A sweet, heavy odor, a smell like of lilies." Mrs. Heart was hysterical, calling for her daughter no one could find. It required several officers twenty minutes searching the house before the eleven-year-old Shirleen was found, by Trowbridge, in a shut-off, unheated part of the house used for storage, wedged beneath a heavy, old-fashioned sofa covered by a white shroud. "You wouldn't have thought anyone could squeeze up into that little space. Not just under the sofa but inside it, where some of the stuffing had been pulled out. The girl was crying, but making no sound. She'd jammed her fingers in her mouth. She seemed to be in shock. When I shone the flashlight into her face her eyes were blank like glass eyes, she might've been blind. Seeing that child, the age of my own daughter, helping her crawl out of the dust and dirt, feeling her hands that were cold as ice, and smelling the animal panic on her, I had a harsh thought for the mother. I thought, 'Ma'am, you hadn't ought to expose your daughter to such ugliness as happened tonight in this house. That's not right.'"

Both Dahlia Heart and Shirleen would be taken to Amherst General Hospital for emergency treatment and retained for observation.

By that time, John Reddy in the acid-green Caddie with the zigzag gold trim and the prominent chrome tailpipe was miles away. He'd escaped the peaceful Village of Willowsville at once. He didn't linger. We envisioned him running down the stairs, grabbing his leather jacket he'd maybe tossed down earlier in the front hall but forgetting the red wool muffler (earnestly if clumsily knitted by Sasha Calvo, then fourteen, for John Reddy's sixteenth birthday, as we would subsequently learn) he'd been wearing wrapped around his neck most of the winter. His leather gloves were jammed in the jacket pocket; he wasn't wearing them; the Colt revolver, still heated from its discharge, clutched in his right hand, would be covered in John Reddy Heart's fingerprints—and no one else's.

John Reddy, run! John Reddy, take care!

We envisioned the wind, our perpetual wind, damp and bone-chilling from the lake, clots of snow and sleet blown into John Reddy's heated face. We envisioned (how many times! singly or together, in reverie or in conversation, stone cold sober or woozily drunk or high on drugs for which some of us admittedly had a predilection in the next decade) the grim determined young face of John Reddy, the stoic-boyish set of his jaws. His oiled black hair romantically disheveled in the wind. The gun—its barrel still heated, smelling of gunpowder—dropped onto the car seat beside him. We saw John Reddy jam his key in the ignition, desperate to escape. *John Reddy Heart ain't gonna stay.* Revving the Caddie's motor. For he would know that Meridian Place neighbors had called the police. He had scant seconds to escape. (Even as Mrs. Bannister was wailing into the telephone, "Those white-trash Hearts! They're killing one another!"—sounding, for the moment, not so refined herself.) We could hear the scream of John Reddy's tires, a thrilling sound rare as a peacock's scream in staid St. Albans Hill. That sound of John Reddy's acid-green Caddie that lodged deep in our collective memories, more familiar to us, we'd one day realize, than any sound of our adolescence in Willowsville, and more prized. "When I hear tires screeching, no matter where I am," Bart Digger once remarked, "—I'm back in Willowsville again. I'm sixteen."

Now came the embarrassing incident. We'd have preferred it hadn't happened but, well—"It happened. A toss of the dice."

To certain of our fathers this was evidence that John Reddy Heart wasn't overly bright. To us, it was evidence that he'd panicked. We could understand. We could sympathize. We did stupid dumb-ass things every day of our lives. Steeling ourselves as we envisioned, yet again, John Reddy in the Caddie turning with screeching tires off Meridian and onto Castle Creek, pressing the gas pedal to the floor even as he pumped the brakes, not wanting to skid on the snowy pavement, slowing as the car thumped across the single-lane bridge over the creek, rolling down his window in haste to throw the gun out over the rail, and into the night; into what he must've believed was oblivion; speeding away as he accelerated, not hearing the gun clatter on ice—not splash into water.

For of course, in mid-March, shallow Castle Creek was frozen solid.

Never mind what our dads, like Verrie Myers's sneering father, thought seeing John Reddy in that famous newspaper photo, captured, handcuffed, in custody. It was our moms who surprised us. Like Shelby Connor's mom saying, incensed, as she studied the photo of a wounded boy caught in a camera's unsparing flash, "To me, that's proof of how unpremeditated it all was—whatever John Reddy Heart did. Tossing the gun out onto ice where even our Willowsville police could find it. It shows how innocent he is. How pure in heart."

9

John Reddy fled to the east.
John Reddy fled to the west.
Sure put them cops to the test!
John Reddy, John Reddy Heart.

In fact John Reddy drove east and north into the Adirondack Mountains by a shrewd circuitous route. Taking back roads, even alleys and unpaved lanes, lurching across parkland and open fields (like the spit of land between Garrison Road and North Forrest where the Caddie's tire tracks would be discovered in the morning) when he could, for the first five hours or so fleeing by night, in sleet, in the acid-green Caddie that by day would have been identified within minutes by cops, for they'd sent out an alert he was wanted, *prime suspect in a murder case. Caucasian, sixteen years old.* John Reddy sped through these towns without registering their names: Lancaster, Batavia, Le Roy, Honeoye, Shortsville, Waterloo, Seneca Falls, Auburn. In the Village of Skaneateles at the northern tip of narrow Skaneateles Lake sometime before four a.m. he abandoned the Caddie, with what grief and regret we could only imagine (for this was the spectacular vehicle that had brought him and his family east from Las Vegas to Willowsville and their new life, and this was the vehicle John Reddy had lovingly repainted and claimed for his own, the flashy vehicle with which he was identified in all our eyes), but of necessity John Reddy abandoned it, for it could too easily be identified, and its gas tank was empty, and John Reddy hot-wired a new-model Jeep to take its place, fleeing then in the Jeep on his panicked northeast trajectory through suburban Syracuse, Phoenix, Parish, Fernwood, Pulaski, Salmon River, now in the Adirondacks through Constableville, Old Forge, Big Moose, Raquette Lake, Lost Lake and Mount Nazarene where, on foot, in a desolate landscape he would be captured two hundred and sixty miles from Willowsville and seventy-two hours after the shooting death of Melvin Riggs, Jr., by two dozen police officers equipped with high-powered rifles, bulletproof vests, tear gas and attack dogs, and taken in shackles to Onondaga Medical Center in Salmon River preparatory to being returned to Willowsville for booking and interrogation. ("They got him! They got John Reddy! But he's alive!"—the cry went out at school from a dozen or more points where we'd been listening anxiously for local news bulletins on transistor radios smuggled into our classrooms. A number of us, both sexes, ninth, tenth, eleventh and twelfth grades, had hardly slept since we'd learned of John Reddy's flight, we refused to eat actual meals with our families, we refused to shower or wash or apply deodorant, brush our hair or our teeth for days and when at last word came of John Reddy's capture several girls fainted dead away including certain distraught girls of the Circle whose ashy faces, sleep-deprived dilated eyes and bloodless lips had made a strong impression on those of us who adored them. And so we would wonder in our radically different ways, in our radically different vocabularies *Will any girl ever keep such a vigil for me?*) In the crossroads town of Parish on Route 22 shortly after five a.m., John Reddy forced the lock of a 7-Eleven store where he devoured two chocolate cream–filled Hostess cupcakes and drank an entire quart of milk on the spot (cupcake wrappers and empty milk carton left behind as evidence); he stuffed into his pockets what he could grab to eat later, in the stolen Jeep or in Mount

Nazarene, a ten-ounce bag of Planter's peanuts, three Milky Way candy bars, the last remaining Italian hero sandwich from the previous day and a quart container of Sunkist reconstituted orange juice from the refrigerated unit; on the counter by the cash register he left $7.60 in small crumpled bills and change, and a hastily scribbled note, in pencil—

> Dear sir or mam,
> I am <u>sorry</u>.

It would be discovered that, at 5:11 A.M., he made a telephone call from the store to his home at 8 Meridian Place. (But no one was there to answer. Dahlia Heart and eleven-year-old Shirleen had been hospitalized and old Mr. Heart and the boy Farley were in a waiting room at Amherst General Hospital where Willowsville police officers closely monitored them. Mr. Heart, disheveled and smelling of whisky, repeatedly muttered, "We ain't seen nothing, and we don't know nothing. And we ain't saying anything." Farley, his clothes pulled on in haste over pajamas, his eyes blurred and blind, wavered between the conviction that his mother had been shot by "that terrible man Mr. Riggs" and was dying, and a childish persistence in wanting to go to school as usual that morning—"You don't seem to realize," the boy said to the cops, "I have a geometry test third period. I can't miss that test!") It would be discovered that John Reddy next telephoned the Calvo residence where as Joseph Calvo would later tell police the phone rang waking him, in the pitch dark, but when he managed to answer it he heard only the sound of someone hanging up—"I didn't know anything about any shooting or John Reddy being a fugitive so I never gave it a second thought, just hung up. A wrong number, I thought. Some asshole." In our booth at the Haven, where we met most nights during John Reddy's trials in the fall, Dougie Siefried snorted in derision when the subject came up of John Reddy's call to the Calvo house and Mr. Calvo's testimony. "Bullshit!

The old wop's protecting Sasha. You wanna bet it happened like this?—John Reddy calls and Sasha picks up the phone on the first or second ring, she's been awake all night because maybe she and John went all the way that night in the back-seat of the Caddie—for the first time—maybe—and she's walking around the house in her nightie (a great-looking girl like Sasha Calvo wouldn't wear pajamas like some dog like Evangeline Fesnacht)—she's Catholic, she's Italian, they believe in premonitions and signs and maybe Dino's been talking to her, John's been confiding in him how fucked up he's getting that this bastard Riggs is banging his mom in more ways than one. Like any guy would who's normal. Like I sure would! So as soon as the phone rings Sasha answers right away and John Reddy says, real quiet, 'Sasha. It's me,' and Sasha says, 'John? What's wrong?' and John says, kind of choking back how he feels, 'Just want you to know I'm O.K. I'm in some trouble, honey, but I'm gonna be O.K., don't worry.' So Sasha says, 'What trouble? What happened? John—' and John says, 'Don't feel you got to lie or anything for me, Sasha,' and before Sasha can ask what he means the old man picks up the phone in his bedroom and hears voices on the line and says, 'Who the hell is this? What's going on?' and Sasha's scared as hell and John Reddy stays quiet and the old man says, 'Who's on this line? Dino? Sasha? Who?' and Sasha sort of stammers and says, 'Daddy, it's me, Sasha, the phone rang and it's a wrong number,' and the old man says, 'Yeah? You sure? Who's on this line?' and Sasha says he's hung up, and says, 'Good night, Daddy.' So the old man slams down the receiver, and Sasha hangs up, and John Reddy out in Parish hangs up. *That's how it was.*"

John Reddy, run! John Reddy, take care!
In the stolen Jeep he wavered in and out of our vision. Sometimes we saw him clearly as in a film close-up (the Jeep swiftly and bravely approaching the camera along a country highway, mountains in the near distance and John Reddy

Heart's face glimpsed through the windshield splotched with reflected sunshine and clouds, haggard, unshaven, the face of someone far older than sixteen and the eyes of someone who has registered this fact), more often not. It was the second day of his flight as a fugitive. Now it was daylight and the sun bright, glaring on snow, he had to be wary of police cruisers, helicopters. In Big Moose, Raquette Lake, Lost Lake. He was running low on gas for the second time. But kept going. Where? By now he might have realized he couldn't make it to the Canadian border. (It was our theory that John Reddy had been headed for Canada but this was a theory never to be confirmed since John Reddy would never confirm it; neither did he deny it. In later years some of us, turned skeptical, would wonder if John Reddy, with only a vague sense of geography, had even known where Canada was. Or, if he'd had a general idea, reasoning it must be north, would he have known he couldn't have crossed for hundreds of miles since the St. Lawrence River was due north, a natural border, and there were few bridges into Canada and these, of course, were monitored by customs officials? He'd have had to drive farther north and east toward the border at Quebec where in a desolate snowy wilderness a wanted man might have crossed, unseen, on foot.) In the Adirondack Mountains in winter there isn't much traffic even on larger roads. These John Reddy tried to avoid. But unpaved, snowy roads led— where? Maybe his flight to Mount Nazarene wasn't shrewd and circuitous as some of us argued but haphazard, desperate. *Maybe he hadn't known what the hell he was doing!* He didn't doubt he might be shot on sight. He'd had encounters with cops in Niagara Falls. He'd seen the same movies we'd seen. He was willing to die (we surmised) but not without a fight. We suspected that by this time he'd begun to consider the strangeness of passing from one category of being to another: for sixteen years he'd been just himself, John Reddy Heart, a kid, and now he was a *fugitive*, a *wanted man*. There had been issued a warrant for his arrest. Police bulletins.

Possibly roadblocks, behind him. He devoured potato chips as he drove, mouth and chin greasy. He tried to listen to the radio which was mainly static. He listened for the sound of his name—*John Reddy Heart*. Which he wasn't sure he might've heard, or maybe not. Mount Nazarene, pop. 412, is north of Lost Lake. Many of us knew Lake Placid, Saranac Lake, Blue Lake, Raquette Lake—these were resort areas. Our families owned lodges—"cottages" as they were called—in those places. None of us knew Lost Lake. None of us knew Mount Nazarene. We'd have to admit that John Reddy had ended up there by chance. You could call it destiny but it hadn't been his choice for you don't have any choice when you're a fugitive, a wanted man, running out of gas. In Mount Nazarene he might've had a vague sense of a post office, a laundromat, a taxidermist's, the log facade of the Mountain Inn on Route 81. Blindly he turned north on a narrow winding climbing road called Cemetery Ridge though possibly he hadn't been aware of the name. Past Cemetery Ridge there was a Sunoco station, a food store, a beer and liquor store and a discount clothes outlet but John Reddy wouldn't have known of these. The sun had darkened. Tall evergreens drifted around him. In the mountains you can't see the mountains, it's mostly timber you see. As Clarence McQuade said cynically, not being a nature lover, the same God-damned tree multiplied a million million times. When the sun isn't out you basically don't want to be in the mountains. A gloomy haze like spent, exhausted breaths. You can see why the locals drink all winter, and hang themselves or blow their brains out, with .12-gauge shotguns, in February. What determined John Reddy's choice of a place in which to hide, or try to hide, a private unplowed lane off Cemetery Ridge to turn onto, no one would know. Even Verrie Myers would hesitate to call it destiny. Evangeline Fesnacht spoke of "random destiny." Dexter Cambrook cautioned, "You can't read too much into these things. You can become 'psycho'—paranoid." Possibly John Reddy was attracted to the lane winding

between evergreens 2.4 miles north of the crossroads of
Mount Nazarene up a considerable hill because, nailed to the
mailbox, there was a weathered NO TRESPASSING sign. He might
have reasoned that he'd be safe there for a while because
intruders were warned off. Because clearly no one had driven
back the lane for a long time. The Jeep had four-wheel drive
and could barely make it. John Reddy must've sweated, gun-
ning the motor, stuck in snow and rocking the vehicle back
and forth in desperation until it skidded forward. He hadn't
thought that, if the Jeep was stuck in snow, it would be seen
from the road and the cops would be alerted to him, this was
a thought he hadn't had, yet so obvious a thought, any asshole might've thought it, he'd have reason now to know he
wasn't in his right mind and couldn't trust himself, his judgment. Yet he had only himself and his judgment. The hazy
light glowered on his skin like the sweat of self-reproach. Yet
he managed to drive the Jeep, churning and grinding and
floundering forward like a frenzied, wounded beast. He managed to drive the Jeep, gas gauge on Empty, a quarter-mile
into the woods, much of it steeply uphill. There emerged
then a cabin out of the sullen gloom, made of logs. Another
faded NO TRESPASSING sign nailed to a tree. This cabin, into
which John Reddy would break by way of a rear screened
window, was a single part-furnished room measuring perhaps
twenty feet by fifteen. (Some of us, the following summer,
would make the pilgrimage to the site out of bold and
unapologetic curiosity. Eleven years later Jon Rindfleisch, by
that time a prominent real estate broker in suburban Buffalo,
would seriously consider purchasing the property, rundown
cabin and five scrubby acres, deciding against it only because
there was no lakefront and because Mount Nazarene "isn't
exactly a chic address in the Adirondacks.") The cabin had a
lavatory, a gas stove and electricity though these weren't
turned on. It had a debris-cluttered fireplace which John
Reddy would use that night; in fear of freezing to death in
subzero temperatures burning cobwebbed firewood and

damp moldy papers to produce little heat but a virulent, eye-watering stink. It would seem that John Reddy chose not to contemplate the risk of sending up smoke where there should be none; or, contemplating it, reasoning that, by dawn, the smoke should have ceased. Possibly he wasn't thinking of the smoke but simply of surviving the night. The next few hours. He had not slept and would not sleep. He had not changed his clothes since fleeing Willowsville and would not. He was hungry, ravenous. He'd devoured all the food from the 7-Eleven store. He drank melted snow and was grateful for it. In a cupboard in the cabin he discovered a few provisions—two six-ounce cans of Heinz's Pork & Beans, the stale and inedible remains of a jar of Maxwell House Instant Coffee. With a rusted can opener John Reddy would attempt desperately to open the cans. He would attempt to tear off the lids with his fingernails. We shrank from imagining his hunger, his trembling hands and the tears of frustration and rage in his eyes. "If only he could have gone to Tupper Lake where our lodge is," Trish Elders said tearfully, "—if only, somehow, he could have known. There would have been things there for him to eat. He could have hidden for weeks."

Instead, this happened: at about ten a.m. of the next day, a Mount Nazarene mailman, delivering mail as usual in his pickup to the few parties who lived on Cemetery Ridge year-round, noticed the churned-up, trespassed driveway, made a call to the owner (who lived in Watertown) and then to the Hamilton County sheriff's office. When two deputies arrived at about ten-thirty a.m. they discovered the abandoned Jeep, whose license plate would quickly be traced, the cabin that had been broken into, evidence of a fire in the fireplace—but no perpetrator. For John Reddy Heart must have had a premonition he was in danger and had fled the cabin, at dawn, on foot.

Within a half-hour a dozen law enforcement vehicles would converge on the scene. New York State troopers, Hamilton County deputies. The manhunt had begun.

For the next seven hours John Reddy Heart, *sixteen-year-old suspected murderer*, *believed to be dangerous*, would be tracked in the wilds of Mount Nazarene, ascending the mountain in a zigzag, staggering course. He moved blindly, without direction. It was a windy, snow-swept, dazzling day. The temperature dropped to −10° F. John Reddy was wearing denim jeans, a leather jacket and biker boots that came only to his ankles and provided little protection against snow. His toes began to freeze. His ears began to freeze. His head was bare. His breath steamed and froze in his eyelashes, nostrils. Tears froze in rivulets on his cheeks. Yet he was sweating inside his clothes. Back in the cabin fainting with hunger he'd devoured the Maxwell's instant coffee mix and now his heart raced and pounded and skipped beats. His lungs were on fire. He heard in the distance the dreamlike howling of wolves, which was in fact the baying of bloodhounds. He heard the shouts of strangers. His name—"John Reddy Heart"—harshly enunciated through a megaphone. *Indicate your whereabouts. Throw down your arms. Surrender. You will not be hurt if you surrender.* We believed that John Reddy would rather have died than surrender. Some of us believed that John Reddy must have regretted impulsively throwing away his grandfather's gun— "He could've taken one or two cops with him, before they mowed him down."

Like a hunted beast John Reddy tried to disguise his trail. He would have waded upstream except the narrow mountain streams were frozen solid. He climbed panting into the branches of toppled trees, lifted himself from the ground. He crawled across rock faces, swinging his legs into space and dangling like a hanged man. On his hands and knees he crawled across ice fields. In the sky a helicopter whined. He hid. His fingers had turned to ice and were in danger of breaking off. His eyeballs had turned to ice in their sockets. Yet his legs carried him forward mechanically. Afterward his pursuers would acknowledge they "didn't know how the hell the kid kept going." They'd been informed that Willowsville police had retrieved the apparent murder weapon but couldn't know for certain that the suspect hadn't another weapon, or two, on his person. Bo Bozer believed they'd wanted to think John Reddy had another gun, that would've given him, and them, a sporting chance. They must've been hot to shoot him down in the snow with their high-powered rifles, to spatter the snow with his blood. "You got to figure—here's this sixteen-year-old kid with long hair, biker leather and boots who'd put a bullet through Melvin Riggs's brain, they'd want to kill him bad enough to taste it. Those guys are only human."

But it didn't happen that way. Instead, John Reddy was tracked down and captured in an ice field halfway up the eastern slope of Mount Nazarene. It was late afternoon of the third day of the manhunt. He'd managed to get six miles from the cabin; in his wavering zigzag course, he must have covered at least ten miles. When they finally found him he'd fallen from a steep, rocky incline and injured his ankle. Bloodhounds converged upon him, howling. A dozen troopers. Seeing he was unarmed they rushed at him, laid their hands on him, and John Reddy who'd seemed barely conscious surprised them by fighting—"resisting arrest." They'd dragged, beaten, kicked and billy-clubbed him into submission, his face that had been frozen like a mask now bloodied like lacework, his left eye swollen shut. They'd practically dragged him by his hair, clumps of it were torn from his scalp. His wrists were secured halfway up his back for maximum pain, so much pain John Reddy fainted, to be then borne down the mountainside in triumph like a hunter's trophy carcass. Of course, John Reddy's wristwatch (we had reason to believe it had been his father's) was broken.

Recounting these facts for us, Evangeline Fesnacht began unexpectedly to cry. It shocked the guys initially—other girls cried often, and our hearts melted seeing them, but Frog Tits? We were embarrassed yet impressed. It was the first clear sign, as Smoke Filer said approvingly, that Evangeline was "an actual female, not a dyke." But we were all in danger of breaking down. We'd been humbled too, humiliated by state troopers in their Gestapo gear. We could taste something tarry, part vomit and part instant coffee mix, at the backs of our mouths. We believed if we'd had a choice, though we never would, we'd have wanted to "go down in a hail of bullets." In waking nightmares for months we would see the glaring ice field, skeletal trees and wind-whipped clouds. We knew what it was to be pursued by hounds, stumbling and falling in the snow, writhing in pain. Kicked in the ribs, in the stomach, in the groin and in the chest and face by Gestapo boots. "You little fucker!"—we heard the furious shouts of adult men, we felt their fists closing in our hair, dragging us along the ground. "Give it up, you little fucker! You're under arrest!" Dwayne Hewson who'd been butted in the head by a West Seneca linebacker in his junior year and had had to be carried off the football field and taken by ambulance to Amherst General said ruefully, "Christ, you never forget it. Being 'concussed.' Like, you never get over thinking it could happen to you again, any time. The earth just opening up like a big black hole and you fall *in*." We would never learn exactly when John Reddy made his single statement to police. We believed he couldn't have made it at Mount Nazarene since they'd beaten him there, and at the Onondaga Medical Center he was in emergency for hours being treated for frostbite, exposure, exhaustion, a sprained ankle, a detached retina in his left eye, plus miscellaneous bruises and lacerations as the medical report would indicate—"Injuries sustained by the prisoner while resisting arrest." Yet there was the famous photo of John Reddy glaring up at us next morning in the *Buffalo Courier-Express* that was delivered before we left for school. The photo to be taped inside hundreds of school lockers, laminated to endure for years! The photo Roger Zwaart would tear out of Suzi Zeigler's fingers and rip into shreds! The photo Evangeline Fesnacht would reproduce in a gilt duotone on the cover of *Death Chronicles*!

The photo about which Mary Louise Schultz's second husband, a deceptively mild-mannered New York State public health official, would say, having discovered it in Mary Louise's lingerie drawer in their mutual mahogany bureau in their suburban Albany home twenty-two years after the morning of John Reddy's arrest, "What—what the hell is *this*?" John Reddy Heart, just a boy, his unshaven face bloody and left eye swollen shut but staring defiantly at the camera as if into his own and our unfathomable future, having made the only statement he'd make to police—even to his own lawyer—"O.K. Do what you have to do."

These words, Verrie Myers confided in us, haunted her for years. In time, they would haunt her through her life. She would hear them—*O.K. Do what you have to do*—as she sank into her most exhausted, fevered sleep. As she performed before movie cameras—"Again, again and again 'proving' myself. But why?" She would hear these words, resigned, fatalistic, yet perhaps hopeful, as, maintaining a serene and beautiful facade, Veronica Myers sweated out the announcement of the Oscar winner for "best supporting actress in a feature film" for which, at the age of thirty-two, she'd been nominated. (Verrie's sole Academy Award nomination. Of course, she hadn't won.) She would hear *O.K. Do what you have to do* at her mother's funeral, at the very gravesite in the Unitarian cemetery in Willowsville. She would hear *O.K. Do what you have to do* as, with a trepidation that would have surprised her old friends and classmates, as well as her Hollywood associates and scattered "fans," she gave herself up, for the dozenth time, to love. (Verrie would be married only once—in her forty-ninth year. But we knew from *People* and elsewhere that she'd had numerous love affairs with actors, directors, writers, artists, most of them dark-haired swarthy-skinned handsome and "fatally unreliable" men.) She would hear *O.K. Do what you have to do* as the anesthetic gripped her when she had her first abortion, and her second. Probably, she anticipated, she'd sink into her deathbed consoled by John Reddy's mysterious words—*O.K. Do what you have to do.*

Even more vivid in our collective memories than these words was the newspaper photograph accompanying the story of John Reddy's arrest. "Like he'd already been taken from us. Like he belonged now to history." At our fifteenth reunion we were drunk and tearful yet happy in our post-coital way (as Art Lutz described it) in the sunken rec room of Art's buff-brick neo-Georgian house on the Common (who among us could've predicted that our Class Clown Artie Lutz whose principal mode of expression had long been the lip-fart would become CEO at the age of thirty-three of his grand-father's multimillion-dollar company Lutz Magic Kleen, Inc.?—and a serious-seeming husband, father, Willowsville citizen?) giddy on champagne and a marathon "The Ballad of John Reddy Heart" in the background listening to our most glamorous alumna, Veronica Myers, confide in us, her oldest friends, that to make herself react emotionally on screen, to lacerate her heart, to weep true tears, she had only to envision that image of John Reddy. So tough, and so vulnerable! So sexy, and so *fated*! To work herself into the mood for a cinematic love scene ("Total nudity now, nothing left to the imagination, but my contracts assure me a body double so at least, while the audience thinks that's me, it *isn't*") she had only to recall that image or, maybe, John Reddy in the school parking lot by the acid-green Caddie smoking a cigarette or yanking a pull top from a can of Coke, or John Reddy as a shadow-silhouette behind the blind of a window down on Water Street. We were moved by Verrie's intense face which seemed to even the most sharp-eyed among us to be hardly older than the face of the girl who'd portrayed Shakespeare's Portia; we were moved by the mournful starkness of her pale blue eyes. *Is she performing? Is she "real"? Is there any distinction?* We'd made every effort to "see" Verrie Myers as just one of us, a girl from WHS, but we were overwhelmed by the aura of her film self, her celebrity, that *Veronica Myers* who towered above us on movie screens like a gorgeous fresco come to life. Yet in Willowsville, Verrie was embarrassed and evasive when the subject of her film career came up. "My career began as a way of saying to John Reddy—'Look at me! Why won't you look at *me*? I'm more than some rich man's spoiled daughter.' But damn him he never did." We protested she couldn't know that for a fact. "I do know! I know for a fact! John Reddy never saw a single play of the eight plays I was in, in school. Not one." "But you don't know about your movies," we pointed out, as reasonable adults, "how could you possibly know?" For John Reddy Heart had abruptly left Willowsville, never to return, a few days after his last exam and though it was vaguely believed he still lived in upstate New York, in the vicinity of Lake Ontario, none of us had seen him again and he was in contact, apparently, with no one. (Dino Calvo? He'd moved away. Sasha Calvo? She'd long since married, and moved away, too.) But Verrie insisted she knew, somehow. "It's as Dwayne used to say—'We didn't, for John Reddy, *exist*.'"

Were we then shocked!—or would have been if we hadn't been drunk—Norm Zeiga had actually fallen asleep on the far side of the fireplace—when beautiful Verrie Myers suddenly pulled down the front of her sleek-fitting summer-knit minidress, tugging at the thin straps and baring her left breast, an amazing breast, lovely in shape, not flaccid, roseate-nippled (a breast we'd seen, in fact, some of us more than once, in Veronica Myers's biggest hit of some years ago), to show us, on the milky pale flesh near her breastbone, a jew-ellike little heart tattoo of about the size of Verrie's smallest fingernail, bright strawberry-red.

"See? You guys are the only people in the fucking world who'd have a clue what this means. *I love you guys*." We hadn't realized how drunk Verrie was until she began laughing, and then she began crying. Afterward we would puzzle over whether the tattoo must have been camouflaged by makeup for Verrie's most spectacular nude scene, with Jack Nicholson; for we couldn't believe that the tattoo was recent. Millie LeRoux Pifer said enviously, "Oh, Verrie! Just like my daughter! But that must've hurt—didn't it?" Ginger McCord Siefried cried, "You had the guts! Verrie, I love you." Guys who'd been crazy about Verrie Myers as long ago as junior high gaped at the tattoo—and at the breast—swallowing like fish out of water though we'd long ago lost our virginity as we'd lost our boyhoods, cruelly transformed it seemed overnight into husbands, fathers, IRS-terrorized adult citizens like Bo Bozer, Jon Rindfleisch, Larry Baumgart, Ken Fischer. Transfixed like Circe's swine we blinked and stared and swayed as if about to topple over, swelling, puffing, swallowing without saliva—"Verrie, my God!" one of us managed to cry in a cracked, reproachful voice. We were astounded then as, suddenly, Ken Fischer, still handsome though ravaged-looking from hours of determined drinking and (it was rumored) marital difficulties back home in Quincy, Mass., fell forward onto his knees and boldly shuffled across the carpet to press his hot tremulous mouth against the strawberry-red heart on the luminous floating breast.

Near dawn at the Hyatt Regency at Buffalo International Airport there was Veronica Myers swooning naked into her former boyfriend's arms: "Oh God, Kenny—maybe I've always loved *you*. All these *years*. *Can you ever forgive me?*"

10

They tried to put John Reddy away.
Man, they tried to put John Reddy away.
Tried tried tried to put John Reddy away.
You gonna try to put John Reddy away?
John Reddy, John Reddy Heart ain't gonna stay.

In all, John Reddy Heart would be incarcerated—that was the official term: "incarcerated"—for twenty months. Twelve months in the Tomahawk Island Youth Camp and eight months in the Erie County Detention Center in downtown Buffalo.

There were those, most of our fathers in fact, even to this day they'd get hot in the face and say *That greaser-killer-kid should've gone to prison for life.* You can't argue with them, so why bother?

Judge Hamilton W. Schor of the Erie County Criminal Court denied John Reddy bail. Even $1 million bail (despite that rumor). The judge agreed with the county prosecutor that John Reddy Heart was a "flight risk"—already he'd fled police and eluded them, making fools of them, for seventy-two hours. It had taken more than thirty of them to "bring him back alive." There was much embarrassment, and outrage, that Willowsville-Amherst police had allowed John Reddy to escape the village on the night of Riggs's death. "A vicious, mad-dog murderer," the prosecutor Dill argued. "His relative youth shouldn't blind us to that fact." Dill was also responsible for insuring that John Reddy would be tried as an adult, in criminal court. Not as a minor, in juvenile court.

Not even Dahlia Heart, pleading personally with Judge Schor, could induce the judge to change his mind.

So John Reddy was locked up. Held in detention awaiting his trial in the fall. That long hot-humid spring and summer. The Erie County Detention Center was a grim weatherworn fortress-building with coils of razor wire strung about it like nasty-glinting Christmas tinsel. Prisoners on trial who couldn't make bail or had been denied bail were transported to the Erie County Courthouse a few blocks away by van, wrists and ankles shackled. Bart Digger who would become a criminologist dated the onset of his interest in such a subject to the summer of John Reddy's incarceration—"It made you think. That's where he is. So what's it like, what *is* it? How does it connect to us?" Most of us just cruised the expressway along the river on slow summer nights, nothing better to do or anyway nothing that drew us. As Ritchie Eickhorn said we got to know the Erie County Detention Center "intimately from the outside." As Millie LeRoux who'd begun writing poetry said, "It's like your soul's some other place." There was a senior guy with a T-Bird who boasted he'd taken, "by a conservative estimate, a dozen" WHS girls, including the most popular varsity cheerleaders, cruising past the detention center with a six-pack and ending up in La Salle Park overlooking the river—"Jesus, something comes over those girls. It's like crying makes them hot. You practically have to fight them off."

There was talk that summer of condoms. Who bought them, or tried to. Condom jokes. Condom anxiety. Out back of the school (where John Reddy's acid-green Caddie was no longer parked) some of the guys fooled around, hoping to befriend the tougher guys like Orrie Buhr, Clyde Meunzer, Dino Calvo and Ray Gottardi. Nosepicker Nordstrom cracked us up blowing up an actual condom like a balloon—or was it a balloon, in fact, long and slender as an eel?—until it burst, spraying a mysterious lukewarm liquid into our faces. Guys packed condoms like chewing gum or cigarettes. Patting their back pockets, sniggering. Somebody, probably Art Lutz and Bo Bozer, raked a mess of used condoms like expired fish from La Salle Beach and brought them back to Willowsville where they were spread out on the school lawn in mimicry of our school insignia:

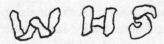

Nice girls shunned us, revulsed. We were virgins waiting to explode.

But not always, for even nice girls like the girls of the Circle needed to be taken on illicit drives into downtown Buffalo, if they wanted to see John Reddy Heart's place of "incarceration" and if they didn't have their own cars. Mary Louise Schultz was seen with Art Lutz because Art had a car, what other reason? Ginger McCord, Bibi Arhardt, Sandy Bangs dated boys who had cars they were allowed to drive into Buffalo or who had parents who didn't know they were driving fifteen miles through the center of gritty Buffalo, cruising the expressway and looping back restlessly to cruise it another time before returning on Delaware Avenue or Main Street to the Village of Willowsville which was, as Ginger McCord said, wiping tears from her eyes as if she'd come a very long distance in only a few hours, "Like something floating in the night—like a beautiful gleaming white yacht anchored in a nasty dark sea."

This was the long hot-humid summer Willowsville girls learned to cry. In that special bittersweet way. "It all began then, but when will it end?"

Not yet sixteen, and so not yet in possession of the canary-yellow Olds birthday convertible, Verrie Myers strained her sensitive relationship with Ken Fischer by hinting she'd be willing to date other boys, with cars, if he wouldn't drive her past the Erie County Detention Center at least once a week, after dark; so that Verrie could flash the car headlights as they approached the grim building, eliciting from its interior, not always predictably or clearly, an answering sequence of flashes like Morse code, from what was probably a hand-held mirror inside one of the barred windows. Verrie responded passionately to skepticism on our part—"How do I know it's John Reddy and not someone else returning my signals? I don't. But I have *faith*." Ken Fischer made no comment. You couldn't even elicit a wink from him, an ironic or disdainful grimace. He was a sap in love with Verrie Myers since, as he'd said, at least kindergarten at the Academy Street School when the bewitching little blond girl had run up to him and, to the delight of all watching adults, kissed him on the nose.

Why had little Verrie Myers kissed little Kenny Fischer that day?—"I don't know, I just did. I *wanted to*."

We'd all expected them to get married someday. But Verrie's career intervened. And Ken, well—Ken married another girl. It never seemed right to us but many years would pass before it was made right.

It's a phenomenon of age, aging. You get to know from repeated experiences what absence means. That, one day, one hour, one minute, someone or something ceases to exist in relationship to you. When you're young, even high school age, you don't get it at once. "It has to, like, *sink in*."

So it sank in upon us in gradual waves of comprehension that John Reddy Heart was gone. Gone from Willowsville. Not permanently but gone. Gone for now. (In fact, maybe gone for good. The rumor was, Dahlia Heart would sell the house. She'd never be able to live in Willowsville again.) The beautiful eye-aching acid-green Caddie was no longer parked conspicuously behind the high school, nor was it sighted on our leafy streets like a quick-darting green flame you fear might singe your eyeballs if you look—but you look. And gone, too, the sound of the Caddie's engine, hoarsened by its aging muffler: whining, gravelly, thrilling to the ear, at least to the adolescent ear, like a deep mock-bass voice, wordless, pushing up through layers of dark earth until you feel, more than hear, its power.

"St. Albans Hill is so damned quiet, my ears *ache*."

"Young lady, don't let your father hear you say such a ridiculous thing! We live here *because it is quiet*."

Abruptly, too, Dahlia Heart was gone from Willowsville. And old Mr. Heart, and John Reddy's younger brother and sister whose names no one could remember. Guys came to realize they'd been gazing along the Avenue of Fashion or glancing up at some white-luminous object in the corner of their eye looking for—*her*. Attendance at basketball games plummeted and not just because the team, missing John Reddy, was bottoming out: there wasn't the possibility of Dahlia Heart showing up and making her grand entrance, shaking the hands of Coach McKeever and other male teachers so that we could observe, we swore, their knees actually *vibrating*. All that was gone. Like a TV program that ends its run, tearing a hole in your heart.

The Hearts had had to move hastily away from St. Albans Hill as soon as news broke of Melvin Riggs's scandalous death in Mrs. Heart's bedroom, while John Reddy was still a "fugitive from justice"—"object of a statewide manhunt"—his name and glowering face on TV countless times a day and in every area paper. Like something bursting, strangers identified as reporters, photographers and TV camera crews swarmed onto prestigious Meridian Place, daring to ascend the drive, ring the doorbell, trample the lawn. Worse yet, these strangers dared to ring the doorbells of the Thruns, the Bannisters, the Kaisers, the Johnstons. Roland Trippe gave a news conference to announce that the family had gone "into seclusion" and would not be available to meet with the media. Willowsville Township provided two police officers to protect the handsome old Dutch Colonial that was still known, in St. Albans Hill, as the Edgihoffer house. Still there were trespassers.

Curiosity seekers from Buffalo and suburbs, yet more media people, freelance and amateur photographers.

NUDE SHOOTING DEATH OF MEL RIGGS
CONTROVERSIAL BASEBALL PERSONALITY
IN AFFLUENT BUFFALO SUBURB

and

16-YEAR-OLD FUGITIVE FROM JUSTICE
SUSPECT IN KILLING OF MOM'S LOVER
ELUDES POLICE CAPTURE SECOND DAY

—such headlines, going out on national news wires, drew people from considerable distances. Motorcycle gangs from Olcott Beach, Yonkers and Erie, Pennsylvania, with straggly greasy hair, beards and black leather and swastika tattoos whose leaders, photographed for the *Buffalo Evening News*, resembled older, coarsened brothers of John Reddy Heart. St. Albans Hill residents were frightened, angered. "I know it's disrespectful to speak ill of the dead," Mrs. Bannister told friends at the Village Women's Club, "but I blame the Colonel! He started it all by taking up with that woman, and left us to stew in his disgusting juices, and *where will it end*?" Photographs and video footage were taken of not only 8 Meridian Place but neighboring houses and grounds as well. Mrs. Thrun's cleaning woman of twenty years, Myrtle Thrasher, who'd never once set foot in Mrs. Heart's house, and had never so much as glimpsed the infamous woman, was nonetheless approached at her bus stop on Main Street and telephoned by rapacious media people offering her as much as fifteen hundred dollars for "inside, intimate reports" on Dahlia Heart and her lovers. Mrs. Bannister's cleaning woman of twenty-five years, Tina Florence, was offered three thousand dollars for similar reports and an "eyewitness description of the bullet-riddled bloodstained bedroom" she was believed to have been hired to clean. Willowsville police were overwhelmed. Trespassers approached the darkened house from the rear, scaling a six-foot stone wall to wander through the weedy, disheveled rock garden that had once been Mildred Edgihoffer's pride; within days of the scandal, Dahlia Heart's controversial lawn ornaments had been spirited away as mementos. Jon Rindfleisch and Steve Lunt encountered, by wind-ravaged moonlight in the lane behind the Heart home, two notorious senior girls who'd long claimed to be secret lovers of John Reddy Heart, and spent much of the night with them in Jon's car in the woods beyond St. Peter and Paul Cemetery—"Don't ask us what those girls are like. Man, we're wasted. Man, there just aren't *words*."

It seemed to us that the Hearts' house, once as distinguished as any house in St. Albans Hill (with the exception of the old Wise mansion on its five-acre lot on the Common) began to deteriorate almost overnight. Cracks began to define themselves between the large fieldstones of which the central, "historic" part of the house was constructed. In bright spring sunshine, the robin's-egg-blue shutters and front door glowed like lurid neon. One of the second-floor windows, believed to be a window in Dahlia Heart's bedroom, was cobwebbed with cracks. When the Hearts first fled into seclusion (somewhere in downtown Buffalo, it was assumed), Pasquito's Lawn Service had continued to tend to the grounds; by mid-June, the lawn service was no longer in Mrs. Heart's employ and the two-acre lot, lush from our torrential spring rains, began to grow rapidly, a tumult of wild grass, dandelions, tall spiky thistles. A violent thunderstorm at the end of June split a giant hundred-year-old elm bordering on Aickley Thrun's property, and Mr. Thrun paid for it to be trimmed and repaired—at a cost of above $2,000, it was believed. Mr. Thrun and other neighbors of the Hearts began to send their lawn crews or groundskeepers over to 8 Meridian Place, since the absent Mrs. Heart seemed to have sloughed off her responsibility; almost overnight, in early July, the property was restored to nearly the distinction it had once had in the old, lost days of Mildred Edgihoffer and repeated awards from the Buffalo

Gardeners' Club. Yet when a reporter and a photographer from the *Courier-Express* came to do a feature on "neighborly compassion" in Willowsville, no one in St. Albans Hill would consent to an interview and all denied any special "compassion" for the Hearts. Aickley Thrun allowed himself to be quoted, photographed grim-faced in the doorway of his handsome English Tudor home: "I happen not to condone murder, and I happen not to condone adultery. Nor do I condone, if you want to go into it, a drunken old derelict scavenging in our midst. But we all have to look at that house, damn it!"

In the weeks preceding John Reddy Heart's trial (in mid-September, six months after his arrest) we began to hear about a beautiful, mysterious woman dressed entirely in white, wearing a white wide-brimmed hat and a white lace veil, white gloves, white shoes, carrying a white handbag, who was observed attending church services in Buffalo churches: Presbyterian, Episcopalian, Lutheran, Methodist, Unitarian, Roman Catholic, Byzantine Catholic. Sometimes the woman was accompanied by an elderly white-haired gentleman with trimmed white whiskers. Sometimes she was accompanied by two children who appeared ill at ease and bored in church, a somber, thin bespectacled boy in his early teens and a somber, plumpish bespectacled girl of eleven or twelve. But usually the woman was alone. She entered church quietly and took an inconspicuous seat at the rear. Though not always familiar with the service, she knelt, she prayed, she sang with the congregation; often overcome with emotion, wiping away tears with a white lace handkerchief. She was said to drop five-dollar bills into the collection but left immediately at the conclusion of the service, before anyone could greet her, or get a good, clear look at her veiled face.

"A vision in white. Like an angel."

When John Reddy's trial began, the media returned to Buffalo/Willowsville in greater numbers than before. At first, we thought it was exciting—"Like we'd all won a lottery," as Dexter Cambrook said.

In those days TV cameras were forbidden in courtrooms. Photographers were forbidden. But press sketch artists were allowed to attend trials, so there began to appear in newspapers and on TV pencil sketches of John Reddy Heart. "That isn't John Reddy! That isn't him at all." We were incensed, disgusted. We were puzzled. Most of the so-called portraits of our classmate John Reddy Heart were of an almost-ugly stranger, much older than sixteen: frowning, simian, malevolent; with heavy-lidded eyes and a sensuous, pouting mouth. As Evangeline Fesnacht had said months before, those were *killer eyes*. These were portraits of the *vicious mad-dog killer* the prosecutor Mr. Dill was trying to imprison for life. Meaning to mock these adult distortions of a reality we knew intimately, someone anonymous (generally believed to be Dougie Siefried but, in fact, as she'd confess many years later, Elise Petko!) thumbtacked the ugliest of the sketches, which appeared in the *Evening News*, on the cork bulletin board across from Mr. Stamish's office, embellished with devil's horns and a red glistening forked tongue; but it was torn down almost immediately by an infuriated Ginger McCord who ripped it into tiny shreds.

TV cameras were forbidden inside the Erie County Courthouse but couldn't be banned from the enormous old building's numerous front steps. We in Willowsville who were forbidden even to attempt to attend the trial were amazed to see, on TV, dozens of teenaged pickets who were totally unknown to us—glamorous girls with teased hair, heavily made-up faces and harsh voices chanting "Free John Reddy! Free John Reddy!" identified as from Cheektowaga—a somber-faced, pious group in suits and dresses carrying signs that read LOCKPORT CHRISTIAN YOUTH FORGIVE US OUR SINS. Naturally the TV cameras for WWBN, WWBF and WWNT favored Buffalo celebrities like Mayor Dorsey who'd been a friend of Melvin Riggs, Jr., and who intoned gravely into the camera,

"Under our law even a hardened criminal is 'innocent until proven guilty' but we all know this is a very, very tragic thing that our friend Mel Riggs who loved Buffalo so much has departed from us." There was Sal Morningstar the popular TV-talk-show host with the rubbery face and glistening eyes—"I can't believe that Mel is gone. I like to think Mel isn't gone. He's here with us, looking down, or maybe"—mugging for the camera—"looking *up*, praying that justice will be executed and he won't have died in vain." There was a procession of Hawks, present-day and past members of the team, interviewed on their way into and out of the courthouse. Shortstop Mick Boyer looking ruddier and fleshier than we remembered who winked into the camera and said in a mock-sorrowful voice, "It's real sad what happened to our beloved boss Mel Riggs. All the guys on the team are taking it hard. Couldna happened to a sweeter fella." Hal West and Buck Sweeney who'd had much-publicized contractual difficulties with Riggs the previous season said, smirking, in the tones of men who'd been warmed by a drink or two, that they were attending the trial "with the hope of seeing justice done." Jimmy O'Grady who'd been photographed trading blows with Riggs three or four years before, and had been fired from the team, said, laying his finger alongside his puffy nose, "Some cruel folks is saying they'd like that kid Heart's autograph. Some folks is saying that kid Heart would get the Buffalo Good Citizen Award this year. *I'm* not saying none of that, I think it's a real sad thing Mel's gone from us." Pitcher Buff Stansell who in fact had been treated well by Riggs, and had managed to stay on Riggs's good side through his career as a Hawk, said thoughtfully into the camera, "Could be, Mel Riggs was a 'murder victim' looking for his murderer. That poor kid happened to be the one to oblige him."

Miles away in Willowsville we were approached by media people, too. "A swarm of locusts—repulsive!" Woody McKeever said, smacking his lips; of the WHS staff, Coach was the most popular target. We'd see him shaking his finger at reporters, delivering angry impassioned speeches. We'd see him, hat in hand, scowling for photographers. Mr. Lepage turned up one day at school looking subtly different, younger—we theorized he'd had his hair rinsed, a lighter, shinier shade of brown. Mr. Dunleddy wore brighter neckties and seemed to have grown more youthful, too; it was believed he'd added a hairpiece to his thinning gray-brown hair. Our principal Mr. Stamish warned us repeatedly over the school announcement system to shun "unwelcome inquiries." Yet he, too, was observed in a new herringbone tweed double-breasted suit, frowning and whistling in the school foyer amid gleaming display cases of brass sports trophies. "We ask you to emphasize that WHS students are good, decent, law-abiding and ninety-seven percent Christian boys and girls from stable families," Mr. Stamish lectured reporters. "John Reddy Heart is the first of his kind, ever, in Willowsville." Off school property we drew reporters and photographers like magnets. The better-looking among us were approached on sidewalks, in restaurants, waiting in line at the Glen Theatre. Seeing we were biased in John Reddy's favor, reporters asked *Do you condone violence? Do you believe in taking the law into your own hands?* and similar crap. We were asked if it was true that John Reddy Heart belonged to the Hell's Angels motorcycle gang, that he "dealt dope," that he'd "bragged of killing some-one else." And what of a high school "sex ring" with which he and his friends were associated?

There was much TV footage, some of it network, of WHS girls wearing black felt armbands decorated with red hearts in support of John Reddy Heart, their sleeves decorated with red sequin hearts. They wore heart-shaped lockets, barrettes, earrings, buttons and pins. Photographers were drawn to the good-looking girls of the Circle, statuesque Mary Louise Schultz, wide-eyed freckled Ginger McCord, Pattianne Groves with her thick-lashed dark eyes and wavy auburn hair to her shoulders. Verrie Myers, the most popular, shocked some of us by posing for *Time* in a sexy, provocative posture, lips moistened, hands on hips, a glittering cascade of sequin hearts in her long blond hair and on both sleeves of her camel's-hair Pendleton blazer, a heart-shaped I ♥ JOHN REDDY! badge on her left breast. Verrie was breathless, feverish; we'd heard she was taking No-Doz as well as drinking black coffee having vowed she "wouldn't sleep or rest or be at peace in my soul" until John Reddy was set free. (Verrie's parents were furious with her when the photo appeared in *Time*, above the caption *Willowsville cheerleader Veronica Myers says she supports alleged killer*. They'd had no idea the story was imminent. They accused her of demeaning herself in public, bringing disgrace to their name. Fifteen years later Verrie would confide to a *Vanity Fair* interviewer that she'd become a "psychic outlaw" when denounced by her parents: "I realized I was free to live my life however I wished and to 'demean' myself however I wished. *I knew I would be an artist of some kind.*") Domestic-minded Home Ec majors like Sarepta Voss, Alice Goff and Sandy Bangs made costume jewelry from mail-order kits advertised in the back pages of *Good Housekeeping*, heart-shaped pins of rhinestones and glass "rubies" to be sold at school and in the Village; though these "heart pins" were not very skillfully made, with a visible excess of paste, as if made by handicapped children, we bought them to wear and to give as presents to our mothers and grandmothers. Miss Bird surprised us by buying one of the larger pins and wearing it prominently on the collar of her tartan coat. A reporter from the *Lockport Union-Sun and Journal* dared to ask Miss Bird, as she was unlocking her car, "Ma'am, does that pin indicate your support of the alleged killer of Melvin Riggs?" and Miss Bird drew herself up to her full height of five feet and said scathingly, "Young man. I hope, as a teacher, I am always in support of my students. 'Judge not lest ye be judged.'"

Miss Bird, too, had become more youthful, energized; she'd taken to wearing spike-heeled shoes that gave her the look of a red-haired, diminutive yet oddly sexy stork. In October,

Sandi Scott's mother would report having seen Miss Bird in the company of Jim Dunleddy at Pumpkin Harvest Day in Newfane, thirty miles away in Niagara County. "I'm sure they were holding hands. It definitely looked that way." Miss Bird and Mr. Dunleddy, having a romance? But wasn't Mr. Dunleddy a married man?

At first we were thrilled to see ourselves on TV and to read about ourselves in local papers and in mass-market magazines like *Time*, *Newsweek*, *U.S. News & World Report*. Our fathers who subscribed to the *New York Times* and the *Wall Street Journal* were surprised, and annoyed, to see articles about John Reddy Heart and Melvin Riggs, Jr., even there. "That S.O.B. Riggs, why couldn't he have gotten himself killed discreetly?" Dougie Siefried's father cursed. "It makes us all look bad." Willowsville mayor Frank Diebold worried aloud on local TV, "We don't want the rest of the country to think our kids are killers and dope fiends. They're *good kids and we love 'em*." We were most amazed at a five-page feature in *Life* with the startling headline

TEENAGE VIOLENCE DOES NOT SPARE
UPPER-MIDDLE-CLASS BUFFALO SUBURB
MURDER, DRUGS, SEX & ROCK-'N'-ROLL
IN WILLOWSVILLE, N.Y.

The first photo in the feature was the now-famous one of John Reddy Heart being arrested by state troopers, blood shining on his battered, defiant face (16-YEAR-OLD DEFENDANT IN LURID MURDER TRIAL). Next came paired photos on valentine hearts of Melvin Riggs, Jr. (CONTROVERSIAL CASANOVA FIGURE, OWNER OF BUFFALO HAWKS BASEBALL TEAM), and Dahlia Heart at her most glamorous in a sleek white ermine coat to her ankles and oversized dark sunglasses disguising half her face (MYSTERY WOMAN IN WHITE, ELUSIVE MOTHER OF ALLEGED KILLER). We recognized familiar village scenes in other photos—the Avenue of Fashion, the One Hundred Weeping Willows Walk beside

Glen Creek, the palatial neoclassical facade of the Willowsville Country Club. We almost didn't recognize our school
seen from the front across an expanse of well-tended lawn, a
building that resembled a temple with slender white Doric
columns, russet-red brick. The caption was shocking:
WILLOWSVILLE SENIOR HIGH SCHOOL, BASTION OF PRIVILEGE. There were
photos of the football team practicing, cheerleaders practicing
on the lawn (sexy senior Bibi Arhardt poised in midair, ponytail flying). But there were other photos of teenagers none of
us had ever seen before, smoking, drinking beer out of cans,
sprawled beside graffiti-defaced trees in what appeared to be
La Salle Park. A scruffy-looking kid in a black T-shirt who'd
identified himself to the *Life* reporter as a student at WHS, but
who absolutely was not a student at WHS, was quoted, smirking, "It's no surprise to hear John Reddy killed that guy. He's
beat the s—t out of plenty of guys."

All of this made us sick, sort of. But we liked it, too. It was
like riding on a roller coaster having stuffed yourself with
hot dogs, Cokes, cotton candy; you're feeling nauseated,
ready to vomit and hoping you will vomit but it doesn't
happen, and you climb back onto the roller coaster for more.

What was most unnerving, we realized, was to see ourselves through the eyes of strangers. We hadn't understood
that we were the children of "privilege"—that we lived in an
"exclusive, affluent suburb." We hadn't realized that our
fathers' average incomes were over $100,000 (and this was
decades ago). We wanted to scream, "Hey! You don't know
us! And you don't know John Reddy Heart, either."

It was at this time that the rock group Made in USA came
out with "The Ballad of John Reddy Heart." Nobody'd
expected this; one day all the radio stations were playing it.
More excitement. The record soared to number one on the
pop singles chart within a week of its release. Local record
stores had to reorder continuously. We sang the lyrics to one
another, we shouted the lyrics out of car windows, we waded
drunk in the duck pond at Tug Hill Park screaming the lyrics

at the tops of our lungs. We were in a din, a frenzy of sexual excitement. Art Lutz who'd had a crush on Mary Louise Schultz since sixth grade but hadn't been encouraged to ask her out, in fact discouraged by Mary Louise's polite dismissal of his jokey-anxious conversation, dared to approach her in the school cafeteria as she sat amid her girlfriends, speaking so persuasively in the manner of the lead singer of Made in USA that Mary Louise had faltered, and said, "Well, yes, I guess so. When?" Our fathers despised "The Ballad of John Reddy Heart" but our mothers, especially younger, more savvy mothers (Mrs. Connor, Mrs. Rindfleisch, Mrs. Baskett) liked it fine. Blake Wells, who played clarinet and was something of a music snob, a pain in the ass sometimes, pointed out that Made in USA had plagiarized the basic melody for "The Ballad" from an old hymn, "Jesus Walked That Lonesome Valley," and given it a cheap rockabilly beat plagiarized from Bill Haley and His Comets. (Not that that mattered, Blake added, since Bill Haley had plagiarized the beat from a Negro musician named Willie Mae Thornton— "It's well known that white rock-'n'-roll has been plagiarized totally from Negro sources.") Mr. Larsen, school music teacher and long-suffering marching band leader, pronounced "The Ballad of John Reddy Heart" to be sickly pseudo-music, adolescent tripe, moronic as Elvis's classic head-banger "Hound Dog." Still, most of us loved it. We still do. *That rush! along our fevered veins! to insinuate itself fatally into our hearts like the heartworm parasite in dogs.*

We had to wonder: how did John Reddy feel, being the subject of a hit single? Made by a rock group he'd never met? His name used without his permission? His life used without his permission? And he never received a penny of royalties? We learned that once you become famous in America, you no longer own your name or your life. "It's like every S.O.B. who knows you thinks he's entitled to a piece of you," Ritchie Eickhorn said, shuddering. "A piece of you stuck in his teeth."

11

John Reddy looked the old judge in the eye.
John Reddy said, Don't give a damn if I die.
John Reddy, John Reddy Heart.

I n fact, John Reddy never said a word at either of his trials.
We all waited for him to speak. But we waited in vain.

Judge Hamilton W. Schor was the presiding judge. Before
him, John Reddy stood silent and sullen as the formal indictment was read charging him with a count of murder in the
second degree. He would be tried as an adult, not in juvenile
court. In a carefully neutral voice Judge Schor asked, "How
do you plead, Mr. Heart?" It was said you could see in the
judge's eyes the contempt he felt for the sixteen-year-old
"Killer-Boy," as the papers were calling him. John Reddy
shifted his shoulders inside his tight-fitting coat and stared at
the floor. It was his lawyer Roland Trippe who answered in a
firm voice, "Your Honor, my client pleads not guilty."

A faint smile or sneer on John Reddy's lips? We imagined
that, we could see that vividly though none of us was present
in the courtroom in downtown Buffalo. John Reddy reflected
the old judge's contempt right back at him. John Reddy's contempt for all authority, his enemies. *O.K. Do what you have to
do.*

Through the first trial of John Reddy Heart, and through the second trial of John Reddy Heart, everyone waited for the sixteen-year-old defendant to take the witness stand. Everyone waited for him to try to persuade the silent, staring jury of his elders in his own words that, as his lawyer argued, he was "not guilty" of murder because he'd fired at Melvin Riggs only to protect himself and his mother from Riggs's violent attack. Or possibly—there was this speculation, too— he was "not guilty" of murder because he'd panicked and pulled the trigger of a gun he'd believed to be unloaded, which he'd aimed at Melvin Riggs only to frighten him off. But John Reddy never volunteered any remarks. He'd never cooperated with police, had never even admitted he'd been the one to pull the trigger, or even that he'd been present when Riggs was shot.

He'd never taken a polygraph test.

The only persons John Reddy was observed speaking with, in the courtroom, in private, were his lawyer Trippe and Trippe's assistant who sat at the defense table with him. And he'd exchanged remarks with the Erie County sheriff's deputies who escorted him into and out of the courtroom, youngish guys he'd gotten to know and who'd gotten to know him, and obviously they got along O.K., being of the same class background and temperament.

Theories differed about why John Reddy Heart whose plea was self-defense wouldn't testify in his own defense. Mr. Zwaart, Roger's father, a lawyer with a downtown firm, said that Trippe, a squash partner of his at the B.A.C., was too shrewd to put that "greaser-killer-kid" on the witness stand to hang himself. Mr. Cuthbert who'd become obsessed with the Heart case believed it would be "suicidal"—"tantamount to admitting guilt"—if Trippe *did not* put John Reddy on the witness stand. (We'd hear Mr. Cuthbert, Miss Bird, Mr. Lepage and other teachers heatedly discussing the case between classes in the faculty lounge when the door was open. The intellectuals among us, Clarence McQuade, Ritchie

Eickhorn and Evangeline Fesnacht, believed that John Reddy was repudiating the American criminal justice system in the tradition of Henry David Thoreau (we'd been made to slog through *Walden* and "Civil Disobedience" in sophomore English). "He's refusing to be a party to his own trial. Why should he conform to the enemy's authority?" With the air of impassioned rectitude with which, as an adult, E. S. Fesnacht would speak at public, literary gatherings, Evangeline hinted to us that she had access to confidential information from John Reddy himself: "He will accept even a verdict of 'guilty'—he's become his own transcendental fate, beyond good and evil."

(Evangeline, daughter of solidly bourgeois parents, startled us with her fiery words. In behavior, she was as reckless, or nearly, as certain of the rebellious boys in our class. She would actually attend a number of John Reddy's trial sessions, though these were declared off-limits to area teenagers and the media was filled with warnings from the county board of education that students cutting school to attend the Heart trial would be "taken into custody" by truant officers. She boasted to us that she deceived her parents into thinking she was going to school as usual; she wrote her own "medical excuse," and signed her mother's name to it; she took a bus downtown to arrive at the courthouse by eight-thirty a.m. and mingle with the adults filing into the courtroom. "I wonder if I look middle-aged? No one gives me a second glance.")

Smoke Filer, Dougie Siefried and Scottie Baskett dared to crash the trial, too. They disguised themselves "as our dads, sort of." After only a few sessions they reported to us how strange it was, that the subject was "John Reddy Heart" on trial for the murder of "Melvin Riggs, Jr." but it was like John Reddy, the actual person, wasn't *there*. Like Riggs, the dead man, wasn't *there*. "That bullshit legal talk!" Smoke said, disgusted. "Guys in suits shooting off their mouths. And the old-fart judge in his big-deal robe presiding. And the jurors sitting there like a bunch of store dummies. And the court-room isn't any big deal either, it's kind of small—it doesn't look like a place anything important could happen."

Smoke's long weasel-face crinkled and twisted as if he'd been confronted with a truth too profound, yet too demean-ing, to be comprehended.

Scottie Baskett said, aggrieved, "John Reddy never saw us. He sits with his back to the room. Anyway it doesn't seem like *him*. Remember how he'd jump, that last split-second jump of his, like he was lifted from the floor by some force, and sink the ball?—and whoever was guarding him dazed like he'd been hit over the head? Well, this 'defendant' being tried isn't that John Reddy."

Dougie Siefried agreed. "Jesus, it's *slow*. Not like TV or the movies, y'know, trials you see—made-up stories. This is more like church. Shit-faced *boring*. It's hard to breathe, people are packed in so tight. There aren't any laughs like maybe you'd get in school, not even dumb laughs. I'd be nodding off, and Scottie would elbow me awake—'The bailiff will make you leave,' he said. I feel so sorry for John Reddy—he's just, like, sitting there. If he made a break for it, he'd be shot. It comes over you he's already in prison. *The bastards have got him*." Dougie startled us by wiping at his eyes. Ginger McCord found herself staring at him, at his wan, freckled, homely-handsome face, with a sensation of falling.

* * *

The People of the State of New York v. John Reddy Heart.

You'd have thought John Reddy was a vicious monster!—the way Prosecutor Dill described him to the jury.

"A precocious moral outlaw . . . a savage killer . . . who has shot and killed a defenseless . . . *unclothed* man." (There was a dramatic pause. In the air above Dill's bald dome of a head there shimmered, only just perceptibly, the naked torso and quivering haunches of media personality Mel Riggs as on an ectoplasmic billboard.) "This young killer . . . did not act in 'blind passion' or as he claims in 'self-defense' . . . far from it! Ladies and gentlemen of the jury, he did *consciously and deliberately* . . . and with *premeditation* . . . determine that the murder weapon was loaded . . . or had, in fact, loaded it himself. As forensics evidence makes clear . . . he dropped to one knee, like an expert marksman, and *fired*"—(Another dramatic pause. Dill may have considered dropping to one knee before the jury box, in awkward emulation of his showy, nationally known defense attorney colleagues; but quickly rejected the notion. His knee joints would have audibly creaked and what if he hadn't been able to straighten up again?)—"fired upward, at an angle, at the victim's head as Melvin Riggs unarmed and *unclothed* . . . in a state of alcoholic inebriation . . . staggering backward . . . let us imagine, ladies and gentlemen of the jury . . . this poor terrified man begging! begging the murder-minded John Reddy Heart for mercy! not to kill him! *Begging for his life.*" (Another pause. Like a TV prosecutor, Dill removed a white handkerchief from his pocket and dabbed at his forehead in a display of corny emotion. While John Reddy Heart at the defense table remained stoic-stony-faced showing no emotion at all. "Say something, John! Tell the old bastard to *go fuck*!"—it was all Scottie Baskett could do, to keep from shouting.) "Nonetheless the defendant fired . . . fired three times! . . . one of these bullets striking and entering Melvin Riggs's skull . . . penetrating his brain and killing him almost instantaneously. The defendant then fled . . . the scene of the crime . . . leaving it to others, neighbors of the Heart family, to summon an ambulance, and police. Guiltily he attempted to dispose of the murder weapon by tossing it out a window of his car . . . into a creek. Except, unfortunately for the defendant"—and here Dill allowed himself a sneer, a mean little smile—"the creek happened to be frozen. This, ladies and gentlemen of the jury, I suggest was *not a premeditated act.*" (Smiles and titters in the courtroom. Even the judge. And John Reddy Heart's back rigid in mortification.) "Police found the murder weapon next morning . . .

covered with the defendant's fingerprints. John Reddy Heart's damning fingerprints, ladies and gentlemen of the jury, *and no one else's."*

Dill drew a deep, satisfied breath. Allowing himself a moment of triumph, glancing about the crowded courtroom. Allowing the significance of this fact to sink in to the twelve silent, staring jurors.

Next, he continued, John Reddy Heart had fled Willowsville by coolly following a route he'd clearly worked out in advance to elude police roadblocks and to carry him, eventually, to the Canadian border and into Canada where, like others of his ilk, draft dodgers, political radicals and common criminals alike, he might have escaped detection for years; in the process he callously stole a vehicle in Skaneateles and broke into a 7-Eleven store in Parish and a private residence in Mount Nazarene; he thwarted a statewide manhunt for seventy-two hours and when finally apprehended by police "fiercely resisted arrest" and injured several officers; in custody, he refused to cooperate with authorities. "To this day, ladies and gentlemen of the jury, to this very minute," Dill said, with the air of an aggrieved schoolteacher, "the defendant has put himself above the law. He has said, in effect, 'I refuse to play your game.' We have here not just a young, vicious killer with a depraved indifference to human life but a young, vicious dissident, an anti-American traitor— I'm not exaggerating!—who would undermine the very foundations of the American criminal justice system in which the rest of us believe and hold sacred."

So the jury, seven men and five women, all Caucasian, most of them middle-aged, stared at John Reddy Heart in his tight-fitting suit, down-looking, heavy-jawed and sullen, and you could see them thinking: *Killer. Traitor-killer.*

"The strange thing is, you sort of believe, yourself. The way words convince."

It was Mrs. Connor, Shelby's youngish, popular mom, who told us this. Mrs. Connor, Mrs. Rindfleisch and a few other

Willowsville ladies attended John Reddy's trial from time to time, if they were in the vicinity of downtown Buffalo and could fit the courthouse into their busy, sometimes frantic schedules of luncheons, club meetings, charitable organizations like Planned Parenthood and the Friends of the Albright-Knox Art Gallery, fashion shows at Berger's. (These visits to the Erie County Courthouse were kept secret from their husbands. We had a sudden fleeting sense of our mothers' secret lives, the lives they lived away from their families, like a door opening, just a crack, and we'd yearned to know more but never would.) Mrs. Connor described the courtroom to us, the way the prosecutor, James Dill, a pinch-faced middle-aged man in horn-rimmed glasses and a polyester suit, with the worst western New York accent she'd ever heard, so nasal, like actual concrete was clogged in his sinuses, seemed to hold the jury in his spell. John Reddy's lawyer Roland Trippe was somehow too attractive, too *smooth*. You could see his suit was expensive, he'd gone to a good law school. Whereas Dill was homegrown, from Buffalo's south side, a local product. One of the jurors, Mrs. Connor said, seemed really to hang on his every word. A plain, prune-faced woman of about forty, Sears-type clothes and hair, staring damp-bulgy eyes, she seemed to be regarding John Reddy Heart as if he was the devil incarnate. "Or maybe she has a crush on him," Shelby's mother said with a high-pitched giggle that startled us.

At the defense table, hour after hour, John Reddy just *sat*. Hunched his shoulders, stared into space. "Like he isn't there, almost. Just his body, not his soul. So different from when he'd play basketball—remember?" As if we'd have forgotten. Those of us who were cheerleaders sighed. We'd never really known John Reddy, not even Verrie, or Bibi Arhardt he'd seemed to like O.K. when he took time to notice her, but there was the expectation in others' minds that we cheerleaders had known John Reddy Heart, possibly even dated him. Or went to parties with him and his teammates. (The truth was, John Reddy rarely dropped by our parties even to celebrate delirious Wolverine victories.) You can bask in the expectations of others, however false, for only so long. Mrs. Connor was describing in her low intense voice a stranger to us. His hair had been cut unattractively short, like a soldier's, and damp-combed so he hardly resembled his pictures. He looked older, perplexed. He didn't look sixteen and a half. The single time that Mrs. Connor and her friends managed to sit near the front of the courtroom, far to the right, on the second day of testimony, they'd noticed that John Reddy hadn't shaved adequately. His navy-blue serge suit, white shirt and necktie looked as if they belonged to someone else, smaller in size and lesser in spirit. Mrs. Connor believed that John Reddy must have been lifting weights in the House of Detention, she didn't remember him so muscular and tight-to-bursting on the basketball court; he'd been more lanky, loose-jointed. Even his jaws looked muscular now. "He never glances around at his mother. That shameless woman. Dressed all in white linen like a nun and wearing dark glasses as if she's been crying. And her hair bleached that preposterous platinum blond like Marilyn Monroe's, Kim Novak's—done up in a French twist as if she's a *lady*. Her! She sits there pretending not to notice how people look at her, staring at John Reddy and touching a handkerchief to her eyes like a woman in a movie, so phony, so staged, but John Reddy won't turn. If he killed Melvin Riggs, he killed *for her*—that's obvious!" We were surprised at the bitterness in Mrs. Connor's voice and the vehemence with which she lit one of her Chesterfields.

Evangeline Fesnacht, agitated as we'd rarely seen her, a rosy bloom in her cheeks, reported that the mood of the courtroom was "electric" and "vindictive." It was a good thing, she said, that New York State had set aside the death penalty. (Decades later, under a Republican governor, the death penalty would be restored.) The jurors looked like "cruel zombie-sheep gathered for a public execution." The judge was clearly a "hanging judge, a right-wing conservative" who favored the prosecution. Dill was a "cruel, cunning old puritan" who knew how to arouse middle-aged anxieties by stressing John Reddy's youth. And Roland Trippe, cross-examining the prosecution's witnesses and raising objections every few minutes, was shrewd, but possibly too shrewd; Evangeline's impressions dovetailed with Mrs. Connor's—"The jury doesn't trust Trippe the way they trust Dill who's one of their own." Evangeline astonished us with the confidence with which she spoke, not only in the cafeteria as we gathered around her, straining to hear, but in Mr. Cuthbert's class; we were forced to realize how intelligent she was, how analytical-minded, mature. Yet she was naive, too: she told us she'd sent letters to Trippe offering legal advice but hadn't heard from him yet. She'd sent a pleading message to Mrs. Heart—but hadn't heard from her yet. "The noblest strategy, I think, would be to allow John Reddy to take the witness stand and tell the court why he killed Melvin Riggs, *and why he feels no remorse*."

We cried in near-unison, "But John Reddy is innocent!"

Evangeline retorted, "Don't be ridiculous. John Reddy is a killer, I saw it in his eyes from the start."

It was obvious that the evidence of the .45-caliber revolver covered with John Reddy's prints had made a profound negative impression on the court. The burden of the defense would be to suggest that, though the gun may have shot Melvin Riggs, somehow John Reddy Heart hadn't shot him—exactly; or, if he had, John Reddy wasn't guilty—exactly—of murder, because he'd shot in self-defense and to protect his mother. (Mrs. Heart's numerous bruises and swellings, attested to by a medical report, would be frequently evoked by the defense.) There was the possibility, too, which Trippe floated past the jurors, that John Reddy hadn't even known his grandfather's revolver was loaded; Aaron Leander Heart had told police, possibly truthfully, that the revolver had never been loaded since the family moved to Willowsville. (Clearly, Trippe was handicapped by John Reddy's refusal to talk about it with him; the lawyer was forced to construct a plausible defense out of speculation about his client's basic actions and motives.) Matt Trowbridge made a strong impression on the court with his damaging testimony delivered in a firm, respectful voice. He and his fellow officers had arrived at the Heart home shortly after ten a.m. of March 19, by which time Melvin Riggs appeared to have died and John Reddy Heart had fled to his car. He'd left only minutes before Willowsville police arrived. There were skidding tire tracks in the driveway that indicated he'd accelerated quickly, veering out onto Meridian Place. When the police officers entered the house lights were blazing and the front door was ajar. Yet there was, Trowbridge said, a "strange silence—like the silence following a thunderclap." He and the other officers encountered, on the stairs leading to the second floor of the house, an elderly, disheveled man, Aaron Leander Heart, the defendant's grandfather, "in a state of agitation, confusion and fear." And the defendant's thirteen-year-old brother Farley, dazed-looking, barefoot and in his pajamas. This boy volunteered to police officers, without being questioned, that his brother whom he called John—But here Trippe rose quickly to his feet, and objected; the objection was allowed; and Trowbridge went on to describe the scene in the upstairs bedroom, Riggs's body on the floor and Dahlia Heart lying semiconscious on a bed "'looking as if she'd been beaten.'"

Dill said suggestively, "'*Looking* as if she'd been beaten'?"

Trowbridge said, frowning, "Yes, sir. Looking as if she'd been beaten."

That afternoon Farley Heart was called to testify by the prosecution. Technically he was what's called a hostile witness. Smoke Filer described how, after hours of police and forensics testimony so repetitious and boring Smoke had about decided to slip out of the courtroom and take a bus back to Willowsville though he'd gone to a hell of a lot of trouble to get there (Smoke boasted how he'd disguised the fact he was high school age and truant, powdering his springy red-blond hair to give it an ashen cast, rubbing darkish-mauve matte makeup under his eyes to look ravaged, wearing a droopy gray mustache borrowed from our school theater supplies—"Man, I looked cool: like shit"), Farley's testimony livened things up. Evangeline Fesnacht, seated closer to the front of the courtroom than Smoke, related how, as Farley Heart approached the witness stand, not frightened so much as in a kind of daze, John Reddy at the defense table looked sharply up at him—"The first time in three days that John Reddy seemed to be *seeing* anyone." At the age of thirteen, Farley Heart might have been eleven. A thin, sallow-faced boy with round owlish glasses that caught the light in fractured nervous winks. His hair was straw-colored and his features so indistinct as to seem partly erased, smudged. When he stepped up to the witness stand, he stumbled. The courtroom was silent. The boy's ears were perceived to be protuberant, and flame-red. "Poor kid," Smoke said sympathetically, "put on the spot like that. I mean, swearing to God to tell the 'whole truth'—like, what's he gonna say about his own brother?" Asked by Dill to give an account of the fatal night, Farley spoke slowly, his voice hoarse; his words seemed pried from his very bowels, one by one, rawly sincere, giving pain. He said he'd been in bed, but not asleep, when he began to hear voices. Around eleven p.m. Men's voices. Quarreling. Then one of the men left, Farley heard him drive away, he didn't know who it was, he hadn't seen, and it was quiet for a while; then, later, possibly an hour later, he was wakened from sleep by a loud noise and again there was quarreling, a stranger's voice, a man's—"I didn't know who. I didn't know Mr. Riggs. My mother has friends, my mother has business friends, but we don't know them. We don't meet them. Grandpa told me this 'Melvin Riggs' forced his way into the house. Nothing like that had ever happened before. Not here or back—where we'd been." Farley spoke falteringly, his eyes fixed on Dill's face with a look of drowning desperation. He looked neither at John Reddy (who was staring intently at him) nor at Dahlia Heart (who was staring intently at him, having removed her dark glasses to sit leaning forward in her seat, lips slightly parted, and moistened, Smoke Filer said, "in a way it's good Dougie didn't see, he's nuts about that broad"). Farley seemed confused, and Dill directed him back onto his account. "I heard a loud sharp noise like a firecracker. I didn't know it was a gun. I heard three shots. I was awake now, and scared. I'd been asleep but doing geometry problems in my head. The noise was mixed up with the geometrical figures, it was like a cube exploding. I was confused at first. I was scared for my mother, and my sister. I wasn't sure if Grandpa was home. I believed John Reddy was not home. He'd gone out that night and he wouldn't come back sometimes till late. Also Grandpa is sometimes away at night. We don't know where. I didn't know that noise might be Grandpa's gun. I didn't know Grandpa still had a gun. Grandpa's got lots of things in his part of the house and we don't go there without his permission. Mother said she didn't want any gun in the house whether it was loaded or unloaded. Grandpa thought we should be protected, though, driving from Nevada to here. He was worried about the car breaking down on the Great Plains. Grandpa said—" Farley squinted in the direction of Aaron Leander Heart who was sitting beside Dahlia Heart in the first row of seats. You could see that Mr. Heart and his daughter Dahlia were kin: Aaron Leander was a handsome old man with sharp cheekbones and a fierce, inscrutable expression behind gray-grizzled whiskers (trimmed for the trial); he'd been made to dress presentably, in a funeral-dark suit, white shirt and checked bow tie; his snowy white hair floated above his head with a cloud, giving him a look of gentlemanly dignity. Dahlia Heart, in a classic white linen suit, a white silk blouse and a string of pearls, wearing pearl earrings and her very blond hair in a graceful French twist, looked like a *lady*. Aaron Leander and Dahlia Heart were gazing at Farley with such intensity you might think *They're sending him a message—but what is the message?* Dill tactfully interrupted the boy, who'd become stuck like a record needle in a groove, asking if Farley had left his room to investigate the gunshot. Farley said hesitantly yes he'd run out toward his mother's bedroom at the far end of the hall but he hadn't known for certain that he'd heard gunshots. "It might— might've been something else. It was just *noise*. I was so—*scared*." Farley began to stammer, his lips trembling. "I was afraid for my m-mother and my s-s-s-sister. My s-sister's just a little girl, she—she gets s-scared, too. She f-fell down the stairs and broke her leg and s-she—hurt herself bad, and—" Again, Dill had to prod Farley to return to his account. He'd come to an abrupt halt as if he'd only just now seen what lay ahead, like a boy running blindly toward a precipice. His forehead glistened with perspiration. He was wearing a suit that fit him loosely, a child's snap-on bow tie crooked at his throat. Dill asked in a kindly voice, "Now, son: did you see your brother John Reddy at this time—emerging from the bedroom, or in the hall, or on the stairs?"

There was a long pause. Farley was staring now at Dill with that look of drowning desperation. "I . . . don't think so, sir."

"You don't *think* so, son?"

"I . . . don't know, sir."

"But what did you tell the police officers when they arrived?"

"I . . . might have told them I s-saw John Reddy. But I might have been w-wrong."

"And later, when you were questioned? And signed your name to the document?"

"I m-might have been wrong. Both times."

"You haven't changed your testimony, son, have you? Under the tutelage of Mr. Trippe?"

"*No, sir.*"

Dill spoke patiently, with an air of barely suppressed exasperation. "Farley Heart, will you simply tell this court: did you, or did you not, see your brother John Reddy *with your grandfather's gun in his hand* immediately after hearing three gunshots fired in your mother's bedroom?"

Farley's lower lip jutted. "I w-wouldn't have known it was Grandpa's gun, sir. If I did see it."

Dill persisted, "But you did see it? The gun?"

"I . . . I can't remember."

"Did you exchange words with your brother John Reddy? As he was rushing from the bedroom in which, on the floor, Melvin Riggs lay dying of a gunshot wound to the head?"

"S-sir, I can't remember."

"Can't remember! But earlier you'd told police, or certainly implied, that you *had seen* John Reddy at that time?" Dill spoke carefully, not wishing to seem to be browbeating a cowed, frightened boy.

(Exactly what was happening here none of us would've known. Not even Evangeline Fesnacht who'd faithfully recorded the exchange verbatim and read it to us at school. It would be Roger Zwaart's father who explained, after the trial had ended: the prosecutor had Farley's statement to the police in his hand, in which Farley, shortly after the shooting, had said that the shooting had been an accident, that John Reddy "hadn't known the gun was loaded." This statement clearly implied that Farley had seen his brother with the gun; that Farley was assuming, or pretending to assume, that John Reddy hadn't known the gun was loaded. "Dill hoped to extract from Farley an acknowledgment that, yes, he'd seen his brother with the gun, but Dill didn't want the boy to sway the jury with the additional statement that, in his opinion, the shooting had been an accident, John Reddy 'hadn't known the gun was loaded.' So Dill couldn't read the statement. So there was an impasse." Seeing our faces, Mr. Zwaart who was usually such a dignified, pained-looking person, actually suffering from bleeding ulcers as Roger told us, laughed. "Look, kids, a trial is essentially a *game*. Law is a *game*. 'Justice' is like a field goal, a winning score; it isn't *just*. They don't teach you that in school?" He laughed, we were shocked. It shocked us as much that Mr. Zwaart was laughing, as what he'd told us.)

Dill made a blunder anyway. In an ironic, almost playful tone he asked, "Son, your vision isn't defective, is it?"

Farley was breathing quickly. He pushed his glasses against the bridge of his nose. "Y-yes, sir. It is."

"But not with corrective lenses, surely?"

"Even with corrective lenses, sir, it isn't twenty-twenty. No."

Like a man who has stumbled into a trap he's only begun to realize he himself has devised, Dill became flustered. He tried to maintain a reasonable tone. "In any case, Farley, you were wearing your glasses, weren't you, when you ran out of your room?"

Quickly Farley said, "Possibly n-not."

"*Possibly* not? But——"

A bright student, Farley pursued his advantage. "I might have run out of my room without my glasses. My glasses might have slid down my nose. They're loose." To demonstrate, he pushed at his glasses as if to adjust them but they slid off his nose and fell into his lap. Exposed, as if in a clearer light, Farley's face without the round schoolboy lenses was a young-old face, the eyes enlarged and myopic, ringed with shadow. Even as Farley's spindly body didn't appear to be the body of a thirteen-year-old but the body of a younger boy, his eyes didn't appear to be the eyes of a thirteen-year-old but the eyes of an older boy. We would recall John Reddy's strange, perhaps devious and certainly unpredictable younger brother Farley on the stand that day when, fourteen years later, his computer software company Hartssoft made front-page headlines in the *Wall Street Journal* and in the business section of the *New York Times*, though unaccompanied by any photographs of "Franklin Hart" as he would then call himself; a *Time* feature on "The Mystery Man of Software" was illustrated by an adult-schoolboy figure with neatly parted

close-trimmed hair and round-lenses glasses and a bland,
blurred face that was in fact an incandescent lightbulb with a
hovering ? at its core. Co-workers of "Franklin Hart" would
claim that they not only didn't know the young genius but
had difficulty remembering what he looked like from one
meeting to the next. *He's always different but the same, somehow.* Farley was saying in an earnest, stammering voice to
Dill, "I wake up from sleep sometimes and I'm still in a
dream. Or, I think I'm awake and I'm still asleep I guess. I
don't know at these times if I'm wearing my glasses. Like I
don't know where I am exactly. Like in a dream you see
objects without seeing them, I mean there's like a blur where
a person's face might be like you can't remember what the
person looks like but the dream tells you who it is, you *know*.
Or you're supposed to know. But the person isn't there, only
the idea. Or it looks like someone else instead of—"

Dill interrupted, exasperated. "Son. Did you, or did you
not 'see' your brother John Reddy at that time? In whatever
fashion?"

"I . . . don't know for certain."

"Well, did you hear him? His voice? Did you by any chance
exchange words?"

Farley was breathing through his mouth. Evangeline
Fesnacht noted how his brother John Reddy, his mother and
his grandfather were staring at him, and how, blinking, fussing with his glasses, he made every effort not to glance in
their direction. "Sir, I look at a thing sometimes and it disappears. A solid object. A person. It's like it turns transparent.
Sometimes I don't hear what other people say. Like in school,
my teachers . . . I think I'm paying attention, but my mind is
somewhere else. My own thoughts intrude. There are days I
think about a problem, a math problem, and it won't let me
go. It's like the problem is thinking *me*. That night . . . that it
happened . . . it was solid geometry. My head was filled with
geometrical figures like blocks and cubes. There's a feeling,
like, of wires—a prickly sharp feeling. So I—"

Dill said irritably, "Son! We're wandering far afield, aren't we? And to what purpose? Is this an attempt to inform the court of your memory of the events of last March nineteenth, or is this an attempt at obfuscation?"

Here, like an athlete who has been waiting patiently for action, Trippe rose to his feet to object to the browbeating of the witness; Judge Schor, though seeming to share in Dill's exasperation, allowed the objection and urged Dill to proceed more civilly, considering that the witness was a child. So Dill said, more patiently, but with subtle irony, "Son, we can sympathize with your reluctance to name your brother as the agent of Melvin Riggs's death. But the facts known to us, the physical evidence we have, including forensic evidence that your grandfather's gun was the murder weapon, suggest exactly that: John Reddy shot and killed Melvin Riggs, fled with the gun, tried to dispose of it in a creek less than a quarter-mile away. If your brother was not the person who carried the gun from the house and threw it onto the frozen creek where it was found next morning, how on earth did it get there?"

This was a question for the courtroom to contemplate, not for Farley Heart to answer. But Farley groped for a new idea. "Someone else—another 'agent'—might have carried it there? It might have been—me?"

At this, Dill gave up on Farley Heart. He may have thought the boy mildly retarded or deranged. He threw up his hands and stepped back with a glance at the jury. *See? The boy is obviously lying to protect his brother.*

Just then, as Evangeline Fesnacht reported to us excitedly, "The unforeseen happened! *All hell broke loose.*"

It was the eccentric female juror Mrs. Connor had remarked upon. The woman with the damp-bulgy eyes and prune-wrinkled face. Incongruously, on this third day of testimony, the woman wore bright red lipstick that glared against her grubby-pale skin; even her fingernails, which looked broken and bitten, had been painted red. Through the previous hours of testimony, as the prosecution grimly presented its case, hammering away at John Reddy's "vicious crime" and "self-evident guilt," the woman had sat leaning forward in her seat staring at John Reddy with a frowning, fixed expression. (We wondered: was John Reddy aware of her? Had they exchanged looks? Mrs. Connor said, "Once you started noticing that woman, you couldn't not notice her.")

When Farley Heart was dismissed by the prosecutor, and stepped down hesitantly from the witness chair, the woman suddenly rose to her feet and pushed hurriedly out of the jury box, stumbling over her fellow jurors and speaking incoherently, her words punctuated by "Judge!"—"Judge!" It was an electrifying moment, Evangeline Fesnacht told us eagerly. You thought someone was sick, or fainting. "Jurors are supposed to just *sit*, like *zombies*. And here was one *jumping up*." Before the nearest of the bailiffs could prevent her, the woman fell to her knees on the floor in front of the defense table, praying loudly for John Reddy's benefit, "O Lord, we accept that this boy is guilty! But this boy is an instrument of Your wrath! Who among us can cast the first stone! Lord have mercy! Lord open our eyes! 'Vengeance is mine, I will repay, saith the Lord.'" As bailiffs hurried to restrain her the woman repeated in a wilder voice, "'Vengeance is mine, I will repay, saith the Lord'!"

Everything came to a halt. The trial's proceedings were derailed. It was the only time, witnesses agreed, that John Reddy Heart looked surprised—agitated. "He was actually wiping tears from his eyes, I think," Evangeline said in a lowered, wondering voice. "I mean—gosh! *John Reddy was crying*."

12

"A *mistrial*? What the hell's that?"

"Is it a good thing for John Reddy, or—not so good?"
We were puzzled. We were fascinated. We'd seemed to
know that any trial of John Reddy Heart's would turn out to
be somehow special, and dramatic, and draw even more
attention to the case, more headlines. But—a *mistrial*?

"It just means John Reddy will be in custody longer. He
won't get out until maybe Christmas."

"Oh, God. You think he'll miss basketball season?"

"If he gets out at all."

The trial halted that day as if a switch had been thrown. It
would never be reconvened with that jury. Judge Schor over-
ruled the prosecutor to agree with Roland Trippe that the
jurors had been exposed to "extreme prejudicial influence" by
the behavior of the maverick female juror; it wouldn't be sufficient simply to dismiss her and name one of the alternates in
her place. For it turned out, as we'd read in the *News*, that the
woman had been a "disruptive element" in the jury room
too. On the second morning of the trial she was agitated,

fussing and complaining, and insisted upon leading the rest of the jurors in prayer that they might "execute God's bidding"; next morning she was the first to arrive, looking as if she hadn't slept all night, yet wearing bright lipstick and finger-nail polish, reading the Bible and showing passages to other jurors who were annoyed by her, or embarrassed, or per-plexed. Since it hadn't been clear, the jury foreman told Judge Schor apologetically, if the woman was for, or against, the defendant, or for, or against, the very concept of a jury trial, they hadn't wanted to report her.

Several disgruntled jurors, all male, middle-aged, com-plained to the *News* anonymously. They felt they'd been cheated. Their time had been wasted. They were bitter that Schor had dismissed them just because a religious kook had gotten it into her head that judging a teenaged murderer is wrong. Juror X told reporters, "I speak for myself. I was keep-ing an open mind. I wasn't going to be swayed by some nutty female." Juror Y said, even more incensed, "It was pretty damned clear to me, and I bet to most of the other jurors, that that kid killed Riggs. We can make up our own minds." Juror Z said, "I wouldn't have trouble even with sending him to the electric chair. I believe in capital punishment. You can trust the cops, right? Why's a cop gonna lie? I am not 'prejudiced.'"

The second trial of *People of the State of New York v. John Reddy Heart* was scheduled for early November.

By that time John Reddy had been in custody for eight months.

We'd begun to lose track exactly of how many weeks, days.

School had resumed without him of course. Fall sports had resumed without him. ("John Reddy didn't play football anyway, that's a break.") By degrees it had become less dis-concerting, except perhaps to certain of the girls, to glance out into the parking lot behind the school from, for instance, the cafeteria, the library or the second-floor girls' restroom, and realize *It isn't there. It's gone.* The acid-green Caddie. Other cars were there, lots of cars including Orrie Buhr's gunmetal-gray Buick with the bared-teeth grill, Clyde Meunzer's black-with-red-stripes Trans Am, and Art Lutz surprised us all by driving proudly to school one day in his brother Jamie's sexy black Dodge Castille, in his use while Jamie was in the U.S. Army on the far side of the earth. But John Reddy's trademark Caddie with the unmistakable throaty engine roar was gone. Nor did you see John Reddy in his black leather jacket and jeans, longish hair whipping in the wind, out there joking with his buddies. Nor would you catch a glimpse of John Reddy in the second-floor junior corridor, taller than most of the other guys, and quicker on his feet, though without seeming ever to hurry.

Coach McKeever who'd begun smoking out a rear exit door, a nasty cigar that smelled like burning hemp, said grimly, "He'll be back for basketball season. You wait."

The team had been so demoralized after John Reddy's arrest last winter, they'd dropped from first place to third in the division.

Girls wrote to John Reddy c/o the Buffalo House of Detention but received no replies. Some wrote to John Reddy c/o Roland Trippe but received no replies. Evangeline Fesnacht hinted she'd been in touch with Trippe discussing "trial strategy" but we doubted this was so. Now we were busier we had less time to drive fifteen miles downtown to cruise by the depressing old ruin of a prison. Except sometimes on weekend nights. After a football game, the West Seneca game for instance which we'd won by a fluke field goal 21–19, and to celebrate we'd been drinking beer at Dwayne Hewson's and in a caravan of horn-honking cars driving to Sandi Scott's on Park Club Lane (where there was an indoor pool, and her divorced mother was out of town), three or four cars with WHS stickers swerving impulsively off to Main to continue along the familiar route into and through Amherst and past Grover Cleveland Park, which few of us had visited since our ninth-grade class picnic and past the darkened campus of the U. of Buffalo many of us were fated to attend while our smarter and more privileged classmates would go to Cornell, Williams, Yale, Harvard and Stanford. In a few miles passing the vast shadowy windswept autumnal emptiness we knew to be by daylight Forest Lawn Cemetery, a staple of Buffalo-area jokes. And so on deeper into the city as if drawn into a vortex until Main Street itself began to alter, wider than we recalled, windier and more riddled with pot-holes and litter. Landmarks were out of sequence or missing altogether like Luigi's Pizzeria at Del Mar, where was it? like the Royale Theater at Perry, where was it? Years later Doug Siefried, by that time a recovered alcoholic, missing a lung, but damned grateful to be alive, would recall with a shudder the beer-blurred signs of cross streets that night he'd have sworn he'd never glimpsed before, such names as Anthrix, Straknel, Bugel. He would wonder if it had been a foretaste of the d.t.'s. And sweet freckle-faced Ginger McCord in her maroon cheerleader's jumper and long-sleeved white blouse beside him, not too close to him and not too far from him, humming along with WWBN-AM turned up deafening-high. Ken Fischer would recall his bewilderment and mounting worry that three quick cans of beer were more than he could handle and he'd somehow gotten lost, and with his girl Verrie in one of her semihysterical moods all evening. Art Lutz and Roger Zwaart in their separate cars had become uneasily aware, crossing Utica, where there'd been an accident, squad cars, an ambulance, red flares and broken glass and a power-ful smell of gasoline, that the cityscape had somehow changed; there were odd surges of traffic, vehicles running red lights, as if the faceless drivers of these cars, vans and motor-cycles (some of whom appeared to be dark-skinned) were mockingly aware of us, suburban kids venturing into down-town Buffalo on a Friday night. We swallowed hard recalling our parents' repeated warnings to which we'd never listened *Don't ever go downtown by yourselves do you promise? Don't ever drink and drive do you promise?* realizing for the first time that perhaps these warnings had been heartfelt and serious and not the mere exertion of petty parental/tyrannical power we'd always believed them to be. But we persevered. Past Bryant. Past North. A diminished caravan of only three cars (despite Suzi Zeigler's protests, Roger Zwaart had decided to turn back) but soon we lost track of one another. It was a gusty October night. The sour chemical odors of downriver factories stung our nostrils. Dougie Siefried and Ginger McCord in Dougie's $750 secondhand Ford V8, Ken Fischer and Verrie Myers in Ken's almost-new Chevy Lancelot, Art Lutz and Mary Louise Schultz in the sexy Dodge Castille. We found ourselves on the nearly deserted expressway passing warehouses, a railroad yard, unfamiliar spaces. At last, the massive weather-stained rock wall of the Buffalo House of Detention which we might not have recognized except for coils of razor wire atop the wall glinting like malevolent teeth. Dougie was sober now, or almost. He shivered. "Christ! That place looks like a what-d'you-call-it—mausoleum. For dead people." Ginger said breathlessly, biting at a thumbnail, "Is that *it*? I didn't remember it so——" But no word came to her. In Ken's car, as they approached the prison, Verrie stared in horror: it was a mound of *rocks*. A *ruin*. But she hurried to flash the car's headlights in her secret code. Ken laughed. Verrie said hotly, "What is so funny?" Ken said, "For Chrissake, honey. He doesn't see you. He never did. There's nobody *there*." Verrie drew in her breath sharply. She shrank away from her devoted boyfriend as if he'd slapped her and would recall, years later, when at last they lay together unclothed and loving in a hotel room approximately twenty miles from their present location, that in fact Ken had slapped her or in any case shoved her away with his elbow. "I hate you," she whispered. Art Lutz was having trouble keeping his brother's car in its lane. Not just the wind from Lake Erie but a perverse willfulness in the car's engine and steering column kept tugging at his arms as if his older brother's spirit, prankish, teasing, slightly bullying, inhabited the car. *Hey Jamie, cut*

it out. That isn't funny. Or maybe—the strange thought flashed
through Art's mind—Jamie had died, he'd been killed that
very day, only a few hours ago perhaps, in what would eventually be acknowledged as a "friendly fire incident," and the
feisty Dodge was sensing its true master had departed. (In
fact, this would turn out to be true. Jamie Lutz, twenty-two,
who'd bitterly disappointed his father by dropping out of U-
B and joining the army, was killed in Southeast Asia at
approximately halftime of the WHS–West Seneca game that
evening in a game that, in its essence if not in its particulars,
had been played five years before by Jamie himself as a gifted
but erratic running back the crowd had adored. But Art
would never dare tell anyone of his chilling premonition,
which he hadn't taken at all seriously at the time and had
almost immediately forgotten.) Driving Jamie's car, resisting
the steering wheel's stubborn drift to the left, Art glanced
sidelong at Mary Louise Schultz. This was the first time they'd
been alone together. What wild good luck, Mary Louise had
agreed to ride with him to Sandi Scott's party; it had been her
idea to follow Ken and the others into Buffalo, to drive by the
prison. Probably she'd assumed that another couple would
ride with them but that hadn't been Art's plan. All the guys
had their plans for tonight, reasoning, as Bo Bozer said
crudely, if they'd beaten West Seneca's ass they deserved some
ass of their own and privacy was essential. Six-packs of beer,
and foil-wrapped Trojans in their back pockets. (Dwayne
Hewson, captain of the team, who'd been hinting for weeks
how far he'd gone with Pattianne Groves already, said with an
evil grin, "Tonight's the night! Now or never.")

It wouldn't quite work out that way. Somehow, it never
did.

Dougie Siefried meekly exited the expressway at gloomy
McIntyre and headed back to Willowsville, stone-cold sober;
Ginger McCord, sniffing and blowing her nose, fussed with
the radio dial until she located, crackling with static, Made in
USA's "Ballad of John Reddy Heart" on an Ohio station. Ken

Fischer angrily exited the expressway at Grindell, jolting and bumping to a stop then speeding with such fury that "burning rubber" was no exaggeration for once. There was nothing he wanted more than to get back to Willowsville to drop off at her English Tudor home on Mill Race the blond mannequin beside him staring stonily out the window to whom he would not, he absolutely would not speak, not only for the remainder of their disastrous truncated evening but for the remainder of his fucking life. Good-bye to the "Original Ice Princess"—as Ken spoke of Verrie Myers to his buddies. We asked why Ken who was one of the most popular guys in our class and would be voted Best-Looking Boy senior year put up with Verrie Myers's shit and Ken said, shrugging, "Well. It *is* Veronica Myers's shit after all, not just any shit." In Art Lutz's brother's car, Art was beginning to perspire smelling Mary Louise Schultz's unmistakable physical presence so close beside him. Like a dog's, his nostrils were rapidly, near-spasmodically widening and contracting. That fragrant girl-smell, hair shampoo possibly, talcumy lily-of-the-valley Arrid-with-just-a-tincture-of-slightly-stale-girl-sweat. (Cheerleaders must sweat too, the way they throw themselves around. But Art had the idea they didn't shower after a game like the team did.) Art and Mary Louise were taking a second pass at the Buffalo House of Detention, at Mary Louise's request. Somehow, the first time driving past, Art had hardly noticed the building in the gloom beside the expressway. Her shiny dark hair sliding forward, Mary Louise sat quivering with tension peering out her window at what appeared to be nothing more than a massive stone wall—a long wall—a very long wall—Christ, it seemed to go on forever!—you could identify mainly by the cruel-looking razor wire strung along its top. Mary Louise seemed to be whispering to herself. (Praying? Mary Louise was one of a number of "good" Christian girls at WHS. She was a Presbyterian and her belief was simple, sincere and unquestioned. She'd long been an officer in Willowsville Christian Youth and a volunteer for Buffalo-area charities organized by a contingent of Willowsville matrons.) Or was she crying? Or both? Art recalled with excitement Smoke Filer saying slyly *If a chick cries you're halfway in her pants*. There was something so sexy about a good-looking girl with a figure like Mary Louise Schultz crying it almost didn't matter why she was crying. And any girl softhearted enough to cry for John Reddy Heart who'd blasted an adult man away with a gun (and who'd screwed more girls and women, including a certain hot-eyed cocktail waitress at the Old Red Mill Inn, Art had reason to believe, than he, Art, personally knew) was a sweetheart, you had to love her.

"It doesn't seem right, does it? For us to be free. To be so happy. Beating West Seneca tonight like we did—*wow*. And *he's* locked inside there." Mary Louise's thin girlish voice sounded hoarse, scraped from screaming cheers.

"I mean—does it seem right?" Art was startled, not knowing what they were talking about. He was thinking of how he might maneuver Mary Louise into being kissed; how, depending upon the circumstances in which they were sitting, how he might touch, or more than touch, her breasts. He said, in a cracked voice, "No. It does not seem right. I feel terrible about it." John Reddy, he supposed.

Art made a lightning-quick decision, a reckless decision possibly, to exit the expressway at La Salle Boulevard. Before Mary Louise knew what was up, he was headed for La Salle Park. Though it was past eleven p.m. and Mary Louise had said something about getting home by midnight. (And the Schultz home, on Sedgemoor Drive, was quite a distance away.) Art had lost track of both Doug and Ken and assumed they were somewhere in the park, too, this vast undistinguished city park no one from Willowsville ever went to, nor even thought of going to, reputed to be dangerous at night, particularly weekend nights, in the *News* and *Courier-Express* were frequent items about beer-can-throwing youths, fistfights and drug dealing, but Art reasoned those incidents occurred in the more public part of the park and he, like

Doug and Ken, was driving in the more private part, cruising Lakeside Drive looking for a place to park. *Tonight's the night! Now or never.* Though in fact Art Lutz and Mary Louise Schultz were so recent a couple, and Mary Louise Schultz had already been asked to the Christmas prom by a well-known senior, and had accepted—maybe that wasn't a reasonable expectation? Yet Art was beginning to breathe quickly. He felt as if he were filling like a helium balloon with sexual desire, need. And with hope. Blake Wells had remarked after an especially titillating biology class that it was pretty clear wasn't it—a single male organism, from the lowly frog to the noble lion to upright *Homo sapiens*, only wanted, modestly, to populate the entire world with the off-spring of his sperm. Art heard a frantic falsetto voice sounding in his ears like the beat of his own heated blood. *Mary Louise I'm crazy about you! Mary Louise you're so—beautiful! So—perfect! I just want to kiss you a little. I just want to hold you. Touch you. A little.* But was this a legitimate voice of Art's, or a subtly teasing voice? Almost, it sounded like Jamie, making fun. How had Jamie's voice gotten into Art's head? *Just want to stick my tongue in your mouth, Mary Louise honey. Just want to squeeze those fantastic breasts of yours in my two hands. I don't think of them as tits. Other girls have tits. Those are breasts. I don't think of what you're sitting on as ass.* There was a pause, and faint, crude wheezing laughter. *I think of what you're sitting on as the vinyl-weave seat of brother Jamie's Dodge Castille and mmmmm! I sure do envy that ol' seat I can tell you.* Desperately Art managed to block out Jamie's sniggering voice by asking Mary Louise what she knew of the upcoming trial of John Reddy. As Art slowed to peer into the shadows, rejecting some spots because there were already cars parked there, rejecting others because they were too brightly lighted, but finding at last a secluded, relatively private place overlooking the choppy, greasy-looking lake, Mary Louise spoke earnestly of how difficult it was going to be to find an impartial jury for the second trial; and the judge, that terrible, cruel man, had ruled against a change of venue. Art murmured a quick agreement. He parked, cut the engine, took a cautious breath. Mary Louise was saying that her mother who was a really close friend of a friend of Laetitia Riggs's had told her that Mrs. Riggs had collapsed when her husband was killed but was strong enough now to testify at the trial; everyone blamed John Reddy's mother for what had happened—"She's a terrible woman, isn't she? To steal other women's husbands. And she doesn't even want them I guess, just tosses them back down. Like Bo's father. Like poor Mr. Skelton. And Mr. Wells was seeing her too, and lent her money I heard—did you? Evangeline was telling us. But Verrie says—" Art murmured agreement. They were parked now, here they were. He'd have liked to lock all four doors of the car. His heart was beating like a tiny fist. *O.K., li'l brother, time to get serious. Down-dirty serious. Whip 'er out, stud. Show this sweet dumb chick what it's all about, eh?* Emboldened, Art slid his arm around Mary Louise's shoulders. She was wearing a wool blazer over her maroon cheerleader's jumper and, around her neck, a long maroon school scarf decorated with wolverine figures. Her head seemed large suddenly—so close to his. Gently he managed to ease Mary Louise against him; she did not resist, though she did not cooperate; there was a sudden wariness between them, and an excited expectation; Art tilted the girl's head to kiss her—to actually kiss her—for the first time! *I'm kissing Mary Louise Schultz for the first time. O Jesus.* Her lips were warm, dry, shy-but-friendly; the lips of a girl who's been kissed before, many times perhaps, and who takes for granted a certain deference, respect. *C'mon stud, let's have some action. Shit!* Art deflected these unwelcome words of Jamie's like Ping-Pong balls. That was the image that surfaced in his head: he'd been the champion Ping-Pong player of the Lutz household, surpassing Jamie at the precocious age of fourteen. So *Fuck you, Jamie: get out of my head.* He was doing all right. He was kissing Mary Louise Schultz. A flame ran swiftly over his body that stung and left him weak.

Possibly Mary Louise sensed this flame for she shifted uneasily in her seat and he could hear her quickened breath. "Artie? What time it is?" she whispered. "T-time? What time? I don't know."

Across the wind-roughed lake lights blinked feebly. Lake Erie, Beach, Ontario. The sky overhead had become porous, heavy. In Willowsville, the night sky had been clear. During the giddy excitement of the game the air had been mild for late October but now, miles away, not long afterward, the lakefront air was agitated and cold. *I said c'mon stud! Get down to basics! We ain't got the rest of our lives, we ain't even got all night.* Art blocked these words by saying, stammering, "M-Mary Louise? I guess you can tell I'm—crazy about you?" but his words were choked and inaudible. Mary Louise turned her chin to avoid his searching, hungry mouth. Politely she said, "Art? I think maybe it's time to go. I'm sorry." Art said, aggrieved, "But we just got here, Mary Louise! It's early." God damn, he might've set the clock in the dashboard back a half-hour, if he'd thought of it. He tried to ease the girl gently against him; she relented, but only partway; like a cat you manage to force into relaxing on your lap, unresisting yet clearly biding its time before it leaps down. "What's that sticking into me?" Mary Louise cried, jerking away, and Art said quickly, "The gearshift. *Sorry.*" He leaned against the shift, taking the brunt of it against his thigh. Already bruised from being tackled and falling heavily that evening, he would discover in the morning a dozen purplish-orange bruises on his thighs. He was calculating how he might unobrusively shift his right arm an inch or so that he might brush the back of his hand against Mary Louise's right breast. Only a touch! The merest touch! It would last him for weeks. He'd given up as unreasonable the hope of actually caressing her breast, as other guys insisted they caressed their girls' breasts (Dwayne, Roger, Smoke, Tommy, among others) let alone cupping it capably in his hand (as in certain dreams he did, often—freely and boldly and without the slightest hesitation as if Mary Louise weren't herself but an obliging rubbery mannequin); he'd put aside the very concept of touching both breasts. Reasoning *The other can wait. One is enough.* It had been years after all: he'd first noticed Mary Louise Schultz's maturing figure in ninth-grade algebra when, seated behind and slantwise from the pretty round-faced girl whose well-to-do parents happened in fact to be golf club acquaintances of his parents', he'd found himself staring at her mesmerized while Mr. Florio droned on in his witty-sardonic manner at the blackboard. At the age of fourteen, Art Lutz was astonished—the ease with which girls like Mary Louise Schultz inhabited their bodies! He wondered if they stared at themselves enraptured in mirrors. (He who shrank from encountering his pimply reflection and scrawny torso in shiny surfaces.) Hesitantly now, Art moved his arm, tremulous to bring the backs of his fingers to lightly graze Mary Louise's right breast even as, with an abrupt nervous movement, the skittish girl leaned forward. "Artie? It's time to go home. I'm *sorry*." Art seemed not to have heard, breathlessly kissing Mary Louise more firmly on the mouth; she seemed to be kissing him back—for a moment. She laughed nervously and would have moved away except Art, inspired, or desperate, took hold of her shoulders and kissed her with more force, nudging at her lips to pry them apart; but they would not be pried apart; they were sealed as if with glue. *C'mon asshole, get hot! We're running out of time! Don't disappoint me.* Jamie's impatient though affectionate voice was being blown to Art from a short distance, perhaps from the waves splashing against the shore. Art's penis was engorged with blood like a thick spicy sausage. Inside his damp, snug-fitting Jockey shorts his erection stirred with a jolt of perverse life. He stifled a sob anticipating yet another night of jerking himself off, jerking himself off, jerking himself off like a man hanging himself compulsively and yet never satisfactorily.

Still he'd have to admit he was relieved when Mary Louise detached her mouth from his. He'd never French-kissed an actual girl before. Though many times in recent weeks he'd slid his wet snaky tongue into an aperture formed by his thumb and curled fingers, but he reasoned that an actual girl, an actual mouth, would present very different circumstances. He wasn't sure how the penetration should be done, or even why. *Jesus, kid! You had your chance. I'm through. You're on your own.* Jamie was withdrawing in disgust, dismay. But Art hadn't time to mourn his brother's departure for Mary Louise was close to wriggling out of his grasp. And the wind was picking up across the lake. A stroke of lightning split the sky above the Canadian shore, thunder sounded like shaken tin, there came a harsh pelting of raindrops across the windshield. Mary Louise surprised Art by murmuring almost suggestively, "It's kind of cozy in here, isn't it? I love the rain." Recklessly then, for he had nothing to lose, Art lunged with his right hand to brush against the girl's breast. There was no resistance. He caressed the breast, and still no resistance. He kissed Mary Louise as his fingers stroked, even squeezed. His forehead was glazed with sweat; the turbulence between his legs mounted nearly to bursting. His life seemed to pass swiftly before his eyes like a Disney cartoon: he was sixteen years, eight months old; a moderately popular junior at WHS; a running end on the varsity football team, as his brother Jamie had been five years before and as his oldest son Kevin would be twenty-eight years later; a math-science major with a mid-B average, he would graduate and attend his father's college, Colgate; he would pledge his father's fraternity, Deke; with his B.A. from Colgate he would earn a degree in business administration from Cornell; he would return to Willowsville part in resentment and part in relief to take his place at Lutz Magic Kleen, Inc., on Delaware Avenue, Buffalo; by the age of twenty-seven he'd be married and by the age of twenty-nine he'd be a father for the first time and this would seem, at the time, a reasonable thing to have accomplished, at least in his parents' eyes. After the first several rapturous months of love-making with his pert, attractive, curly-blond wife, a Chi

Omega elementary ed. major from Cornell, he would find himself evoking at such times the painfully vivid memory of Mary Louise Schultz as she'd been in Jamie's car that night. Mary Louise's prim pursed lips, Mary Louise's firm, pear-sized breast he'd actually held, or believed he'd held, in his hand. *I loved her. Love her. Jesus!* His orgasm like raw silk tearing inside his guts. As he'd never experienced once, not a single time, with the actual Mary Louise Schultz though they would date, intermittently, through their junior and senior years of high school until Mary Louise went away to Vassar and Art went away to Colgate. He'd hear of her marriage, her children. He'd dream of her, or of someone resembling her leaping into the air, shiny dark hair flying and arms spread in a victory cheer. And years later, separated from his curly-blond wife, bored to oblivion by his curly-blond wife, Art Lutz would find himself dozing on long headache flights from Buffalo to L.A., from L.A. to Buffalo, dreaming of Mary Louise Schultz's perfect girl-breasts, cupping them gently in his hands, his reverent worshipful hands. As Flight 283 from L.A. due to arrive at Buffalo at 7:40 P.M. of a sleet-riddled February evening shuddered nineteen thousand feet above Springfield, Ohio, and the forty-one-year-old Art Lutz shut his eyes clinging to a vision of sixteen-year-old Mary Louise Schultz even as, like the other passengers on the plane, he tasted the terror of imminent dissolution.

Mary Louise jerked away from him, self-consciously adjusting her blazer, lifting her hair from the damp nape of her neck. It was then that Art realized that it hadn't been Mary Louise's breast he'd been holding but her bunched-up wolverine scarf and the lapel of her blazer. Quickly he removed his arm from her shoulders, chagrined. His arm had gone partly to sleep, numbness radiated outward from his right armpit. And his armpit was slick with sweat.

"Artie? Please. I want to go *home*."

"Y-yes. Sure. Sorry."

He'd have agreed to anything. Blindly, he started the car. He was humbled, humiliated yet elated. He'd played on a winning team that night, the home crowd had screamed for them, and even if he hadn't been one of the first-string stars, not like Jamie "The Bull" Lutz, he'd been on a winning team. Seeing the look in Art's face when Coach pulled him from the game after less than ten jolting minutes in the final quarter, Coach had said kindly, *We can't all be scoring field goals. We can't all be Dwayne Hewson.* Mary Louise Schultz liked him, obviously. She'd let him kiss her and he'd be kissing her again. And again. He'd French-kiss her someday, too. He'd tell her how he felt about her. She would blush, she'd laugh, embarrassed. But she might say *Artie, I kind of love you, too.* She might say that. It was possible. He would carry the possibility with him like a flame cupped in his hand, precious. He cast a lovesick sidelong glance at Mary Louise as they drove north and eastward now on Main Street returning to Willowsville; he saw that the pretty round-faced girl was peering at herself in a compact mirror, hastily repairing the damage done to her lipstick. Such intimacy!—as if it was the most natural thing in the world. Art thought of John Reddy Heart with a flood of gratitude.

Thank you, John Reddy. You made it all possible!

13

The second trial of *People of the State of New York v. John Reddy Heart* would move far more swiftly than the first. After nine days of testimony both sides would complete their cases and the jury would adjourn to deliberate for a full day, and a second day, and part of a morning. In a state of almost unbearable tension we listened to illicit transistor radios at school, hidden in lockers and desks. We sat in one another's cars for long hours, smoking, listening to our pop-rock station WWBN-AM, awaiting the interruption of a news bulletin. *And now from the Erie County Courthouse—the verdict is in on John Reddy Heart! Friends, are you re-ady?* Our disc jockey Smilin' Jack Daniel teased us cruelly. Yet we could not not listen. We convened for vigils and stayed up much of two nights. Sudden new friendships formed among us while older and seemingly stable friendships shattered. We were in a state of ecstatic suspension. Our parents and teachers shouted at us; we were deaf. It did not seem possible that John Reddy Heart might be found guilty of murder and sentenced to life in prison—"God wouldn't let such a thing happen. I just know He *wouldn't*." But Evangeline Fesnacht said with her melancholy smile, which some of us misread as a smirk, "If he's guilty, he's guilty. John Reddy knows that. He expects a just fate."

Each side, prosecution and defense, had clearly learned from the first practice run. Judge Schor whom we believed to be our enemy was brisk and matter-of-fact and must have learned to disguise his repugnance for John Reddy. Police and forensics testimony were pruned and condensed to minimize boredom in the courtroom; Dill, a wiser man, would not call Farley Heart to the witness stand. Roland Trippe's cross-examinations were less tinged with sarcasm. He dressed less stylishly. He seemed to be competing with his opponent Dill to appear earnest, sincere, without guile. Often he addressed the jury as if they were alone together, his peers, "embarked upon a mutual quest for justice tempered with mercy." At the defense table, John Reddy Heart appeared less wooden than previously. Several of us who attended sessions reported back that "he doesn't look like himself exactly but you could still recognize him, sort of." His skin was a sallow curdled color. There were deep shadows beneath his eyes as if he'd been thumbed. And twitches in his eyes. Frequently during testimony he licked his lips (Bibi Arhardt wished she could've passed him her lip balm!) and shifted his tightly muscled shoulders inside the snug-fitting blue serge suit coat but not once (so far as we knew) did he turn to look at Dahlia Heart or old Mr. Heart seated almost directly behind him nor did he glance in their direction when guards brought him, handcuffed, his head held defiantly high, into the courtroom.

Still at this time, most of us were waiting for John Reddy to take the witness stand. It was painful for us to realize that, for whatever reason, he never would.

Just won't play their rotten game. Good for him!
He's guilty as hell. It would all come out.
He's just a kid. Frankly, he's scared.
Him? A kid? You see those eyes?

I know killer eyes when I see them.

It was a wild, giddy time. Rumors circulated in Willowsville like haphazard gusts of wind. Now from one direction, now from another. It wasn't even mid-November but already—we were perversely proud of living in the "Snow Belt" tucked between two massive, brooding Great Lakes— we were ankle deep in snow from a flash snowstorm that had knocked out power in parts of rural Erie County. At school, one of the rumors was that Sasha Calvo had returned to Willowsville to testify at John Reddy's trial. She would testify that John Reddy had been with her at the time of Riggs's murder—he was innocent. (Which left—who?—to have committed the crime. Maybe Dahlia Heart. Maybe old Mr. Heart—"It was his gun." Better yet, as Bart Digger suggested, "Mrs. Heart's other boyfriend, Mr. Rush, who might've come back after Riggs thought he'd chased him away.") It was also a possibility that Sasha had been subpoenaed by the prosecution and would be forced to divulge incriminating evidence against John Reddy. Though Sasha hadn't returned to school, suddenly everyone claimed to be sighting her. Sandi Scott said she'd seen Sasha and her parents "hurrying sort of shamefaced" into Mr. Stamish's office. Ken Fischer and Bonnie Patch, leaving the Glen Theatre, late, reported they'd seen Sasha in a car driven by one of the elder Calvo brothers, on Main Street. (Ken and Bonnie were a startling, controversial new couple. Bonnie was a senior who drove her own Fiat sports car and boasted of "making it" with good-looking younger jocks.) A more disturbing rumor was that Sasha was pregnant. ("Oh God. Will he have to marry her? I'll kill myself," Verrie Myers cried, heartbroken.) Evangeline Fesnacht, contemptuous of all rumors except those initiated by herself, reasoned calmly that it was unlikely that Sasha could be pregnant since John Reddy had been in custody since mid-March—"If she'd been pregnant, which there's no evidence for at all, she'd have had the baby by now." But this, in turn, was transformed into a new rumor which even our teachers and parents circulated. In fact, the rumor at school could be traced back to Trish Elders (already on the verge, as she said, of a total nervous breakdown—it was the second week of John Reddy's trial) who happened to overhear her mother on the phone with a woman friend, saying in a shocked murmur, "Sallie, did you hear? That Calvo girl had a baby. That's why the Calvos sent her away—to Brooklyn, I think. Or back to Italy. A baby boy they say looks *exactly like John Reddy Heart.*"

The rumor that most upset our parents was an old one, resurfacing. That Dahlia Heart had been keeping an "intimate diary" of her friendships with Buffalo-area men. Quite a few men. And prominent men. Skip Rathke at the Village Food Mart was a font of excited information on this subject: he'd heard from an "absolutely reliable source" in the Willowsville Police Department that Mrs. Heart had been involved with just about every prominent man you could name. "Mel Riggs, that sap, was merely one." There was Buffalo's Mayor Dorsey, there was Buffalo's TV personality Chris Durrell. There was the Hearts' neighbor Aickley Thrun, a retired businessman and philanthropist who'd been reported trespassing on Heart property the day following Riggs's murder, in clear violation of the yellow crime-scene tape. It seemed to be an open secret that the Buffalo chief of police had overridden the authority of suburban Willowsville police, ordering Mrs. Heart's diary "suppressed" because prominent local citizens were named in it. Roger Zwaart's father speculated, "There have been payoffs, certainly. We're waiting to see if some names will be leaked to the press and others withheld." An uncle of Scottie Baskett, also a lawyer, hinted that several potential "names" had contacted him in anticipation of being exposed. "This 'Dahlia Heart' situation may involve not only payoffs but blackmail and extortion as well." It seemed to be general knowledge that Bo Bozer's father, separated from Mrs. Bozer, fired from his job of many years and seriously in debt, "but still in love with Dahlia Heart," had tried to commit suicide in a motel in Batavia by swallowing a large quantity of barbiturates; this was why Bo played football like such a demon, amazing his teammates with his endurance and recklessness, and why, it was believed, Coach had arranged for him to have sessions with "some kind of 'adolescent psychiatrist.'" Shelby Connor astonished us by saying bitterly, one evening at Verrie's when a gang of us was watching the six o'clock local news in the Myers's family room, on about the fifth day of John Reddy's trial, that her father had left the house at five that morning supposedly to fly to New York but she really believed, having overheard her mother on the phone, talking with friends, crying, that her father had been involved with Mrs. Heart and he'd decided to confess before it hit the newspapers—"My mom was just devastated. She's like somebody hit her on the head with a sledgehammer."

In the luridly glamorous made-for-TV film *The Loves of the White Dahlia*, the beautiful blond actress who played Dahlia Heart was presented as icily calculating; under the pretense of establishing herself in a semi-mythical suburb of Buffalo called "Williamsville" as a businesswoman, she inveigled loans and gifts from a number of naive, smitten middle-aged men; managed to be invited to join the most prestigious country club, where one of her lovers was on the executive board (one of the film's numerous steamily erotic scenes was in, appropriately, a Jacuzzi tub); out of a pure love of evil (there were numerous provocative close-ups of this "Dahlia Heart" gloatingly admiring herself in a full-length mirror) she set her lovers against one another, broke up marriages and neglected her own family; to our horror and disgust, she was depicted as a near-incestuous mother, in several scenes approaching her terrifically handsome teenaged son in erotic circumstances. The film was advertised with suggestive copy: *A Mother's Ultimate Temptation—A Son's Ultimate Revenge.* And: *She led men—men of power, men of passion—to their doom. And she never looked back—but once.* The most disappointing part of the film was its depiction of John Reddy as a hellion teenager involved in a motorcycle gang, drugs, fights and sex with leather-wearing girls meant to be teenagers but played by actresses who more resembled hookers. This John Reddy was *too handsome*. One of the film's few elements with any historical veracity was an action in which John Reddy leads members of his motorcycle gang, the Avengers, in a milling fistfight in a park with affluent, suburban-type boys to revenge the honor of a beautiful young Italian girl who'd been raped by one of them. But the John Reddy of the film (played by a young soap opera star to have a brief career in Hollywood films, and die of a cocaine overdose at the age of twenty-three) wasn't our John Reddy. And he played, in fact, a relatively minor role in the film!

In *The Loves of the White Dahlia* there was only one trial. John Reddy did not take the witness stand, as he hadn't done in real life. But when Dahlia Heart took the stand, at the film's climax, her perjured testimony was interspersed with slow-motion flashbacks to the shooting scene, so that the viewer could see that, though Dahlia Heart was claiming not to have seen what happened, all the while implying that of course her son was the killer, in fact it was Dahlia Heart who'd handed the gun to her son and urged him to kill her lover—"If you're a man, prove it!" (The plot involved Dahlia Heart's shadowy financial dealings and her insistence that Melvin Riggs divorce his wife and marry her, which he'd resisted.) This evil "Dahlia Heart" resembled the original physically, to an uncanny degree, but there was no attempt in the film to convey a vulnerable woman, a confused woman, an affectionate girl-woman, in her way naively trusting and hopeful. There were many of us who believed John Reddy's mother to be more than the sum of her glamorous appearance and behavior. We never hated her like our mothers did. Though we weren't enthralled by her like the guys. (Decades later, Dougie Siefried would confess he still dreamt about Dahlia Heart. "Though she's become more of an abstract idea, you know? Like an actual erection gets to be an idea at a certain point in a man's life.") The grown girls of the Circle would recall, thrilled, the time they'd eavesdropped on Dahlia Heart and her little girl (whose name we could never remember—Shirley? Kathleen?) in the Crystal. Those teasing words she'd said to the waitress: *I know what it's like to be on your feet all day, Gloria—it's hell.*

We wondered what happened to Dahlia Heart after the trial. Much of what we heard was contradictory and vague. She'd moved away, of course. She'd disappeared. Even John Reddy didn't know where she'd gone. She'd changed her name—and the color of her hair. She'd gotten married. She'd returned to her old life in Las Vegas as a blackjack dealer. She'd returned to her old life in Las Vegas as a hooker. She'd died there of a drug overdose. She'd died in Los Angeles of a drug overdose.

She'd married a rich man, and gone to live in New Mexico on his thousand-acre ranch, happily ever after.

* * *

On the fifth day of the trial, the prosecution called Dahlia Heart to the witness stand.

Though in *The Loves of the White Dahlia*, the perjured testimony of "Dahlia Heart" would be the climax of the film, in actual life, Dahlia Heart's testimony, delivered in a hushed courtroom, was brief and inconclusive. She was, in legal terms, a hostile witness—a witness for the defense, but pressed to testify by the prosecution. Dill, who'd learned his lesson exposing Farley Heart to the jurors, was overly cautious questioning Dahlia Heart. "You can't trust any witness in a trial," Roger Zwaart's father told us. "But you sure can't trust a hostile witness."

Everyone stared greedily at Dahlia Heart. The mother of the "alleged killer." The woman who had brought Melvin Riggs, Jr., to his "untimely end." The surprise was, Mrs. Heart didn't resemble a voluptuous Marilyn Monroe or Kim Novak, but a more fragile, vulnerable, *ladylike* beauty like Grace Kelly. Her clothes were carefully chosen (by Roland Trippe?): she wore a white linen suit with a silk blouse beneath the sheathlike jacket; her flared skirt fell decorously to midcalf. Pale glimmering stockings. Around her slender throat, a single chaste strand of pearls. Her blond hair seemed to have a silver sheen and was worn in a French twist. Her makeup was subdued, minimal: a "natural" look. Her nails, of moderate length, were frosted silver. When she removed her dark glasses to face her interrogator, it was perceived throughout the packed courtroom *Here is a grieving mother!* For her beautiful eyes were melancholy, ringed with fatigue. *Here is a grieving, repentant mother!* Dill began his questioning carefully. He would hint at, but could not pursue, for this was inadmissible evidence, Mrs. Heart's shadowy "business relations" with men besides Melvin Riggs; he would hint at, but could not pursue, Mrs. Heart's ambiguous, some would say outright suspicious relationship with the late Colonel Edgihoffer. If Dill asked too probing a question—"Exactly how would you characterize your relationship with the late Melvin Riggs, Mrs. Heart?"—Dahlia Heart quivered as if he'd raised his hand to strike her. "It was like a stage play," Verrie Myers reported excitedly, for at last she, Trish Elders and Millie LeRoux had dared to skip school to attend the trial, cleverly disguised as older, matronly women in theatrical makeup and dowdy clothes secretly borrowed from their mothers' closets, "—the only thing that was real was what you could *see*. It's all happening *now*."

The girls were riveted by Dahlia Heart's testimony, though they were seated near the back of the courtroom, at the extreme right, and their view of the witness stand was partly blocked. They were distracted by what they could see of John Reddy at the defendant's table—the back of his head, his short-trimmed black hair. (Fearful of being caught by county truant officers, the girls tried to be inconspicuous. They were able to catch only a fleeting glimpse of John

Reddy's face, or profile, at the close of the day's session, when guards led John Reddy away and he'd seemed, almost, to turn, to glance around like one who has heard his name called—"I swear, John Reddy saw me. Our eyes locked. Just for a fraction of a second. I didn't dare wave of course. He didn't. But—" Verrie murmured. Trish believed this might have been so but Millie, the most phlegmatic and doubtful of the girls of the Circle, said bluntly that John Reddy hadn't even turned his head.)

Dahlia Heart spoke in a faltering voice, so softly that Dill had to ask her to please speak louder. She insisted she'd been "entirely surprised—shocked" that her friends Mr. Rush and Mr. Riggs had come to her home on the night of March 18, uninvited, separately, for neither had been there before, and her relationship with Mr. Rush had been "purely business, and recently concluded." Melvin Riggs, she hesitantly confessed, was a different matter. Yes, she'd been "romantically involved" with this gentleman for several months. He had told her from the start that he was legally separated from his wife and when she learned otherwise, she'd insisted upon breaking off the relationship—"I'm not the kind of woman who sees another woman's husband. I respect the institution of marriage. I respect personal integrity and fidelity. I could not live with myself ever if I did not."

Dill asked, with a hint of irony, "You've never before been 'romantically involved,' Mrs. Heart, with a married man? You expect the court to believe that?"

Dahlia Heart said, hurt, "Sir, not *knowingly*! But men— you must know—don't always tell the truth. Especially to a woman."

Dahlia Heart continued her testimony, saying that, at first, Riggs had seemed to respect her feelings; he'd ceased telephoning her as he'd been doing at all hours of the night. He'd lent her a sum of money—less than five thousand dollars, in cash—for "purely investment purposes"—and she was hoping to repay him soon, as he knew; but for some reason he showed up, unexpected, drunk, at her home, by coincidence at the time Rush was leaving, and the men quarreled, and she made a mistake, "a tragic mistake I wish to God I could undo," in allowing Riggs to stay with her as he'd pleaded. "That man had a certain power over me—he could be so charming, so warm, so convincing—and so cruel." Within an hour Riggs had turned abusive and threatening. He'd begun by saying he loved her and wanted to marry her; when she demurred, saying that she could never trust a man who'd betrayed his wife, he turned nasty; she had to admit, to her shame, they'd both been drinking whisky— "Mel liked his whisky neat. Once he started, he couldn't seem to stop." What happened after that was a nightmare of threats, blows, shouts, screams—"and next thing I knew, someone was trying to revive me. A paramedic! I seemed to be lying across a bed, in a place I couldn't recognize though it was my own bedroom. My face was swollen and bleeding and my head was ringing with pain. I was terrified. I knew that something terrible had happened but I didn't know what it was." Dahlia Heart had begun to speak so faintly, Dill had again to urge her to speak louder. She said, pressing a hand against her chest as if she were short of breath, "I hadn't heard any gunshots. I swear. It was all mixed up with that terrible man shouting at me. And my head being pounded. I saw these strangers—paramedics, police officers—and couldn't comprehend why they were there. I was frightened for my children—my little girl especially, she's so sensitive, shy of strangers—I hoped nothing had happened to her, or my other child. I mean—my other young child, Farley. I must have seen Mr. Riggs's body on the floor, but—I don't remember seeing it. I didn't see John Reddy at any time that night. I guess I would have thought he wasn't home, he'd gone out with his friends and he did stay out late sometimes, even on school nights, he's a mature boy, he's had to be mature most of his life, growing up in a household without a father. So far as I know, John Reddy had never met Melvin

Riggs. He had never set eyes on Melvin Riggs. I—don't believe he shot Melvin Riggs. I don't . . ." Her voice trailed off miserably. She'd begun to cry, and was dabbing at her eyes with a handkerchief. "I can't believe that my son would act in such a way except possibly—possibly—to defend himself, or to defend—me."

There was silence in the courtroom. John Reddy Heart was sitting at the defense table with his head in his hands, the tips of his fingers pressed against his shut eyes. You could see, Trish Elders said afterward, the tension in his back and neck. "Everyone was staring at Mrs. Heart and trying to figure out—what had she *said*? That John Reddy had not shot Melvin Riggs but if he had, it was for a good reason? *Wow.*"

Dill hadn't any choice but to continue his questioning, and to risk seeming rude, ungentlemanly. He said, dryly, "Mrs. Heart, you claim not to have seen your son with a gun in his hand? At any time, before or after Melvin Riggs's death? No? Nor did you exchange words with him before he ran out of the house with the gun?"

"I don't see how I could have, sir. If I was unconscious."

"If you were unconscious."

"I was. I'd been beaten. Punished. Oh God, it's all I deserve."

Dahlia Heart began to sob. Dill said quickly, "Thank you, Mrs. Heart, you may step down." Mrs. Heart rose unsteadily, but immediately began to sink, to faint. Dill clumsily caught her and for a moment it looked as if the two—the beautiful blond woman in dazzling white linen, the balding middle-aged man in a dull gray suit—were embracing.

There was a shout. John Reddy had jumped up to rush to his mother, but two uniformed guards immediately restrained him. He pushed and shoved against them; they deftly wrestled his arms behind his back and handcuffed him within seconds.

Some observers claimed that John Reddy had called, "Mother!" Others claimed they'd heard him curse. "It was all over before we knew that anything had happened," Verrie said breathlessly. "Poor John Reddy! We almost had heart attacks, we'd thought he was going to be *shot*."

Aaron Leander Heart, whose age was given in the *News* as seventy-two and in the *Courier-Express* as seventy-six, was also called to testify as a hostile witness. Though Dill must have known from police reports that the old man would have nothing conclusive to offer. How Mr. Heart had aged since last March—it was shocking to see. He'd lost weight and his cheeks were gaunt and creased; wattles of flesh hung from his neck. His hands shook as if with palsy. His eyes were shrewd as ever but sunken and lusterless. When he took his seat, unsteadily, in the witness chair facing the courtroom, Trish whispered in Verrie's ear, "Is that *him*? Our Mr. *Heart*?" We realized we hadn't seen him in months, prowling our village with his sack of bottles over his shoulder. He'd become a familiar sight and had not, we would have sworn, changed in the slightest since arriving in Willowsville years ago, as the five-foot red plastic Santa Clauses that festooned our downtown during the holiday season never changed from one year to the next. Some things are so familiar, so boring and comforting, you never need to look at them, exactly. You just need to know they're there.

But now, for sure, John Reddy's grandfather was *old*.

On the witness stand, Mr. Heart spoke in a slow, quavering voice. No sir, he told Dill, he hadn't seen John Reddy on that night, he hadn't exchanged any words with John Reddy and he wasn't sure he'd even heard the gunshots—"If I did I might've thought it was thunder, sir. It was a thundery time if I recall right. This is a stormy thundery region of the U.S. Between them big lakes like we are. They say it's too much electricity generated. Mankind wasn't made to tolerate too much electricity in the air. It has to discharge, and many's the victim. If I'd heard it, and I ain't saying I did, only if, 'cause I wasn't anywhere near that part of the house, I would've thought it was thunder, sir. Yessir, I would've said, 'It's thunder.' And placed my money on that."

Dill asked a few more questions but it was hopeless. Old Mr. Heart could no more be herded along than a loose pack of cats. When Roland Trippe took over, he used the opportunity to read to the court a note from Aaron Leander Heart's doctor—"'Mr. Heart is suffering from a neurological impairment that affects both his memory and his thinking processes. The impairment is exacerbated by stress and is probably related to advanced age but is not to be confused with Alzheimer's.'" So Aaron Leander Heart was excused from testifying, and helped down from the witness stand by Roland Trippe.

Whatever had happened, or hadn't happened, on the night of March 18–19, that left Melvin Riggs permanently dead was revealed to be, so far as the Heart family was concerned, a blank.

The surprise testimony of the trial, and the trial's turning point, was that of Laetitia Riggs, Melvin Riggs's widow. A witness for the prosecution.

Laetitia Riggs took the stand with more apparent confidence than the previous witnesses. She was a short, compact woman with solid cheeks and a small determined rosebud mouth. Her skin was high-colored as if with permanent embarrassment. She appeared breathless. Bibi Arhardt described her as looking "like a girl hockey player thirty years later." She wore black—a boxy woolen suit with wide shoulders, black patent leather shoes. A vivid contrast to the "White Dahlia." It was observed that, when Mrs. Riggs testified, Mrs. Heart sat very still, dark glasses hiding half her face and hands clasped piously in her lap. Everyone in Willowsville knew that Laetitia and Melvin Riggs were one of those couples, and there were many such, who led very different, separate lives. Melvin Riggs the owner of the High Life, Melvin Riggs the co-owner of the Buffalo Hawks, Melvin

Riggs the county politician—the aggressive glamour of Riggs's public personality had little to do with Laetitia, the daughter of an old moneyed Buffalo-area family. "Of course, that man married Laetitia for her money. What can she expect?" There was pity, but little sympathy. Melvin Riggs had two grown children from an earlier marriage but he and Laetitia were, in Laetitia's forlorn word, "childless"—so she'd naively told her Women's League friends. Mrs. LeRoux told the story of suggesting to Laetitia, delicately, that she and Melvin might explore the possibility of adopting a child—"And, goodness! Laetitia stared at me and said, 'Are you serious? To take such a risk? Not knowing a child's ancestry? It would be like Melvin to take such a gamble, the man loves gambling, but, thank you, not *me*.'" It was believed in Willowsville that since Riggs's murder, and the public scandal, Laetitia had had a nervous breakdown and had gone into seclusion with relatives in another part of the state, but the woman who appeared in court that afternoon did not seem ravaged or sickly. "What we saw in Laetitia Riggs, though we were too young to identify it at the time," Trish Elders would marvel years later, "was the glisten of passion—pure womanly rage."

Dill began his examination by making sympathetic reference to Mrs. Riggs's recent widowhood and apologizing for the necessity of "reawakening the pain of grief." Courteously, he asked Mrs. Riggs to describe to the court what she knew of her late husband's business transactions and "personal relationship" with Dahlia Heart in the months preceding the shooting. Mrs. Riggs, a handkerchief clenched in her fist, spoke carefully, a little sharply, as if reciting rehearsed words. From time to time she glanced toward the jurors as if gauging what effect her words had upon them. (They were imperturbable, unreadable. A jury resembling the jury of the first trial—mostly middle-aged men and women, all Caucasian. No one looked obviously crazy.) Vehemently Mrs. Riggs denied all knowledge of her late husband's business transactions and "personal relationships." She denied absolutely that he'd asked for a divorce or even a separation. She insisted that, though they were not often seen together in public, because Melvin was so deeply committed to his work, they'd had a "deep, spiritual marital bond" based on "twenty-six years of mutual trust and understanding." They had been married in the Lutheran church and both had observed its fundamental beliefs. She accepted that, as a man of the world, a highly competitive businessman and politician, her late husband had accumulated some enemies, but that was only to be expected. "There was a saying of Melvin's—'I'm a businessman, I'm not running a charity.'" Mrs. Riggs laughed sharply. She dabbed the handkerchief against her eyes, fumbled and dropped it, and as Dill stooped gallantly to retrieve it, her handbag slipped from her lap and fell, too, with a clatter, spilling some of its contents onto the courtroom floor. This wakened spectators and those jurors who'd been on the verge of dozing off. Mrs. Riggs blushed. She seemed suddenly about to cry. As Dill retrieved the handbag for her, in a moment of confusion, Mrs. Riggs spoke incoherently, on her feet as if to leave the witness stand; then she sat heavily back down as if she'd been pushed. She said loudly, "Oh why don't I tell the truth! For once! My husband Melvin Riggs, Jr., was a brute. If ever a man deserved to die *Melvin Riggs deserved to die*." Dill, appalled, tried to cut Mrs. Riggs off, but she continued in a high, aggrieved voice, addressing the jurors, who stared at her in amazement. "Yes, my husband was a brute! It was my secret, and I'm sick of secrets! Having to pretend—it's exhausting, half the women of Willowsville are exhausted, we keep up the effort for years, for decades, then, one day, we *stop*. I want to tell the court that if that woman sitting over there—'Mrs. Heart'—says that Melvin beat her, and threatened her, it's probably true. I don't doubt he threatened that boy—that poor boy sitting there, John Reddy Heart—I've heard him threaten his own children, his grown children." Mrs. Riggs was speaking rapidly, her face glistening with hot, angry tears. Her fists were clenched in her lap. "Melvin Riggs was my husband in name only. I endured the humiliation for pride's sake—like many another woman. If Mrs. Heart believes he was her lover, she's a fool—he was not her *lover*, as he was not my *husband*, for the man was incapable of love. 'A woman is a cow.' 'A woman is to be milked.' For twenty-six years I pretended not to know. Melvin married me for my money—I wasn't a woman he'd have glanced twice at, otherwise—I knew, but I pretended not to know. 'A woman is a commodity or she's nothing.' I suppose I loved him. In the beginning. Already on our honeymoon—in Italy—which my family financed, of course—I pretended not to know—certain obvious facts. Later, when I confronted him with one of his infidelities, he turned on me and—he struck me. 'My private life has nothing to do with *you*.' What contempt he felt for me! And what contempt I deserved! Melvin could be a charming man—of course. Most men can. If they wish. If you're rich, or pretty. If there's a good reason for the charm. And Melvin could do things, public things, with a certain flair—he knew how to get attention. You *wanted* to like him. The way people, weak people, *want* to like brutes and bullies, to have them on your side. Melvin claimed to love baseball— 'The soul of America'—but everyone knows he treated his players, even his best players, like 'chattel'—that was his word for them. It's been noted that the Hawks rarely hired Negro players. And for a good reason—Melvin hated Negroes. He hated Jews. He hated women. He was a selfish, ignorant, intolerant man. No one knew—I hid the shame well—that Melvin struck me sometimes. Not often in recent years because I'd learned. Only just slaps, cuffs—'To keep you in line, Lae-titia.' The way you'd cuff an old dog you knew wouldn't bite." Again, Dill tried to cut off his witness, but Mrs. Riggs raised her voice louder. She said, sobbing, "Sometimes I wished he'd kill me, I couldn't bear the shame of divorce, and everyone feeling sorry for me. It was always my pride. I knew he was seeing a woman—the 'blackjack woman' people called her—but I didn't dare confront him. I was terrified of his temper. A few years ago he put his hands around my throat and squeezed—his big, brute hands—and I almost fainted—and he laughed at me, and said, 'Just kidding, Laetitia, just to show you what I can do'—he laughed in my face—'and I can finish it any time.' And next day a relative called, an aunt, and I could hardly speak on the phone my throat was so hoarse, and she said, 'Laetitia, is something wrong? You sound ill,' and I said quickly, 'Oh no, nothing's wrong, of course nothing's wrong, I'm fine.' And that was how it was, Mr. Dill. All of my life as Mrs. Melvin Riggs, Jr. All of my life. I've been *fine*."

"Mrs. Riggs, please—you may step down."

"Oh yes may I? May I? May I, sir, may I *step down*? Yes?"

Mrs. Riggs began laughing shrilly. Her face shone as if every part of it had been rouged. Dill reached out to assist her, she slapped at his arm, rose to step down from the witness stand and lost her footing, or became light-headed, and began to fall; Dill and one of the bailiffs caught her; there was an outcry somewhere in the courtroom. (Bibi Arhardt and Sandi Scott who'd crashed the trial reported afterward they believed it must've been some scandalized relative of Laetitia Riggs's, some male, trying to shut the old woman up. But things were so confused, it was doubtful Laetitia was even aware of anyone calling to her.) Judge Schor, disgusted, tapped his gavel loudly, and ordered the court cleared and the session adjourned until the next morning. To Walter Thrun, Jenny's uncle, a fellow judge and an old buddy he saw frequently at the B.A.C., Schor reportedly said a few days later, "That asshole, Dill! Blindsided by two female witnesses in two days! I nearly burst a gut laughing at the look on his face. Any attorney who doesn't know what the hell his witness is going to say before a jury deserves whatever verdict he gets."

(Jenny Thrun told us she was shocked, she hadn't known that judges spoke that way—"So crude! Like guys our age." Roger Zwaart, son of a lawyer, who, since Suzi Zeigler had begun dating Norm Zeiga had become disturbingly crude himself, where once he'd been one of the nicer, more courteous boys in our class, laughed at Jenny. "Hell, judges talk like anybody else, only nastier. A judge is a *lawyer*, right?")

John Reddy tried to hang himself in his jail cell last night with a torn bedsheet. Two guards pulled him down, he was revived and beaten. Under his clothes, where no one can see.

Sasha Calvo visited John Reddy in the detention home last night—they're engaged. The wedding is planned for New Year's Day.

Tomorrow, John Reddy will testify at his trial. He'll tell the true story of what happened on the night of Riggs's death!

14

The prosecution completed its case. Declaring that John Reddy Heart was a murderer—"A vicious, precocious, *anti-American subversive murderer*. Ladies and gentlemen of the jury, you have only to look at the defendant to plumb his soul: he sits silent, contemptuous of our law, *utterly devoid of remorse.*"

The defense completed its case. Declaring that John Reddy Heart was no murderer but a confused youth of only sixteen caught up in a drama not of his own making, and not of his comprehension—"John Reddy Heart is himself a *victim*. A victim, ladies and gentlemen of the jury, of his own gallant impulse to protect his mother, and his instinctive impulse to protect himself."

Those of us who attended the trial in the closing days compared notes with those who'd attended earlier. There was much confusion which even Evangeline Fesnacht's voluminous notes could not clarify. It seemed strange to us, that, another time, testifying now for the defense, Dahlia Heart and her father Aaron Leander Heart were summoned to the witness stand, and encouraged to amplify their previous statements. Where Dill had tried to curtail testimony, Trippe encouraged it. For now John Reddy was a "serious, good-hearted boy who never had a father"—"a respectful grandson, blessed with a native intelligence"—"though 'book-learning' didn't come easy to him, he's always been *smart*." Still, Dahlia Heart and old Mr. Heart were vague about what had actually happened on the fatal night. Neither seemed to have *seen*. Or *heard*. "It was as if," Evangeline Fesnacht said wonderingly, "a mist or something pervaded that part of the house. An amnesiac mist. Things *happened*, but no one seems to have caused them to happen."

It was noted that Roland Trippe didn't recall Farley Heart to testify, nor did John Reddy's younger brother return to court to observe the trial. There was a rumor, unsubstantiated, which came to us from Cynthia Swann, a sophomore, whose father taught junior high social studies, that Farley had had a "nervous collapse"—which wouldn't have surprised us. (How close were John Reddy and Farley? Most of us assumed they weren't close at all. They neither looked nor acted like brothers.) Nor did Farley's sister (whose name none of us could remember) appear in court; the child was said to be in a state of "nerves"—"traumatized"—by the violence in the Heart household; there was talk, we heard circuitously from Frannie Reid and Carlotta Schoppa, Mr. Schoppa's wife, of her being placed in a foster home, or perhaps a Catholic convent school (?), removed from Dahlia Heart's custody should Mrs. Heart be ruled an "unfit mother."

(After the trial, it would become common knowledge that Farley and his sister, whose name was Shirleen, were living with both their mother and grandfather in a "quiet, residential apartment neighborhood" near Delaware Park during the trials. They'd been pulled abruptly out of their Willowsville schools, of course, and both were provided tutors for the remainder of the school year. Roland Trippe made these arrangements. Three decades later, as Sister Mary Agatha of St. Anne's Sisters of Charity, a Roman Catholic order, John

Reddy's sister would be nationally acclaimed for her "revolutionary, inspired, empathetic work" in unlocking certain of
the secrets of autism in children and of the effect of childhood
trauma upon the developing brain, yet never in any of the
rare interviews this remarkable, reticent woman granted
would she speak of her own life. As Barbara Walters said
admiringly of her, on network TV, "You find yourself taking
for granted that Sister Mary Agatha is a 'pure soul'—one in a
million, or millions, among us with no private history, no
'personal baggage' at all!")

There came a succession of "character witnesses" to take
the stand, urged by Trippe to speak in support of John Reddy
Heart. It was amazing to see Coach McKeever as "Woodson
Earl McKeever, Jr.," in a suit and tie, nervously speaking, at
length, of John Reddy's "diligence and fair-mindedness" in
sports. There was petite Miss Bird remarkably composed,
flamey-red-haired and wearing spike-heeled shoes, speaking
of John Reddy Heart's "essential shyness, sobriety." There
came Mr. Lepage in tweeds and distractingly bright-polished
brown shoes. Also Mr. Cuthbert, Mr. Dunleddy, Mr. Schoppa
with his twitchy smile and raspy smoker's voice. Even prissy
Mr. Stamish we'd believed had disapproved of John Reddy—
"Basically a decent boy, despite the length of his hair and his
'biker' gear. I am certain." There was Miss Crosby our guidance counselor with her frowning potato-plain face and
dignified manner, speaking as if she were an aunt of John
Reddy's—"I counseled John Reddy on certain private family
matters, and urged him to concentrate on 'vocational arts' in
our curriculum, and found him, on the whole, a mature and
responsible individual for his age . . . thrust in the midst of *a
volatile domestic situation.*" (With a meaningful, disapproving
glance in the direction of Dahlia Heart whose face was partly
obscured by dark glasses but who seemed to be staring,
abashed, at her hands clasped in her lap.) There came Mr.
Hornby who taught vocational arts—"The boy might be a
little impatient now and then, but that's his age. It's my

impression he tried to stay out of fights. He has a real gift with his *hands*." There came even Alistair the school custodian to declare in his thick Scots accent—"John Reddy is a boy who cleans up after himself, you'd never find rancid food stinking up his locker, or filthy old sneakers, mildewed gym clothes. There sure ain't many boys like that these days."

We were proud of the WHS staff for supporting John Reddy, we had to think it impressed the jurors. (Who must've been wondering why John Reddy, an accused murderer, refused to speak in his own defense; sat day after day at the defense table looking sullen, or sad, or pained, or pissed, or half-asleep in a trance like he couldn't be bothered to listen.) We had to revise our opinions of certain characters like Dunleddy, Schoppa, Stamish—"Maybe they're not so bad after all." Blake Wells, editor of our *Weekly Willowsvillian*, would write in an editorial, in his eager, slightly pompous style, "A trial can bring out the worst in a community. But it can bring out the best, too. Sometimes. WHS can take pride in . . ." (This was both true and not so true. For though Roland Trippe had approached a number of John Reddy's classmates, including boys on the basketball and track teams, only Orrie Buhr and Clyde Meunzer agreed to act as character witnesses. The others, among them Dwayne Hewson, Bo Bozer and Ken Fischer, were embarrassed to have to decline—their fathers had forbidden them to get involved. There was the fear that these boys of good Willowsville families would be contaminated by the association with John Reddy Heart and his notorious mother, and wind up blackballed by the most prestigious fraternities when they went to college, or lose out on job prospects after graduation. As Mr. Hewson told us sagely, "It's a harsh world, kids. The only people who think it's 'live and let live' are losers.")

John Reddy's friends Orrie—"Orson"—Buhr and Clyde Meunzer came through for him, though. It's doubtful that they made favorable impressions on the jury: they were uncomfortable in cheap-looking suits and snap-on ties, "looking like off-the-rack at Sears," their duck's-ass hair slick with grease and their lips swollen and mumbly. Tough guys who'd sneered at us since seventh grade, pushing us around on playgrounds and intimidating us with their big-knuckled fists. Orrie's skin was clam-colored and sweaty; he'd grown a mustache on his upper lip that looked like he'd smeared it on with a charcoal stick. Clyde, whose braying-threatening call ("Gonna fuck you up real good, fuckface") had terrified some of us since the boys' locker room in junior high, was revealed to have a stammer. Seeing his friends at the front of the courtroom, John Reddy was said to have squirmed in his seat and pressed the tips of his fingers against his eyelids. His own mouth worked, silently. Both Orrie and Clyde swore that in all the years they'd known John Reddy he had not mentioned, not once, the name "Melvin Riggs"—nor had he said much about his mother's men friends or private life. "John Reddy keeps to himself, y'know? He don't ask questions neither," Orrie said. "Except John might w-worry about his mom, the way you do, y'know, if she ain't m-married," Clyde said, squinting at Trippe. "Y'know what I'm saying?" Both boys denied that John Reddy had a violent temper, as Dill had repeatedly suggested—"No more than anybody else. Maybe John got in a few fights, you wouldn't want to cross him, he can hit real hard and he's, like, *fast*, like a snake, y'know? But no more than anybody else."

Like a snake. The words hovered in the courtroom, you could almost feel the vibrations.

Frank Farolino was a character witness for John Reddy, and so was Caleb Burnham of Burnham Nurseries for whom John Reddy had worked one summer—"Quiet kid. But sometimes impatient." There was, unexpectedly, Willowsville's mayor (this was a largely honorific position paying a token $1500 annually) Mr. Diebold, for whom John Reddy had done handyman chores and lawn work—"John had to grow up fast in that household. He wasn't a typical Willowsville child. He took on certain of the qualities of an adult, I think, at an early age. If he gets impatient sometimes it's because of being *misjudged*." There came Mrs. Rhona Buhr, Orrie's mother, a glamorously made-up redhead of about forty, who told the court a little too assertively (you could see the women jurors disliked her, the prissy little mouths beneath their pinched nostrils) that John Reddy was the most considerate of her son's friends—"Like the time last spring my car got stuck in the mud in our driveway and it was mainly John Reddy who helped push it out. Hardly minding he got mud all over his nice-looking leather boots. And another time—" There were no Calvos in court. Not even Dino. Certainly not Sasha. We were disappointed; we'd begun to doubt that Sasha had even returned from Brooklyn, or wherever the Calvos had sent her.

Honestly there is a baby! A little boy looking just like John Reddy Heart. The girl Sasha is going to raise him in Milan, that's where the Calvos come from. Lots of Calvos there.

No they won't be married. No the Calvos hate his guts.

They'd had to send Dino away, too. So Dino wouldn't try to kill John Reddy Heart and wind up on trial for murder himself.

Years later, as adults, calmly discussing the mysterious saga of John Reddy Heart over drinks in a dim-lit cocktail lounge of the Kenawka (Minnesota, north of St. Paul) Marriott, the novelist Evangeline Fesnacht would confide in the poet-professor Richard, once "Ritchie" Eickhorn, her old classmate, that she'd been so obsessed with the Heart trial, she'd hardly slept; couldn't concentrate on anything except the case; fasted from the time the jury began to deliberate until they announced their verdict nineteen exhausting hours later. "It seemed to me, in my madness, the least I could do for John Reddy." Evangeline confessed that she'd also brashly volunteered to be a character witness—"Fortunately, Trippe politely declined my offer. I was going to speak of John Reddy's 'killer eyes' and 'destiny'—I was going to quote D. H.

Lawrence—'The American soul is hard, isolate, stoic and a killer.' My God, I might have gotten the poor kid sentenced to life imprisonment. How crazy can love make you!" Evangeline sighed, and ran her hands brusquely through her short-cut mannish hair. Richard Eickhorn whose adulthood had become possible only by way of a continuous reimagining and reconstituting of the past, as if he himself were the "epic American poem" he'd once determined to write, was amazed at such a disclosure. E. S. Fesnacht—the only writer of their WHS class to have achieved anything like a national reputation. He'd been aware of Evangeline's literary career since her first novel, *Time Travel*, was published, to generally admiring reviews and modest sales, when they were in their mid-twenties; he'd read everything she'd published since then, envious of her talent, resentful of her reputation, yet, he had to admit, proud of her, and happy for her, the homely girl certain of the boys in their class had called Frog Tits behind her back. Had it helped, Richard wondered, that Evangeline had been slightly loony in high school? With her fixation on John Reddy Heart, her voluminous *Death Notebooks*, or had it been *Death Chronicles*? Even now, so many years later, speaking of her adolescent self with an air of pained embarrassment, Evangeline's small, lashless eyes shone. Richard confessed, "Evangeline, at least you went to John Reddy's trial. I'd wanted to, but I didn't dare. I was such a meek kid—I read Dostoyevsky in high school, I identified with Raskolnikov and the 'Underground Man'—but I took the truant officer threat seriously. I was afraid of being *arrested*." Evangeline laughed, and signaled for another round of drinks: they were both drinking vodka martinis. She said, wiping at her eyes, "We took everything seriously in those days, Ritchie. We were fucking *alive*."

I saw John Reddy his clothes stripped from him, naked and bleeding. His forehead, his hands and feet. They had impaled his body on iron spikes and these had been driven through a wooden cross of aged rotting boards. He was panting, groaning in pain. My eyes were seared with the wonder and glory of his face! Who has done this to you, John Reddy? I cried. For the cross hung crooked as if in mockery. And there was mocking laughter like thunder. Ugly angry laughter rolling from the underside of the earth. I approached John Reddy in horror, I could see the gaping wound in his side. The blood glistening like pearls. I could see the terrible spikes driven through John Reddy's hands and feet. I could see his ribs straining against his pale, tight-stretched skin. I could see the damp, dark hairs of his body. Between his legs his genitals at which I did not dare to look yet somehow saw gleaming with a fluid like tears, the flesh red-tinctured and smooth like something that has been skinned alive. I understood that it was my task to save John Reddy from death. It was my task to bring him water to drink, but I had none. It was my task to bring his limp penis to life, to caress it between my fingers, but I could not reach him. I wasn't tall enough. I wasn't strong enough. I wasn't fierce enough. I fell to my knees, my hair hung in my face. I was crying, ashamed. I smelled the rank odor of my body. John Reddy! Forgive us! We never knew. These words were torn from me, words I could not comprehend. I felt such helplessness, such sorrow. John Reddy's eyes opened and he fixed his bloodshot gaze on me in suffering, and pity—pity of me. Though John Reddy did not utter a word, I understood that he forgave me. He forgave me my weakness, my cowardice. He has forgiven us all. Like flame a sensation of love swept through me. A sensation of warmth, infinite joy. John Reddy! John Reddy! As my body is pierced and torn open like his nailed to the cross in mockery and humiliation, as one day I will give birth out of my pain-racked body, this would be my secret, John Reddy's and mine.

Katrina Olmsted. Katie. Such a dream, to have come to her.

We were astonished. We were in awe. We weren't jealous. (We believed we weren't jealous.) During the long hours of our vigil. As John Reddy's fate was being decided by strangers. We fasted, we prayed. We were happiest on our knees praying

for John Reddy like the good Christian girls we were. Katie
Olmsted was the most feverish of us, it was the onset of her
terrible illness perhaps, we would recall that night in Trish
Elders's room and think *Did it begin then?*—*poor Katie* but at
the time of course we could not have known, we were astonished by the quivering passion in her voice, Katie's little-girl
voice we'd known since grade school, we held her, we wept
with her, we prayed, "Heavenly Father, don't abandon John
Reddy Heart in his hour of need," for such were the childlike
prayers we uttered, Verrie pressed her gaunt hollow-eyed
beautiful face against Katie's round burning face, Trish
wrapped her arms around Katie and hid her face in Katie's
neck, "Almost, I could believe in the devil, to make a deal
with him—you know?" someone whispered, we were
shocked, yet sympathetic, we wondered *Is this how evil
begins? out of desperation.* Pattianne held and caressed Katie's
icy fingers, none of us was jealous but perhaps we were envious, we yearned to be Katrina Olmsted that night, to have had
Katie's amazing dream, we did not doubt it was a dream-
vision from God, on the eve of the verdict in John Reddy
Heart's murder trial, one of us cried, "Oh, Katie—what?" for
in her ecstasy Katie had dug her fingernails so deeply into the
tender palms of her hands, both palms began to bleed.

"Why does it matter so much to you if that little bastard is
found guilty or not? What is he to you? What the hell is he to
you? Or any of the Hearts, to us? What's going on here? Look
at me, I'm talking to you. Look at me, answer me, God damn
you, *I happen to be your father*."

Mr. ———— was shouting at his daughter. For the nineteen
hours of the jury's deliberations she'd refused to sit at the table
with the family as she'd refused, in stubborn outrageous silence,
to eat anything except liquids (fruit juice, skim milk, Tab and
Diet Coke), nor had she shampooed her hair, or even brushed
her hair in long loving strokes as ordinarily she was obsessive
about doing. *Don't touch me. Don't look at me. Don't speak to me.*

You know nothing of me. This beautiful girl Mr. ——— loved. This beautiful girl Mr. ——— adored. Looking as if she'd been sleeping in her clothes, a mental patient, ashy-skinned, gaunt-eyed, her lips pale, she'd neglected even to apply Hot Pink or Watermelon Gloss or Blackberry Wine lipstick, peevish as a martyr. Yet her serious error was: glancing disdainfully at Mr. ——— as if he, the head of this costly and exhausting household, owner of house and grounds assessed at $375,000 in Willowsville's St. Albans Hill district (which property would be assessed at beyond $1 million at the present time), a successful businessman in a frantically competitive field, the second-youngest trustee of the Albright-Knox Art Gallery, had no more substance than a dissolving cloud of cigarette smoke or an actual bad smell. And a sudden fury overcame him, and he rushed after her, gripping her by a shoulder and shaking her, his daughter who weighed only one hundred five scrupulously monitored pounds, and she screamed, and pushed at him, Mr. ——— who weighed one hundred ninety-six pounds, and Mr. ——— shoved her from him, even as he continued to grip her shoulder, shaking her, she would later claim striking her, with his fist, his closed fist, his face red and contorted as a demon's—"I was on the floor, and he was standing over me shouting. I'd fallen hard I guess, I didn't know what had happened, the glass of skim milk was broken on the floor, I was trying to crawl to get away from him, under the kitchen table, I was on my hands and knees trying to crawl, to hide, to escape from him, I remember thinking I didn't know how to crawl any longer, my legs were too long, I didn't realize that my wrist was sprained, I didn't feel any pain it was so weird, I had to get away from Daddy, *I was in terror of my life.*"

* * *

At 10:20 A.M. of the third day of deliberations in the trial of John Reddy Heart word came at last from the jury that they'd reached a unanimous decision. The trial's principals were hurriedly reassembled in the courtroom, Mr. Dill and Mr.

Trippe and their assistants, Judge Schor and assistants, stenographer, bailiffs, Erie County sheriff's deputies escorting the defendant John Reddy Heart who was looking dazed as if he hadn't slept in a long time. It was observed that Heart had a man's face now, no longer a boy's. His skin was coarsened, sallow; his jaws were bluish with stubble. He had a habit of rubbing at his left eye, which watered. Though obviously aware of the jurors in their polished wooden box, he took care not to glance in their direction. His hands might have been trembling. *You can sit in judgment of me but you can't make me acknowledge you.*

Just as Judge Schor commanded the defendant to rise to hear the jury's verdict, a door at the rear of the courtroom opened, and there came Dahlia Heart, hurrying, breathless, an unlit cigarette between her fingers. Mrs. Heart was not dressed so stylishly as usual, though perhaps as conspicuously—a white scarf, dampened with snowflakes, covered her seemingly untidy hair; she wore a cream-colored woolen cape over a white woolen suit, white leather gloves and white leather boots disfigured by salt stains. John Reddy did not glance back at her as she hurried into the room, then halted, as if she'd been forbidden to come farther, staring in frightened silence. (It was noted that Mr. Trippe glanced back at Mrs. Heart, with an unreadable look: anxiety? tenderness? concern? For it had been rumored for weeks in certain Buffalo circles that the notorious Mrs. Heart and the respected criminal lawyer had become lovers, though Trippe was believed to be happily married, the father of two young children.) Judge Schor was posing his ritual question, "Mr. Foreman, has the jury reached a decision?" and the foreman replied gravely, "We have, Your Honor. We find the defendant John Reddy Heart—not guilty of the charges brought against him."

There was a beat of startled silence.

Not guilty.

A woman cried faintly, "Oh Johnny. Oh my God."

John Reddy's head snapped up as if he'd been struck. His eyes were clear, and alert, and he acknowledged the jury, now. Trippe was shaking his hand, grinning like a boy, congratulating him; Dill, stunned, turned away in defeat, fumbling to thrust a sheaf of papers into his briefcase. Several rows behind in the courtroom Dahlia Heart staggered and pressed the back of her hand against her eyes as if she'd become faint.

But John Reddy Heart, a prisoner for so many months, "in custody," remained where he stood, motionless, staring at the smiling jurors as if he hadn't heard the verdict clearly, or hadn't understood. His left eye brimmed with tears.

Not guilty?

If I am not guilty—who is?

15

America, I hear your heart breaking.
America, my soul is you.
America, you've betrayed me.
I adore you.
    —Richard Eickhorn, *America I Hear Your Heart Breaking*

John Reddy Heart was declared NOT GUILTY—yet he spent the next twelve months in prison, and twelve months beyond that on probation.

John Reddy Heart was expected to be freed, and return to us—yet he spent the next twelve months behind bars in the Tomahawk Island Youth Camp.

We were shocked. We were incredulous. "Pissed as all hell." We knew we'd been cheated. It was shitty adult logic, adult vengeance. We hated it. As soon as news of the acquittal came to us we rushed from our classes, drove in a horn-honking procession from school to Tug Hill Park, a dozen cars crammed with screaming kids—HEART ACQUITTAL CELEBRATED IN WILL'VILLE, the *Buffalo Evening News* headline would read, above a photo of Smoke Filer driving his T-Bird, our arms stuck out every window like tentacles, fingers flashing the V-for-Victory sign. Tommy Nordstrom's notorious party was that weekend, at least sixty of us crowded around, and in, the Nordstroms' fantastic heated indoor swimming pool—where some of us, as we'd ruefully reminisce, first learned to drink seriously, to get *smashed*. And six days later we learned John Reddy, instead of coming home, had pleaded guilty to a catalogue of charges ("possession of a deadly weapon"—"leaving the scene of a crime"—"obstruction of justice"—"vehicular theft"—"two counts of breaking and entering"—"burglary"—"resisting arrest"—and more), and had been sentenced to twelve months in a maximum-security youth facility and twelve months' probation, immediately remanded to Tomahawk Island Youth Camp on a scrubby island in the Niagara River associated in the minds of Willowsville residents with, as Dwayne Hewson's dad said scornfully, "Negro dope pushers, drunk Indians sticking up gas stations and white trash blowing one another's brains out. Losers."

It wasn't just the shock of it but the shame. For Tomahawk Island *was* a place for losers—guys who couldn't be classified as juvenile delinquents any longer but weren't adults either. Dangerous characters.

John Reddy Heart?

Roger Zwaart's dad tried to soften our hurt and disappointment by explaining, with lawyerly logic, that since John Reddy had shot and killed Riggs—"And I don't think anyone seriously doubts he did, yes?"—the Erie County prosecutor's office wasn't going to let him walk away free. "Trippe understood this perfectly. I've heard that, without the Hearts knowing it, Trippe had been negotiating for a reduced-sentence deal all along. Except his client wouldn't plead even involuntary manslaughter—he wouldn't plead anything, at all. Which is why the official plea was 'not guilty.'" Mr. Zwaart shook his head as if, in Trippe's place, he might have handled things differently; yet, if he hadn't handled things differently, his client wouldn't have been acquitted. "But if there'd been a second trial on these lesser charges, the Heart kid would've been found guilty and sent away for a long time. A judge would've taken one look at him and at the case and sent him away for twenty years minimum. The jurors at his trial obviously decided that Riggs, the victim, deserved killing. Trippe helped them see to that, but so, inadvertently, had Dill. Punishing a deserving victim posthumously makes sense to some citizens, and that's what they did. But the Heart kid wouldn't have had such luck a second time, and believe me it was sheer luck, I mean like getting struck by lightning, that Dill was stupid enough to allow Laetitia Riggs to sabotage his case. And Trippe knew it. So Trippe advised his client to plead guilty, for a reduced sentence, and the kid went for it, and got a terrific bargain, believe me. For a killer." Mr. Zwaart laughed soundlessly. He saw the sick, sad look in our eyes, and our knowledge, the gift that one generation yields to another, the sweetest gift wrested from us against our wills, that he was right.

(Why did we waste so much time and energy as kids, we'd ask one another in our flaccid-fitting adult disguises, in our balding-creased maturity, resisting most of what our fathers had to tell us? For they were right, like Mr. Zwaart. And even if they weren't right the substance of what they told us would become what we'd tell our children, more or less, fumbling and faltering to recall the very cadences of speech that, at the time of its utterance, we'd despised.)

* * *

At about this time in November of that exhausting year a memorial service was held at the high school for Art's older brother Jamie, James Michael Lutz, Private First Class, U.S. Army, who'd graduated from WHS a few years before and who'd been killed "in the line of duty"—"serving his country"—"protecting the cause of freedom and democracy" in some desolate spot in Vietnam that may have been mispronounced by Mr. Stamish at the ceremony, or misheard by Willowsville residents whose ears could not accommodate combinations of consonants and vowels not already known to us—"Cameron Bay" it sounded like. The WHS staff and most seniors recalled Jamie Lutz but younger students were vague about which of the good-looking jocks he'd been. There would always be a scattering of transfer students who would confuse, over the decades, to our exasperation and their own perplexity, the deceased Jamie Lutz with the still-living John Reddy Heart, or the still-living John Reddy Heart with the deceased Jamie Lutz.

16

Where you gonna go when there's no goin' farther?
Who you gonna love when there's no love for you?
John Reddy, John Reddy Heart.

Twelve months imprisoned at Tomahawk Island we in Willowsville tried to imagine but could not. Even Evangeline Fesnacht our chronicler of disaster, devotedly accumulating her *Death Chronicles* in her locker until it spilled out onto the floor. Even our broody intellectuals Ritchie Eickhorn, Clarence McQuade, Dexter Cambrook, Elise Petko. Even Art Lutz, Bo Bozer and Tommy Nordstrom (sporting his new, truly weird "convict crew cut") who drove out to Tomahawk Island one rainy Saturday afternoon to check out the facility from a short distance—"Jesus. What a depressing place. You drive over a nightmare bridge. You come along this crappy road. There's a tall fence like high-tension wires. Signs warning RESTRICTED. NO TRESPASSING. OFFICIAL BUSINESS ONLY. A 'camp'—yeah! A concentration camp." The guys had had a vague idea of visiting John Reddy but hadn't been able to get within fifty yards of the mustard-colored building: a "Gestapo guard" turned them back.

Shelby Connor, hearing this, burst into tears. We were excited, seeing this frail pretty bird-girl dissolve like a watercolor.

Bibi Arhardt, hearing this, crammed in our booth at the Haven, pressed her hands against her ears and screwed up her glamour face into the baby-pig face that'd made us laugh since third grade. "Guys, shut up! My heart's broken enough *as it is*."

Dwayne Hewson said menacingly, "Somebody should break John Reddy *out*. Like a revolution in, y'know—Mexico. Paris, 'Bastille Day.'"

We didn't forget John Reddy Heart through those twelve months but there were some of us, maybe even the majority of us, for whom he became, in Bart Digger's words, "increasingly abstract. Like a geometry theorem."

Not a day off for good behavior?—that sucks!

John Reddy won't play their ass-kissing games.

So? He's locked up, isn't he? The bastards have got him.

Nobody's got John Reddy. Nobody ever!

Where were the other Hearts? Living in Buffalo? But where?

We never saw him with our own eyes but there were frequent reportings of old Mr. Heart on local roads, prowling Tug Hill Park and the One Hundred Weeping Willows Walk beside Glen Creek, usually in the very early morning, emerging out of the mist, a tall bony white-haired and -bearded apparition tirelessly searching for discarded bottles. "You can hear the bottles clanking like chimes. Even if, when you look really closely, you can't see Mr. Heart anywhere."

Another report, which we didn't want to hear, was that Aaron Leander Heart had died. After his testimony at his grandson's trial. The strain had been too much for him. Speaking the truth had been too much for him. Lying ("Lying through his beard—what a character!") had been too much for him. An aunt of Chet Halloren's who was a friend of Mrs. Roland Trippe had said the pity of it was, the old man had died, of a massive coronary, after John Reddy's case had gone to the jury but before the verdict had come in.

"The Hearts have caused tragedy in others' lives. But they're not immune to it, in their own."

Dahlia Heart's Willowsville men friends, humiliated by the publicity, insisted that they knew nothing of her whereabouts. "She'd been here, now she's gone. Like a tornado. What more is there to say?" Herman Skelton, divorced and living alone in the Blackbridge Apartments facing Willowsville Green, said bitterly. "What a gal! She's reinvested the money she got from Riggs. Which was a helluva lot more than five thousand, let me tell you. She's right here in Buffalo, she hasn't gone anywhere. That babe is tough as nails," Frank Diebold, our mayor, said mysteriously. The *Courier-Express* column "Out Our Way" noted that **Dahlia Heart has been spied in the company of none other than—Buff Stansell, the Hawks' fairhaired boy. Could it be, our Buff is "looking to be a victim"?**

Like old Mr. Heart, Dahlia Heart was occasionally sighted in Willowsville. Always at dusk, or after dark. Frequently in the company of an unidentified man, a stranger to our village—"an older gentleman driving an exotic European sports car." Dougie Siefried insisted he'd tracked Dahlia Heart one Thursday evening at the Amherst Hills Mall through several department stores, losing her finally in the Designer Collections on the fifth floor of Saks—"She went into a changing room behind some mirrors and I waited and waited and she never came out, I mean I waited like an hour, I *swear*." The elder residents of Meridian Place often called one another excitedly claiming they'd just seen Dahlia Heart close by. She and her gentleman friend with the sports car, variously identified as a Porsche, a Fiat, a "sinister black Jaguar," arrived at 8 Meridian Place, stayed for several hours but (apparently) didn't spend the night—"Next morning when I came downstairs, at about six-thirty, which is my usual waking time now, my brain just switches to *on*! and I can't switch it to *off*! so I might as well get up, I figure—I looked over, and their car was gone," Aickley Thrun reported. He and his wife and the Hearts' other nextdoor neighbors the

Bannisters complained bitterly at their clubs to whoever would listen—"Why don't those terrible people *sell*! Everyone on the Hill is waiting for them to *sell*! Even ignorant white trash, you'd think, could comprehend when they are *not, not, not wanted*!"

It became a time of cruising past the Heart house though no one was home or likely to be home. At dusk, or after dark. When we figured we wouldn't be noticed. As some of us, girls, would later cruise past John Reddy's lonely-romantic apartment on Water Street. We dreaded a real estate agent's FOR SALE sign at 8 Meridian Place. We took heart from the fact that, though no one was (apparently) in the house, lights burned deep in the interior. If we parked and if we were patient we began to see shadows through the near-opaque draperies and venetian blinds, fleeting silhouettes of human figures. We heard raised voices. A woman's scream. Gunshots. Parked one night at the foot of the driveway amid a slow silent snowfall that would, by the time they left, entirely cover the car to a height of two inches, Suzi Zeigler and Norm Zeiga saw vividly reenacted the entire drama of the shooting of Melvin Riggs—the flight of John Reddy Heart—the arrival of squad cars, an ambulance—as if it were a shared vision; they solemnized the occasion by making a kind of love that left them dazed, breathless, frightened and exhilarated—"And we vowed never, never to tell, it was so *sacred*."

At school, there were unexpected encounters. Verrie Myers, lonely for John Reddy, restless and reckless, began dating, in a tentative way, unknown to her parents, a senior named Jake Gervasio (his dad owned Gervasio's Lawn Service), tough and sexy in John Reddy's style, a vocational arts major who scorned the preppie–jock–St. Albans Hill clique to which Verrie belonged but who had the distinct attraction of being a buddy of Orrie Buhr, thus a buddy of John Reddy; Verrie confessed, shivering, she was "scared stiff" of Jake and never went anywhere with him in his car "that might be remotely dangerous." And Jake treated her, she said, "like a lady. I'm *serious*." But then one day Verrie found herself cornered in a restroom in a part of the school she didn't ordinarily visit, there rushed at her several senior girls including Lulu Lovitt who'd been Jake Gervasio's girl off and on since ninth grade, and Verrie was shoved, poked, pinched and slapped by the furious Lulu—"I was so terrified! I didn't know what was happening! I walked in, and they were on me like ravenous birds! Crazy Lulu was wearing a leather vest and studs in her ears and her hair was teased like a banshee's and she slapped my face and screamed, 'You hot-shit cheerleaders better leave our guys alone or you'll regret it.' And she called me—she called me—" But Veronica Myers who would one day on stage and in films utter any words, perform any actions, so long as they were prescribed for her by another, could not bring herself to pronounce the crude monosyllabic word that Lulu Lovitt had called her: we were left to imagine it, blushing.

Relations were even more strained among the boys. None of us understood how bitter friends of John Reddy's were about those members of the basketball and track teams who hadn't testified as character witnesses for John Reddy at his trial until, one afternoon as school was letting out, shortly before Christmas recess, Clyde Meunzer in black T-shirt, oily jeans, duck's-ass hair and an unlit cigarette clamped between his teeth deliberately collided with Dwayne Hewson. There was a quick exchange of words, and before Dwayne knew what was happening Clyde swung at him, saying, "Fucker, you let John down!" Dwayne staggered backward, taking the blow with a look of total astonishment, too surprised to defend himself. Though Clyde was shorter than Dwayne by at least an inch, and lighter by as much as fifteen pounds, he was built like a fire hydrant and knew how to fight; as the larger boy gaped at him, already bleeding from the mouth, Clyde threw another mean, hard overhand right at Dwayne's unprotected face, knocking him back against a row of lockers. There were cries, girls' squeals and screams. Chet Halloren, shoving his books into his locker nearby, said, "It just didn't seem like what was happening was actually happening. It was so *fast*." For possibly there hadn't been an exchange of serious blows, nothing resembling a "fistfight," at Willowsville Senior High, in our collective memory. Chet, a tall, thin, honor-roll boy with a sardonic temperament, as he'd characterize himself in our yearbook "a Diogenes-class skeptic," nonetheless tried to pull Clyde off Dwayne, and Clyde responded by butting Chet expertly in the head, opening a two-inch gash above Chet's right eye, the jagged scar of which he'd proudly exhibit for the remainder of his life—"A memento of my adolescence on the 'mean streets' of Willowsville, New York." Seeing both Dwayne and Chet sprawled on the floor, and Clyde Meunzer with clenched fists cursing them, Ken Fischer was drawn into the melee, which, despite the confusion, he'd swiftly and accurately interpreted as *us versus them*, and before he could lay a hand on Clyde Meunzer there came out of nowhere, silent as a pit bull, Orrie Buhr who grabbed him in a vicious hammerlock, threw him to the floor, and stood kicking his ribs and groin with steel-toed biker's boots. Ken would recall, afterward, how both Orrie Buhr and Clyde Meunzer were grinning. Even as they cursed their fallen, dazed victims. "They called us 'fuckface white boys'—what the hell? They're white themselves, aren't they?" Ken who'd imagined himself well-liked, a popular guy who in fact liked most other people, was profoundly shocked. Hulking boys whose names and even faces were unfamiliar to most of us, whose yearbook captions would consist of a single terse line, *Major: Industrial Arts*, rushed out of Mr. Hornby's shop classroom to join the fight, screaming revenge for John Reddy as they punched, elbowed, kicked and wrestled preppie-jock boys like Smoke Filer, Jon Rindfleisch, even Bo Bozer who more than Ken Fischer might've had reason to believe himself a friend to such guys, bloodying faces, knocking bodies against lockers and onto the floor, attacking even Bart Digger and Ritchie

Eickhorn who'd wandered naively into the danger zone, breaking Dexter Cambrook's nose, loosing Ketch Campbell's buck teeth and smashing Petey Merchant's new horn-rimmed glasses. "Stop! At once!" There came Mr. Lepage in his English tweed coat and paisley tie, clapping his hands as if the brawling six-foot boys were young children. He so startled Ray Gottardi, who was his student, by grabbing Ray's collar and dragging him backward, that Ray ceased his vicious pummeling of Ritchie Eickhorn. But then Mr. Hornby rushed up and grabbed Mr. Lepage by his coat lapel, swinging him around, growling, "What the hell's going on? You better keep your hands to yourself, Frannie." (Mr. Lepage's first name was Francis. None of us had realized until this encounter that Mr. Hornby so despised Mr. Lepage and the knowledge, like a family secret, both thrilled and disturbed us.) Blake Wells who'd begun to bring a camera to school was snapping photographs of the fight when Jake Gervasio noticed him, wrenched the camera from his fingers and smashed it against the row of lockers; when Blake dared to protest, Jake slammed him against the wall, too. ("I never knew what it meant—to 'have the wind knocked out of you,'" Blake said wonderingly. "Now I know.") Mr. Stamish came running, shouting, "Order! I command you! Now! *Boys!*" but he must have stumbled, or been pushed, for he fell sprawling to the floor, his glasses, too, thrown from his face and his necktie twisted like a noose. Ray Gottardi said afterward, laughing, "Jesus. I looked down at this guy clawing my ankles, and it was Stamish. Lucky for me the old fart can't see without his glasses."

The brawl only came to an end when Willowsville police arrived, summoned by Mr. Stamish's secretary.

Clyde Meunzer, Orrie Buhr and several other boys were singled out as ringleaders and expelled permanently from school; the rest of the vocational arts boys who'd been "actively aggressive" were placed on probation; boys who'd been victims were reprimanded, some of us thought unfairly, for "participating in barbarism and chaos" instead of seeking

help from faculty or staff. Most of us never saw Clyde
Meunzer or Orrie Buhr again. (We'd wondered where Dino
Calvo was at the time of the brawl and learned afterward that
Dino had quit school and gone to work at a factory in
Lackawanna.) Though Bo Bozer would recount for us at our
fifteenth reunion how, the previous year, he'd come back to
Willowsville with his family (a wife, two children) to visit his
mother (Bo's father, long estranged from the family, had been
dead for six years by this time); they'd driven out to a popular
farm stand on the Millersport Highway, and Bo was hauling
baskets of apples and peaches to his car when he happened to
see a man in the parking lot who looked familiar. "A tall husky
guy about my age with a fattish kid of about ten, Denny's age,
they're walking past me and the big guy sees me and a look
comes over his face—a strange look. And a few minutes later
I'm loading my car trunk, my mother and family are buckling
up in the car, and I feel a tap on my shoulder and I turn and,
Christ!—it's Orrie Buhr. He's heavier by possibly thirty
pounds. He's losing his hair as badly as I am. He hasn't shaved
that day and he's looking a little hung over. Though his acne's
cleared up, like mine, and that ratty little mustache is gone.
He's wearing a Buffalo Hawks baseball cap and so am I. I say,
'Orrie! Hello.' Whenever I run into someone from high school,
from those days, I feel so happy, so excited—hopeful, somehow. And almost a kind of dread, that there's so much emotion
I might not be able to handle—you know what I mean? Yeah.
So I'm extending my hand to shake Orrie's big hand and he
just stands there staring at me, and at my hand, like he's
smelling a bad smell, but sort of enjoying it, and he smiles and
says in a low voice so nobody else, my family in the car, his
kid standing a few yards off, can hear, 'Bozer, you fucker—you
let John down.' And Orrie shoves me with the flat of his hand
against my chest, knocks me back against the opened trunk
lid, and it *hurts*. And I have to admit, in that instant I'm *scared*.
My mother, my wife and kids are in the car possibly observing
this incident, I'm not sure, they won't mention it to me and I

won't mention it to them. What's Orrie Buhr do but turn and
walk away. Not in any hurry, either. His kid that's been waiting
and watching is looking scared, too, but proud of his daddy,
and the two of them saunter off together. I'm standing there,
by my car, shaking. I mean—seriously shaking. So flooded
with adrenaline it's like an electric current is rushing through
me, and already I know I'm going to be exhausted. I wanted to
run after Orrie Buhr and tell him, "Look, normal sane people,
adult men, don't behave like this. They don't nurse a grudge
for almost fifteen years. Like high school was yesterday. Like
'John Reddy Heart' was yesterday. I'm going to call my lawyer,
and I'm going to sue you for assault, you son of a bitch." But
I was kind of hurt, too. I'd always been John Reddy's friend—
I thought—and I'd wanted to be a character witness for him
but, God damn, my parents wouldn't let me. My mom was all
upset because of the divorce anyway, and my dad falling apart
over John Reddy's mother like he did, so I couldn't upset her
any more, but I did feel like shit over it, and maybe, just
maybe, Orrie Buhr had a point, which is why I didn't run
after him; but mainly, I have to admit, I was scared as hell of
the guy. I didn't say a thing, just shut the car trunk and
climbed into the car, behind the wheel, hoping nobody
noticed. The bottom line is, I didn't want my nose bloodied
like the other time."

* * *

Faithfully during the long year of his absence we wrote to
John Reddy Heart c/o Tomahawk Island Youth Camp. We sent
Christmas cards, birthday cards (John Reddy's birthday was
February 8). We sent small gifts including complimentary
subscriptions to the *Weekly Willowsvillian* with its columns of
febrile print celebrating our myriad activities and achieve-
ments, and to the literary journal *Will-o'-the-Wisp* devotedly
co-edited by Evangeline Fesnacht and Ritchie Eickhorn.
Though we seemed to know beforehand that John Reddy
would never respond, still less thank us. His silence did not

deter us. His indifference, his probable contempt. For there was a thrill, an actual physical tremor certain of the girls felt, composing diarylike letters of startling intimacy to a boy at Tomahawk Island Youth Camp in the late-night secrecy of our beds, when our parents believed us safely asleep, or, more recklessly, at school. *Dear John Reddy, I have been so unhappy. I think of you all the time. I think you must be lonely in that terrible place. I am so lonely here!* Our faces were bright and fever-struck. Our eyes shone defiantly. None of our friends at other high schools could make such glamorous claims— "Corresponding with a convict! A murderer!" our parents said, disapproving. Some, like Mr. Myers, were angry. Some were worried. We told them that John Reddy was no *murderer*, how could he be a *murderer*, hadn't he been *acquitted*?

It had been a jury of adult men and women who'd acquitted him, after all.

That winter there came, out of nowhere, a compulsion to knit among the more high-strung, nervous and moody girls of the Hill. One of our mothers taught us ("It's better than smoking, it gives you something to do with your hands that's useful") and within a week the fad had spread through the high school. Of course, we were in a frenzy to knit things for John Reddy Heart. Though few of us had the skill or the patience to finish the scarf we were trying to coax into being, or the gloves, or the sweater, and fewer still would dare to wrap this item and mail it to John Reddy Heart in prison. It often seemed that the agitated flashing and clicking of our metallic knitting needles, the repeated "knit, purl"—"knit, purl"—our lips shaped like a mantra, the woolen material perpetually damp from our sweaty hands, had nothing to do with an actual product, an article of clothing, or even with John Reddy. One day at a rehearsal of *Our Town* Mr. Lepage lost patience with his favorite Verrie Myers who, when she wasn't in a scene, snatched up her knitting and began agitatedly to knit, saying, "Veronica, for God's sake! What is that thing you're knitting?—whoever do you imagine would willingly wear something so *ugly*?" Verrie, lost in a trance of knitting, woke to the sound of laughter; Mr. Lepage was cruel, but funny. She began to stammer: "I'm—sorry, Mr. Lepage. I don't know what it is. It began as a sweater, a 'Scots heather cardi-gan'—but now"—Verrie stood, shaking out the thing she'd been knitting feverishly for weeks, a misshapen rectangle of mud-green wool that did not immediately suggest an article of clothing—"it's become something I'm doing because I can't stop. My fingers can't stop. I wish I could stop but I can't. *I don't know what it is*." To our drama coach's astonishment, beautiful Verrie burst into tears.

(It was that evening, Verrie would confide in us, years later, that Mr. Lepage first "touched" her—just the back of his hand, at first, against her wrist. He'd frowned at her, grave as a physician. He'd taken the misshapen sweater from her, noting with a flicker of repugnance that it was damp, and smelled of damp, from her sweaty hands; he'd set the thing aside, positioning the silver knitting needles in such a way that the knitting wouldn't slip loose. He hadn't kissed her then, but he'd framed her face in his hands and regarded her with kindly myopic eyes. Had she known at the time that the man was crazy for her, we wondered; and Verrie said, embar-rassed, "Oh, Francis was never what you'd call crazy for me, that's all been exaggerated.")

In the end, Verrie's disgusted father took the "sweater" from her and burnt it in the fireplace of their home. What became of the other girls' knitting? At our big thirtieth reunion, at a cookout at the Zwaarts', Janet Moss of all people made us laugh by showing up with a "muffler, I think," she'd been trying to knit for John Reddy; she'd found it in a trunk in her mother's house. The fad for knitting died out abruptly, leaving us exhausted, our poor fingers so strained they could hardly function as fingers.

It was known that Miss Bird regularly sent reading mater-ial to John Reddy Heart in prison, purchased from her own modest teacher's salary. She'd initiated a remedial reading course for him to take with her by mail, with the approval of the Tomahawk Island warden. She'd never gone to visit him. Perhaps he would not have consented to meet with her. She told us, hesitantly, yet with an air of quivering excitement like one betraying an old lover, "John Reddy had difficulty reading. He was probably dyslexic. That would help account for his quick temper, too. But no one knew 'dyslexic' in those days. It was believed that young people so afflicted were 'rebellious,' 'uncooperative.' 'Antisocial.'" An honored guest at our Tug Hill reunion picnics, Miss Bird spoke gravely. "My most tragic pupil."

We exchanged glances. The wistful way in which Miss Maxine Bird, now in her late sixties, spoke of the long-ago John Reddy Heart suggested she'd been in love with him, too.

17

Says John Reddy, Come ride with me!
Says John Reddy, Mmmmm baby come ride with me!
In my Caddie we'll travel the highways and we'll travel the sea!
John Reddy, John Reddy Heart.

In fact when John Reddy Heart at last returned to Willowsville, in November of our senior year, having "maxed out" at Tomahawk Island, we saw less of him than we'd seen before. He wasn't on any sport team, he wasn't assigned to any homeroom. "It's like he's in quarantine or something. Like they think he's gonna poison us." Instead of the acid-green Caddie burning rubber when John Reddy traveled certain stretches of road, he drove a beat-up Mercury purchased from his employer Mr. Farolino that was the color, as Chet Halloren meanly said, of "barely dried puke."

The surprise was, John Reddy's family didn't return to Willowsville with him. We'd expected them all to move back as if nothing had been changed, but our expectation was, as we came to realize, unrealistic. "After all he killed a man, right? His mom's lover. You can't just erase that." John Reddy didn't live in the house at 8 Meridian Place which continued to remain empty but in a rented apartment, rumored to be "pretty sad, just two small rooms" above the North China Take-Out on Water Street. (Eventually, in January of our senior year, the Heart house was sold to a Merrill Lynch executive transferring to Buffalo from Cleveland. The controversial robin's-egg-blue front door and trim disappeared as if they had never been, replaced by a tasteful dark green. Much of the lawn was dug up and replaced with sod. The executive's wife was swiftly accepted in Willowsville social circles, invited to join the Village Women's League within a month of her arrival; polite and well-mannered, she nonetheless expressed "frank exasperation" with the numerous elliptical remarks made to her about the Riggs shooting, the scandal and so forth about which she and her husband had known nothing whatsoever at the time they'd bought the house.)

It was rumored that the Heart house had been sold to pay John Reddy's legal fees. It was rumored that the Heart family was "scattered."

John Reddy worked after school and on Saturdays at Farolino's Cabinets & Carpentry as he'd done before his arrest and imprisonment. He never remained on WHS property beyond 3:20 P.M. when his last class ended. He'd been provisionally allowed by the district board of education to return as a special student who would not be participating in sports or extracurricular activities; he was even exempt from gym class. ("It's like they're trying to keep him from *me*," Coach McKeever complained bitterly. "Like maybe he hasn't been punished enough.") John Reddy had lost a year and a half of formal schooling but he'd accumulated some credits at Tomahawk Island, plus the remedial English course with Miss Bird ("He earned a B—he's a hard worker") so he was enrolled in our senior class. At the age of almost eighteen he seemed older. His features were severe, his skin coarsened. There was a scar in his left eyebrow and his left eyelid drooped slightly where, it was said, he'd been injured at the time of his arrest on Mount Nazarene. ("That eye is so sexy!" Bibi Arhardt shivered. "It's permanently bloodshot like *it sees too much*.") John Reddy no longer wore a black leather biker's jacket ("They say it was blood-splattered, he'd had to get rid of it while he was a fugitive") but a red plaid wool jacket of the kind worn by the workmen our fathers hired for carpentry or lawn service. His hair was savagely trimmed at the nape of his neck, yet grew long and uneven at the sides and top, starkly black, lank and without lustre as a horse's mane. When quills fell into his face, John Reddy was observed snapping his head roughly back, or brushing at his head with a hand, or both hands, in gestures that seemed to us both brutal and beautiful. ("It's like he wants to hurt himself," Pattianne Groves observed. "He's angry.") At Tomahawk Island, we were told, John Reddy had been beaten and "persecuted." By guards? By guards and fellow prisoners, older guys. Why? we asked and the boys told us, exchanging cryptic glances with one another, "Resisting." Resisting what? we asked. Bo Bozer moved his shoulders uncomfortably inside his WHS letter jacket, saying, "Just *resisting*. John Reddy's the kind of guy you'd have to kill to make give *in*."

Now he wasn't on the basketball or track teams, now the cheerleaders didn't scream *John Reddy we're ready! John Reddy we're rea-dy!* he was naturally known to fewer people. Even seated beside us in class, frowning hunched over a notebook, or striding through the halls, he seemed to exist on the far side of an abyss. He walked swiftly as before except now he seemed taller and more intense and few of us would have dared to fall into step beside him to attempt a one-sided conversation. So many girls called out, "Hello, John!"—"Good morning, John!"—he seemed often not to have heard, though, with a quick forced-smiling courtesy we didn't remember in him before his troubles, he'd glance up, with a nod or an inaudible murmur that sounded like "H'lo." His former teammates tried to engage him in casual conversation, saying they'd missed him, everybody'd missed him, things hadn't been the same without him, and John Reddy ducked his head, you couldn't tell if he was embarrassed for himself, or for them, and mumbled, "Yeah. Thanks." Dwayne Hewson who'd been feeling, he said, like a shit for a long time, for giving in to his old man and not testifying as a character witness for John Reddy, said, "We, uh, thought about you a lot. Last year. We . . ." His voice trailed off miserably. Bo Bozer said awkwardly, "Yeah, John. We were damned sorry about . . . you know. All that shit." And Bo Bozer too fell silent. John Reddy was at his locker, turning his combination in fierce deft spurts until it clicked open. It almost seemed he hadn't heard Dwayne and Bo, lost in his own thoughts, or was going to ignore them, his jaws clenched, his mouth working silently, then he turned, and bared his teeth in a smile, a forced-friendly smile. He seemed to be making it a point, Dwayne thought, to look them in the eye. ("And that one eye of his so fucking *bloodshot*.") He said, "Yeah. O.K. Thanks. I missed you guys, too."

Later, Dwayne told us how he, Bo and a couple of other guys from the basketball team just stood there like assholes not knowing what to say next, or whether to say anything, they'd been planning vaguely on asking John Reddy to a party that weekend but clearly he didn't want to talk, at least not at the moment, in the school corridor where people passed glancing at him, staring at him when he wasn't aware of them or even when he was, and that hurt the guys' feelings kind of, "Even assholes like us have feelings, y'know?," so they repeated to John Reddy they were glad he was back and *Let's get together soon O.K.?* and John Reddy nodded already stooped to reach into the cluttered interior of his locker, the plaid wool jacket straining across his shoulders and the nape of his neck flushed as if with emotion. Dwayne said, "It hit us that John Reddy was an adult, and we were kids. He was humoring us. He was being fucking *polite*. And him, a guy who'd blown a man away with a bullet through the skull!"

It was Katie Olmsted in her new aluminum-and-chrome wheelchair who'd been the first of us to meet John Reddy Heart when he returned, in mid-November, to WHS.

Mrs. Olmsted had driven Katie to school that morning, as she did most days now. When Katie was having a bad day it was important for her to get to school early. For months her M.S. (as Katie called it, casually—"M.S." sounded less terrifying than "multiple sclerosis") hadn't been so severe, she'd had good days when she could walk almost normally, and bad days when she needed help getting out of bed, but in the fall of our senior year she'd been pretty sick, and was using a wheelchair much of the time, entering the school "via the cripple ramp at the rear." (Katie spoke jocosely of her illness as if daring her friends not to laugh with her. "M.S." had strangely altered her personality.) It was a fact: most of us who'd been friends with Katie remained friends, girl friends that is, but most boys, especially boys who'd dated her (Larry Baumgart, Jon Rindfleisch, Ray Gottardi—that bastard) kept an awkward distance. If boys couldn't avoid speaking to Katie they were self-conscious and abashed. We were shocked to hear Katie call out, with her newfound boldness, to a knot of boys in the cafeteria one noon, "Hey guys—I'm not contagious, really! This isn't leprosy." The boys laughed nervously, embarrassed. But quickly slipped away. Verrie Myers said, incensed, "They're assholes. Don't pay any attention to them." Katie said, laughing, "Half the human race is assholes? And I'm not supposed to pay any attention to them? That might be difficult."

Mrs. Olmsted had left Katie at the rear entrance of the school just inside the door, at Katie's request. Katie had learned to operate the wheelchair with a certain flair, determined not to ask for help unless she truly needed it. We respected her independence but she tired easily sometimes, a look of fatigue came into her face that was terrible to see but, still, you had to be careful—you had to be tactful. Everyone, even teachers, had learned to wait for Katie to ask for help. "So there was this person behind me, he'd come out of Mr. Stamish's office and I sensed him looking at me, I could almost feel him about to touch me, I mean the back of the chair, and I said, 'No thanks! I'm fine!' before he could do anything or even say anything. 'O.K.,' he said. Actually there was a doorway coming up I'd possibly have trouble with, so I looked around to see who it was—and it was him. It was John Reddy Heart." Katie paused, breathing quickly. Her fair, thin skin had heated and her eyes, which were ringed with tiredness, were shining, too. Before M.S.—before John Reddy had been sent away to prison—Katie had been one of us who'd adored him from a safe distance. And she'd had her dream-vision of John Reddy after his trial, of which we'd been jealous. She'd written letters to him, intimate diary-letters which possibly she hadn't mailed, and she'd knitted for him, doggedly and devotedly and not without a sense of humor, a gnarly misshapen muffler in the school colors, maroon and gold, which certainly she hadn't sent. She was telling us, breathlessly, the words rushing from her, "It was his first day back. He'd gotten here early, too. He has to report to Mr. Stamish's office every morning at eight-thirty—he isn't assigned a homeroom. Or a study hall. As if he'd contaminate us! He won't be going to assemblies, he said. Or pep rallies, or games. Anything 'extracurricular.' He just wants to get enough credits to graduate next June. They've given him a 'desk' in Miss Crosby's office, he told me, just a table he can use to work at. In shop, where he's learning carpentry, auto repair, drafting, he has a workbench at the back of the room. 'You sound like a leper, John, just like me,' I said. (Yes, I called him John. By now he was pushing me in the chair, sort of gliding me along, and it was O.K. It was like magic. Like I could do it perfectly well myself, which of course I can, but was allowing him to push me, like a favor between friends.) 'Hey, don't say that about yourself, Katie,' he said—I'd told him my name quickly so it wouldn't come out he didn't know my name and we'd both be embarrassed—'that's not a good thing to say.' His voice sounded hurt. It's a low, serious, somber voice not like a kid's but a man's. I said, 'Who cares what's a "good" thing to say, since getting sick I've had enough of "good" things said to me that are ninety percent phony.' I couldn't see John Reddy's face but I sensed he didn't like this, either. We were almost at Miss Bird's room. He'd gone out of his way to push me there, I guess, though that wasn't clear to me at the time. I guess I was sort of—excited. Upset. Maybe crying a little. He came around in front of me and took my hands, lifted my hands from my lap where I was holding my books, I was too surprised to pull away, I was too surprised to say anything, John Reddy turned my hands over and saw the palms, the little scars in my palms, I could hardly look at his face, his eyes were so bright it hurt me to see them. He said, 'You are not a leper, Katie, and neither am I.' I was crying now I guess. I was saying, angry, 'Yes yes I am, God damn it I am, I am a leper, John Reddy, and so are you,' and John Reddy said softly, 'Do you think Jesus was a leper, Katie? Maybe Jesus was a leper, too.'

"He'd opened Miss Bird's door so I could roll myself inside, he said goodbye and when I looked around he was gone."

* * *

Do you think Jesus was a leper? immediately began to be whispered among us. Even by those who didn't know that John Reddy Heart had uttered the words, or in what circumstances. (Of course, Katie Olmsted would claim the circumstances: "It was a revelation to *me*. Like Jesus was speaking to *me*." Never again would she surrender to "dark desolating despair. Never!") Clearly, John Reddy's words were a riddle. They were our responsibility to cherish if not to fully comprehend. *Maybe Jesus was a leper, too.* Secret talismanic words fastidiously recorded in school notebooks, scrawled inside lockers and in flaming lipstick in the toilet stalls of girls' restrooms not only at school but throughout the village and into Amherst as well. In those days, a surprising number of us prayed. We must have believed that God was attentive and basically sympathetic. We shut our eyes, our lips moved silently. *Was Jesus a leper, too? Like me? Maybe Jesus was a leper, too.* Of all of us, only Blake Wells, in his late twenties a Peace Corps medical worker in Kenya, assigned to a leprosarium, would resist the metaphor—"Lepers are just sick people. Nothing special."

Months after John Reddy Heart had pushed Katie Olmsted in her wheelchair, in May of our senior year, Reverend Ogden, the youthful middle-aged minister of the Willowsville Unitarian Church, preached a poetic sermon titled "Maybe Jesus Was a Leper, Too"—one of Reverend Ogden's most stirring and inspirational sermons, the consensus was.

Unknown to our parents we'd begun, in November of that year, to cruise the lower village after dark. Where we had no more purpose in being than we'd have had in gritty downtown Buffalo. Like guys cruising the strip looking for Cheektowaga girls to pick up. Looking for trouble. Except we weren't looking for trouble but seeking John Reddy Heart.

"Oh God! I'd want to die if anyone found out. If *he* found out."

"*He* wouldn't ever tell."

We were sick with apprehension, for we were good girls. We were breathless! ashamed! thrilled by our own audacity! Our destination was Water Street, south of Main. The shadowy downside of the jewel-box village. Where, above the perpetually steamy windows of the North China Take-Out which no one we knew ever patronized, John Reddy Heart, our classmate, lived alone as no other student at Willowsville Senior High lived alone. As no other seventeen-year-old of our acquaintance lived alone.

"It wasn't just that. Not just him. It was"—the wounded middle-aged woman with the girlish lined face who'd startled us by insisting she was Shelby Connor, "Shelby Connor formerly Simms," would one day attempt to explain to us a mysterious facet of our own experience—"it was being drawn like moths to that tender, almost inexpressible moment at the end of the day when lights come on, headlights, streetlights, store-window lights, lights inside houses, the moon, the stars—and the world isn't a place of solids any longer, not

brick, not stone, not concrete, not wood, but a place of magic
held together by lights. Remember?—we'd drive down from
the Hill into John Reddy's neighborhood and there everything
would be *dark*, would be *night*. And, if his window was
lighted—"

Unknown to our parents. Unknown to our fathers who
loved us too much to trust us, or to trust the world with us.
Virgin daughters of Willowsville, New York, soon to leave
home but, that final high school year, living still beneath their
protective roofs. In their heavily mortgaged homes in tree-
lined residential neighborhoods, on costly soil. "If Daddy
finds out about this he'll *kill me*. I'm *not joking*." "*I'm* not
joking. *My* dad would *kill me*!" We laughed together. We
shivered. In the crowded back seat of Verrie's car, four of us,
or were there five of us, clutched at one another's icy fingers.
Descending south on Main Street, passing the seductively
lighted store windows of the Avenue of Fashion, those glimmering mirages with the power to evoke in our dreams of the
next forty years, and beyond, that quicksilver emotion of
hope, elation, certainty and well-being perhaps found solely
in dreams. We'd been talking of John Reddy Heart, what we'd
heard of him in recent days. How at Farolino's Cabinets &
Carpentry he worked in silence at the back of the shop for
hours. Mr. Farolino, who tended toward garrulousness, had
learned not to bother him. But there were customers who
came into the shop, inquisitive, cruel. Staring at him.
Whispering to Mr. Farolino ("Is that the boy who—? Is
that—John Reddy Heart? *Here?*") and sometimes even speaking to John Reddy themselves, asking how his mother was?
his family? what his plans were for after graduation?—and
John Reddy muttered a reply, or continued working in "dignified silence." One asshole, it was told to us by Bart Digger,
actually asked John Reddy "what's it like at that place you
were in?—'Indian Island'?" but it wasn't known how John
Reddy responded. There was a report that came to us from
Mary Louise Schultz's mother who'd heard it from Agnes

Scroop who was a close friend of our guidance counselor Miss Crosby: evidently John Reddy had hoped to join the Air Force after graduation, his father had been in the Air Force and died in active duty—"But that's out of the question now, of course. The U.S. armed services don't allow anyone in with a *criminal record*. An *ex-convict*." Hearing this cruel, crude bit of news, we wiped angrily at our eyes. "Oh God. John Reddy. They're making a martyr of him." "A leper, you mean." "A leper! Yes."

And there was another report of a curious remark of John Reddy he'd allegedly made in Mr. Salaman's geometry class that morning—"Just to prove something doesn't mean it's true." Mr. Salaman had spent fifteen minutes at the blackboard working out the solution to a Byzantine homework problem in his flamboyant, ironic manner, and when he'd finished, gloating at the expressions of bewilderment and panic in his students' faces, John Reddy, who was seated, as in all his classes except shop, in the first row, extreme right, to be under the teacher's eagle eye, shifted his long legs violently beneath his desk and muttered skeptically, "Just to prove something doesn't mean it's *true*." Mr. Salaman had stared at John Reddy, as rarely he glanced in John Reddy's direction, disliking him, or fearing him, his adult presence amid adolescent presences: Mr. Salaman seemed to be debating a reply, one of his quick quippy put-down replies, then thought better of it. None of his WHS teachers cared to confront John Reddy Heart in their classrooms.

Richard Eickhorn would record John Reddy's enigmatic remark in *America I Hear Your Heart Breaking*—"Just to prove something doesn't mean it's true." Ritchie didn't credit John Reddy Heart with the statement but it was set off in quotes at the start of a section and we all recognized it of course. In fact, Ketch Campbell whose desk was close by John Reddy's claimed that John Reddy had actually said, in exasperation, "Shit. Just to prove something doesn't mean it's *true*." Ray Gottardi had claimed that John Reddy had said, loud enough for everyone in the room to hear, "Bullshit! Just to prove something doesn't mean it's *true*." Steve Lunt who was in the class that morning, one of only three students who'd been able to crack the homework problem, dismissed John Reddy's remark as "illogical. Nothing can be 'proved' as true unless it is true." But Clarence McQuade who was taking advanced calculus with Mr. Sternberg, another WHS math teacher, claimed that John Reddy's remark was "profound—if Heart knew what he was saying."

Later that night it would rain, and the rain would turn to sleet but now a bone-bright moon glowed overhead.

How the moon drew us. And the wind!

We were impressed that Verrie drove her new car so capably. Not missing a single green light on Main Street. We weren't envious of Verrie, we loved her car: the four-door canary-yellow Olds convertible her parents had given her for her sixteenth birthday. It glittered like a sleek Christmas-tree ornament. Its interior was butterscotch-colored leather soft as skin and smelling of newness so rich and so sharp it took your breath away. "A beautiful car for a beautiful girl," Mr. Myers had said, winking at us, as he'd handed the keys to Verrie in our presence. We knew that, in time, we'd all be given cars for our birthdays. This was Willowsville, we were Willowsville girls. Our fathers strove, like suitors, to please us even as they despaired of controlling us. So we weren't envious of Verrie Myers, we loved her car and would remember it all our lives: the plush seats, the low seductive hum of the motor, the dashboard lights like code, the radio turned low to WWBN-AM "Radio Wonderful" playing the Top Pop Fifty hour after hour, a new hit single "Broke Heart Blues" we sang at the top of our lungs. Verrie, teary-eyed, shouted, "Somebody pass me a cig, will you?—*I'm dying for one*."

We were passing Spring Street. The darkened Sunoco station with its wind-whipped banners. Darkened Burnham Nurseries where, one summer, some of us had glimpsed John

Reddy Heart shirtless, tanned dark as an Indian, working in the sun. And now we were passing North Long, and now turning onto Water Street, narrow, potholed, leading downhill to a bumpy plank bridge above Glen Creek. Mist rose from the creek like dread in our bowels. "It's kind of—crazy, isn't it? Maybe we shouldn't—" "Will you please just shut *up*." We were not thinking of our fathers whose voices murmured warnings of impotent rage in our ears. *If I ever catch you. If I ever hear of. That boy. That criminal. That white trash. If you disobey me. If you, my daughter. If.* Instead we were thinking: Would John Reddy Heart be home? Upstairs in his apartment? If home, would he pass by a window? If he passed by a window, would he look out? Look down? At the street, at us? Would he recognize us? Should we call to him? Would we dare call to him?

There was the shabby sandstone apartment building, there the North China Take-Out. There, John Reddy's battered old Mercury at the curb. "He's home."

His windows were lighted. No turning back.

Verrie jolted the car to a stop at the curb. We stared as a shadow-silhouette passed fleetingly by the window. "It's— him." "*Him.*" "We'd better leave. We—" Yet we were outside on the sidewalk. Frantically we whispered, clutching at one another; the wind blew our words away. We laughed. Hysteria touched us like quick-darting flames. One of us, it might have been Verrie, framed her mouth with her cupped fingers and called out softly, thrillingly, "John? John Reddy?" One of us slapped her. One of us backed blindly away and collided with something, a trash can, which toppled, making a clattering noise on the sidewalk. A couple leaving the North China glanced at us before driving off. Had we been recognized? We hid our heated faces. John Reddy's window overhead had been yanked up by six inches. "Who the hell's there?"—we saw him leaning out the window, looking down. His hair hung forward partly hiding his face. We huddled together to hide our nakedness. Verrie fumbled for her car keys, they slipped through her fingers to fall to the pavement. We panicked hearing John Reddy's footsteps on the stairs. And the door opened and he leaned out, staring at us. He scratched with a thumbnail at his chest. He wore a T-shirt, jeans. Bluish stubble covered his jaws. He was breathing quickly, his breath just perceptibly visible as steam. When had it begun to rain, when had the rain turned to sleet, when had the bright moon disappeared? A jocose wind blew grit and scraps of paper into our pretty-girl faces. John Reddy stared at us, each in turn, possibly recognizing us, possibly not. It was inconceivable that several of us, varsity cheer-leaders, had once boldly chanted, in the company of hundreds of screaming spectators as well as John Reddy Heart and his sweaty teammates, "John Reddy we're ready! JOHN REDDY WE'RE RE-ADY!" for we were not ready and could not, outside the lighted basketball court, outside the contained delirium of the game, have dared such an invitation.

There was nowhere to hide. In his warm bemused Texan drawl John Reddy said, "Well, shit. C'mon up. I sure wasn't expecting company tonight, but—" As if practiced in this maneuver, John Reddy didn't lead the way up the narrow flight of stairs to his apartment but stood on the sidewalk herding us, one by one, before him. We were silent, terrified. We could not even glance at each other. We fled upward like birds whose wings have failed them. At the top of the stairs we stepped into a bright blinding space—"Like the way you feel taking nitrous oxide at the dentist's. That terrible sick-excited sensation of letting go. Of not being able to not let go. You're not asleep but you're not conscious, either. You're paralyzed. You're not yourself. You're deeper somehow." John Reddy Heart closed the door behind us so gently we failed to hear the *click!* of the lock. Or, if we heard it, we heard it belatedly, as an echo. There was a faint throbbing sound of music. Not words, only music. Already he'd taken one of us by the hand. Drew her to him, and took both hands. "Hey look. Don't be scared. Nobody's gonna make you do anything you don't want to do, O.K.?" The light was blinding but warm and comforting. You seemed to understand that, though everything was bathed in light, you would not be seen; you would not be recognized. John Reddy laughed at us but in a kindly way. He led one of us, possibly Verrie, though it may have been Trish Elders, into the next room, we understood that it was John Reddy's bedroom. Quietly, the door was shut behind them. Frightened, not daring to glance at one another (as in the girls' locker room at school some of us shrank from glancing at one another out of modesty or out of an emotion stronger and less definable than modesty) we hurriedly removed our clothes. Our sweaters, shirts, skirts from the Tartan Shoppe. Our rayon panties, our white cotton bras. Only then, trembling, did we dare raise our eyes to one another. What beautiful bodies! Our faces were blurred but our bodies were curiously illuminated, pearly-pale, slender yet well-shaped, breasts, nipples, the rosy-brown aureole surrounding the nipples, the crescent of shadow beneath each breast. We stared at our perfect bellies, the lovely curve of our thighs and hips. The fluffy tracery of pubic hair—pale on several of us, dark on others. We hadn't guessed how beautiful we were. John Reddy had returned, and was leading another of us into his bedroom. "Anytime you want me to, I'll stop. O.K.?" We were laughing, clutching at one another. We couldn't seem to catch our breaths! There were more of us here in John Reddy's apartment than we'd believed. Six of us, or seven. Maybe eight. Ten? A dozen? One of them was Bibi Arhardt who was like a sister to us, the kind of sister you quarrel with, but you love, though Bibi wasn't a member of the Circle and never could be. Another was Katie Olmsted, on her feet, not in her wheelchair, her body as healthy-looking as any of ours though she moved unsteadily, needing to support herself on our arms. John Reddy was in the room with us, and John Reddy was gone from us. John Reddy kissed us gently each in turn and led us one by one into the other room. There too, unexpectedly, was a blinding warm light. One of us halted just inside the doorway, stammering, "I'm afraid. I—" and John Reddy said gently, "O.K., then we won't, honey." She whispered, "Don't send me away, John Reddy," and John Reddy laughed. "O.K., honey. You bet I won't send you away." John Reddy's warm mouth, John Reddy's warm hands, John Reddy's warm lean muscular naked body covered in dark hairs swirling thick and damp on his torso, at his groin and thighs. John Reddy's erect blood-engorged penis sprouting like a strange, ripe fruit at his groin. "I'm afraid, don't hurt me, don't send me away, John Reddy? Please?"

It went on like that, through the night. A November wind blew wild and pitiless sweeping across the lake from Canada and making John Reddy's windows shudder in their frames.

18

John Reddy jumped in that ol' Caddie and floored 'er.
John Reddy said, Man I'm gone from here.
We looked   we looked   we looked
John Reddy was gone from here.
John Reddy, John Reddy Heart.

Not the Caddie of course which he'd lost to the cops and to the natural course of oblivion, instead the low-slung rustbucket no-color old Mercury he'd bought from Mr. Farolino, his employer, for (Ray Gottardi told us, marveling) just $250—"Of course, John did a lot of work on the fucker." Essentially, though, the words of the song got it right, he drove out of our lives without saying good-bye, didn't even come to graduation to accept his diploma and shake hands with Mr. Stamish. Nor did John Reddy come to the senior prom. We waited, waited, we're still waiting. "We'd elected him King. Even if it didn't work out. And if it had worked out, he wouldn't have been there. *I'd have a hard time forgiving that.*" It was a delirious time. A roller-coaster ride. Some of us, three of us, fell off, died. (Smoke's date survived, with "extensive facial cosmetic surgery.") That final year at WHS, senior year. Our final year as our truest selves "spilling gold coins from our pockets" (as the poem says). Couldn't catch our breaths! Some of our teachers chided us: *Slow down!* We were dazed, mesmerized. The future rushing at us like a windstorm—dazzling blinding light. We were excited, we were terrified. "You kids. Sweet dumb kids. If you only knew. But—you don't." Suzi Zeigler was catatonic with humiliation when her dad drifted into the rec room, drink in hand, watery-eyed, in what looked like flannel pajama top, wrinkled Bermuda shorts, none of us knew how to answer, smiling miserably *H'lo, Mr. Z., how's it going Mr. Z., yes sir things are O.K.* We figured Suzi'd been keeping it a deep dark secret her dad had been canned from his lawyer job at Lackawanna Steel, you had to feel sorry for her but that didn't make it any easier on us. It was harder to figure out Bart Digger's attitude—his father was being transferred to Peoria, Illinois, which sounded like a bad joke, and Bart was telling his friends he didn't care, he was going away to college next year anyway, he'd been admitted to Yale, why should he give a shit if his family moves to Peoria, Illinois—"It isn't as if things won't be coming to an end in Willowsville anyway," Bart said bitterly. (Why was Bart so bitter? His closest friend Clarence McQuade knew: he'd fallen ridiculously in love with the most elusive, inaccessible girl of the Circle—Veronica Myers. "One of those girls who wouldn't piss on you if you were on fire," Clarence said with a mean grin.) Bo Bozer's dad was gone from Willowsville. Shelby Connor's dad, only forty-four, had a minor heart attack and was back home again with his family, and Shelby was enthusiastic about that—"At least, now, we know where Daddy *is*." Irma Skelton and Laetitia Riggs shocked their women friends by entering into a partnership to open the Hat Box, a boutique selling "quality ladies' hats" in Amherst. The saddest news was of Elise Petko's mother, a PTA officer, ovarian cancer at the age of forty-six and she was gone within six weeks, already in a coma when news came of Elise's full-tuition scholarship to Barnard—"Mom would've been so proud," Elise said, stunned with grief. "Maybe, somehow, she knows?" We comforted Elise whom we'd never liked, much, until now; we invited her to have lunch with us in the school cafeteria, even to join us in our booth at the Crystal, shielding her thin tearstruck face from inquisitive eyes. In time, we'd cajole Dexter Cambrook into asking Elise to the senior prom guessing that neither would have a date anyway and why not the two of them, Elise and Dexter, class brains with chipmunk teeth, horn-rimmed glasses and halitosis? We laughed fondly imagining the two trying to kiss good night holding their breaths. It was an era of erotic fever and confusion. From the first day John Reddy Heart returned to us, pushing Katie Olmsted's wheelchair along the hall to Miss Bird's homeroom, there was a sense of excited disorientation of the kind one might imagine on a sinking, shifting ocean vessel. Rumors of kissing, petting and "going all the way—almost" circulated continuously, often detached from specific individuals, identities. As if such actions, committed in privacy, might be anonymous; or attached to anyone. You would hear, Monday morning, that, Saturday night, half the basketball team had made out with half the cheerleading squad in Sandi Scott's swimming pool—"Most of the water was splashed up onto the *tiles*. Rubbers were floating *everywhere*, even outside on the *lawn*." Yet you would hear that Sandi Scott was one of several girls involved in "practically an orgy" at Roger Zwaart's house, while Roger Zwaart, or some guy who looked just like him, and Millie LeRoux, or some girl who looked just like her, were "all over each other, shameless" in the back row of the Glen Theatre during the late showing of *Bonnie and Clyde*. Mr. Stamish was overheard pleading with the youngest secretary in his office, for a date; Coach McKeever and Heidi Flechsenhauer, the girls' gym teacher, were overheard in a lovers' quarrel in the gym after hours; Miss Bird, her hair ever redder and her high heels ever spikier, was reportedly sighted with certain married male colleagues, Mr. Lepage, Mr. Dunleddy, even white-haired Mr. Sternberg, who walked with a cane, in such obscure public places as the Erie Canal Historic Museum in Lockport and the *Maid of the Mist* excursion boat at Niagara Falls. It was reported to us by Jenny Thrun, who played flute and often attended chamber music concerts in Buffalo, that, one

evening, Miss Bird, Mr. Dunleddy and John Reddy Heart were
together at Kleinhans Music Hall for an evening of Beethoven
quartets. Another evening, Jon Rindfleisch's parents saw Miss
Bird, Mr. Dunleddy and "that Heart boy, the murderer" having
dinner together at the Hungarian Village, a popular restaurant
on Swan Street, Buffalo—"The Bird woman Jon says is so
eccentric was gripping both the men's hands and looking at
them with such intensity! Like they were some strange sinister *family*." Larry Baumgart was leaving his dentist's office in
the Amherst Dental Center when, he claimed, he saw Miss
Bird and John Reddy entering another office—"Sort of hurrying inside like they didn't want to be seen. It makes sense,
John Reddy's teeth would be in pretty bad shape after
Tomahawk Island, right?" One afternoon in the late fall
Dexter Cambrook was half hidden behind a fence casually
watching the girls' hockey team practice behind school, the
sky was like a gray washboard overhead, there was a cold
breeze yet the girls were perspiring, galloping along the field
like Valkyries in their maroon shorts and hooded school jer-
seys, calling and laughing to one another, Dexter was certain
he wasn't spying on the girls though perhaps he'd singled out
Pattianne Groves to follow with his admiring eyes, how
impressive a hockey player she was, in her position as forward, her long wavy auburn hair pulled back into a ponytail
swinging wildly as she ran, the straight-cut bangs across her
perfect forehead blown by the wind, Dexter's heart lurched as
he noted winglike patches of damp on Pattianne's back, soaking delicately through her jersey, he was gazing dreamily at
the girl who'd seemed to have emerged angellike out of the
stampeding horde of her teammates, an angel of wrath with
her flashing hockey stick, her luminous eyes narrowed to
slits, her lovely knees flashing points of light, her sturdy, long
feet in grimy white ankle-high sneakers thudding in the frost-
stubbled grass, Dexter felt her charging spirit rush through
him with the happiness and certitude of love, *I have no need to
tell her, I have no need to tell anyone, I have no need to be loved*

in return—and in the next instant he was on the ground, out cold. "Something hit me on the side of the head and I was down. It felt like a small rock. A rock traveling at the speed of light. They said I had a concussion, I must've been out cold, but I seemed to know what was happening, I heard cries and screams, I heard *her* voice—'Oh God, it's who? Dexter Cambrook!'—she was crouched over me panting and staring, her hockey stick clutched in both hands, she was saying, 'Oh my God, is he dead? Did I kill him? Dexter, wake up!' I saw tears in her eyes, I saw her bite her lower lip, poor Pattianne was so frightened, so sorry, I tried to smile, I was able to move my lips, 'It's O.K., Pattianne, if you killed me, I don't mind, I love you.' And then Miss Flechsenhauer took over, and the rest is history." Dexter was carried in to school and revived and afterward taken to Amherst General for X rays. It would seem to him that, judging from Pattianne Groves's subsequent behavior, her polite, slightly embarrassed friendliness, that she hadn't heard him declare he loved her; perhaps he hadn't spoken aloud; though he was certain he'd been conscious. In recounting the story, years and eventually decades later, Dexter would insist he remembered Pattianne kneeling beside him and touching—"Stroking, almost"—his forehead; and that it had been worth it, the pain, the shock, the swelling that would be the size of an auk's egg; but a more reliable witness, Bunny Cornish, Pattianne's teammate, flatly denied that Pattianne had touched Dexter—"Pattianne's dad was a litigator, she'd have known not to touch her victim. Anyway, poor Dex was out *cold*. His eyeballs had rolled around in his head so what you were looking at was *white grapes*. Ugh!" Though angry at Mary Louise Schultz for dropping him, to resume dating suave Smoke Filer who now drove a sexy red Thunderbird, Art Lutz continued to dream helplessly of her and to stare after her, at school, with such an expression of dopey longing, his own buddies hadn't the heart to laugh at him. Art was desperately dating a succession of girls, purposefully not-nice girls like Tessa Maypole who'd reputedly put out for the entire first-string football team; he parked with Tessa in his dead brother Jamie's Dodge Castille for hours; but though Tessa would allow Art to touch, caress, fondle and occasionally stroke her breasts, which had the bouncy texture of melon-sized rubber balls, she never allowed him to proceed any further, and he had to content himself with trying to pretend she was Mary Louise—"You'd think, abstractly, that if girls' breasts are approximately the same size they'd be identical breasts for all practical purposes but, God damn, they're *not*." Of his hurt, frustration and adolescent fury Art Lutz would cultivate such sidesplitting hilarity we'd elect him class clown by twice as many ballots as his nearest rival Nosepicker Nordstrom; as many as thirty-five years later certain of his ex-WHS classmates, female as well as male, would still impulsively telephone Art with the plea, "Make me laugh, Artie! I'm scared I won't make it through the night. Can you still do 'Daffy Duck Stamish at assembly'? Please." Jon Rindfleisch, whose father owned Rindfleisch Realtors, Willowsville's premier real estate agency with which Dahlia Heart had listed the house at 8 Meridian Place, "borrowed" the keys to the notorious house from the office in the brief interval after the Hearts moved their furnishings out and the new owners from Cleveland moved in; though Jon warned her never, never to tell anyone, "my old man would break my ass if he knew," his girl Deedee Drummond, a gumcracking business major junior from south of Garrison Road, boasted to her girlfriends of how Jon, a rich man's son, took her on a tour by flashlight of the big old mansion on the hill where Mel Riggs had been shot dead, and made love to her not once but several times on the very floor of Dahlia Heart's bedroom where there were, Deedee swore, "actual bloodstains in the wood you could see if you knew what to look for! It was *far out*, it was *sick*, but it was *fantastic*." (Jon must have taken Polaroids of this allegedly bloodstained floor for, for a week or so, pictures of bare floorboards were passed among us with an air of lewd if puzzled excitement, described as "the place where *it happened*." In the dim lighting, it wasn't clear whether there were bloodstains in the floorboards or simply stainlike shadows.) In December, at a performance of *Our Town*, Dwayne Hewson, captain of the football team and class vice president, came to the stunning realization, watching Verrie Myers in her luminous portrayal of the girl-heroine Emily, that he was probably in love with her, and not with Pattianne Groves, his pretty, devoted girlfriend; he'd probably been in love with Verrie since kindergarten at the Academy Street School, when the willful little blond-headed girl had stolen his Crayolas, torn his coloring book and made him cry; but, shrewdly, for Dwayne was a quarterback by instinct, he decided to remain at a distance from her—"I knew how that neurotic doll had fucked up poor Ken, and I didn't want it to happen to *me*." And it didn't: through the decades, Verrie never guessed. "And that's the best way." For there was brainy Dexter Cambrook mooning over Pattianne Groves, who half the time made Dwayne restless, she was so normal, so healthy, so *good*, and there was Dougie Siefried stuck on Ginger McCord who was stuck on John Reddy Heart, staring at the guy glassy-eyed in Mr. Cuthbert's fifth-period social studies class; there was poor Roger Zwaart, Dwayne's friend he'd about given up on, determined to date any slut who'd put out for him, or possibly just jack him off, or allow it to be believed that such was occurring, and regularly, to exact revenge on Suzi Zeigler for dropping him for, inexplicably, Norm Zeiga the transfer from Niagara County everybody thought was "kind of weird but O.K., maybe." There was Ritchie Eickhorn, a brain like Cambrook, writing embarrassing love poems, mooning over some girl you had to know wouldn't "piss on him if he was on fire" as the guys laughingly said, a favorite expression, so Artie Lutz cracked us up at the Haven jumping up in the booth and protesting loud enough for every other patron to hear, "Yes! Yes she would! Mary Louise Schultz thinks that much of me, you assholes, she would piss on me if I was on fire, you just ask her!" There was that cynical shrimp Bart Digger in love with, probably, like Ritchie, one or another of the snobby girls of the Circle. There was Ken Fischer himself, Dwayne's good friend, who'd "given up on other girls, I kind of think Verrie needs me," though it was clear that Verrie, flying on diet Coke and (possibly) diet pills, was obsessed with John Reddy Heart, hinting that something meaningful had passed between them, "I can't say," despite the fact that, at school, she and John Reddy were never seen together, and if Verrie hurried breathlessly between classes to pass by John Reddy and flash him an anxious muted version of her trademark cheerleader smile, John Reddy took no notice. It was believed that Ken Fischer was the only individual of more than four hundred WHS students who seemed not to have heard titillating rumors of "something weird going on" between Mr. Lepage and his star actress Verrie, angrily denied by Verrie's girlfriends but promulgated by others including Sandi Scott who surprised the guilty couple in the rehearsal room late one afternoon— "The lights weren't exactly out in there but *almost!*" Sandi told us breathlessly. "Mr. Lepage and Verrie were standing in a funny way, sort of too close together, and when I came in both of them *jumped*! Verrie's lipstick was gone, I swear, and Mr. Lepage, you know how his hair's so perfect, it was kind of mussed, and his necktie was crooked, and he was breathing funny and his *eyes!*—I said, 'Uh, gee, excuse me!' and backed out. *And nobody called after me.*" Art Lutz and that greaser Stan Kurschman got into a fistfight, allegedly over Tessa Maypole, and Art's nose was broken. Deedee Drummond's older brother Seth who'd graduated a few years ahead of us and worked at Curtiss Wright showed up to "beat the shit out of Rindfleisch" but failed to find him—Jon was hiding terrified in the trunk of Smoke's Thunderbird. And the guys wouldn't spring him for hours, driving all over hell hitting potholes, laughing like hyenas. Sallie Vetch, a junior business major, quit school abruptly—"She's p.g. You wanna bet?" We started a rumor that Ketch Campbell whose prick was approximately the size of, in Chet Halloren's cruel words, "a tumescent snail," was the father. Ketch cracked us up vigorously denying it. Blake Wells decided not to kill himself by overdosing on his mother's barbiturates when he was turned down by Harvard, Princeton, Yale in a single hellish mail delivery but accepted by the University of Michigan (where he'd excel, win awards and fall seriously in love); instead, as an *acte gratuit*, he sent one dozen long-stemmed yellow roses anonymously to his rival Evangeline Fesnacht who'd recently won a *Buffalo Evening News*–sponsored high school essay contest in which Blake himself had placed fifth. "I figured, what the hell. The universe is without meaning anyway." Katie Olmsted woke to good days, and to bad days. The course of her disease, if it was a disease, was wayward and capricious. Sometimes she walked "almost normally—you could hardly tell" and sometimes she had to use the damned wheelchair. "I need to believe that Jesus has faith in me. That He still loves me." On those days when Mrs. Olmsted delivered Katie to school fifteen minutes early, in the wheelchair, Katie was observed lingering in the first-floor corridor near the principal's office; but John Reddy seemed rarely to appear; instead there was, unexpectedly, little Petey Merchant whom Katie had never given a second glance at when she'd been well. "Isn't it *sweet*! It won't matter that Petey's practically a midget, he towers over Katie in that chair." The air in the boys' and girls' johns grew porous, bluish with smoke. We broke our fingernails trying to shove up the window in the upstairs girls'. Smoking was forbidden on school premises except for the faculty lounge where the air was blue with smoke. You could hear old Schoppa hacking halfway down the hall—"That's a rhinoceros?" And Dunleddy clearing his throat like he was bringing up gravel. Mme. Picholet smoked a classy gold-packed French brand. Even ruddy-cheeked Miss Flechsenhauer smoked: Bo Bozer boasted she'd bummed a cig from him one day when they were leaving school at the same time—"Like one guy to another. The broad's *cool*." We smoked surreptitiously in the cafeteria. We smoked in our cars. Butts were strewn everywhere on the parking lot pavement. They floated, swollen like grotesque white worms, in puddles. Alistair in his thick Scots accent fumed that butts were tossed down the basement stairs—"It looks like the inside of a vacuum cleaner bag. D'ye rich spoiled brats live like this at home?" We smoked surreptitiously in Friday morning assembly, if the lights were dimmed for a film. We smoked while necking, exhaling smoke in one another's mouths with languorous sensual abandon. We smoked while petting, to use the clinical expression, to climax, groaning and scattering glowing ashes over one another's disheveled clothing. Sometimes our cigarettes leapt from our fingers to tumble, to roll, to smolder invisibly beneath car seats. Between the cushions of rec room sofas. The tale was told through school on Monday morning of how, on Saturday night, Babs Bitterman's hair caught fire in the back seat of Art Lutz's funky Dodge. Unless it was Jenny Thrun's hair, in the back seat of Smoke Filer's Thunderbird. Scottie Baskett complained with a clumsy wink that his Corvette had a "real disadvantage—no backseat." We loved being addicted to nicotine. It made us adults overnight. It made us into our parents yet it was our secret from them—it was perfect! In Verrie Myers's canary-yellow Olds convertible cruising lower Willowsville at dusk, at night, in rain-pelting November wind, in yellow-tinctured fog, in a brisk falling snow, in snowfall like clumps of white blossoms, in subzero crystalline air that froze your eyelashes, like a ghost ship under a spell to forever cruise the lower village, Water Street south of Main, in Verrie's beautiful birthday car, we smoked. Avidly, anxiously. Passing a pack of Winstons. Passing Verrie's platinum-plated lighter. "I guess we thought we'd live forever." "So what? You don't live forever." Even Ginger McCord whose surgeon-grandfather, a three-pack-a-day man for thirty-eight years, who'd died of lung cancer—"Such a long time ago, I was just a baby. I really don't remember Grandpa too well." Even Roger Zwaart whose father had had a lung removed in September and would die twelve days after Roger's graduation in June. Even Norm Zeiga whose father had emphysema. "It's something to do with your hands. It's cool." Bo Bozer and Tommy Nordstrom picked up some weed, as they called it, in downtown Buffalo, and overnight half the senior class was smoking dope. You could buy it at the Wheatfield Mall, at Transittown, at a half-dozen places near the U-B campus and along the strip. Within a decade junior high kids would be buying it in Willowsville, plus acid, speed and selected downers, but not just yet. Tommy Nordstrom told of easing up to John Reddy Heart who was washing his hands in one of the lavatories at school, meaning to be friendly, offering him a joint, and how John Reddy "cut his eyes at me like I'd farted or something. He says, 'Get away from me with that shit. That shit is illegal. You could get into serious trouble with that shit.' I started laughing, and Bo's with me, he starts laughing, we're naturally thinking John Reddy must be kidding, this guy who'd offed Melvin Riggs, but he isn't kidding evidently, he turns and walks out of the john. Jezuz." Tommy wiped his face on his sleeve as if he'd come close to some sort of grave danger. Ken Fischer said, "He's on probation, isn't he? He's scared of going back to prison." The word *scared* hovered strangely in the air, we did not associate John Reddy with *scared* in any way, and so the word was not acknowledged. Possibly, we resented Ken for uttering it. John Reddy did smoke, of course. When he was on the basketball and track teams he'd "cut down"—like other guys on the teams who smoked—but in general he'd smoked Lucky Strikes since sixth grade at least. We remembered, some of us, from the Academy Street School—"John Reddy had a cigarette in his mouth when he climbed up onto the roof, didn't he? That time he freaked us all out by *disappearing*." We would've liked to ask John Reddy if Luckies were the brand of choice for inmates at Tomahawk Island, but we were wary, thinking that such a question, however well-intentioned, might be misinterpreted by John Reddy. For it seemed possible to insult John Reddy without intending it. He was cool, he was detached from us, but, for sure, nobody wanted to insult him. "Frankly, we were scared of him. Nobody wanted to admit it. I was looking at John Reddy's hands one day in social studies class, his nails edged with grease, hairs on his knuckles, and the thought came to me, 'He could beat me to death with those hands.'" A rumor circulated that, at Tomahawk Island, John Reddy had spent weeks in solitary confinement because he'd gotten into fights "and hurt his opponents pretty bad." Sarepta Voss, one of those Home Ec girls no one ever noticed, drew a measure of excited attention for several days telling a story relayed to her by a cousin who lived in Olean and knew a guy who'd done time at Tomahawk Island when John Reddy was in—"Everybody knew that John Reddy had actually killed a man, with a knife made out of some metal. Everybody was afraid of him, even the guards." We wondered if he was armed at school: a switchblade knife would've fitted in his jacket pocket, no problem. "We'd get to school a little early, 'cause John Reddy was required to get there early and check in to Stamish's office, so we'd sit in Bob's car having a smoke and watching for the Mercury to arrive, and John Reddy, it was, like, *a thing to do*. We really got dependent on it, the last month or so." Dougie Siefried recalled, embarrassed, "I'd try to catch him, mornings, coming out of Stamish's office where they had him in, like, quarantine, and I'd say, 'How's it going, John?' and he'd look at me like almost he didn't know me, we hadn't played basketball together for two years, then he'd sort of see me, he'd smile, or make his mouth smile, and say, 'O.K., how's it going with you?' like that was an answer." Evangeline Fesnacht agonized over such an irrevocable, heart-baring act but in the end, succumbing to her fate, pushed a tensely handwritten note, on thin blue stationery, through a slat in John Reddy's locker:

You are right to scorn us, we are ignorant spoiled children of the doomed bourgeoisie. But know that there is one who plumbs your heart. You had no choice but to—KILL YOUR OWN SOUL.

Sincerely,

your friend through life,

E.S.

John Reddy seems never to have acknowledged this peculiar communication, as he never acknowledged, so far as we knew, any of the notes numberless infatuated girls left for him in his locker, in his classroom desks, under the windshield wipers of his Mercury parked out in the lot, or brazenly shoved at him, even jammed into his jeans pockets, as he passed us in the halls; nor did he even glance in Evangeline's direction when amid a crowd of others they were in close proximity to each other. But three days after she'd left the note Evangeline received, at home, one of the astonishing surprises of her life, one dozen beautiful long-stemmed yellow roses—"'Evangeline, first among equals'—and no signature," Mrs. Fesnacht said, reading the card, excited. "But you must know who it is, Evangeline? Don't you?" *My soulmate. Though we never acknowledge each other in this life.* More than a year after the trial in which John Reddy had been acquitted of murder, people continued to ask us, with leering eyes, "What's it like to go to school with a *murderer*?" A female reporter for the *Niagara Herald* came snooping by with a camera, seeking "candid, unposed shots" of students mingling with John Reddy Heart. We responded coolly. We'd had enough of the media—its distortions, lies. "John Reddy is just like anybody else." In fact, John Reddy was like no one else. We kept waiting for that to happen, for John Reddy *to become one of us* but it never happened. New to the faculty of WHS was a history teacher, Mr. Feldman, who didn't have John Reddy in any of his classes and knew of him only from scandalous articles and faculty gossip. This guy would lecture us in an ironic, scolding tone that pissed us, so superior, like he was bringing wisdom to unwashed aborigines. "There is an undeclared war between the ninety-nine percent of human beings who persist in believing in fairy tales and 'myths' and the valiant one percent who use their intellects, reason, analyze, come to independent conclusions," pacing at the front of the room with a piece of chalk in his fingers, a youngish-fattish guy with thick glasses and thick lips and skin that broke out in hives if he got too excited which he did often, we stared coldly at him sending thought-waves of dislike, defiance, "The human instinct to create myths seems to be as deeply rooted in our species as the instinct to bond, to mate, to reproduce, it just *is*, but, students, it's dangerous in so technically advanced a civilization, it's a primitive remnant that doesn't belong in such a civilization, like the paranoia of the ongoing Cold War, it's up to you, a younger generation, to break the cycle of superstitious thinking, you must learn to question all assumptions, all murky thinking, you must ask, 'Is it so? Why?' the way scientists examine their material," we continued to stare coldly, some of us frowning, a little anxious, arms crossed, working our mouths in resentful silence that this guy, this jerk, reported to be completing his Ph.D. at Syracuse University, headed for university teaching, had the right to lecture us about our souls, speaking more and more rapidly, waving the piece of chalk, "Students! It's up to you. The yearning for mythic origins must be exposed as infantile, 'nostalgia' for what never was, ludicrously out of place in a civilization founded upon scientific progress, linear time, ceaseless change—*history*." From the look on Feldman's face you'd think that *history* was some big-deal balloon he'd blown up to dazzle a bunch of morons, he's presenting it to us, a gift—and from canny Art Lutz at the rear of the room, a brilliantly timed lip-fart executed as only Art could do it, his lips seemingly pursed together, innocent and unmoving, and the rude hilarious noise seeming to come from all directions at once. *The look on Feldman's face.* "Like, welcome to WHS, man." Forty years later we'd still be laughing. In Mr. Cuthbert's social studies class the mood was completely different. Mr. Cuthbert liked John Reddy and was respectful of him. And maybe just a little scared of him. The way Mr. Cuthbert's eyes shifted behind the lenses of his plastic glasses, tugged in John Reddy's direction. *Killer-Boy! In my classroom.* Scottie Baskett swore he'd seen our teacher's hands trembling with the thrill of it—"For sure, Cuthie's got a crush on John Reddy." The usually skeptical-minded Carolyn Cameron, one day to be a distinguished oncologist at the Mayo Clinic, a smart, practical-minded girl who intimidated most of us, spoke of how she'd gaze at John Reddy Heart for most of each class period, unable to break the spell—"I tell myself that he's only a guy. I can see him breathe. I can see veins pumping in his throat. I can monitor his complexion over days, weeks—the arrival of a pimple, its gradual eruption, disappearance. I've seen him scratch his underarms, his crotch, pick his nose behind his hand if he thinks no one is looking. (But someone is always looking.) He sweats taking tests and quizzes—literally. I see his grades when Mr. Cuthbert hands them back, and they're mediocre—seventy-four, sixty-eight, seventy-seven. I tell myself, 'He could be my brother.' But he turned to ask me, once, if I'd lend him a pen—and I almost melted. I began to stammer. My heart kicked against my ribs. There's no getting around it—John Reddy Heart isn't like anybody else. He's—*only himself*." Carolyn shook her head irritably, for there just weren't words. In this class there were two girls of the Circle. Ginger McCord and Shelby Connor. The intimacies they'd shared with John Reddy Heart set them apart (they believed) from others in the class; yet John Reddy, seated at the very front of the room, in the extreme right row, rarely glanced in their direction. Ginger McCord was in the habit of staring glassy-eyed at John Reddy in profile, at his scruff of shaggy black hair, his right shoulder, right bicep, which was about as much as she could see of him leaning forward in her desk in the approximate center of the classroom until her midriff ached from the pressure of the desktop and her slender neck felt as if it had been stretched. (Some of us, guys, gazed at Ginger with the same sort of helplessness with which she gazed at John Reddy.) If you told Ginger you loved her, like Dougie Siefried, or Ginger's own parents and grandparents—"*Bor*ing! They don't know me at all." She was convinced that only John Reddy Heart knew her while conceding, for she wasn't a stupid girl, that John Reddy Heart didn't give a damn about her. "I accepted this. But for those months in my life there was the *possibility* that John Reddy would suddenly take notice of me, in public, in Mr. Cuthbert's class for instance, he'd turn in my direction as if my thoughts had summoned him at last, and our eyes would lock. This *possibility* of something—of happiness, or more than happiness—has stayed with me all my life. It was my way into others' hearts—others' secret hearts." Shelby Connor, who, seated even farther from John Reddy's corner of the room than her friend Ginger, had to content herself with what she could glimpse of him through a maze of intervening heads and shoulders of no more consequence to her than department-store mannequins, told us passionately, "I thought, 'The only way to justify life is to help others.' I never saw John Reddy as tough, invulnerable. I understood that he was suffering. He'd shot a man without meaning to. He'd gone to prison. He'd lost his family. He lived alone above a Chinese takeout. I thought, *He's suffering. Inside, where no one can see*. At that moment I was filled with a great happiness. I seemed to know my life's vocation. *My destiny stretched before me like a road only I, Shelby Connor, could take*." Yet there were disquieting tales even then which neither Shelby nor Ginger, nor any of the enraptured girls of the Circle, wished to acknowledge: Sasha Calvo, a year older, more savagely beautiful than ever, with thick wavy dark hair to her waist, had returned to Willowsville after a year's exile and, though forbidden by the Calvos to see John Reddy, was in fact John Reddy's secret love. ("But where can they meet?

Not after school—Sasha's brother Giovanni comes and picks her up. They all watch her like a hawk.") ("If Sasha Calvo had a baby, she gave it up pretty easily! Wouldn't you think, even for an Italian, she'd be ashamed to show her face?") Janet Moss, in despair that "nobody ever looked at me—if you weren't in a clique, you didn't *exist*," shocked her parents by dyeing her hair black, darkening her eyebrows and letting them grow across the bridge of her nose, wearing tight skirts, tight sweaters and crimson lipstick, despite her plans to attend Wells College in the fall, and within days was invited by not one but three guys to the senior prom—"I said yes to Larry Baumgart. I figured he didn't know any more about making out than I did, and I was right." In his private journal, hidden beneath his mattress in the book-strewn bedroom in which he'd lived nearly eighteen years of his "essentially tragic" life, Ritchie Eickhorn observed *High school life is our metaphor for life that devours what remains of the remainder of life. Help me!* Blake Wells, who would one day be president of Williams College, one of our class's high-profile achievers, yet again, and again reconsidered suicide for *What is life*, Blake wondered, writing in his journal which he, too, kept hidden in his room, *what is life but the perpetual pushing of a bean with one's nose across a vast filthy floor without end—its "center everywhere, circumference nowhere."* Millie LeRoux told us solemnly, in confidence, that Frank Farolino had told her mother in confidence that poor John Reddy was sending most of his paycheck to his family—"Old Mr. Heart isn't dead, he's living somewhere on Lake Ontario. Some Indian-sounding place. Where Mrs. Heart is, or his brother and sister, Mr. Farolino isn't sure. 'Ask me, they're a buncha leeches, the whole family. Sucking the poor kid dry.'" We donated money for a secret fund for John Reddy, it was fantastic how we collected $230 almost right away, and Verrie Myers was saying half-seriously she could sell her car, it was her car to dispose of as she wished, a few of the guys like Ken Fischer, Pete Marsh, Smoke Filer you wouldn't have expected it of, were pretty generous, too—"Hell, I can afford twenty-five bucks. My grandma's always slipping me checks, every time we go there." In the end, we decided against giving the money to John Reddy, it was an agonizing decision and we quarreled over it, the prevailing logic was "John Reddy's got his pride for God's sake, we'd be destroying his *pride*," so the money, by this time it was almost $300, we sent by money order to the American Red Cross—"It was about the only place we could think of. We didn't want to spend a whole lot of time thinking." Who instigated the plan to elect John Reddy Heart our King of the Senior Prom isn't definitely known. Who provided the caption beside his name in the yearbook (there would be no photo)—*His ways are the ways of mystery*—isn't definitely known. Babs Bitterman, whose ashy-blond pageboy was rumored to have caught fire in the backseat of Steve Lunt's car, and who could not have anticipated how, one day soon, she would die in that car, in the front seat, thrown partway through the windshield, asked John Reddy to be her date for the senior prom—"Like, why not? I'm figuring he can only say no." A startled-looking John Reddy, approached by breezy Babs as he was opening his locker, apparently mumbled, "No. Thanks." It was a fact that, through our senior year, John Reddy pissed off a lot of us, especially his ex-teammates who liked to think they had a special relationship with him, by declining their invitations to get together—"For a few beers." Not once but, hell—a dozen times. Our dance parties. Pool parties. Even parties at the country club he could've come to—as our guest. John Reddy's expression was polite and deadpan and possibly (some of us thought) ironic. He'd shift his shoulders in that way of his, sort of twist his head like a boxer slipping a slow, dumb punch, and say, "Thanks! but I guess not. Gotta early morning next morning." That series of notorious senior parties to which half our class would trace the source of our "chronic drinking problems," culminating in prom night, when Smoke Filer would lose control of his racy Thunderbird just down the hill on

Garrison where he'd sped a hundred times and some of those times pretty smashed, or high on weed, and this time Smoke's luck ran out and he lost control of the T-Bird and swerved into the side of an oncoming car at seventy-five miles an hour, a cool forty-five miles an hour over the speed limit—"*Totaled.*" And worse yet was graduation night, *tragic* as the papers would exclaim, *teen graduation turns to horror*, *grief* when Steve Lunt in his Buick LeSabre, driving from Coke Smith's house to Tommy Nordstrom's, at about one a.m., five drunk kids crammed into the car, skidded on wet pavement on North Long and crashed head-on into an abutment. "It's a miracle, only two of them died. God must've been looking out for the others." Where John Reddy Heart was on prom night, let alone graduation night, only John Reddy knew. "Yeah, we were disappointed." "Something he'd said to someone, I forget who, made it sound like, yeah, he might be showing up at the prom." A confused tale would circulate that Sasha Calvo had been elected Queen of the Prom, along with John Reddy Heart as King, but that was erroneous, as well as preposterous, for Sasha was only a sophomore, and anyway none of us would've voted for her, especially the girls—"What's he see in *her*? She doesn't even wear makeup." Petey Merchant agonized for days, it may have been weeks, should he ask Katie Olmsted to the prom—"It wasn't that she might be in her wheelchair right then, I could handle that O.K. We'd just sort of be together. It was as if she was on her feet, and wanted to dance. That scared me"—and in the end drew a deep breath and asked. The head custodian at our school, Alistair whose last name nobody knew, whose dislike of us, and of most of the WHS staff, shone in his whisky-colored eyes, was rumored to have arranged for John Reddy and his girl Sasha to meet in the school basement where he had a cozy if smelly (windowless, overheated) office between the mammoth furnaces and the hot-water tanks. Alistair's most urgent responsibility was to check the pressure gauges on the furnaces when they were in operation—"Without me, the whole friggin place *goes*." He spoke with mordant satisfaction, snapping his fingers. Surely Alistair would have lost his job if he'd been caught arranging for Sasha Calvo to slip down the basement stairs from the east, sophomore wing of the school, make her way along a shadowy corridor to his cave of an office to which John Reddy would have come, eagerly slipping down the basement stairs from the west, senior wing of the school. There was said to be music playing, a radio turned low. A shaded forty-watt bulb. Shabby yet still colorful carpet remnants laid on the concrete floor, curling up onto the walls to a height of several inches. And Alistair's old sagging cushioned sofa. "Oh, God. A throbbing *womb*." We were uneasy, anxious, seeing the lovers below us, oblivious of us and of danger. How famished they were for each other—kissing, embracing, their hands clutching at each other's bodies. No time for words, only murmurs, groans, choked cries. Their lovemaking was tender, yet passionate. Possibly a little rough, bringing tears to Sasha's beautiful eyes. As, at the foot of the basement stairs, smoking his foul-smelling pipe, Alistair stood watch. "S'pose Stamish comes down? What's Alistair gonna do?" Some of us were convinced that John Reddy and Sasha met like this only a few times; others, that they met every weekday afternoon through the winter and spring. For these were the only times they could meet, we reasoned—the Calvos guarded Sasha so closely. In our dull rows of seats, in our classrooms on the floors above. The red second hand of clocks in every classroom, positioned uniformly above the blackboard, ticked urgently onward. "What're they doing now, d'you think? *Now?*" "Do you think they do it bareassed? Or some quicker way?" "Shit, John Reddy wouldn't do anything *quick*." Boys, aroused and anxious, tried to hide their gigantic erections with notebooks, or textbooks, which occasionally slipped from their clammy fingers and clattered to the floor. Girls, short of breath as if they'd been running, a faint flush in their cheeks, dabbed at their eyes with tissues and sat very still, feet flat on the floor and legs uncrossed. Our

most innocent, unknowing teachers like Mme. Picholet and
Mr. Sternberg were observed mysteriously agitated, a glisten
of sweat on their brows. The *throb! throb! throb!* of furnaces
was reportedly felt as far away as the music practice room on
the third floor of the annex. In Mr. Alexander's fifth-period
physics class, always a drowsy class, dazed eyes blinked
rapidly to keep in focus. "Excuse *me*? Is this class *awake*?"
Mr. Alexander inquired in his hurt, chagrined way, staring at
us with his hands on his hips. "Peter Merchant!—how would
you approach this problem?" Petey Merchant's physics text
crashed to the floor. His cheeks flushed crimson. Yet there
were those, among them Verrie Myers, who vehemently
denied that John Reddy and "that Calvo girl" were lovers at
all. Nor had she believed that there'd ever been a baby—
"That's *sick*." In time, Verrie's view prevailed. More disturbing
tales were being spread of John Reddy on those evenings
when his windows were darkened down on Water Street,
when the girls of the Circle, or any other girls who sought
him, discovered he was gone. At such times John Reddy was
cruising in his funky-sexy Mercury in Cheektowaga,
Tonawanda, Lockport or downtown Buffalo, restless and
looking for action. "Even on probation, John Reddy's set for
action." Often he was seen with a glamorous girl, or an adult
woman, pressed up close beside him, head on his shoulder
and fingers, though not visible from the street, caressing the
inside of his thigh. John Reddy had gone out with Mr.
Stamish's youngest, pretty secretary Rita, that seemed to be a
fact. Scottie Baskett came to school pale and haggard and
stunned by an experience he could bring himself to share
only with his closest buddy, Roger Zwaart, and that after several days: Scottie had returned home a little early from swim
practice to discover his own mother, her hair damp from a
shower, in slacks and a sweater clearly thrown on in haste, no
bra beneath, and, of all people, John Reddy Heart!—"In my
own house. He was there laying tile, supposedly, in our guest-
room bath. Farolino's truck was out front, I don't pay much

attention to what my folks do so I was surprised to see it there, but, O.K., I walk in, and there's—*John Reddy*. 'We're laying tile in the guest-room bath,' Mom says. She's trying to sound cool but she's trembling, I can see her hands. Her face is all pale—no makeup. And you never see my mom without makeup. They must've heard me come in so John's hammering away innocently in the bathroom like somebody on TV and Mom's like rushing at me in the kitchen, her boobs bobbing, asking if I'd like a snack? chocolate milk? butter-crunch cookies? like for Christ's sake I'm ten years old and fucking *blind*." Two days later, Art Lutz had a similar experience, returning home after school to discover John Reddy on the premises, and "My mom acting wound-up and hysterical, saying 'We're having these beautiful new cabinets put in, Art, see?—aren't they beautiful?' and there's John Reddy on a kitchen stool hammering away, in a sweaty T-shirt and ripped jeans, his prick practically hanging *out*. And fuck-smell all over the house like steam from a shower. He looks at me with this shit-eating grin and says, 'How's it going, kid?' and I realize I got to get out of there fast before I get violent. So I slammed out again, climbed into Jamie's car and floored 'er." Bibi Arhardt was wakened in the middle of the night by gravel thrown against her second-floor bedroom window. Frightened, she knelt by the windowsill without turning on the light and saw, below, the figure of a man, or a boy, signaling impatiently to her. 'Though I couldn't see his face clearly, I knew it was him—John Reddy. And there was the Mercury out on the street. At once, I had no will to resist. I knew it might be a mistake, but—" Bibi hurriedly dressed, and slipped out a side door into the night, which was a bright moonlit gusty night smelling of damp, greening earth—for it was late March by this time, and the long winter was ending. There came John Reddy, his eyes burning, to seize Bibi in his arms and bear her, feebly protesting, to his car. In silence they drove to Tug Hill Park which was larger, more desolate and wild than Bibi remembered. How many hours passed there, in John Reddy's car, Bibi could not have said; how many hungry kisses passed between them; how many caresses; how many times, with gentleness and sweetness, yet control, John Reddy made love to her, bringing her to tears of ecstasy—"It wasn't like you would think! It wasn't like you would imagine any guy could *do*." A few nights later, in her bedroom on the second floor of the Zeiglers' Georgian colonial on Castle Creek Drive, Suzi, though wearing Norm Zeiga's onyx signet ring on a chain around her neck, was wakened by a sound in her bedroom and looked up to see a tall figure standing over her bed—"I was too scared to scream. I seemed to know, even before he knelt beside me, and kissed me, who it was. 'Don't be afraid, Suzi, I won't hurt you,' John Reddy whispered. 'And if I do, forgive me.'" Evangeline Fesnacht came to school pale, moist-eyed, strangely silent. When Mr. Lepage tried to engage her in their customary witty banter, as the rest of us looked on, Evangeline sighed, lowered her gaze meekly and made no reply. "Have I, Miss Fesnacht," Mr. Lepage said in a voice heavy with sarcasm, "a rival for your thoughts this morning?" In the backseat of his brother's Dodge Castille, as Art Lutz kissed her eagerly with his opened mouth, and awkwardly tried, with his left hand, to unhook her bra beneath her sweater, Tessa Maypole burst into guilty tears, saying, "Oh, Artie, I can't. I can't. I'm in love with someone else, it wouldn't be fair to you." Lee Ann Whitfield, our fat girl, was observed in the school cafeteria pushing around, on her plate, a large portion of macaroni and cheese, with the look of one who has lost her appetite, or her soul. Ritchie Eickhorn noted in his journal, under the new, heady influence of Pascal, *We yearn for eternity—but inhabit only time*. Miss Flechsenhauer noted with suspicion an unusual number of girls asking to be excused, with "cramps" or "migraine," from gym, swim class, team practice. "What is this, girls, an epidemic?" Miss O'Brien, our school nurse, a chesty, dour woman with a perpetual sinus snuffle, noted, with suspicion, an unusual number of girls requesting Bufferin and Midol and to be allowed to lie, with heating pads on their lower abdomens, on cots in the peaceful, darkened infirmary. "What is this, girls, an epidemic?" John Reddy Heart was said to have been seen at a nine a.m. Sunday church service at the United Methodist Church on Haggarty Road. "But nobody goes *there*, who would've seen him?" John Reddy Heart, as spring progressed, was looking, at school, more and more exhausted, as if he no longer slept at night. His eyelids drooped as our teachers droned on; he was having trouble, it seemed, staying awake in his classes. His left eye was bloodshot and leaked tears. His jaws were sometimes stippled in tiny cuts from careless or hurried shaving. Some mornings, he didn't shave at all, evidently. His longish hair, separating in greasy quills, exuded a frank, pungent odor, sharp as that of his body. Girls swooned if they passed too close to him. It was known to be particularly dangerous to pass close by John Reddy on the stairs: several sophomore girls nearly fainted. In fourth-period English, Miss Bird, leading a discussion of Robert Frost's "After Apple-Picking," stared at John Reddy Heart who was gripping his textbook and frowning into it as if the secret of life might be located there, in a few teasing lines of poetry; she sniffed his scent, and for a long embarrassing moment lost the thread of her thought. We'd realized for some time, uneasily, that Miss Bird no longer wore her hair skinned back from her face in that unflattering style but curled and fluffed out, "feminine" in the way that women are "feminine" in late-night movies of the forties. Her small, pursed lips were a savage red. Her slightly bulgy brown eyes, fixed on John Reddy, who may have been glancing shyly up at her, appeared to be shifting out of focus. "Miss Bird? I'll open a window," Ken Fischer said quickly, leaping to his feet. "It's kind of stuffy in here." It was in such abrupt and seemingly unpremeditated gestures that Ken Fischer, blond, blandly handsome, a "nice" guy, would continually surprise us: we'd recall his gallantry in coming to Miss Bird's rescue many years later when he came forward suddenly to kiss, in homage, our drunken Verrie's beautiful bared tattooed breast. For a precarious moment—"I held my breath, oh God, she's going to faint!"—Miss Bird swayed groggily in her spike-heeled shoes. Then she smiled wanly at Ken, touching the back of her thin hand to her forehead, and the sinister spell was broken. Yet the following morning in Mr. Dunleddy's biology class, where John Reddy sat in his prescribed corner, first row, extreme right, Sandi Scott, usually so poised and droll, astonished us by bursting into tears in the midst of a recitation of the steps of mitosis: "'Prophase'—'metaphase'—'anaphase'—'telophase'—oh God, it's so relentless! So *cruel*." Mr. Dunleddy, short of breath even sitting, overweight by fifty pounds, who would be the first of our teachers to die, a few years later, of a stroke at the relatively young age of fifty-six, stared at the weeping girl with middle-aged eyes of dolor and regret. That night, Evangeline Fesnacht typed the first line of what would become, eventually, after numerous metamorphoses, her first published novel ("wild, dithyrambic, dark, riddlesome") *I woke from a dream so vivid I would search the world for its origin—in vain*. Ritchie Eickhorn noted in his journal *We inhabit time but remember only "eternal moments." God's mercy*. Dexter Cambrook impulsively called Pattianne Groves. He was flooded with excitement as with an intoxicant in his normally calm veins— "My acceptance just came from Harvard!" He waited with sweaty palms, pounding heart for Pattianne's kid brother to call her to the phone and asked her point-blank if she'd go with him to the senior prom and was met with, after a moment's startled silence, "Oh, Dexter? Did you say— Dexter? *Cambrook*? Oh gee, thanks. I mean, that's so thoughtful of you, Dexter. But I'm sorry, I guess I'll be going with—" Verrie Myers and Trish Elders, closest friends since kindergarten, who, in recent weeks, had scarcely been able to look at each other, each feeling a deep physical revulsion for the other, found themselves walking swiftly, then breaking into a run, like foals, onto the vividly green playing field behind school. Each girl grabbed the other's hand at the same instant. Their uplifted faces were luminous, radiant. Their eyes shone. We watched, a haphazard and unknowing trapezoid of (male, yearning) observers, one of us from a second-floor window of the school, another from the parking lot and the third as he was leaving the building at the rear, as the girls in maroon gym shorts and dazzling-white T-shirts ran, clutching hands; at that moment the sun burst through storm clouds, and a diaphanous rainbow appeared in the sky, near-invisible, an arc of pale gold, rose, seablue shimmering over open fields beyond Garrison Road—"like a wayward, tossed-off gesture of God" (as Ritchie Eickhorn would one day observe). It was John Reddy Heart toward whom those girls were running, we knew. Yet we were resigned, not bitter; philosophical, not raging with testosterone jealousy. *He won't love them as we love them. One day, they will know.* We were hurt, and we were incredulous. Some of us broken-hearted. Quite a few of us, frankly pissed. "John Reddy wouldn't just— leave? Would he? Without saying goodbye? Without coming to the prom? To graduation? Just—leave? Drive away? *Out of our lives forever?*" Of course we'd believed that John Reddy would attend the senior prom for it was unthinkable he wouldn't. Rumors circulated among every clique and seeped down to loners and losers alike that he was "definitely, definitely coming" for he'd purchased two tickets, he'd be bringing Sasha Calvo who was having her wild mane of hair trimmed and styled for the occasion, though there was a rumor he might be bringing Verrie Myers (whose comment on this rumor was a tight-lipped, "No comment"). *To realize that you are truly going to graduate from high school* Ritchie Eickhorn noted in his journal with tremulous fingers *is to realize that one day, inescapably, you must die.* Of course we had less hope that John Reddy would attend graduation since you weren't required to attend the actual ceremony to get your diploma, it would be mailed to you courtesy of the school district, but, as Dwayne Hewson said, "Not attend graduation? That's like not attending your own *funeral.*" Who was the genius who thought of electing John Reddy Heart our King of the Senior Prom? Improbably, considering his rabid anti-Heart bias, which he'd claim well into his forties—and fifties!—wasn't based on simple male jealousy, oh no, it was our class skeptic, Chet Halloren. His brilliant brain employed in organizing the infamous semi-secret campaign to elect our Killer-Boy ex-con classmate King of the Senior Prom meaning John Reddy Heart would get his picture in all the papers again and WHS would leap back into headlines. As Chet chortled, "Hey look, what a fantastic way to burn Stamish's ass. What's he gonna do about it, sprout a hernia?" In fact, Stamish royally fucked our asses. The shrewd old fart must've learned of the plan, the plot, before we'd hardly got started. Last week of school he called an "emergency assembly" of all seniors (except John Reddy who wasn't going to vote anyway) and told us, white-lipped, sort of blowing and puffing his cheeks, it'd been called to his attention that "certain of you are contemplating a defiant, self-destructive act." We sat there bug-eyed gaping at him as if we didn't know what the hell he was talking about. Which, at that point, some of us didn't. Stamish is saying, "Students, this is a sacred time for you. It is a time that will never come again in your lives. It is a time you will revere for the remainder of your lives. You would not wish to sully it for a mere prank. You would not wish to make a mockery of it. You would not wish to call unwanted *media attention*"—and here Stamish paused, puffing, allowing us to know he knew exactly what was up—"to your beloved school. Therefore, you must take care to vote for appropriate individuals in the senior balloting. You must respect your classmates who have earned certain honors. The Queen and King of the Senior Prom—these are high, high honors. The local papers—" We stared, we frowned, we were mightily impressed. You could hear a pin drop in that auditorium. There was Art Lutz sitting on his hands, gravely nodding. Even Nosepicker Nordstrom was subdued. Those guys who would've been strong contenders for King, if we weren't going in an avalanche for John Reddy, Dwayne Hewson, Ken Fischer, Blake Wells sat sort of embarrassed and down-looking. So Stamish is yammering away. If they talk long enough, they think you're convinced. And one of the good-girl girls, Millie LeRoux, raises her hand and inquires, "Mr. Stamish? It's a democracy, isn't it?" and there's titters and laughing and Stamish doesn't like it but he likes Millie LeRoux who's an officer of Student Council and the daughter of J. Gordon LeRoux of LeRoux, Saxon & Trimme, Inc. He can't figure if she's being ironic or sincere—Millie's got these big beautiful brown cow-eyes to die for. So he says, "Quiet, the rest of you! Millie, yes, it *is* a democracy. Of course. I would never interfere with our democratic process. But there is, you know, an old, revered tradition at Willowsville Senior High, a sacred tradition certain of your parents cherish from their days here, too; a sacred tradition of excellence, integrity, honesty, good sportsmanship—" We applauded the old fart and he went away thinking he'd won. Or we thought he thought he'd won. Then when we voted in the cafeteria on the last day of classes, we assumed the prom committee would count the ballots as usual; but Stamish's old-biddy assistant from the front office shows up and carries the box away. So, though we calculated we'd elected John Reddy our Prom King by a wide majority, at least ninety ballots out of one-thirty, when it comes time for the announcement, at midnight of the prom, everybody excited, apprehensive, a kind of fever in us, looking for John Reddy (who'd been sighted since nine p.m. every ten minutes entering the dim-lit gym, with his date Sasha Calvo or some other gorgeous girl)—the news is, read off by the prom chairman Pete Marsh from a sheet of paper provided him by Stamish, "Queen—*Veronica Myers!* King—*Ken Fischer!*" and we're fucked. And there's nothing we can do but applaud. Because the ballots for John Reddy were probably destroyed as soon as they were counted. And it's over, it's history. And we're thinking, *Well shit, John Reddy never showed up, never much chance he was going to show up at our prom, and Ken*

Fischer's our friend. In a cream-colored tux and powder-blue cummerbund to match Verrie's strapless powder-blue chiffon formal. Ken is blushing like a kid, understands he didn't really win the election—"Hell, I voted for John Reddy myself." Verrie's beautiful face is mottled with a kind of complex shame. "What a childish fantasy it was, to think John Reddy would be our King. That one of us would be his Queen. That John Reddy Heart would show up here—in our 'romantically decorated' *gym.*" Cameras flash as Veronica Myers and Ken Fischer, that terrifically good-looking WHS couple, are crowned with silver tinsel crowns. Verrie is given a bouquet of long-stemmed white roses, and Ken a white carnation for his lapel. The girls of the court embrace their Queen, the boys of the court shake hands with their King. One of us, drunk on vodka-spiked punch, slips on the polished floor and falls heavily, amid peals of laughter. Bo Bozer, belching toxic beer fumes, growls, "That broad's so sexy you want to tear her apart with your *teeth*," meaning our new Queen. Bo's friends, and Janet Moss who overhears, laugh uneasily. Some old song from our parents' era, or maybe our grandparents', "Tenderly," is being played by the band, and the King and Queen, our royal couple, move out onto the dance floor. We're all dancing, sort of. "What's there to do but fucking dance, it's a dance, Christ's sake," Dwayne Hewson (who'd been given reason to think that, if John Reddy was eliminated by Stamish, he'd be crowned King, now he'd be dancing with Verrie Myers instead of who he was stuck with—terrific Pattianne Groves) mutters, mildly drunk. Verrie's face is streaked with tears. Ken's eyes, too, appear damp. Among the faculty chaperons, Mr. Lepage is conspicuously absent. It's an open secret—"Verrie had some sort of thing going with Mr. Lepage." It's an open secret—"Verrie had some sort of thing going with John Reddy Heart. But *he* dropped *her*." Girls who'd made tender, passionate love with John Reddy Heart would forever afterward bear the scars of his ardor, but invisibly. For even our hymens grew back—"The weirdest thing. That tough little sinewy tissue, he broke and it bled and I cried, cried. But afterward, a few weeks later, I noticed it had grown back across the split, sore place, and anatomically *I was a virgin again*." In the years ahead our lovers would not believe we'd had a high school lover, nor would the numerous gynecologists (exclusively male) who examined us. Our husbands humored us, condescended to us and pointedly changed the subject. We remained confused over the issue of whether John Reddy had used condoms. In that era, the very word was repugnant. "Oh my God," Shelby Connor murmured, fingertips fluttering, "—I'd have been mortified to *look*." Yet not one of us got pregnant. (Sallie Vetch, a junior no one knew, certainly didn't count.) Jenny Thrun reported a "pregnancy scare"—which utterly baffled us since she'd never been singled out by John Reddy Heart for any attention, and the boy she sometimes dated, Chet Halloren, for all his worldly-wise poise, was shy and stiff when alone with a girl, and would've had to summon all his courage just to ask Jenny if he could kiss her goodnight. In her flutey reproachful manner Mme. Picholet inquired of us, "*Mes amis*, will you never wish to *think*? To slow this mad pace, to gaze inside, to contemplate who you *are*?" Now the band is playing Lollipop's "Die Lovin' You," the decibel level is deafening. It's frantic, fantastic. Even gawky Dexter Cambrook and his nemesis Elise Petko are dancing, giddily stumbling over each other's feet. Smoke Filer, who hasn't more than two hours to live, is grinning, sweating, shaking his ass as if he knows his number's coming up. Pete Marsh (who won't die for another several years) is happily dancing with Trish Elders in pale green chiffon who's watching the crepe-paper-festooned doorway in vain, waiting for John Reddy Heart to appear. "He can't just stay away—can he? Don't we mean anything to him at all?" Miss Bird, one of several prom chaperones, glamorous in shimmering green taffeta that clings to her hipless body, has cooly declined Mr. Dunleddy's request for a dance to retreat to the faculty women's lounge on the second floor of the darkened school to ponder, with a bitter smile, her pale mirrored reflection— "The nature of heartbreak never changes, Maxine. Only its elusive object." Evangeline Fesnacht who hadn't a date for the prom is at home in the seclusion of her room in a passion of a new discovery—Franz Kafka. *As E.S. awoke one morning from uneasy dreams she found herself transformed in her bed into a gigantic beetle!* It's an open secret that Veronica Myers and Ken Fischer will be splitting up after graduation. Tonight, the glittering prom that's the highlight of the happiest four years of our lives, graduation and a final frenzy of parties— "After that, it's permanent. We'll always be friends, of course," Verrie has said. Stoic Ken has made no commentary. "That neurotic doll," Dwayne Hewson, shiny-faced, mutters, "she'd never get away with that shit, with me." Pattianne Groves, gorgeous in strapless dusty-rose tulle, long gleaming auburn hair in a French twist at the back of her head, stares at her date. "Excuse me? *What?*" Ginger McCord in strapless yellow chiffon turns upon her date Dougie Siefried in a rented tux and sky-blue cummerbund—"Damn you, Dougie, John Reddy Heart is not a murderer. *He is not.*" We're amazed, thrilled as a tearful Ginger slaps Dougie's freckled face, bloodies his nose and the starched snowy-white front of his tux. Years later, guilt-stricken Verrie Myers, by this time a moderately successful film actress, wouldn't be able to recall why she and Ken Fischer had broken up at graduation. When she was told of Ken's apparent suicide, at the age of thirty-nine, during a business trip to Stuttgart, Germany, Verrie reacted with as much emotion as we'd seen in her in any of her movies: she burst into tears, tore at her hair and face until we restrained her—"Oh God. Oh no. Ken Fischer is *dead*? I'd always thought—"—*we were destined to marry* we wanted to finish Verrie's stammered sentence for her. But possibly this wasn't what Verrie meant to say. Possibly, Veronica Myers, who has told interviewers she's at peace only when following a prepared script, uttering words others have prescribed for her, when she isn't forced to improvise for herself out of the "banality, exhaustion and terror" of her soul, hadn't a clue what she meant to say. *O.K. Do what you have to do* is probably the wisest course. We gather together to recall prom night, graduation and the parties that followed. (Those notorious parties not all of us survived. Babs Bitterman, Steve Lunt— "It's so ironic, they weren't even a couple really. They didn't love each other much." Smoke Filer. "But who was Smoke's date for the prom?—I keep forgetting." "Half her face ended up, the cop at the accident site said, on the broken windshield, like a putty mask. But she didn't actually *die*.") *Our youth O America like gold coins spilling from our pockets* as the poet Richard Eickhorn would one day write. *So many coins! such riches! no need to stoop to pick up what you've dropped.* Waiting that night, the night of the prom, for John Reddy Heart who was our uncrowned King. And he never came. Until the last dance was danced, we were staggering, kissing, hugging, crying, girls' mascara streaked on their youth, flushed faces like ink, guys goofily grinning and wobbling in their too-tight polished black shoes, vomiting in the boys' john, a madhouse scene like kiddie bumper-cars in the parking lot. But John Reddy didn't show, as two weeks later he didn't show at graduation, either. And it was revealed to us he'd moved out of his Water Street apartment. "He couldn't just—leave? After living here for seven years? Not saying good-bye to *anyone*?" We tried to determine who'd seen John Reddy Heart last in Willowsville. There had to be a pair of eyes that, knowingly, saw him last. (No contesting who'd seen him first: Ketch Campbell.) Sometimes we counted adults, sometimes not. Like his boss Frank Farolino who told us he'd said good-bye to him weeks before—"He'd given me notice early. He was quitting the job on June first. I had a sort of idea he'd be leaving town, he was vague about that part of it. Mostly he was anxious about passing exams, getting his diploma. You have to hand it to him. Poor bastard." His teachers Dunleddy, Hornby, Salaman must have seen him walk out of their exams, might have waved to him not knowing it was a final good-bye. Hornby said, "I spoke to John about going to Erie County Tech. The tuition's low, he could get a loan. I urged him to study drafting, he's got some real talent. But he said, 'I'd get too restless. It fucks me up to *sit*.'" Many times Woody McKeever would recount how he'd met John Reddy in the parking lot on a scorcher of a June afternoon—"I asked the kid how things were going and he sort of winced saying he hoped O.K., he was worried he might flunk geometry and not get his diploma. I said, 'John, I bet you passed, wanna bet?' putting out my hand, and he backs off like he's scared of being touched, and says, 'Coach, I lived too long in Vegas, I never *bet*.' I'm kinda hurt, I didn't know it would be the last time I'd see him." It was under similar circumstances that Miss Bird said good-bye to John Reddy, after our two-hour English exam in the gym. A dozen of us, groggy from the ordeal, eager for the punchy jolt of nicotine tinged with smoke, were filing out at the end so Miss Bird could only call out "Good-bye" across rows of desks, and John Reddy who was sort of with us, though not with us, waved goodbye to her in his offhanded way: you could see that the exam ordeal had been roughest on him, he appeared distracted, sweaty as if he'd been sleeping in his clothes (which maybe he had), T-shirt stained across his back and his lank, thick, black hair disheveled from running his hands through it despairingly. Miss Bird would declare afterward, her pursed lips trembling with hurt and indignation, "Never did I suspect John Reddy wouldn't be coming to graduation! Or that, so abruptly, he was leaving Willowsville. He never hinted. And I had a graduation present for him—Walt Whitman's *Leaves of Grass* in a beautiful facsimile first edition. I've kept it for twelve years, wrapped." That last day of exams was a Friday. By Wednesday of the following week, John Reddy was gone.

He'd passed all his courses with average grades of 75 percent, 73 percent, 79 percent except for Vocational Arts III: Mr. Hornby had given him a grade of 94 percent.

None of the girls of the Circle, searching their hearts and consciences, being truthful, mostly Christian good-girls, could lay claim to having seen John Reddy following exams in the gymnasium. Except Katie Olmsted in her sweetly dogged way insisted she'd "caught a fleeting glimpse" of him, Sunday morning, 9:48 A.M., as he was driving the Mercury (at a moderate speed) south on Haggarty Road; the Olmsteds, en route to the First Presbyterian Church, were driving north. Katie said eagerly, "I wonder—where was John Reddy going? To church? In a white shirt, so handsome, so neat, a long-sleeved white shirt with the cuffs buttoned, but no necktie that I could see, and his hair wetted and combed, like a tamed wild animal? I'm sure it was *church*. I'd been hearing talk of John Reddy attending services at the United Methodist, and the Church of God, but nobody actually saw him; there were no eye-witnesses; people brushed it off saying such a notion was far-fetched—'John Reddy, in *church*? *Him*?' But his mom used to go to church, I've heard. The Hearts may be a good Christian family, who can judge? It's sinners who need church, not the rest of us." Katie acknowledged she got a little excited, and leaned out the window to wave at John Reddy rushing past, and "maybe, just maybe" John Reddy waved back; though it wasn't clear whether he'd recognized her. Sexually rapacious, stylishly dressed Mrs. Rindfleisch, Jon's problem mother (a "nympho-mom" we'd been hearing lurid rumors of since we were all in sixth grade), her hunter-green Mazda parked crookedly, idling at the curb, hurried swaying into Muller's Drugs to pick up a prescription (for Valium: Mrs. Rindfleisch described herself as a pioneer of state-of-the-art tranquillizers in Willowsville in those heady years) and nearly collided with a display of hot water bottles, staring at the tall rangy classmate of her son's, what was his name, the Heart boy, the boy with the astonishing sexy eyes, the boy who'd plugged Melvin Riggs, Jr., through the skull, darling Mel Riggs who'd once, a decade ago at a New Year's Eve party at the Bozers', danced her into an alcove, knee between her red-spangled lamé skirt, and murmured into her burning ear words of breathy endearing obscenities—"The last I can reasonably expect in my lifetime, I think." Mrs. Rindfleisch heard her husky voice lift lyrically, "John Reddy! Hel-*lo*." She somewhat surprised herself, cornering a boy Jon's age who so clearly wanted to escape. (What was John Reddy doing in Muller's? Some of us speculated he was stocking up on Trojans for the weekend, he must've run through rubbers like other guys run through Kleenex.) John Reddy appeared startled that Mrs. Rindfleisch knew his name. Or maybe it was the lilt of her voice, her gleaming predator eyes and shiny lip-sticked lips. He must not have recognized her though he and Jon had been on the varsity track team together and she'd come to a few meets, eager to see her son excel and to be proud of him even if, most times, unfortunately, he didn't, and she wasn't. "Well, um, John—lots of excitement imminent, yes?" Still he regarded her blankly. "I mean—the end of the school year. The end of—high school. Your prom, graduation. Such a happy time, yes?" Politely John Reddy murmured what sounded like, "Yes, ma'am." Or possibly, "No, ma'am." Mrs. Rindfleisch queried brightly, "And will your family be attending your graduation, I hope?" John Reddy shook his head, pained. "Why, that's too bad! No one?" Mrs. Rindfleisch moved closer, emanating a sweet-musky scent like overripe gardenias. She tried not to lick her lips. "Why don't you join us, then? I'm hosting a lavish brunch that day. Family, rela-tives, friends, scads and scads of Jon's classmates—your classmates. Will you join us? Yes?" Not looking at the woman's heated face, John Reddy mumbled he might be busy that day, but thanks. Flushed with her own generosity, Mrs. Rindfleisch said, "Well, John Reddy, know yourself *in-vited*. *Chez* Rindfleisch. Anytime. In fact—" Her second Valium since lunch, or was it her third, had just begun to kick in. That delicious downward sensation. Sliding-careening. A spi-raling tightness in the groin. In the juicy crevices and folds of the groin. She had a quick, wild vision of how her pubic hair (not graying for the same shrewd reason the hairs on her head were not "graying" but shone a fetching russet-red) would appear to John Reddy Heart's staring eyes, flattened like italics glimpsed through the pink-satiny transparency of her panty-girdle and believed it was a sight that would arouse him; she laughed, effervescent. Teeth sparkled. Asking the edgy boy if, um, would he like to join her in a Coke? a cup of coffee? a beer? a slice or two of zingy-hot pizza with all the trimmings? next door at the Haven or, better idea, her car's right outside, ignition already switched on for a quick get-away, they could drive to Vito's Paradiso Lounge on Niagara Boulevard, no trouble there, him being served. "What d'you say, John Reddy? Yes?" But John Reddy was mumbling, not meeting her eye, "Ma'am, thanks but I gotta go, I guess. Now." Mrs. Rindfleisch was astonished to see her hand leap out, as long ago that very hand might've leapt out to forestall her swaying, toddler-age Jonathan from falling and injuring himself, now it was a beautifully maintained middle-age hand, manicured, Revlon-red-polished nails scratchily caressing the boy's hairy forearm, brushing against the boy's taut groin, she saw a flicker of—what?—helpless lust in his face?—or childish fear?—"Ma'am, thanks, *no*." Quickly then he walked away, about to break into a run. Mrs. Rindfleisch stared after him, incensed. How dare he! What was this! As if everyone didn't know the brute animal, the lowlife fiend, sexy Killer-boy! As if she hadn't one of her own, a handsome sexy teenage son, at home! Watching him exit Muller's as if exiting her life, steadying herself against a rack of Hallmark greeting cards. His lank black greasy hair was long enough for her to have seized into a fist, and tugged. God damn she should've. The way he'd insulted her. A hard-on like that, practically popping out of his zipper, and cutting his eyes at her, sending her unmistakable sex messages with his eyes, staring at her breasts, at her (still glamorous, shapely) legs in diamond-black-textured stockings, then coolly backing away, breaking it off teasing like coitus interruptus, the prig. Like all of them,

Goddamn prigs. Tears wetted Mrs. Rindfleisch's meticulously rouged cheeks. Tears wetted Mrs. Rindfleisch's raw-silk champagne-colored blouse worn beneath an aggressively youthful heather suede vest ideal for mild autumn days and nights. She stumbled in her high-heeled lizard-skin Gucci pumps to the door, or what appeared to be the door; she'd forgotten— what? Some reason, some purchase to be made, she'd come into Muller's for, what was it, God damn who cares, that beautiful boy was slipping through her outstretched fingers *like my very youth, my beauty, you wouldn't believe how lovely I was, my perfect little breasts so bouncy and so free-standing, just hated to strap myself into a bra.* Oh but there, he was waiting for her— on the sidewalk—he hadn't stalked off, after all—no: it was her son Jon, glowering Jonathan, he'd sighted the Mazda crooked at the curb, motor running, left-turn signal crazily winking. "Oh Jesus, Mom, what the hell are you *doing*?" this boy yelled, grabbing at her arm, and Mrs. Rindfleisch who was crying screamed, "You! You and your dirty foul-minded 'John Reddy Heart'! *Don't any of you touch me.*" A few hours later, Smoke Filer and Bo Bozer, high on weed, cruising Smoke's T-bird along the Cheektowaga strip, swore they sighted John Reddy driving the Mercury with, Smoke said, Sasha Calvo squeezed up so close beside him she was "basically riding his cock" but Bo disagreed—"That wasn't any high school kid, that was a woman. A broad. Somebody who knows the score." Smoke tailed John Reddy's car for miles but eventually lost it in traffic. Blake Wells argued, most convincingly, that he had to be the one to see John Reddy last—"I saw him with the U-Haul." He'd been cruising through Tug Hill Park on his bicycle, fighting the senior-year malaise that had been seeping into his soul "like squid ink" for months, looping along the One Hundred Weeping Willows Walk by Glen Creek and through to Spring Street, and North Long; from North Long to Garrison. He carried his camera in the bicycle basket and frequently stopped to take pictures. "Preserving the time before graduation. Like it was our pre-posthumous time. Our time yet of innocence. I guess, like a lot of the kids, I was feeling kind of lost and scared." And suddenly he saw, passing through an intersection, a familiar sight—was it John Reddy Heart in his battered car, a U-Haul attached? Blake almost toppled from his bicycle, he was so surprised. He stopped, snatched up his camera. "I seemed to know this might be a historic moment." Blake waved, but John Reddy didn't notice. Or, if noticing, didn't respond. The car and the wobbly U-Haul were moving away. Quickly, Blake snapped several pictures. Of the twenty-four exposures on the film, only these four would turn out blurred, dreamlike. "God damn!" Many times we examined the pictures, in the months and years to come. We held them to the light, turned them at hopeful angles, as if they were visual riddles like the artwork of M. C. Escher, or children's games in which shapes secreted in clouds or foliage suddenly leap out at the viewer. But these were not riddles to be solved. These were merely blurred snapshots. Blake said, disgusted, "I don't know what went wrong. I steadied the camera on the bike handlebars, I sighted the car perfectly in the viewfinder. *I know I did.*"

But we could see only blurred movement along a familiar roadway that might've been a car, or a U-Haul. "Like background in a picture in which the foreground, the actual subject, is missing."

19

Said John Reddy, You never knew me.
Said John Reddy, Ain't got a clue of me.
John Reddy, John Reddy Heart.

Kenawka, Minnesota. One of those American places, and there are many such, where you wind up, living your life, *your actual once-only life*, though you can't recall having chosen it or why, in the first flush of what delirious or drunken or deluded exhilaration you might have thought *Yes! I can do it. I will.*

His name in this place was Richard A. Eickhorn. Yet to himself Ritchie. In his soul, seventeen years old.

He woke to a painfully dry mouth, veins pinching like wires at his temples. It was so early—7:40 A.M.—there was no sun. And perhaps it wasn't a season for sun. He was in his Thermopaned but still drafty first-floor study where he'd slept what had remained of the previous vodka-blurred night on a sofa bed he hadn't tugged open, in his clothes he hadn't removed, only his boots shoved off and left to fall, spread-eagled, on the floor. He was about to pick up the phone and dial her number she'd scribbled on a Marriott Inn cocktail napkin when the phone rang and he answered it, instead. He seemed to know it would be her—Evangeline Fesnacht. The last voice he'd heard the previous night. A woman's husky voice, that air of urgency. When they'd been together, those intense hours, he'd felt himself drifting into love as a small tethered boat drifts with the current to the end of its capacity for drift and then is brought up rudely short. *No. Too late. I'm a married man and a father. A once-promising poet who has lost his youth, and his ambition. Too late.*

He was thirty-seven years old. His father had died at the age of forty-seven. That was considered young. Set beside eternity, forty-seven is young. You could argue, Ritchie had ten years remaining.

He held the receiver to his ear. He heard the voice, wonderfully nasal, intimate, the unmistakable accent of his upstate New York boyhood, lifted in girlish contentiousness as if they'd been arguing only a few minutes ago—"I have a question for you, Ritchie: *Why weren't there any fingerprints on that gun except John Reddy's?*"

II. Mr. Fix-it

1

*What I believed to be broken things of no more connection
with one another than mounds of trash were pieces like
those of a shattered mirror I could fit together again. Because
God created the wholeness and mankind has shattered it and we
are given the power to piece it back together again.* On Mount
Nazarene in the blinding ice slope this vision came to him
that would be completed twenty-two years later beside the
Glass Lake.

2

MR. FIX-IT. Says so in white balloon letters on both doors of his shiny sky-blue Ford pickup.

MR FIX-IT. HAVE TOOLS—WILL TRAVEL! In the yellow pages of the Oswego County telephone book, where he'd placed a small cheery ad under both *Carpentry* and *Handyman*.

MR. FIX-IT was of an age difficult to guess. In his late thirties—but he seemed younger. Lean, dark, hungry-looking—women loved to feed him meals, or to try. Men liked drinking with him because he was a good listener, or gave that impression. A man of few words, himself. As if distrustful of speech. Though not shy. Much of the time he wore work clothes, faded jeans, T-shirts, old battered paint-splotched boots, but sometimes he'd show up at a customer's house in a white shirt and necktie beneath his denim jacket. Or a good-looking fedora instead of his usual grimy baseball cap. He was frequently unshaven but never cultivated a mustache or a beard. His black hair, threaded with silver like mica, was long enough to be tied back in a ponytail sometimes, and in warm weather held in place by a red headband stained with old sweat. There was an air of unconscious swagger about him, a just-perceptible favoring of his left leg. In addition to the pickup he rode a Honda motorcycle. He tinkered with both vehicles himself. He lived in a secondhand trailer set in a lush ruin of an apple orchard on what remained of a fruit farm on Barndollar Road, Route 37, a mile east of the country town of Iroquois Point, New York. Within the memory of most neighbors the fruit farm had been a working though not thriving farm, but it had been allowed to sink into dereliction for the past twenty years, like many small farms in the countryside south of the eastern shore of Lake Ontario. Of the outbuildings, MR. FIX-IT retained, and energetically repaired, only a small barn for professional use.

MR. FIX-IT
HAVE TOOLS——WILL TRAVEL!
Carpentry   Painting   Odd Jobs   My Specialty

was prominently advertised on the front of the barn, two-foot-high white balloon letters on a sky-blue background. There was a cartoon optimism to the sign. Customers asked, "Did you paint that sign yourself?" and MR. FIX-IT shrugged affably and said, "Ever need any signs painted, big or small, I'm your man." There was a boyish-anxious defensiveness to this response. As if MR. FIX-IT believed he might be challenged in his authority, and you hadn't better challenge him. He had a carpenter's look of being carved from wood, a darkish stained and carved wood, gnarly muscled forearms, compact hard-looking muscles in his shoulders and chest. He was restless standing still, shifting his shoulders, flexing his fingers. Though he'd be smiling, too. As if reminding himself every few minutes *Smile!* It was quite a dazzling smile. Women melted at that smile. Men found themselves smiling back. MR. FIX-IT's voice was deep, throaty, hoarse and slightly cracked as if, maybe, his windpipe or larynx had been injured. The impulse was to ask *Have you been hurt, MR. FIX-IT?*

But no one ever did. For there was something edgy about
MR. FIX-IT, too. Your heart might begin to beat more quickly
in his presence as if, who knows why, for what unfounded
reason, you felt unease, even danger. But there was the man's
smile, quick and boyish. And, for sure, you'd find yourself
smiling back.

When John Heart, who was MR. FIX-IT, purchased what
remained of the fruit farm, five acres of wild-growing apple
trees, falling-down buildings and overgrown meadows, it was
said he'd paid with a single check, not requiring a bank loan
or a mortgage. The check was from an Oswego bank but
where the man had come from most recently wasn't clear—
"Up farther north. Different places." Meaning north in New
York State, or north elsewhere? There was a drawl to his
accent that suggested not north but south and west. The real
estate woman, from Oswego, who sold John Heart the property liked to say he reminded her of Montgomery Clift as a
sexy cowboy in *Red River* which played sometimes on late-
night TV.

It was late May when John Heart took possession of the
farm and by this time wild lilac, pale purple, dark purple and
vivid white, had grown to a height of eight feet or more
hiding most of the rotted old farmhouse from the highway. A
rich, sweet, intoxicating lilac smell pervaded the air. John
Heart, the new owner, blinked like a man waking in a dream.
Or was he a man waking from a dream. He sniffed deeply,
half-shut his eyes, said, "Smells like heaven would be." In the
years he'd live on the property, in a nickel-colored Cruiser-
Craft trailer on cinderblocks amid the orchard, he was never
to trim back the wild lilac trees or haul the debris of the collapsed house. He was never to do anything serious about the
apple orchard, just let the trees grow more and more wild. He
was a good-looking but elusive and mysterious man, apparently a bachelor, with no family. Or none he mentioned.
(People sometimes asked if he was related to "that old man

Leander Heart, that artist or whatever you'd call him—the one who collected all the glass bottles? The 'Glass Ark' up in Shawmouth?" John Heart would shake his head curtly, no.) If you stood close to John Heart you could see a small hook of a scar in his left eyebrow and a droop to the eyelid if he was tired and, attached to the dark liquidy iris of that eye, a tiny, almost invisible drop of blood. You might be distracted by this drop of blood, talking to him. Until finally you might ask, "What happened to your eye, John?" And the man who frequently introduced himself to strangers as MR. FIX-IT, as if that might be his actual name, or as much of a name as you'd require from him, or he'd merit, touched the eye with his fingertips, annoyed or embarrassed as if he'd never been asked about it before, and said, with his affable shrug, "Just lucky, I guess. It wasn't gouged out."

In Iroquois Point where everyone knew everyone else, rumors naturally circulated about MR. FIX-IT living out on Barndollar Road. He'd spent time in prison, it was believed. Auto theft? No doubt he'd been a kid at the time. His reputation through the county was for scrupulous honesty, first-rate and exacting work, never a complaint or surly remark. No one was apparently close enough to John Heart to know the details of his background or to wish to ask. In any case, in Oswego County, it wasn't uncommon to know men, many of them good family men, who'd "spent time," as kids, in one or another prison facility.

3

Thirty-eight years old and not a day passed, not a night (unless he drank, nights could be long), even an hour he didn't reflect on how he'd survived—so many years beyond the time, the hour, when he'd believed he would be killed, beaten and stomped to death by New York State troopers who must've had good reason to hate him, or to fear him, as if seeing the very image of Satan in him, and he'd accepted this, his fate. *Yet I didn't die.*

Sometimes, though he loved his life, he felt regret. A good, clean death it would've been in that glittering ice field and his family would remember him kindly.

Since then he'd always been vigilant. Always prepared to defend himself. He didn't want to hurt other people, other men, though he knew how. (It was inconceivable to him he'd ever hurt a woman.) Many years ago the dark-tanned, squinting-smiling man who'd been Daddy had squatted before him instructing him "don't punch—counterpunch"—"let the other guy swing first and get off balance then you step in: *pow!*"—and he believed his father had taught him, too, to avoid such confrontations when he could, where he could, so

long as it was only pride and vanity, his pride and vanity, that
might suffer, and no other person dependent on him. "You
can always back out of a fight, Johnny. Unless someone else,
like a woman, will get hurt if you do."

It seemed clear to him as a child of scarcely six that Daddy
must be speaking of Mommy. Who else?

"Hey, 'Fix-It'—asshole!"

This windy-bright March morning John Heart was walking
quickly in the corridor outside family court, at the first-floor
rear of the Oswego County Courthouse. It was 10:20 A.M.
The custody hearing, *Leavey v. Leavey*, was still in session
and would continue through the morning. And then it would
be adjourned and rescheduled for another morning, probably.
A decision from the judge was expected next week. John
heard footsteps close behind him and saw in the corner of his
eye the hulking figure of Leavey, his pursuer, who'd left the
courtroom just after him. Leavey repeated, in a low, jeering
voice, "'Fix-It'—asshole!" John Heart gave no sign of hearing.
He continued walking, headed for the exit. He didn't want a
confrontation with the former husband of the woman with
whom he was in love, and with whom, in a manner of speaking, he lived. Not anywhere, not at this stage in his life, and
especially not here in the county courthouse with sheriff's
deputies posted in the halls alert for sudden eruptions of violence—"domestic case violence" it was called. Nola Leavey
had told him it was about the only kind of violence that
occurred in the courthouse and that it invariably centered
around family court—divorce and child custody cases. People
killed, and were killed. Men were the killers, women the victims. Usually.

"I'm talking to you, asshole. Just a minute—"

Leavey's voice was loud and aggrieved. People glanced at
him warily. He sounded and looked as if he'd been drinking.
John Heart was nearly at the exit, calculating how he'd make
a run for the pickup as soon as he got outside, when Leavey

grabbed at his jacket sleeve, then at his arm. Strong, angry fingers. They scuffled together, panting, Leavey cursed him as John managed to wrench his arm free, biting his lower lip, damned if he'd get into a shouting match with this guy another time. Though wanting to grab Leavey around the neck and shoulders to quiet him, comfort him—"You don't want to do this, brother. Let the judge decide, don't screw us all up." One of the guards was approaching them, right hand casually touching the butt of his holstered pistol. "Hey? You two? What's the problem?" The guard was someone John knew, a name and a face he knew, though not well, not well enough to save himself from getting pushed around if it came to that, possibly he'd done some work for the man's wife, or his parents, they'd seen each other around at the Lakeside Inn maybe, at the County Line, at Capuano's, weekends. John said, "No problem, Officer." Jordan Leavey said loudly, laughter in his voice, "*Noooo* problem, Officer." He might have been mimicking the buffoonish speech of a TV personality, or he might have been mimicking John Heart.

John pushed through the exit door, and Leavey followed close behind. Bright, gusty, cold air. Swaths of sky vivid as the sky blue of MR. FIX-IT's pickup parked on the far side of the lot where, God damn, he'd never get to it in time. Leavey kept pace with him, laughing, cursing, shoving at him with the flat of his hand, pushing him off course. They were stumbling together, swaying like drunks. John ducked, swung around in a quick lateral movement as if, on the basketball court, slipping a big, aggressive guard, but Leavey followed, a man about to lose control. John thought *Don't fight him: don't make that mistake*. He hadn't realized his face was burning until the cold air struck. His face had begun to burn in the courtroom, he'd had to get out, had to get to where he could breathe, knowing he was innocent, he'd done nothing to incur punishment yet knowing too that he would be punished and would bring punishment, and grief, upon others close to him. Nola had turned anxiously toward him as he'd suddenly stood, muttered, "Excuse me!" and left the room. He was an involved third party in this suit, as Nola's lawyer described him, but not a principal. *Leavey v. Leavey. Child custody, dangerous emotions. Loving another man's wife* even if, in fact, she wasn't the other man's wife any longer, hadn't been his wife for several years.

Yet John could understand why Leavey was risking so much, following him. Demanding to know what John Heart was doing with his wife, his kids, *his*. Nola had said, *I hope to God he hasn't been drinking this morning, it will be terrible for us all if he's been drinking*, and in fact Leavey smelled of alcohol, unmistakably. John tried to calm the man down though he was excited, too. "Jordan, come on. You're only making things worse." Leavey said, "Fuck *you*! Who the hell are *you* telling me what to do?"

John heard his father's voice of thirty years before. *Don't punch—counterpunch*. He was broken out in sweat, trembling with the adrenaline rush. But he didn't want to fight Jordan Leavey, he was finished with fighting, even to protect himself. Jordan's face was blotched with emotion, rage. He was younger than John Heart by a year or two but looked older, with bloodshot slate-gray eyes, eyes of hurt, bafflement, indignation beyond speech. A stocky man, formerly an athlete—college football. Now thickset as a steer, with sloping shoulders, tall as John Heart at six-two, heavier by at least thirty pounds. There were vertical creases like knife marks in his flushed cheeks. His graying red-brown hair was thick at the sides, thinning at the crown. He wore a suit, a white shirt and tie, cuff links. As a younger man he'd been vain of his looks, Nola had said, but as an ex-husband who was restricted by a court order to visiting only on alternate weekends, for a carefully delineated number of hours, he'd lost his vanity, his masculine pride. Nola had spoken of her husband's hands, his strong hands that could be so gentle but sometimes "struck out" as if of their own volition. A vortex of heat, quick pummeling blows. *We'd be left stunned. Both of us, and*

*the kids, crying. But I was the one on the floor with the bloody
mouth.* Leavey currently had a managerial position with a GM
auto parts manufacturer in Lockport, New York, a well-paid
job as he described it. But since the divorce it wasn't clear
what the man's life was.

Sometimes, John Heart lost the logic of his own life. The
life he'd scraped together out of the trash heap of his boyhood. He wanted to commiserate with Jordan Leavey, who
stared at him with such hatred. Not fight him. *I know what it
is. Once your family breaks up, you're fucked. What's lost won't
return, brother.*

"No! Stop! *Please!*"

A woman's voice—Nola's. From the rear entrance of the
courthouse she emerged, coatless. Her voice was shrill, frightened and angry, the wrong voice, triggering Leavey's fury.
Now it begins John thought *now it can't be stopped.* Leavey
swung at John, grunting, a clumsy roundhouse right that
would have sunk John to the ground like a dead weight
except somehow he managed to avoid the force of the blow,
crouching, but losing his balance, slipping on a patch of ice.
Leavey charged after him, cursing. All was confused, chaotic.
As if the parking lot was tilting. Earth and sky tilting. Long
ago Dahlia Heart had thrilled and frightened her children by
excitedly describing an earthquake, "a madness of God," in
Guadalajara, Mexico, her beautiful eyes widened, hands flur-
ried, unnerving the younger children for what reason no one
could know, even the eldest, John Reddy, who'd prided himself on not being susceptible to his mother's exaggerated,
dramatic tales; he would recall this sorry episode in the parking lot of the Oswego County Courthouse, being harassed,
mocked, struck by the enraged Leavey, not wanting to hit
back, as a kind of earthquake. Picking you up, throwing you
down. Blows raining on all sides. The strength had rapidly
faded from John's legs. He was thirty-eight, the legs are the
first to go in an aging boxer, blood pulsed in his eyes, darkening his vision, a roaring in his ears, Nola screamed, trying

to pull Leavey away, "No! Stop! God damn you, Jordan, you promised! You—" A knuckled fist struck John's cheekbone beneath the right eye, so hard the bone must've cracked. Another blow to the side of the head, Leavey was grunting, "Fuck! Fucker! Get out of my life! My wife's life! My kids'! Ex-*con*!" At Tomahawk Island you couldn't back up in a fight, if you backed up you were finished, but John staggered backward, left ear ringing, the eardrum maybe broken, oh Christ. He'd never fully recovered from the beating the state troopers had given him on Mount Nazarene, fists, feet, billy clubs, resisting arrest was the charge, the provocation, he'd tasted his own death, black bile at the back of his mouth.

Leavey was shouting at him. Nola was pleading. The woman's deathly-white face, not an attractive face now, her damp frightened eyes. *Do you love me enough to risk getting hurt by that madman* Nola had inquired of John Heart frankly, flirtation and dread in her voice, and John Heart had laughed carelessly. *Sure*. And so it was true. All of it.

"All right. Break it up."

The scuffle, one-sided, hadn't lasted more than two or three minutes. Two sheriff's deputies pulled Leavey off John Heart and Nola and another man, a stranger, helped him to his feet. Nola was crying, not in sorrow but in anger, frustration. She wasn't a woman who cried readily, and never in public, strangers watching at the courthouse entrance, whispering to one another. Leavey shook off the deputies, cursing them. They were speaking quietly with him, repeating a few simple words. It seemed clear now that he'd been drinking, he was desperate, a hunted man. A man who wanted only to see his two children more, to have more hours with them, more days with them, more custody, he'd filed for full custody, a measure of his desperation but also his love, a father's love, that might be argued. His face was shiny with sweat and he was breathing hard, his breath steaming, as if he'd been running uphill. "You O.K., mister?" one of the deputies asked John Heart.

"Need somebody to look after that?"—meaning his bleeding face. Quickly, annoyed, John said, "No." It was nothing, a scratch. He just wanted to get the hell out of there. He had the distinct idea, Nola would want to talk him out of it, that the deputies were eyeing him with astonishment, contempt, that he hadn't fought his opponent at all, letting himself be hit, called names, what kind of a guy's this?

They watched him, how many eyes, limping to the sky-blue Ford pickup. His left knee aching. Left eye, where the retina had come detached, years ago, blinded with tears. MR. FIX-IT, that's who this guy is? Carpenter, handyman? HAVE TOOLS—WILL TRAVEL! The hopeful telephone number beneath: (716) 737-9542. Six-year-old Ellen had helped him paint bright yellow sunflowers on the sides of the truck and these looked, in the unsparing light of a cold March morning, like goofy grinning decapitated heads. Nola called hesitantly after him, "John?—wait." But he wasn't going to wait, and she knew it. He was in one of his moods and wouldn't talk, he'd sulk off to nurse his wounds. The aftermath of fury pumping his heart for he was a man of pride born to fight, to use his fists, or a tire iron, a claw hammer, tools he carried right there in MR. FIX-IT's pickup. *But I won't. Because I am strong enough to resist. Because, whatever is believed of me, I can overcome it.*

Nor would he press charges against Leavey. He guessed that the deputies wouldn't arrest Leavey, they'd let him off with a warning, poor bastard, they saw it at the courthouse, in family court, all the time, a divorced father, custody suit, he's desperate to see more of his kids, discovers after he loses them how he loves them, and the wife, too. The woman's got a live-in boyfriend, in this case, as everyone seemed to know, an ex-con.

Sure, the deputies would be sympathetic with Jordan Leavey. If you didn't know about the drinking, and the abuse, hearing his sad tale of being kicked out of his own home, you'd be sympathetic with him, too.

4

He hadn't prayed. That hour, that night his life was changed forever. Hadn't known yet about praying. Emptying yourself, being filled with God. A rush of brilliant blinding light. A rush of certainty. What people called in their groping fumbling way "God." He hadn't prayed, praying was beside the point. It had happened so swiftly—a fraction of a second. *Do what you have to do. And what you do, you look back and say,* I had to do that. *And so I did.*

They hadn't wanted him to sacrifice his life. Aged sixteen. They'd wanted him to sacrifice his life. Aged sixteen.

No, they'd loved him. Her, especially. It was his idea, not theirs.

All of it, John Reddy Heart's idea.

Not that they would speak of it. Ever. As words, printed words on a page, columns of print, sometimes confused him, dazzled his brain, so spoken words, uttered words, his own words especially halting and inadequate in his ears, embarrassed him. *I had to do that. So I did.*

Sure there was pride in it, vanity, that he'd been man enough, strong enough, just a kid of sixteen at the time. And the years to follow. And the long nights. *Why? Because I am strong enough. I did what I did, and grew into my strength.*

Rushing up the stairs to Dahlia's bedroom, knowing what he'd find. Or nearly. He'd heard the gunshots. And stooping to pick up the gun. Grandpa's gun. A gun he'd held many times in his hands, as a boy. That instant, that swift irrevocable decision—he'd done it, and so it was done.

Grandpa's gun. Dropped onto the floor after it had been fired, discharged three times, lying now at the edge of the beautiful dusty-rose thick-piled carpet already beginning to soak with blood. The gun that would be referred to, forever afterward, as the *murder weapon*.

One of those mysterious word-terms. Like *God*. Sounds you hear, and hear, so many times. You lose the meaning. If there was ever a single coherent meaning.

A *murder weapon* means there's *murder*, means there's a *murderer*.

He hadn't wanted to sacrifice himself, aged sixteen. But it had happened.

Wanting only, since his father's death, to keep the family together. Nothing terrified him more than being lost, scattered. It wasn't that he might lose the others, or be lost by them—if he lost them he'd lose parts of himself. He believed this. For it was so easy to be broken apart. For they'd traveled so often, those early years. From Lubbock, Texas, where his father was stationed at the Reese Air Force Base and where John Reddy Heart was born, to Gila Bend, Arizona, and the air force base there, where Farley Heart was born, at last to the base at San Angelo, Utah, where his father was killed in a plane crash on a routine flight. (So through his life he would envision his airman father's death in a glittering silver attack jet falling out of the cobalt-blue desert sky to smash on earth. "Mechanical failure." Yet the pilot hadn't ejected himself— why? Had he refused to surrender the plane? Imagining he could bring it under control? The wreckage, on an isolated mountainside, yielded no secrets.) After San Angelo there was Sparks, Nevada, there was Reno and at last Vegas where his grandpa Heart came to live with them. Wanting only that their lives wouldn't unravel like one of the cheap sweaters their mother bought them at Sears. Fall apart like her cheap high-heeled shoes—the heel suddenly detached from the shoe so that poor Mommy, flushed with shame, had to limp back home. Wanting that their lives wouldn't be shattered like glass, how the desert at the edge of the city was littered with broken pieces of glass and other debris, cellophane wrappers, metal scraps. *This world is filling up with the shit of mankind one day to choke us as we deserve* Grandpa Heart observed with vehement satisfaction raising his glass of bourbon in a toast to such a fate. *Oh Dad-dy!* Mommy would cry, exasperated. *Stuff it.* Wanting only that their lives wouldn't glitter melting in the sun the way, suddenly bored with her own drink, or maybe the drink had turned tepid, ice cubes melted to thin crescents and the whisky too diluted to taste, Mommy would toss the contents of her glass out onto the sandy soil beyond the porch of the shabby little bungalow on Arroyo Seco, Vegas, and whisper, *Oh shit.* Stretching and yawning like a big cat. By this time Mommy was "Dah-lia Heart" and her voice was throaty, shivery. It was a voice that invited you to look at her, to admire.

I am a woman who can do anything, no one can stop me.

When news came to her of her husband's death she had not been that woman, a younger sister maybe, naive, a fool, anyone who has such rotten luck has got to be a fool was Dahlia Heart's judgment. Her eldest son John Reddy, John, could recall only vaguely the circumstances of those days, the news of the death, Mommy stunned, stupefied, hair in a coarse pigtail between her shoulder blades, barefoot, her skin tight-stretched and sallow, arms and legs oddly thin beside her distended belly which resembled a watermelon shoved up inside her clothes. For when her husband Lieutenant Lamarca was killed, Dorrie Lamarca was seven months pregnant with the baby girl who would be Shirleen.

She'd screamed, waking John Reddy and his brother. She'd fallen into a faint, hurt her head. Later she would beat at her great belly with her fists, hysterical, weeping, as a child might weep. She tore at her hair, raked her hands and arms with her nails. Other women on the base had cared for her. And for the little boys John Reddy who was six, Farley who was three. The baby girl, Shirleen, would be born prematurely, in another month, in the emergency room of a Sparks, Nevada, hospital to which, reeling from a combination of tequila and speed, bruised from a fall, or a scuffle, in a bar, Dorrie Lamarca had been brought by a man in a creamy-white cowboy hat who disappeared immediately afterward and was never heard of again. *Twenty-five when my husband died. My handsome air force husband. My hero-husband. A lieutenant. A fighter pilot. Flew an* A-10 Thunderbolt *at the San Angelo Air Force Base. And that was how he died—a crash, two hours into a mission, something wrong with the engine, he'd been on many missions, he was thirty-one years old. Oh, God—I loved him. I will always love him. Tony was my first love. We met when I was fifteen. There is no love like your first love. He died, and I was only a girl. I'd married him so young. He'd come to get me, I had to go with him. I hadn't any choice. I was just a girl, in Lubbock. Tony made me have babies. His babies. I loved him, I wanted to have his babies. Seven months pregnant when he died. I can't forgive him for dying. Can you imagine—three children, and I was twenty-five. Yes, I wanted to die. But I did not die. I loved my babies, I love my babies. Tony didn't believe in birth control. Wouldn't speak of it, it disgusted him. I didn't know any better. I did what he wanted. What he wanted, I wanted. There is God pushing through us seeking to be born, Tony said. He'd get excited especially if he was drinking. You learn to stay out of their way. My own father. Other guys at the base. Tony was Catholic but that wasn't it. He argued with other Catholics. I don't hate my babies. I love my babies. The Messiah might be born, Tony said. He was Catholic but never went to mass. He had ideas he'd elaborate. For instance—Jesus needs to be born again, and again. It wouldn't be only one time. He'd get in crazy arguments. He liked to get a rise out of people. I don't hate my babies I love them. All I have left of their father. Especially my Johnny. My little love. He's promised to take care of his mother who's a widow. All our life.*

Those long nights before the baby was born. Just the two of them in Mommy's bed.

She'd held him, her Johnny, locked safe in her arms. Safe, and tight. She'd given him Daddy's Air Force wristwatch with its large flat face, its greeny-glowing numerals and hands—"But you're too young to wear it yet. Someday." But sometimes he wore the wristwatch anyway, on his slender forearm, grimy adhesive tape wound around the band to make it fit. His warm face pressed against Mommy's heavy breasts lightly perspiring, smelling of talcum through the nylon lace of her nightgown he would lie very still listening to the minute *tick-tick-tick* of Daddy's watch.

This was in the motel with the rainbow neon in Sparks, Nevada, where they rented a room by the week. Most nights were sultry, the desert sky rippling with flashes of heat lightning. Sometimes the TV was on, only the picture not the sound. The old movies Mommy liked best weren't in color but in black and white—"Things were more serious then." So he'd come to believe that the past, the time before he was born, had been just black and white. On the bedside table was Mommy's tumbler of whisky, her black plastic ashtray heaped with cigarette butts and ashes. She'd let Johnny sip from the tumbler, she'd let him draw a puff on her cigarette and smile when he coughed. "Take your time, hon. There's plenty of time waiting." He was fascinated, a little frightened, feeling the baby kick inside Mommy's tight-stretched belly. "Your little sister, Johnny. I know she's going to be a girl. Feel her? Shirleen."

Shirleen. He'd helped Mommy choose the name.

Always he would feel he'd had a hand in the making of her.

His sister. One day she'd change her name, taking the veil as it was called, a bride of Christ. But always she was Shirleen. Always he would remember her in Mommy's belly kicking against his amazed outspread fingers. "Baby? Hi! It's me. Johnny." And Mommy would laugh liking him when he was funny not sad. When he said kooky unexpected things like people do who've been drinking.

He was six, almost seven. He'd lost interest in playing with children his own age. And anyway there wasn't time. At the San Angelo base he'd had to drop out of first grade to be with Mommy. In Sparks, five or six weeks in the motel, he went to school not at all. Nor in Reno. Though in Vegas he'd start school again, reluctantly. In the Sparks motel his little brother Farley slept on a vinyl sofa covered with towels, a single sheet and blanket. Whimpering and snuffling in his sleep. Farley who'd had bronchitis for five months. Farley who was forever sniffing, snuffling. Poor kid, a hairless rat. No rival for Johnny who looked like their father. "Your eyes exactly like his! Oh, God." Those nights she woke him repeatedly from sleep to take his hands in hers, spread the fingers and press them in wonder against her belly that was always burning-hot to the touch. Her young face, a girl's face, swollen, lumpy, glaring with tears. Her face that was the last thing he saw as he drifted into sleep, too exhausted to keep his eyes from clos-ing, and the first thing he saw when she nudged him awake, needing him she said, not wanting to be awake and alone she said. "Because I'm afraid. I just don't know what might happen if I'm alone too much." Mommy's face and Mommy's belly that shimmered pale through the gauzy fabric of the nightgown. "Johnny, d'you know you come from here, too? When you were born. Your daddy put you inside me, his seed, out of this," touching his quivering penis gently, almost shyly, though his body was entirely her possession yet allow-ing him to know how special this part of him was, and how special he, Johnny, was, "—and inside your mommy and you grew there, like your baby sister is growing now. That's why no one can love you like your mommy loves you. Because you came out of Mommy when you were born. And you can love no one like you love your mommy. Understand?" It wasn't noted that Farley too had been born out of Mommy's belly, put there by Daddy. It was possible to believe, those nights, that Farley didn't exist. And through his life John Heart would recall his young, enormously pregnant, whisky-smelling mother he'd adored and feared. How many times running his hands in reverence yet in utmost familiarity over a woman's body. Of course he had the right, of course the woman wanted him. Never any doubt. How could there be doubt. Running his hands over Nola Leavey's body and knowing she loved him, beyond the range of his love for her though he did in fact love her and wished to marry her if marriage to John Heart, an ex-con, would not endanger her custody of her children. For always it comes to the matter of children. *A child is someone you love more than yourself. And a hell of a lot more than you love your own happiness* Nola had said.

She'd recognized him, maybe: a man who loved women, and was loved by women. A man in awe of women. A man wary of women. Without asking him, she'd known.

Of course the child Johnny had adored his baby sister Shirleen when she was born. A wizened red-faced little monkey sputtering with what seemed like indignation. "Oh, God. I've got to keep this one alive, too. I'm so *tired.*" Mommy was a long time recovering from the birth. Mommy cried a lot. There'd been some worry that Shirleen might not live. Or, living, might not be "right." The fact was, Mommy had disappeared from the motel for two days before the baby was born, she'd gone drinking with a man and left Johnny and Farley alone in the motel room. That was O.K.: Johnny had twenty dollars she'd left for him, there was a 7-Eleven store across the highway and a vending machine just outside the door. There was TV through the night to keep them company. There was the telephone that, though it didn't ring, might ring, at any moment. "Johnny baby? Hi! it's Mommy checking in, sweetie. Everything under control?" One day Johnny would learn from a mean remark of Grandpa Heart's that Shirleen had been born with "poison" in her blood. Alcohol? Drugs? She'd weighed less than five pounds. Born six weeks premature. At first her eyes were slightly crossed. She hadn't much appetite yet was capable, as Mommy marveled, of vomiting up more than she'd consumed. "We could get her in Ripley's 'Believe It or Not,' you think?" She was colicky, fretful. Worse than Farley. (Johnny had been her dream baby, for sure. Slept for six hours straight the first weeks home from the hospital.) Shirleen cried feebly, like a sick cat. Yet she could cry for hours. She could cry, Mommy said, like the Chinese water torture. When you couldn't hear her, if you actually went to listen closely, she'd be crying. Mommy tried to nurse Shirleen but Mommy's breasts ached. Mommy drank as she nursed but it didn't seem to help. Mommy said, puzzled and resentful, "It's like this one isn't Tony's. It's like she's somebody else's." Sometimes Mommy was panicked, her hands trembling. "What if I can't keep her alive? What if she dies, will I be to blame? Who'd take care of you kids if—?" At other times she joked about leaving the baby in the Dumpster, adding with a wink, "Just kidding!" Johnny helped feed Shirleen, learned to prepare formula to exactly the right temperature. He came to believe that his baby sister knew him, smiled at him. He was special in her eyes. If Mommy's hands shook too much to risk bathing Shirleen, Johnny bathed her while Mommy watched from a chair. Johnny toweled the tiny body dry, sprinkled talcum, diapered her. He liked it that Shirleen was a little girl, and that little girls hadn't penises like little boys. He liked it that he was special. He was in charge of bathing Farley, too, and could almost believe that Farley was a girl. Yet Farley could be a tough little bugger for his size. Hated having his hair washed. Screamed like he was being killed if soap got in his eyes. Actually—this was funny!— tried to fight his older, bigger brother who could pin him in three seconds, like a TV wrestler, flat on the floor with the palm of one hand.

At the age of only seven, Johnny was brusque, bossy. If you had to take charge, you took charge. Seeing him walk with his dead father's swagger, Mommy stared and laughed weakly. "Oh Johnny. You're the one." There were sudden fierce kisses and hugs of Mommy's, and bouts of tickling that left Johnny hot-faced and trembling. Farley, sullenly sucking a thumb, watched from a corner. Or, turning his face to the wall, did not watch. Shirleen slept her thin fretful whimpering sleep. Mommy often came back to the motel room at dawn, a rose-sepia light like neon breaking across the desert beyond the blind-slatted window, through his life John Heart would recall the ache of excitement, almost unbearable excitement, when his mother returned to them, back from her waitress job, or her casino job, or a dinner-date as she called such appointments with a man friend whose face they would never see and whose name they would never hear, greeting them in a whisper, for usually only Johnny would be awake, kicking off the spike-heeled shoes she hated, flopping onto the hastily made-up bed, reaching for the bottle of Early Times and the cloudy tumbler already on the bedside table from the previous evening, a cigarette already bobbing in her mouth. Sometimes Mommy was in a good mood, sometimes Mommy was in a bad mood. But always Mommy would pull Johnny onto the bed beside her, hug him close against her. And tell him her stories, which often had to do with how close, how heartbreakingly close she'd come to winning a sizable amount of money that night. *If only I could get a decent stake, if somebody would please come along and set me up with a decent stake, is that too fucking much to ask?* Mommy allowed Johnny to sip her glass of whisky, it was a taste that stung, that burned, that brought tears to his eyes but he liked it. Mommy allowed Johnny to draw a few puffs on her cigarette as she smoothed his damp spiky hair off his forehead. Mommy said so much air-conditioning everywhere in Nevada her bones were chilled to the marrow, it was Johnny's duty to warm her.

By Greyhound they moved, the four of them, to Vegas. It was the New Year and Mommy'd had a vision, you could call it a vision from God though it was on TV, crowds of screaming, laughing revelers in tuxes, low-cut gowns, masks lifting their champagne glasses to toast the New Year as in the sky above fireworks and sparkles exploded like those wild, crazy things at the end of the world promised in the Book of Revelation. (In Lubbock, Texas, Mommy'd gone to church with her family, United Methodist. When she tried to think of those days, already eight years ago, a heavy sensation came over her brain.) She'd snapped her fingers and declared, "Our lousy rotten luck is due to change. I *promise*." The biggest surprise was that, out of nowhere it seemed, Grandpa Heart came to live with them. Not in a motel room as Johnny expected, but in an apartment. And afterward in a rented house. There were checks from the U.S. Air Force, there was money from Mommy's jobs and friends, there was money sometimes from Grandpa Heart's poker skills and occasional jobs, never really enough money but, as Mommy promised, at least they wouldn't starve. Grandpa Heart promised that would be so, too. It was he who regimented the household, as he called it. He described himself as an Old Testament ascetic in the wrong time and place. He believed in discipline, in no-nonsense and everybody pulling his own weight. He was a drinker but took pride in holding his liquor unlike some persons of his acquaintance who set a poor example for the young and impressionable. The first week of living with Mommy, Johnny, Farley and Shirleen, Grandpa Heart lectured Mommy on her "ramshackle white-trash ways." He would not tolerate it, he said. He was accustomed to orderliness. A towering, imposing figure, with flowing white hair and a thick white beard and severe eyes, like heated balls of glass. With a quick temper, harsh and comical by turns, in cowboy hat, vest and cowhide boots, the Lamarca children's first grandparent. Their only grandparent. "Children, your mother summoned me in her hour of need. I will never abandon you." Yet Grandpa Heart was often gone for a day or more, pursuing his "poker skills." When he returned, he was upset if the household was messy. He lectured Johnny, who was fascinated by the flamboyant old man, in the necessity for strict schedules, things in their rightful places, no clutter. He perceived the world of both nature and humankind as a "galaxy of blind chance" you could nonetheless bend to your will as you might dam a river, pour concrete over the earth, spray insecticide through the rooms of your dwelling, gestures that would prove in time futile for the river will one day rise up and destroy the dam, vegetation will push up through the concrete cracking it like ice, roaches and ants will return as they wish in biblical plenitude. "Yet the wise will persevere, for it is only they who will survive." Grandpa Heart insisted that meals be served at regular hours even if he, Aaron Leander, or Mommy herself wasn't present, even if the food set on the kitchen table was heated-up frozen dinners, soup out of cans, canned beans or Spaghetti-Os, slices of slick processed cheese on slices of Wonder Bread, potato chips. Even if breakfast was stale doughnuts, frosted cereal sprinkled with just-rancid milk, more potato chips. "Regular hours. Three times a day. Every day."

Even if there wasn't a Lord God the kids should be trained to say grace—"say grace" in Grandpa Heart's Texan drawl was a prissy, jeering yet severe commandment—before these meals, in preparation for the day when the children would find themselves in the blessed company of those who said grace because they abided in an America in which the Lord God was no stranger. Of course, it fell to Johnny to lead these prayers, as it fell to Johnny to prepare most of the meals. *Bless this food O Lord and bless us who are about to partake of it. Amen!* It was easy to do, it made Johnny feel important and who knew, maybe there was a Lord God fussy enough to care that somebody thanked Him three times a day like clock-work. (So through his life John Heart would utter this prayer silently. One day coming to believe in God if not in the Lord God of the Bible he'd imagined as a child, in the image of Aaron Leander Heart.) It was Grandpa Heart who insisted that Johnny return to school. Sure, Johnny was quick, sharp, like no other kid his age, but he needed schooling, too. Grandpa Heart scolded Mommy saying, "Girl, you've got no right to make this child into an adult long before his time. You had you one husband already. It's selfish, it's wrong, it's *unnatural*. And you could get arrested." Mommy said, flush-faced, "'Unnatural'?—you'd better watch your mouth, Aaron Leander." But before Grandpa Heart's bristling authority even Mommy had to give in. At least about school and other visi-ble matters the vigilant old man could monitor.

It was in Vegas that Mommy who was "Mrs. Lamarca"—"Mrs. Anthony Lamarca"—"Dorothy Lamarca"—"Dorrie Lamarca"—came to realize how much pain she had to endure hearing the name of her lost love casually uttered by strangers. In the startling lucidity of a sober afternoon (she'd had to go to the dentist, and was ashamed to turn up smelling of whisky) she came to the revelation that it was damaging to her to continue bearing that name. She wasn't strong enough, or good enough. Now that Tony was dead forever, her hus-band was dead and would never be her husband again and possibly it'd been her own fault for running off, marrying an Air Force pilot so you could argue she'd gotten what she deserved, there were those in the Heart family including her mother and sisters who might argue that but must it be for-ever? "I'm not thirty years old yet for God's sake! This is Vegas not fucking Lubbock, Texas." Grandpa Heart raised his glass and said he'd drink to that—"One hundred percent right, girl. Took you long enough to catch on." He told her she was too young, too damn good-looking and too smart to be a widow. "What kind of man wants to meet a widow? What kind of employer wants to hire a widow? If Aaron

Leander Heart, a wise, practical no-nonsense man, had a choice of hiring a woman who wasn't a widow, and a woman who was, you can bet your socks he'd hire the woman who *wasn't*." Grandpa Heart said he'd never met this flashy Lieutenant Lamarca anyway. (Grandpa Heart had long been estranged from his wife and family in Lubbock. Whether he and Mrs. Heart were officially divorced wasn't clear.) It was Grandpa Heart's idea that Mommy reinstate her maiden name which happened to be his name, and change the kids' name to Heart, too. "That way we're all family. On the books like in the blood. I'll rest easy knowing the Heart lineage will persevere through time. For we are of pioneer stock, settled in north Texas in the sacred year of her independence 1835." Mommy thought this was a great idea. Mommy said she was proud of the name "Heart" which was, to her ears, a beautiful name. So she went to the Las Vegas County Courthouse to arrange for the change and while she was at it, filling out forms, providing copies of birth certificates, paying a fee, she decided, impulsively, what the hell, she'd change her first name, too—to Dahlia. She'd always hated Dorothy, the name put her in mind of some squat ugly old aunt, and Dorrie was even worse, some squat ugly old *boat*. She chose the name Dahlia because dahlias are such beautiful flowers, she'd tried to grow dahlias in San Angelo until the slugs got them. So "Dorothy Lamarca" became "Dahlia Heart" and Grandpa Heart took the family out to Caesars Palace for a celebration supper and even snuffling Farley and fretful, startled-eyed Shirleen, now eighteen months old, fell in with the mood. Of the children, Johnny was the one not so happy about changing his name because he remembered his daddy and loved his daddy and believed with a part of his mind that his daddy might one day come looking for them and how would he know how to find them if their name was changed?—but after Mommy kissed him, and teased him, and let him sip her drink, and staked him to five dollars to play the slots (surreptitiously, since he was too young by thirteen years) and he won $68.50 within a few minutes, he conceded it was a pretty good idea. The name Heart seemed beautiful to him, too.

Next, Mommy peroxided her hair which was a fair, wavy brown to a sunny, silky blond and eventually to platinum blond which, she said, was the classiest blond, and worth the extra effort. Their little adobe bungalow on Arroyo Seco stank for days. Ever afterward, Mommy would have her hair done in a beauty salon. Next, she went on a crash diet of low-cal sodas, raw vegetables and canned tuna, and dry white wine, slimming down in less than a month from a size ten dress to a size six. Grandpa Heart took her shopping with his latest poker winnings, a cool $855, to purchase a new wardrobe and numerous pairs of shoes. ("We were mistaken for some lecherous old Texas oilman and his youngest wife!—what a hoot.") With puttylike pancake makeup of the kind the Vegas showgirls used she began to make her face more exotic. Always she'd taken her healthy good looks for granted, not bothering with moisturizer, foundation cream, eye makeup. Since junior high she'd been noticed by boys and men, often more noticed than she could accommodate, but Grandpa Heart warned, "This is Vegas, girl. And you're not getting any younger." Vegas was a challenge, all right, and Dahlia Heart meant to meet it. Johnny observed her covering her face with steaming-hot cloths, plucking at her eyebrows, rubbing cream into her skin until it glowed. Rouging her cheeks, outlining her lips with a special gloss to make them appear larger, more sensuous. Eyes like the iridescent-glittering "eyes" of peacocks' tails were painted on over Mommy's own eyes, and these too appeared enlarged, shimmering with emotion. "What 'Dahlia' is, I intend, is some mysterious story not yet happened." There was a season in which Dahlia Heart wore exclusively black in the evenings: black silk, black satin, black chiffon, clinging black jersey and see-through black lace. There was a season in which Dahlia Heart wore exclusively red. "How does 'Dahlia' look, Johnny?" "Real nice, Mommy." "'Real nice' is for saps, Johnny." "Mommy, you're a *knockout*."

Mommy laughed delightedly and kissed him. Seeing Mommy's transformed face, Shirleen squealed in excitement and alarm, crawling beneath a table. Nearsighted Farley blinked without recognition. Johnny, sighting his mother in the street by chance alone, or in the company of a man, a stranger, her bone-white hair ablaze with light, her mouth a savage red slash in her perfect face, in her snug-fitting clothes and spike-heeled shoes, followed her for blocks as if mesmerized. *You grew there. Inside your mommy. That's why no one can love you like your mommy loves you. And you can love no one like you love your mommy.* Johnny saw how men stared at her. It was a mystery why.

"What you see isn't what you get in this world," Mommy had told him, with the air of one imparting a secret. "You never get what you see, you only get to see it."

And she laughed happily, showing the moist darkly red interior of her mouth.

Now Dahlia Heart, in her early sixties, was living with her third husband, a retired stockbroker, on a thousand-acre ranch in Casa Adobes, north of Tucson, Arizona. If the snapshots she sent her son John were reliable, she was still a platinum blond, very beautiful, with a nearly unlined face and a jauntily serene smile. "This woman is your mother?" Nola Leavey said to John Heart, astonished. "She looks about forty years old." Dahlia was posed in a white bathing suit and wide-brimmed straw hat beside a pool of aqua water bright as neon. Dahlia was posed in jodhpurs, silk blouse and smart riding hat on a sorrel horse with a long silky mane—*Miss Thunderbolt & me* written on the back of the snapshot. The photo John Heart studied the longest, as if it were a puzzle to be decoded, showed Dahlia posed beside a smiling, darkly tanned and handsome older man in shorts and T-shirt, a riding crop in hand; in the background, in a corral, were several horses. *Christmas Greetings from Dahlia & Raymond, Casa Adobes. Come visit anytime!*

But John hadn't visited Casa Adobes. He had no plans to visit Casa Adobes.

According to wistful remarks of Dahlia's, neither Farley nor Shirleen had visited Casa Adobes, or was likely to do so.

Every several months Dahlia called John, leaving a message on MR. FIX-IT's answering machine. Because John rarely answered his phone directly. *Johnny? Please call. I miss you, it's been so long.* John would return his mother's call, though not immediately. He'd wait for a good day—a carpentry job, a paint job that had gone especially well. Something he could feel proud about. Or things were going well with Nola Leavey and her children. So he'd open a beer and call Dahlia out in Arizona, and after they spoke for their usual fifteen–twenty minutes he'd be too restless to remain indoors, he'd drive on his motorcycle for hours along the shore of Lake Ontario, stopping at a familiar sequence of taverns, and drinking. It wasn't purposeful but it happened. Nola dreaded these episodes. Now that she and John were more or less living together she couldn't help but know John's personal life, as much of it as he chose to reveal to her. Nola said, urgently, taking both John's hands in hers, stroking the callused fingers, "Stay home tonight. Don't go out. You lose yourself when you drink, and it's like I don't know you. It scares me." John wasn't a man comfortable with women telling him what to do even when he knew what they told him was good practical common sense. But he liked his hands held in that way by Nola Leavey, he loved the way her quick nervous fingers stroked his, as if that was a way of calming him, taming him, keeping him with her, as in his deepest self he did truly want to remain with her and not risk death riding his motorcycle, bare-headed, at ninety miles an hour along the lakeshore road. He said, bending to kiss her cheek, "O.K., honey, I won't. This time, I promise. I mean, I'll try." But, after a typical conversation with Dahlia, it happened.

Stranger yet, from Nola's perspective, was the frequency with which, during these conversations with his mother, John fell silent. If he'd made the call from Nola's house, and if Nola happened to be in another room, unaware that John was still on the phone, she might call to him, or lean in the doorway—"John, honey?"—and he'd hold his hand over the receiver, indicating he was on the phone and couldn't reply just then. Nola would express surprise. She'd whisper, "How can you be so quiet on the phone? Is your mother doing all the talking?" In fact, Nola didn't know that Dahlia too was likely to have fallen silent at such times. Except for the ice cubes tinkling quietly in her glass, two thousand miles away. Their silences were tense, a strain. *Will you never speak of it? Never accuse me? Oh, Johnny.*

When John hung up at last, Nola would look at him expectantly. Why didn't he ever speak of his mother? What had happened, or hadn't happened, between them? There was that clouded look in John's eyes, he'd shift his shoulders meaning he was restless, in another minute he'd be out the door and on that damned motorcycle racing along the lakeshore highway and he might not be back until dawn and then he might be drunk; he might not return at all, but drive out Barndollar Road to his trailer, where he'd fall on his bed, too exhausted to pull off even his shoes. He laughed at Nola's worried face and said, "Yes, right. My mother does all the talking."

5

They hadn't wanted him to sacrifice himself.
They'd wanted him to sacrifice himself.

He would not think of it. Rarely thought of it. He wasn't the kind of man to dwell upon the past, his own or anyone else's. Anyway, it had happened a long time ago. He'd been acquitted.

Frankly, he was too busy. MR. FIX-IT, in his sky-blue Ford pickup. HAVE TOOLS—WILL TRAVEL! A familiar sight, in and around Iroquois Point, New York, population 2,200. Never without work, sometimes with too much work. Working through the night in the converted barn, radio turned up high, whistling with the music, a can of beer turning luke-warm as he lost himself in the task at hand. Sawing, planing, sanding, inhaling the lovely smell of fresh-cut wood, rubbing linseed oil into wood, with the grain.

"You're happiest when you're working, with wood. I wish I could make you so happy," Nola said.

"You make me a lot happier than wood ever does. And you know it."

But she didn't know it, did she. Constantly needing reassurance.

And the children, who'd become frightened of their father. Beginning to trust their mother's friend John Heart. "They're beautiful kids," John told Nola. Hesitating as if he had more to say, but couldn't find the words. Or couldn't risk them.

Do you think you'll ever find the right woman? Dahlia had asked wistfully, the last time they'd spoken on the phone. *You've been spoiled—John Reddy Heart.* The very sound of his name, the old glamour name of his youth, the name of scandalized headlines, made them both laugh. The ice in Dahlia's drink made a sharp tinkling sound as of laughter too.

In Vegas, you'd see a van in the streets with MR. FIX-IT painted on the sides. A pale yellow van with a look of cheery optimism. The child Johnny would gaze longingly at it. MR. FIX-IT—who was he? Handyman-carpenter-plumber. 24-HOUR SERVICE. A glimpse of a tanned, muscular forearm leaning against an opened window. Rock music blaring out of the van's windows. Johnny wished his mom could call MR. FIX-IT and set things right. For always there was something not-quite-right, something needing "fixing." It hadn't occurred to him that MR. FIX-IT was just a man like anybody else, an individual, or possibly a team of individuals, workers, hustling, trying to make a living in what Johnny's grandpa cheerily called the rat race to oblivion, trying to *get by*.

Dahlia once said, with angry defensiveness, as if someone had hurt her feelings and she felt the need to explain to her children, *Everybody's trying to get by, selling themselves in different ways! Some of us just do better than others*.

Now he, John Heart, John R. Heart as he sometimes signed his name, was the MR. FIX-IT of Iroquois Point and environs. He wouldn't have needed to advertise much, any longer. Word of mouth brought him more customers than he could handle. In fact, MR. FIX-IT had so much work backed up, he should have hired a team of MR. FIX-ITs himself.

Not a good idea, he'd decided. One MR. FIX-IT was enough for Iroquois Point. "And I'm it."

That was how John Heart had met Nola Leavey two years before, and fallen in love with her. MR. FIX-IT was responsible!

There he was installing maplewood kitchen cabinets in a house in town, one of the large brick homes on Iroquois Avenue, owned by a public-school principal, and Nola Leavey, a teacher, and a friend of the family, dropped by with her two young children; a few days later, MR. FIX-IT was summoned to her house, a much smaller, more modest wood-frame house on the edge of town, a dwelling MR. FIX-IT quickly saw to be in need of major repairs: front porch and steps, shutters, clapboard siding, shingles. The house hadn't been painted in more than a decade and had faded to a dusty sparrow-brown, peeling in strips like a plane tree. But it was the roof Nola believed she wanted repaired, reshingled; at least, she hoped that John would give her an estimate so that she could decide if she could afford it. "The roof is our priority, inescapably. It *leaks*." Nola's laughter was resigned yet cheerful. She shook hands like a man, or like a woman of independent mind and character who imagines she shakes hands like a man—brisk, quick and to the point. MR. FIX-IT who wasn't of a class in which women shook hands with men, or men commonly shook hands with one another, was startled. But intrigued. He said, "Well, a house like this, built probably after World War II, not too carefully kept up—it'll *leak*."

Was his remark funny? Nola laughed again, showing small pearly teeth and a comma-sized dimple, or dent, in her right cheek. John blushed, and laughed too. He hadn't meant to joke but if it came out sounding that way, that was fine.

He liked hearing women laugh, especially women he didn't know well.

Nola Leavey was a junior high school teacher, new to Iroquois Point, a woman who appeared at first glance to be in her mid-twenties but was probably a decade older, despite her young children. She was small-boned, hardly more than five feet tall, with dark alert eyes and an intense manner, an edginess that seemed to John attractive, sexy. She wasn't a beautiful woman, nor even pretty. But he thought her a striking woman, an unusual woman, a woman of quality, with those eyes, an oddly furrowed, crinkled forehead, the rest of her face unlined, her straight-cut mahogany-dark hair parted in the center of her head and brushed severely back to give her an Old World hauteur that must have intimidated her students, and possibly her colleagues. She wore an unfashionably long skirt, a long-sleeved blouse with a high collar, a distinctive leather belt that emphasized the remarkable smallness of her waist. Black ballerina flats, shoes without heels. Female vanity, John supposed. A woman who needs to make men tower over her, that's her advantage. Somehow, this made him feel affectionate toward her. Protective. Yet what an odd way the woman had of pacing restlessly about, gesturing as she spoke, elbows pointed as if she didn't want him, a visitor in her house, a stranger, dark-haired MR. FIX-IT in denim jacket, paint-splotched jeans, biker boots, a man of virtually no speech, to get too close.

Nola introduced him again to her children—Ellen who was four, dark-eyed like her mother, very pretty; Drew, a toddler, an excited chatterer, who lunged at John Heart immediately and tugged at his sleeve. "Do you remember MR. FIX-IT?" Nola asked. Ellen nodded vehemently, "Yes, Mommy!" and Drew gaped at John, thumb in mouth. He had fair hair, plump cheeks, slate-blue eyes, an almost perfectly round face like a baby moon. John wondered if he resembled the absent father.

Where *was* the father? John had noted, at their first, brief meeting, that Nola Leavey wore numerous rings on many of her fingers yet no wedding ring. He guessed she was divorced, probably recently divorced, which would account for the edginess in her manner, the pointy elbows, that air of *Don't come too near!* yet *Help me, please!* Briskly she led him through the house, which was a small, crowded house with a creaking pinewood floor, antiquated ill-fitting windows, ceilings that needed repainting, water-stained wallpaper that needed replacing, electrical wiring (he was imagining this, with his professional X-ray eyes) that needed replacing. He noted bookcases neatly filled with books, mainly paperbacks with colorful covers, a Scandinavian-style sofa with needle-point cushions, a Shaker-style hickory rocking chair with a slat back and rewoven splint seat. "Hey. This is nice," he said, tapping the chair, setting it to rocking. "Yes, it *is* nice," Nola said almost primly. Had he insulted her? Suggesting that the rest of what he'd seen wasn't so nice? Well, that happened to be true, she was a smart woman and must know it.

They trooped through to the backyard. "Oh, please don't *look*," Nola said, laughing uneasily. The yard was surprisingly deep, running back about sixty feet to an open field, a tangle of weeds. Near the house were beds of drooping asters, deli-cate cosmos bent on their thin stalks nearly to the ground, hollyhocks nearly devoured by aphids, roses turned leprous with black spot. Nola Leavey was clearly one of those gar-deners who begin with hope and enthusiasm in the spring but by midsummer are overcome by weeds, insects, fungi, too much rain or too little. Most of the yard was dandelions, twisty knots of green tough as wire. One of MR. FIX-IT's side-lines was lawn work and this lawn would have to be totally dug up and reseeded to look like anything at all. "Just the roof," Nola said with an anxious little laugh, "—what do you think of the roof? Is it—as bad as it looks?" John pretended to be examining it, frowning; no need to climb up onto a ladder to look closely, it was obvious the shingles were thoroughly rotten. Lichen and thistles growing in the eaves! A tilting brick chimney down which, in a rainstorm, rain must plunge like a waterfall. John avoided Nola's eye. He might have asked such a smart-seeming woman why she'd bought such a house, had she bought it with her eyes shut, her mouth taped shut so she couldn't have asked the simplest questions, had she told herself it was a "fantastic bargain at the price," was she escaping with her children from another, dreaded house? John Heart had known other divorcées, he wouldn't have wanted to count how many divorcées he'd known since the age of seventeen, and they'd all been a little crazy, or more than a little, at the time of their divorces. Desperate to take their lives in hand again, but desperate also to fall in love again. Staring at him, John Heart, with their hungry eyes.

But Nola Leavey wasn't looking at him. She was pacing about in the weeds, brushing away gnats from her face, waving her pointy elbows. "It's an old, melancholy house, we've discovered. It seemed charming at first, from the outside, Ellen thought it was a house in one of her storybooks—a gingerbread house! It's a house with secrets, but not the kind you'd be interested in. Ellen says it's haunted. 'It has that smell,' she says. 'Haunted? What does a haunted house smell like?' I asked her. She said, 'Like this one.' She isn't a skittish child, I actually think she's practical-minded. Takes after me. Do you have children, John? No? Well." Nola had been speaking rapidly, nervously. Glancing sidelong at John Heart who as MR. FIX-IT stood with hands on hips, squinting up at the roof where, he saw, a number of shingles were missing as if they'd been blown off in a windstorm. The more a woman talked, even a woman to whom he was attracted, the quieter MR. FIX-IT became. He'd been known to pass entire meals in moody silence. Entire nights in silence, and in the early morning before dawn to slip away from a sleeping woman, or a woman feigning sleep, without a word. Nola said, "I've been divorced, you see. That's why the children and I are here—alone. Maybe you've been wondering? Or maybe not? But—you're divorced, too? I think I've heard—"

"Yes. Right."

He hadn't meant to say this, it wasn't true, yet he'd spoken. Sometimes words came out impulsively, he'd hear himself say something he didn't mean; yet, having said it, he wouldn't contradict it, or explain. His face throbbed with blood. He'd been with, and parted from, so many women, he felt divorced enough.

One day, he'd explain that to Nola Leavey. But not just yet.

Nola was staring at him. "How recently?"

John shifted his shoulders inside his denim jacket, annoyed.

"I don't mean to pry. It's just that—" Nola sighed, her voice trailing off. Inside the house, a phone began ringing. But she made no move to answer it.

John said, in a neutral voice, "Did you want an estimate for the roof, ma'am?"

Nola laughed. "'*Ma'am*'! You're calling me '*ma'am*'? Are you serious?"

"Mrs. Leavey."

"That's not funny. I still use the name for legal purposes, but you know I'm divorced."

John felt his face burn, his mood was turning sullen. This conversation had gone into a swerve, a skid, like a motorcycle hitting gravel. He said, "I sure as hell didn't mean it to be funny. *Nola.*"

"Well, I should think so: *Nola.*" Nola wiped her eyes, smiling, turned away. She'd become agitated suddenly. Even her hair, straight-cut and thick, like a glossy helmet, with that severe, defined part, had become disheveled. "Well. Give me the bad news, MR. FIX-IT. I'm prepared."

"Bad news?"

"The damned roof."

MR. FIX-IT, with relief, put on his professional face as if slipping on a mask—you could almost watch him do it. He pretended to be studying the rotted shingles a final time, backing up in the grass, silently calculating figures. He gave Nola Leavey an estimate based on materials alone, without labor, which would have approximately doubled the cost.

Nola's eyes widened in panic. "What? What did you say?"

MR. FIX-IT mumbled another price, not meeting the woman's eye, lowering the original by one-third. So smoothly you almost wouldn't notice it.

"That's a little—high. Isn't it?"

"Sorry, ma'am."

"But I suppose—it has to be done."

"If there's leakage, probably."

"Or maybe, just the worst parts could be done? Where the leaks actually *are*? Next time it rains I could mark the places from inside."

MR. FIX-IT said, embarrassed, "Ma'am, the whole roof needs to be reshingled. If not by me, then someone else."

"You're suggesting I should get another estimate?"

"O.K."

"Or should I simply go with yours, with you? Maybe I could get another bank loan."

"That's O.K., too."

"You're hard to talk to, MR. FIX-IT. John Heart. You're so damned *agreeable*, it's like nothing has gotten said."

Plenty has gotten said, John Heart thought.

He murmured he had to leave, he had another customer to get to, walked away leaving the woman staring after him. "You're rude," she said. "Good-bye!"

A few days later as he might've predicted there was a contrite-sounding message from Nola Leavey on MR. FIX-IT's answering machine. *John Heart? This is Nola Leavey, could you please call me? About the roof?* MR. FIX-IT had no secretary or assistant, wanted no hired help, depended upon his answering machine to keep him in business. There was a comfort in it, a sense of safety; and a measure of voyeurism— like watching someone, this woman for instance, this woman he understood was sexually attracted to him, through a window of her house as she's on the phone, earnest, ill-at-ease, probably smiling and gesturing as she speaks, unaware of being seen. And when John returned the call and Nola answered on the first ring she sounded confused, embarrassed. "I did call for another estimate. I mean—another man. But yours is so much lower, I think there must be something wrong?" John Heart was standing in his CruiserCraft trailer kitchen, drinking from a can of beer, feeling good, muscles aching but essentially he was feeling good, he'd accomplished something that day of which he could be proud, floor-to-ceiling custom-built shelves and cabinets in one of the big old brick houses on the lake that were being bought by rich businessmen from Syracuse, Rochester. He'd made money. More money, with this job, than he'd made for any other comparable job since MR. FIX-IT had set up shop here in Iroquois Point. There was a part of his mind that was contemptuous of making money, as the hotheaded kid John Reddy he'd thought grubbing for money, selling yourself, was absolute shit, but as an adult he'd come to see by degrees that you had to have skill, talent, as well as crude luck, to make money, even just enough to get by. (Not the kind of money his kid brother Farley was making with HARTSSOFT, his computer software, which was beyond John Heart's capacity even to imagine; not even the kind of money their mother had always believed she'd needed, which was essentially as much money as she could get, as a buffer against being poor, sinking back into the desperation of their early Nevada days.) So he was feeling good, liking the way Nola Leavey was speaking to him, not the bright-controlled teacherly manner she'd started off with, yet not pleading either, but sincere and matter-of-fact. She said, "John? Are you there?" and he said, "Sure." She said, "I'm just concerned that—Ellen, help Drew up, will you, honey?—I'm a little worried that, your estimate is so much lower, and there's so much work, this other man, this roofer, was telling me, and last night—wasn't that a terrible rainstorm?—living by the lake, I guess—I should be used to it by now—well, I'm worried that you must feel sorry for me, or pity, or—I don't know, exactly, I w-wouldn't want you—or anyone—to think that—" John interrupted, "Do you want the fucking roof done, Mrs. Leavey, or not?" and Nola said, "Yes, John Heart, I want the fucking roof done. Thank you."

Reshingling the roof of Nola Leavey's bungalow was more work than MR. FIX-IT, for all his expertise, had bargained for. And the weather turned prematurely warm, for June. He wore a red sweatband around his forehead, and still sweat ran in ticklish rivulets down his face. He removed his shirt, his muscles gleamed damply, attracting gnats. Late each afternoon, Nola Leavey in a skirt to midcalf, or a neat shirtwaist dress with long sleeves, came out into the yard and complimented him on how wonderful the shingles looked, how much he'd accomplished, but wasn't he working too hard? too long? She called up to him, "John, stay for supper tonight? The kids asked me to ask you." MR. FIX-IT grunted a reply that might've been yes, or might've been no. It must have dismayed Nola Leavey, a junior high English teacher, to learn that she'd hired one of those handymen who play a radio as they work, turned to a local pop-music station, so that hammering and rock music permeated the neighborhood at about the same decibel level.

At the curb, MR. FIX-IT's sky-blue Ford pickup shone proudly in the sun. He had the idea (maybe an offhand remark of Nola's made him think this) that people in neighboring houses, especially women, were alert to how long, how late, the truck remained at the curb each day.

If there was one thing MR. FIX-IT maintained, even if he didn't invariably shave, shower, launder his clothes or get his hair cut as frequently as he should have, it was a shining-clean vehicle.

Nola, accompanied by Ellen, and little Drew who stumbled excitedly in the grass, like a baby goat, came around the side of the house to where MR. FIX-IT was hammering and called up brightly, "John? Didn't you hear me? Stay for supper tonight?"

Ellen mimicked her mother, cupping her hands to her mouth. "Mommy's making roast—" It sounded like *chickchick*.

Nola said, "Roast chicken. But not an actual roast, not from scratch. From the grocery store, a barbecue chicken, in one of those aluminum foil bags? MR. FIX-IT? You must get hungry sometime."

There was that eager, hungry, slightly crazed look in the woman's eyes. Beautiful eyes, and her mouth was beautiful. He'd fallen into the habit when he was away from her of trying to envision her: the swinging straight-cut hair, the pointy elbows and small-boned fingers, rings. A way she had of laughing at herself that invited him to laugh with her except he held back, afraid somehow. If ever he touched her, or she touched him—"Jesus. That's it."

So MR. FIX-IT evasively declined her invitations to stay for a meal, saying he hadn't time. It was true he worked most evenings, sometimes into the night. MR. FIX-IT had a backlog of furniture to repair, restore. Methodical work, some of the pieces of furniture were what you'd call challenging. Nola said, "Insomnia? You, too?" John said defensively, "No. Insomnia's when you want to sleep and can't. When you've got plenty to do, and are happy doing it, that isn't insomnia." Nola said, "But it comes to the same thing. You don't sleep."

On the fourth, final day, when at last the shingling was done, John agreed to have supper with Nola and the kids. He drove home, however, to shower and shave and change his clothes. He wore a white shirt, seersucker trousers, even a necktie. (A hand-painted, expensive tie that had been a gift from a well-to-do woman customer when MR. FIX-IT had lived in Watertown. "When you wear this, John, will you think of me?" MR. FIX-IT had long forgotten her name.) He brought Ellen and Drew a surprise: a wooden rocking horse from a flea market in Shawmouth he'd bought when his grandfather was still alive. For years he'd had no use for it, one item among many in MR. FIX-IT's barn. Now inspired, he repaired the horse, repainted it, a warm golden hue. It was a friendly-looking horse, a miniature, standing about three feet from the ground on a flat wooden platform; when it rocked, it creaked. The children were ecstatic. "He's a palomino pony," John told them. "His name is 'Pal.'" Nola's eyes shimmered with tears, she'd had to turn aside. She said, "I'm sorry. I can't help it." She burst into tears, her shoulders shaking.

John stared at her in dismay. "I'm not used to people being nice to me. I mean—so nice." John said, "Bullshit, Nola." Nola laughed, laying a hand on his arm, yes it was bullshit but she couldn't stop crying.

* * *

In MR. FIX-IT's sky-blue pickup he drove home from the Oswego County Courthouse, eleven miles to the nickel-colored trailer in the ruin of an apple orchard on Barndollar Road, Iroquois Point. *What our lives come to! How God tests us*. Dripping blood from a cut above his eye. For a while, driving, he'd pressed a wad of tissue against the cut, soaking up blood, then gave up in disgust. Sure, those deputies had looked at him, John Heart, with contempt. A man who hadn't defended himself. A man who'd let himself get hit in the face. Who wouldn't press charges against his assailant.

Probably the deputies knew he was an ex-con, too. Everyone seemed to know.

If anyone had asked him point-blank, he wouldn't have denied it. Tomahawk Island Youth Camp wasn't a maximum-security prison for violent adult offenders like Attica, Sing Sing.

Nothing to be ashamed of. Not now.

Nothing MR. FIX-IT couldn't fix.

But since Jordan Leavey had initiated his custody suit—his blackmail as Nola called it—more of John Heart's private life, his long-ago teenaged life as John Reddy Heart, was emerging. Not just the conviction for auto theft, to which he'd confessed, and the other accessory crimes, but the indictment for second-degree murder. He'd seen the look in Nola's face when Jordan Leavey's attorney alluded to Nola's "current live-in companion," a man who'd been tried for murder in Buffalo as a sixteen-year-old and had had a "controversial" acquittal. And those twelve months at Tomahawk Island without a day off for good behavior.

He'd seen the look on the judge's face, too. A frowning

middle-aged woman with conspicuously rouged cheeks, chunky bifocal glasses.

John had told Nola about his past, some of it. Not all. Though he believed he loved her, and would one day marry her, he would never tell her everything.

She'd said quietly *I'll just have to trust you, I guess. Since I love you.*

He'd said *That's up to you.*

But maybe it was time to move on. HAVE TOOLS   WILL TRAVEL.

Possibly, if things worked out, if the custody suit was settled favorably, Nola would come with him. Nola, and the children. There was the eastern edge of the state he'd never lived in: Lake Champlain, on the far side of the Adirondacks. A beautiful region, beside another Glass Lake. He was the owner and executor of Aaron Leander Heart's estate in Shawmouth, an hour's drive from Iroquois Point, but he'd hired someone to deal with it, finances, maintenance, publicity, he hadn't any need to live close by. He had money saved, though he'd never accepted a dime from his brother. Nor from Dahlia the rich man's wife who was always hinting how much more money she had to spend than she ever would spend, always trying to calculate how deprived his life was.

MR. FIX-IT could move! The idea began to interest him. He'd built up a solid reputation in Iroquois Point, he was hired on a regular basis by contractors renovating the spacious old nineteenth-century houses on the lake, he had friends here, and numerous friendly acquaintances—so, why not move? He'd lived in Iroquois Point for almost five years, the longest period of time he'd lived anywhere as an adult.

When he'd mentioned to Nola how many places he'd lived, just in New York State, she'd said, "My God, John. You sound like the Flying Dutchman."

Flying Dutchman? Who was he?

Seeing John's carefully neutral expression, meant to mask his ignorance, also his defensiveness about living with a woman more educated than he, Nola said quickly, "A man accursed by fate. Condemned to sail the seas until Judgment Day unless"—and she paused, her face slightly coloring— "he's redeemed by a woman's love."

John laughed. "How's about a woman's cooking?"

It was true, John Heart had lived in so many towns after fleeing the Village of Willowsville he'd already forgotten some of them, and the people he'd gotten to know, even the women he'd loved. The women who loved him. Sodus, Fair Haven, Lycoming, Red Creek. Briefly in Oswego, and in Watertown and Sackets Harbor (in a fishing shanty on the lake). For eight lonely months he'd lived in Ogdensburg on the St. Lawrence River bordering Canada, the vast province of Ontario he'd once desperately studied on a road map found in a stranger's Jeep, fantasizing how he might escape into such vastness where no one would have known him and *it would be just life, a flame of a life, setting itself down in that new place*. But he'd never made the crossing into that other country.

His years in Willowsville had passed in a blur like a land-scape glimpsed from a speeding car. He'd been anxious about his family, keeping the family together, monitoring his mother's crises. Her drinking, her drugs, her errors in judg-ment. Her childlike dependency on him. Even his basketball playing hadn't been real, somehow—it was a way of focusing his energy, he'd had so much nervous energy, he'd thought sometimes he might explode.

After graduating from high school he'd gone to live in Shawmouth to be near his grandfather Aaron Leander Heart who was all that remained, for him, of his family. (Farley and Shirleen had been placed with foster families and were said to be adjusting reasonably well. Dahlia had had a "nervous collapse" after he'd been sentenced to prison, she'd gone into seclusion yet not long afterward, exactly how he'd never learn, she found a new, well-to-do man friend and fled to— was it Palm Springs? Sun Valley, Idaho?) As strange a time as any in John Reddy Heart's life, his plane crash of a life, his life strewn with glittering wreckage. He was barely eighteen, desperately lonely for his family yet not always on the best of terms with Grandpa Heart who'd become increasingly eccentric since the "days of vengeance." John loved his grandfather, and his grandfather seemed to love him, but living with the old man on a daily basis was impossible. Grandpa Heart believed himself ordained by God to create his "wondrous Glass Ark beside the Glass Lake" and no reasoning could shake him from his conviction. (For all his grandson knew, maybe it was true. God did work in mysterious ways.) It was Grandpa Heart's unshakable belief, too, that he'd bargained personally with God to spare John Reddy's life. "Except for me you'd have died in the electric chair, Johnny. Deserving or not, that was your fate in the world of human justice." It had seemed beneath John's dignity, as well as a waste of breath, to argue that there was no capital punishment in New York State at this time. The expensive lawyer Dahlia had hired for John, who'd thoroughly disliked him, and who'd never thought he might be acquitted, had told him to be prepared for a sentence of twenty years to life—"Which isn't as severe as it sounds, you'd be up for parole in ten years unless you screw up again."

John Reddy had been prepared for this. Almost, he'd been at peace. When a murder is committed someone must be punished, that was only fair. He felt, in his heart, that he'd already begun his sentence, a life sentence, when he fled the police that night, slipping into his life as an outlaw, a fugitive from justice, as you'd slip on a glove that doesn't quite fit at first, and then does.

Then, the jury had acquitted him.

Acquitted!

His life handed back to him, in that moment of grace.

(Several of the jurors, interviewed anonymously afterward for the *Buffalo Evening News*, said they'd voted to acquit because they believed the defense's argument that John Reddy Heart had acted to protect his mother and himself. His action

had not been premeditated, but only instinctive. "A boy, protecting his mother, even if the mother's a you-know-what—he
isn't guilty of murder in my book." "That Melvin Riggs, Jr.—
we didn't have any trouble believing he was a brute. The way
that S.O.B. treated his baseball players, you wouldn't be surprised at anything a man like that might do, including getting
himself killed.")

The phone was ringing when John unlocked the door of
the trailer. He let it ring. He went into the closet-sized bathroom, turned on the cold-water faucet, splashed water
carelessly on his face, which was burning, aching, beginning
to swell. The answering machine clicked on, it was Nola.
"John? Are you there? Will you pick up the phone? Please."
He stood very still, as if she might hear him. She was saying,
pleading, "Will you call me as soon as you get home? The
hearing has been adjourned until tomorrow morning, I'll be
home in a half-hour. I need to speak with you. You're coming
over tonight, aren't you? I'm so worried. Did he hurt you?
What did he say to you? Will you go to a doctor? Please? I
feel so responsible! Jordan has revealed himself now, in
public, he's a desperate man, everyone can see what he is. A
man like that, so out of control, demanding full custody of
the children! The judge knows what happened and my lawyer
is going to move that this ridiculous suit be dropped, it's bla-
tant blackmail, it's an act of cruelty, of harassment. That
bastard!" Nola paused, breathing quickly. "Oh, John—I love
you so much. But I don't know what to do."

John winced, poking at his swelling eye.

She wants me out of her life. Doesn't even know it yet.

The message tape ran out, cutting Nola off abruptly. John
hoped she wouldn't call back.

Since Leavey had initiated the custody suit, threatening to
take the children from her, Nola had lost her good spirits, her
wry and unpredictable sense of humor. She'd become, in a
way, more feminine. But less of a person. Calling John often,

leaving messages on the machine. She clutched at him hiding her face against his chest—"I know! I'm a little crazy right now." Her pale skin exuded an air of frantic heat. Yet she was perpetually cold, shivering. She was susceptible to colds, sore throats, flu. Her pockets were comically crammed with used Kleenex, there were stiff little wads of Kleenex beneath her bed pillow, littering the floor beside the bed in the morning. She moved like a sleepwalker, eyes open but unseeing. She'd had at least one minor accident driving her car of which John was aware. When John didn't stay the night, she allowed Ellen and Drew in her bed, one on each side of her, and their tabby cat Pretzel at her feet—"Protected like a fortress!" If John was late to arrive at her house, and John was often late, he'd discover her anxious and pacing, her forehead creased with worry. "I'm sorry. I can't help it. I wish you didn't ride that damned motorcycle." Where she'd rarely spoken of her marriage, except to say that she and Jordan had married young, had respected each other at one time but had stopped loving one another, now she spoke of the marriage, and of Jordan, with more bitterness. When they made love, in Nola's bed, sometimes in John's bed in the trailer, what had been tender, sweet, piercingly lovely had become something of an ordeal for them both. John seemed to see without wishing to see the woman's delicate face contorted into a masklike expression of enormous strain. Her skin turned slippery with sweat. Her lips were drawn back from her teeth in a savage grimace, her jaws were clenched and eyes shut tight. A woman straining for orgasm, like a woman straining to give birth—the ordeal was too private to be shared with another person. Even a lover.

He remembered the evening he'd brought the palomino rocking horse for Nola's children. The look in their eyes. And in Nola's eyes. Like a flame coming up, the first rush of love. He'd gotten drunk that evening on a few beers, so excited, so deeply moved. Nola told him, "Once you have children, you're no longer unique. You give up 'uniqueness' pretty quickly. You want to be ordinary, and you want to do the right thing. You want to be *good*." John told her he'd never wanted anything much else than to be ordinary, and do the right thing, and be *good*—"The rest of it, whatever it is, is just bullshit, I think." His words were stammered, stuttered. He never could express himself if he tried to think, it was like trying to write, to set down words on a page, sweating over a few sentences as he'd done in high school, a tall lanky kid cramped in a desk, head bent to his examination bluebook and a ballpoint pen clumsy in his fingers. They'd begun to make love almost without knowing it, Nola's fingers trailing along his arm, Nola's liquidy yearning eyes turned up to his, Nola's mouth that seemed to him beautiful, smiling against his, talking and laughing even as they kissed. He remembered being surprised at the smallness, lightness, delicacy of her body. Her small hard breasts pressed with such intimacy against his chest. How startling, and how sad—she was so thin, he felt her ribs against his outstretched fingers. He was fearful, almost, of hurting her. Kissing her, running his hands over her, how good it felt, how happy he was, Nola Leavey in his arms, a woman in his arms, like coming home.

He felt a stab of love, of responsibility, guilt. But he didn't call Nola back, not that afternoon.

Washed up, stuck a square flesh-colored bandage against his swollen eye, changed his clothes. Fed the mewing, anxious cats, who were semiwild barn cats, as many as eight of them, back of the trailer. Scattered seed across the ice-stippled ground for wild birds, and corn for wild deer. A herd of twelve white-tailed deer, does and yearling fawns, wintered in a nearby woods and were close to starving at this time of year. He whistled thinly through his teeth though his mouth was slightly swollen. His breath steamed, he moved briskly about outside without a jacket. There was a curious pleasure in his throbbing face, his beaten face, blood quickened beneath the lacerated skin. It was a cold windy March day, now overcast, clouds like rippled gray concrete scudding across the sky from the north, above the lake. That sharp, metallic smell of snow. From the highest point of his property you could see, a mile to the north, a rim of pale, icy blue. Lake Ontario stretching to what could be seen of the horizon, large as an inland sea. He didn't want to leave this place but if forced, he would find another place beside another lake. For it seemed that he, John Heart, had fallen under the spell of the Glass Lake of which his grandfather had spoken with such stubborn passion. *The Lord has demanded a Glass Ark! Beside a Glass Lake! My mission that must be fulfilled.* An afternoon of carpentry work awaited him in the barn. And possibly he'd see Nola that evening, and stay the night with her, and possibly he wouldn't. Maybe that was why he felt so good. Whistling, smiling to himself. Such moods swept upon him suddenly. He didn't question them, he wasn't cynical about happiness. He recalled Grandpa Heart of the old reckless days, in Vegas—"When things are going to hell in a handbasket, and you're rushing right along in that basket, hooo-*eee*! A Heart will always feel *good*."

John laughed. The old bugger'd had the right idea.

6

The first time John Heart lifted the .45-caliber Colt revolver that would one day be tagged the *murder weapon* in the shooting death of Melvin Riggs, Jr., he was Johnny Heart, nine years old.

"Go on, boy. Take 'er up. Time you learned to respect firearms." Grandpa Heart, basking in the white winter-solstice sun of the Nevada desert, was in one of his good whisky moods. (He had bad whisky moods, too, in about equal measure, but that's another story.) He was filled at such times, he said, with the bounty of the Lord and wanted to share his happiness. His handsome ruin of a face was flushed with inspiration and love of his favorite grandchild. His eyes, netted with broken capillaries like cobwebs, shone. His big-knuckled hands had been steady enough that morning for a careful trim of his rakish white beard. Sometime the previous day at a private poker game in town Aaron Leander Heart had won an undisclosed amount of money with a stake of only $249—possibly as much, Dahlia had thrillingly hinted, as $4,000! Already he'd brought Dahlia an enormous floral bouquet—"To my Beloved Daughter"—and presents for the

underfurnished house including a brass floor lamp with an
American eagle icon and a full-sized refrigerator with a self-
defrosting freezer to replace their rattletrap midget refrigerator
that was always breaking down and turning the children's
cereal milk sour. And for the protection of the household, as
he told Johnny solemnly, a smile of boyish excitement twitching at his lips, the metallic-gray .45-caliber Colt revolver to
replace one he'd lost long ago.

"Your momma's dealing blackjack till late tonight, she says.
So let's go." Grandpa Heart slid the bulky revolver into an
inside pocket of his fringed rawhide jacket with a wink.

Arroyo Seco, a narrow street, paved only in the downtown
area of glittering casinos, high-rise hotels and neon-lit restaurants, disintegrated into gravel and red dust as it ran out into
the desert. Grandfather and grandson made their way up the
street and across a railroad track and through a littered vacant
lot to the edge of the desert. Their targets would be discarded
Coke and Coors cans, bottles, strips of metal. A Styrofoam
slab, ghastly white, of the approximate size and shape of a
human torso. Johnny's heart was beating quickly. He looked
anxiously about to see if anyone, kids from the neighborhood, had followed them. Grandpa Heart, sipping from a
bottle carried in his pocket in a paper bag, whistled unper-
turbed. Nevada was a gunowner's state, he said. He had a
permit for this firearm, which he'd purchased in a real gun
store, not a pawnshop or through a friend. There was no
danger in firearms if you knew what you were doing. Firing a
gun was not nearly so risky as driving a car the way some
fools drove, and women drivers. "Stop that blinking, boy!
You look like a scared rabbit. Just trust Grandpa and you'll be
fine." He took another quick sip from his bottle, smacked his
lips and sighed. His whisky-colored eyes gleamed. Johnny
had overheard him tell Dahlia a while back how happy he was
he'd hooked up with them in Vegas, not just he was tired of
wandering on his own but he'd discovered he liked being a
granddaddy, never would've guessed it, and Dahlia laughed

her husky-wistful laugh saying she was glad he loved his grandkids since he'd never much seemed to love her and her sisters. Grandpa told her to hush, that was ancient history.

"Now. Stand here by me, Johnny." Johnny came to stand close beside his grandfather, trying not to tremble. He was excited! Grandpa Heart opened up the revolver with a click, showed Johnny the bullets, turned the cylinder and clicked it shut, and took aim at a brown bottle stuck upright beside a stubby cactus about thirty feet away. How slowly, with what dignity Aaron Leander Heart raised the gun in his right hand, steadied by his left. You could see that firing a gun was a solemn task that conferred a true importance upon this hour. "One, two, *three*." The noise was deafening, the child jumped and whimpered as if he'd been shot. The smell of gunpowder was a surprise. "God *damn*." Grandpa sucked at his mouth seeing he'd missed his target by a good six inches. He raised the revolver, counted three and fired again. Another miss. The bullet went skidding along the crusty surface of the sand. Grandpa took a sip of his drink and said thoughtfully, as if confessing a secret, "Marksmanship, like a man's ability to throw a lethal punch, is not a 'talent' to be taught. You must be born with the gift. Few are. If you have a willingness, you can be taught competence. You can improve from a state of total ignorance at least. Always know, Johnny, a man can *improve*." As he spoke, he'd been approaching the target; at a distance of about twenty feet he took aim and fired again, and this time the bottle shattered, bits of glass flying and winking in the sun.

Now it was Johnny's turn. He took the revolver from his grandfather, saying, "Thank you, sir." The Heart children were taught to be polite Texas-style. His first surprise was the gun was so *heavy*. So *real*. He played wild screaming games of cowboy-and-Indian and war with boys in the neighborhood, shooting guns from Kresge's, play-rifles and cap pistols, he was one of the toughest of the kids, a natural leader, but this— this was the real thing!—a grown-up's gun, and no toy. In that instant Johnny lost his interest in kids' games. "Now. That

Coors can over there. Blast 'er." Johnny's hand was trembling, he couldn't get his eyes to stop blinking. He was remembering a night a long time ago, at the air force base, when he'd been a small boy, waking to hear adult voices outside, his daddy's voice, his mommy's, others', they were talking about someone who'd had an accident with a gun, or maybe he'd shot himself with a gun, his daddy was saying what a terrible damn-fool thing, why the hell, why would anybody, Jesus what a surprise, and a woman was crying, and it came back to him now, which was why his hand, both his hands, were trembling, and his eyes damp with moisture. Grandpa Heart was standing behind him firmly gripping his shoulders so he'd stand straight and tall—already at nine the top of his head came to his grandfather's mid-chest, and his grandfather was a tall man—and murmured instructions. "Raise the gun, lad. Both hands. Now—steady! Regulate your breathing. Sight your target. Take care to note if there's anything between you and your target, or anything beyond your target. Now draw in your breath—slow. No need to fear, the bullet goes *out*, away from you and not *back*. *You* are the one in control. Draw breath—squeeze the trigger, don't pull it—one, two—" Johnny shut his eyes and jerked the trigger. There was a deafening crack, the gun leapt in his hands like a live thing. Except Grandpa Heart caught his swaying hand, he might have dropped it.

He'd missed the beer can by who knows how many feet. But his grandfather said cheerfully, "That's just the first shot of many hundreds. Like I said, a man can *improve*. Only just stop that blinking."

The lesson continued. Forty minutes passed in a blur. It was a surprise that Johnny wasn't enjoying this adventure as he'd thought he would. He couldn't get used to the noise and he didn't like the smell of gunpowder, it made him sneeze and every time he sneezed his eyes leaked tears and his nose ran. He was conscious of disappointing his grandfather. Every time he lifted the gun, sighted a target tremulously and pulled the trigger, even if he didn't miss, he understood that something was wrong. And Grandpa Heart sensed it, too. It was strange, he just didn't like his grandfather's gun the way he'd expected he would. Though he liked being with his grandfather, loved being with him in fact, and there wasn't much doubt that Grandpa Heart loved him the best of the grandchildren. It would be the surprise of Johnny's childhood, how he'd failed to take to firearms. Despite Grandpa Heart's pep talks. "With firearms, you must show who's master. You must not be mastered. It's said that firearms are dangerous to those who own them because some fools allow their guns to be wrested from them and used against them. But even a cop will suffer such an indignity, sometimes. Usually only once." He laughed, and Johnny tried to laugh weakly with him. "A gun is unforgiving, Johnny. You must win its loyalty or never pick it up."

Johnny mumbled, "O.K., Grandpa." His eyes ached and his nose was running, he wished the lesson would end.

It ended, but not as he'd wished. Grandpa Heart was having him set up targets at ever-farther distances, which made sense of course, but made hitting them harder. He stood watching glumly as his grandfather fired and missed, fired and hit, fired and missed, fired and missed, fired and hit, he couldn't help thinking that the difference between a hit— "Bingo!"—and a miss—"God *damn*!"—was ninety-nine percent accidental. *Lucky Strikes* was the name of the cigarettes Dahlia smoked, and *lucky strike* was all it was. Why did it matter so much? Weren't you the identical person if you *hit*, or *missed*? When Johnny managed to hit one of the targets, sent it flying or shattered, he felt he'd performed a trick of some kind, that was all. It puzzled him that Grandpa Heart who was a grown-up and should have known better chortled with delight and clapped him on the shoulder telling him he was "coming along." The only part of it that made sense, some sort of sense, was that, when he did well, Grandpa Heart smiled. The way, when he behaved in a way that pleased his mother, she smiled, sometimes laughed, kissing him. *Oh, Johnny! You're the one.*

He'd only just wanted to make her happy. After his father had disappeared from their lives and she'd never be happy again really.

One more round of shots, three bullets each. Grandpa had reloaded the gun several times, with bullets loose in his pocket. Then they'd be finished for the day. (Johnny, whose ears were ringing, hoped they'd be finished for a long time. He was feeling the way he felt after taking care of the younger kids when they were both whining and whimpering for Dahlia, staying up late waiting for her to come back home. Having to smile, and pretend to be O.K. Just so *tired*.) "Now, lad. *Pièce de résistance*." Johnny wasn't sure what this meant, he hadn't been paying attention. Grandpa Heart was having them shoot at some metal strips, looked like chrome torn off a car, placed in strange, human-like postures against some stunted Joshua trees. Something glimmered beyond them— probably flies. Grandpa Heart got off three shots in rapid succession, only one of which struck a chrome strip, with a sharp *ping!* Then it was Johnny's turn. Wanting only to be finished with the ordeal, he raised the gun in both hands, squinted along the sight, drew in a jagged breath and fired— one, two, three shots. His ears rang. He sneezed. When he opened his eyes he saw that he'd missed the chrome strips but seemed to have hit something else—something living?

He ran to investigate. His grandfather called after him. He poked in the debris and saw something that made his stomach sink. "Oh. Oh, geez." He'd shot a hummingbird. He knew it had been a hummingbird though nothing remained of the creature but a few bloody silvery-green feathers with a strip of darker gray, on the ground a few feet beyond the rusted chrome strip. When she was in the mood, Dahlia set out hummingbird feeders in the side yard of their little rented bungalow, and cried out happily, "Kids! Come look! Hurry!" when the silvery-green hummingbirds, with red throats, often in pairs, came to drink from them with their long needle-like beaks. The tiny birds were so small, hardly more than three inches long, their wings so finely vibrating, it was easy to mistake them for wasps or dragonflies. Johnny choked back a sob. He felt terrible. The fact that he'd killed by accident made it worse, somehow.

They headed back to Arroyo Seco. Grandpa Heart tried to joke the boy out of his crestfallen mood. But Johnny was quiet, down-looking. For a boy of nine he sometimes didn't seem . . . nine. "Have a sip, Johnny. You're looking peaked," Grandpa said, wiping his lips and handing the bottle in its wrinkled paper bag to Johnny, but Johnny said numbly, "No thank you, sir." The old man saw that the boy was troubled, and laid a warm heavy hand, an almost too heavy hand, on his shoulder. "Well. Keep in mind there's lots more hummingbirds in the world, Johnny. Lots more."

When, next day, Dahlia learned of the target practice in the desert (Farley must've told, he was turning into a tattletale), she was furious. "Daddy, how could you! He's only a child! Were you drunk? Were you crazy! Getting my Johnny started on that road that's one-way to—you-know-where. Just like you."

They were in the kitchen of the little bungalow. It was a confused time—not morning, for Dahlia never woke before noon, yet it was breakfast time, some of them were trying to eat. Grandpa Heart, his cowboy hat already on his head, was putting on a white shirt, a new purchase, and became so upset by his daughter's words that he misbuttoned the shirt so that it hung on him crooked, like a bad joke. Dahlia had uttered unforgivable words. It was like firing a gun in this small space. Johnny could almost smell the gunpowder. "Hush about that, girl," Grandpa Heart said in his morning-hoarse, whispery voice. "That's ancient history."

"Not so ancient. A criminal record is *forever*."

It was rare for Dahlia to speak so to her father. Her father she adored, but also feared. (For the old man had quite a temper. When he stopped smiling, you knew to keep your distance.) She was reckless when barefooted, no makeup on her pale, young-looking face, last night's mascara rimming her eyes like an owl's eyes, her bone-white hair bouncy-curly on one side of her face and matted on the other. She was wearing a filmy red nylon wraparound shift that didn't entirely cover the tops of her breasts which looked agitated, too, loose and swinging inside the cheap fabric. A cigarette burned in one hand she didn't recall having lighted.

Grandpa Heart overturned one of the kitchen chairs, causing Farley to cringe, and little Shirleen, eating a rolled-up slice of Wonder Bread with grape jelly, to stare wide-eyed. "Insulted in my home! By my own daughter! In front of my own grandchildren!" The old man did look aggrieved. He looked as if he'd been kicked in the stomach. He turned on his heel, stomped out of the kitchen and got a few things from his bedroom (including the .45-caliber Colt revolver he kept between his mattress and bedsprings) and slammed out of the house, marched up the street, with Johnny trailing after him until he turned to curse the child, waving a fist and telling him to get the hell away—"*You*, couldn't keep your mouth shut, eh? Had to tell Momma! Momma's *boy*!" He was gone for four days and they believed he would never return. Dahlia wept, cursed herself, made telephone calls and searched Vegas in the company of a man friend, a bouncer at Caesars Palace happy to drive her in his big boat of a Caddie east and west, north and south, traversing the city, looking for her father she feared might not only have abandoned the family forever but might even, if drinking, hot-headed and quarrelsome, come to harm. For an hour or more she stood outside a police precinct agonizing if she dared go inside to file a missing-persons report—"I'd worry they might not let me out again. Then what, you kids left all alone?" Even the speedy diet pills she took to keep her weight down didn't give her sufficient courage to face the police. It was Dahlia Heart's terror, laced with shame, that, one day, her children she loved more than life itself would be taken from her and placed in the custody of the state, she seemed to know beforehand that this would be her fate as a mother, for of course she was a bad mother, a careless mother, a drunk-mother, a slut-mother, she knew this, accepted this, yet wept and raved against it as unfair, unjust—"I wasn't meant to be a widow, so young. God has treated me like shit." When Grandpa Heart did return to the little rented bungalow on Arroyo Seco, early one morning, sullen, exhausted, in his stocking feet, missing his smart cowboy hat and, you could surmise, his poker earnings, Dahlia kissed him and asked no questions, she and Johnny prepared the old man his favorite breakfast of eggs, grits, ham, hot buttered biscuits, and no mention was made again, ever, of what she'd said. And Johnny forgot. Or almost forgot. Until a year or so later when they started on their journey east, to the Village of Willowsville, New York, like a TV comedy family embarking upon a wild new adventure that had to turn out well, seeing it was a comedy, and TV, on their way to a big expensive mansion they'd seen only snapshots of, a gift to Dahlia from a "sweet, sad, sort of pathetic old gentleman" known at the casinos as the Colonel, who'd fallen in love with her and begged her to marry to assuage the terrible loneliness of his life, though older, and much older-looking, than Grandpa Heart, and she'd been deliberating such a radical step (the advantages were obvious, Colonel Edgihoffer was a rich old man not likely to live long, but there were obvious disadvantages, too—Dahlia enjoyed male companionship of a certain kind, a not-gentlemanly kind, and this she might have to give up at least for a while), there was debate about whether Grandpa Heart should take the Colt revolver along with them in the car, for possibly there were laws against carrying concealed weapons in the states through which they had to pass, Utah, Colorado might be safe for these were Western states, but beyond that—Kansas, Missouri, Illinois, Indiana, Ohio, a stretch of Pennsylvania? What of New York State in which they'd be living? Dahlia agreed they might need protection on such a long journey into the unknown, the Great Plains particularly filled her with worry, but she was fearful of highway patrols, police questioning, so maybe her father had better leave the gun behind; and Grandpa Heart declared if he had to leave his gun behind he sure as hell wasn't going, that was that. It was an impasse. There were hot words exchanged. Another time, Dahlia hinted of something in the old man's past—"you-know-where, and you-know-what." But when Johnny asked her if his grandfather had been arrested, ever, if he'd been in prison, she turned on him and slapped his face. "Such a thing, to say of your own flesh and blood. Certainly *not*."

Only after John Reddy Heart was himself arrested for murder, at the age of sixteen, did Grandpa Heart reveal to him, shamefaced, that he'd "done time" at North Texas State Prison for Men—"I was just a damn-fool kid, nineteen. Had me a gun, and this buddy of mine had his, we got drunk and went out and stuck up a gas station and came away with fifty-eight dollars I swear, though they'd claim five hundred. I was in for three years, paroled for good behavior. We're talking ancient history, son. And none of it has anything to do with *you*."

John Reddy understood that it did, though. Anything the Hearts did or had done or contemplated doing had everything to do with him. Especially if it involved the .45-caliber Colt revolver originally purchased at a Vegas gun shop by Aaron Leander Heart.

* * *

During the fall and winter months, well into spring, John Heart would hear gunshots in the distance. Sometimes on his own property. These were deer hunters. His five acres of land, like much of the farmland in the area, was posted against hunters and trespassers, but hunters ignored the signs. There was a local tradition of ignoring such signs, this was deer-hunting country. When he'd first moved to Iroquois Point, John Heart was advised not to order these trespassers off his property, not even to try to speak with them, it just wasn't done, he could get into trouble—"There've been barn fires, livestock shot, gun 'accidents.' You can't win." John knew he couldn't win, he'd lived in other hunting counties in the state.

Most counties were in fact hunting counties. He'd have to endure it, waking at dawn to the sound of gunshots, his nerves like tight-strung wires, he'd begin drinking beer before he was fully dressed, needing to anesthetize the sick hurt, the memory, the sound of three rapidly fired gunshots, so close, in his own head they seemed, always there, echoing and re-echoing. *Always I knew it would happen, someday. That gun. But not when, and not how.* He hated the hunters with their glaring orange Day-Glo dickeys worn over bulky camouflage jackets. He hated even those men he liked, friends of his, guys he might work for, drink with. But he had to endure it. Live with it. Men loved guns, men loved hunting. Men loved killing living things, hauling them back home as trophies. MR. FIX-IT wasn't a hunter (everybody knew who hunted, who didn't, as they could name the names, occupations and addresses of the few blacks who lived in the area, not inevitably with prejudice, but simply as a statement of fact, information) but he wasn't one of the local antihunters, troublemakers writing angry letters to the *Iroquois Point Sentinel*. From his trailer windows, from his workbench in the barn, MR. FIX-IT was likely to see hunters at the edge of his woods. In his shiny blue pickup he was likely to see their pickups parked by the sides of local roads, sometimes on his own property. He drove past. He might wave. The hunters sighted him, grinned and waved. MR. FIX-IT who was John Heart was well liked, a little strange maybe but lots of people were strange, guys who appeared outwardly normal with kids, families, could be strange if you got to know them. For there's a solitary soul in most men you don't find in most women. MR. FIX-IT was clearly one of those solitary souls. Never spoke about his private life, rarely asked personal questions. A loner. Had more carpentry work than he could handle but he didn't seem to want to hire any assistants. Sometimes he played poker at Capuano's Tavern, not a very methodical player, trusting to luck, cards. During hunting season he wouldn't offer any comment when the talk shifted to hunting. He'd never ask hunters how they'd done.

He was a good drinking companion, a good listener. His brooding, serious eyes. Passing no judgment on others, possibly wanting no judgment passed on him.

The worst of it was after a day's barrage of gunshots, hiking out in the silence, in the gathering cold just before dusk, to discover a wounded deer, sometimes more than one, dying up in the woods. These were likely to be does, even fawns. Illegal game so hunters let them lie where they fell, or crawled. He might have recognized some of the very deer he fed through the long winter, though he tried not to. He found himself squatting over them, a witness to their deaths, his mind empty of intention, even of thought. He could not have said why he was there. He never killed the deer to put them out of their misery. He wouldn't have had the strength. He couldn't even bury them, the ground was usually frozen.

It seemed such a sad fate, to die alone. With no witness.

As sad a fate as to live alone.

Some of this he'd told Nola Leavey after they became lovers. He found himself telling her things he hadn't told other women. He worried that one day, one night, in a moment of weakness, out of his terrible loneliness, he might tell her too much.

Nola hated hunting, too. Despised hunters. She told John how shocked she'd been, her first year as a teacher in Iroquois Point, when as many as one-quarter of her junior high boy students stayed out of school at the start of hunting season in November. "Their fathers take them hunting. Can you imagine? They're only *boys*." She told him that her ex-husband Jordan owned at least one rifle, a .22-caliber Winchester. He'd gone hunting as a boy, he had fond memories of those years. He'd owned a .12-gauge shotgun at one point, she'd asked him please to get rid of it or she would refuse to allow the children to visit him in his home and he said he would, he had, but she didn't know if she could believe him. She talked for a while of how Jordan had changed during the course of their brief marriage. She wasn't a woman to speak indiscreetly, she despised self-pity and swore she would not succumb to it, but she'd been badly hurt by that man, he'd been unfaithful to her while she was pregnant with Drew, telling her afterward it hadn't meant anything to him, the woman hadn't meant anything to him, it was just something that happened, it had nothing to do with her, and nothing to do with their marriage. "But, for me, it was all over then. The marriage." John listened in silence. He had begun to love Nola, it seemed to him he loved her seriously, yet also helplessly, and he didn't like that feeling, it reminded him of Dahlia's helpless loves, the brutal, manipulative men she'd been involved with, her curious failure of will, a perverse sort of enthrallment. *I know this one's a shit, but I can't help it. Only for a little while.*

"That gun. The rifle. I think he still has it. I can't know, but I think so. He's become a desperate man."

Nola spoke rapidly, angrily. Clenching and unclenching her fists which was a sign of nerves in her. John was quiet, listening. He understood that there was a secondary layer of meaning here, but he wasn't quite sure what it was.

Once you were sleeping with a woman, so much was this secondary, lower layer. Often the woman wasn't aware of it herself.

It was the evening of the day Jordan Leavey had attacked John Heart with his fists in the parking lot of the Oswego County Courthouse. Through the day, traveling in MR. FIX-IT's sky-blue pickup, he'd kept seeing the contorted face of his enemy. *Not enemies but brothers. Loving the same woman, the same children.* His own face, he thought, looked comical, swollen and meaty where he'd taken more than one hard punch. Nola said, gravely, "I think you should make an appointment to speak with the judge in private. I think she should see you, what he's done to you. What he's capable of. And what kind of man you are."

It was a surprise to Nola, an affront, deeply disturbing, that the family court judge, though a woman, a plumpish woman of youthful middle age, evinced no evident sympathy for her. Judge Whitfield was professionally neutral, coolly matter-of-fact. Frequently, with admirable calm, she interrupted the quarrelsome male lawyers, urging them to move on. She wanted the quarrelsome parents to settle. The term "settle" sounded, on her lips, like a directive issued to a malingering waiter. Why was she reluctant to make a decision? Wasn't that her role (Nola fumed) as a family court judge? Nola speculated that the woman might be unmarried, and thus not sympathetic to the problems of marriage; or if married, childless. Though she certainly looked maternal: bosom, hips. A somewhat sensuous face made up in the elaborate manner of another era. (Maybe that's it, Nola told John meanly. She's jealous of me, of us. She's old. Too old for sex.) It was true, John saw, that the judge, regarding Nola, contemplated her without warmth. She contemplated Jordan Leavey who breathed noisily, sighed frequently and shifted about in his chair, with polite, barely disguised disdain. It was doubtful that John Heart could have made a positive impression upon her, a man with a criminal record. A man who'd been tried as a teenager for a serious felony—second-degree murder. Judge Whitfield appeared to be in her early forties, and so she might well remember John Reddy Heart in the headlines, the vulgar glamour that had gone on, and on. But John didn't want to argue with Nola, not at this time. The woman was exhausted, he'd never seen her so disconsolate, her head resting on his arm, in the crook of his arm, in an odd, awkward pose as of abnegation.

Between them they'd finished a bottle of red wine at dinner. The children were in bed, the house was quiet. (But Ellen, anxious and edgy and not always obedient since the onslaught of the court hearing, was probably not asleep.) Again, Nola hadn't invited him to stay the night. He said, "The gun. The rifle, if he has it. Do you think you're in danger from him? In that way?" and Nola said, not lifting her head, "No. But I think you might be."

7

He didn't feel that his life was in danger. Who would want to hurt MR. FIX-IT? That was the point of MR. FIX-IT—who'd want to hurt *him*?

Throw your life like dice. Be brave! As a child he'd learned. A wild light of hope and yearning in the bone-blond woman's eyes as she stood at the craps table swinging her fist beside her head preparing to release the dice, tumbling rolling dice.

"Hey, Heart—*mail*."

A horn sounded importantly at the end of the drive. He could barely hear the shouted words. Unloading a heavy mahogany table from the rear of the pickup backed to the barn door, he squinted to see who it was, and waved. Martindale the mailman in his low-slung magenta Chevy, splattered with a winter's accumulation of dirty snow like lace, waving as he drove away.

John felt a stab of dread. That childlike rise of hope, yearning—you learn to beat down, it's so often disappointed.

John Heart, known for his promptness and reliability as MR. FIX-IT, had a strange habit of neglecting to bring in his mail for days at a time. Why? Just forgot. "Didn't get around to it." Until finally the box was stuffed, the lid fallen open like a gaping mouth. An eccentricity like refusing to answer a telephone ringing at his elbow or a question put to him point-blank. Nola said, "Such behavior, in certain quarters, might be interpreted as rudeness." She was only partly joking.

When John Heart had first moved to Iroquois Point several years ago he was approached one day in a local diner by a beefy youngish man with a sandy crew cut, a stranger, who shoved out his hand, "John R. Heart? 'FIX-IT'? You live out Barndollar Road, right? I'm Terry Martindale, your mailman. Sometimes you don't take in your mail for days and I notice your truck's parked there, you're actually home so I'm won-dering—is something wrong?" Martindale looked so genuinely concerned, John apologized and made an effort to bring in his mail every day for weeks. Then, gradually, he began to forget.

He hiked down the driveway now, his breath steaming. It was another cold bright-blue windy March day. And that smell of the lake—icy, metallic. His head had ached much of the night. He'd slept some, a jolting rocky sleep, the way a bowling ball might sleep between bouts of rolling and crash-ing. To dull the pain he'd swallowed a dozen aspirins. He might've had a beer or two during the night. Living alone, sleeping alone, you do crazy things. Aspirin washed down with beer was an old bad habit of his—started when he was a kid. One of his back molars was rotted and aching like hell and he'd had to do half the driving, if not more, those exhausting days, day following day, two thousand miles bringing the Hearts and their belongings in a thumping U-Haul from Vegas to Willowsville, New York, and they hadn't wanted to stop and Dahlia guiltily fed him aspirin, cans of lukewarm beer, promising they'd find a dentist for him soon. *I'll make it up to you, hon. All of it!*

A kid of eleven, Johnny'd been proud of his driving. He'd only just learned, instructed by one of Dahlia's man friends.

He looked older than his age, he was quick to catch on, fearless behind the wheel of the big old glitzy-orange Cadillac Eldorado where another kid his age would've been terrified.

While Grandpa Heart was still alive, up in Shawmouth, John would receive cards from him every eight or ten months. *Johnny, boy. Still kicking here. Can't complain. Life is good. Come see Grandpa soon or it's too late. Bless you, boy. Our love to you.* The signature was "Grandpa H." and below it a stamp in green, AARON LEANDER HEART, as if John might need further identification. These cards were slick, full-color reproductions of THE GLASS ARK at Shawmouth, N.Y.—*A world-renowned collection of more than 30,000 bottles and other glass items open to the general public 365 days a year*. Aaron Leander Heart's Glass Ark was a bona fide tourist attraction seventy miles beyond Oswego on the lake. Listed in the *New York State AAA Tour Book* for the Oswego-Watertown region. Ten years before there'd been a two-page feature in *People* showing the stately old white-haired and whiskered "native-grown seer and artist" posed proudly before the glittering Glass Ark he'd constructed, piece by piece, in the backyard of his shanty-house in Shawmouth. There'd been numerous other features in regional magazines, newspapers, tourist guides. John Heart was occasionally asked if he was related to "that old man named Heart, the one with all the glass bottles, or whatever" and he said no, he wasn't, his reply curt and embarrassed and probably so transparent a lie no one believed it, including Nola Leavey who backed off and never brought up the subject again.

What a character, Grandpa Heart! Johnny had always loved him, no matter what. As an adult, John Heart had loved the old man, too. But not quite so unconditionally. Not entirely trusting him. He'd driven up to Shawmouth every few months to visit, enjoying the old man's company, all that remained of his family by that time. They'd talk circumspectly about Dahlia, Farley, "little Shirleen"—it seemed that Aaron Leander Heart's memory of the family was set, perhaps deliberately, in a time predating Willowsville. It was as if Willowsville, where they'd lived for seven years, where John Reddy Heart had come of age, hadn't existed. But mostly they talked of the Glass Ark, how many visitors had come recently, this was a seasonal tourist attraction of course, though Grandpa Heart kept it open daily—"As God has ordained." They talked of the future of the Glass Ark, beyond Aaron Leander Heart's lifetime—"You will take it over, Johnny? You're my sole executor, my only heir." John mumbled a reply. He couldn't think of a less likely fate. He couldn't think of the old man dying. All that remained for him of his family.

But Grandpa Heart had died last November. Already four months had passed. The Glass Ark was being managed by a woman friend, a former assistant of Aaron Leander Heart who lived in Shawmouth. John Heart kept his distance. He didn't want to think about it. He had too much to think about in Iroquois Point—his MR. FIX-IT work, his connection with Nola Leavey and her children. What he missed was Grandpa Heart's cards in the mailbox. Those cards with their enigmatic messages in that handwriting he could recognize at six feet had ceased forever.

He'd fetched his mail from the box and slammed the loose-fitting lid. MR. FIX-IT was painted in bright blue above JOHN R. HEART in matte black on both sides of the handsome aluminum box.

Quickly he scanned the envelopes, advertising brochures and flyers in his hand, seeing, yes, he'd been expecting it, the envelope, computer-addressed, JOHN R. HEART, BARNDOLLAR RD., IROQUOIS POINT, NY 13016 from HARTSSOFT, PALO ALTO, CA 94303. "Fuck it." Every six months like clockwork a dividend check came to him. He'd never cashed one of these checks yet they kept coming, following him from one address to another. Through the galaxy of instant information available in cyberspace to his brother Farley he could be tracked anywhere on earth, he supposed. Not Farley but one of Farley's numerous assistants. Though probably it was done entirely now by machines. For it was all clockwork. What had once been emotional, vivid as a dying man's glistening blood.

At the barn, in his workshop, the phone was ringing. A woman's voice clicked onto the answering service, asking when MR. FIX-IT could drop by to repair a broken window. Quickly John sorted through the mail, tossing away most of the advertising brochures and flyers, setting aside the weekly *Iroquois Point Sentinel* he'd read diligently to absorb the mysterious life of the community in which he lived. There were two or three checks for MR. FIX-IT from customers who'd owed him for weeks, maybe months. He never put pressure on anyone to pay him, never telephoned. He might send a second bill, eventually. Some people waited to be billed twice before they paid any bills. He'd encounter these people in town, at the mall, catch their guilty evasive smiles, he'd just smile back, wave, walk by. It was more important, MR. FIX-IT had always believed, to be liked and respected than to be paid on time. His own bills, he paid as soon as they came in. Kept his finances in scrupulous order. It was easier, in fact, than the other. (The Hearts! Dahlia and Aaron Leander. They'd left Vegas owing hundreds of dollars. Maybe more. Driving away in the middle of the night from the little rented bungalow on Arroyo Seco where they'd owed two months' rent. Grandpa Heart might've owed money to gambling acquaintances. Dahlia might've borrowed from friends to buy the Caddie Eldorado from another friend. Though he'd wanted to marry her, and he was a rich man, Colonel Edgihoffer hadn't given Dahlia any money, it was all to come when they were legally "man and wife.")

John examined the envelope from HARTSSOFT without opening it. His hand shook slightly.

Resist ye not evil. He'd never understood what Jesus meant by that remark.

Not that he, John Heart, was a man who brooded, trying to decode what isn't decodable. He'd read the Bible, the New Testament mainly, at Tomahawk Island. Frowning over the

verses, sometimes moving his lips as he read. He'd been John
Reddy Heart then, kind of a brash smart-ass scared kid, he'd
thought that if he could've met Jesus Christ face to face a lot
of the mystery, the murk, would've been cleared up.

One day four years ago when John was living in
Watertown, working as a carpenter for a local contractor, a
rare personal letter had come to him, certified mail.

Dear John,

One hundred shares of HARTSSOFT have been
purchased in your name and dividends will be processed
and sent to you in due course.

Please note that my legal name is now Franklin S. Hart.

I hope you are well, as I am.

                              Sincerely, your brother
                                    "Farley"—

                              (dictated but not read)

John was mystified, mildly annoyed. He didn't need his
younger brother's charity.

Later he would learn that identical letters had been sent to
the rest of the family. Aaron Leander in Shawmouth, Shirleen
who was Sister Mary Agatha of the St. Anne's Sisters of
Charity in Kansas City, Dahlia Heart in Casa Adobes, Arizona.

He put away the letter, forgot it. Then the first of the
checks arrived—at his new address, in Ogdensburg. He'd
opened the envelope to discover a check made out to JOHN R.
HEART for $460.73 and for a long moment couldn't figure
what it was, who it was from. When he realized, a burn
seemed to spread across his face. He hadn't spoken to Farley
in years but he managed to get through to him, for in those
days you could get through to "Franklin Hart" if you could
convince an assistant of his that you were in fact the man's
brother, with an urgent message. "Hey Farley, if you'd given

me this by hand, as a gift, I'd cash it with thanks." (Not that that was true. John wouldn't have cashed it in any case.) Farley stammered some sort of reply, taken by surprise, as if no one ever spoke to him in such a familiar, intimate way any longer. He'd sounded exactly like the boy John had known, the shy quiet startled-seeming brainy kid brother of whom no one took much notice, even his mother. John, not very comfortable on the phone himself, congratulated Farley on forming his own computer company, he'd heard from Dahlia that Farley was doing really well, he'd patented some new invention?—or more than one?—"microchips"?— "neurological-cybernetical microchips"?—and how did he like California? There was an awkward pause, and Farley said, his voice almost inaudible over the breadth of the American continent, that he wasn't much aware of California yet—"It's just the place I live and do my work." After this the conversation between the brothers had quickly died.

John had assumed that his call would cancel the checks but six months later a second arrived, for $512.91. He tossed it into a drawer and forgot it. He might've assumed, since he hadn't cashed either check, that he wouldn't receive any more, but, six months later, the third arrived, for $623.14. It had followed him to Iroquois Point though he hadn't left any forwarding address with the Ogdensburg post office. "God *damn*. I don't want his charity!" The next check was for $1,772, and the next for $6,829, and when he'd torn open an envelope to discover a check for $26,336 he vowed he wouldn't open another envelope from HARTSSOFT, it wounded his nerves, spoiled his mood for the rest of the day. To be a carpenter-handyman driving a bright sky-blue Ford pickup at the beck and call of customers scattered through the county you had to maintain a good mood, you couldn't be susceptible to upsets, shocks. Your soul couldn't be in thrall to a man you'd have to confess you scarcely knew, a man you hadn't seen in twenty years and possibly would never see again.

Nola had asked about John's family, had he any brothers or

sisters. She knew of his mother in Arizona. She wasn't a woman to pry, even elliptically, but she'd sensed John's hurt. He said, shrugging, "We're scattered. Younger brother on the West Coast, younger sister in the middle of Missouri. And me in Iroquois Point."

He never cashed the checks but he saved them, tossed into the lowermost drawer of his battered filing cabinet in the barn. He forgot about them, the accumulation of how many thousands of dollars, from the jarring arrival of one HARTSSOFT envelope to the next in his mailbox. *Go on, cash the goddamn checks. You fucking well deserve it. If not you, who?* Within the past two years the value of HARTSSOFT stock had steadily risen; even people (like John Heart) who knew and cared nothing about the stock market or high-tech computers knew the name and had possibly heard the name "Franklin S. Hart"—a multimillionaire, a man of mystery, rarely photographed, only in his mid-thirties. It had crossed John's mind more than once since meeting Nola Leavey that he could put his brother's charity-money to good use. Nola's teaching salary at Iroquois Point Junior High wasn't much. Now she had to pay her attorney legal fees—in itself a form of harassment by her ex-husband. John could help her. She'd say no at first, no thank you, but she'd give in. He didn't doubt he could persuade her to give in. They could buy a house together. Move in together. He was fed up with living in a trailer, like living in a submarine. He wasn't in his twenties any longer. His next birthday, next February, he'd be— what?—thirty-nine years old. He and Nola knew just the house they wanted, they drove by it often, a slightly run-down clapboard-and-fieldstone house on the edge of town, it would be on the market soon and MR. FIX-IT was the man to take on the task.

The trouble was, money like Farley's was too much. Like winning a lottery you hadn't known you'd entered. Like a fairy tale. It took away the incentive, the fun. You didn't need to buy a run-down house, you could buy a new house. You could build your own house. You could change your life if you could figure out another life to change it into.

After Farley was placed with a foster family in Elmira, New York, his foster father a professor at the state university there, he'd excelled at his high school studies, won a scholarship to MIT and after graduation done advanced work there and at Caltech on computer technology. He'd earned a Ph.D. by the age of twenty-three. He'd begun a company of his own by the age of twenty-seven. By the age of thirty, he'd founded an early version of HARTSSOFT. John Heart, during the same years, hired himself out as a manual laborer, a carpenter's assistant, a housepainter, a truck driver. He was happy for Farley, for what he knew of Farley, relayed to him by their mother who was happy, too, and proud, but, if she was drinking, susceptible to sudden remorse—"I lost them. I gave them up too easily, didn't I? Johnny? You can be frank with me. You can tell the truth to me. I wasn't well in those years. I couldn't have been a responsible mother. Farley needed a stable home. Shirleen needed a stable home. A healthy environment. I couldn't provide it. I was a weak woman. I know I was a bad mother. I let that man into our lives, into our house. I brought doom onto us. I mean as a family—I destroyed us. 'The Hearts.' Can you forgive me, Johnny? Say you forgive me." John, scowling, opened a beer and watched foam bubbling up and onto his hand. "Fuck it." "John, what? I couldn't hear." "I said sure, Mom. Sure I forgive you. We all do." There was a pause. He'd been cruel, and he wasn't a cruel guy in his heart. When Dahlia spoke, her voice was almost inaudible and her words were slurred. She tried to say, "T-thank you." She'd begun to cry. There was another pause and a man's voice, pleasant but firm, came on the line. "John? This is Raymond. I'm afraid your mother will be hanging up now. Thank you for speaking with her."

John wasn't jealous of Farley, he'd been relieved that Farley had turned out so well. The kid might've cracked up.

Witness, or almost a witness, to a murder. (John hadn't ever learned just how much Farley had seen.) He might've been sick the way Shirleen had been sick. At that time John Reddy had been imprisoned at Tomahawk Island and none of the Hearts had visited him except his grandfather on the first of each month. John had to fight back tears when Grandpa Heart appeared in the visitors' room. He'd wanted desperately to grip his grandfather's hand, just hold it, and be held by it, but that wasn't allowed in the facility. No touching. They'd spoken to each other in lowered, shamed voices, seated on opposite sides of a sticky counter. All John could think to ask was "How is Mom?"—"How is Farley?"—"How is Shirleen?"—"How are you, Grandpa?" Again and again like a cracked cuckoo clock. For no answers Grandpa Heart could give him, in mere words, were enough.

He hadn't believed that Dahlia had abandoned him. He would never believe that, exactly.

The night of Melvin Riggs's death, it was Farley who was waiting for John when he came home, after midnight. Farley told John about Dahlia's men friends arriving at the house uninvited. Their angry quarrel in the front hall. The one who'd gone away, and the one who'd stayed. The one who was with Dahlia upstairs in her bedroom. John hadn't liked any of this. It pissed him off that Riggs (though he hadn't known it was Riggs at the time) was in the house, in such circumstances, because, until that night, Dahlia hadn't brought any of her Willowsville "business associates" home. In Vegas, men had stopped by the house at any time. Some of them were welcome, greeted with hugs and kisses, some weren't. Some who'd been welcome at one time weren't welcome at another time. A few pounded at the doors, even at the windows. More than one stood in the front yard calling for Dahlia, cursing and threatening Dahlia. Grandpa Heart cursed in return, waving his gun. He fired a warning shot. Two shots. Vegas police came to 837 Arroyo Seco. It might have been a night Dahlia Heart herself wasn't home, for there were many such nights. Two patrol cars were parked in the street, head-lights glaring. Neighbors were wakened and came to stare. The child Johnny stood in his shorts peeking around a corner of the house to watch in scorn as a youngish man, beaten about the head by cops, dripping blood, was cuffed, shoved roughly into the rear of a patrol car and driven away. Those nights of sirens, gunshots. There was a carnival mood, a mood like fireworks. You were excited to see some poor bas-tard beaten about the head, even kicked. But the Village of Willowsville wasn't Vegas. There was an entirely different mood here. The Hearts had risen considerably in the world. No one could mistake them for white trash now. They were, as Dahlia instructed them repeatedly, "residents of the upper middle class." She'd learned the word "bourgeoisie" and uttered it in three equally stressed liquidy-sensuous syllables. They lived in a beautiful house, a small mansion. In an exclu-sive neighborhood—St. Albans Hill. Dahlia had purchased outright (or maybe it was a gift?) a tasteful Mercedes of the hue of silver mist and had given the eyesore Caddie to John Reddy. She was a frequent guest at private Willowsville and Buffalo clubs and had reason to expect she'd be invited to join these clubs soon. She'd teamed up with local businessmen who were guiding her investments. It was her dream to own a small business one day, a beauty salon possibly. A boutique selling high-quality imported merchandise. It was her dream to be a "purely self-capitalized" businesswoman not depen-dent upon any living soul except herself. Except there were men who interfered with this vision, like Melvin Riggs, Jr. Riggs wasn't the only one, only the most conspicuous one. The one who'd ended up naked on the floor of her bedroom, a bullet in his brain.

At John Reddy's trial, Farley Heart was called to the witness stand as a hostile witness by the prosecution. It had been a bizarre episode. Farley had seemed dazed, drugged; his skin was the sickish color of curdled milk; his eyes swam behind the lenses of his schoolboy glasses. *He's lying. For my sake. My brother!* John would not be able to recall afterward the details of Farley's stumbling yet passionate testimony; a dull roaring as of Niagara Falls in his ears obscured much of the trial for him. He'd appeared an outlaw, a dissident, a vicious young murderer in the eyes of others yet had been to himself stunned and helpless as a patient under anesthesia. Farley had been a brother-patient, as helpless as he. Saying, his eyes snatching at the prosecutor's, *Sir, I look at a thing sometimes and it disappears. A solid object. A person. My mind is somewhere else. My own thoughts intrude. . . . Someone else—another "agent"—might have carried it there? It might have been—me?*

No one in the courtroom had believed his testimony of course. But the feeling behind it, the desire to spare his brother John Reddy—that was unmistakable.

It hadn't mattered. That trial had ended in a mistrial. Farley hadn't been called to the witness stand again. John hadn't been able to tell him how grateful he was for the testimony, how much he loved him. *My only brother.*

Twenty years later. "Franklin S. Hart." HARTSSOFT. The pioneer of Virtualized Reality.

Click into the event from X possible points of view. Soon your perspective will be multiplied to infinity. Limitless as the universe. Mankind will truly become as God, having information access from an infinite number of perspectives! Dahlia, proud if more than a little baffled, sent John an article her husband Raymond had clipped from *Scientific American*. The brilliant new discoveries that had been made within the past eighteen months alone of the possibilities of cyberintelligence. The explorations of cyberspace. "Franklin S. Hart" about whom little biographical information was known was one of a dozen young men renowned in the field, not the most famous perhaps, nor the wealthiest, but an individual, a loner, about whom the others spoke with respect. (There were five very young-looking men photographed for the article, but Franklin S. Hart hadn't been available.) HARTSSOFT was known for its rapid advances. The computing power in their new chips was doubling, on the average, every fifteen months. John read the article word by word, frowning as he read, feeling a wirelike band tighten around his head, he'd wanted so badly to understand his brother's work if only conceptually; he'd never had much of a mind for math, though he'd liked geometry, the actual visualization of space bounded by lines you could draw yourself, but beyond that—trigonometry? calculus?—he'd been a vocational arts major in high school, he hadn't had to take such courses. Dahlia was enormously proud to own one hundred shares of original stock in HARTSSOFT and couldn't resist boasting to her Casa Adobes friends, that the mysterious Franklin S. Hart, president of HARTSSOFT, was her younger son. "'Why has he changed his name?'—they ask. I tell them, 'My son is an American. But an American born in the West, right here in Arizona at Gila Bend. We believe in revolution. We believe in starting over, rebaptizing ourselves. We're *optimists*.'" On the phone with John, this was Dahlia's usual tone—upbeat, cheery, just slightly defensive but good-natured. It was rare in recent years she'd break down.

The other Hearts were grateful for HARTSSOFT's dividends, too. Aaron Leander said humbly, "This is truly God's blessing! It will go into the further development of the Glass Ark and to its maintenance, and publicity—for the Glass Ark must be seen by as many men, women and children as possible, for its beauty to be known." Sister Mary Agatha, formerly Shirleen, accepted the dividends as she accepted any and all contributions to help support her work with learning-disabled and autistic children at her Kansas City school—"For the greater glory of mankind, which is identical with the glory of God."

(Shirleen never failed to call her brother John twice a year: on his birthday on February 8, and on Christmas Eve. If he wasn't home to take the call—and usually he wasn't—she left a breathy, rambling message wishing him a happy birthday or happy Christmas, asking after his health and spiritual well-being and his work and moving on then to speak not of herself but of her recent work, about which she was invariably enthusiastic, excited. Alone of the Hearts, Shirleen retained the nasal, curiously hollow-sounding accent of western New York. Her voice was cheery and upbeat as Dahlia's yet rang with a girlish innocence that had never been Dahlia's. You envisioned, hearing her, a tall gawky self-conscious girl with glasses, slightly crooked teeth, a habit of wetting her lips as she spoke. So far as John knew, though he hadn't seen his sister face to face in many years, this was in fact how she looked; she'd never gained back the excess weight she'd lost at the time of her illness aged eleven and twelve. She spoke at length, interlarding her remarks with *Bless you, John!* and a catch in her throat as if she was about to cry but she did not cry, only continued, until the answering machine abruptly cut her off in mid-sentence. When John tried to return the call, she was never available to come to the phone. An assistant would say in a hushed voice, "Oh, Sister Mary Agatha is out!" or "Sister Mary Agatha is with one of her children!" They hadn't spoken together, so far as John could calculate, in ten years at least. *But we think of each other every day of our lives. My sister.*)

He stooped to open the lowermost drawer of the battered old filing cabinet and tossed the HARTSSOFT envelope inside. A dozen unopened envelopes. More. He'd never counted them. Checks never cashed, how many thousands of dollars' worth by this time? His brain shut off, he didn't want to think. *Resist ye not evil.* But he'd resist evil. He had that strength.

Already panting, sweating inside his clothes. He'd run up the stairs. Past Farley in his pajamas, glasses halfway down his nose as if he'd been hit in the face. The deafening-loud gunshots. The vibrating of the air. So that what you heard once, twice, three times you would hear yet again, and again, again. Through your life you would hear. At the farther end of the corridor in his underclothes was the white-haired, white-whiskered old man now unmistakably old. A hand pressed to his chest stricken in astonishment, pain. He was calling, shouting—what? There was Shirleen in her flannel nightgown crawling on hands and knees like a panicked animal, bumping her forehead against the floor. There was Dahlia through the doorway fumbling to wrap around her loose-seeming, soft helpless body a filmy negligee. There was the man, the body, fattish, naked, on the floor, on his back, head turned to the side as if he was trying to see over his shoulder. Dead or almost-dead, dying. Blood seeping into the dusty-rose carpet Dahlia had thought so elegant. The .45-caliber Colt revolver on the floor. Where it had been dropped. It was Dahlia's eyes he met, blank and glassy with horror, he would not afterward believe there'd been any command in those eyes Pick up the gun, Johnny! Take it! Take it out of here! Johnny, save us! *yet there was no protest when he did so, nor would there be in the weeks, months and even years to come, he'd acted out of instinct, his John Reddy–instinct, fastest kid on the basketball court, eyes in the back of his head, reacting without thinking, without needing to think, as one might leap into freezing water to save another person with no regard for one's own safety, no regard for any time beyond this terrible moment.* Throw your life like dice.

8

MR. FIX-IT didn't feel that his life was in danger. But he had a premonition that his life was going to change radically.

So he kept in motion. Ten hours on the road. The shiny sky-blue Ford pickup MR. FIX-IT HAVE TOOLS—WILL TRAVEL! looping about the back roads of Oswego County, servicing customers as far to the northeast as Port Calumet on the lake, as far to the east as Waukeega, as far to the south as Bridgeport on the Erie Canal and as far to the west as Sodus (where once, in another lifetime it seemed, he'd lived, aged twenty, an apprentice carpenter and roofer who'd fallen in love with his boss's wife). He replaced a bedroom window someone seemed to have smashed with a boot. (The boot was lying on the floor amid shards of glass. No explanation was offered, and MR. FIX-IT wasn't one to inquire.) He repaired, in three deft minutes, for no charge, a rusted old toilet that wouldn't stop flushing. With loud rapid rhythmic blows of his hammer he laid in speckled green-gold tile linoleum in a ranch-house kitchen, he loaded onto the rear of his pickup a brass-colored leather sofa with broken springs to

be repaired in his shop. For an edgy hour he worked with a
chainsaw, a treacherous implement he distrusted and feared,
clearing storm debris from around a house. He whistled atop
a stepladder repairing loose shutters, he replaced another
window, painted a child's closet-sized room (pale pink walls,
creamy-white ceiling—his heart ached, he thought of Ellen
peeking at him through her fingers when they'd first met). He
shimmied his way into a cobweb-infested crawl space to
retrieve, for an anxious elderly woman, an obese elderly cat
who'd perversely hidden away from his mistress—"He could
hear me calling and calling, begging him to come out and *eat*,
and he *wouldn't*." Expertly and cheerfully he hammered,
sawed, sanded, painted and shellacked. He repaired a sump
pump standing in three inches of dirty water. He accepted a
beer, two beers, from customers who urged him to sit down,
stay a while. Stay for lunch. Stay for supper. Thanks, MR.
FIX-IT told them. But he had to keep going—"My next customer's waiting." A Bridgeport housewife in her mid-thirties,
ash-blond, good-looking, pushy and nervous and practically
falling into MR. FIX-IT's muscled arms, laughed heartily at
this saying, "Hmmm. I don't doubt she *is*."

It was a day to wear him out, a day of exhaustion. A good
day. Before he'd left home that morning at seven-thirty a.m.
he'd fed the mewing cats, scattered seed for the wild birds and
dumped corn in a fifteen-foot trail for the white-tailed deer
who waited hungrily at the edge of the clearing. He'd learned
to spread the corn like this since otherwise, if he dumped it in
a heap, the deer would fight one another for it, butting with
their heads, slashing at one another with their sharp hooves.
There were no mature bucks in the small herd but in their
absence two or three does dominated, aggressive as males.
And in the act of spreading corn from a plastic bag he happened to glance up to see several deer panic and bound away
through the orchard—what was wrong? What had they seen?
In that instant he felt a stab of panic himself; he imagined the
back of his head, hatless, in a rifle scope; the hunter, his

enemy, would be crouched at the corner of the barn having approached stealthily through a meadow, avoiding the driveway where he would've been seen from the trailer.

But John Heart gave no sign of alarm. Continuing his spread of the yellow corn-kernels as the rest of the herd, less skittish than the others, watched with their grave, liquid-dark eyes. "Of course, it turned out to be nothing. My nerves. Probably they were spooked by a hawk"—he rehearsed telling Nola.

Except what could be his motive in telling Nola? Did he want the woman to worry that her ex-husband might kill him, or did he want her to know that he, her lover, wasn't worried in the slightest?

No. Keep your mouth shut.

There was no hearing in family court that morning. Nola had returned to teaching her classes. Later in the day she was to meet in her attorney's office in Oswego with Jordan Leavey and the two attorneys, directed by the judge to work at a settlement. Nola had protested in the judge's office, "Your Honor, it isn't possible, we've been over and over the same—" and her attorney interrupted, saying quickly, "Your Honor, my client means *yes*. We'll certainly *try*."

Furious, shaken, Nola called John; called him several times, leaving messages on his machine; at 6:40 A.M. his phone rang in the trailer and, guessing it would be her, John answered it; Nola hadn't been able to sleep most of the night, she said, she was trying to hide her agitation from the children, she'd assumed that her ex-husband's preposterous demands would simply be rejected by family court, what was she going to do? "I really think I could kill him. I could kill him! Imagine—I, a junior high English teacher, mother of two, a perfectly ordinary, civilized woman, a not-mad woman, *could kill another human being*." John was impressed by the vehemence of Nola's words but wasn't sure how to reply. She continued in her rapid, excited breathless voice, telling him she missed him, she missed their nights together, she needed him, the hell with family court, if the decision went against her maybe she'd run away with Ellen and Drew as in some TV movie of the week, she could live in a van like a Gypsy, she could be MRS. FIX-IT, Ellen and Drew adored him, he was their MR. FIX-IT they adored and they were always asking her when he was coming over, if he was having dinner with them that night, she was convinced they were truly frightened of their father but frightened to say so. "I can only guess what he's telling them. Poisoning them. If I could afford a better lawyer! If I'd thought this through better, at the start! He's just an Oswego attorney, specializes in child custody, he and Jordan's attorney apparently know each other, they might be in collusion, how would I know? The man gives me advice I haven't solicited. He's researched *you*. His aftershave is virulent enough to scare away mosquitoes. I'm wondering—could I sue for malpractice? And he's charging me by the hour! If I call him on the phone, it's 'billable' time! My students and their parents can call me at any time, and they do, and I'm happy to speak with them, I consider it my professional responsibility, and I like my students or anyway most of them, imagine—'billable time'! That bastard. All of them. And the judge—'the Honorable Ms. Whitfield.' She doesn't like me and I don't know why. I have to admit, I'm hurt. I've been a damned good mother and my ex-husband is the one who's had the drinking problems, the 'abuse problems,' I'd gotten an injunction against him when we were living in Lockport and all this is a matter of the public record, doesn't that ridiculous woman *see*? He's saying that I moved away deliberately so he has a long drive, getting the kids, bringing them back, he wants them to live with *him*—can you imagine? 'What's best for the children'—as if these people, these strangers, could know what's best for my children. As if it could be that clear, that impersonal. As if what a frightened, confused child might say impulsively is what that child actually means—Jordan keeps saying the kids tell him 'We miss Daddy'—it 'breaks his

heart to hear it' he says—and that's why he's suing me for custody, not out of malice or revenge, oh no, not out of sexual
jealousy now he's seen *you*. John, they've actually asked
neighbors of ours, colleagues of mine at school, for statements. Some anonymous source allegedly told Jordan's
attorney that I 'see men'—'men stay the night' at my house. 'A
man on a motorcycle'—'a man driving a van.' 'A man with a
ponytail.' Can you believe it? It's been said that I don't take the
children to church. And Jordan *does*. Suddenly out of
nowhere he's gotten religious—Lutheran. He and his mother,
taking the children to church in Lockport, Sunday school, it's
Mrs. Leavey's church, she's sincere I suppose, a kind of well-
intentioned woman, she and I got along very well until the
marriage started coming undone and now she's my enemy,
she's enlisted this pious Lutheran minister 'Reverend
Steinbach' whose remarks are actually being quoted! John, am
I losing my mind? This isn't me, honey, is it? You know me,
this isn't me. Did I tell you they've questioned Ellen's and
Drew's teachers, and the baby-sitter—that little high school
girl Linda! Judging *me*. Suppose Linda and I hadn't gotten
along? Suppose I'd caught her stealing, or sneaking a
boyfriend in—what then? Would I lose my children? I can't
believe this is happening. I thought the custody arrangement
was final. Jordan agreed—how can he disagree, now? I've
been awake for nights. I can't work. I want to cry all the time.
Which is why I'm smiling constantly. Damn it, John, why do
they accuse me about *you*, haven't I a right to—" She began to
cry. John, pacing about in his cramped kitchen as he listened
to this long disjointed speech, felt a stab of love for the
woman, and guilt; he didn't know what to say but had to say
something. "Nola? That was a long time ago. I was a kid, sixteen. I was tried, yes it was for murder, and I was acquitted."
Nola said excitedly, "I know you were acquitted, honey. I
know all about it. I mean—I've seen clippings. I wasn't living
in New York at the time, I mean my family was living in
Illinois, I wasn't aware of the case at all—'John Reddy Heart.'

I know you don't want to talk about it. I respect that, I understand. None of that is *you*. But—" "Yes?" "—you were acquitted, but—did you?—" There was silence. John wanted to slam the receiver down. *What business is it of yours, you don't know me, you have nothing to do with me and my family, go to hell.* He was shaken by his own reaction. He muttered, "Look, I was acquitted. I can't talk any longer right now."

Since then, he'd kept in motion.

A moving target.

* * *

Johnny's grandfather kept promising, in defiance of Johnny's mother, another target-practice session with the .45-caliber Colt revolver. But months passed, eventually years. The two never went out again.

In Vegas, he'd been wakened by arguing in the next room, his mother's raised voice; he'd gone to investigate and saw Dahlia in one of her casino costumes, black satin, low-cut across her breasts, a miniskirt to mid-thigh, high-heeled red shoes and textured stockings, she was wild-eyed, grappling with Grandpa Heart for the gun—"Just let me have it, Pa, God damn you! I won't use it on myself, I promise." The heavy gun went flying out of their hands onto the sofa, bounced and clattered to the floor, Dahlia screamed fiercely as she and her father lunged for it, but cunning Johnny, ten years old, whom they hadn't noticed, rushed to snatch up the gun, ran away with it into the backyard, both Dahlia and Grandpa Heart cursed him, "You, boy! You, Johnny! Get back in here *now*." He crouched in a ditch at the back of the property, hidden in the shadows, thinking if they came out to get him he'd throw the Goddamned gun as far as he could into someone else's yard. But chasing Johnny in the middle of the night was too much for the elder Hearts, the excitement ended there.

After a while, seeing the house was quiet, he returned. With the gun.

Another time, Vegas. A dry scorching heat. The little
rented bungalow on Arroyo Seco. The TV was on loud and
five-year-old Shirleen was watching it in her rapt, staring
way, seated eighteen inches from the grainy screen, and
Farley was doing his homework at the kitchen table, Grandpa
Heart was out playing poker and Dahlia was at her blackjack
job at Caesars Palace and Johnny drifted into the kitchen for
a Coke, saw a lone can of Mexican beer at the back of the
fridge and debated taking it, decided he hadn't better, just one
would be missed. He returned to the living room and there
was the TV loud as before, a jeep bounding over a desert
landscape, machine-gun fire, and—where was Shirleen? He
found her in their grandfather's cluttered room at the rear of
the house, a room forbidden to the three children. She'd
switched on the bedside lamp. She was holding, in both
hands, the .45-caliber Colt revolver. It looked like an oversized toy too heavy for a child to carry. Johnny broke out in
a sweat. "Hey, Shirleen. Hey, no. Give it to me, hon." He was
in charge of these kids! Shirleen blinked at him calmly. She
was an unpredictable, often obstinate child. Dahlia spent
little time with her but Grandpa Heart brought her treats
nearly every day, pockets of cashews and pistachio nuts taken
from cocktail lounges on the Strip. Ordinarily both Shirleen
and Farley obeyed their older brother without resistance. He
had a quick temper, like Dahlia's. Though he tended to be
fair, even kind. He wasn't mean to them, or capricious or
unpredictable like the adults of the family. But now Shirleen
gripped the gun and smiled, a strange twitchy smile. "I know
what this is. I know how it *works*." "So you know it's dangerous, huh? Come on." Johnny's legs were shaking as he
approached his sister. He'd seen a gunshot victim only the
previous week, carried away moaning on a stretcher, his face
and neck netted with blood. Damn Grandpa!—he kept the
gun hidden beneath his mattress, but everyone knew where it
was. He'd promised Dahlia that it would be kept unloaded
but somehow Johnny knew it was loaded. Clumsily Shirleen

raised the barrel in his direction, she was holding the gun in
both her pudgy hands, without a finger on the trigger;
Johnny ducked and came at her swiftly from the side, snatching the gun from her. He felt in that instant that he would
never complain again in all of his life, God had blessed him!
Not that he believed in God exactly. There was a little adobe
church up the street he'd sometimes drifted by hearing
singing inside. . . . Johnny said, "If I was Mommy you'd be
slapped silly. You're lucky it's me." Shirleen giggled, sticking
a thumb into her mouth. Johnny wondered how she'd been
able to pull the gun out from beneath the heavy mattress.
Such a little girl. A strange little girl. He believed she was
intelligent yet she behaved sometimes as if she was retarded,
or hard of hearing. He spoke to her as you might speak to a
dog, kindly but no-nonsense. "*Bad.* Go on out of here now.
You know better." She rushed past Johnny, who opened the
cylinder as he'd seen his grandfather open it. His fingers
trembled. Six bullets, dully gleaming.

He told Grandpa Heart about Shirleen and the gun. He
told Dahlia. They were both astonished. Grandpa Heart
vowed it would never happen again.

Those years. His childhood in Vegas, fleeting images as in
a film he'd only seen and had not experienced. That kid not
himself. Street-wise, a smart-ass, dark-tanned as a Mexican.
Somehow stronger, smarter, more stubborn and more desperate than he knew himself to be. By the age of eleven he'd
begun to be obsessed with keeping the Hearts together for it
seemed to him that anything could happen at any time to
break them up. He was not the only child of his acquaintance in the neighborhood who worried about his family,
what remained of his family, but he believed himself to be the
one canny enough to do something about it. *It won't happen.
It won't!* Not the way his father had vanished. If he, Johnny,
could've prevented the plane falling out of the sky. Possibly it
had been "sabotaged." Struck by missiles. God's wrath. An
explosion, flames. Fire and smoke trailing the sky He looked

up, hearing jets overhead. Flying in formation. The camera would follow the plane, and would cut to the ground to the terrible crash. Dahlia had begun to say, when she'd been drinking, that their father had brought it on himself, so proud of being an Air Force pilot.

You were punished beforehand for what you hadn't understood you would do until you did it.

Dahlia understood, she and Johnny were on the same wavelength. Wired on speed which was her truest self. Alcohol fuzzed her up, made her sleepy and delicious and ready for love but speed sharpened her intellect like a razor. Eyes glowing like coils on a stove. *I know I'm damned to hell. I can't help it. Someday one of them will kill me, I'll have to accept that. It says in the Bible the whore gets what she deserves. The bad mother.* They'd beaten her, some of the men. The ones she'd liked best. But none of them had killed her.

How many times after they'd left Vegas for their new life, he'd never kept track, she'd call him from taverns, motels in Buffalo and Niagara Falls and one memorable night from U.S. Customs & Immigration at the Peace Bridge after her friend Mr. Skelton sideswiped a railing on the bridge and had to be taken away by ambulance. *Johnny, help me! Come get me!* Each time was the last time, she promised. Possibly it had to do in some way with him. For he had girls of his own now. And women. Even before he had his driver's license to legally drive the glitzy Cadillac Eldorado she'd given him, that fantastic car the color of a blazing neon peach. He shaved, often twice a day. His thick black sideburns grew into his cheeks. His eyes were thick-lashed as a girl's. His genitals swelled with blood. His penis like blood-sausage hot and hard to the touch. But Dahlia was wary of touching her Johnny now. He's slap her hand away, and he wouldn't laugh. He locked the bathroom door so she couldn't intrude half-dressed, her hair in her eyes. Still she teased, she rolled her mascaraed doll-eyes. *Mmmm Johnny Heart! Tell the family why every girl in this Village is chasing after you.* Farley, overhearing, blushed crimson.

Shirleen blinked and stared, smiling with clumsy lewdness as if she caught on. Johnny slammed out of the room. *Fuck you, Mom!* and Mom laughed in his wake, *Sweetie, I wish.*

The Belle View Motel on Niagara Falls Boulevard where he'd almost died. If the beer can opener had sliced into his jugular vein instead of his cheek. He hadn't a driver's license yet, he was only fifteen. Driving through pelting rain at three a.m. praying he wouldn't be stopped by any cops. Cursing and sobbing. He'd never been to the Falls before by himself and certainly he'd never been there at night. In such rain. Couldn't find the fucking motel, driving up and down the Boulevard, fuck her she must've babbled the wrong address. Terrified and whimpering over the phone. *Johnny, help me. I made a bad mistake. He isn't the man I thought he was he's going to kill me I'm so afraid Johnny will you bring Grandpa's gun?* When at last he found the motel, went to room eleven and she opened the door an inch, hair in her face, haggard-look- ing, stinking of sweat, sex, whisky, she demanded *Where's the gun? Where's Grandpa's gun?* and he told her he hadn't brought it for Christ's sake. He tried to pull her out of the room. His car motor was running. She was barefoot, in black bra, black half-slip and no stockings. Gusts of hail like machine-gun fire raced across the asphalt parking lot. A crimson neon sign blinked moronically overhead BELLE VIEW MOTEL LUXURY ROOMS $18 & $25 WITH POOL. Dahlia balked, cursing him. Out of the dark- ened room behind her a man suddenly rushed at Johnny, cutting him in the face. They fought, he managed to drag his mother out into the Caddie and skidding and swerving they escaped. *Don't you judge me God damn you you have no right to judge me.*

Those years. He'd been a high school student, a basketball player. Worked after school as an apprentice carpenter. None of it was very real to him. Only the family was real to him. He was tired much of the time, exhausted. Never got enough sleep. Could've slept for ten, twelve hours at a stretch and sometimes he fell asleep at the high school, leaning his forehead against the aluminum locker and nodding off on his feet even as his fingers turned the combination lock, laying his head down abruptly on his arms at his workbench in shop class and dying, it felt like dying. What was the teacher's name, Hornby—poking him cautiously to wake him. Where he would've yelled at another boy. *John? Hey. You O.K.?* (It was believed he was a heroin addict. One of his friends informed him.) They watched him as you might watch an upright snake. Fascinated but wary. The nice boys, the nice girls. Dahlia hadn't had to warn him not to fool around with any of those girls. He went home never knowing what to expect. Entering the "Edgihoffer mansion" to—what? Farley who came home directly from school would give him a dour report. Unless there was nothing to report. For sometimes, to be truthful it must've been most of the time, things were all right at the Hearts'. Most of the time their mother was fine. A woman of energy, passion, cunning intelligence and a fierce self-devotion he was never to encounter in any woman, or man, afterward. Dahlia Heart was certainly a terrific-looking woman, people stared at her in the street, her dazzling platinum-blond hair, her impeccably made-up movie-star face. Sheerly an invention. But an invention like a fine-tuned auto that worked. *Why're you frowning at me like that, Johnny? Think you've got the right to pass judgment on me? I gave birth to you out of this body, eleven hours of labor you smart-ass son of a bitch.* She laughed like a man sometimes, deep belly laugh no one ever heard outside the Hearts. Johnny couldn't help but laugh with her. What a joker. His mom had learned comic turns, droll squinchings of her eyes, a way of wriggling her breasts from the Vegas lounge acts. Her raw-lewd humor she didn't dare reveal to her Willowsville "business associates." No truth so profound, so crushing you can't turn it into a joke—that's the Vegas philosophy. At the Hilton she'd seen poor Elvis perform in the last year of his life, once-handsome Elvis bloated as a corpse that'd been floating in water for a week. Fat face made up pearly-white as a geisha's. She could

do an Elvis routine, actually. *Love me ten-der, love me tru-e.*
Even Farley giggled. Yes she took seriously the challenge of
being a good mother, a responsible resident of the upper
middle class. Intermittently she made an effort to take notice
of the younger children. Farley bewildered her, he was so
damned smart, but quiet, "still waters run deep," in fact she
was proud of Farley's high grades, and one time astounded his
teachers by turning up at an open house at his school. Yes,
she tried to love her daughter, too. They all tried to love
Shirleen. A sad pudgy not-pretty child. A slow-learning child.
A clumsy stumbling yet stubborn child. A child who stared at
her mother as if watching TV. A child who flushed with pleasure if her mother noticed her, said a kind word to her. Yet a
child stupid enough or reckless enough to have made the
error, more than once, of shrinking from Mommy when in
one of her wired moods Mommy swayed in her direction
zealous to hug her, and to kiss. The child's beady lashless
eyes blinking, narrowed as if she feared being struck. By her
own mother. So fearing, in the face of Mommy's proffered
love, naturally she was struck. Anyone of the Hearts could see
that coming. Mommy's slashing hand. The sharp edge of
Mommy's twenty-five-carat diamond ring in its platinum setting that was in fact a flashy zircon with the diamondlike
power of shearing into the child's flesh just the same. *Damn
you! Nasty little thing! You do it on purpose to break your
mother's heart don't you!*

And the time Shirleen fell, or was pushed, from the top of
the stairs. Though Dahlia who'd been at the top of the stairs
shaking the child by her shoulders would not be able to comprehend afterward how the accident happened, how it could
possibly have happened, denying responsibility even as she
wept for forgiveness. Farley, shaken as Farley rarely was,
described to John how their young sister fell fifteen thumping
steps without apparent resistance. Her legs and arms limp,
head banging against the steps which were carpeted but still
ungiving, she fell doggedly, as if out of spite, as Dahlia

screamed from above. Her right leg was caught beneath her and cracked in two places and would require a hefty cast for eight months. It was Shirleen who volunteered to the emergency room physician, stammering with excitement, that she'd been "reading *Alice in Wonderland* and didn't know I was on the stairs, and the words made me dizzy so I fell." For weeks afterward Dahlia was sober, "stone cold fucking sober" as she described the state. Shirleen, her leg in a white plaster cast that soon became unaccountably filthy, was allowed to stay out of school much of that winter. She was indulged—pushed in a wheelchair when she should have been walking with crutches. Swinging and lurching on crutches when she should have been walking. Her brothers saw with alarm that she sometimes *crawled*—thumping along on her hands and knees, dragging the clumsy cast. A glum satisfaction in such infant behavior though Shirleen was a solid-bodied girl of ten and in other respects said to be in good health. Though Farley sought out John Reddy one day to tell him he was worried that Shirleen was "mentally ill." John Reddy relayed this information to Dahlia without comment; Dahlia slapped her hands over her ears and began to hum loudly. Then she burst into tears. "None of us ask to be born, Johnny. It's smart-asses like you who rub it in." Sustained sobriety was exhausting, Dahlia had discovered. Where others were forgetful when they drank, and perhaps drank to be forgetful, Dahlia was forgetful when she didn't drink. Possibly, with the world so diminished, as if glimpsed through a soiled scrim, there were fewer things worth remembering. Fucking hard some mornings to muster up the energy, she said, to breathe. Yet you have to slap on makeup, eyeliner. And there came Shirleen, the afflicted daughter, crawling in the corridor like a six-month infant, banging her cast against the floor. Shirleen explained that her leg, when she stood, "scared her" because she could see it. When she crawled, she couldn't see it. She crawled with surprising dexterity up the stairs and would have crawled down the stairs like a slithering snake if

she'd been capable. Evidently she wasn't capable. (No one
had seen her practice.) There was Shirleen noisily sucking at
her fingers. There was Shirleen refusing to speak. Shirleen
refusing to sit and eat with her family. (Though she ate ravenously at other times, alone in the kitchen through the day
and sometimes at night.) When at last the soiled cast was
removed from her leg of course she limped. The doctor recommended physical therapy but Shirleen refused. She
preferred to limp. You could see the satisfaction in her eyes,
quivering in her mouth. With stubborn pride she would limp
through life bearing the irrevocable sign of her mother's
excessive love. Sister Mary Agatha of St. Anne's Sisters of
Charity whose pronounced limp from a "mysterious childhood injury" was unfailingly noted. Sister Mary Agatha
suffered migraine headaches, shortness of breath, occasional
tachycardia, frequent indigestion; she spoke frankly, even
cheerfully, of her "congenital dyslexia"; the world would be
amazed when it was revealed that this indefatigable woman
fasted virtually every day of her life, subsisting on a few grains
of brown rice, minuscule quantities of raisins, solitary let-
tuce leaves, unleavened bread, watery skim milk and vitamin
supplements. (Her superiors in the Order of St. Anne insisted
upon the vitamin supplements.) In truth, Sister Mary Agatha
subsisted on prayer and work in equal proportions: prayer
from three a.m. to eight a.m., work from eight a.m. to six
p.m., prayer from six p.m. to midnight, with approximately
four hours eked out in the interstices of this schedule for
sleep and other unavoidable physiological functions. "The
way of the penitent," Sister Mary Agatha described herself,
"—but the penitent who puts her shoulder to the wheel."
But it was rare that the white-clad, wimpled, bespectacled
nun with the perpetually windburnt girlish face spoke of herself, or spoke at all. She'd been known to lead interviewers
through her workday at the Kansas City school without a
single word, so fierce was she in her concentration on her students. Eight days before the death of Melvin Riggs, Jr., which

would shatter the Heart family forever, Shirleen, eleven years old at the time, sought out her older brother Johnny to ask anxiously, "Do you remember your dreams when you wake up? Do you still hear the voices? I do! I'm afraid of them. My dreams don't stop when I open my eyes, they keep on and *on*. They have so much power. They sift through me like I'm nothing—a strainer. It's like in school when the teacher talks through your thoughts, you don't have the power to not-hear. I know, though—I can't make things happen so I need to make myself want the way things happen. Is it like that with you, too? Do you think it's God talking to us? But we don't understand? I was so happy—in a dream last night a voice said, 'I am God. You are my daughter. I love you.'"

9

Rock of Ages, cleft for me.
Let me hide myself in thee,
Let the water and the blood,
From thy riven side which flowed,
Be of sin the double cure,
Cleanse me from its guilt and power!

They were singing the old hymn military-style. Not begging but commanding. Sometimes John Heart didn't join in, sometimes he did. Singing was one of those things he'd never learned to do with much pleasure or even comprehension, why it meant so much to so many people, not to listen but to *sing*. It's like your soul catches flame, someone told him. In another lifetime, Dahlia Heart had hoped to sing. Her breathy-sexy Eartha Kitt impersonation. But singing, true singing, true music, required not just talent with which you might be born but training, discipline, doggedness. At the Apostles of Jesus Christ Risen, John Heart told the minister he was embarrassed to sing, he hadn't any voice. Reverend Andy Shaffer said snappily, "Eh what? I hear your voice, son. What's that if it ain't your voice?"

A few Sundays of the year, depending on his mood and the weather, John Heart rode his motorcycle twenty-five miles to Watertown, to the storefront church whose minister, Reverend Andy as he was called, had hired MR. FIX-IT a few years ago to repair rotted shingles and drainpipes. A few Sundays of the year, John Heart rode his motorcycle thirty-two miles to Port

Calumet to the Unity Love of God, another small church he'd
discovered through his job. There was a Free Methodist
church in Pulaski, and there was a Catholic church with a
predominately Portuguese congregation in Shawmouth. He'd
never stepped into any church in Iroquois Point. He'd never
told Nola Leavey of his itinerant churchgoing, she wouldn't
have known whether to be mystified or to laugh at him. "You,
John? A Christian? Come on!"

Well, he wasn't sure, either. About the most fundamental
principles of his life, the innermost secrets of his heart, he
wasn't sure.

All night fighting sleep because his dreams were grating as
pebbles. Hurtful to his brain like splinters of glass. Ice-pellets.
He understood that he was John Heart, thirty-eight years old,
MR. FIX-IT of Barndollar Road, Iroquois Point, New York,
but at the same time he was a boy, a kid, hunted like an
animal. Running, stumbling, spraining an ankle. Crawling
(as his poor sister had crawled) on his hands and knees. He
was lost in an ice-field. He'd wiped the gun clean of all fingerprints save his own. Covered the gun with his fingerprints.
He'd tossed the gun over the railing of the little bridge onto
the ice. It was not this ice, not the ice of the Glass Mountain,
but it was ice, since November, covered with a powdery film
of snow. He would be surprised at the ease with which the
deception worked. *They want to believe it's me; it's me they
want to hunt down.* And that was true. He was only a kid, sixteen. But he hadn't been a child in a long time. He knew
certain truths only adults knew. And not all adults know.
There are those among us we want to hunt down, and kill if
we can. There are others, most others, we would spare, We're
good people, we don't want to hunt and kill. Except sometimes. So they were hunting him on Mount Nazarene.
Sighting him through their riflemen's scopes. That was their
privilege, he'd given them the privilege. But he meant to make
a run for it, climbing, slipping, sliding. His ankle throbbed

with pain. Pain could make you into an animal. They were hunting him like an animal, that was their privilege. The brilliant winter sun blinded him. The steep ice-field. He didn't have his dark glasses, or his gloves. He was in terror of going blind. Beneath the ice-crust was a bluish haze. Grasses like frozen ripples in water. He'd believed they might be human beings like himself somehow reduced, shrunken. He was losing his ability to coordinate hands, arms, feet, legs. His ability to think. He was panting. He began to cough. Rock of Ages, its crust frozen. *Cleft for me* but it would not. *Let me hide myself* but it would not.

God shouted at him through a megaphone. Called him by name. Hunted him down like a wounded animal. Captured him, kicked and billy-clubbed and brought him back in shackles. His face bleeding, his eye punctured. He would be much-photographed. Much-memorized.

John Reddy Heart we would've died for you.

* * *

He heard himself telling Nola Leavey that he was better out of her life. Her children's lives. She knew this, obviously. There was silence at the other end of the line. "Nola? I'll come by tonight, pick up whatever things of mine are there. All right?"

She'd begun to cry. She managed to say, over a confusion of noises in the background, "It's not as if I have much choice, John, is it."

When he arrived, later than he'd planned, Linda the freckled high school girl was with the children in the kitchen. John didn't want to say good-bye to them, nor did Nola, who was looking shaky, think it was a good idea at this time. She'd work it out with them somehow. If he could call in a day or two and speak with Ellen first and then Drew . . . "I want to spare them as much hurt as I can this time. But I don't want to lie to them." She wiped roughly at her eyes. She blew her nose. She laughed. "God, I want to be so virtuous! It's as if I almost died, this past week, my life was spared by a miracle, I'm so weak and so absurdly grateful. Though, losing you, I did die, I guess. Let's go to the Lakeside and get drunk."

"You can't get drunk if you drive."

"Why am I driving?"

"You drive your car, I'll meet you there."

Nola considered this. In the other room, Drew was chattering excitedly. "That's right. You're right. Separate cars. Of course."

At the Lakeside they sat in their usual scarred booth at the rear of the bar, as far from the jukebox as possible. The old inn was a popular local place, distinguished in summer by a lengthy open veranda overlooking the lake and a grayish pebbled beach below. John Heart had come here with other women, but not in a long time. Nola ordered a whisky-and-water, rare for her, and began talking rapidly. Now that it had been decided, there was no danger of her asking him another time about the trial. Was he a murderer. Had he been "protecting" another person. He wouldn't have to say *I was acquitted*.

Twenty-two years ago. Long past.

"All he basically wanted, he claimed, was to live closer to the children. I mean—to have the children live closer to him. The way it had been before I moved us to Iroquois Point. Before I upset the balance," Nola said. Quickly she used up all her tissues, and what John had in his pockets, which wasn't much, then began to wipe her eyes and nose on cocktail napkins. "So he's dropped the suit. He's started back at AA in Lockport, he says. He asks me to apologize to you and to thank you for not pressing charges. He swears he didn't want to cause trouble, or grief for any of us—'I'll never hurt you again, Nola,' he says. 'That's right,' I told him. 'You won't.' I don't think he knew I'd had an offer from a school in Bolivar, about twenty miles northwest of Lockport, at the time I accepted the position here. It's still available. A former teacher of mine, who'd been a teaching assistant at SUNY–Albany when I was in graduate school there, is principal. I called him yesterday. It's virtually set. I'll be resigning here. So fast! My head is spinning. But, as I said, Bolivar is only twenty miles from Lockport where Jordan lives and he could move closer if he wants, it's up to him. Now we have no emotional claims on each other maybe at last we can be, what's the word, 'amicable.' Another word for 'indifferent.' This will be so much more convenient for Ellen and Drew, of course. It was selfish of me to make them have to ride so far, so long, in Jordan's car—a hundred-and-forty-mile round trip in a single weekend. And poor Jordan—two hundred and eighty miles. I hadn't been thinking I guess. I don't believe it had been out of spite. He'd complained bitterly but I didn't seem to hear him. I mean, the justice of what he said. His voice got in the way. He says he wrote me letters and his mother wrote me a letter but I have only the dimmest memory of this. I must have torn them up without reading them. John, do you know Bolivar? It's about the size of Iroquois Point. It's inland from the lake about ten miles. Just a small town. The school is approximately the same size as Iroquois Point and I'll be teaching more or less the same subjects, at a slightly higher salary I hope. And this time I'll rent a house before I buy. I won't make the same mistake twice. God, this is embarrassing. Like hemorrhaging." Nola meant her runny nose, her bloodshot tear-brimming eyes. She laughed. "What a way for you to remember me, John. What romance. But maybe you won't remember me."

The more a woman talked, the quieter and more withdrawn MR. FIX-IT became.

Thinking how like blows of a hammer. One! two! three! Pounding nails into fresh-sawed wood. Blunt and deft as a master carpenter the woman was, not noticing, or not seeming to notice, the mild dazed look in his face.

He'd mumble, "Sure." And, "O.K." And, "Another drink?"

She talked. Seated not beside him but across from him, a subtle rearrangement of their usual positions side by side nudging each other's shoulder. It had been John Heart who'd slid into the seat opposite Nola's and he guessed (the Lakeside was local, everyone knew everyone else) this rearrangement had been noted by the waitress, by the bartender and the cashier who was the bartender's wife. Noted, decoded. One of those unmistakable rearrangements of the expected that signals profound and probably irrevocable change.

MR. FIX-IT, dextrous with his hands, you might say generous with his hands, wasn't very dextrous with words. Not his own, nor others'. Sometimes, where emotion was involved, and surprises, he had difficulty comprehending. His English teacher Miss Bird, that pushy, kindly woman who'd seemed to like him, as if seeing, in him, a boy other than the one others saw, had said with sparkling impatience *Oh John Reddy, express yourself! What you feel, what you want to say, just write whatever comes, or you could talk to me, tell me, and I'll write it down for you, c'mon don't be silly just try!* But he couldn't. For sure, he couldn't. He'd let her down, hadn't wanted to know how badly he'd done on his final English exam, the essay question a cobweb maze of X's, for sure he'd disappointed her, he'd disappointed them all. For it was one of the mysteries of his life, that, in the Village of Willowsville where he'd passed among inhabitants like a ghost, they'd seemed to like him, to see some elusive promise in him—*John Reddy Heart*. And Nola Leavey had, too. Until now. This past week. Then he'd let her down. She loved him but not enough. You couldn't blame her of course—she'd been a mother before she'd become John Heart's lover. Still, he was stunned. Had to admit, stunned. Like he'd taken several hammer blows to the head. A new teaching job? A town called Bolivar? A friend, a school principal? Nola Leavey who'd confided in him so much of her personal life had never told him any of this, nor even hinted at it; she'd told him repeatedly how much she loved Iroquois Point, what a good decision it had been to move as far from her former home as she could—"To break those depressing connections." And how often, how sincerely, she'd told him she loved the little wood-frame house she'd bought on impulse, especially now that MR. FIX-IT had reshingled, reshuttered, rewired, repainted most of it for no fee except meals, kisses, etc. *I won't make the same mistake twice.*

Nola was saying, "I was awake most of Thursday night trying to work a way through this maze. I've never been such a wreck. I'm so ashamed—I must have left twenty messages on your machine. I realize I'm a little light-headed now, it hasn't sunk in yet, but it feels right. Morally, in my heart—it feels right. Adults have to compromise. 'Settle.' Judge Whitfield, I'd resented her so, was right all along. I see that now. Oh, John." She began to cry again. She'd been nervously twining her fingers through his and impulsively she lifted his hand to kiss the knuckles: her mouth was surprisingly cold. "Forgive me, forgive me, I love you." John disengaged his hand from hers. "O.K., Nola. It does feel right, I guess. We'll keep in touch." He shoved out of the booth and grabbed his jacket. Apparently he was leaving. Nola stared up at him startled as if he'd slapped her. Her forehead was finely creased and there were thin white lines at the corners of her eyes. "You're leaving—so soon? It's so early. I thought we were going to have dinner, John?" "Some other time," John said, backing off. He had the look of a man who's finished with a conversation; a man who's hung up a phone.

John paid the bright-brassy cashier for their drinks with a twenty-dollar bill and told her to keep the change. The woman called after him in a way meant to be cheery, jocular—"Thanks and g'night, MR. FIX-IT. Come back real soon." Outside in the drizzly dusk he was hurrying to climb into his pickup when a burly man in a sheepskin jacket passed, face almost-familiar—"'FIX-IT,' huh?"—and John said, "Right now, friend, no."

10

It was always a surprise to see the first of the signs—

THE GLASS ARK!
World-Renowned Spectacle!
SHAWMOUTH 5 MI. AHEAD
Open to the Public

The signs, designed by Aaron Leander Heart himself, were bottle-shaped, a vivid glossy green, with glow-in-the-dark white letters. They were of various sizes, the largest at least six feet high, set at a short distance from the highway. As you neared the home of the glass ark, the signs came at decreasing intervals: 1 MI. AHEAD, 500 FEET AHEAD (TURN RIGHT). At last, at the bumpy end of the Shore Road, a bottle-sign lying on its side to point you into the parking lot: THE GLASS ARK ➔ Visitor Parking Free.

John had to smile. His grandfather had certainly been optimistic, and enterprising, in the last decade of his life.

He'd told John that The Glass Ark, upon which he'd worked for almost twenty years, had begun as a vision ordained by God for no purpose other than itself, but, as time passed, and he, the creator of the Ark, deepened into wisdom, he understood that it was "a way of redeeming my sins, and the sins of anyone who glances upon it. But a way, son, of beauty, not repentance."

Well, good. John Heart thought there wasn't much point in repentance, this far along in history.

When Grandpa Heart was living, John made the seventy-mile trip up to Shawmouth on the lake at least twice a year. (Aaron Leander Heart never left Shawmouth—"On principle.") After his death, and his burial in a nearby nondenominational cemetery, the previous fall, John hadn't been back, though he'd promised Nola Leavey to take her and the children for a visit when the weather turned warm. (As now it had, finally, in late April. But John Heart wasn't seeing the Leaveys any longer.) He hadn't much wanted to think about The Glass Ark, as he hadn't wanted to think about the checks from HARTSSOFT accumulating in his file drawer. But he was now the legal owner as well as the executor of Aaron Leander's estate. The last time he'd seen Grandpa Heart alive, this past October, the elderly man, now in his mid-nineties, had walked with difficulty, leaning on an ivory-handled cane (a gift from an admirer of the Ark) and on John's arm, leading him through the shimmering radiance of the Glass Ark, reassuring him that, though he'd made the bequest in his will to "John R. Heart, my beloved grandson," it was a bequest made in love, not obligation. "Johnny, you do *what you do*. For your grandpa, that's enough."

But was it, really? Was any human effort ever *enough*?

It made him resentful to contemplate a responsibility he didn't feel equal to, and one he'd never requested. And since Aaron Leander's death, the HARTSSOFT checks made out to his grandfather were continuing, flowing into an account established in an Oswego bank for the maintenance of The Glass Ark. MR. FIX-IT was being stuck with finances, IRS forms, hiring an accountant. At the same time he was restless in Iroquois Point, preparing to move several hundred miles east and north to Rouses Point on Lake Champlain, close by the Quebec border; he needed freedom like he needed oxygen to breathe!

"Damn." As soon as he turned his motorcycle in to the parking lot beside the entrance to the Ark, he saw that the asphalt pavement had begun to crack and the first tough weeds were poking through. In a few months they'd make cobweb cracks everywhere. The twelve-foot plank fence, painted a flat oyster-white, with a sheen to make it glow in the dark, would soon need repainting. (Aaron Leander had never wanted a fence around his property but his assistant Tildie Manchester, fearing trespassers and vandals after the *Life* feature made such a local fuss, had insisted. MR. FIX-IT liked the idea of fences, and he liked most fences, especially if he put them up himself, but this one, a tall picket fence, was impractical for Shawmouth weather, so close beside Lake Ontario.) And the local tree service Tildie hired, to repair winter storm damage, had pruned the row of poplars above the lake cliff so brutally it looked as if a giant child had hacked at them with a cleaver. John felt his heart sink—he was being drawn into the folly of the Ark.

It was 10:10, a weekday morning. He'd made the trip from Iroquois Point in less than an hour. There were three vehicles in the parking lot: a Winnebago camper with Ontario, Canada, license plates, a burgundy-colored Lexus with New York plates, and Aaron Leander's decade-old Buick he'd left to Tildie Manchester. The asphalt was still wet from last night's rainstorm. Sunshine reflected in puddles. There was a dizzying mirror effect. John parked his Honda beside the Buick and went to the front entrance of the little house, which had been hardly more than a shanty for most of the time Grandpa Heart had lived in it, and rang the clapper-bell, and Tildie Manchester opened the door for him, breathless and anticipatory. She must have been waiting just inside. "John Heart! Welcome! Come *in*!" John hadn't known what his grandfather had told the woman about him. Long before he'd become her employer she'd gazed at him with a peculiar sort of intensity and seemed confused when he asked the mildest questions of her—"How're you doing, Tildie?" and "How's business these days?" MR. FIX-IT's manner was frank and outgoing and friendly and he wondered if Tildie Manchester expected something more exotic from him. She was a plump, easily embarrassed woman in her late fifties with a girl's face, tight-permed hair tinted a hopeful russet-brown. She was a recent widow: her husband had been the Shawmouth postmaster, and both Manchesters had been friends and admirers of Aaron Leander Heart whom they'd believed to be, as Tildie said, an "amazing" man, a man "not like any you'd see around here," a "prophet." It was John's vague recollection that, when his grandfather first came to Shawmouth to construct his Glass Ark beside the Glass Lake, on one-third of an acre behind an uninsulated old house, local residents had believed him crazy; probably there were some who were still convinced he was, and The Glass Ark, though a tourist attraction on a par in the *AAA Tour Guide* with historic sites, small museums and flea markets, and evidently something of a moneymaker, was a monument to craziness. But, with the years, most Shawmouth residents had come around to being proud of it. Aaron Leander had been moved by the fact that some of them, including schoolchildren and friends like the Manchesters, had supplied him with bottles and other items for the Ark after he'd become too crippled by arthritis, and deteriorating vision, to continue scavenging for himself. He'd hired Tildie Manchester as his assistant after she'd volunteered to work for him for nothing; when, after his death, John Heart kept her on in a position he called permanent manager, she'd burst into tears with gratitude.

Not that Tildie Manchester was so very efficient a manager, or smart. Probably, if John had tried, he might've found someone better. But Tildie was trustworthy, devoted. Grandpa Heart had liked her. ("Anyway, she's the best we can get in

Shawmouth.") She was saying, excitedly, following after John, "Your grandfather never wished to believe that the Ark might need to be protected from the elements, but I'm afraid he was mistaken. If I hadn't put a canopy over it this winter, I don't want to think what kind of damage we'd have right now. Hail the size of *baseballs*. But we were spared. Now, tourist season is starting. Last week, Easter, we had more visitors than we'd had all winter. One family had eight children! They were from Quebec. And there was a sixth-grade class from Oswego, they came in a school bus. Your grandfather never wished to 'police' visitors but I think it's best to hire this nice reliable young man I know, my neighbor's son, to help out here on weekends and busy days. With these schoolchildren, for instance, there were two teachers and they assured me they'd keep watch over the children but I didn't let any of them out of my sight, of course. And there's souvenir hunters. Senior citizens are the worst! It's such a temptation to pry off some little glass jar, some tiny little thing you're sure nobody will miss, and suddenly it's gone. And with your grandfather no longer around to continue with construction—" Overcome by emotion Tildie broke off and John didn't pursue the subject.

No matter how many times John had seen The Glass Ark, he was never prepared for its strange glittering beauty.

The Ark was a shock to the eye. Then it was a shock, or at least a puzzle, to the mind: what did it mean? why did it exist?—not a single ark, in fact, for Aaron Leander had added to his original vision, but five arks of approximately the same size. Why had an aging man with no prior interest in art, or in craftsmanship, devoted so many years to piecing these fantastical structures together out of discarded bottles, glassware, strips of shiny metal, tinfoil, "gilt," stones collected from the beach? How did Aaron Leander Heart, who'd been a problem drinker until the last decade of his life, have the skill to create such elaborate, intricate designs? Had his vision really come from God?—but what was "God"? When they'd all lived in

Vegas, John's rakish cowboy-styled grandpa had applied himself to poker playing and gambling schemes that rarely worked out. He'd been something of a ladies' man. He'd had an Old Testament temperament (as he liked to boast) but no religion—"Belief is for suckers, kid. The game is, to be what the suckers *believe*."

Tildie said, "The Ark is very beautiful this morning, isn't it? After rain it always sparkles in the sun."

It was one thing to have a vision, John thought, but The Glass Ark was *work*. His grandfather had collected as many as fifty thousand bottles and other objects, according to printed estimates; he'd carefully assembled them with mortar and wire into stylized arklike structures that rose to about twelve feet at their highest peaks and were arranged in geometric figures, over a third of an acre. Each ark was predominately a single color—shades of greens, reds, blues. There were mosaic patterns of transparent glass inset in colored glass. Bottles of all sizes and shapes, jars, vases, chinaware were placed vertically, horizontally and at precisely ruled angles. Within these boundaries there were crazy-quilt patterns. A trash heap come to life. Cast-off broken and repudiated things. Scorned things—cheap plastic clock faces, picture frames lacking pictures, dime-store mirrors, two-thirds of a grotesque ceramic turtle that might have once been a soup tureen. The arks were soaring and magical, as in a children's storybook. Their prows were elaborately ornamented. Elsewhere were archways, columns, spires, towers. There were tunnels no more than six inches in diameter and shards of mirror positioned in them as to reflect one another as in a labyrinth. Where the arks' prows came together there was, built up from large bottles (whisky, bourbon, cheap wine), an elaborate throne with a high back and armrests, decorated in gold. The throne was on a foot-high pedestal and rose to a height of six feet. When John walked with his grandfather here back in October, the old man nudged him, pointing to the throne—"You have a place in

the Ark, Johnny. Your sacrifice is enshrined here." John felt
his face flush in dread of what his grandfather might mean.
He couldn't think of a reply and so stood silent for a long
time, gnawing at his lower lip.

He'd been pissed at the old man, but by the time he left that
afternoon he'd forgotten, they were saying good-bye in the
parking lot and he had an impulse to hug Grandpa Heart but
it didn't quite happen. Aaron Leander and John Heart had
never been sentimental with each other and weren't about to
start now. The old man regarded his grandson with crinkled,
cloudy eyes. He was smiling, brooding. John recalled their
target practice in the desert, how many years ago. He wondered if Grandpa Heart was remembering, too—what they'd
hoped might happen between them, whatever it was supposed to be, that hadn't happened. Johnny hadn't liked his
grandpa's gun, and he had no special talent for target shooting. All he'd shot was a tiny hummingbird.

A hummingbird! He was preparing for the rough, windy
drive back to Iroquois Point on his motorcycle. Strapping on
his crash helmet which he never failed to wear—MR. FIX-IT
was one for safety precautions. The sky was a mass of dirty,
broken concrete oddly floating in pale blue vapor. Wind
churned the lake's surface to a boil. *Maybe I won't see him
again. Maybe this is it.* Grandpa Heart had had only a single
shot of whisky since John arrived, and he'd been short of
breath as they walked through the Ark. But now, as John
climbed onto the Honda, he broke their somber mood by
slapping him on the shoulder. "Better to whistle in the wind,
son, than piss in it. A head wind, I mean." Grandpa Heart
uttered this remark as if it was ancient wisdom though John
had never heard it before and doubted his grandfather had
either. He laughed. "I bet."

"That's a crown he has floating there, hanging from that
wire. I mean—the idea of a crown. See it? Above the throne.
I thought it might be a bird, a seagull, the shape of the wings,

you know your grandfather used to stand on the cliff and watch seagulls for hours, so I told him, I said, '*I* thought that was a bird,' and he said, 'Make it a bird, then, Tildie.' And just laughed. But it was meant to be a crown so I suppose that's what it is." Tildie had taken a tissue from the pocket of her slacks and was dabbing surreptitiously at her nose. John said, "Hell, it looks like a broken piece of ceramic." He'd meant to be funny but Tildie sniffed, "It's the idea of what it is, it *is*. Not what it's made of."

John walked on, alone. He didn't like the way he was feeling. Not-himself. A tall lanky guy in biker's gear, greasy biker's boots, dark-tinted glasses, a day's growth of beard. But feeling shaky, sad as a kid. This was the first time he'd visited Shawmouth without his grandfather close beside him, keeping up a running commentary like John's own subterranean thoughts, and touching him. In his old age, Aaron Leander had taken to touching people more; his eyesight had deteriorated. John didn't want to imagine how the world, even The Glass Ark he must've memorized, looked to him. It seemed wrong that the Ark should outlive Aaron Leander who'd been the only human being in history inspired enough to create it. "Yet it's so. Has to be." John wasn't aware of speaking aloud.

More visitors were arriving. A middle-aged couple fussing with a video camera. A young mother with two children. John felt trapped. He was trapped! When Grandpa Heart first envisioned The Glass Ark he hadn't envisioned a site, an actual place, winding paths, staring strangers with cameras. He hadn't envisioned paying customers—$3 adult, $1.50 children & senior citizens. (In fact, Aaron Leander hadn't wanted to charge admission at all. It was Dahlia, on her single visit to Shawmouth, when the Ark had been open to the public for a few months, who insisted. "If Americans don't think something is worth paying money for, they won't think it's worth a moment's glance. And maybe it isn't.") But this was what the Ark had become, and this was what John R. Heart had inherited. MR. FIX-IT was trapped. For he couldn't help but see that the paths required regraveling. Pink limestone was attractive, Grandpa Heart's stubborn preference, but it was impractical. MR. FIX-IT might as well do the job, instead of Tildie hiring some local contractor probably a relative of hers. And the parking lot—the damned asphalt needed resurfacing. That messy job, MR. FIX-IT couldn't do himself. "Shit!"

A thin young woman in a rumpled olive-green trench coat was taking photographs nearby, and may have heard this. Though she'd been absorbed in her intricate-looking camera, using a light meter like a professional photographer, John had the impression that she'd been watching him sidelong, too. He hoped she hadn't overheard his conversation with Tildie and hadn't deduced that, somehow, he was connected with the Ark and not just a casual visitor about to drift away. She turned to him, smiling nervously. What was there about the Ark that provoked strangers to speak to strangers?—but John couldn't be rude on his own premises. The spirit of The Glass Ark was supposed to be *happy*, *uplifting*. The woman photographer caught John's eye and said, with a strange breathlessness, "This is my first time at the Ark. It's beautiful! The photographs of it I've seen don't exactly suggest its atmosphere. Its complexity. People say, 'Oh, folk art—I know what that is.' But the eye can't really absorb all this at once." John, startled, stood with his hands shoved in the pockets of his leather jacket. He nodded gravely, warily. When women talked like this, with an air of head-on, plunging eagerness, a woman in her mid-thirties (he saw, she wasn't so young as she'd seemed) speaking in the cadences of a fifteen-year-old, a part of him turned off. And when women talked too much, a part of him turned off. There was something else about this woman that made him uneasy. Her nasal western New York accent. Her rich-girl manner. The Lexus out front must've belonged to her: a $60,000 luxury car. Hers wasn't new, he'd noticed a slight dent in a front fender, but it had been new a few years ago. She had money, she was educated. Even her windblown sand-colored hair, her rumpled trench coat, suggested a quality of life far removed from Shawmouth and Iroquois Point. But he wouldn't have thought she looked familiar until she said, with a pushy sort of shyness, "Excuse me? We know each other, I think." John looked at her blankly. She said, extending her hand, "We went to the same high school. I'm Kate Olmsted. You're—John Reddy Heart?" Even after the passage of so many years her voice quavered. John wanted to turn abruptly away but he forced a smile, a MR. FIX-IT smile. "My name is John Heart. That was all a long time ago." He managed not to shake her hand, which was possibly rude, but there are times, fuck it, when they force you to be rude, that was John Reddy's problem in those days. He spoke flatly enough so she'd get the point he wasn't interested in pursuing the conversation and he was obviously edging away yet she persisted, "Do you—remember me?" and smiled an anxious smile showing too much gum. John said ambiguously, "I might." This woman's face was familiar though it had no distinct association for him. One of the rich Willowsville girls. One of the nice girls. None of them had been real to him and he'd kept his distance from all of them. (His girlfriends had been older, and out of school. Except for Dino's little sister Sasha he'd taken out a few times, she'd knitted a red muffler for him, had such a crush on him the Calvos asked him please not to encourage it, please avoid her all you can, and he'd honored that, that made sense. Italians took virginity seriously. Dino would've shoved a knife in his heart.) "I used to have," the woman photographer was saying, embarrassed, "—I mean, I still have, it's been in remission for years—M.S." Seeing his blank look she said, "Multiple sclerosis. I used to come to school sometimes in a wheelchair. You pushed me, once. You were kind to me. You gave me advice I've cherished all my life. I'm sorry—of course you don't remember me." The woman's voice had become alarmingly emotional. John shifted uncomfortably. What was this about? He didn't like the way this woman, for all her quavering, held that fancy camera in her hands. Her hands weren't trembling. *If you take a picture of me, lady, I'll smash that thing. Try me!* He saw Tildie at the entrance greeting more visitors. "I'm a freelance photographer now. I live in Buffalo. Here's my card." John had no choice but to take the stiff little card from her, importantly engraved KATE OLMSTED, PHOTOGRAPHY, with an address and telephone number in Buffalo. "If you're in the area, ever, will you drop by? Or call? Do you ever get back to Willowsville?—no? I'm helping organize our twentieth reunion for next July—would you come? It's the second weekend of July." John laughed, the idea was preposterous, but not wanting to seem rude he said, "Maybe." He was walking away. He'd forgotten the intense woman's name. Nonetheless she followed behind him saying, "I came here to photograph The Glass Ark for a book I've been commissioned to do on 'folk art' in New York State and—it's a coincidence meeting you, John! I know—Aaron Leander Heart was your grandfather. What a remarkable man. When we lived on Glen Burns Lane he used to walk past in the early mornings, my sister and I still talk of seeing him, we'd peer out the window and there, like a ghost—" John escaped from the woman, the appeal in her face, her voice. *I can't. Don't look at me like that. I'm exhausted, I have nothing left.*

Tildie Manchester was surprised at John Heart's manner. He wasn't broody and indecisive as he usually was on these visits, sitting in the office at the rear of the house she'd made over, since Aaron Leander's death, into a combination kitchen–sitting room with a big console TV on a shag rug. (Long dark winter days Tildie, sole proprietress of The Glass Ark, watched daytime soap operas and drank coffee to keep awake.) It was as if he'd made up his mind about something and felt good about it. Relieved, and sort of reckless. Agreeing with her on just about everything where, in the past, he'd frown and try to speculate what his grandfather would've wished. Tildie was feeding him hot cross buns she'd baked solely for him that morning. She worried he was too lean, a bachelor who didn't feed himself right, very likely drank a little too much, the curse of the Hearts as Aaron Leander spoke of it. She'd tried to get him interested in her sister's daughter and other Shawmouth girls but none of her effort had ever taken hold. There was the danger, too, of a man who rode a motorcycle—even if, like John Heart, he wore a helmet. You had to figure one day he'd have a crash. One day, if you loved him, you'd have your heart broken. You'd lose him. She was saying, rattling on nervously, "About hiring this boy I mentioned?—to help out on busy days? Like a security guard except he wouldn't have a gun of course, or even a badge. Or a uniform. Just to help out on busy days in the summer." John said, "Sure, Tildie. Hire 'im." "I wasn't sure what to pay—" "A fair wage," John said. "What you'd pay a carpenter, for instance." "A carpenter!" Tildie was shocked. "You mean, like you? A carpenter is *expensive*. Almost as bad as a plumber." "Well, pay him a fair wage," John said. "What does the Ark pay you?" He was serious, he didn't remember. He'd hinted to Tildie that Aaron Leander's estate had more money than she might suppose, admissions were a small fraction of its revenue, it was subsidized by some mysterious relative who'd never even come East to visit it, and never would. Tildie stammered and fell silent for nothing mortified her more, as it mortified anyone she knew, as frank money-talk of any kind. It was as discomfiting to her as talking of sex would've been, with this restless young man.

He said, as he left, strapping on his motorcycle helmet, "Tildie, use your judgment. You're the boss."

Tildie laughed, feeling almost hurt. "I'm not the boss, and I don't want to be. The idea."

She followed him outside. There were five visitors' vehicles in the parking lot now. The camper was still there, and the burgundy-colored fancy car, those people had stayed quite a while. The Glass Ark had such a hold on certain folks. John Heart climbed onto his motorcycle and kicked the noisy thing into starting, fixed his aviator-style sunglasses on his face and waved smiling at Tildie, "O.K., boss, see ya." Tildie scolded after him, having to laugh, waving good-bye, you never knew when you might see John Heart again, he'd spoken of moving MR. FIX-IT to the farthermost corner of New York State though possibly that was one of his jokes. "Good-bye! Come back soon! Bless you!—you know your grandpa would've, and God, too."

III. Thirtieth Reunion

It was a delirious time. It was a profound time. A time to celebrate, and to cast one's thoughts within: "It's, like, in my deepest heart, you're all *me*." A time for hilarity and a time for gratitude. A fun time—but also a tragic time. A time none of us is likely to forget.

And, historically, once-in-a-lifetime: our thirtieth WHS class reunion.

"Who'll be missing this time, d'you think?"
"Missing, or dead?"
"Dead *is* missing."

High as helium balloons and as combustible a record *eighty-seven* of us out of a graduating class of *one hundred thirty-four* converged on the first weekend in July upon the Village of Willowsville. By plane, by car, practically by foot we came. (For a number of us lived close by in Willowsville and environs—"We never left home, you might say.") We came from the farthest corners of the U.S. (i.e., Alaska) and two of us (separately, unknown to each other) from Europe. "Why'd

I come back?" *Washington Post* political cartoonist Chet
Halloren brooded. "To discover if life is truly so random as it's
come to seem in middle age. Or whether there's a pattern, a
design. In which somehow I fit. And you guys, my old buddies and classmates, can help me find it." Willowsville is a
sociable suburb where weekends are like riding the surf, party
after party, as local socialite and cochair of Thirtieth Reunion
Committee Millicent LeRoux Pifer thoughtfully observed, "I
scare myself when I'm alone. I'll be alone enough in the grave
for heaven's sake." Amen, Millie! Being so sociable, and, it's
true, socially competitive, we Willowsville residents draw lots
to see who'll entertain for our out-of-town visitors at our
reunions; and some of us arranged to meet at Tug Hill Park at
four p.m. Saturday to kick off the weekend with a WEL-
COME BACK BEER FEST! The weekend was crammed with
social events: cocktails on Saturday evening at the home of
Jon and Nanci Rindfleisch on Brompton Road, our traditional
pig-roast buffet held this year at the Pifers' in Amherst Dells,
and a post-midnight swim and all-night disco at Willowsville
Mayor Dwayne Hewson's house on Mill Race Lane; Sunday
morning a champagne brunch at eleven a.m. at Trish Elders
Carnevale's lakefront studio-home on Fleet Farm Road, and
afterward an open house at Willowsville Senior High courtesy
of the current principal and his friendly staff, and an afternoon doubles tournament on the courts there, plus our
traditional softball game (with cheerleaders!), followed by
cocktails/beer at Art Lutz's house on the Common and, for the
hardy, a farewell cookout at Jenny (Thrun) and Roger
Zwaart's new house on Castle Creek. To most of these events
we'd invited our former WHS teachers as guests of honor—
those we believed to be still living.

"What if they all show up? Doesn't Stamish have
Alzheimer's?"

"No. McKeever."

"Coach, Alzheimer's? God. What'd I hear about Stamish,
then?"

"Dead."

Dead! Seemed just yesterday the sweet old guy'd come to our twentieth reunion. One of our guests of honor.

At Tug Hill Park just above the lagoon, a half-mile or so beyond General Washington on his horse we'd festooned in pink toilet paper after our final homecoming victory over arch-rivals Amherst, we'd arranged for a local caterer to set up a beer tent. Glossy maroon and gold stripes, our WHS colors. Six kegs of imported beer, spicy Buffalo wings, nuts and nachos. "It's you guys I learned to drink with. Your faces! Sometimes, I'm having a drink on a plane? alone? we're maybe encountering 'turbulence' and I'm thinking *Jesus this is it*, I shut my eyes seeing you guys again, sweet sappy kid-faces, guzzling beer so it's running down our chins, eyeballs rolling back in our heads and who was it, Dougie Siefried? maybe Art Lutz? puking his guts out the back door where next morning who-was-it's dog—Smoke's?—that beautiful dumb border collie—Jesus, think: *Smoke's been dead thirty years*—would woof it down? And I'm not drunk but in that state of surpassing lucidity belted in my seat thirty thousand feet above the earth hurtling through what's called the sky and there's tears running down my cheeks so the person seated next to me must think I'm en route to a funeral but no, in fact not, it's *I'm so happy*. Whatever age I am, I was a kid with you guys, in our hearts we're all kids together, *the most profound truths never change*." Planning the BEER FEST somehow we'd imagined, don't ask me why, we'd be the only WHS reunion in the park that day. In fact, there was something annual called OLD HOMES DAY TUG HILL PARK—a youth festival. Hundreds of WHS graduates back home from college. A pandemonium of youth. Gorgeous in tank tops, T-shirts, cut-offs, miniskirts, some bare-chested, barefoot, hair cascading down their backs. And some with shaved heads. We middle-aged revelers were easy to spot amid slim bodies and smooth faces and hair. Eyes darting and snatching at one another like frightened fish. "Hey! Here! How the hell are

you?" "Jax, is that you?" "Bo, is that *you*?" We stared at Bibi
Arhardt in short shorts and a red bikini top drinking beer
thirty yards away with strangers, beautiful-brazen Bibi as we
remembered her, one of our WHS personality-plus cheerleaders a few of us had actually dated, made out with, or
believed we had, we couldn't figure out why Bibi was with
those strangers, not us, until Jax Whitehead slapped his forehead, saying, "Jesus, that isn't Bibi, that's just a girl. A girl
maybe eighteen. Bibi's our own age now—remember?" We
laughed uproariously. We spilled our drinks, laughing. Sweat
beaded on our faces, our bifocal tinted glasses slid down our
noses. We were being jostled by a gathering crowd. A swelling
crowd. Bare-chested college kids muscled like body builders
bullied their way past us demanding beer from our bartender,
beer we'd paid for, forty dollars per person payable by check
in advance, foamy liquid sloshing and spilling out of waxed
paper cups onto our shoes. "'Scuse me, Pops, lemme in here,
O.K.?"—we were nudged aside repeatedly. Amplified rock
music blared from all corners of the park making it impossible for us to talk to one another without shouting. Even
shouting, we had difficulty being understood. The summery-
muggy air vibrated with sheer sound. The lagoon's usually
placid surface gathered in agitated ripples as during an earthquake sending panicked snow-white swans paddling to the
farther shore. "It never used to be so noisy here. So *littered*."
"Are we in the right place? *This* is Tug Hill?" A dark-tanned
elfin-faced middle-aged man resembling Art "Class Clown"
Lutz in a sports shirt fitting his paunch snug as a bandage,
gray-grizzled locks, tufted eyebrows and a moist grin, was
cracking us up with his well-seasoned Stamish–Daffy Duck
imitation. "'Kwaaa-kwaaa B-b-boyz! B-boyz and girlz! Order!
I kwaakwaakwaamand you! *Now!*'" (Who could have predicted that Artie Lutz would one day be CEO at Lutz Magic
Kleen, Inc.? One of our class's bona fide millionaires? Whose
secret wish, according to our yearbook, was "To climb the
highest mountains, explore the deepest seas, and be the first

Willowsville astronaut in history.") Girls showed up, a few
with dazed-looking husbands but most with one another,
except they weren't our girls exactly but brave-smiling
streaked-blond women with sinewy golfers' legs and flaccid
upper arms, necks that would require artful arrangements of
scarves in another few years. There came rushing at us in an
explosion of perfume, in high-heeled open-backed shoes, a
mustard-bright mini-sundress, a thick-waisted woman with
shiny red lips resembling Sandi Scott—"That's *Sandi*? Sandi
Scott? Who used to be so pretty? Jesus God"—squealing with
nervous excitement as she vigorously hugged, and was
hugged by, a balding round-shouldered character in white
linen blazer, maroon carnation, ascot, who'd just emerged
panting out of a crowd of kids—was this our old classmate
Pete Marsh we hadn't seen in thirty years, we'd believed to be
dead? Or, no—was this Tommy "Nosepicker" Nordstrom
we'd heard owned a TV cable station in Palm Beach? No mystery who this was: that jerk Ketch Campbell perspiring and
hopeful in a maroon WHS T-shirt and new blue jeans that
fitted his womanish hips oddly, like cardboard, and a straw
boater hat with a perky red feather, trying to look festive,
elated, though as usual no one wanted to get stuck with him.
Poor Ketch had been faithfully attending each of our reunions
since the first and we'd come to see it was impossible to discourage him; he lived close by in Buffalo and was on our
mailing list, and so forth. Later that night at Millie LeRoux's
Ketch would surely tell the story another time of how he was
the first of us to set eyes on John Reddy Heart and his family
on Main Street, Willowsville, thirty-seven years ago this very
month, but not just yet, for under cover of the deafening rock
"rap" music we managed to elude him as we managed to
elude other forgotten classmates Charlie Swiss ("Lawn sprinklers, Akron, Ohio"), T. R. Krueger ("Haywood, Mimms &
Krueger, Accountants, Troy, New York"), and a sleek sealish-
looking individual who called himself Jocko ("Vista
Investments, Piscataway, New Jersey") all claiming to have

taken part in the notorious fight our senior year in the corridor outside Mr. Hornby's auto repair class when John Reddy's
greaser buddy Orrie Buhr attacked Dwayne Hewson without
warning, or was it Clyde Meunzer who attacked Ken Fischer
without warning, and friends of Dwayne's and Ken's rushed to
defend them, and guys poured out of auto repair, and Mr.
Lepage got kayoed by Mr. Hornby, and Smoke Filer got
knocked on his ass, and Mr. Stamish was cold-cocked, and
somebody pulled a fire alarm, and cops were called to break
it up—"I still got this chipped tooth in front here, see? One of
those hard-knuckle greasers slammed me."

It was a mystery, some of our classmates managed to get
lost trying to find the BEER FEST tent. Some got lost trying
to find Tug Hill Park! Which we would've believed we'd
memorized in our very cell-tissue. In the deepest recesses of
our brains. "Who's missing? What time is it?" "Who's got
the list?" "What list?" There were only twelve Porta-Johns for
what must've been twelve hundred beer-guzzling revelers
waiting in lines thirty deep. We middle-aged celebrants
hadn't any choice but to use the johns, or to try to, some of us
needed to use one every half-hour it seemed. Kids kept pushing ahead of us, even girls. "'Scuse me, Pops, gotta go, it's an
emergency." Sandi Scott and T. R. Krueger, arms around each
other's waist, wandered off searching for Jax Whitehead
who'd disappeared on his way to a Porta-John and got lost
themselves. Waiting in a long jostling line of U-B undergrad-
uates Art Lutz was appalled when, directly in front of him, a
pretty glazed-eyed redhead in a Deke T-shirt falling off a
naked shoulder suddenly squatted, lifted her miniskirt and
urinated on the ground, so drunk she nearly toppled into
the wet mess she'd made as onlookers cheered, whistled and
applauded. Art was appalled, and aroused. A flash came to
him of his high school sweetheart Mary Louise Schultz suddenly squatting in exactly that way, lifting her maroon
cheerleader's skirt and urinating through her white cotton
panties (when the cheerleaders leapt and kicked you could

see up their skirts, they wore identical white cotton panties) on the ground before him, exclusively *him*. He was forty-eight years old, he'd been married to the same woman for at least a quarter-century, had three near-grown children yet in that instant he was weak with sexual desire. Knock-kneed! "Jesus God, if this generation had been *us*." Art felt a metaphysical conviction so powerful it registered in his very gut: the injustice, unfairness, *he'd been born too soon for the fantastic freedoms that were now*, casually, enjoyed by youths to whom (he knew, he was paying for such services in his kids' college tuition) condoms were doled out like sticks of gum. As, years ago as a boy, he'd known the bitter injustice of having been born as himself, Arthur Lutz, and not a few years earlier as fate might have arranged, as his older brother James—their parents' clear favorite, a star football player and adored by all the girls. *Born too late. God damn!* We'd wonder what became of Art, he didn't return from the Porta-John, instead decided to leave the park and drive to Rindfleisch's cocktail party which had begun by this time, for it was already past six p.m., he could use a bathroom there, possibly Mary Louise was there, he'd heard she was flying from Albany for the reunion in her husband's private jet. His lips moved numbly. "Still the most beautiful girl I've ever known, Mary Louise. Hell, I still dream about you. Me, Lutz-of-no-illusions. Your eyes, your mouth, your hair—Your—" He squirmed, miserable with happiness. Others of our classmates never showed up at the BEER FEST or, if they did, swarms of young people beat them back, kept them from us. And now time to move on to Jon Rindfleisch's million-dollar showplace. (Did we resent our old buddy Jon who'd been such a clumsy fuck on the basketball court, and hit the water, diving, like concrete? No. We were happy as hell for the success of Rindfleisch Realty he'd inherited from his old man just when the real estate boom took off.)

Yet we were reluctant to leave. As if at our besieged BEER FEST we awaited a revelation that hadn't yet arrived.

(Scrawny-necked Fred Falco, another of our forgotten class-mates? with his simpering-cute little wife Cyn Swan dressed like a teenybopper? No *thanks*.) And then—"Hey look: that's who I think it is?"—it arrived. Barreling their way through the kids, rudely pushing them aside like ships cresting the waves of a choppy sea, were two individuals we didn't recog-nize at first—a massive two-hundred-twenty-pound darkly tanned man of vigorous middle age, a more slender but ropey, and mean-looking, Italian-looking man of middle age, the one resembling an ominously transmogrified Orrie Buhr and the other resembling—who?—Ray Gottardi, or Jake Gervasio?—and within minutes we were quarreling with these boorish uninvited guests (not only hadn't the two paid their forty dollars, they'd been expelled from school and hadn't graduated with our class, *they didn't belong among us*) who'd showed up, we knew, just to harass us—"Where's Hewson?"—"Where's Bozer?"—"Where's the rest of you?"—"Fuckers, you let John Reddy down!"—tossing lukewarm beer into our faces, shoving and jeering, laughing, one of us tripped and fell against the bartender's table, another would claim to have been lifted (by Buhr, it must've been, with those ape-muscles) and flung inside the tent, against the pole, there were shouts, screams, fists, furious elated faces, bulging eyes and carnivore teeth and flailing legs, and the sudden whoosh-ing collapse of the tent like a helium balloon rapidly deflating. It would be glimpsed by an exhausted, infuriated Clarence McQuade arriving two hours late for the BEER FEST, having managed at last to park his rented Volvo in a distant parking lot and hike through protoplasmic swarms of young people, grinding his teeth preparing the speech with which he'd greet us, his classmates he hadn't seen in thirty years, "'Who the hell's responsible! I sent a check for forty dollars, nobody ever acknowledged it or sent me directions how to find this fucking beer tent! All that crap about "We miss you"—"We love you"—"We want you"—and I fell for it like a sucker. Me, McQuade, a *sucker*.'" But he halted dead in his tracks staring

and blinking as, fifty feet ahead, the festive striped tent collapsed, sank, and was sucked down out of sight—"Like
matter sucked into a black hole, in an instant invisible, and
extinct."

· There'd been a time, many years ago when we were in our
early twenties, when Clarence McQuade was dead. That is,
we'd been led to believe he was dead. Elise Petko, a graduate
student in English at Columbia, telephoned Dexter
Cambrook, a graduate student in molecular biology at
Harvard, to tell him the tragic news: Clarence, Dexter's closest friend in high school, had killed himself on a bad acid trip
diving, or possibly he'd been trying to fly, from the Golden
Gate Bridge. Elise had heard he'd been brooding over his
mathematical research which wasn't going well, and experi-
menting recklessly with drugs. Flatly Dexter said, "No. That
can't be."

Shortly afterward, the story was modified, corrected: it
hadn't been Clarence McQuade who died, but Pete Marsh!
Pete who wasn't an intellectual like Clarence though intelligent enough, and diligent in his first year of law school at
Berkeley. But Pete had taken LSD and dived, or tried to fly,
from the Golden Gate Bridge. Died at the age of twenty-one.
The first of our class to die other than by vehicular accident.
"Don't you wonder what Pete would look like if he was with
us tonight? After all these years? His skin would've cleared up
by now. He'd be *handsome*." "Pete! He'd look at us and whistle through his teeth in that way of his, 'Cheeze guys, what
the hell *happened* to you? You're *old*.'" We laughed, we could
hear Pete's voice after thirty years and it hadn't changed at all.

When we have a few drinks we always do Smoke Filer imitations. We miss Smoke, too. We miss all you dead guys.
Smoke's weasel-pouty face the girls considered handsome,
his lewd snorting laughter. The kiss-kiss suck-suck noises
he'd make in Miss Bird's class that seemed to come from all

directions at once, poor Miss Bird didn't know where, cracking us up. (At one of our early reunions, it might've been our
tenth, Miss Bird was invited for dinner, and we apologized for
Smoke's behavior, and Miss Bird said, "No, no—that was the
way you children *were*. You can't change the past by an apol-
ogy any more than you can heal a wound that's long scarred
over. So why try?") On our way to the Rindfleisch party on
Brompton we drove past Smoke's old house, Willowsville's
sole Frank Lloyd Wright house and quite a landmark now.
"When we knew Smoke, it just seemed kind of weird.
Remember, we'd be inside and it felt like a cave? Smoke hated
it. He said, 'It's like living in somebody's goofy idea.'" That
house of poured-concrete slabs, horizontal planes and narrow
columns of glass shimmering at twilight. "Gosh. We don't
even know who lives there now, do we? Their names." In
fact we hadn't known for fifteen years, Smoke's family had
long since moved away. Willowsville was filling up with the
houses of our old friends, houses we'd visited as kids but
were barred from now forever.

Kate Olmsted was telling us she'd met John Reddy Heart in
the spring and he'd "vaguely promised, almost definitely"
he'd try to make it to the next reunion. This was ten years
ago, at our twentieth. Some of us had believed Kate, who can
be very convincing, and some of us hadn't. Now, at our
thirtieth, with its record number in attendance, and its atmosphere of frenetic celebration, it seemed even more plausible
that John Reddy Heart might show up. Millie LeRoux, co-
chair of the reunion committee, said eagerly, "We sent him a
handwritten invitation c/o the address Kate gave us. 'The
Glass Ark, Shawmouth, N.Y.' We told him he'd be a special
guest of honor—he could stay in anyone's house he wanted.
But we don't know if he received it." Trish Elders said, half-
joking, lifting her hands in protest, "He can't just stay away
forever, can he? Don't we mean anything to him at all?"

———————

Cocktails at twilight, the sweet-dampish fragrance of fresh-cut suburban grass, a sickle moon floating above the tall evergreens of Brompton Road. At the rear of the dazzling split-level home of Jon and Nanci Rindfleisch—"The very house in which Melvin Riggs lived at the time of his death. Imagine!" But we were disappointed, those of us who'd never been in the house before, for it was explained to us that Jon and his young, stylish second wife Nanci, an interior decorator trained at the Parsons School in New York, had so obsessively transformed the five-bedroom stone, glass and redwood house that it bore only a minimal resemblance to the showier house in which Riggs had lived and where, in his day, which seemed to us a remote, corrupt era, he'd entertained so lavishly. By the time of our thirtieth reunion, many of the Rindfleisches' neighbors on Brompton Road claimed not to know who Melvin Riggs was. Some vaguely recalled a "controversial" individual who owned the Buffalo Hawks baseball team and a long-razed Buffalo nightclub, and had something to do with township politics. Had he been arrested for embezzlement? Taking bribes? You could believe anything of that older, less ethical generation, even in ethical-Protestant Willowsville. "Or did he die in some violent way? *Murdered?*" There hadn't been a murder in Willowsville since the night more than thirty years ago when Riggs was blown away by a .45-caliber bullet. We stared in dismay at individuals who asked such questions. Some of them were newer residents of the Village, and others, in fact the growing majority, were simply young and ignorant.

Some of us, spurred by Roger Zwaart who loved plotting, intrigue, surprises, tried to rent the old Heart house on Meridian Place for one of our reunion events. But the current owners, a rich middle-aged couple with no ties to our crowd, turned us down coolly. Nor had they heard of any Melvin Riggs or John Reddy Heart—"You must have the wrong address. We've lived here twenty years and we've never heard of any scandal. *Sorry.*"

On display at the Rindfleisch party, and at Millie LeRoux's, were old yellowing yet lovingly preserved copies of the *Weekly Willowsvillian*, the *Will-o'-the-Wisp* and our handsome pearlescent-covered *The Yearbook*. Our smiling teenaged faces, feckless, freckled, open-eyed, peered up at us in faint incredulity we'd so aged, so changed. Yet—had we changed at all? "Seeing you guys again, Jesus it's like, it's—" we weren't sure who he was, that earnest smooth flushed bulb of a head, oyster-pouchy eyes, maroon sport coat and white fishnet pullover, he hadn't been able to manage affixing his name tag to his lapel and had shoved it into his pocket and it seemed awkward to ask him who he was for he knew us, seemed to know us intimately, shaking our hands and retaining them in a moist grip, "—it's like, dying almost—dying and waking in some new dimension where the solace is—old familiar faces. *Faces like lost souls that're your own soul—y'know?*" Our host Jon Rindfleisch (who we'd been kidding we wanted to stuff in a car trunk and haul around town over bumpy roads— "Remember, Jon? Deedee Drummond's brother was after your ass?") stood on the terrace that had once been Melvin Riggs's terrace looking like his own, old dad Mr. Rindfleisch greeting guests with crushing handshakes, embraces and kisses for the good-looking ex-girl classmates like Ginger McCord, formerly Siefried, in a backless pale green dress that set off her pallid redhead's skin, how wan Ginger was looking, but beautiful as we hadn't seen her since Doug's alcoholic collapse, cancer operation (a lung removed, Dougie'd been a four-pack-a-day man for twenty years) and their divorce and bitter child-custody case, we'd heard rumors that Ginger herself had been hospitalized, attempted suicide by barbiturate overdose, but her old friends Trish Elders and Shelby Connor loyally refused to talk about this, or about Ginger; and it was difficult to believe that Ginger had suffered any profound malaise of the soul as she slipped her bare, slender arms around Jon's thick neck and kissed his startled mouth with wet little-girl kisses as Jon's wife Nanci stared smiling a few yards away. "Oh, Jon. What's happened to us, what kind of spell is this, we're so suddenly *old*."

All weekend, Kate Olmsted took our pictures. Making us scream with laughter and in protest. Though her group pictures of us would be prized by all and that of poor Dwayne Hewson gaily kicking and flailing, being carried buck-naked to his own swimming pool by the drunken girls of the Circle, would be the last photograph of Dwayne's life—a collector's item, you might say. Chet Halloren, former *Willowsvillian* cartoonist, was up to his old tricks, quick-sketching hilarious portraits of us, caricatures of varying degrees of cruelty and accuracy depicting jowls, pouches, dents, wrinkles, excess weight and deficient hair and too-glaring dentures with the slapdash skill of the pro hit-man. "Chet, this is hideous. This is libelous. Oh Chet—*how could you?*" Sandi Scott tore the offending portrait into confetti and tossed it into her old boyfriend's face.

"Why did I come back? To determine the answer to a question that's been haunting me since that night a bunch of us guys from Chess Club got drunk out behind Burnham Nurseries waiting to learn that John Reddy Heart had been shot down dead. *Is life serious, or not?*"

"Why did *I* come back? I live over on Fairway Drive, *I never went away.*"

"Did you hear? John Reddy Heart is definitely coming! Millie says she expects him at her house for dinner, by ten. He's staying with Kate Olmsted. Did you know they're friends?"

We were puzzled to see Mrs. Schultz, Mary Louise's attractive mother who used to drive us around in her station wagon after school, being greeted and warmly hugged by Jon Rindfleisch; and Mrs. Connor, Shelby's pretty mom, was here, too, nervously laughing in a group that included at least two of her daughter's ex-steadies; then it was pointed out to us— "Those aren't our classmates' mothers, *those women are our classmates.*"

It was definite—E. S. Fesnacht was coming. She'd sent in her check, a name tag had been prepared for her: *Evangeline Fesnacht*. Never once had this mysterious WHS classmate of ours, dubbed in our newsletters our "most renowned literary light," attended a reunion, or even answered our queries— "But the thirtieth is an exception. Vangie told me personally, *she'll be here.*"

At last, exhausted and embittered, Clarence McQuade stumbled onto the Rindfleisch terrace, an hour and forty minutes late. We recognized him immediately: that narrow intolerant head, those perpetually bulging eyes with their expression of barely suppressed fury at others' stupidity and slowness, even at his good, fellow-brainy friends in Chess Club; the tall spindly frame in off-the-rack queer-textured clothes, like Velveeta cheese; except for his thinning hair worn long, lank, Clarence, one of our class geniuses such teachers as Mr. Alexander and Mr. Salaman used to defer to, hadn't changed in thirty years as if embalmed in Palo Alto cybertech research (for megasuccess corporation HARTS-SOFT) as in a time-warp. Without greeting us whom he hadn't seen since graduation Clarence protested in the whiny nasal western New York accent of his boyhood, "Who the hell's responsible! I sent a check to the reunion committee, nobody ever acknowledged it or sent me directions how to find these fucking events! All that crap about 'We miss you'— 'We love you'—'We want you'—and I fell for it like a sucker. Me, McQuade, a *sucker*. I tramped all over Tug Hill Park and by the time I located the BEER FEST the tent was down, vanished. I drove all around Willowsville hitting one-way streets and streets I didn't recognize! And the signs aren't readable! It's exactly as outsiders used to say of Willowsville—it's a closed, private community! A community of privilege! Immediately on Transit Road I got lost, it's become a mega-highway like something in *Road Warrior*. Why didn't one of you prepare me for Main Street! Where there was farmland, woods, there's wall-to-wall minimalls, gas stations and car washes and McDonald's. Where we used to go sledding, off Haggarty Road by the ravine, in grade school, remember?—there's this obscenity Zwaart Shopping Center—is that *Roger Zwaart*? The guy we knew? Couldn't get calculus through his thick skull? Why didn't somebody warn me that Garrison is a four-lane highway and you can't make turns from the left lane? I ended up in 'Fox Hollow Estates' lost like a rat in a maze! And Burlington has *overpasses*? We used to live just off Burlington, for God's sake. And there's a roundabout—a *roundabout*, like England!—in the center of town where there used to be the green! What the hell happened to downtown? Where's the Bookworm? Where's the Haven? The Sport Shop looks like it's taken over the block. Where's the Glen Theatre? What's this 'Glenside Medical Center'—I don't even remember what used to be there. It took me five minutes to figure out where I was, like a stroke victim, Burnham's Nursery is gone and all the land beyond, all that open land and woods, it's the campus of some monstrosity—'Niagara Technological College'—why didn't anyone tell me? Why are you all staring at me? *Who are you?*" Clarence jammed the black plastic glasses frames he hadn't changed in thirty years against the sweaty bridge of his nose, blinking at us, his old classmates, in horror. We were impressed, we'd never heard any geek-guy express himself in such a way, one of us offered a glass of champagne to poor Clarence and made him welcome.

Not three minutes later, as in a rehearsed comedy routine, which made some of us laugh uproariously, there came another of our class brains, snobby Carolyn Cameron, Doctor of Oncology at Columbia-Presbyterian Medical Center (as Carolyn never failed to indicate when updating her lengthy biography for our newsletter), stumbling onto the terrace, in breathless reproach—"What a shock! Why didn't any of you warn me! I haven't been back in sixteen years and the village is virtually unrecognizable! The skyline is high-rise office buildings and condos! What happened to our municipal zoning? What happened to the old library? What happened to the green? Where's the Bookworm? Where's the Glen Theatre? Where's the Crystal? Is it true, Dwayne Hewson is *mayor*? A football player—*mayor*? The worst is, oh God I couldn't believe it, I'm sick to my stomach—all the willows are *gone*. Our famous beautiful one hundred weeping willows—*gone*. And Glen Creek—*gone*. How can an actual creek be paved over, *gone*? What is this hideous 'Glenside Mall'— boutiques and restaurants and a Cineplex where the creek used to be! Oh how could you, some of you must be responsible, Willowsville has lost its *soul*." Carolyn astonished us by bursting into tears, we resented her high moral tone but liked her better than we'd liked her in a long time.

A few of us had driven around the village before the Rindfleisch party and we, too, had noticed these changes. Except to some of us, who'd been returning to visit our families over the years, the changes weren't so extensive, or so shocking. Certainly, the disappearance of our village's One Hundred Weeping Willows Walk, and the paving-over of Glen Creek, had been controversial issues in Willowsville a few years ago. "Unfortunately, progress is a law of nature. Economic progress is even more coercive because, as any businessman knows, if you're not actively developing, you're stagnating; if you're stagnating, you're dead. Glen Creek is a sentimental icon we simply can't continue to afford." (An excerpt from Mayor Dwayne Hewson's speech at the unveiling of the lavish Glenside Mall which Dwayne, Jon Rindfleisch, Roger Zwaart and a few others had built.) We were saddened to see the Village Tartan Shoppe gone, replaced by a stylish Banana Republic. Pendleton and Jonathan Logan were gone, replaced by Gap and Hermès. The Bookworm had been taken over by the Village Sport Shop which had a complete section devoted to skiing and mountaineering. The Haven, totally renovated, was now an elegant French restaurant, L'Auberge. The Glen Theatre had long ago been razed and was now Village Video Sales & Rentals. Even Muller's Drugs had vanished, we weren't certain where it had been. Most distressing to us was the gentrification of what we'd known as the lower village, sometimes called the "Italian zone." Water Street was handsome two-story brick office buildings, medical suites and hair salons. Wherever Glen Creek had been, all was pavement, meticulously maintained green grass and ground cover; the old row houses must have remained, behind gleaming facades and freshly painted shutters and front doors, but were totally transformed. "My God, where's John Reddy's old apartment building? How can it be *gone*?" Pattianne Groves whispered. "It's gone," Trish Elders said, "and the North China, years ago. I wish I'd come over and taken some pictures before the block was demolished but I had an art exhibit, I was distracted. Kate took some, I think. Ask Kate." Pattianne said, "If Verrie comes this weekend, I hope she won't see this. She'll be heartbroken. She's had a difficult time lately, I've heard. That nasty piece in the *National Enquirer*. And she seemed, what?—drunk, or drugged, on the *Late Show*. And this is *so sad*." "More than sad," Mary Louise Schultz said, rubbing at her eyes, "—*tragic*." We parked Trish's pale yellow Acura which reminded us of Verrie's beautiful canary-yellow Olds convertible of our girlhoods. We stood on Water Street at the approximate location of the North China Take-Out and gazed upward, not at the bland, boring brick facade of a new office building, but at, how vivid in our memories, the smudged old sandstone building in which the seventeen-year-old John Reddy Heart had lived in what we'd come to see, in retrospect, was his year of exile, expiation; a boy bereft of his family in our village of families and good, decent, law-abiding citizens. "Remember?—John Reddy's silhouette on the window shade? My God." "His window would be open. Those October nights. We'd hear music—his. He'd stand there in his undershirt, maybe bare-chested, smoking. *God*." "John Reddy!—just think, he was younger, then, than our own sons are now. It doesn't seem possible." Pattianne who'd come to our reunion from Oslo, Norway, where her ambassador husband of whom she rarely spoke remained at the American embassy, cupped her hands to her mouth and murmured slyly, "Killer-boy! Oh Killer-Boy!" Mary Louise, since her surgery eighteen months ago inclined to random surges of emotion, laughed wildly, cupping her hands to her mouth, too, and calling, "Killer-*Boy*! Hey! Are you home, are you ready John Red-dy? John *Red-dy*!" Two youngish men in suits, looking like lawyers, passed us by with quizzical looks. Trish cautioned her friends with a forefinger to her lips, "Shh!" but they'd had a glass or two of wine on the way over, they were laughing, arms around each other's waist and clumsily grasping at Trish too, they paid her no heed. "'John Reddy we're ready! John Reddy we're rea-dy! Mmmmm JOHN REDDY WE'RE REA-DDYY!'"

Veronica Myers was in fact expected at our reunion if her "complex schedule," as her assistant called it, making arrangements with us over the phone, allowed. We hoped, if she wanted to make a pilgrimage to Water Street, it wouldn't push the poor woman over the edge.

Like his old friend and rival Clarence McQuade with whom he'd lost touch twenty-seven years before, Dexter Cambrook, though a former Princeton professor and more recently director of the National Science Foundation in Washington, D.C., had gotten absurdly lost on his way to the BEER FEST in Tug Hill Park—"And my folks used to live on Beechwood. This just makes no sense." Three hours late for the gathering, his anxiety mounting, Dexter decided to go directly to Jon Rindfleisch's cocktail party but was having difficulty now finding Brompton Road; he didn't recall Willowsville so mazelike, the street signs so obscured by shadows and foliage. "What did they call us—'A bastion of privilege.' So our world appears to an outsider." Growing desperate, he drove for a while by instinct, his was a personality perhaps overly determined by logic, rationality, analysis, but he found himself now approaching a staid colonial house with dark shutters, on Sedgemoor Lane—"God damn. Jon's family's old house. Am I in a time warp?" Was he going to miss this party, too? This was Dexter's first reunion—was he fearful of meeting his old classmates? Or too hopeful? (His excitement was mounting at the prospect of seeing, after so many years, *her*.) The Nissan Altima he'd rented at the airport, unable to get a Honda Accord like the car he drove at home, handled stiffly and he was in terror of having an accident. Like Clarence McQuade he'd been overwhelmed by traffic on Transit Road and had in fact been swept miles out of his way, north on that thunderous highway, thwarted from making a left turn. When at last he managed to find Main Street, Willowsville, he hadn't recognized any landmarks— there were no landmarks, only minimalls and fast-food restaurants—and wondered if this "Main Street" was in another suburb unknown to him. The wisest thing would be to stop and telephone for directions—"But they'll laugh at me. Hewson, Bozer, Siefried. Lutz. Nordstrom. That clique. At least Smoke Filer and Steve Lunt are dead. *They* can't laugh." He felt a thrill of satisfaction that Smoke Filer in particular wouldn't be at the reunion weekend. That jeering-snorting laugh of Filer's he'd heard since the Academy Street School (most cruelly in the locker room, as commentary on smaller boys' genitals) had echoed through the years like a premonition of Hades. He was forty-eight years old yet seized with a powerful emotion of the kind that routinely overcame him in adolescence. "Fucker! Glad you're dead. I'm director of the National Science Foundation in Washington, D.C., and you're *dead*."

The pale sickle moon, an icon of romance, was rising in the night sky. A muffled roar as of malevolent thunder wafted in our direction from OLD HOMES DAY   TUG HILL PARK where thousands of young people had gathered. Seeing her husband staring wistfully across the crowded terrace at the middle-aged girls of the Circle, Nanci Rindfleisch who was fourteen years younger than anyone else at the party, except the caterer's assistants, said in a lowered voice, "For God's sake, Jon—what's so special about those women? That black-haired woman over there, talking to the bald man with the carnation in his lapel—*she's* truly beautiful. A Botticelli. Who is she?" Jon looked away reluctantly, wiping his face with a paper napkin. At first he couldn't comprehend whom Nanci meant. "Oh—her? Janet Moss." Jon's voice was pleasant enough, yet dismissive. Nanci said impatiently, "What do you mean—'Oh, her.' I said, that woman is beautiful, and interesting. I was talking to her a few minutes ago, did you know she's a research geneticist? At the Rockefeller Institute in New York? Working on a cure for certain kinds of brain cancer? She and her teammates are rumored to be on the shortlist for a Nobel prize? And she's an amateur pilot, just got her license? And she has four children of whom three are sled-dog racers? Her husband's a geologist and the entire family goes to Alaska every winter for the sled-dog tournament?" But Jon found it difficult to concentrate on his wife's remarks. We knew that Janet Moss was only Janet Moss, her family had lived in a small wood-frame Victorian house on lower Mill Street and her father was middle management at Niagara Trust, the Mosses belonged to none of our clubs and no one had missed them. What did it matter who Janet Moss was *now*?

In a horn-honking flotilla of shiny cars we would wend our way to Millie LeRoux Pifer's home in Amherst Dells three and three-quarter miles away as, years ago, after football and basketball victories, we would wend our way through Willowsville wild and intoxicated and disturbing the peace, never doubting the peace was ours to disturb. It's true some of us had been drinking steadily since the BEER FEST at four p.m. in Tug Hill Park and most of us were stuffed to the gills—that fantastic seafood bar, giant shrimp, raw oysters, crab legs and chunks of Maine lobster, spicy Buffalo wings, salty cashews and grape leaves, the Greek caterer's specialty. And Rindfleisch's generous bar. "It's so hard to say no. These reunion weekends are like wombs." "Wounds?" "And it's so hard to *hear*." Half the men in our class were hard of hearing in their left ears, and the other half were hard of hearing in their right ears. "It's my rotten luck always to be seated between two of these guys, on their 'bad ear' sides." But where was Bart Digger, the distinguished criminologist now advisor to the Attorney General whom we glimpsed frequently, proudly on CNN, and were eager now to remeet? And where was our film star Veronica Myers who'd promised to join us, at least for part of the weekend? And where was E. S. Fesnacht our most renowned (if controversial) literary light, "Vangie" to her dearest, oldest friends? Where was broody Ritchie Eickhorn our class poet? Where was sharp-tongued Elise Petko our valedictorian, and where was her sweet-gawky prom date Dexter Cambrook our salutatorian? Where was computer science theorist P. F. Merchant whom we fondly recalled as little Petey Merchant, shy to the point of muteness, practically a midget, with watery spaniel-eyes and acne-skin?—another high-tech cyberspace explorer in the hire of HARTSSOFT of Palo Alto, CA? (We'd been hearing, too, a rumor unsubstantiated for the past fifteen years that the mysterious founder of HARTSSOFT, by the time of our thirtieth reunion one of the most successful computer software companies in the world, was none other than Farley Heart, John Reddy's younger brother not one of us could remember!) Where was our cosmetic surgeon Dr. Scott Baskett, and where was his friend Blake Wells, our class's single college president, who'd played the clarinet so well?— "Whenever I hear a clarinet, or it could be a trombone, I suppose—I'm no expert on these things—I think of Blake, and wish I'd tried to be nicer to him." Effervescent Suzi Zeigler, the WBEN-TV *Nightly News* anchor, had just arrived—"You guys! I couldn't stay away from you! You're the only people on earth who know me as I *am*, not as I *appear*!"—but where was her friend Sandy Bangs we'd heard had become a feminist documentary filmmaker? And where was Suzi's old exotic boyfriend Norm Zeiga who'd stolen Suzi away from Roger Zwaart in our senior year? "Sure, I was angry. Suzi and I planned on getting married since first grade practically. It wasn't that I loved her, though I guess I did, or even that I wanted to get married at all, but, like, it was fate. And fate was thwarted." Roger, of course, was here in Willowsville; he'd married one of our pretty, rich-girl classmates, Jenny Thrun; with his father-in-law's financial backing and his own dad's shrewd legal advice he'd become one of the Niagara Frontier's premier real estate developers, a rival and sometime partner of Jon Rindfleisch with whom he played squash and golf at the Willowsville Country Club—"For what's 'developing' but a way of countering, that's to say 'thwarting' fate? Taking revenge, you could say, on nature." Roger and Jon! Zwaart and Rindfleisch! And in high school they'd hated each other's guts since Jon had allegedly pulled a fast one on Roger, rigging a Student Council election so he was elected treasurer in Roger's place. Of course our Willowsville mayor Dwayne Hewson was among us, rakishly good-looking as he'd been at the age of eighteen, though forty pounds heavier, with a blood-dark high-cholesterol face and hoarse smoker's voice. In fact, Dwayne was honorary chair of the Thirtieth Reunion Committee and had been involved in our reunions from the start. Senior Prom King Ken Fischer who'd killed himself for some tragic personal or professional reason years ago couldn't be among us of course, but where were his old buddies Bo Bozer, Tommy Nordstrom? There was Art Lutz, another local CEO, gazing across the crowded terrace at chic, still-terrific-looking Mary Louise Schultz who stood laughing amid a circle of male admirers oblivious to him; but where was his old friend Dougie Siefried? (Ginger McCord who'd divorced Dougie three years ago had become cruelly unfeeling, we felt, on the subject of poor Doug. "Why ask me? We're out of touch. I never think of him. I have grown children, I have my own complete life now. *I'm a human being not Dougie Siefried's girl.*")

And where was John Reddy Heart after all these years?

"After the age of forty, déjà vu is as good as it gets."

At our lavish twentieth reunion, too, there'd been the giddy, excited expectation that John Reddy would turn up at the pig roast. As Kate Olmsted told us breathlessly— "Probably for just an hour or so. He'd be driving from somewhere upstate on his motorcycle. Yes, John Reddy is his old, elusive self, you know—damned hard to pin down. But he smiled at me when I introduced myself—remember that smile?—he hasn't changed. Or, hardly at all—his hair is threaded with silvery gray, and he still wears it long. He's still good-looking, sexy. He said, 'My name is John Heart. That was all a long time ago.' But I was flattered—he remembered me! Pushing me in the wheelchair, I suppose. He seemed surprised that I was walking, so I explained about remission. The mystery of remission. 'Our lives are essentially in remission,' I said. 'Our lives are in a perpetual state of grace. We are no more lepers than Jesus Christ was a leper—or, if we're lepers, so was Jesus Christ. *You* taught me that, John Reddy.' I didn't mean to embarrass him but I figured, we're adults now. Adults talk frankly to one another. I could see he wanted to talk more but the circumstances weren't quite right, so I invited him to visit my gallery, which he hasn't yet done, and I invited him to our reunion as a special guest. He said he'd try to make it, he practically promised, and I believe him."

"Oh, Katie. Did you shake hands with—?"

"Katie, *is he married*?"

"Did he ask anything about—any of *us*?"

Kate touched a forefinger to her smiling lips as if to chide us. Like a magician pulling tricks out of the air, marvels to astonish, she began passing around a dozen or more remarkable photographs of The Glass Ark, which Aaron Leander Heart (oh, we remembered *him*!) had constructed out of thousands

of bottles; and two intriguing if blurred photos of a man in
biker's black-leather gear and a crash helmet, his back to the
camera, on a motorcycle speeding away. "You can't see his
face, unfortunately, but it's unmistakably John Reddy."

We wiped our pork-greasy fingers on napkins, examining
the photos for long brooding minutes. Finally, one of us said
quietly, "Yes. It's him."

"Are you serious? You expect him to come to this party,
after thirty years, when he's snubbed every party we've ever
had, including even our senior prom? It's just too *improbable*."

Yet, we persisted. For it was just *possible*.

We stared, astonished. Who?

Conversations faltered. She was standing at the edge of the
Pifers' elegant redwood deck cantilevered over a sparkling-
waterfall ravine in the portaled, privately policed Village of
Amherst Dells, due west of the Village of Willowsville, gazing
at us, her old classmates, with a look of defiance, and deference. Her hair was a handsome shade of gray, fastened neatly
at the nape of her neck. She was taller than we recalled and,
though hardly slender, no longer fat. In fact she'd become, in
our absence, a woman of character and presence. A woman of
professional achievement. One of us whispered—"She's a New
York State family court judge. Lee Ann Whitfield is a *judge*."
Incredulous, we recalled our fat girl hunched at the misfits'
table in the cafeteria. Her twin breasts ballooning against her
cafeteria tray. Her plump blushing cheeks. The shyly hopeful
movement of her lowered gaze as we swung by, a pack of us,
ignoring her, in fact not seeing her, as we didn't see the trash
bins and the colored cafeteria workers behind the counter. Lee
Ann Whitfield whom we'd had to vote into the Honor Society,
Miss Bird our advisor insisted, she had the grades. *Lee Ann
Whitfield*. You could see she was new to our reunions, she'd
hauled a husband with her, a professional-looking man in a
suit and tie, who was hanging back, already dazed. (We'd all

ceased bringing our spouses to these reunions. Not one of them had survived more than the first two hours.) We'd gone silent, the noisy pack of us, smiling at the Honorable Lee Ann Whitfield as she forced a smile, a brave smile, at us. In that instant we moved to greet her, to make her feel welcome in our rowdy midst.

"Why, Lee Ann!" gracious Millie LeRoux warmly cried, lifting her arms for an embrace, "—it's been too *long*."

("The poor woman was afraid we'd snub her. Imagine. A New York State judge, forty-eight years old. As if we aren't all adults now.")

High thin cries as bats cry in the depths of a haunted cavern in that House of Death where the burnt-out wraiths of mortals make their home. And I trembled inwardly, knowing I was of that company and could not turn back.

"What a crowd! Who are all these middle-aged people?—*us?*"

There were nervous jokes about the redwood deck cantilevered with such architectural bravado over the rocky ravine.

When Scottie Baskett arrived, direct from the airport, his old friends applauded and rushed to greet him for we'd read with pride, or we'd been told, of an article on Dr. Baskett of the Westchester Clinic for Aesthetic Plastic Surgery and other New Wave cosmetic surgeons in *Vanity Fair*; we had urgent questions to ask of our old classmate, of a semipersonal/semiprofessional nature; the most aggressive was, to our surprise, glamorous Ginger McCord who pulled Scott off into a lighted area inside the Pifers' house before he'd had a chance even to get a drink so that he could scrutinize her face—"I just had collagen injections last week and they're *lumpy*. Oh God, Scottie! *Feel.*"

Scared kids' eyes inside rubbery adult masks. Stragglers kept arriving, many of them alone. "If you have to read the name tag, it's probably no one important." "God damn, the names seem always to fall just at the seam of my bifocals." Some names, *Brenda Rhinebeck*, *Pokie Renke*, *Sonny Deidenbach*, were unrecognizable even after we did a quick check of the yearbook.

Artie Lutz, our beloved Class Clown, lived up to his reputation as usual. Wearing his old football jersey which gave him a "sort of watermelon-pregnant chic" he threw a bevy of onlookers into alarm by leaning over the redwood deck's railing—leaning far over—so that Mary Louise Schultz and the mysterious unknown (but not bad-looking) Brenda Rhinebeck seized him by the belt to haul him back—"Ar*tie Lutz!* Are you crazy!" Artie reported gravely that he couldn't see the bottom of the ravine, it was too dark—"Or too far *down*."

Millie LeRoux's husband, Mack Pifer, our host, kept disappearing into the California-style Normandy château as if our din was too much for his ears, then he'd reappear, wiping his beaming face, to reassure us that, yes certainly the redwood deck was perfectly safe, the architect who'd designed it was a famous Buffalo architect and the contractor who'd built it was the best in the business—"But, still, if you didn't all congregate at one end? Sort of spread your self around? There are tables on the lawn, too. And inside the house. And if you didn't stomp your feet, friends, at least not in unison?"

We laughed, we applauded Millie's rich, smart, sweetly funny-looking husband ("Kind of like a penguin, but shrewd"). There was beautiful cow-eyed Millie laughing, too. (We were thinking of how, in tenth grade, when we were lined up on the edge of the pool, buck naked, at the start of swim class, poor Millie had come wandering in looking for her wristwatch.) A few of us, bold, whistling, the usual bad-boys and goof-offs, though chafing inside our middle-aged-body costumes, may even have "stomped" our feet in unison.

But the redwood deck, though quivering, as with its own vengeful life, at that time of evening, 9:48 P.M. (Ritchie Eickhorn nervously checked his watch), still held.

The HARTSSOFT cyberspace explorers regaled us flat-footed civilians with the wonders of what they called "VR"—"VIRTUAL REALITY"—"A wholly computer-generated reality"—"Reality without randomness. Reality with a purpose, a principle, an intelligence, an evolutionary blueprint in which mere 'contingency' and 'catastrophe' have no role." (Was this Petey Merchant, speaking with such authority? We were relieved to see his acne had cleared up.) Ginger McCord who'd hardly been an intellectual in school called out with flirty belligerence, "What then of 'tragedy'? Will you eliminate 'tragedy'?" Petey Merchant frowned, and replied, "If we eliminate 'tragic persons' we will eliminate 'tragedy.'" Clarence McQuade chortled, "We may have to eliminate 'persons.' The revolution is at hand!" We had no idea what these guys were talking about but we liked it they'd made good in the world beyond Willowsville, we applauded, whistled and stamped our feet. Jax Whitehead cried, "'VR' for Prez!" A blissed-out mood just as Reggie Edgihoffer arrived with, literally, an armful of crimson and orange gladioli for his hostess whom he hugged, and who hugged him—"Oh, Reggie! We'd been wondering where you were." And a flurry of a false alarm, sudden excitement that Veronica Myers was arriving just behind Reggie, by limo (he'd said, unless in the din we'd misheard) direct from the airport, a white stretch limo with dark-tinted windows—"Verrie? Verrie's here?"—we rushed about looking for Verrie, we had our cameras poised to flash—where?

It was a time of squeals, screams, rib-cracking hugs and wet ravenous kisses. Tongues probing tongues like eyeless sea creatures frantic to touch, to couple, to mate. "There was Katie Olmsted we'd heard was crippled, an iron lung. She's on her feet lunging at us!" "There was Ketch Campbell we'd heard was *dead*. And his wife what's-her-name, looking *pregnant*." "There were the Zwaarts we'd heard were deep into therapy to save their marriage—poor Jenny, she's a zombie on Xanax." There was Molly Enzeimer in her maroon cheerleader's jumper and starched white blouse, leading a raucous group of us in cheers—

> Wolverines! Wolverines!
> You're the team   of our dreams!
> YAYYY!

("Molly's still cute, for a woman of almost fifty, but, in that uniform, with those hips, she looks like a hot little sausage.") There was a tall Amazon-looking female, bronzed skin, granite-gray hair, not of our generation—"Miss Flechsenhauer? Wow." There was elderly Mr. Larsen with flesh-colored plastic hearing aids in his ears, dazedly shaking hands with a totally bald, stoop-shouldered but pugnacious old gent in a Hawaiian shirt and plaid shorts— "Mr. *Horn*by? Wow." There was Mr. Cuthbert in his sixties, still teaching at WHS, smiling, trying not to spill champagne on his seersucker blazer, offering us witty remarks on the occasion of our thirtieth reunion and pretending to remember us, with that embalmed look of the veteran teacher across whose increasingly impervious gaze so many generations of adolescents have passed that he'd acquired a vaguely beneficent patina, like a weatherworn statue. There was Miss Bird, now retired, in her late sixties? early seventies? still with her brave carroty-red perm, in "stylish" clothes of a bygone era cupping her hands to her mouth to inquire, as she does at every reunion, "Do any of you ever hear from him? John Reddy? That poor, doomed boy?" (We know better than to speak to Miss Bird of Mr. Dunleddy. Her watery eyes blink rapidly, her thin lipsticked mouth trembles, she'll pretend not to hear and ask again, "Do any of you hear from him?—John Reddy?") In fact there came, stumbling onto the redwood deck, an elderly liver-spotted gentleman with tremors in both hands, some of us believed was Mr. Dunleddy—"Look, it can't be. Mr. Dunleddy is *dead*." Well, was this Mr. Stamish?—Mr. Sternberg? There came a stiffly smiling oldish man in a striped sport coat and ascot, wearing a starkly black-dyed toupee—"I almost burst into tears seeing him, I'd had such a crush on Mr. Lepage!" But Mr. Lepage, hard of hearing amid the party noise, wasn't his "old self"—you could tell—so it was a relief when he asked Millie to lead him away. None of our teachers (except Miss Flechsenhauer who was laughing uproariously with a half-dozen girls from the field hockey team) endured the party for more than a few minutes—"I love our old teachers but thank God they leave early, we can relax and be *ourselves*." There was busty Sandi Scott breathing into the ear of mysterious Jocko ("Vista Investments, Piscataway, New Jersey") asking with wistful coquettishness if he remembered her from high school?—"Just any stray memory, any glimpse, anything," and Jocko peered smiling at the name tag on Sandi's heaving left breast and murmured, "Sandi. Of course. You were, to me, the most beautiful, fascinating girl in our class. I stared at you opening your locker—I had a wild fantasy, your fingers turning the combination of your lock were turning *me*. Always I'd wanted to date you but—I was too damned shy." A Mystery Man in a baggy summer suit came pushing up to the bar, shook hands all around, bland hairless face and gleaming globe of a head, eyes pouched in wrinkles like an ancient tortoise's, he'd lost weight, obviously, once a heavy man and now weighing not more than one hundred twenty pounds, his fingernails ridged and rippled and his breath metallic as damp copper. Despite the muggy midsummer air and the heat of our bodies we shivered and tasted cold. He seemed to know all our names—"Trish!"—"Art!"— "Shelby!"—"Pattianne!"—"Roger!" Our sports, activities,

class offices. Where we'd lived in Willowsville, and which of
our families were "vanished" from the area. This individual
was our age presumably but looked decades older. His features had bleached out like paper left too long in the sun. He
had no eyebrows or lashes. No hairs in his ears or in his
enormous black nostrils. ("Chemotherapy," Carolyn Cameron murmured.) Dwayne Hewson, in his capacity as one of
the reunion hosts, came over and shook the Mystery Man's
hand briskly—"Who'd you say you were, I didn't quite
hear." The Mystery Man smiled gloatingly. "*Did* I say? *I*
didn't quite hear." Others gathered near. We made a game of
trying to identify him—"Well. You're not Rindfleisch, he's
right over there. You're not Zwaart—he's over *there*. You're
not Norm Zeiga—you don't speak with a weird accent.
You're not Larry Baumgart, he's a big fella. You're not Pete
Marsh—he's gone from us. You're not Bo Bozer—ditto.
Nosepicker Nordstrom?—nope. Or—" Janet Moss
screamed, "Larry Baumgart! *My date for the senior prom.*"

We stared, astonished. Who?

She was standing hesitantly at the edge of the party. A
dark-haired owl-eyed individual with a narrow, pinched
nose, the nostrils rapidly expanding and contracting as she
inhaled the aroma of roasting pig. So peculiarly dressed, in a
white shirt of some shiny synthetic fabric, black satin bow
tie, black tuxedolike jacket and black rayon trousers with
two-inch cuffs that flowed, visibly dusty, over her clunky
orthopedic-looking black patent-leather shoes—you couldn't
blame Millie for discreetly scolding her, even as Millie maintained an icy, composed smile, asking why wasn't she helping
to clear the glasses, etc., with the other caterers' assistants?
why wasn't she helping with the suckling pig? or preparing
the corn? why was she simply standing there doing nothing?
and Trish Elders, embarrassed, discreetly nudged her friend
Millie to indicate that, just possibly, this odd-looking woman

wasn't one of the hired help, but—"My God. Is it—*Elise Petko?*"

It was.

Even before arriving at the reunion some of us had begun nervously fingering our faces. And, at the reunion, it got worse. *A new pimple? Pimples?* We were alert to that deep-rooted throbbing that, overnight, could erupt into reddened pustulated boils. Some of us anxiously checked to see if our braces were back on our teeth. *It couldn't be possible, and yet—!* We'd been taught that humankind is essentially spirit, were we mistaken?

In memoriam. Bo Bozer's third wife, we weren't certain of her name, his widow in fact whom none of us knew, a glamour-girl type with coarse skin, couldn't have been more than twenty-five or -six, showed up unexpected staring and blinking moistly at us. "We'd been doing Bo imitations just a few minutes earlier! No one knew Mrs. Bozer was coming." Poor Bo, we hadn't seen him since our twentieth reunion, he was a vice president for some swimming pool manufacturer in New Jersey and he'd died one of our ambiguous deaths. He was in the habit of calling his old teammate Dwayne Hewson from time to time, usually drunk, maudlin and despairing and "just like Bozer, hilarious—except for the coughing," and he'd complained to Dwayne last time they spoke that the powerful pills he had to take for his blood pressure were making him impotent so he'd risked a stroke stopping them and "poor bastard, you know Bo he cracks me up—'I'm even more impotent without 'em. Go figure.'" Bo had died in a Days Inn motel room only a few miles from his East Orange, New Jersey, home and none of us would've felt right asking his wife or relatives (there were some Bozers still living in the area) about the circumstances, nor did any of us, even Dwayne Hewson and Art Lutz, manage to get down for Bo's funeral a few months ago. So Bo's third wife, a girl with big, crimped hair like a country-and-western singer, a stranger to us all, showed up with no warning carrying what she called "Bo's urn"—"Bo's ashes"—"Actually not all of them, only a few ounces"—asking Millie LeRoux if she could place the urn in some unobtrusive spot at the party, for instance a windowsill overlooking the deck. The urn didn't seem like an urn, it was a square box of black plastic textured to look like stoneware, about five inches cubed. Mrs. Bozer was wiping at her eyes— "Bo just loved you all so. He didn't love many people, that wasn't in his heart, but he'd look through your yearbook, he'd talk about basketball games he'd been in, and football— 'Dwayne,' 'Doug,' 'Ken,' 'Smoke,' 'John Reddy'—high school was the happiest time of Bo's life he'd say: 'It wasn't a happy time but it was my happiest time.' I always felt I got to know Bo too late. You're the ones who really knew him. He sort of understood he'd be going to die soon, hints he'd made, things he'd told me, how possibly he wasn't going to make his thir-tieth reunion with you guys but he hoped you wouldn't forget him so I thought I'd do this for him, O.K.? I mean, I hope it isn't morbid or anything?—" There was so much noise at the party, our old classic rock tapes turned up high, so Millie had to ask Bo's weepy widow to repeat some of this, then with her usual composure Millie said, as the rest of us stared appalled, "Why, no. But make sure you take it away again when you leave."

He was trying to avoid her. His date for the senior prom. Her myopic eyes snatching eagerly at his. "As if we'd been lovers. As if the intervening years hadn't mattered." It seemed to him, he must be imagining it, Elise Petko still had braces! He recalled their awkward dancing at the prom, sur-rounded by those glamorous-sexy others. The virulent-sweet gardenia that drooped from her meager left breast encased in chill royal-blue taffeta. Her breath that smelled, to his sen-sitive nostrils, yeasty. (He'd imagined with horror scummy back teeth teeming with bacteria. Her forced smile, teeming with bacteria. He was a biology major, and knew all about bacteria.) He'd been tricked into asking her, brainy Elise Petko, homely Elise Petko, his rival Elise Petko, to the senior prom. "Elise's mother has died, Dexter. It would be so sweet of you! I'll save a dance for you, and so will Trish, Mary Louise, Verrie—we promise." But they'd forgotten. He hadn't seen them all evening. Now Elise Petko, nearly fifty years old, a waxy ravaged girl's face, a disappointed face, her surprisingly hard, thin fingers gripping his wrist— "Thank God you're here, Dexter! Isn't this hideous? These people? Their values? They haven't changed at all. They're still adolescents—look at them flirting and fawning! Look at those two—they're practically 'necking.' They can't keep their hands off each other—it's disgusting. Tell me about your new position—director of the National Science Foundation. I'm proud of you, Dexter. Did you get my note? I'm happy for you. I'm not happy, but I'm happy for you. I won't ask about your wife, your family. You needn't ask about my 'personal life.' *I don't have a personal life.* I'd thought women had no more need of personal lives. I lived for my work. I still do. It isn't fair, it should never have happened, life is a gigantic lottery, I'm the one, valedictorian of my graduating class! SAT scores in the highest percentile! scholarship to Barnard, graduate fellowship to Columbia! tenure track at Michigan! and then—I'm one who slipped through the cracks. I'm not bitter, please don't misunderstand. Don't look at me like that, you don't understand. Maybe we could slip out of here, this ridiculous 'suckling-pig roast,' and talk quietly? I'm staying at the Matador Inn. At the airport. What about you? I didn't want to stay with relatives. My parents are dead. I'm not close to my relatives. Why was I denied tenure?—because people in my field were frankly jealous of me, frightened of me, my original research, my independence. My reputation for being an iconoclast—" Elise laughed shrilly, her teeth shone. Dexter believed he saw braces but surely he was mistaken. "Excuse me," he murmured, disengaging the woman's fingers from his wrist, "—I have to use the b-bathroom."

She was a young woman covering our Thirtieth Weekend Reunion for the *Buffalo Evening News* Style section. So young, we were stunned to learn, she'd never heard of John Reddy Heart, let alone Dahlia Heart or Melvin Riggs, Jr. ("Wasn't Riggs some old-time baseball player? Like, I don't know— Babe Ruth?") She took photos of us, singly, in small groups and in large; she seemed fascinated by us, in that way a certain kind of sharp-eyed anthropologist-type young person can be fascinated by her elders, or can give that impression; she asked us what was the origin of our famous tradition of roast pig?—and we were stumped how to reply. "It's what we do. We started with roast suckling pig, and we continue." "It's a quirky tradition, but it's ours." "Even those of us who never eat meat, and especially dislike pork, including hard-core vegetarians like Kate Olmsted, Mary Louise Schultz, health-food fanatics, have said they'd be 'terribly upset' if the tradition was broken." "Why? Who knows why? If you have to ask, you're outside the tradition." "None of us, we discovered by a newsletter poll, ever eats roast pig except at these reunion feasts. *Many never eat ham or pork at all.*" "We're the only WHS class that roasts a pig, and we're the only WHS class, we've been told, that has such strong emotional ties with one another." "Our reunions are, on an average, the best-attended of any in the history of the school. That's a fact." "That is a fact, and we're proud of it. It can be verified at the school office." "Every year the pig gets larger. We began with a seventy-five-pound pig—a long time ago. Tonight's, Millie tells us, is a one-hundred-six pounder. That's a lot of pig!" "And we're a lot of appetite. *That's our tradition.*"

And so we fell under the spell of the Pig. For every year as the Pig increased in bulk, the time required for its roasting increased, and we ate later, and were more famished. And drunker. *Roast pig turned slowly on a spit over smoldering embers. Naked hairless body. You stare appalled, fascinated. Why is any naked body, so trussed, so gutted, vacant-eyed, a female body? You breathe in the rich succulent aroma, mouthwatering to the point of pain. Perfect pig, perfect victim, mute, eyeless and unresisting.* "This is my body and this is my blood." *Slowly turning on the cruel spit. Tenderly tended by young servants in altar-boy white uniforms. Even those of us who'd stuffed ourselves earlier in the evening are panting with desire by the time the Pig is served.* With a bugle-like call husky Dwayne Hewson, co-chair of the weekend, summoned us: "Hey guys! Grab plates, get in line! Dr. Baskett's our carver again this year—our resident surgeon. *Dig in.*"

Even the glamorous among us. Even the money-minded. Even the "socially conscious." Even the embittered. Even the several rationalists fiercely debating Virtual Reality, cyber-space and -time and the future course of evolution ("It can only be by way of the machine! Human brain-circuits transformed by microchips into computers! *Homo sapiens* will be to the next species as chimpanzees were to *Homo sapiens*"). Even the lawyers. The investors, the business-minded. The plotters. The romance-minded. The besotted, and the near-suicidal, and the religious. Even broody Ritchie Eickhorn drifting at the periphery of the party feeling estranged from his old Chess Club buddies and vigilant for Evangeline Fesnacht, *E. S. Fesnacht* with whom he'd fallen in love eleven years earlier—"A night of madness in Kenawka, Minnesota, where madness is rare & exquisite as a hummingbird in winter"—fell under the spell of the Pig.

Even Bart Digger who'd left us scornfully thirty years ago vowing never to return, nor even to cast his wistful thoughts in our direction. Even Elise Petko our valedictorian who'd planned for weeks, she didn't yet know how, some sort of "class-action revenge." Even Dexter Cambrook our chagrined salutatorian who'd arrived at the party an hour late, anxious and infuriated. Even snobby Carolyn Cameron, even Blake Wells, president of Williams College, and waifish Shelby

Connor (formerly Sims) soon to embark upon a career as a psychiatric social worker in the slums of our nation's capital—all fell under the spell of the Pig. Even the serious drinkers. The Xanax- and Prozac-sedated. Jokey Jax Whitehead who'd been slipping into a guest bathroom to vomit up beer, spicy Buffalo wings, grape leaves and blood. Jon Rindfleisch who'd left his own party to arrive at the Pifers' without his glamorous wife, swaying-drunk like a man with one wooden leg, striding across the redwood deck to again greet slinky Ginger McCord in such an embrace, you'd swear the two hadn't seen each other since our twentieth reunion. Art Lutz who confessed to having had so much pig ("Totally pigged out!") at our rowdy-raunchy twentieth, the very smell of roast pig made him gag. (Still, Art ate. You know Art.) Even Lee Ann Whitfield our fat girl in disguise. Even Sarepta Voss who was undergoing radiation therapy for breast cancer and whose appetite was depressed— "Everything tastes like foam rubber except wine, which tastes like axle grease." Even Kitzie Cox and Marge Flemm, Home Ec majors who'd braved Millie's party guessing we would, if but innocently, snub them. Even Lulu Lovitt scarcely recognizable as a late-forties suburban housewife with blond-tipped bouffant hair and a silent, sullen husband who stared at us unsmiling. Even Ginger McCord whose cat-eyes were electric. Even Pattianne Groves who confessed to being "neurotically obsessed with my weight." Even Mary Louise Schultz who spoke of her recent fear of meat—"The additives. The toxins. The way they may activate matching toxins, 'cancers,' in our cells." Even Kate Olmsted who followed a quasi-mystical regimen to maintain her M.S. remission, and thus never ate meat—"Our karma is what we *eat*, and *are*. The pig's terror at being slaughtered will be communicated through its flesh." Even E. S. Fesnacht our controversial literary light, as we spoke of her in our newsletter, who'd slipped into the noisy gathering unnoticed, declining to pin a name tag to her purple satin jumpsuit, a trim, hipless, boyish figure with striking prematurely white hair shaved close to her head, and furtive eyes—all fell under the spell of the Pig.

Even, at last, Veronica Myers!—we'd given up expecting her—who arrived at 11:08 P.M. by limo, alone, gaunt-cheeked, eyelids like tarnished coins, in a backless cerise summer shift that showed much of her still-buoyant breasts (just the tip of the tattooed ♥—you had to know it was there to see it), tousled blond hair to her shoulders, our celebrity Hollywood actress (though she'd been doing mainly made-for-TV films since turning forty), glamorous, distracted and magnetic to the eye as always—Verrie, too, sniffing the mouthwatering aroma, fell at once under the spell of the Pig. Eating ravenously the morsels we fed her, not taking time to use a fork, panting, "Mmm! Mmmm! *Mmmm!*" as in the throes of cinematic sex. We poured champagne for our precious Verrie, we toasted her miraculous arrival. The middle-aged girls of the Circle, her former boyfriends and admirers, the rest of us gathered around her on the Pifers' redwood deck so boldly cantilevered above a shadowy, perhaps a rocky, treacherous and unfathomable abyss. ("An abyss," Ritchie Eickhorn was thinking, "—as of Time itself.") Our knees bumped Verrie's bare lovely knees. We saw that she'd kicked off her glamorous high-heeled shoes, her bare toes wriggled with happiness, nails bright cerise. Plates of food were passed, and more plates. Wineglasses were drained, and refilled. The servants at the spit helped serve the exquisite carcass Dr. Baskett had so expertly carved. One hundred six pounds of pig. Except for bones and gristle, we would devour it all. On our plates, steaming pork fumes rose out of the lacerated flesh. We noted how Bart Digger we'd recalled as one of the quiet, brainy guys, now a renowned criminologist, Northwestern Law School, advisor to the U.S. Attorney General, was surprisingly aggressive, managing to shoulder out former quarterback Dwayne Hewson himself—fetching for Verrie more champagne, and a second lavishly buttered

cob of fresh-steamed corn. We noted how Dwayne stared at
Verrie, licking his greasy lips. And Roger Zwaart, having
coolly avoided his old, recently divorced sweetheart Suzi
Zeigler all evening, sprawled snake-like at Verrie's naked feet.
Kate Olmsted ("We try to love her but frankly Kate's a pain in
the ass") kept intervening, taking flash photos. And others
were taking flash photos. Verrie cringed, and cried, "But this
is private life! I'm *eat*ing." That luscious mouth. We speculated that Veronica Myers had been starving herself,
mortifying her flesh in homage to her fading career. Even
those of us who adored her searched her face for signs of
encroaching age. But though she complained of exhaustion
("It must be chronic fatigue, I can't fucking *sleep*, not just my
fucking career keeps me awake, my 'personal life' that's in
ruins, but for weeks now anticipating this reunion, how
much it means to me, you guys I love, my only friends, the
only people in the world who know *me*. And knowing, oh
God, Ken won't be with us tonight") when she glanced
around at us with those eyes, greasy lips gleaming, we had to
acknowledge that Verrie Myers was our Prom Queen still.

During this time "The Ballad of John Reddy Heart" had
been playing on the Pifers' tape deck. It had been repeated so
much through the evening, we'd ceased hearing it. Though
we felt it: the percussive beat, the edgy-sexy rippling in our
blood. Trish Elders whose lovely mouth, too, gleamed with
pig-grease, shouted at her old friend Verrie, "John Reddy's
possibly going to drop by tonight. At Dwayne's. The all-night
disco. Isn't that great?" Verrie's shadowed eyes brightened.
She'd been grieving for Ken Fischer, but now she said excitedly, "He's alive, then? I knew it. I had a dream of John Reddy
the other night, the first in years. He held my hands in his and
was telling me something urgent but there was too much
noise, static, I couldn't make out the words."

When the redwood deck collapsed beneath our weight, at
12:12 A.M., it wasn't "The Ballad of John Reddy Heart" that

was playing but another, later hit single by Made in USA, "Hunger Hunger." By this time, Mack Pifer had retreated to one of the farthest rooms of the California-style Normandy château to listen, through headphones, to one of his favorite Callas recordings—*Tosca* performed by the La Scala Orchestra and Chorus. Though he'd turned the volume up as high as he could bear, still Millie's husband could hear, or perhaps feel, the powerful seismic throbbing of "Hunger Hunger" like a vibration of the earth's very crust. Mack Pifer had long considered himself a "tough player" in the competitive world of high-stakes medical insurance, and he and Millie had endured the protracted adolescences of three typically American children, but his nerves were close to shattered by this party. "Even if the deck hadn't collapsed, it's likely the Pifers were going to separate soon. The way Millie was dancing with some of the guys—she'd never have behaved that way back in high school. It wasn't just she'd been drinking, our Millie was *hot*."

The pig-carcass had been stripped clean of all save gristle by this time. The long buffet table profusely stocked with other meats and seafood, salads, breads and desserts looked as if a rampaging wave of locusts had struck. Numerous cases of champagne, wine and beer had been consumed. For hours, the white-uniformed caterers' assistants had labored grimly to clear away debris and garbage. In the Pifers' gleaming kitchen with its myriad new-model appliances, the garbage disposal unit had broken, defeated by the heavy use to which it had been put. How many of us were on the deck at the time of the accident? "A conservative estimate, counting incidental spouses and the hired help, is somewhere beyond one hundred. And some of these were *big fellas*." Our former athletes, for instance, except for Blake Wells who'd been a swimmer, must have weighed on average two hundred twenty pounds. Many others had put on weight, including a number of the women who'd been, as girls, obsessed with dieting.

There followed then a boisterous interlude of after-dinner

speeches and jokes. Dwayne Hewson and Jon Rindfleisch, arms around each other's broad shoulders, "our WHS Tweedledee and Tweedledum," were witty if not always coherent masters of ceremonies. We applauded and stamped our feet, informed that these notable WHS alums had donated a generous sum of money to the school—"To the Woody McKeever Memorial Fund." We applauded and stamped our feet, informed that Veronica Myers had donated money for the construction of a theater wing of the school—"The Francis C. Lepage Theater." We applauded and stamped our feet, informed that E. S. Fesnacht and Richard Eickhorn, former co-editors of our literary magazine *Will-o'-the-Wisp*, and apparently still good friends, were donating money for the "enhancement" of the magazine. Our former *Willows-villian* cartoonist Chet Halloren was establishing an annual award for most talented cartoonist in the graduating class, and our local artists, photographer Kate Olmsted and painter Trish Elders, were establishing awards in their respective fields. HARTSSOFT men McQuade and Merchant announced that they'd acquired a "seed grant" from their notable employer to establish a state-of-the-art computer laboratory at the school. Our millionaire cosmetic surgeon Scott Baskett was establishing a pre-med scholarship, and our National Science Foundation director Dexter Cambrook was establishing a science scholarship. Not to be outdone, Artie Lutz heaved himself to his feet to declare that he'd tried to establish an award, funded by "big bucks," for annual Class Clown—"But the assholes at the school turned me down. So I said, 'What the hell's wrong with a sense of humor? Why's brains so important? People blow their brains out, in fact, for lack of a sense of humor. Every day people are dying for lack of a sense of humor. (Of course the joke is, the schmucks would die anyway. But they don't know it.) I said, 'Give an award for once at commencement to some poor dick, yeah he's gotta be a guy, only a guy can be a true dick, a girl who's a dick is too pathetic for any award, some poor dick who never succeeded at anything much through high school, but never failed, either; some guy everybody kind of likes, or say they do, but nobody, y'know, gives a profound shit about, if he lives or dies. Even his own wife and kids. *Even his old girl-friend he'd die for.* I said—" We applauded and stamped our feet drowning out Artie who looked a little hurt, and abruptly sat down.

There were prizes for who'd come the farthest distance, who'd had the most children, who had the youngest child (made posthumously to Bo Bozer and accepted tearfully by his young wife, who had a ten-month-old back home in East Orange, New Jersey), who among the men had the best-preserved hair and, among the women, the best-preserved figure. Our controversial award—to the individual who'd made the shrewdest use of the bankruptcy law since the last reunion—had been squelched at the last minute as "not in the spirit of the occasion." Then came our bittersweet toasts to the departed. Every reunion, the solemn recitation of names becomes longer. "Jesus. It's like you look over your shoulder and there's somebody rolling up a carpet right behind you. Brrr!" We passed around well-worn copies of *The Yearbook* opened to black-bordered photos. We passed around school pictures, snapshots. We made one another weep with old memories, cherished anecdotes—"'So Smoke offers a roach to John Reddy of all people, John Reddy who'd been doing weed, maybe LSD and heroin, back in grade school, and John Reddy looks at Smoke like he's never seen such an asshole, and says, 'Man, get that shit out of my face, I'm on fucking probation, man.' And Smoke says—" We were deeply moved, we were thrilled to hear our old departed classmates' names evoked: Dickie Bannister ("Our first—ninth grade"), Smoke Filer, Babs Bitterman, Steve Lunt, Pete Marsh, Bert Fox, Ken Fischer, Bo Bozer, and—were there others? "Hell, I'm think-ing—Nosepicker. I have a premonition." "What? How do you know?" "It was looking pretty grim last time I checked in." "And Janey Plummer?" "Who?" "Oh, you know—that kind of cute little cross-eyed girl with the bangs, in Mme. Picholet's homeroom? In chorus? French Club?" We looked up Janey Plummer in the yearbook, sure enough she'd been in our class, but no one knew of her whereabouts thirty years later— "I don't know, I just have some sort of idea she's, I guess, dead. In maybe a car crash? Batavia?" "And what about Dougie?" "Who?" "Dougie Siefried, how many Dougies are there?—how's *he*?" We tried not to turn in Ginger McCord's direction knowing how her face would have stiffened but it was hard to resist. And Ginger was crying. Poor Ginger, she'd loved Dougie so, when they were kids at least—"It was just one of those tragic mismatches, as adults. *All they had in common was they'd been high school sweethearts and could never love anyone else.*" By this time the girls of the Circle were sobbing, holding Ginger, and Verrie who was crying as if her heart had broken, we knew (we believed we knew) that Verrie and poor Ken had had a brief love affair after our fifteenth reunion but we weren't certain what had happened: Ken had attempted a reconciliation with his wife, from whom he was subsequently divorced, but possibly he'd been rebuffed by Verrie who'd had a love affair (at least, *People* so reported) with John Travolta, her co-star in a film many of us had purchased in video. Following this, on a business trip to Europe, Ken, a corporate lawyer, a "troubleshooter" for Motorola, Inc., had allegedly killed himself in a hotel room in Stuttgart, Germany. There was some debate over the actual method of suicide—"It just wasn't like Ken to opt out like that. On the team, he'd never let you down. He'd get kicked in the gut, in the groin, he'd be staggering after a foul or a tackle and *he'd never let you down*. Ken Fischer."

Made in USA's "Hunger Hunger" was whining, thumping, panting like a living thing. The dense foliage of the Pifers' giant maple trees, incandescent in the moonlight beyond the redwood deck, shook in sympathy. Verrie hastily stood, upsetting her glass of champagne. Her face was gaunt, ghastly. Her beauty drained out of it like blood. Staring behind us, hands to her cheeks in the pose of Edvard Munch's *The Scream*, she cried—"Ken? *Ken?*"

We believed that Veronica Myers had snapped. Under the strain of so many memories. Under the strain of her fading, failing career. She'd eaten ravenously, she'd drunk too much too quickly. She was giddy and groggy under the spell of the Pig. But when we turned to look, in astonishment we saw— Ken Fischer? A handsome, trim, graying man in his late forties, his face relatively unlined, his smile diffident, yet playful? He was wearing, like one or another of his ex-teammates, a WHS maroon and gold T-shirt beneath a summer blazer. Could it be—Ken Fischer? Alive after all? Not dead? We stared, some of us screamed, a few staggered as if about to faint. Yet the man was obviously real, as real as any of us. Politely he made his way past us, to Verrie. *Ken Fischer returned to us as if he'd never been away.*

We made a little circle around the lovers. Ken rushed to Verrie, gathering her in his arms. She was beginning to faint, lovely bare arms swinging limp, windswept blond hair nearly brushing against the floor. Ken said worriedly, "Verrie, darling! Forgive me! I didn't mean to frighten you." Some of us helped Ken revive Verrie by pressing a damp cold cloth against her burning forehead. She moaned, and her eyelids fluttered. She was staring at Ken, yet could not speak. He murmured, "Verrie, it's me. It's Ken. I've never been away, darling. Someone has been spreading ugly rumors about me but I've never been away, and I've never stopped thinking of you. Not for a moment. Not for a heartbeat. Oh, Verrie!"

Verrie recovered, and twined her arms around Ken to kiss him full on the mouth as she hadn't done, at least in our presence, at our Senior Prom. She cried breathlessly, "Ken! I love you. Don't ever leave me again, Ken. Please." Ken said, "Of course not, darling. Never again." We applauded and stamped our feet. We rushed at the lovers, eager to touch them. Tears streamed down our cheeks. Even embittered Elise Petko was weeping. Even our class cynic Chet Halloren. Even

Bart Digger and Dwayne Hewson who'd been in love with Verrie for decades. We were overjoyed for them, we wished the fated lovers well. In the stampede to get close to them we must have caused the cantilevers beneath the deck to buckle; with no apparent warning they collapsed, and the deck tilted violently beneath us. We screamed and flailed at one another, thrown together, tumbling, desperate, as the elegant redwood deck splintered and crashed into the abyss and Made in USA yelled in seeming sympathy, "Hunger hunger! I gotta hunger! Hunger ain't never gonna be fulFILLED!"

On the windowsill, out of range of our disaster, Bo Bozer in his black plastic box brooded upon us, untouched.

At Dwayne Hewson's, things really got *wild*.

Reports of what happened at Dwayne's residence on Mill Race Lane printed in the press were confused and misleading, and overly sensationalist. LURID W'SVILLE 30TH REUNION. TRAGIC END CLAIMS POPULAR W'SVILLE MAYOR. ACCIDENT-PRONE 30TH WHS WEEK-END: "YES, WE PLAN A 40TH." Probably it's most accurate to say that no one really knew what happened at the swim-disco party through the remainder of the night—"It was like being picked up and flung around by a tornado, you know something sure happened but you don't know *what*."

Originally our traditional swim-disco all-nighter was scheduled to begin shortly after midnight but, due to unavoidable circumstances at Millie's house, it was past one-thirty a.m. by the time a depleted crew of us, in a giddy horn-honking flotilla of about nine cars, departed for Dwayne's. Dwayne himself led the procession in his sleek mint-green Porsche, head bandaged as with a rakish white turban after he'd struck it on a railing at the Pifers'. Quite a few of us had decided to retire for the night, worn out by the excitement—"Jesus. At home, we're in bed by ten p.m. We haven't watched the *Late Show* in years." We'd all been shaken by the collapse of the redwood deck, and several of us had been injured seriously enough to be taken by ambulance to

Amherst General, sirens blaring—poor Lee Ann Whitfield with a shattered femur, Bart Digger with a nasty head wound, someone named Fred Falco who'd been knocked unconscious and pinned beneath the buffet table, and a plump, heavily made-up woman wearing the name tag "VAL POMEROY" whom no one knew, sobbing hysterically. Clarence McQuade had crawled out from the wreckage and limped away, cursing, refusing paramedic treatment. Ken Fischer had carried a fainting Verrie Myers out of the ravine and, though dazed by head-blows, had gone back to get other victims. "Thank God, the damned deck fell only eighteen feet." "Eight feet." "That was *enough*." We'd lingered at the Pifers' to help the paramedics with our injured and to soothe distraught Mack Pifer who seemed intent upon blaming us when (as Roger Zwaart dryly remarked) he'd have better been worrying about a barrage of personal-injury suits. Millie, by contrast, was a good sport, and climbed into Dwayne's Porsche with him and other friends to drive off as if nothing, or almost nothing, had happened. "I'm a co-chair of this weekend and damned if I'm going to let anything spoil it. *This is our thirtieth, guys!*" Millie's beautiful brown eyes blazed and her milky skin, only just visibly lined with age, exuded a heat we'd never observed back in high school.

At our twentieth reunion Dwayne Hewson had hosted a swim-disco party at his house, one of the big old eighteenth-century colonials on Mill Race Lane, St. Albans Hill, which had been, in high school terms, which were yet the most accurate terms, "a blast"—"fantastic." He was determined that this thirtieth-reunion swim-disco be just as much fun— "And yet meaningful, too. We'll each carry away from tonight something special." We stood about the pool drinking, laughing, a little breathless. Rock music was playing, alternating with dreamier old-timey dance music. Dwayne had strung mirrored disco-balls overhead and a strobe light pulsed and throbbed like frantic lightning. ("The sort of thing that can cause convulsions if you have an epileptic predisposition,"

Scottie Baskett observed.) Dwayne urged us to make our own drinks, make ourselves at home. There were swimsuits in the bathhouse—"One size fits all. Plus robes and towels. Plenty of towels." Some of us kicked off our shoes to lower our toes in the shimmering aqua-bright water of the Olympic-sized kidney-shaped pool: the water was warm as blood, so inviting. On the tape deck the Shrugs' classic rockabilly lament "Broke Heart Blues" was playing. Why were some of us oddly shy, reluctant to get into the pool, or to dance? "It's like I wasn't sure suddenly if I had my body. Like some parts of it were dead, or had fallen off." A small talky group of us stood reminiscing about the accident at the Pifers' as if it had taken place years ago and not less than two hours ago. We'd all been impressed and exhilarated by the way most of us had rallied to help one another. "Emergency situations can bring out the best in people, and that one did." "Nobody panicked. Well, almost nobody. Some of the guys, like Ken, were true heroes." "And some of the women, too. Shelby Connor's got *muscles*." "And the paramedics—they looked like kids but were they terrific! Even with our cars blocking the road they managed to get their vehicles through. And fast." "That's why we pay the taxes we pay," Jon Rindfleisch gravely observed, dabbing a tissue over his gleaming, flushed face. "If Willowsville-Amherst is prime real estate, the Gold Coast of western New York, it's for a damned good reason."

Our gregarious host Dwayne Hewson, passing by in a maroon Wolverine T-shirt and snug-fitting plaid swim trunks, his white bandage-turban cocked over one eye, barefoot, said, "Friend, I'll drink to that!"

We all drank. "Broke Heart Blues" ended on a melancholy whine and the Hoors' "More More More!" came on loud, fast, hot and humping.

It seemed, at poolside, beneath the revolving disco-mirrors and pulsing strobe lights, that there were as many of us as there'd been earlier, possibly even more. Kate Olmsted, now barefoot, padded about taking flash photos—"For posterity. For *us*." We noted that the fall into the Pifers' ravine had bruised our stalwart Katie but hadn't slowed her down. Petey Merchant who'd had a crush on her thirty years ago but had been too shy to ask her to the Senior Prom was saying in his stubborn-pushy manner, as if he expected Kate and others to disagree, "Our only hope for the salvation of our civilization is to diminish randomness. Randomness—'accident'—is our enemy. Cyberspace is the dimension of calculation and control and certainty. The only dimension of certainty. There are too many local dialects in the lexicon of *Homo sapiens*—that's why the earth is soaked in blood. The twenty-first century will require a new, universal lexicon, and computer science will supply it!" Verrie Myers in her backless cerise dress was dancing in the arms of Ken Fischer, her blond head nestled dreamily on his shoulder; Ken had tossed aside his powder-blue linen jacket, and was seen to be wearing his Wolverine T-shirt of thirty years ago, maroon with the gold numeral 3 on its back. We noted Millie LeRoux laughing loudly whirling by in the muscled arms of—who? A tall looming fellow in swim trunks, Wolverine T-shirt and bristling chest hair like iron filings—Tommy "Nosepicker" Nordstrom? He'd come to our reunion after all? There was Pattianne Groves looking slightly dazed, giddy-drunk, her russet-brown hair in snarls and mascara smudged and mouth shaped to a startled "Oh!" whirling and stumbling by in the arms of her old ex-steady Dwayne Hewson whose face was, by strobe light, a smoldering demon-mask of lust. ("At the prom, Dwayne got drunk and made a maudlin asshole of himself over Verrie and Pattianne broke up with him that night and never spoke to him again—I mean, until we were all grown up. And they were both married to other people.") Roger Zwaart was dancing with Suzi Zeigler whom he'd lifted out of the wreckage at the Pifers', the two pressed so close together that Suzi's thickish breasts were flattened against Roger's bare, grizzled chest; they kissed, and their breaths melted together in a sticky, palpable substance like gum; Roger moaned with desire, blood pumping between his legs as it hadn't in how long he couldn't recall, he shut his burning eyes and saw Suzi's sweet face lifting to his, lips poised to kiss his, as they clutched in a sweaty embrace in their usual seats in the back row of the Glen Theatre; Suzi shut her eyes and saw, with a stabbing thrill, John Reddy Heart sitting a few rows ahead, his profile outlined against the insipid Technicolor of whatever Hollywood fantasy, strong-boned face and thick dark hair like a noble, heraldic head on an ancient coin. "I love you! Oh my God." "I love *you*, Suzi." Bibi Arhardt we hadn't recognized earlier, a stout earnest attractive woman with oddly frizzed hair and lavender-tinted bifocals, was telling of the night John Reddy had "come for me—taken me from my father's house—it wasn't like you would think—it wasn't like you would imagine any guy could *do*." Kate Olmsted was showing photos of The Glass Ark and of John Reddy Heart, or someone who closely resembled him, on a motorcycle speeding away, to those of us who hadn't seen them before, including Petey Merchant who gnawed his lip, staring in helpless envy—"'My name is John Heart,' he said," Kate recited, "—'That was all a long time ago.' So, if he comes tonight, please—we won't bring up the past, all right?" Petey Merchant saw his hand in slow motion, his blood emboldened by alcohol, he who never drank, reach for one of the photos, snatch it from Kate and tear it into shreds—"Yes, we won't! We won't! We won't bring up the fucking past!"— though somehow his hand hadn't moved, he hadn't ripped up the photo nor even spoken his despairing words but stood mute, stricken with shame. Yet exhilaration, too: for he was a HARTSSOFT man, a cyberspace explorer, one of the elect. *He would conquer the only world that mattered—the world inside the brain.* Trish Elders who'd been trying to cool off in the pool, except the bright aqua water was blood-warm, paddling about fretfully in diminutive white panties, her bare smallish breasts floating like chunks of melting Ivory soap, she who'd been so self-conscious when we were girls she'd hidden behind her opened locker in the girls' changing room—Trish was arguing with an unidentified individual crouched on the pool rim with a bottle of beer in hand, rivulets of water streaming from his ape-hairy legs, genitals like a swollen goiter barely constrained inside Jockey-style swim trunks, in a hurt, little-girl voice she argued, "Please. I resent that tone. Whoever you *are*. You might've graduated with us but you don't know *us*. John Reddy wouldn't just stay away again, Kate invited him and he said he'd *come*. He knows how we miss him. We were sort of close, John Reddy and me. He'd drive me home after school sometimes in his Caddie. We never exactly dated. He had his own girl. 'Sasha Calvo.' We all wanted to be Sasha Calvo. We all wanted to be sort of— savage. Italian. And John Reddy looked sort of Italian, too. Kate said he more or less promised he'd come, she sent him Dwayne's address here and a special invitation signed by the reunion committee and by coincidence we're only about a block from John Reddy's former house on Meridian Place. I'm an artist, a painter. I'm not famous but my paintings sell. They aren't realistic though they spring from 'realism.' Old pho- tographs. I take images that haunt me and enhance them. They're dream-images actually. My first was of John Reddy's car—salmon-colored, then parrot-green. I painted those cars for ten years. I could never paint John Reddy—any image of him wasn't *right*. He's someone you *feel*. Though he enters you through the eyes, he's someone you *feel*. Why are you staring at me like that? I'm not drunk. I'm perfectly lucid. I've had a baby, in fact two babies—I'm 'real.' I believe that John Reddy will come tonight. He wouldn't stay away again—like we didn't mean anything to him at *all*." She'd begun to cry, tears falling into the festive aqua water and vanishing at once.

Out of the phosphorescent foliage above the pool amplified guitars, drums, wailing androgynous voices fell upon us and made the water tremble. Zappa's old-timey classic "Why Does It Hurt When I Pee."

Lulu Lovitt was her old, high school self again, squealing

and splashing at the other end of the pool as Jax Whitehead
wrestled with her, a burning cigarette in his mouth, trying to
untie her red polka-dot bikini top; we couldn't remember if
those two had dated, but it sure looked as if they had. There
was Chris Donner swinging through the crowd on those
metal crutches that make him look like a giant, feisty insect,
there was a fattish Stan Aquino we hadn't seen since our tenth
reunion when he'd gotten into a drunken fight with Roger
Zwaart, there was brainy, embittered Elise Petko in a stained
tunic-and-pants costume slipping away to be sick to her
stomach in one of the downstairs bathrooms of the Hewsons'
grand sepulchral house; noting to her disgust that the lavishly
appointed bathroom already smelled, despite the exertions
of a fan, of vomit. And afterward wandering the Hewsons'
house pinch-faced and contemptuous, these bourgeois hyp-
ocrites, these crude characters out of what crude juvenile
comic book scorned by Elise Petko even as a child, she found
herself in an upstairs bedroom massed with gigantic furniture, canopied king-sized bed, mahogany bureau with
ceiling-high mirrors reflecting a gawky and eager fourteen-
year-old girl so strangely betrayed by life. "Betrayed by
America. Promising 'you can do it alone.'" There was Elise's
hand inside a lacquered jewelry box on a glittering vanity,
seeking "some small restitution, some emblem of what's owed
me"—a loop of cultured pearls, a single silver earring thrust
into a deep pocket of her tunic. In a bathroom there was a
mirrored medicine cabinet opening, like a treasure chest, to
reveal among the usual toiletries an astonishing quantity of
prescription drugs, Elise helped herself to two chunky white
tablets of oxycodone prescribed for "Constance Hewson" and
three tablets of methocarbamol prescribed for "Dwayne
Hewson—for muscle spasm," carefully replacing the plastic
bottles yet they slipped from her fingers, fell to the floor scattering pills, tablets, what the hell. Elise stumbled to the
canopied bed the size of a football field and pitched head-on
into a deep, seething, churning night only to be awakened,

how many hours later that morning, by paramedics from Amherst General—"It must've been a world record. Two unrelated emergency calls, to the same private residence, within ninety minutes!" (Indeed this would be noted in the local press gloating over our ACCIDENT-PRONE 30TH REUNION WEEKEND.)

Outside, on the terrace, amid the deafening though catchy strains of The Splats' "Why Do Fools Fall in Love?" shading into the Elvis classic "Heartbreak Hotel" there was brainy, dazed Dexter Cambrook, his right eye swollen and bruised from a clumsy fall into the Pifers' ravine, trying, and, we saw, failing, to summon up the nerve to tap Dwayne Hewson on a burly shoulder to ask if he might at last dance with a fleshy, bronze-haired Pattianne Groves, wife of our ambassador to Norway, with whom he hadn't danced at their Senior Prom though he'd been inveigled into taking Elise Petko to the prom for solely that reason. "Pattianne? Excuse me? You remember me, I hope—" But Dwayne spun Pattianne away in an iridescent aura of perspiration like full-body halos. (Some of us recalled, with smiles, fierce Pattianne charging down the playing field behind school, ponytail swinging, knees flashing, to unleash from her hockey stick a wooden ball to fly into Dexter's head like fate and knock him cold—though we doubted that, so many years later, and her ponytail long vanished, replaced by stylishly streaked and "electrified" hair, Pattianne herself would remember. "There's a girl who has knocked lots of men cold. Better believe it!") A number of us were intrigued, if skeptical, to learn from Ken Fischer that he hadn't committed suicide in Stuttgart, Germany, nor even attempted it: instead, involved in a traffic accident, he'd been rushed to a hospital where, by the sheerest coincidence, another "Kenneth Fischer" had just been admitted, also an American businessman who'd been drugged, severely beaten and robbed, and the two "Kenneth Fischers" were somehow confused in the press, and—"The rest is history. Or, rather, fiction. *He* died, *I* didn't. One of you spun the rumor completely out of control for Christ's sake," Ken said, glaring at us, "—*almost as if you wanted me dead.*" We laughed uneasily, Verrie loudest of all, an edge of hysteria to her laughter we recalled from her cheerleader days, the team only just barely scoring to win, possibly not to win, our throats raw with screaming. "Well, you're back with us now, darling," Verrie said, lavishly kissing Ken's face, "—so don't do it again, ever." Ray Gottardi of Gottardi Fences was talking excitedly with wary Jon Rindfleisch who (it seemed: we couldn't hear very clearly over the music) owed him somewhere beyond $30,000. Ketch Campbell had left poor Bonnie (we hadn't even known she'd been injured in the redwood deck collapse!) at Amherst General to join us, glassy-eyed, disheveled yet eager to celebrate, and to tell us another time his tale of having been the first of any of us to sight John Reddy Heart and his family on Main Street thirty-seven years ago almost to the day—"You could tell immediately that these folks were from somewhere else. Somewhere *far else.*" There were still a number of us who listened to Ketch's tale avidly, as if for the first time, for, as Shelby Connor stumblingly expressed it, in her slurred, blear-eyed way groping for a profound metaphysical truth, "The way Ketch tells it, it forces you to realize: what if the Hearts hadn't come to Willowsville at all? What if their car had broken down in Nebraska? Or Colonel what's-his-name had died before giving Dahlia the house? Our lives would be irrevocably altered, but—*what lives would they be*?" E. S. Fesnacht who'd been listening to Ketch (with a furrowed brow, pursed lips, was it possible she'd never heard the story before?) appeared shaken by this query, but at a loss how to respond; Blake Wells, ever the intellectual, said with a shrug, "Cutting-edge philosophy posits 'counterworlds' in which, in theory at least, and, we have to assume blissfully, 'counterselves' of ours exist. Now and then they wonder about us but, for the most part, *they don't give a damn.*"

On the tape deck was an anomalous sloozy-sludgy "Can't Get Enough of Your Love, Babe" by Barry White and to our amazement there was Ritchie Eickhorn, drunk as we'd never seen him, spiky-haired, glasses askew on his horsey, almost-handsome middle-aged-boy's face, one of those seeming-shy types obviously in a secret clamor for attention, clambering up onto the diving board fully clothed, waving his arms and shrilly declaiming what we surmised was poetry, since it rhymed:

> O Corporate America!
> Your love-need misconstrued as greed!
> Your hunger for sanctity misconstrued as rapacity!

There may have been more but we interrupted to applaud and stamp our feet. We were proud of Ritchie, we were proud of all our classmates who'd "made names for themselves" in the world beyond Willowsville. Grinning Larry Baumgart whom none of us remembered as a prankster leapt up wheezing onto the diving board and stamped his skeletal feet so vigorously, as he continued to clap, "Bravo, Walt Whitman! Son of the cosmos, bravo!" that a startled Ritchie Eickhorn lost his balance on the board and fell, arms and legs pathetically flailing, into the pool. What a splash! And how he sank, like a laundry bag weighted with rocks. Art Lutz yelled, "Can he swim? Who is it? Jesus—one of the geeks. Don't let 'im drown, grab his hair or something. Never mind, I'll get 'im." Art was shirtless, barefoot, and quickly stripped to his paunchy boxer shorts to dive into the pool, quite a respectable dive, so we applauded him, too, and stamped our feet; and Dwayne Hewson yelled, laughing, "If you fucks crack my terrace, I'm gonna sue *you*." Art hauled poor limp Ritchie up onto the tile where he vomited aqua water and choked and coughed so miserably some of us decided we should practice "artificial respiration" on him—pumping his arms, pressing hard on his soft midriff, as we hadn't done since our Mom's First Aid classes at the Willowsville Country Club when our kids were babies. "So we helped save Ritchie Eickhorn! Another emergency rescue operation. It felt *good*."

Zappa's *Hot Rats* was playing, loud and funky. Next, Made in USA's "The Ballad of John Reddy Heart"—our all-time favorite we could identify within a nanosecond, the first striking of an amplified guitar chord. We'd memorized the interminable stanzas of the "ballad" decades ago and now we shouted, bawled, wept them as, like electric eels, we thrashed about in the pool, on the terrace and on the dewy lawn. In unison we shouted, stamped our feet at our favorite stanza:

> John Reddy looked his man in the eye.
> Said John Reddy, *Time to die!*
> John Reddy, John Reddy Heart.

A single thought swept through us like an electric current: would it be too much to hope for that John Reddy would show up at our reunion *at the very moment this song was playing?* We asked Dwayne please to play the ballad again, and he did, but, well—John Reddy didn't show up just then. ("What time is it? Oh, Christ—three-twelve a.m.") It was then we noticed how excited, or more than excited, Evangeline Fesnacht had become. In the old days she'd scorned "The Ballad of John Reddy Heart" as "exploitative kitsch" but now she grooved with it like the rest of us, that was clear. We'd noted how, all evening, this mysterious classmate of ours had been watchful and silent ("We just knew, she's taking all this in, she's going to write about us!") and we were given the impression she still believed herself superior to us, but had come around to liking us, somehow. In fact most of us were damned impressed by "E. S. Fesnacht," the career if not the woman, though we weren't certain that we liked, or even understood, her peculiar prose. Hurriedly we skimmed a new novel of Fesnacht's seeking traces of ourselves, our shared Willowsville past, and invariably we were disappointed— "What's this stuff *about*? What's it *mean*?" Some of us persisted in defending E. S. Fesnacht, out of loyalty, while others, the majority, had long ceased reading her. "My daughter who's in college reads Fesnacht," Dwayne Hewson said grumpily, "so she's quizzing me on her. Like that's Daddy's claim to fame, he knew Frog Tits in high school." Chet Halloren said, more thoughtfully, "Fesnacht's is a perverse cosmos. You're drawn in, the landscape looks familiar, but it isn't. 'Spiritual' people come to destructive ends while seemingly 'evil' people are redeemed and rewarded. As if she's turned our human wishes upside down. I'm proud of her." At the reunion what impressed us most about Evangeline was her totally changed appearance: we remembered her as a dumpy, middle-aged adolescent girl with a blemished skin and weird, weird ways but now, in middle age, she more resembled an adolescent, androgynous figure of surprising attractiveness. That hair! We couldn't decide if our Vangie had gone prematurely white, like some of the fellas in the class, or if she'd bleached all the color out of her hair for some mysterious symbolic (or dramatic?) purpose. It was strange to see her photo in the paper, or in a magazine, or on the back cover of one of her books, and think, "Is this the 'girl' I went to school with?" knowing it couldn't possibly be, though in literal fact it was. The organizers of our Thirtieth Reunion Weekend, hearing that E. S. Fesnacht was planning to attend, worried she'd be writing a satire on us—"You can't trust writers. Any more than you can trust cartoonists." But maybe they'd misjudged her! Evangeline Fesnacht had been friendly, if quiet; she'd smiled, and she'd laughed; she'd certainly eaten roast pig with the rest of us—the front of her purple satin jumpsuit was stained and spotted with grease. We thought it was sweet as hell that Ritchie Eickhorn, our poet, had a crush on her after all these years ("But isn't he married? Out in Minnesota, or Dakota?") and had been following her about all night like a puppy; the two of them had tumbled together into the Pifers' ravine, and seemed to have escaped unscathed. But now there was a strange, urgent luster in the woman's eyes as she took up the topic of John Reddy Heart, and we recalled how, in high school, she'd been possibly the most obsessed of us all, with

her brimming *Death Chronicles*. She was saying, pleading,
"Excuse me? Will you listen? Why would only John Reddy's
fingerprints have been on that gun? 'The murder weapon.'
Obviously there should have been other prints. The gun
belonged to John Reddy's grandfather. But there weren't other
prints because John Reddy wiped them off. *He was protecting
the true killer of Melvin Riggs.*" "For sure! 'The White Dahlia.'
She killed Riggs. I always knew." Who was this?—Dougie
Siefried? He'd come up stealthily in our midst, a nervy,
intense figure in Wolverine T-shirt, numeral 11, his boyish
freckled face familiar to us as our own but ghastly pale and
his tall lanky frame almost as wasted as Larry Baumgart's.
There was a rush to greet our Dougie we'd feared was no
longer with us, one of our most popular jocks, we grabbed his
hands, we hugged and kissed him; though, conspicuously,
Dougie's former wife Ginger McCord kept her distance, as
startled as we were but trying not to show it. Evangeline tried
to regain our attention but there was a new distraction: poor
Mack Pifer, haggard and distraught, and clearly in a rotten
mood, had come to bring Millie home with him, and Millie,
indignant, for no one told Millicent LeRoux what to do,
refused to budge; standing barefoot at the edge of the aqua-
shimmering pool like a figure in a lurid film still, in a
borrowed fuchsia swimsuit with a flounced skirt that emphasized her matronly hips and the veins and dents in her lardy
thighs, saying calmly, "How dare you. I'm not a child. Go
away, please. I'm with my friends, my oldest friends, I love
them and they love me, you scarcely know me, there's a deep
spiritual bond between these people and me you couldn't
comprehend, who cares if your precious deck collapsed?—it's
nothing but a material object *and who cares about material
objects*? Go away and leave me alone, damn you!" Mack Pifer
whom we'd believed to be one of your good-natured gregarious fellas, a shrewd businessman but a creampuff when it
came to women, the kind of man Willowsville women marry
for their money and social position and come frequently, in

time, to love, said harshly, "Millie, you're drunk. This is disgraceful. You're not yourself, you'd better come home at once." He reached to take hold of her wrist, and Millie backed away from him screaming. It was at this point that Dwayne Hewson, glowering and menacing, fists raised in a classic boxing stance, moved protectively toward Millie—we were led to wonder if Dwayne and Millie, who hadn't dated in high school, were closer friends than any of us knew? Poor Mack Pifer exchanged a few words with Dwayne, then retreated humiliated and quivering with rage; Millie ran off weeping to the bathhouse. By this time only Ritchie Eickhorn was listening to Evangeline Fesnacht—"I believe you, Evangeline," he said earnestly. "I know you must be right."

Ritchie had managed to recover from his near-drowning, clothes soaked and plastered to his thin, somewhat round-shouldered frame, and his thin mouse-colored hair plastered to his head. "Excuse me, please," Evangeline said, raising her voice. "Will you listen?" We tried, some of us, though we'd been drinking for hours and overhead the mirrored disco balls winked and glared as if with a malevolent life of their own. And a thin high whistling marred the next set, a heavy-breathing rhythm-and-blues number by Muddy Waters —"Just Want to Make Love to You." Desperate, Evangeline managed to get the attention of Verrie Myers and Trish Elders, raising her voice, pleading, "Not only did John Reddy wipe the killer's prints off the gun, he tossed the gun on a frozen creek so it would be found. Obviously! He sacrificed himself for someone in his family—maybe the mother, maybe the grandfather. Or the brother Farley. It might even have been the sister. The one who's a nun, who's made a life of 'ministering unto the needy and the troubled.' All along *John Reddy Heart was innocent*." Verrie cried angrily, "I knew! He wasn't ever a killer in his heart." Trish cried, "*I* knew! Just to look in his eyes, to be close to him and look—you knew." Sandi Scott who hadn't heard all of this clearly said, in a passionate voice, "John Reddy did what he had to do. 'Looked his man in the

eye, said *Time to die!*' We've known this for thirty-two years."
Others came forward, gallantly, like Ken Fischer—"I'd do the
same for my mother, or any woman—if a man was abusing
her. I'd blow him away and take the consequences." Dougie
Siefried said eagerly, with a furtive glance at Ginger McCord
who stood stiffly close by, "Right, Ken! Any man would do as
much for any woman. At sixteen, when the rest of us were
popping zits in the bathroom and trying to scrounge more
allowance out of our dads, John Reddy was a *man*." Poor
Evangeline Fesnacht was a plaintive sight in her purple satin
jumpsuit which was now stained and spotted, her too-white
hair lifting from her scalp like quills, and her eyes hollow and
intense. Impatiently she said, "No. You're not hearing me. It's
like high school—you don't *hear*. I don't mean that John
Reddy killed Riggs to protect his mother from Riggs. I mean
that John Reddy took the blame for the killing—to protect the
true murderer. All these years! And I was the most mistaken,
I believed he had 'killer eyes.' *I wanted him to have 'killer eyes.'*"
But the music was too loud and our mood too frenetic, no one
seemed to be listening; even Verrie Myers who'd have sworn
she was in love, still, with John Reddy Heart (for didn't she
cherish her secret ♥ tattoo on the creamy soft flesh of her left
breast?) found it difficult to concentrate on Evangeline
Fesnacht's words. And there was another confrontation at
poolside: a young man in khaki shorts and WHS track T-shirt
came charging into our midst, clearly disdainful, disgusted, to
lead a glassy-eyed and disheveled Bibi Arhardt away with him
stumbling in her high-heeled shoes, humbled but unresisting.
"Who was *that*?" "Bibi's son Vince. He's a senior at the high
school." "Bibi's *son*? Since when? Is Bibi married?" "Are you
kidding? *We're all married*." Evangeline cried drunkenly, "I
wanted him to have 'killer eyes.' Nobody in Willowsville had
'killer eyes.' John Reddy, forgive me!"

On the tape deck there came Black Banana's "Love Like a
Beast (Die Like a Saint)" none of us had heard since junior
high.

This was a funky but danceable song and to Evangeline Fesnacht's dismay many of us began to dance again. "As if our legs, our haunches hanging like sides of beef began to twitch to the music, and we hadn't any choice but to follow. *Wow*." Even sniffy Carolyn Cameron the oncologist we'd guessed might have gone home hours ago was dancing, shaking hips and breasts, head flung back, with horny Jax Whitehead. And who were these greaser-guys we hadn't seen in years—Clyde Meunzer? Jake Gervasio? Orrie Buhr?—who'd evidently crashed the party, swinging and stamping with certain of our "good" girls? Emboldened by the late hour and the frenzied music and a glazed look in Mary Louise Schultz's tawny-golden eyes, Art Lutz at last asked her to dance, and they sank into each other's arms like long-distance runners who've rushed over the finish line just in time, or almost, to collapse. Mary Louise breathed, "'Loooove like a beast (diiie like a saint),' yes yes!" into Art's burning ear. He stumbled but retrieved the rhythm. Since cocktails at the Rindfleisches' he'd been gazing at this woman and now, close up, his mouth loosened into a foolish smile, he noted how, except for a net of fine wrinkles around her eyes, and a slight puckering of her mouth, she was exactly the girl he'd loved long ago. Mary Louise laughed quietly. "Artie? Remember? That drive we took together? You got hopelessly lost, and we were late getting home? My father was furious." Art said eagerly, "The night we drove by the Buffalo House of Detention where John Reddy was being kept, and we parked by the lake—" "We were with Roger and Suzi and coming back from Crystal Beach you took a wrong turn, we got lost in rural *Canada*—wow." Art said, with a hurt smile, "I guess that was some other time, Mary Louise. Must've been some other guy." "Oh, no. I'm sure it was you, Artie. In that car of yours? I remember that *car*." Mary Louise gave a little shiver, and bit her lower lip in a naughty little-girl smile. "It couldn't have been my brother's car," Art said, puzzled, "—unless Jamie was your date? You went out with Jamie? You *did*?" Mary Louise laughed, and snuggled closer. He inhaled the wan, spent fragrance of an expensive perfume and the more immediate odor of a woman's body after hours of eating, drinking, dancing. "Hmmm. Like I said, I remember that *car*."

Blake Wells had been contemplating Evangeline Fesnacht all evening. At the pig roast, he'd wanted to sit beside her, but Ritchie Eickhorn was always there. Now he made his move, seeing the woman staring disconsolately about. He came up to her and shook her hand, reintroduced himself after thirty years, in case she'd forgotten him; though not wanting to seem to boast, Blake felt that he had to bring his old rival up-to-date, for she was surely one of those who tossed out the class newsletter without glancing into it; so he rapidly recited his major career accomplishments ending with the fact that he'd recently been inducted as president of Williams College. He told Evangeline that he "very much admired" her novels (though possibly he'd only finished two or three of the eleven she'd published) and wondered "if you might accept an honorary doctorate from Williams next spring?—we'd all be so honored." The white-haired woman seemed to be listening, with a polite, neutral expression, her pale face drawn in fatigue and the corners of her pug-mouth drooping in disappointment. This was remarkable: didn't the woman care that Blake Wells was speaking to her? Inviting her to Williams to be honored? After a moment she murmured what sounded like *Yes thank you* or *Maybe, thank you* and Blake leaned closer to confide, over the grunts and groans of "Love Like a Beast," "Evangeline, I've never told a living soul but, our senior year, I was terribly depressed—'fucked up' as kids say today. Then, I'll never know why, just a gesture of friendship, I sent you a dozen yellow roses—'To Evangeline Fesnacht, first among equals'—and somehow it was like the sun shone again in my heart. I wanted to live, and to excel, and by God I did." At this revelation, Evangeline's face tightened like a fist. Indifferent a moment before, her eyes widened in a look of incredulity, fury. "You—what? You sent me those roses? *You?*" "But you must have guessed. How many others could have written 'first among—'?" But Evangeline Fesnacht hissed at him these words he could scarcely believe, afterward, he'd heard from the mouth of a woman of culture and breeding, "You duplicitous S.O.B. *Fuck-er!*"

For having offered the woman an honorary doctorate? *But why?*

The headbanger Lollipop's "Pops You Gonna Gimme the Car Keys (Or Am I Gonna Have to Take 'Em from You?)" came on fast, funny and furious.

It was then we heard a sudden roaring noise. Louder even than Lollipop. Thunder? An earthquake? (we'd been conditioned by the collapse of the redwood deck, we expected the worst). A motorcycle? Speeding along Mill Race Lane, of all unlikely Willowsville roads? From somewhere came the despairing female cry, "It's John Reddy!—he was here, and he's gone." "What?" "Who?" "It's John Reddy, I'm sure!—*he was here, and he's gone.*" Confusion, and near panic. We rushed at one another clutching arms, hands. "Who? *Who?*" "John Reddy. He was *here.*" "*Here?* Where?" We collided with one another in our hurry to run out to the street, some of us rushing through the Hewsons' house, others taking the long way around through the wetted grass and a prickly boxwood hedge. Upstairs in a guest bedroom into which they'd stolen to sit on twin beds and clasp hands, whispering, kissing, laughing, weeping, Jenny Thrun (who was in fact Roger Zwaart's wife but knew divorce was imminent now he'd found Suzi again) and Chet Halloren (married too, and "innocuously happy") would claim to have seen outside the window the passing motorcycle, and the cyclist—clearly identical to the blurred photos Kate Olmsted had shown us earlier. John Reddy Heart had come to Dwayne's party after all and knocked at the front door and in the din no one had heard! And so he'd gone away again.

John Reddy Heart had come to our thirtieth reunion, and now he was gone.

Clyde Meunzer, eyes reddened from drink, a day's glinting-gray beard on his thickset jaws and chin, shouted at stunned Dwayne Hewson, "You sent John Reddy away, Hewson? Didn't let him in your house? You cheap fuck, you!" Clyde would've rushed at Dwayne to batter him with his fists but his friends restrained him. Dwayne protested, "I didn't even know he was here! I was the one who invited him for Christ's sake! John Reddy was more my friend than yours, Meunzer, *we were close as brothers*."

One hundred feet away on Mill Race Lane, unknown to any of us, in his parked, darkened Ford Escort with rust-flecked Pennsylvania plates, there slouched Norm Zeiga, groggy from whisky and cigarettes, a newly purchased .38-caliber Smith & Wesson revolver in his jacket pocket; Norm was wakened by the deafening roar of the passing motorcycle, a rarity in St. Albans Hill, whose driver he hadn't seen clearly except to know it was a mature man, not a kid, wearing a black T-shirt and a crash helmet; he saw the noisy, milling crowd on his ex-friend Dwayne Hewson's sloping front lawn, and was confused and panicked thinking somehow that police had already been called, and decided not to go through with the desperate kamikaze act of vengeance he'd been plotting for months.

Leaving Suzi Zeigler and Roger Zwaart alive, and reasonably healthy, destined to marry at last in their fiftieth years.

Stunned into silence, we returned to Dwayne's back lawn and to our "celebration." We were demoralized, aggrieved. It was now 4:20 A.M.—"My God! How did it get so *late*?" It was in fact Sunday morning. On Dwayne's increasingly defective tape deck, the Freaky Five's hit single "Gonna Sneeze Antifreeze" was chuffing and roaring like old times. It struck us as perverse: the mirrored disco balls continued to wink and leer, the strobe light continued to pulse lewdly in our absence—"A vision of earth after mankind has vanished. Beyond all sentiment and nostalgia. Brute *Existenz*." Suddenly we began to laugh. Even those who'd been sobbing as if our hearts had broken began to laugh. What the hell! John Reddy Heart had been here, and was gone, and how did that alter our condition from what it had been only a few minutes before? We resumed our frantic dancing. Shaking shoulders, hips, breasts. Arms swinging, legs blurred with speed and heads flung back, long hair flying. Aureoles of perspiration framed our heads like crowns. Some of us leapt screaming and flailing, or were pushed screaming and flailing, into the shimmering Olympic-sized swimming pool. From the icy depths of a second, enormous refrigerator in his enormous kitchen our indefatigable host Dwayne Hewson produced, like a magician, more beer. We'd greedily depleted the pista-chios and other snacks but Sonny Deidenbach whom we were getting to know, and like a lot, had impulsively ordered a half-dozen party pizzas (twenty-inch diameter) which were delivered by a wide-eyed black kid in a Cornell T-shirt who ventured with comical caution into our midst like Odysseus descending into the Land of the Dead, aghast at the swarms of wraiths rushing at him. Sonny and Dwayne quarreled good-naturedly over which of them would pay, for of course each wanted to pay; most of us tossed down bills and coins, as the kid in the Cornell T-shirt smiled nervously at us, but it *was* a smile at least, and then waving and retreating hurriedly he thanked us for our generosity (part drunken carelessness and part drunken good spirits, we must've tipped him a hundred bucks) and was gone. ("You think he lives in Willowsville? Is it, um, integrated now?" "Of course it's integrated! What d'you think this is, apartheid?" "But where exactly in the vil-lage is it 'integrated'?") Though some of us had heard this tale before in a number of differing versions, we listened enthralled as Scottie Baskett told us of having discovered, on a back street in Las Vegas, a modest adobe house in which Dahlia Heart and her family had lived before emigrating to Willowsville. "What an adventure! Later I'd be warned at the hotel not to walk around in such neighborhoods by myself, even in daylight—'Everybody has a gun permit in Vegas.' But no one approached me, I wasn't afraid in the slightest. No one was home at the Hearts' old house—I remember the address perfectly: 47 Arroyo Seco Street—but there was a next-door neighbor, a true 'spirit of the West,' clearly part Native American. At first he was suspicious of me but when I introduced myself as a friend and classmate of Dahlia Heart's son John Reddy, the old man's face came alive. His eyes, cloudy with cataracts, shone. He told me of the time, a long time ago now, when Dahlia Heart was just a young woman, a girl really, living in that house; he described her in such detail—! I could've kicked myself not to have brought along a tape recorder. And a camera. He really opened his heart to me, the poor old fella. (He knew he hadn't long to live. It was touching, how he recognized me as a doctor!—as if he'd had a lot of experience with doctors.) Some of what he told me was about Dahlia Heart, 'the most beautiful, glamorous woman' he'd ever seen, and some of it was about being young in those days in Vegas. 'Son,' he said, his voice quavering, 'it's not the same now. You kids don't know what passion is. You've got to want to die for a woman, and to kill for her. If you lack that passion, son, you have not lived.'" Scottie paused. Except for the deafening Freaky Five sound, you could've heard a pin drop. "I could see this great-souled old man, of another era almost, a vanishing America, had loved as much as any man can love a woman. Obviously, he'd been her lover. The thirty or forty years that had passed were nothing to him, Dahlia Heart existed for him so vividly. And it came to me in that instant with the illumination of a lightning flash that *I was in the presence of John Reddy Heart's father*."

Inside the pounding beat of the Kinks' "Tongue in My Heart" was a poignant silence. Some of the girls were crying. Even Jon Rindfleisch who'd been laughing uproariously all evening wiped at his inflamed eyes. Ken Fischer was holding Verrie Myers's white-knuckled hands in his; Ritchie Eickhorn was holding Evangeline Fesnacht's white-knuckled hands in his; Dwayne Hewson scowled, as if in pain—"Navajo, I bet.

That hair, and that look in John Reddy's eye." Tears shone on
Kate Olmsted's face with a startling radiance. She said, gently
reproachful, "If only you'd had a camera, Scott. If *only*."

The red sickle moon had long disappeared, sucked over the
edge of the earth and into the void. We shivered.

Somehow, who knew how (for we all protested we were
stuffed to the gills with succulent roast pig), the enormous
party pizzas, thick with slices of pepperoni and Italian
sausage, had been devoured. Crusts sharp as broken glass if
you happened to step on them with bare feet lay scattered on
the terrace for the Hewsons' disdainful maid to clean up, with
other garbage, later that morning. Still, there was a hunger for
dancing! A ferocity for dancing! "Like we'd been bitten by
one of those giant poisonous spiders—a tarantula? And, to
sweat the poison out, had to dance, dance, dance till we
dropped." Blake Wells was blowing his clarinet as we'd never
heard him blow it back in school—wild screeching breathy
wavering notes. Scottie Baskett was playing trombone, a
clumsy instrument, something was wrong with the mouth-
piece but Scottie managed to blow a few notes loud, piercing,
terrific! There was Jax Whitehead (taking Pete Marsh's place)
at the drums, eyes shut, rocking in a swoon as he slammed
his fists drummer-boy-fashion against a metal table top—Ka-
boom! ka-*boom*! ka-*boom*! There was Chris Donner, inspired,
on cymbals—except these were caterers' aluminum trays
Chris was crashing together. Had these guys ever played
"Tongue in My Heart" before?—they seemed to know the
music, anyway the wild percussive beat. With a little cry,
Verrie Myers leapt up and hauled Ken Fischer laughing to his
feet and—there they were again, our Queen and King of the
Senior Prom, dancing before our enraptured eyes, swaying
and stumbling together, like spent boxers, groping for the
Kinks' slam-dunk beat. Lulu Lovitt, blouse falling off her
shoulder, was dancing with her old steady Jake Gervasio,
slither-bumping with the frenzy of copulating insects. Trish

Elders, her pale, pettish face tightened in a knot, was dancing
with a grinning, gyrating Sonny Deidenbach whose forehead
was beaded with sweat of an eerie reddish hue. There were
Roger Zwaart and Suzi Zeigler twined together like drowning
creatures, murmuring and laughing softly into each other's
avid mouth. Ketch Campbell we'd thought had gone home
hours ago was dancing with clumsy abandon, swinging head,
shoulders, chunky ass, with a panting, perspiring Sandi
Scott—"My God. Sandi would never have stooped so low in
real life." Our cyberspace whiz Petey Merchant we'd thought,
too, had long since slipped away was dancing like a puppet
jerked on a string with hot-eyed Kate Olmsted who stamped
the tile terrace with bare, wounded feet as if trying to injure
herself. Ritchie Eickhorn, maudlin-drunk, was clapping his
hands, chanting—

> O youth O America like gold coins falling from our
>   pockets!
> So many coins! such riches! no need to stoop to pick
>   up what you've dropped.

(We clapped for Ritchie, we were proud of Ritchie—America
needs poets!)

Yet it was disturbing to see how, at the edge of the terrace,
pale-skinned languid Ginger McCord had been drawn at last
into the arms of her sweetheart Dougie Siefried, though
Dougie's arms had lost their sinewy-muscular definition, in
fact they were skeletal-thin, and his freckled boy's face
showed veins, arteries, spidery nerves through translucent
skin. Tall, a basketball forward, Dougie leaned over Ginger,
smiling into her uplifted, heart-shaped face, teasing, making
her laugh as he'd always done, kissing the tip of her pert,
perfect nose even as he swung them away, turned and gyrated
them away out of the lighted poolside area and into the shadows and we called after them—"Ginger? Ginger, come back!
Don't go with him! *Ginger!*" Beneath the frantically revolving

disco mirrors, alternately exposed and annihilated by the powerful strobe light, Babs Bitterman, page-boy hair glistening on her shoulders, and Steve Lunt with his tough-guy Marine-issue crew cut were pressed tight together grinding chests, bellies, pelvises. As they turned, we saw in speechless horror the glass-pellets like stitching in their young faces. A triangular patch of Steve's skull missing above his right ear. And Babs who'd been so vain of her good looks, always rushing to the lavatory to freshen her lipstick, pat powder across her face—what was wrong with her right eye? They lifted their tight-clasped hands to wave at us, with wan, mildly mocking smiles.

There was Smoke Filer dancing with a girl whose face we couldn't see. Whose name we didn't know. We'd forgotten! In the yearbook, where her pretty, dimpled-smiling face was positioned, her curled hair and wavy bangs, we'd see nothing, a blank. There was Smoke Filer winking at her, and, over her head, at us. His handsome weasel-face crushed, pulped. His chest (he'd been a little anxious about, not so thick with kinky hairs as his teammates', naked as a child's set beside John Reddy Heart's dark-haired muscled chest) crushed. "They said the T-Bird steering column had pierced him like a spit. Through his chest, out his back. Those were the reckless defiant days after seat belts had been installed in most cars but before the era of seat-belt laws." His face a glowering demon-mask of lust, the soiled white bandage-turban askew on his head, Dwayne Hewson was dancing with not one but two sexy, desirable women, mature women with breasts and asses, hurtling them around, grunting, cursing—"God *damn*, who stepped on my toes?"—as they shrieked and pushed at him, hair in their faces, stumbling out on the lawn. On the tape deck was playing a strangely distorted "Die Lovin' You," another hit single by Lollipop. The wind had risen, rocking the disco mirrors. One of them had shattered, pieces of glass lay underfoot. The surface of the aqua water shivered, quaked. These were damned fine-looking women, Pattianne

Groves, Mary Louise Schultz, Shelby Connor whose white panties we'd glimpsed at pep rallies when she leapt, twisted, turned, spread her legs as in an embrace of multitudes—where had Shelby come from, so suddenly? We feared she'd left the party, slipped away in disgust. And now came rushing at them—"'Gonna die lovin' you!'"—hot-skinned Millie LeRoux, and there was—wild!—little Trish Elders he'd dated only once, tenth grade, took her to the Glen Theatre that smelled mouthwateringly of stale buttered popcorn to see *2001: A Space Odyssey* and poor Trish was so freaked by the movie, by the nightmare ending, she'd begun to cry on the way home and Dwayne had to comfort her like a goddam older brother, what a letdown, what a bummer, he'd heard from Jon Rindfleisch you could kiss Trish if you went about it in the right way, she wasn't all elbows and nervous giggles like other girls, but he'd screwed up, never told any of the guys, in fact he'd entirely forgotten since this moment, hadn't even tried to kiss her in fact, green-eyed Trish Elders who'd gone riding (it was enviously reported) in John Reddy Heart's Caddie. Pattianne was Dwayne's steady, a good kid but Christ he was bored with her, "necking" was the limit, she'd gone about it like homework, but no French-kissing—not once. Not once! Anyway it was sexy Verrie Myers he'd been crazy for since kindergarten, Verrie Myers he'd dreamt of touching, gripping in his hands, kneading and squeezing and sort of twisting (like clay, like dough—weird!) in his strong eager hands, perennial tease Veronica Myers you couldn't help wanting to tear (as old Bo memorably observed) with your teeth. "Hey—Verrie?" Dwayne was startled to see she'd come to join them, running barefoot across the lawn and leaving, for once, crestfallen Ken Fischer behind. (Why the fuck wasn't Ken dead? Dwayne had adjusted, like most of us, to Ken's death, he'd shook his head over the "riddle" of another's suicide, in fact he'd helped to promulgate the rumor, he'd felt sick at heart by the loss of his old friend and teammate but he'd gotten over it and now Ken was back *which was just like*

him.) "Hi Dwayne!" Verrie cooed in the throaty contralto of
her film successes, immense partly clad Blond Goddess hovering on the screen with that sly-seductive smile, perfect
heaving breasts, "'Gonna die lovin' you! lovin' you baby!
lovin' you-uuu ba-byyy!'" No exaggeration, every hair on the
nape of Dwayne Hewson's twenty-one-inch bull-neck stood
up.

He was a hefty, thunderous billy goat with tufted ears,
horny feet stabbing the grass. He'd have said he was chasing
these part-nude shrieking girls, tearing at their soft, melting
skins, their flyaway hair and glistening lips and peek-a-boo
nipples, but somehow it seemed to be he, Dwayne Hewson,
star Wolverine quarterback, Willowsville mayor and well-
respected local businessman, a husband and a father of four
kids, and damned fine kids they were, he was proud of them
and of himself—somehow it was he they were chasing, he
staggered panting, heart leaping in his chest, on his hands and
knees in the spiky evergreen hedge at the rear of his expensive Mill Race Lane property, the girls' fingers tore away the
soiled bandage-turban, there it flew across the grass like a
wounded bird, now their bold hands stroked his amazed body
teasing, tugging, pulling, as his good dull wife Constance
would've never done, and—"Hey: my trunks!"—they'd
thrown him down, flopped him over like a big fish and
tugged, torn at his trunks, managed to pull off the tight-fitting
trunks (that invariably left an angry red mark at his fatty
waist, God damn he hated that) so suddenly he was naked,
his soft, limp genitals exposed, though trying to laugh, "Hey
girls! This isn't funny. What're your husbands gonna say
about this, girls?" But they showed him no mercy. It was
worse than a football scrimmage. Worse than every guy on
the other team jumping on you. Truly he was surprised: these
good girls? Millie LeRoux who'd taught Sunday school was
fantastic! Since her hysterectomy a few years ago she'd told
Connie she was convinced her life was over or maybe, who
knows, maybe just begun? Plucking, tearing at his penis,

laughing at the look in his face. But Pattianne too was laughing, as he'd never heard her laugh before, wicked sly laughter, and sweet Mary Louise Schultz biting her lip, pink snaky tongue protruding between her lips, and witchy Trish Elders, and Veronica Myers straddling him like an Amazon, prodding a naked knee into his naked belly—"No mercy, Dwayne! We got the ball, the ball is *you*!"

The surprisingly strong middle-aged girls of the Circle managed to hoist their squirming prey aloft, and how Dwayne kicked, squealed, shrieked with laughter—"Girls! Have mercy!" We stared in amazement as they bore our buck-naked hairy host like a pig to the spit across the dewy grass and into the swimming pool, tossed him in with screams of female triumph, tore off their clothes and leapt into the water themselves. A gaping observer would afterward claim that actual steam rose from the pool when Dwayne and those girls hit the water—"They were so *hot*."

It happened so quickly! Like the collapse of the redwood deck, and John Reddy's sudden appearance and departure! But Kate Olmsted, that intrepid photo-historian of our class, was already scrambling for her camera. Quite a few of us would be uneasy with Kate's use of the prints next fall at her gallery opening, but Kate was adamant that Dwayne wouldn't have minded—"You know that wild sense of humor of his. He'd have wanted a memorial exactly like this."

We whistled and applauded and stamped our feet. Several of us couldn't resist jumping into the pool ourselves, part- or fully-clothed, joining Dwayne and the scandalous women paddling and splashing, playful as amorous seals. Lollipop's "Die Lovin' You" was still playing, a defective tape marred by high thin batlike whistles. The wind was up. The eastern sky was lightening. A new day, already? Too soon! It was 5:20 A.M. How we laughed, laughed and applauded, sure, Dwayne was a little out of condition, that belly, that torso, some of us guys embarrassed of our own guts were gratified to see Dwayne's, and that something swinging between his hairy legs like sausage, he was definitely puffing hard, flailing to keep afloat as the girls poked and tickled him, his bug-eyes bloodshot and he had a raw head wound we hadn't noticed till now, poor Dwayne Hewson, Mayor of Willowsville, looking fifty-nine rather than forty-nine, but the fact remains: *Dwayne Hewson was one blissed-out fella in that pool, and if you can't die young you can at least die happy, eh Dwayne?*

* * *

At dawn, on Mill Race Lane, a small flotilla of vehicles, greatly reduced from the number of the previous night, moved away from the Hewsons' handsome old colonial.

Already in our memories Dwayne's house, the swimming pool and the orgiastic dancing and nude-Dwayne-tossed-in-the-pool-by-nymphs, were beginning to fade.

As Richard Eickhorn would write in his posthumously published masterwork, the dithyrambic poetry sequence *Broke Heart Blues*—

> You never lose what you never had.
> Never have what you hadn't lost.

There'd been no intention to drive in a kind of funeral pro-cession!—somehow it just happened. "Ken in the new Jag, and Verrie snuggling close beside him, naturally took the lead. The rest of us followed."

In fact, Trish Elders and Shelby Connor, giddy with an exhaustion that would have seemed to any suspicious hus-band post-coital, hair stringy-damp and smelling of chlorine from Dwayne's pool, were riding with Ken and Verrie in the miniature back seat of the robin's-egg-blue sports car. (Which many of us had admired at the curb outside Dwayne's. Classy! Must be that "troubleshooting" for Motorola's big bucks, eh Ken?) Trish who declared herself "wrecked" was in no con-dition to drive home to wherever she was living—on the lake shore? She'd have had difficulty saying which husband lived there with her unless they'd already decided to separate, but no—this *was* a new marriage, to a man who respected her art, or said he did, *this marriage would last.*

Behind the Jag was Art Lutz at the wheel of his feisty Dodge Grand Caravan. Sleepy Mary Louise Schultz snuggling close beside him, her head on his shoulder.

Next was Ritchie Eickhorn in his airport-rental Toyota, a silent Evangeline Fesnacht beside him staring into space with the look of one granted a vision at the cost of being struck blind.

And last, perky Kate Olmsted who'd surprised us (Kate was always surprising us) lasting through not only Millie LeRoux's tumultuous party but Dwayne Hewson's. Kate drove her battered wine-colored Lexus with, beside her in the passenger's seat, P. F. Merchant, our Petey, dead asleep, snoring softly, a fine line of spittle running down his chin.

In the windless hush before dawn, the beauty of the Village sobered us. Our old, lost hometown. We moved like a procession of spirits purified by death.

"God, it *was* beautiful, wasn't it? And no dream."

Eighteenth-century colonials, Georgian brick homes set back in wooded lots. The great elms of our childhood had long since died and had been torn out of the earth by their roots but the rich citizens of Willowsville had replaced them with near-mature oaks, maples, plane trees, evergreens. From Mill Race to Glen Burns and Castle Creek ("That creek!"), Spring Green Lane, Lilac Lane and so to Meridian and Meridian Place, to bring us to the old Heart residence, an ugly house really, though impressive, "historic"—fallen now into the possession of strangers who claimed not to know the name John Reddy Heart.

Ken drove the Jaguar slowly, at fifteen miles an hour. Not just he was stoically fighting a headache like a balloon filled with iron filings in his head but this would be the final time Veronica Myers, Ken's wife-to-be, would see the old Heart house.

Unexpectedly, Verrie was silent. She bit at her fingers like a disturbed child but said nothing.

Her trademark blond hair, now damp and matted from Dwayne Hewson's pool, smelled of chlorine commingled with a sweetly astringent perfume. Her backless cerise gown was wrinkled across the thighs, and stained. Somewhere, she'd lost her shoes. Her feet were dirty, scratched.

In the rear of the Jaguar, staring at the old Dutch colonial barely visible through a stand of evergreens, Trish Elders and Shelby Connor were silent too. It might have been that they scarcely recognized the house. Where was Dahlia Heart's controversial rock garden with its gnomes and frogs?—"Vanished for decades." The lapping splashing aqua-winking surface of the water in which they'd recently been immersed would seem to have done something irremediable to their memories.

For a long grave moment no one spoke. Nor did Ken Fischer, a model of tact, indicate the slightest restlessness and a wish to be gone. Then Trish sighed, half a sob, "Let's drive past the school? Then we'd all better get to bed."

Shelby said, quickly, "But don't take Castle Creek, Ken, this time? Just cut on through to Glen Burns."

None of us wanted to see the notorious creek—"Just a ditch, really"—that had betrayed John Reddy and exposed him to the derision of our fathers.

The Jaguar moved on, its exquisite motor nearly silent. A delicate light, the sepia of earliest dawn, played about its flawless chrome fixtures.

In Art Lutz's heavy-duty family vehicle there was an embarrassing odor of sweat-stained clothes, old jogging shoes, his teenaged kids' crap. And crap of his own. He'd taken the Caravan to the reunion parties instead of his sleek white Acura, it hadn't been a formal evening. He hadn't anticipated Mary Louise Schultz driving away with him! He wondered uneasily if he should apologize to her for the condition of the van; except, snuggling against him as if mistaking him for her husband, or for a husband, Mary Louise didn't seem to mind.

She murmured, "Artie? Where're we going? I thought you were going to take me to—" Her voice trailed off, she'd forgotten where she was staying for the weekend, possibly at Trish Elders's new place on the lake? A half-hour drive at least. (Did Trish have a husband now, named "Carnevale"?— was he someone Art was supposed to have met, and to know?) "I'll take you anywhere you want, Mary Louise," Art said. "Tell me." Mary Louise murmured, "Mmm." She'd been the only woman not to have flung off her clothes to leap into Dwayne's pool with his naked, flailing body; more decorously, Mary Louise had hoisted the skirt of her Laura Ashley frock and splashed about shrieking with laughter in the shallow end. What a sight! Art Lutz and the other men had stared in disbelief. The skirt of Mary Louise's dress was damp and her olive-bronzy skin exuded a faint, flirty chlorine smell that mingled, like a dream crosshatched by another dream, with a trace of perfume—or possibly deodorant. Art, following his friend's car, felt a wave of elation so profound he almost rammed into the pristine rear of Ken's car. *Anywhere you want, Mary Louise. Anywhere!*

Behind him Ritchie Eickhorn followed hesitantly in the rented Toyota. His eyes ached as if he'd been staring into the sun and he felt a touch of panic that his vision had deteriorated over the past twelve hours. Had he really been awake all night? Drinking, laughing, shouting until his throat was hoarse. Drinking until he'd gotten sick to his stomach sometime after arriving at Dwayne's. And maybe he'd blacked out for a few minutes. His guts were churning now and yet, Evangeline Fesnacht beside him, that mysterious, eccentric woman of genius, that woman like no one he'd ever encountered intimately before in his life, he felt an irrational surge of hope, happiness. "I wonder where Ken's going? Should I just follow, or—?" By chance, Evangeline was staying at the same Comfort Inn on West Main Street in which he was staying. He would drive her to the reunion events. He had an idea that she, too, had been sick at Dwayne's, locked away in a downstairs bathroom to emerge, at the time of the hilarious immersion of Dwayne Hewson in the pool, deathly-white, dazed. In distress she'd looked to *him*. She'd called him, in a surprisingly timid voice, *Ritchie*. In high school, Evangeline Fesnacht had barely acknowledged him, her co-editor of *Will-o'-the-Wisp*, hadn't condescended to call him by any name at all that he could remember. Mr. Lepage had encouraged her to feel superior, he'd puffed her up with pride; almost, Ritchie yearned to confide in this woman who would be (how keenly he felt this!) the soul-mate of his middle years—*Evangeline! I hated you then*.

As if she'd been hearing his thoughts Evangeline said quickly, "Yes, follow. I think I know where they're going."

In the wine-colored Lexus at the end of the procession, Kate Olmsted deliberated waking her sleeping companion to ask if he'd like her to drive by his old family house—hadn't it been on Seneca? Or Garrison? A small, undistinguished house by Willowsville standards of which (you had to assume) Petey had probably been ashamed. She decided not to wake him. He slept so profoundly, head lolling against the seat back, his skin clammy-pale as an infant's, Kate cast him a fond, protective glance. "To what purpose, Petey? Now's *now*."

She wondered: would they become lovers? Or would he simply disappear back into cyberspace, in California, from which, so unexpectedly, he'd come?

The flotilla of cars, survivors, moved along Seneca, beyond Turnberry and onto Main Street. How deserted the Village seemed. Many lights were still burning. Ken turned into the high school grounds and there was Willowsville Senior High so suddenly—somehow larger, more impressive than we recalled. Verrie cried, "Look at the bell tower! That golden light." The bell tower did appear golden, lit from within. The giant clock hands were poised precisely at 5:49 as if there were a secret message, a profound coded meaning, in the juxtaposition of slender black clock-hands and black Roman

numerals; by the merest coincidence, as we'd afterward discover to our horror and grief, this was the approximate arrival
time of the Amherst General paramedics at Dwayne Hewson's
house, summoned to treat a middle-aged male for "acute cardiac arrest."

Yet he'd known bliss. God in a fireball exploding in his
chest.

"It's something we need to believe. Please don't take our
beliefs from us."

Slowly the flotilla of cars moved onto the deserted school
campus. An eerie predawn light hovered at ground level, like
mist; above, the air was turning golden. We stared at our
beautiful school we'd never seen when we were students. We
were humbled by its redbrick respectability, its churchly calm.
The broad white portico, the white Doric columns and broad
fanning granite steps. A three-foot-high gleaming plaque set
in the ground proclaimed "WILLOWSVILLE SENIOR HIGH SCHOOL Est.
1911." Ken Fischer said quietly, "God. They must've loved
us—our parents. To have spent so much on us." It was a profound realization, we didn't know how to absorb it. Verrie
said, "It's like we were their dreams. We never knew." Trish
Elders said, "It makes me feel so strange! As if I'm seeing my
own, what is it—sepulchre. But it's a happy sight. It fills me
with happiness. That our parents loved us. Even if they didn't
know us."

In middle age we'd begun to speak of our parents as if they
were dead whether in fact they were already dead or not.
Literal death seemed somehow beside the point. "After high
school in America, everything's posthumous."

We parked. We admired the new science wing, the new
tennis courts, the new track course and the new football stadium. Verrie proudly pointed out the likely site of the Francis
C. Lepage Theater. She'd been communicating by phone and
fax with the school architect for weeks. Art Lutz in the gun-
metal-green Dodge Grand Caravan pulled out around the
Jaguar, grinning and waving, on his way to the stadium.

Beside him sat a dark-haired woman we might not have recognized as Mary Louise Schultz though she lifted a hand to us in greeting, or in farewell.

Art was saying earnestly to Mary Louise, "I loved football. I loved my teammates. I never played a really good game in my three years on the team, I was one of those players who did well in practice then kind of freaked out in the game. 'Existential angst,' Coach called it. 'The will to fail.'" Mary Louise protested, "That isn't right. Don't say such things. I remember you playing very well, Artie. I do. We led cheers for you—didn't we? Of course we did." This wasn't true, but Art was deeply moved to hear this woman, who'd been a varsity cheerleader, say it. After thirty years, maybe it didn't matter what was true or not, only what was remembered as true. "I love you, Mary Louise. Not that I want to embarrass you." "Oh! I guess you are, a little." "I realize you're married, and I'm married. You've got—kids?" "Oh Artie, it's all right." "What's all right?" "Our other lives. 'Real' lives. They don't matter, do they?" Trembling with excitement, Art parked the van smelling of his family on the far side of the stadium, where the air was sharply shadowed and smelled of recently mown grass. Overhead the sky was a pale washed blue. He killed the motor, his heart was beating so rapidly he thought it might burst, he turned to Mary Louise—half-expecting she'd be gone. So often in his dreams he'd turned to her in such a way, in such raw yearning, and she'd vanished. Sometimes he'd actually touched her breasts, or the shimmering air close about her breasts, and, in that instant—she'd vanished. But Mary Louise smiled now and said, almost shyly, "Artie? Will you do me a favor?" "A favor? What?" "Let's neck." "—'Neck'?" "You know. Kiss. Like in seventh grade." "—'Seventh *grade*'?" Art laughed awkwardly to disguise his alarm. "I never had a girlfriend that young. Not till tenth grade." Mary Louise wrinkled her nose, chiding, "Don't be so literal, Artie! I'm speaking of the principle." Boldly she moved into his arms and kissed his opened, startled mouth. He was breathing through his mouth, panting like an aging dog; sweat had broken out ignominiously on his forehead and beneath his arms as in the old, dread days of high school football, his Wolverine jersey, his jockstrap, underwear, pants and most of all his socks stiffened with sweat and mineral salt. Mary Louise hugged him happily around the neck, kissed him again, giggling and nudging her forehead against his. She whispered, "I've had a crush on you for—well, a long time." In a swoon Art hugged this amazing, mysterious woman against him, and kissed her in return. A long impassioned vertiginous kiss like falling down an elevator shaft in a nightmare of childhood. Emboldened, he nudged his tongue against her lips to open them, and to enter her warm moist mouth, and was blocked by her playful, practiced tongue—if this was seventh-grade kissing, it was of a virtuoso sort. Mary Louise lightly scolded, "*Artie*." His hands too were eager and hopeful as a boy's, for perhaps they were the hands of a boy; he'd shut his eyes and fallen into the vivid memory of this girl in his arms in Jamie's car, the sexy Dodge Castille—how happy he'd been! "Miserable, yet happy." His hand cupped Mary Louise's left breast, a mound of amazing female flesh, and she stiffened at once, murmuring, "*Artie. Can't we just neck?*" He understood her implication: they were mature individuals who'd been married for years, to whomever they'd been married for years, and they'd done enough of *the other*, possibly too much. (Half the time, with Reeny, Art wasn't what you'd call aggressively potent. The rest of the time his mind was on other matters—for instance, Mary Louise Schultz in her maroon cheerleader's jumper, "Wol-ver-ines! Wol-ver-ines! You're the team—of our dreams! Yayyyy!"—leaping and throwing wide her arms as if to offer her breasts to him, and those white panties flashing. *That was it. Every time.*) If Art had been an articulate man like certain of his classmates, Blake Wells, Dexter Cambrook—even Dwayne Hewson could speak persuasively, if not always sincerely, at Village council meetings—he might have explained to Mary Louise that, yes, there was a purity in necking, a philosophical first principle, kissing was so like speech, "necking" a kind of conversation unknown in any other mode, beside which sexual intercourse seemed both crude and impersonal, yes this was so, still, he yearned to run his reverent hands over the woman's warm, wonderful body, he loved her and, loving her, had he not the right, in fact the obligation, to love her body? If he kissed her mouth avidly, and hungrily, wasn't it natural for him to wish to kiss her breasts? Her body, everywhere? He was forty-eight years old, would he be living forever? "But Mary Louise, darling—you must know that I love you." "Well, can't that be enough?" "No!" He spoke in anguish. She was like one of his own children when they'd been young, stubborn, exasperating, alarmingly willful, so he'd wondered *What are the origins of such willfulness? such opposition?* as in Mr. Dunleddy's class he'd been confused by the ironclad procedure of mitosis—*prophase! metaphase! anaphase! telophase!*—and still more by the eventual adversarial nature of certain split cells as if, in the very molecular constitution of unanimity, there was, somehow, tragically, or farcically, opposition. Yet he, Art Lutz, whose only distinction at WHS would be Class Clown, could hardly have posed such a question, had he been able to articulate it—everyone would have laughed at him, including Mr. Dunleddy. He repeated, grimly, "No." He'd managed clumsily to undo the first half-dozen lavender pearl buttons of a row of myriad buttons on the high-necked Laura Ashley frock, reaching inside in triumph to cup Mary Louise's breast in its tight elastic bra. At first Mary Louise feebly protested, pushing at his hand, breathing hotly, then, sighing—"Oh, all right." Nearly overcome with excitement, his hands trembling, Art managed to undo more of the buttons, it's possible that one or two were ripped off, flying and bouncing into oblivion, or onto the gritty floor of the Caravan to be discovered, a few days later, by quizzical Reeny whose sharp eyes invariably detected what she called "household mystery items"—for what's a household, like human history, but a concatenation of unsolved mysteries? At last Art was holding, caressing, stroking both of Mary Louise Schultz's amazing breasts, and yet—"Mary Louise, is something wrong?" He tasted cold, for there was something wrong, the woman's breasts were somehow wrong, though ample as he'd imagined them, and buoyant. Mary Louise hid her face in his neck. He felt her tremble, as on the brink of tears. "Oh, Artie. I should have told you, I guess." "Told me—what?" "I've had—last year—the surgeon recommended it—a mastectomy. A double mastectomy." "What!" "My breasts are foam rubber. I was afraid to have more surgery, to replace them, I'm still afraid, and anyway—these are adequate to my purposes, at my age." Mary Louise spoke hotly, and unapologetically. Art, stunned, couldn't think of a reply; his fingers had frozen on the foam-rubber protuberances encased in their sturdy bra, in fact it was a sexy lavender bra, as if they, too, were paralyzed. Mary Louise said, "My husband won't even look at me, he says it's too sad. The scar tissue. I know he means sad for him, not for me. I spend a lot of time in the bath tenderly washing myself, like I'm a baby, my own baby I'll never have again, you know?—it must be like that with a man, too, sometimes?— you'll never have another baby, and the babies were the best part of marriage, and your babies are all grown up, and if you touch them they practically throw off your hand like you're a child molester?—anyway, I spend a lot of time in the bath, and I look at myself in the mirror, and I remember— well, never mind! So I thought I'd come to the reunion, I was so happy in high school, I was so really, really fond of you, Artie, and I'm sorry now, I guess—" Art said, "It's O.K., Mary Louise. I still love you." "You do?" "I couldn't just stop, you know—it's too late." "Well, I love you, too. Oh, Artie!"

You've got to want to die for a woman, and to kill for her. If you lack that passion, you have not lived.

In Ritchie Eickhorn's rented Toyota, indecisively parked near the front walk of the school, by the monumentally tall flagpole that rose virtually out of sight, flagless at this hour of the day, Evangeline Fesnacht had at last begun to speak, with such emotion, such seeming anguish, Ritchie was deeply moved, and gripped her icy fingers in his. Such childlike, stubby fingers for a woman of her stature! As if the ravages of the long night and the startling iconic beauty of their old school had partly unhinged her, she confided in Ritchie that she was, nearing fifty, at an impasse in her life, her professional and personal life which were virtually identical; she was gripped in a paralysis, like Odysseus who'd been in sight of Ithaca suddenly blown out to sea by a wrathful god. "I can see my 'home'—but somehow I can't get to it. Always something blows me off course. I'm practically a homeless person, Ritchie! You were wise to fall in love, and marry, have children—a 'real' life. While 'E. S. Fesnacht' has no existence apart from the spines of a few books. And 'Evangeline'—that was my girlhood name, and that girl is *gone*." Ritchie protested, "My 'real' life isn't anything I'd actually chosen, Evangeline. It was more like it *happened*. I was standing there, and it happened to *me*." "But you're happy, aren't you? I mean—happily married?" "Yes, of course," Ritchie said vaguely, though he wasn't sure if this was so, and imagined his wife Annie overhearing, with her sardonic, *I-know-your-bullshitter-heart* smile, that devastated him even in contemplation, "—but what's so profound about happiness? Most of the time it lacks depth, texture"—he groped for a word, as if he'd spoken these words before, possibly in a poem, yes, an early poem of his zestful twenties, "Happiness: An Elegy," one of the few poems of Richard Eickhorn to appear in *The New Yorker* and to have been actually read by numerous old classmates—"timbre. It might even be claimed that happiness, as an existential condition, can't be 'real' but only provisional." Evangeline said, "But to write, to truly write, to exhaust your heart in the effort, you have to feel that someone cares. That someone's heart will be moved." Ritchie said, shocked, "You? You're saying these things? 'E. S.

Fesnacht'?—you've won a National Book Award for Christ's sake. Every one of your books is *in trade paperback for Christ's sake*. While my three books, which sold a grand total of two thousand four hundred and six copies—" He heard his adolescent, adenoidal voice in alarm and disgust. Evangeline Fesnacht seemed to have recoiled from him, wiping at her blood-veined eyes, faint with exhaustion. Her curdled-pale face that had looked, in other circumstances, striking as the face of a Greek statue, now was merely curdled-pale, like slightly rancid cottage cheese; there were sharp indentations beneath her eyes, and her starkly white hair, so brutally short, seemed to betray, at its roots, a penumbra of brunette. Of course, Evangeline Fesnacht had had brown hair like everyone else. Yet Ritchie felt a surge of sympathy for the woman, his exact age, for perhaps she was, this old co-editor of *Will-o'-the-Wisp*, himself somehow: his soul-mate: as weak, confused, insecure and undefined as he. He said, "Evangeline, I'll read what you write. Anything you write. My heart will be moved. I *know*." "You—will?" "Of course. Why do you think I'm with you in this ridiculous place?—at our old high school, thirty years after graduation, at six in the morning? Both of us wrecks from last night? Why do you think I came to this ridiculous reunion weekend, except in the hope of seeing you? Since you seem never to answer my letters." Evangeline stared at Ritchie in alarm. She'd begun to cry, her face crinkling like crumpled tissue paper, fumbling for a Kleenex but couldn't find one in the zipper-pockets of the stained purple jumpsuit, fumbled in her bulky canvas totebag imprinted with the words *Black Oak Books Berkeley*, but gave up, swiping at her nose with the back of her hand, as Ritchie too searched for a tissue, all the tissues in his pockets wadded, stiff, God damn. Evangeline said, "And to think—John Reddy Heart was here, just a few hours ago, in Willowsville. And like fools we missed him." "You think—he really was here?" "Don't you?" Evangeline stared at him belligerently. "Well—no one saw him, exactly." "Yes, Jenny Thrun and Chet

Halloren told me they'd seen him. On the front walk at Dwayne's. He'd parked his motorcycle and was approaching the house and—maybe he heard that ludicrous rock music? He'd outgrown? Changed his mind and—he's *gone*." Evangeline said ferociously, "I hate our classmates, don't you, Ritchie? They never read *Will-o'-the-Wisp*. Once in the cafeteria Smoke Filer was reading a poem we'd published to the guys at his table, cracking them up, it might've been a poem of yours, in fact—that's what they are. They ruin everything. I've never come to any reunion but I came to this reunion for—well, I don't know. But they've ruined it, and I hate them. John Reddy was here, and he's gone. I wanted to tell him, 'I know you're innocent, you were innocent all along.' I wanted to tell him—" Ritchie took hold of Evangeline's hands again, suddenly inspired. Never in ordinary life, in ordinary circumstances, could he, Richard Eickhorn, have behaved so decisively; having survived the long night, he felt his consciousness ascend to a dizzying, visionary plane. "I have a plan, Evangeline: we'll redeem John Reddy Heart's name. You and me. Together." "What do you mean?" "We'll write to the district attorney of Erie County, whoever he is. Dill's retired, or dead. We'll insist that they reopen the case, which they bungled. They arrested and tried the wrong person, and the true murderer was never punished." "Actually, I've thought of that," Evangeline said, "—but after all, John Reddy was acquitted. It's hopeless." "Why is it hopeless? We want to redeem a man's name. We could get our classmates to sign a petition." As he spoke, as Evangeline Fesnacht gazed at him with doubtful, yet admiring eyes, he felt enthusiasm swell in his heart; that old, nearly lost sensation as of burgeoning love; the sensation that once signaled the onset of a poem. Small bluish flames like the flames of a gas jet licked about his brain. Flatly Evangeline said, "Ritchie, there's no evidence. The law requires evidence. Mere ideas, theories, even if correct, aren't enough." Ritchie protested, "But if the true murderer *confessed*—" "The 'true murderer' might no longer

be alive. And a confession, in such circumstances, so many
years later, without evidence, probably wouldn't be enough,
either." "But, Evangeline, we have to *try*. If we want justice for
John Reddy Heart." Already Ritchie envisioned the dense,
difficult poem that would spring from this effort: Richard
Eickhorn's longest and most ambitious poem, in lush
Whitmanesque cadences, *Broke Heart Blues: An Elegy*. Or,
Broke Heart Blues: A Love Song. He would pour everything in
him into it—he would empty his soul. Evangeline was regarding Ritchie with startled, respectful eyes. Her fingers that had
been stiff and ungiving all evening now clutched at his. Still
she said doubtfully, "He might not want us to do this, Ritchie.
'John Reddy Heart.' *He* might not be alive. And we couldn't
give him back his youth in any case." Extravagantly Ritchie
said, "Maybe he doesn't want his youth back, Evangeline. Do
you?"

It was 6:16 A.M. None of us (except Ketch Campbell who'd
remained behind at Dwayne Hewson's for a final nightcap, at
Dwayne's insistence, and was there at the time of Dwayne's
collapse, thank God, to dial 911 and summon an ambulance)
could know that another of our classmates had died, and
would never be seen by us again.

"Here. He used to park *here*."

"Wasn't it more over here? Closer to that sign."

Ken Fischer had driven them around to the rear of the
school, Kate Olmsted in his wake, and now several of them
were trying to determine where precisely John Reddy Heart
had usually parked the Cadillac. "When it was its original
salmon color, I think he parked it farther back," Trish Elders
said pedantically, for she alone of the Circle had actually
ridden in that car, "but after he painted it that green so sharp
it hurt the eyes, I believe he parked closer in. About here."
"Yes, but more to this side," Verrie said pettishly. Extricating
herself from the Jag as from a stranglehold of an embrace,
Verrie'd been so light-headed she'd almost fainted but now,

with that resilience for which, even as an amateur actress, she'd been known, she seemed to have made a full recovery. In fact, she stood tall and splendid on bare, slender, swordlike legs, her feet bare, too. In the stained cerise dress that exposed her lovely back, and a good deal of her breasts, blond hair tangled past her shoulders, she yet retained an exotic glamour; Ken Fischer stared at her mesmerized. Of course, his beloved Verrie was *real*, and yet—? Might her smudged makeup, her grimy feet and that embarrassing pig-grease stain at about the position of her navel be part of a performance? "I had to ask myself, not for the first time—'How real are *any of us*?'" Parking her Lexus close by, Kate Olmsted reached for her camera, as if reaching for a part of her body, and emerged already snapping—"I had a premonition that this would be one of those radiant moments—an epiphany." Shelby Connor was saying, with a lyric drunkenness, "Ohhhh *no*. You're wrong, Verrie. I used to look out that window, right there"—pointing to a second-story window of the school, "in Mr. Cuthbert's class, my desk was beside the window and every day I saw John Reddy's car. I mean, every day he was here. Days he wasn't, and the space was empty—well, you know how that felt. But when John Reddy was on the premises, the Caddie was *here*."

Verrie turned hot-eyed and vexed to Ken, as to a (male) arbiter of fact. "Darling, of all the guys in our crowd, you were closest to John Reddy. *Where did he park his car?*" But wily Ken Fischer, running a hand over his gray-stubbled jaws (he hadn't shaved since flying from Frankfurt more than thirty hours before) backed off, smiling, "Hey, I wasn't John Reddy's friend—really. I hardly knew him, and he sure as hell didn't know *me*."

Verrie whispered, "I love you anyway."

She'd left her handbag in the car, went to fetch it and seeing we were her old friends, no one to judge her harshly, she dumped its contents out onto the asphalt. Wallet leaking credit cards and carelessly wadded bills, liquid makeup in small jars, loose-powder compact, dented lipsticks, vials of prescription pills, multiple vitamins, calcium and melatonin, address book and cellular phone and a half-dozen felt-tip pens, and—what was this? An empty aluminum Coke can. A dented Coke can of a design and hue we hadn't seen, without realizing we hadn't been seeing it, in decades.

Shelby cried, "Is it—?"

Trish cried, "It *is*."

Verrie snatched up the Coke can, held it aloft and with a flourish placed it on the pavement, where Shelby had said John Reddy parked his Caddie. "*There*. I'm done with it."

It could have been only a coincidence but at that moment, on the other side of the stadium, Artie Lutz gunned the motor of his sports vehicle and drove away. "Back to the 'real world,' I suppose," he said, stealing a sidelong glance at Mary Louise who was serenely repairing the damage done to her makeup; but Mary Louise merely gave him a sidelong glance in return, enigmatic as the Mona Lisa. Ritchie Eickhorn and E. S. Fesnacht had already driven away—where? We were never to know. In Kate's Lexus, poor Petey Merchant we'd somehow imagined had been dead for years, continued to sleep, lost in a virtual dream-reality that compelled him to grind his back teeth. Hard not to feel a tinge of exasperation, if a guy like Petey is your sole romantic hope for the future, as he was Kate's—"Oh, why do these 'brains' miss everything crucial? Always in their damned *brains*."

It was then that, across the high school lawn and playing fields, dozens of sprinklers suddenly switched on. Across the campus a startling iridescent play of water appeared; translucent-aqua Willowsville water subtly tinged with the colors of the rainbow; a dozen rainbows simultaneously; miniature rainbows no more than eight or ten feet in length. Verrie gave a shout of laughter and seized Trish's hand (no matter that just now Trish had been seriously pissing Verrie off with her self-important talk of John Reddy's Caddie) and pulled her along, running across the lawn through sparkling skeins of water toward the hockey field. Both were barefoot, bare-legged. Laughing and shrieking like young girls. Kate limped after them, snapping her camera, while Ken and Shelby watched rapt in admiration. What an exquisite sight, the women's uplifted faces!—luminous, radiant, in the moist early-morning light. Ken said, sighing, "I've been in love with Verrie Myers since kindergarten. It's a curse—I mean, my destiny. Can you keep a secret, Shelby? In Stuttgart, it's possible that I did contemplate—but only for a minute!—hanging myself, in my four-star hotel. First the minibar, and then—oblivion. But I gave myself a pep talk in Coach McKeever's toughguy voice—'How the hell would that improve your lot, Fischer?'" Ken laughed happily, wiping at his eyes. He was terribly jet-lagged, sympathetic Shelby could see. Weren't the Germans six hours ahead of our American time? "Sometimes I wonder, Shelby, what my life would have been if that little blond girl hadn't stalked over to me, first day at the Academy Street School, and kissed me on the nose." Shelby said, startled, "But that wasn't Verrie, Ken. That was me."

Across the distant hockey field, through the sprinklers, Verrie and Trish ran, ran. The Coke can in the foreground had toppled and was forgotten, mere teenage litter. America is filling up with teenage litter. Verrie in her water-splotched cerise dress, Trish in her tattered gypsy costume that looked as if it were made of cobwebs. Already it was nearing six-thirty and there was a champagne brunch scheduled for eleven at Trish's lakefront house/studio on Fleet Farm Road but not one of us, including the hostess herself, would make it; Trish, totally wiped out, would sleep for fourteen hours straight, missing the remainder of the reunion weekend—the Open House at the school, the tennis tournament, the softball game, drinks at Art Lutz's and a farewell, and somewhat anti-climactic, cookout at the Zwaarts' (from which Jenny Zwaart would be conspicuously absent). A time of joy, if a time of sorrow; a time of bittersweet laughter, and a time of tears. Our thirtieth reunion. And already some of us were planning our thirty-fifth, and our fortieth. We loved seeing those of you who came but we missed those of you who stayed away and as always we couldn't help but wonder *where were you*?— Carol Banks, JoAnn Windle, Jack Schmidt, Gordie Stearns, Tommy Nordstrom, Jean Windnagel, Jerry Hugar, Rev. Matt Watkins, Mary Alice Glass, Perky Ensminger, Marietta Bongiovannia, Emily Jane Paxson, Steve Meguin, Al Riggs, Marilyn Mason, Gary Stranges, Janey Plummer, Jori Fullenweider and "Buck" Weisbeck, Wayne Butt, Bruce Burnham, Linnea Ogren, Gail Gleasner, Alice Goff, Nancy Catena, Patti Ann Rathke, Gregory Dickke, Hilde Faxlanger, Faith Ryan, Sandy Bangs, Bette Pancoe, Kevin Koehler, Marvin McClenathan, Dottie Palmer, Chris Carr, Sandy Slosson, Deanna Diebold, Molly Eimer, Ray Kaiser, Rick Ludlow, Corky Castle, Charley Chriswell, Marian Mattiuzzio, Dino Calvo, Johnny Olinger, John Reddy Heart—we miss you, we're thinking of you, we want to see you again, *we love you.*